A Novel

Imperfectly Perfect & Royally Yours

B. Montgomery

ISBN: 978-1-7365667-2-5 (Paperback)
ISBN: (Hardcover)

Cover design by: Author using Canva App
Other Images: Canva App and Microsoft Word
Drawings: Brianne Maijala
Library of Congress Control Number: TXu002254171
Printed in the United States of America

To my beautiful daughters who keep me on this journey...

To my best friend, there are no words for the love and gratitude I have for you and your love and support with another book. As a tribute to you, "BriaLynn's" singing voice is in honor of you and your beautiful singing voice!

"True love is purest when the love is truly unconditional."
~ BriaLynn

"For unto whomsoever much is given, of him much shall be required." ˜ Luke 12:48

"When one has a much-privileged life, one has a much-privileged responsibility to the people."

Imperfectly Perfect & Royally Yours

INTRODUCTION TO BOOK 2
The Imperfectly Perfect Alternate World

Please remember, the world within this book is a world very much like ours, but it's still a fictional world. The story of book two takes place mostly in *The United Kingdom of Provinces*. This 'UK' is ruled by a monarchy, with a parliament running the government 'at the leisure of The King.' Those members of parliament are voted into office by the citizens of the country. However, because this country is ruled by a monarchy, The King has the power to override anything at *any* time; it's a power rarely used. When putting things into law, it is similar to signing a bill like The President of the United States, who also has the power to 'veto' a bill and send it back.

The Queen Mother has her hands deep in how 'The King' rules, which he does to protect his brother and sister. He's become numb to her tirades; her demeaning and abusive nature is just a part of his life. The enthusiasm for The Royal Family has dwindled and would have gone dormant if it weren't for a few favorites.

This past year, the love and excitement the people have for their royals and nobles is getting the surge its needed, with the help of a Scottish-American Marchioness who is quickly becoming popular with the people. Articles and society pages have pictures of BriaLynn with David or with Jack, and ones with all three; clearly showing they genuinely love and care about each other. The only articles and pictures becoming more popular are the ones with The Marchioness and The King!

The rumors around The King visiting Newhaven often, have the people elated and hopeful The Marchioness will be "The Royal Consort!' They not only wonder if The King has his sights on a 'Direct Bloodline' for his 'Heir to The Throne,' *but* wonder if her influence will be a change for good *for everyone*, perhaps especially, for The King?

CHAPTER 1
Imperfectly Perfect Insights

On the tarmac of a private airport in Newhaven, Katie and BriaLynn are at an impasse. Katie is *fuming* with anger and jealousy and has just blurted out to Bri, "Still think you're not a glorified prostitute?! Ask David about The King wanting *you* for *his* 'Royal Consort' and have *his* baby!" Katie glares at them with a smug look when she sees an angry David clenching his jaw.

Bri had responded emotionless, "I know."

At that moment, David and Jack look at Bri in shock, while Katie's mouth falls open. Jack and David can't believe it! All this time, *Bri knew*? How?!

Katie turns up her nose in disgust. "So, you *want* to be a baby mill?! Have you no shame in being passed around?!"

Bri's face shows her own disgust with Katie as she says, *"You don't."* Katie is temporarily silenced since she has nothing to come back with.

Jack, still in shock, asks, *"You knew?!"*

"Technically, I knew when I was in the coma, but I wasn't allowed to remember when I woke up. It was only later when Jessica gave me those memories back. It's odd..." she contemplates, "I received *all* those memories *after* I accepted David's proposal and of course, I was also accepting Jack as my 'Noble Consort.' *However,* you would think I wouldn't have gotten those memories about Herst back yet..."

David is curious. "Why do you think you got all of them back at once?"

She looks from David to Jack as the answer comes to her... "Because my first decision was accepting David's marriage proposal, *knowing* I was also accepting the tradition that comes with it..." she gestures and smiles at Jack, "having a 'Noble Consort.'"

"Which opened you up to the possibility of being 'The Royal Consort.'" Jack follows along.

Bri nods and asks him, "Is it customary for someone in my position to be expected to accept being 'The Royal Consort' when it's offered?"

"Generally speaking, yes." He replies.

Her eyes flick to David. "*Explain.*"

"This kind of 'opportunity' doesn't really come around. In centuries past, kings would've tried to snatch you from me the moment it was discovered you were a 'Direct Bloodline.' Had we been married, family would've jumped at it because it would elevate an entire family name to royalty status, regardless of their social class—."

"A goal a lot of families have around the world, noble or not." Bri notes.

"Right, but Bri," Jack turns her to face him, "David would *never* force this on you!" Katie scoffs and rolls her eyes. Jack ignores her and tells Bri, "He loves you too much for that!"

"I know that, too." She lovingly looks from Jack to David.

David reminds her, "My rule of love applies here, just as it did with Jack and you. Herst knows I *won't* back down from that, but he's never asked me to reconsider either."

Jack tells her, "David wanted the both of us to talk to you about it after our honeymoon and we'll still do that, but a little later. Right now, I'm going to let you and David have a minute. Alright?" She nods. Jack hugs Bri before stepping away.

David and Bri move further away for more privacy from Katie. David steps closer to Bri and looks at her with so much love, she can't help but smile back with teary eyes and a slight lump in her throat. He kisses her firmly. When he looks into her eyes again, he sees her adoration for him and smiles.

"That, *right there,*" he points to her eyes, "is why I could *never* force this decision on you. I want to keep you looking at me like that, *not destroy it.*"

"Kiss me again, then." She smirks. He smiles back and gives her a very fierce kiss, dipping her back a little.

"Bri, I *can't* stress this enough! The only way this will work is with love. I want you to be loved by Herst, *and* for you to love Herst. But I'll never lose sight that this is *your* body, *your* choice, and *your* rules! Just like Jack won't forget and I've also told Herst, who completely agrees!"

"David, from an American perspective, Katie's right! I'll be seen as a baby mill, a prostitute, a wh—."

"*Stop right there!*" He holds his hand over her mouth. "You're *no* such thing because this *isn't* about sex! It's insulting to me, too, Love, since I wholeheartedly support your relationship with Jack! The same goes for Herst! If you find that there's nothing there, *or you just don't want to do this*, I'll support that, too. All I ask is you give this careful thought as you get to know Herst." He gives her his own loving smile. "Herst, Jack, and I were raised differently than you, and I'm expected to honor certain traditions—."

"Because you'll be 'The Duke of Newhaven.'" She finishes and he nods. She tells him, "I get it, *I do*! That's why I've been considering this because I'll be 'The Duchess of Newhaven' right alongside you, having those same expectations to certain traditions!"

He lovingly smiles. "And even though *we're* expected to honor certain traditions, I refuse to ever force anything like this *on you*!" She kisses him. He then tells her, "Like Jack said, we'll talk about this more later. *Right now, we do need to take care of some things first.*" He takes her hand and laces their fingers together, then kisses the back of her hand. She knows he's implying 'together' and she nods with a sweet smile.

They walk up to Jack and she sees he's clenching his jaw, glaring at Katie over something she said. She puts a hand on his forearm, and he turns to look at her. His eyes quickly fill with love for her and his face softens. He takes Bri's free hand and softly squeezes it.

"What would you like to do about Katie." Jack asks.

When Bri sees the extra car and the two additional people, she realizes David has a plan. Bri looks at David and he tells her, "Love, we'll support whatever *you* decide." She sees Jack nodding in agreement out of the corner of her eye.

She walks up to Katie who's telling her, "I meant what I said. Whether you want to admit it or not, you are a whore!"

Bri asks with a humorless laugh shaking her head a bit at the ridiculousness of it all, "What do you hope to accomplish, Katie?! Because jealousy has you acting like a neurotic fool!"

"Jealous of what?!" Katie sneers. "Jack will come running to me when he gets bored with you, because I won't be chasing after him anymore and let's face it, men are more interested in me, not 'good girls.'"

Bri raises her eyebrow. "Which is it, Katie? You call me a 'whore' in one breath, but a 'good girl' with the next. I can't be both."

Katie scoffs, "I'm referring to the bedroom and with your lack of *talent*. He'll find out you're a total *snooze fest* and seek for passion between the sheets with me!" Bri keeps a straight face, even with Jack bursting into laughter. "Jack, you can't fool yourself forever, but make no mistake, you *will* get bored with her and you'll come to me for fun and excitement!" Jack rolls his eyes.

"Do you really think Jack doesn't know what he wants by now, or what trash to stay away from because of the stench?!" Bri asks.

Katie glares at her. "You *bi*—."

Jack grabs and jerks Katie's arm with a grip that *almost* hurts telling her. "*Don't* finish that sentence!" He seethes with anger and disgust; Katie jerks her arm free. "I do know what I want!" Jack looks at Bri still talking to Katie, "*And I want* what I have with Bri!"

Something snaps in Bri and she does something she normally wouldn't do. *Normally* she would've walked away, but this time...after recent events in Rome and now, combined with the past 'event,' she wanted *a little* payback.

She winks softly at David, then fully turns to Jack. Jack sees the hint of playfulness in her eyes as she gets closer to him. She keeps her eyes locked on his as she runs her hands under his shirt and feels his abs and pecs. He catches on with a big smile spreading across his face. He holds her face and pulls her in for a slow, seductive kiss. He wraps his arms around her, while her hands feel his toned back, under his shirt. He deepens the kiss, running his hand down to her bum and pulls her closer to him. Katie fills with more envy because she sees what everyone else sees: love *and* passion.

8

David mentions to Katie, "That's what you're missing, Katie, and you'll *never* find it the way you're going about it. Jack and I should know! We've had more than enough empty sex with various women before meeting her."

Jack says to Katie still looking at Bri, "I'll always choose passionate love with Bri over empty sex with any other woman *every time!*" Bri taps another kiss to his lips.

Bri, still looking at Jack, says, "David, would you please send Katie home? It's time to let go of the Katie I thought she was, and the friendship that ended 'once upon a nightmare.'" She turns to David and tells him, "My life, our lives, will move forward *without her in them.*"

Katie is shocked. She didn't think the consequences would be her deepest fear, because of Bri's big heart! She never considered there was a limit to how much Bri would take until that moment! David and Jack hide their relief. They watch Katie's surprised look, but her disappointment can be seen.

David steps closer to Katie. "You heard Bri. It's time for you to leave." He reaches into the inside pocket of his suit jacket and pulls out a commercial airline ticket, but hands it to one of the two men he's brought with. "These two gentlemen will make sure you don't miss your flight, *and* you get on the plane. Unless specifically invited and security knows about it, you'll not be allowed on The Worthington Estate; you're no longer welcome on our family's property, Ms. Barnes." Katie's glaring at Bri, so David gets closer to her to get her undivided attention, "Lastly, if you *ever* do anything that threatens *our wife* in *any* way, Jack and I will come after you and bury you legally, even financially, if we have to! *Am I clear?*" Katie was going to be defiant and not answer, but he lifts an eyebrow with anger on his face.

She rolls her eyes and says, "Yes."

"Good." David says.

He gestures for her to get into the car and he shuts the back door once Katie is inside. The two men climb into the car as well; one drives, while the other sits in back with Katie and they go to the airport in Edinburgh. David, Jack, and Bri crawl into their SUV bound for The Worthington Manor.

David holds her hand with a sweet smile, "Ready to go home, Mrs. Worthington?" He kisses her hand and watches her face light up being called 'Mrs. Worthington.'

She teases, "After the past month, I'm *so* ready to go to bed! I could sleep for a week!" She grins and adds a slightly exaggerated wink. David and Jack chuckle a bit.

CHAPTER 2

An Imperfectly Perfect Year Goes By

BriaLynn is in her corner office on the top floor of The Worthington Corporation Complex in Edinburgh, Scotland. She sits at her desk thinking about the past year or so. She first thinks of the evening at The Manor after she had David send Katie home and out of her life. The three of them were in the living room in David and Bri's quarters where she explained a few things to them regarding what she knew about being 'The Royal Consort.'

"I was told I would always have a choice, but like all good and bad choices there are good and bad consequences." She replies and they nod. "Can either of you think of what a very serious consequence would be if I didn't do this?" David and Jack were thinking, but Bri helps them get there faster, "Consider you already know I saw three of our children yet to be born and you both know you're each a father of one of them." They start to see where she is going. "I didn't know right away, but when it finally hit me who the father of the third child was, I realized that to refuse being 'The Royal Consort' would not only deny one of our children to be born into our family, but it would deny them their destiny." She looks at David and Jack as more things connect together and their eyebrows shoot up with that realization. She adds, "I would deny our family and The Worthington's as a whole, a part of their destiny as well!"

David caressed her cheek, then holds her jaw. "Even with all that said, I don't want you to feel compelled to go right into this. I want to be absolutely clear; I won't allow this to happen if you two are not in-love with each other. I mean that! All this won't work otherwise, alright?"

She smirked, "You say that as if you'd actually be able to deny The King his choice of a 'Royal Consort.'"

"You're forgetting there are rules Bri, there always has been. The spouse picks The Consort, or at the very least approves of the choice. I won't agree to this, nor sign anything, unless this is for love. Anything less will have an effect on all of us and our relationships with each other. Keep in mind there are other ways to have a baby if you and Herst don't fall in-love that will still bring us all your babies!"

She takes a deep breath and replies, "I keep having the beginning of the third chapter of Ecclesiastes play over and over in my head: To everything there is a season, and a time to every purpose..." she squeezes a hand of each of theirs.

"There's more but I can't tell either of you, not because I don't want to, but because it isn't time yet."

David asks, "So there's more to Herst and The Royal Consort?"

"Yes, and also in a roundabout way, not exactly." She grins at them.

Jack snorted a laugh. "That's fantastically clear!"

David is genuinely concerned about her safety. "Will you be in danger?"

She says plainly, "My Love, I'm considered a 'Direct Bloodline,' so my life will always be in danger until I'm not able to have children anymore." The guys reluctantly agree with that.

Bri's present thoughts go to a time with Jessica...it's right after David's proposal and before the wedding when she was talking with Henry in his study. It's the time when Jessica appears and gives Bri her memories back from when she was in a coma, including those with Herst. She is told:

'...The King needs your love to help him heal...ultimately helping to heal his family...You'll bond with The King in a way, like no one else, not even Jack or David, but your bonds and love for Jack and David won't be any less meaningful than the one with The King.'

She's never told them about the overwhelming feeling of evil that somehow surrounds the family and she's not sure how she's supposed to help The Heathherst Family to heal. *Healing with love is one thing, but how's she supposed to help them heal surrounded by some sort of evil?* She asks herself. She also remembers telling them that evening Katie was sent home and out of her life:

"I keep thinking I chose to come back to David knowing that it comes with a price; yet I was also told I would live an 'extraordinary life' and that would seem to include Jack and Herst. I need to honor my choice to come back, but Jessica has stressed numerous times to trust my sensitivity to the Spirit and let it guide me! I feel I need to continue in faith on this spiritual path I chose and trust there is a reason for all of it."

David asks, "With all that Katie's done, what good reason could there possibly be for what she did?!"

"If nothing else, I can let it continue to strengthen me! I can also trust that it will all work together to some greater purpose that we don't see yet and perhaps won't until after we die. There are lessons she needs to learn as well." She smiles. "One thing I know for sure is my faith hasn't wavered!" She wipes a tear about to fall. "I committed to this course of my life when I chose to come out of my coma. I not only owe it to myself to see it through; I especially owe it to our family and all of our children! I'm not ready to jump into anything with Herst, but I also have faith to start the journey by getting to know him, and trust I'll know which steps to take when I get to them."

Bri thinks back to when she and Katie first visited The United Kingdom of Provinces...when she first stepped onto The Worthington Estate as a tourist to stay at The Worthington Inn, well over a year ago. It feels like her life in Washington, D.C. was a different lifetime altogether.

 She turns back to her desk and looks at the scrapbook she had opened earlier to add a few things. She flips through it and smiles as she sees a picture of Artemis and remembers the pull she had to David, and still does, with it growing stronger every day. They both felt drawn towards each other, and yet they both fought against it.

There were loose pictures from the first Black-Tie Party. Photos of Katie and Bri, and a couple with Katie and James. There were glued photos on the page of her with Jack, who was her date that night. One of her favorite pictures is of her and David at the end of the evening, after their very heated face-off not too long before the picture was taken, only now she notices how in-love they both were when this was taken. She wonders how many couples have a photo to mark when they first admit their love to each other?

The more she contemplates her life and all the events leading up to her life in Newhaven, it's plain to see there has been a 'Divine Plan' with a 'Divine Hand' in it *all along*, because of the countless blessings in her life! Certain things being put into place centuries ago, for a life that really is uniquely hers...

Bri knew she had strong ancestral ties to Scotland and knew they reached and stretched throughout Europe; she just didn't know how deep. Nor did she know how serious the upper-class society takes their lineage *and all social classes take hers*! So much so, the people of Newhaven loved her when she married David and embraced her having a Noble Consort, and essentially marrying Jack, too. Those two being 'two peas in a pod,' or 'Two Musketeers,' have shown Bri how well it *can* work when true-love exists between Bri and David, as well as Jack and Bri, and a brotherly-best friend-bond between Jack and David. They assured her this would work because they trust that she loves each of them and her love for them is separate from the other. Their love and adoration for her only makes her love grow so much more for them; in fact, she's overflowing with love for them. David had noticed this 'surplus of love' again, which was one of his arguments for her to *at least consider* being The King's 'Royal Consort.'

Yes, she's *overflowing* with love for Jack and David, but she wonders if she'll have enough love for Herst... She contemplates this as she picks up the pendant on her necklace, running it back and forth along the chain. A smile spreads across her face when she pictures Herst and his dimples, then she catches herself in *how* she's smiling at her thoughts of Herst...*with affection?* Her heart squeezes for him. They've been seeing each other this last year, taking it slow and have gotten to know each other on their various low-key dates. Only now, she is wondering if she has unknowingly fallen in-love with him...

She remembers Herst is currently at a summit in Switzerland and would be back and forth to London for a few weeks; he wasn't sure about being able to see her. Herst didn't ask her to go or meet up with him during this time, which she suspects is because he has a 'party regular' there. This doesn't bother her because, even if they do decide to go down the road of her becoming 'The Royal Consort,' she won't sleep with him until it's official and she would feel like a hypocrite expecting him not to 'see' anyone else, when she has her relationships with Jack and David.

Bri hasn't really seen, nor met, Lawrence's parents, but she has seen enough in pictures through the media to know his looks come from The King Father's side of the family! Lawrence has brown, clean cut hair; sometimes there's a ruggedness with facial hair he only lets those closest to him see, but he isn't able to do that very often being king. He has *beautiful* blue-green eyes, and a slightly wider frame than David and Jack, and she assumes he's just as fit as the other two.

The Queen Mother has mousy stringy dark-brown hair, brown eyes that sit into slightly sunken sockets with dark circles. She has a 'skin and bones,' gaunt look, overall. Unfortunately, she can be difficult to look at and Bri scolds herself for thinking that way.

Bri turns back to the pages in her scrapbook. She finds a newspaper clipping about 'Heirloom Wool.' When Bri's twin girls were visiting at various times throughout this past year, Natty and Emmie liked to walk the shops in The Village. On one particular day, they had walked into a fabric shop and came across some wool samples that were oddly *super* soft. The shop owner told them it was 'Heirloom Wool' and it had its start right there in Newhaven. That was the actual beginning of the textile's comeback.

NEWHAVEN NEWS
CHRONICLES

Newhaven Heirloom Wool Makes a Comeback!

By: Francis Chapman

For those of you who are new to Newhaven, or those of us who don't remember our Newhaven history, here's a quick history lesson. 'Heirloom Wool' was first made in Newhaven from 'The Heirloom' breed of sheep, which was first found in The Scottish Highlands around the middle of the eighteenth century. Over the years, the process of 'Heirloom Wool' was perfected to make the already soft wool, feel more like liquid silk. They accomplished this with a highly guarded recipe that includes adding 'essential oils' at certain times during the process.

Foreign markets got ahold of the product and worked on their own processes, cutting steps to be able to mass produce it cheaper with a 'soft enough' synthesized product. Eventually, 'Heirloom Wool' went out of production and the textile mill closed soon after. That economic hardship had a long-

lasting effect on Newhaven in various ways ever since.

Being a journalist this day in age is cutthroat! I'm ashamed to admit that I freely climbed onboard the bashing of the American who married The Marquee of Newhaven. Many of us in the media, myself included, never stopped to consider that *maybe* she married the man she loves, who *happens* to be 'The Heir to The Duchy of Newhaven.' A marriage that discovered she's a rare 'Direct Bloodline.' With that discovery also came the shift of the tradition of 'The Noble Consort' to her, when she married 'The Marquee of Newhaven.' Some of us doubted an American would respect our long-held traditions, but we were wrong.

It was truly my honor to sit down with the *wonderful* Worthington Family and meet this American for myself. I learned *our 'American-*

Scot' was thinking of Newhaven and our economy before she was even a citizen!

Lord Newhaven planned just about every last detail of their wedding; except, he didn't pick her wedding dress. He thought she would look for a dress while still living in Washington, D.C., before moving to Newhaven only days before the wedding. He found out his fiancée had a much better idea! She would be inspired to contact a few dress shops in Newhaven to see if they would be interested in making her dress. Well, she ended up loving two dresses: one for the ceremony and one for the reception.

Now, these designers are forever linked to Newhaven history! Their shops have seen an increase in business that has had a rippling effect throughout The Duchy. Lady Newhaven allowed each dress to take residency in each designer's shop until The London Museum added them to their 'Newhaven History' section. Plus, the designers continue to dress Lady Newhaven for the various events she attends.

Her Grace, The Duchess of Newhaven tells me, "I already knew Bri would be *perfect* for David and would one day make a *fantastic* 'Duchess' beside him; however, when she explained how she went about finding her wedding dress, she was already *thinking* like a duchess!"

You may be asking yourself, 'what do wedding dresses have to do with 'Heirloom Wool?'' It simply shows Lady Newhaven has had the well-being of Newhaven on her mind from the beginning, so it shouldn't be a surprise what she's doing now! From the moment Lady Newhaven learned the history of 'Heirloom Wool,' her mind was thinking about how to bring it back!

Lady Newhaven explains to us, "Originally, my goal was to help tourism, even if it was just a small item to go along with its history. Best case, in time, we would grow the production of it. Lord Carlisle, being the 'financial guru' he is, saw the potential of this venture and wanted to be my business partner. He wanted to help me pull all this together, to get it up and running, and have it be so much more than a little souvenir. I'm so blessed he did, *and so is Newhaven!*"

 Lady Newhaven and Lord Carlisle researched and tracked down descendants from the *original* Heirloom sheep and found some were still in The Scottish Highlands, but also in The Midwest of the United States. "The timing seemed to be lining up because when we wanted to buy a farm and land for this in, or near, Kingsbury, there was property right next to The Worthington Estate already on the market!"

Lady Newhaven has formed *The New Beginnings Foundation* to work with *The Newhaven Textile Mill* in helping individuals who need a fresh start, or a 'new beginning,' to get back on their feet. Whether it's with employment, providing housing, rehab, counseling, and/or other services, *The New Beginnings Foundation* will provide a way to give someone their best chance at starting over.

 It's an interesting logo for The New Beginning's Foundation. There's a heart at the center of the lotus representing the desire someone would need to have, to want to start over and the bee represents the hard work that person will need to put forth. The lotus flower to show someone can bloom beautifully from the murkiest of waters, or troubled life.

As Lady Newhaven and Lord Carlisle pull all this together, they have the full support of Lord Newhaven. "I couldn't be prouder of the work Lady Newhaven and Lord Carlisle are doing for Newhaven!"

The Duke of Newhaven adds, "The intelligence of Lady Newhaven is astonishing! The Duchess and I are proud to have her in our family! Teaming up with Lord Carlisle, who's financial intellect is legendary, Newhaven couldn't be more fortunate to benefit from both of their talents!"

We should all be grateful for The Worthington Family's continued efforts to see the people of Newhaven grow and prosper!

Bri smiles after she reads that article and then thinks about their visit to the property next to The Worthington Estate. David joined her and Jack to look at the property that included a farm and a cottage house, which was bigger than the pictures made it look. Jack had pulled her aside and asked if he renovated it, would she want to make the house *their home*? She thought it was a great idea and happily agreed!

Jack has made some beautiful improvements to their home! She finds it's closer to a 'normal life' and a nice change of pace. He spared no expense with the structural updates and changes, but he does honor her request of simple decor. Jack understands her wanting to have a more relaxed environment, which suits them as a couple; he's told her he wants to be her 'calm in the storm.' Jack definitely is that, but the amazing thing is, when she's with him she also feels she can do anything, *even fly*!

The next thing Bri comes across in the scrapbook is a pressed rainbow rose. She reads the card that came with a dozen of them. It reads:

 I wasn't sure what your favorite flower and color is. Roses may be a bit cliché, but they're a classic! However, the rainbow color isn't typical either, just like you. ~ L

Bri remembers sending him a 'thank you' text for the beautiful roses telling him she absolutely loves roses and these were her new favorites! She also tells him she had heard of rainbow roses, or 'kaleidoscope roses,' but always thought they were dyed, which she *hates* dyed flowers. She is pleasantly surprised they are real and very beautiful!

Bri had no way of knowing her text meant a lot to Herst. He had wanted to do romantic things for her and with her, but he wasn't sure where to begin. He saw an ad for flowers on a website for something he was working on, and he was inspired to send her some. He felt good when she said rainbow roses were her new favorites. He also thought it was interesting that she loves all colors of roses, but she hates dyed flowers. Then again, she's the genuine article; it makes sense she wouldn't like dyed ones.

Bri reads her journal entry about the discussion the four of them had about 'The Royal Consort' the week after she sent Katie out of her life...

JOURNAL ENTRY

Herst came to visit today and the four of us sat down to talk about what he wants for a 'Royal Consort.' He explained that his brother, Prince Seth, and Queen Genevieve fell in-love when they were sixteen and fifteen. The arranged marriage of Prince Lawrence to Lady Genevieve came as a surprise for all three of them, which caused heartache that he is sure was a huge reason why his mother arranged the marriage in the first place.

Watching Seth and Genevieve all this time, Herst knew his parents were wrong to do what they did, so he encouraged Seth and Genevieve to continue in their relationship. King Lawrence went as far as making Prince Seth, Queen Genevieve's 'royal consort' because being forced into an arranged marriage with the woman his brother loves, well, there's no way that arrangement would work! Herst told Genevieve and Seth he'd find love with the woman he'd choose to be his 'Royal Consort.'

Herst said he was intrigued by the relationships I have with Jack and David. It was obvious to anyone that not only was I madly in-love with David, but I was also crazy in-love with Jack! Herst told me he doesn't expect me to blindly go into this, we need to get to know each other first. If it ends up where there's only friendship, no hard feelings. If we do fall in-love, and I agree, he'll officially make me The Royal Consort.

I told him that was a great start, but there's something additional we needed to discuss: a baby, or in other words, his heir, 'THE Heir.' I needed to know if he expected me to leave my baby behind with him at The London Palace to be raised by a nanny? He quickly said, "Absolutely not!" He must've seen the relief on my face because he told me he'd want his baby to be with their mother and any other siblings, "to grow up and be raised together." There was also no way he'd allow his parents to have any influence on his child, especially his mother, The Queen Mother! It'd be alright with him if his child never knew their grandparents!

I asked him if the order of babies mattered because David and I were just letting things happen as they may. Herst said he doesn't expect David and I to change things for him, especially when we haven't figured out what kind of relationship this will be: hopefully, love, but it could just be a great friendship with a baby (like invitro). Jack suggested that his baby with me would come after one with Herst, because if we do this, there's a two-year-deadline with 'The Royal Consort.' I would be expected to conceive within two years, or the title is essentially revoked. Herst told me not to worry about that and we could discuss additional time if it became necessary. A time limit was set long ago allowing a previous king to move on to the next woman if his current Royal Consort didn't bear a son.

I then asked him how Queen Genevieve feels about all of this. I remember his sweet smile as he held my hand telling me she's family and he loves her, just as he loves Seth and Abby.' Genevieve and Herst have a mutual respect and family love for each other, but they're hoping to correct their arranged marriage in a way that all of them can be happy. I worry about all this imploding...then again, if this could work, this just might be the way...with the now 'Three Musketeers'...!

P.S. Later, I would tell Jack that I wasn't comfortable pushing him out and making him last in line for a baby. He said he'll enjoy each baby we have in our family. I'll never forget his megawatt smile as he says, "We're saving the best for last!" But that's Jack for you! One of the many reasons I love that man! And one of the many reasons why I love David is how much he wants me to be loved...and he only wants me to do this with Herst if we're in-love with each other. He is absolutely adamant that this is nothing less than true-love, or it won't work! He said I needed to open up my heart; to be open to follow this wherever it goes...like I did with Jack.

Part of the next journal entry catches her eye...

JOURNAL ENTRY

David reminded me today that he doesn't lose anything when I love Jack, just as Jack doesn't lose anything when I love David; and they won't lose anything if I were to love Herst. He says it's actually the opposite! They will gain more love when I love all three of them; because my heart just continues to grow in love.

A nagging concern is time...There's only so much time in a day, and a lot of things to do; however, that list will only get longer as I learn more of the duties with The Duchy... I'm having Luke 12:48 come to mind a lot.

"For unto whomsoever much is given, of him shall much be required."

With the love I have for David and Jack, and the duties that will come don't feel they're so much requirements as the need to do right by the people...as well as David and Jack...and our family. Then I felt the earlier verse change just a bit:

"When one has a privileged life, one has a much-privileged responsibility to the people."

Anyone in the public eye should be held to those words.

Bri stares out the window, lost in thought again, when Herst's text chimes on her cell phone. It startles her a little, snapping her out of her memories.

> Herst: "I'd like to come see you again! I've missed you! If I arrange a dinner at The Estate this weekend, would you join me?"
>
> Bri: "I'd love to and I've missed you, too! But our multi-city European tour is starting tomorrow. Raincheck?"
>
> H: "Certainly!"
>
> H: "Better yet, would you want to meet up and we can do something together?"
>
> B: "Absolutely! I love spending time with you!"

He smiles when he reads that and it makes him that much more determined to put something wonderful together. He has been wanting to get serious about their relationship and when he mentioned this to his brother, Seth thinks he's already fallen in-love with Bri. Herst has been thinking hard about that... He thinks of a particular woman, Dominique, he has been seeing most often at the various parties he attends. She told him at their visit she was getting married and moving somewhere in the South of France. As they stood next to each other and talked, there was an empty feeling. He wants something meaningful, lasting...he *needs* to talk to BriaLynn to see where she might be at in her decision to become 'The Royal Consort.'

> H: "If you're okay with it, I'll call and talk with David and Gabriel about your itinerary."
>
> B: "Sounds good. Can't wait to see you!"

21

H: "I can't wait to see you!"

Bri puts her phone down, just as David comes in with his things. "Ready to go, Beautiful?"

Bri smiles at him, then looks at the clock. "*Wow!*" She exhales as she stands up to gather up her things. She tells him, "Herst just texted and said he wants to meet up with me on our 'European Tour.' He said he'll reach out to you and Gabriel."

"I think we can arrange something..." he smirks.

She rolls her eyes with a smile. "I'm curious to see what he has up his sleeve...dinner somewhere fancy, or in the middle of a park, or the top of a mountain..." she giggles.

David laughs. "Have any requests I can steer him towards?"

She gives him a determined look. "*Don't you dare!* You know I'll be happy with whatever *he* plans, as long as *he* plans it!" She picks up her bags.

"I know, but..." he points to his lips, "you may need to seal my lips shut with a kiss..." smiling his beautiful smile that works on her. She walks over to him, drops her things, and cups his face, then gives him her best, passionate, and hottest kiss...*aaand* it works a little *too* well.

He pulls back just enough to say, "We either leave now or you'll be naked in less than thirty seconds!"

He didn't care one way or the other. Mary had left for the day, not too long after everyone else, so they were all alone on their floor. If not here, they'll pick up where they left off when they get home.

"I'm ready to go!" She smirks pulling away to get her things. He takes her computer bag for her, adding it to the shoulder where he already has his. He holds her hand, lacing their fingers as they leave.

In the car, he holds her hand and kisses it every now and then; here and there he runs his lips across the soft skin of her hand just to hear her breath catch. When they pull up to The Manor, Bri gets out of the car after David and they walk inside together. Everyone is gathering in the dining room, but when Bri starts to follow, David pulls her back.

"Oh no, Mrs. Worthington! *We'll* be fashionably late!" He doesn't take her up to their quarters, but to The Billiards Room and locks the door.

Bri gasps and whispers, "Seriously? Here?" David doesn't say a word, backing her towards the pool table with a smoldering look...

David and Bri join the others and no one even noticed their late arrival, *except Jack*. He's smirking with a quiet chuckle leaning over to kiss Bri on her cheek.

CHAPTER 3

Imperfectly Perfect Royal Getaway

David, Bri, and Jack spend the next week-and-a-half traveling Europe. Towards the end of the tour, Herst flies Bri to Budapest, Hungary, to meet up with him. He shows her around after a foreign policy meeting. As they walk around, Bri notices all the dreamy eyes and pointing with whispers, even giggles when 'King Lawrence' acknowledges them with a friendly nod and smile. Bri is surprised when she realizes they're mostly whispering about him *and her.*

Bri has gotten good at having a friendly smile glued on, but she has also gotten good at being in the moment with whoever she is with at the time. Herst senses she isn't totally relaxed and has learned holding her hand seems to help calm her. Whenever he holds her hand, he tucks her arm up under his, making her somehow feel better, safer, *protected.* Every so often he would squeeze her hand and arm, helping Bri relax into all this even more.

Later that afternoon, Bri shares her smoothie before they go to the airport. Lawrence flies them to a small Mediterranean island between Italy and France to stay at a beachfront hotel. He found this place on his own for them to have more quality and private time together. He is hoping to find the courage to tell her he wants to work towards her becoming 'The Royal Consort.'

"There's a hotel that has an almost complete five-star review. I looked for five-star reviews, but there just wasn't any on this island."

Bri could tell he was nervous. "Herst, *relax.*" She holds his cheek. "To me and the rest of us commoners, a four-and-a-half star is still a five-star rating because *no one* can please *everyone* with everything; it just isn't realistic."

He gives a 'that's true' facial expression. He takes her hand that's holding his cheek and kisses the palm of it, giving her a nice smile as the helicopter comes around, bringing the beach front of the hotel into view.

Bri turns to the window and asks with excitement, "Is this it?!"

He leans over to see out the window. "That looks like the 'Sunset Paradise' from the pictures."

"Lawrence! This place is *fantastic!*" She teases with his accent. He quietly chuckles as the pilot announces they're about to land.

 Lawrence points to a cabana on the other side of some trees. "That must be for us. I was hoping to watch a sunset together while we're here." He tells her. She sees there's a rug under the canopy with a bed and large pillows.

Bri looks at her watch. "We should be able to do that."

"We have a few days, My Darling."

"Really?! How'd you swing that, *Your Majesty?!*"

He laughs. "I believe you just answered that yourself." He winks. "Plus, Jack is helping us out by covering for you. We'll meet up with them at the airport in Téseau, France."

When they land, they're greeted by hotel staff, which Bri would be used to, except there are three times as many than when she travels with David or Jack! She whispers to Herst, "*Are all these people really necessary?*"

He whispers back surprised, "*This doesn't happen when you travel?!*"

"Yeah, but there's usually only about a third of what's here!" She quietly replies.

"Really?"

"Herst, seriously," she gestures around, "there are people just standing around? They must have better things to do than watch us walk!"

"You can't possibly *not* understand?" He gives her a skeptical look.

"*Oh, I do!* And *clearly* they haven't met you, or they would've stayed at their posts!" She teases. "Maybe we just need to get the word out that you're not *that* exciting."

"Oh-ho!" He laughs. "Is that your perception?"

"Of course not! And therein lies the problem...no one else would believe it either!" She gives him a saucy wink. He chuckles and shakes his head a bit.

When they enter their hotel suite, there are two master bedrooms. "Which one would you like?" He asks and she takes a look around as he has hotel staff pause inside the living room for a moment.

"These are both the same, Herst." She says, but he's been watching her and it seems she does favor one over the other. He has her things brought to the room that has an all ocean view out its floor to ceiling windows. The other room overlooks the resort in the corner of its floor to ceiling windows, but the rest is the same ocean view as the other room.

"You want me to have this room?" She asks.

"You seem to favor this one." He smirks.

"I do?" She's surprised.

"I'm learning 'the art of you,' Darling." He says. "There's a swimsuit hanging in the bathroom for you," he throws his thumb over his shoulder, "I'll get changed, too, and then we'll go out to the cabana."

She smiles. "Interesting, isn't it?"

His eyebrows come together as he asks, "What's that?"

"You already had a swimsuit for me in *this* bathroom..."

"Ha-ha! No, Darling. I'm *hoping* the right swimwear is in there, so you may want to check right away."

She goes to the bathroom and checks. She's relieved when she sees a one-piece. She stays inside the bathroom and says, "We're good!"

"*Fantastic!*" He tells her and he leaves to go to his room to change.

She looks at her swimsuit and the top third of the swimsuit, her chest, is royal blue that twists in the middle, and the rest of the two-thirds is black. It also has thick straps, rather than spaghetti straps. When she's ready to put it on, she is pleased to find it has a bra built inside. That, with the thicker straps, will help give her the support she likes to have. Then there is a black, short sleeve, soft fabric cover-up dress she puts on. She sees the flip flops and smiles as she puts them on thinking, *He thought of everything.* She walks out into the living room where he's waiting for her. She watches a huge smile spread across his face when he sees her.

"I can't believe you thought of sandals!" She smiles. "Thank you." She gestures her beach attire. "I'm glad you knew to get a one-piece, or a tankini would've worked, too."

"I didn't, the one piece is for me!" He bites his lower lip and shows some of his white teeth.

"Oh, *really?*" She giggles.

He walks over to her. "*Darling,* I may be 'The King,' but as you're well aware I'm still a man and seeing you in a one-piece will be hard enough, but a bikini..." He steps behind her. "Well," he runs his hands down her shoulders and arms, "let's just say I know my limits and I'm trying to honor your request of nothing physical until you're officially mine to have." He kisses just under her ear. He hears a light gasp and her breath catch; he smiles to himself. He steps back around to face her again with a knowing smile.

He hands her a straw hat and her sunglasses. "I don't want to scare you, but even though this is supposed to be a private beach, we can never be too sure about the paparazzi. I'm perfectly happy to be photographed with you, and David and Jack are fully aware of that possibility. I believe Jack's words were, 'Better to happen when 'The King' is actually enjoying himself on holiday!'"

She softly laughs, then smiles sweetly at him. "My *only* reservation with being photographed together is that I don't want either of us to feel pressured one way or the other. It *has to be* our choice and David's right; *it has to be* for love, or it won't work, because it won't last." She smiles genuinely and he smiles back, caressing her cheek.

"Agreed." He cups her cheek. "And I'd like to talk to you about that..." He takes her hand and they walk out the patio door of their suite and out to the beach. He stops them. "Don't say anything yet, but I'd like to change our relationship status to something more...'Royal Consort' focused."

She doesn't answer but looks out at the horizon...where the ocean meets the sky. The sun was getting low and turning the sky shades of orange with the sunset colors glistening on the water; small waves were lapping along the shore. They were on a private section of the beach, away from other guests, with large boulders and thick trees blocking the resort from their view and the view of them from the other guests. To the other direction is bare land and beach with a privacy fence covered in green foliage and more boulders.

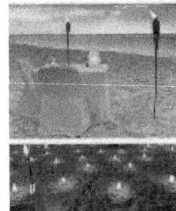 They walked around the cabana and there was a dinner for two set up in front of it. Bri quietly gasps at the beauty of it. A candle was lit in the middle of the table, but the tiki lights scattered around it and the cabana were being lit, along with tea lights in the sand, all creating more of a romantic feel.

"This is so beautifully romantic!" She kisses his cheek and his arm goes around her waist. "Thank you!" He gives her a small smile and she pauses a moment, seeing love in his eyes for her and her heart squeezes.

A young gentleman pulls out her chair for her and she sits as Herst sits next to her. His guard is down, and she still sees the love in his eyes for her as he reaches to take her hand and lightly laces their fingers in an upward angle on the table. They stay like that, staring into each other's eyes until the food comes and breaks 'the spell.'

They eat for a minute before Herst asks, "So, Bri, what would be something no one would ever be able to guess about you." He takes a drink of his wine.

"*Ooo*, I don't know if you're ready for that answer." She smiles as she takes another bite.

"You're not serious?! After all this time?!" He's surprised. "We've been seeing each other for a year and it feels like we've talked about everything else!"

"I *am* serious!" She laughs. "It's been a year because we've gotten to know each other, plus our schedules have been difficult to line up visits. Besides, you keep me from The Palace, so we talk *a lot* by phone, videoconference calls, or text messaging!"

He's chuckling some more. "Okay, I'll give you that, but now I'm *very* curious about your answer to that question!"

"You just said you wanted to change our relationship status, but we've only been getting to know each other; *we haven't even kissed yet*! Wouldn't that suggest maybe there's nothing really between us?" She asks him.

He catches the twinkle of playfulness in her gaze. He says, "Oh, I think you know as well as I do there's *a lot* between us." He smiles a beautiful smile with his dimples, the one that makes her melt. She holds his gaze as she takes a drink of her water. He studies her trying to think of what to say to get her to spill more about herself. "Wouldn't it bring us closer together to know something that I'm assuming is *so personal*, it's a secret to almost everyone else? It would be a great start to taking our relationship to a deeper level."

"Then wouldn't you know how fond I am of you when I *finally* share it with you?" She grins.

He teases being hurt, "You mean you're not fond of me *now?*"

"Touché!" She giggles. "*Fine*, then. *You first!*" She points with her finger but it's more with her water glass. "And it better be *super* good for me to reveal mine!" His eyebrow raises and she smirks putting the glass to her lips, "Just saying..." she adds before taking a drink.

He simply states. "I hate being king."

Bri spits out her water, spraying Herst. "Oh my gosh," she's embarrassed putting her glass down, wiping her mouth with her napkin. "I'm *so* sorry!" He stands up to dry himself off with his napkin. "I did *NOT* see that coming!" She gets up and steps over to him, wiping his face with her napkin.

He watches her and she pauses when she sees him studying at her. She feels his arm wrap around her waist and his other hand holds her hand that's wiping the water from his face.

He has a faint playful look on his face as he says, "I think the only way to make this right is for *you* to kiss *me!*" He playfully hugs her a little tighter.

She smiles playfully back. "How do you figure?!"

"*That*, or I'll have to get *you* wet," he tips his head to the water with a mischievous grin, "to even the score."

She looks towards the water and back at him again. "You know, if you really wanted to kiss me you could've *long before now...*"

"As you pointed out, we were getting to know each other. Maybe I was waiting to see if you were interested in taking this relationship further?" He tells her.

"You seriously expect me to believe that line?! Mister *I always get what I want?*!" She retorts.

He smirks. "This *is* getting what I want!"

She studies him, then purses her lips as she smiles getting an idea... She wraps her arms around his neck, with one hand going up into his hair and brings his head down to hers, but she softly kisses the corner of his mouth. She hugs him expecting him to do what he does; he pulls back and looks at her smirky smile. She goes to step away, but he holds firmer.

"Oh, no, Darling! That wasn't a kiss, it was more of a peck."

"What?" She asks coyly. "You said *a kiss* would make this right."

"That, right there," he points to her face, "tells me you know *exactly* what kind of kiss I was referring to in the first place!"

"You've made it clear you always get what you want, so not specifying *exactly what you wanted*," she says with his accent, "leaves it up to me to decide..." she gives him a pointed look challenging him.

He finds his attraction growing for her, along with his need to win. "Making amends means I should feel how sorry you are, or your apology would be empty, would it not?"

He feels her surrender and he surprises himself with how much more attracted he is to that. She runs her hand into his hair at the back of his head again. She pulls his head down and meets his lips in what starts as a soft, sweet kiss, but they feel the passion starting to heat up. Her arms wrap around his waist and he moves his hand to the back of her head to keep them kissing; he wasn't ready to stop. The passion is growing hotter and hotter to where she *has to* break the kiss and they're out of breath!

"That," he has a cocky smile, "was a *great* amends!"

She rolls her eyes, smiling and shaking her head a little. "Shall we finish eating?" He nods with a soft smile and they take their seats.

When they finish eating, they walk over to the cabana and crawl onto the bed. He lays on his side, propped up on his arm; she sits so she can look directly at him.

"Alright, Ace," she exhales, "out with it!"

He raises his eyebrow. "Abby and Gen call me Lawrence; Seth goes back and forth between Lawrence and Herst. And honestly, you can call me anything you'd like..."

She giggles. "You sound like David." With an apologetic, sweet smile, she replies, "It's hard to call you 'Herst.'"

"Really? Why?" He wonders.

She shrugs. "It's fine for David and Jack, but for me I feel like have to force it out." She doesn't say that it makes her think of a coffin carrying hearse.

"Alright, then why, 'Ace?'"

She smiles wide. "You're absolutely wonderful, excellent, and *brilliant* even!" She teases with his accent again and he chuckles. "An 'ace' can be a high or low card, and it's also used as a 'wild card,' making any hand better!" She sees people walking around them, cleaning up. When they are all alone again, she asks, "So, I can call you *anything* I'd like?" She raises her eyebrow.

He matches her eyebrow and cautiously replies, "*Yyyeeesss...*"

"So 'Sweetheart,' 'Honey,' I can call you? Then there's 'Darling,'"

"*Anything.* But I have to admit, 'Ace' is quickly growing on me since no one I know has that nickname." He runs thumb along her lower lip. "*And* I like the thought of being a 'wild card.'"

She lightly laughs. "Well, pet names may have to wait until we're official, so I won't get into trouble addressing you in such a casual way."

"And what if that's what *I* want?" He smirks.

"Oh-ho!" She laughs, a sound he loves to hear. "Are you seriously playing the '*I'm The King*' card with me again or is it '*I get what I want*' card?!"

"*For* you, Darling! Playing either card *for you*!" He teases her.

She kisses him firmly. "For the record, I love hearing you call me 'darling' with *your* accent!"

"Noted!" He taps another kiss to her lips.

"Now, as I was saying, *Ace*, you need to explain your comment a little bit ago that caught me by complete surprise."

"Alright, but this could take a while." He admits.

She happily smiles and lays on her side to get comfortable, propping herself up on her arm, too. He puts up a finger looking around at those cleaning up. He looks at her and smiles; feeling so good when he's with her...*he* feels safe enough to tell her anything! '*And now to be able to kiss her...everything is perfect!*' He thinks to himself.

They watch the others walk away. When it's just the two of them again, she says, "You're on, Handsome!"

He exhales with a whistle. "Answering that question is a matter of where to begin, Bri." He thinks about it. "A small history lesson: my grandfather stole the kingdom from his older brother. He raised my father to be cruel and ruthless; my father modeled himself after the more horrible kings of our past. The Duke of Devonridge, my mother's paternal uncle, was *instrumental* in the overthrow. My grandfather 'encouraged' the marriage of my father to my mother, the niece of The Duke. My father didn't care because he couldn't marry the commoner he wanted to marry...*at least not directly*—."

"Ah, *she* became your father's 'Royal Consort.'" Bri notes.

He nods. "But she wasn't 'The Royal Consort' long before she died."

Bri sadly replies, "How sad?"

He agrees. "My brother, sister, and I were raised by two very loveless people, but somehow we managed to be some of that love and support for each other." He looks at Bri for a long moment. "I sometimes wonder if his Royal Consort lived longer, would he have been a different father? Then again, if they would've had children, then maybe nothing would've changed for us

32

anyhow? He would've had a family with her, separate from us." He feels the end of a ringlet of her hair. "*So soft...*" he whispers to himself.

"I sense you're holding something back..." She smiles sweetly, running a hand in his brown hair and he closes his eyes to the feeling of it. "It's okay if you are, you'll tell me when you're ready." He furrows his eyebrows as he opens his eyes to look at her. "*Lawrence, no judgements.* I promise you! Hearing things like your father being raised 'cruel and ruthless' makes me sad on one hand, but curious about this man before me because *thankfully* his parents have failed raising him that way! You talk about your mother most, so it makes me think she's the cruelest of the two."

There is a sadness in his voice. "My parents stepped down so that Gen and I could rule, but Mother hasn't really stepped down. I'm the one caught in the middle between her need for power and control, and my siblings...it's just all so tiring because it's not me, or at least it's not 'The King' I want to be..." He takes a deep breath.

"Caught in the middle?" Bri urges him to say more.

He reaches for the lock of her hair again to feel the softness in his fingers. "Essentially, she uses Seth and Abby to make me do what she wants by threatening to hurt them."

She reaches for his hand and lays her hand on top of his. "For what it's worth, I'm sorry for what you, Abby, and Seth went through and are going through."

He gives her a weak smile. "It wasn't your fault."

"No, but I want to do everything I can to help you see you can trust me. No judgements. Just compassion and—." She stops herself, trying to hide her embarrassment of almost saying 'love,' but she's also surprised that she almost said it...then she realizes and thinks to herself, '*It's because I feel it?!*'

"What?" He smiles encouraging her to say it, but she quickly shakes her head.

She moves on. "You know my rule with Jack and David is 'what happens behind bedroom doors, stays behind bedroom doors.' I feel that's something you need to hear..."

He nods. "It is." He'll let her change direction *this time*. "David and Jack have some idea, but that's as far as I've gotten. Not that I didn't trust them—."

"You wanted a disconnect when you were with them. You wanted to keep them separate from that part of your life, just as you keep me away from The Palace." She follows along.

He studies her, almost in awe of her, "*Right...*" He gives her a little smile and kisses her hand again. He continues to study her, amazed at how perceptive she is and incredibly genuine.

"Now," she tells him, "I'll give you some relief *for the moment* and we can shift the focus to me."

He laughs. "Go on!"

Bri tells Lawrence her story. They somehow ended up with her telling him how she had fallen in-love with David, how she felt when David explained Jack being her Noble Consort. "Marrying David was, and is, the crucial piece because without him, Jack, *nor you*, would be romantically in my life.

"*That* definitely makes sense!" He agrees. They always talk for hours because he's so easy to talk to and he feels the same way about her. He comments, "I can't imagine going through what you three went through with Antonio!"

"It was Jack and David who had to wait around for three days, not knowing if I was going to live or die, until I actually woke up. To me, that would've been the hardest part!"

"Any lasting effects like droopiness, twitches, or whatever?" He teases.

"Ha-ha! No, nothing like that." She says, staring out at the last bit of the setting sun.

"Then like what?" He asks.

She looks back to him and scrunches her eyebrows together in confusion, "What do you mean?"

"You said, 'nothing like that,' so is there something?" There's silence as she contemplates telling him. "Bri," he pulls her chin so he could see all of her face, "keeping secrets goes both ways, whether we're, as you say, 'behind bedroom doors' or not, your secrets *are* safe with me. And I can stand up to a lot of torture!" She lightly laughs, knowing that was meant for humor, but she senses there's more truth to it. "You have to know by now I'll protect those I love and care about, *including* their secrets."

"I do, it's just that we've never really discussed spirits before." She studies him a moment... "Jack and David were open to the spirit world...*are you?*"

"Like...do I believe in Heaven?"

"Well, I *do* know that already!" She lightly giggles. "We covered that some time ago, that you believe in God and Christ; that the challenges we face are for a reason. What I'm asking is more, do you believe someone can actually see and talk to spirits."

"I guess I never really thought about it. If they honestly could see them, I think it'd be pretty fantastic!" He tells her.

He looks at her expectantly. She closes her eyes and blurts out fast, "*I can see spirits and ghosts.*" She braces herself for his reaction.

"Really?!" He asks, only he goes quiet as he thinks about what she said.

Her eyes pop open when he doesn't say anything more. She nervously says to him, "Ace, I need you to say more..."

He has a huge smile spreading across his face. "Bri, that has to be the most *fantastic* thing I've *ever* heard! How does it work?"

She's relieved and explains, "When I was in a coma, a messenger, Jessica, told me that since I was 'touched by death,' I had two options: stay and become a messenger like her, and thus *ending* my mortal life; *or* I could return, but returning would come with a price, as well as some gifts. Obviously, I returned and while the price isn't completely known yet, nor all the gifts; one thing is for certain, I'm able to see spirits. As for those other 'gifts,' I have no idea what that 'power' entails, nor to what extent...I only know that I have power over spirits and I've gotten more empathic, which is frustrating because it's hard to control the tears. *Oh!* And love somehow controls everything."

"*Love?*" He asks.

She smiles so lovingly at him, *his* heart squeezes. His question is innocent, yet it tells her he has been told by his parents, probably more his mother, something like 'love is a weakness,' to keep him under her control. *Which means...*she thinks to herself...*he may still need to learn that true, abiding love is a* powerful *strength...*

"Lawrence, my guess is you were probably told that love is a weakness...a crutch that makes you vulnerable to outside influences." She sees him nod, but he's staring out at the water. "What they don't know is that when genuine love exists between two people, that true and pure love solidifies their bond." She takes a deep breath. "When I was with Jessica, I can remember hearing, 'The love of a true mother' which is 'pure love,' and somehow, I possess this 'pure love'...so, I've surmised thus far that 'pure love' controls my power because of the compassion and understanding I feel reinforced by my empathic power..." He looks back to her as she says, "Not wanting to force people to do what I want them to do, yet wanting to help and protect others, there's a fine line not to cross in order to know the precise moment of when to intervene." She takes another deep breath. "The love between David and me, as well as Jack and me, only makes our love grow, *binding us together.*"

Lawrence scrunches his eyebrows together as he thinks about what she just said... "*How* would it bind?"

"Picture two people standing together, encouraging, and supporting one another; however, they're still two individuals. But what happens if you take those two people and wrap them together with something simple, like regular tape. They're a little stronger together and have a *type* of bond, like working together for the same company or teaming up for a project or some sort of collaboration partnership—."

"Seems like a lot of marriages." Lawrence inserts. She has a facial expression of 'true' expression as she nods.

She continues, "Now, if we use, say, duct tape and secure them to a post, those two people would be strongly bound, working as one unit; loyalty is a strong bond. However, if there is pure, true, and adoring love between them, it would create such a solidifying kind of bond that one could only get by soldering, or melting, two pieces of metal together. *They're actually two halves of the same relationship, solidified as one;* and work together *as one!*"

"If true love is as powerful of a bond as you say, then it brings new meaning to the phrase 'when two become one!'" He lovingly looks at her. "The love that's obviously in your heart that's seen when you look at David and Jack the way you do..." he touches her cheek with the side of his finger, "because it's the love I see in them right now." Her eyes get teary as she realizes the significance in that statement...even though they haven't said, 'I love you' to each other, yet, he *sees* the love in her eyes for him.

She slightly shifts the conversation. "I *wish* I always had that kind of love to express. I love my girls more than words can describe; however, I've always felt like I had more love to give but it was locked up tight and I didn't have the key to unlock it..." She looks out to the ocean thinking about how different it is now with David and Jack; how all this added love has made her heart grow *and it continues to grow...* She doesn't hear Lawrence right away.

"Bri?" He tucks a strand of hair behind her ear to get her attention. "What came into your mind just now?"

She smiles sweetly. "That falling madly in-love with David was the key. It unlocked the love that has me crazy in-love with Jack, which all that love has grown to encompass——." She freezes and looks past his shoulder.

Lawrence catches it and squeezes her hand for her to look at him. "I rather like the sound of your heart opening up to love me..." He kisses her hand and looks adoringly at her.

She gives him a little smile and feels she needs to explain more. "What drives almost every person on this planet is to be needed, wanted, to be desired, *to be loved-unconditionally.* Unfortunately, the fear of being alone can be so loud for a lot of people, they make quick and hasty decisions because of that fear and possibly desperation. Sadly, to be wanted and desired is depicted with sex, which confuses people and they interchange love and lust. Just look at how 'The Goddess of Love' is depicted! Lustful, *not loving.* What people fail to understand is what actually binds and keeps people solidly bound together is to be loved and accepted without judgement for who they are, but also encourages them to be better and reach their potential; all of which comes from unconditional love! That someone knows them inside and out, all the good *and all the bad,* and *still* wants them in their life; 'warts and all.' In today's judgmental world, that's hard to come by and it takes time, but add sex into the mix and lust confuses things!" She looks at him and asks, "When you think of the women you've been with and then think of me, what differences come to mind?"

"You're a lady," he cups her cheek, "I see a chance at forever..." He gives her a sweet smile. "Sadly, I really didn't have an interest in anything more than the physical with the others."

She softly nods. "We're surrounded by the media constantly substituting lust for love and there's a *huge* difference between being 'a play toy' versus 'a keepsake!' If a woman truly values herself, she won't present herself as 'a play toy' because she would want to be treasured as 'a keepsake.'" She kisses him a little more than a tap of their lips.

"That's true. You and the women who are 'keepsakes' are truly beautiful and timeless on multiple levels!" He cups her cheek and she softly smiles.

"There are women out there that demand to be treated as men's equals. Personally, I want to be treated better than that!" She tells him. "I don't want to be considered just 'one of the guys.' I like being a woman!"

He softly laughs. "I like that you're a woman, too!"

She snorts a little laugh. "I like how we're all different and we should embrace it!" She takes a deep breath, then continues, "Another piece is that people don't know what 'true-love' is or they don't believe in it, *perhaps a little of both*, so they settle; being driven by that fear of being alone for the rest of their life; which can be overwhelming!"

"Begging the question: if a person can't stand being alone with themselves, how can they expect someone to *want* to be in their company, let alone married to them?" He asks.

"Great point!" She replies. "That kind of alone, is different. A person may take time for themselves to find themselves, to figure out what direction they want to go with their life, and some may do so to heal from something that has happened to them. That kind of alone is different because it isn't meant to be permanent." She senses Jessica near her and turns to find her standing at the end of the bed; Lawrence thinks she's looking out at the water.

Jessica encourages her, "Keep going, Bri. He needs to hear it all to help him more later."

She also explains, "After a failed marriage or relationship, some people will get to the point where they convince themselves they're happier alone." She raises her hand. "They feel they're protecting themselves from making another mistake, or getting hurt, or whichever reason, leading to another failed relationship."

"*Fear* being the root of all that as well." Lawrence adds.

"Fear *is* an incredibly powerful emotion!" She states. "It can do many things, even convince us true-love doesn't exist, or is super rare, or whatever limitation someone wants to put on it. *Although* hope can be paralyzing, too."

He tells Bri, "Seeing Seth and Genevieve all these years, and now you with David and Jack, it's *obvious* true-love exists."

"And you're drawn to that, to me, because you're drawn to it like every other person...*you want to be loved unconditionally*!" She shifts back to him. "A mother is where someone should feel true and pure love first, but sadly, there are many children who never feel that kind of love from their mothers." She raises her hand again." I suspect one reason is because some babies are not conceived between two people who *truly and deeply* love each other. The world not only teaches love is *conditional* but having sex whenever is okay between two consenting adults, while casually overlooking the chances of some *really* significant consequences, including emotionally." She puts her hand on his cheek. "I don't think even a little prince, destined to be king, felt the love he should've felt from his mother growing up." He puts his hand on top of hers and closes his eyes. She adds, "Unconditional love is where someone feels safe to reveal their hopes and dreams, even their deepest and darkest secrets, without fear of judgement; without being made to feel dumb, stupid, or inadequate in *any* way. Love encourages, uplifts, and perseveres through the many challenges of life. Once we find it, we never want to live without *them* again! *True love is purest when the love is truly unconditional*."

He holds her cheek as he now understands the deeper meaning of waiting to have sex. "That's why you want to wait until we're officially together before we're *intimately* together! Because the only way to make sure lust isn't getting in the way, or driving our relationship, is to keep it out of the initial equation altogether!"

She smiles lovingly. "And letting love grow and thrive, if it's going to at all, without the murkiness and fog that lust would bring into it."

Lawrence stares at her and holds her hand. "You're amazing, BriaLynn." He smiles and squeezes her hand a little, feeling his love reaching deeper in his heart for her. "What happened that Jeff let you walk away?"

"It wasn't like that exactly. We were good friends, but there wasn't any adoring love. We dated and marriage seemed like the next 'logical' step. When it's said a man will change for only one person, the woman he truly loves, it's true! Plus, I didn't like myself through his eyes." She takes a deep breath. "With Jack and David, I feel loved, adored, worth *everything* to them. If I'm upset with them or they're upset with me, we don't twist it around in our heads to make things out to be worse than they are. They don't make me out in their minds to be a mean, spiteful person. No matter how upset we may be, love *always* wins out! I *hated* how Jeff chose to see me when he was upset with me or in a bad mood; it was frustrating and expressing frustration is never a pretty look for anyone, *including myself!*" She admits. "I know this might sound weird, but when he was in a sort of 'foul mood,' I got to the point where I could sense darkness around him. It was uncomfortable to be around him and I tried to keep my distance whenever I could. Now when it was a normal day, he was fine. He really is a good guy and now, being with the right person, Olivia *really* brings that out in him!"

"So maybe Jeff *couldn't* see, or do things differently, until he actually felt true-love for someone?" He asks.

"I hadn't thought of it like that, but yes!" She tells him, "Love drives a person to have their loved one's feelings and well-being be their main concern. That constant concern for their happiness is there for every decision that affects them because the last thing they want to do is hurt the person they love, even when they're angry about something. If they do hurt them, they're quick to make things right!"

"I look at you and knowing what I already know of you, I figured the man had to have been standing in a *bloody black hole!*" He holds the back of her jaw. *"I've been feeling your light breaking through the darkest parts of my soul for some time now..."* They stare into each other's eyes. Lawrence pulls her into a tender kiss. They pull apart and Lawrence rests his forehead to hers. He tells her, "Part of me is also scared."

"Of what?" She whispers.

He lifts his head to look into her eyes. "Because I've fallen in-love with you and if you didn't feel the same, it would be impossible to walk away——." She kisses him firmly.

He feels her fingers in his hair behind his head and she holds him tighter with her other arm. He hugs her firmer, too, and forgets everything else. Any other time, just kissing a woman would seem like a waste of time and he'd begin feeling her body to initiate sex, but not with her. He understands now, *more than ever*, what she has been saying! He knows *this love is real* because lust hasn't been mixed in!

It gets really dark outside and she stops their 'PG' make-out session. "It's getting late."

"Sadly..." he says with a hint of playfulness as he kisses her again.

She breaks their kiss and gets up telling him, "You three have 'incorrigibility' in common!"

"Then I hate to break it to you, Darling, but that would mean *we* aren't the problem!" He smirks.

"Oh really?" She laughs. "How do you figure?"

"You're the 'common *factor*!'" He teases her.

She rolls her eyes smiling. "Don't you mean 'common *denominator*'?"

He laughs, "*Of course not!*" He takes her hand and starts to walk back to their suite, with a couple of Royal Guards, and McMasters only a few paces behind them. "Darling, you *multiply* David, Jack, *and me.*"

"I'm afraid one doesn't multiply anything. However, we know that two, doubles and three, *triples!*"

"Then you need to double check your figures because from where I stand, you forgot to add the endless zeros *behind* the one!" Lawrence grins. He sees her mouth open to respond, but he beats her to it. "*And no.*" He puts the side of his forefinger to her lips. "There is no decimal point until *after* all those endless zeros!" He kisses her again, noticing the moment she relaxes into his arms, and he tips her back a little bit.

She giggles, "Let's not get a headache from arguing." The guards, as well as McMasters, try to stifle soft snickering.

After their suite is secured for their safety by McMasters and another Royal Guard, some take up a post for a shift while the others go to bed. Lawrence and Bri say goodnight with a small kiss and a hug at her bedroom door.

CHAPTER 4

Imperfectly Perfect & Royally Fun Time

The next morning, after Lawrence has exercised and showered, he orders room service before waking Bri. He cracks her door and asks if he can come in and when there's no answer, he says, "I'm coming in."

He does wait another moment for her to reply before he goes in. He walks over to the bed and sees her sleeping so beautifully, he *almost* hated to wake her. He climbs onto the bed and kisses her shoulder. She stirs a little and he lays down next to her.

He whispers, "*I just ordered breakfast and thought you might want to eat with me? You have time for a shower, if you can make it quick...*" he listens for a reply...instead he hears her breathing has gone steady. He smiles and softly shakes her, "Bri?"

"*What time is it?!*" She faintly whines with her voice cracking.

"*Time* for breakfast!" Lawrence replies.

"Are you *seriously* trying to be cute right now?!" Half her face is planted into the pillow.

"I prefer *charming*..." He says.

She is unamused. "Uh-huh...*riiight*..."

"Is it working?" He smiles and she feels him smiling against her cheek.

"*Not* in the slightest, *King Charming*!" She bluntly answers.

"How about..." he kisses her cheek, "our time is limited, and I'd like to spend as much time with you as I possibly can?"

Bri starts to sit up saying in a groggy voice, "*That works!*" She rubs her face and yawns, then crawls out of bed. She sees another swimsuit and cover up laying on the foot of the bed. She looks at Lawrence. "I think I actually have a swimsuit in my things for the European Tour already. You shouldn't have bought me any, let alone two."

"I wasn't sure." He smiles adoringly at her. "Jack and David seem to enjoy buying you things, so I thought I'd give it a try. I can see why they do; it *is* rather fun!"

"Why is that?" She dully asks. "Shouldn't just being with '*The King*' be the *ultimate prize*?" She snips.

He lifts his eyebrow. "Are you always this cheeky in the morning?"

"No, only when I'm woke up." She semi-playfully glares at him and goes into the bathroom.

He laughs. "Glad to see it goes right into feisty!"

After her shower and she is ready for their day on the beach, she looks around for Lawrence and sees he is on the beach with breakfast for two set up. He is sitting and staring out at the sea. When she touches his shoulder, he looks up at her smiling. He goes to stand up for her...

"Sit." She says, stopping him. "I love chivalry, but it's not necessary this time." She holds his face and leans down. "I believe I need to give you this..." She kisses him tenderly. "I needed to brush my teeth first." She taps another kiss to his lips. "Good morning."

"Good morning!" He smiles. "That makes it worth the wait..." He puts his hand on her jaw and pulls her in for another sweet kiss. She smiles at him and he kisses her hand before she takes her seat.

She sees the food. "This looks *so* yummy!" She places a napkin in her lap and asks, "Is it private? I ask because I wanted to go back to what we were talking about last night, *about you?*"

"Of course." He smiles a bright white smile at her.

She quietly says, "You never fully explained *why* you hated being king? You said you're not the king you want to be, but I was hoping for more information."

He takes a deep breath. "My mother not only tells me what I have to do, but I also hear her call me every demeaning thing there is that basically tells me

I'm worthless. I'm not the only one, the staff are treated far worse! What's that saying? She would 'make a sailor blush?'"

"Oh, Lawrence..." Bri's heart squeezes for him. "That's *horrible...*"

"She's hoping, because she's a mean and hateful woman, treating me like this will have me becoming just like her and all those before me. If she isn't taking it out on me, she'll target Seth and Abby, only Abby will have it *so much worse!*"

"Wait. Abby? Why Abby? She's *super* sweet—*riiight...*" Bri catches herself because that's the point.

"*And* Seth and I protect her! Which makes Mother see her *more* of a weakness..." he replies.

"I get wanting to protect them *and that's enough of a reason*, so I'm simply curious if she has any real power being 'The Queen Mother?' Does she somehow 'outrank' you, so-to-speak, that I'm missing?" Bri asks him.

"In the general sense, it's just a title. In the hierarchy of things, the titles afford them the power the reigning monarch *allows them to have...*" He stares down at his plate thinking about that. "She has supporters all over because they're scared to death of her and don't want to be in the way of her wrath, or they want her protection."

"So, if you were to cut her off—."

"She'd retaliate." He states. "Putting Seth and Abby in that much more danger."

Bri had finished and stands up to go over to Lawrence. She moves his napkin so she can straddle him. He's confused and places his hands on her hips. Normally, she'd only straddle David or Jack because this is a very intimate move, but with him, at this moment, she wanted him to *really hear* what she was going to say to him.

She holds his face. "I know this is a bold move, so forgive me. I'm sitting like this because I need you to hear me, I mean *really* hear me!" He has a small smile on his face and nods. She tells him, "YOU are an *incredible* man, Lawrence Alexander Heathherst, and *my* life is already so much better for just knowing you!" She kisses him lovingly, but firmly. "*That's* the man my heart fell for!" His mouth opens, a little surprised. "*I love you!*"

Hearing that stirs his emotions for her that he can only express by fiercely kissing her. She wraps both her arms around his neck as his go firmly around her waist and upper body. When they pull apart, she rests their foreheads together and he closes his eyes, feeling so much love *for* her and *from* her. She lifts her head and looks into his eyes, but he speaks first.

"Bri, there have been women in my life, women I've cared for but for the first time in my life, I can actually say 'I've fallen *in*-love' with you! I know you're told how incredibly *amazing* you are *and it's true*! I want you in my life, *if* you'll *have*—." A lump closes off his throat.

"I want you in my life, too." She kisses him again before she gets up.

When they're done eating, Lawrence takes her hand as they walk to the beach canopy, where they lay in comfortable silence. She had fallen asleep and wakes to find Lawrence sleeping, too. She watches lunch being set up on a table next to the bed. She whispers a 'thank you,' and the staff smile and nod, then she watches everyone leave.

Bri smiles as she watches Lawrence sleep. She gently kisses his lips and he moans, "Mmm, I like waking up to that."

"Hungry?" She asks.

"Oh, I'm hungry..." He smirks.

"Ha-ha! Not yet, Ace! They set up lunch for us." She waits for him to open his eyes. She looks at him seriously. "I'm going to say something to you, and I want you to respect me enough to *not* answer me."

He rolls to his back and his eyebrows come together, studying her. He puts a hand behind his head, "Alright..."

"I can see you regretting either answer you would give to me and I just want to keep this out there. I think David has told you I'm not the sharing kind?" He nods. "*However*, it's unfair for me to ask you to wait until we're official when I have my relationships with David and Jack. If you choose, you can *discreetly* continue to see whomever you've *already* been seeing."

He gets an embarrassed look, "Bri—." She covers his mouth.

46

"As I was saying, my relationships with Jack and David make it unfair to ask you to—." He kisses her and pulls her to lay next to him, so he can partially lay on top of her.

He looks down at her and says, "I'll honor your request *not* to answer, but I'm going to tell you that when you become 'The Royal Consort,' I accept *and will honor* those *same* terms David and Jack have accepted *and honor*." She nods and kisses him. He purposely changes the subject. "What would you like to do today?"

She teases, "Am *I* not enough for you?"

"I just want *you* to enjoy your time with me."

"Then you, *My King*, haven't been paying attention! I'm here *with you*, enjoying this time *with you*!"

"But still!" He chuckles.

"Lawrence Alexander, I'm not a morning person, but what did you say to me that made me get up without thinking twice once you said it?"

He thinks back, "Something about having only so much time to spend with you." He smiles at her. "Then, could I make a request?"

"*Sure!*" She says with a smile that flows up into her loving eyes.

He plays with the shoulder of her cover-up dress. "We go out into the water...I'd ask you to take this off here, but in these positions..."

She giggles as she gets up. She stands on the rug and locks eyes with him as she takes the cover-up off. She sees him looking her over and holding his breath. She tosses the cover-up dress at him. It hits his eyes and part of his nose, but he's smiling with his dimples as he falls onto his back again pulling the cover-up off his head. He sits up and watches her go out to the edge of the water. He gets up and as she turns, she sees him take off his shirt.

"Whoa, whoa, *whoa!* THAT'S *way too much hotness*, Ace!" He smiles, tossing the shirt on the bed before walking towards her. "*Put your shirt back on!*"

47

He gives her an incredibly determined and smoldering look, "That's funny…" he pulls her close, wrapping his arms around her, "the same could be said about you!"

"Oh! Well, I can go put *your* shirt on!" She teases, stepping in that direction.

He stops her. "Oh no!" He grips her firmer at her waist with one arm and runs a finger along her collarbone. "I have to *earn* you wearing my shirt and…" he leans in, "that won't be happening…" he ghosts her lips, "…until you become *mine*."

She clears her throat. "We need to change the topic of this conversation!" She fans herself with one hand and blows out her exhale. She sees a playfulness in his eyes that makes her tell him, "I have a *deathly fear* of water where I can't touch the bottom, other than a pool."

"Good to know!" His playful smile gets bigger. "Now I know you won't swim away when I do this!" He picks her up and puts her over his shoulder then takes her out into the water. "Global warming won't be to blame for the oceans warming up after I do this!" He tosses her in and she playfully squeals.

 She stands up laughing. The water is below her knees and gets higher as the waves come through. She splashes him and the water fight commences, with a kiss or two in between, until they're both out of breath; laughing so much their stomachs and cheeks hurt.

"Ceasefire!" He says, wiping the saltwater from his eyes.

Bri's wiping water from her eyes when she feels Lawrence scoop her up, only this time he carries her back to their cabana. She has her arms wrapped around his neck and she's close to his ear to whisper, *"I love being with you."*

He smiles as he sets her down and wraps a towel around her. "But…"

"What makes you think there's a 'but' coming?" She asks as she dries her face with two of the corners of her towel.

"Most women enjoy the luxuries when they're with me, but that's about as deep as it goes."

She worries. "*And is that what you sense with me?*"

"Not at all!" He cups her cheek. "My apologies, Darling."

She sweetly smiles. "I won't lie to you, luxuries can definitely be fun, *buuut,*" she winks and he softly chuckles, "it's really only fun for me when there's someone to share it with." She gestures around, "All this, by myself...*boring;* but with you, it's enjoyable! I love that I get *you* all to myself because if we step one toe outside of this secluded place, I'll have to share 'The King!'" She fights a lump forming in her throat by swallowing hard. "I just want to soak in our time together." The lump takes over and she looks down with a 'tsk' in frustration at herself, tears form in her eyes. She swallows hard again, then looks back up into his beautiful blue-green eyes. She tries again. "I fell so fast for David! I didn't realize I loved him until *after* I stood up to him at the Black-Tie Party and we were in the gardens the weekend when he, Jack, and James first met Katie and me. Jack was easy to fall for, but I'm sure with his charisma he's had quite a few ladies fall for him over the years." Lawrence nods. "With you, it may not have been immediate, but I've fallen *very* hard for you...it's a little scary, considering I haven't seen 'The King' in action yet."

What she doesn't tell him is it's also scary because of the danger she senses with him at different times. Something about her vulnerability has him grabbing her in an embrace as he kisses her passionately. After a solid minute, they rest their foreheads together in such a way that when a picture of them is snapped from the privacy trees and hits the tabloids in the next editions, royal and noble watchers know, *beyond any doubt*, exactly who King Lawrence is romancing for his 'Royal Consort.' But that's tomorrow's headlines. For the rest of the day, they go back and forth between the ocean and the cabana. Followed by an evening tucked away on the couch, snuggled into each other watching movies and listening to a thunderstorm roll through.

CHAPTER 5
Imperfectly Perfect Detour

After breakfast the next morning, they're airborne again and on their way to Château de Téseau. David and Jack are waiting for them on the tarmac of the small airport in Téseau, France. As the flight attendant opens the door, Lawrence pulls Bri into a hug.

"David and Jack suggested we start a rotation so you and I can spend time together more regularly. Will that be alright with you?" He asks.

"That sounds *brilliant!*" She teases with his accent to make him smile and he does. "If you want me to come to London, though, then we may need to juggle a little in the beginning, but Gabriel will make anything work!"

"For the time being, I'll travel to you." Lawrence holds her cheek. "I don't want my mother interfering." He is his mother's king and he does exactly what she wants, even being downright cruel to anyone and everyone around him, or Seth, or Abby, pays the price. He doesn't want Bri to witness that any sooner than she has to!

When Bri steps off the plane, she sees Jack and David and has a huge smile go across her face for them. Jack and David greet them at the bottom of the stairs with a hug for Lawrence, and a hug and kiss for Bri.

"Okay, all this handsomeness is overload for me." She fans herself.

Jack wraps his arm around her waist. "Here it takes three of us to have that effect on you and only one of you have that effect on each of us!"

"It *could be* that I'm not able to conceal the now *triple* effect you have on me *all at once!*" She smirks.

Lawrence chuckles a bit. "Jack and I are flying back to London. There's an estate and finances I want to talk to him about, as well as an item I'm hoping he'll find on an auction block for me." David goes and waits by their car as Bri says her goodbyes to Jack and Lawrence.

"Jack, I'll see you in a few days, Amore Mio."

He smiles. "You can count on it, Amore Mia! I love you!"

"And I love you!" She holds Jack's cheeks and kisses him so lovingly. Lawrence notes the beauty in it and remembers those moments he had with her. Jack heads up the stairs and into The Royal Jet.

Bri turns to Lawrence. "I had an absolutely wonderful time, Ace! Promise me that we can do something like that again!"

"I'd move mountains to make that happen, if that's what you want." He smiles, but there's a hint of shyness in it.

"I don't need mountains moved, only you...and a cabana, on a beach, *sometime in the future*!" She winks and then kisses him, wrapping her arms around his neck and hugs him tight; he lifts her feet off the ground. She whispers, "*You are an amazing, wonderful man!*"

He hugs her tighter before he walks her over to David and their car. "I'll see you soon." He taps a kiss to her lips and firmly hugs her again. He and David pat each other's shoulders before he walks back to the jet, waving as he climbs the stairs.

David and Bri get into the backseat where Bri finds a printed newspaper article from the internet. "Thought you should see one of these...sort of ease you into this as we go along." She's confused as she looks from David to the article and begins to read the first part.

NEWHAVEN NEWS
CHRONICLES

Lord and Lady Newhaven Tour the Major Cities of Europe with Lord Jack Carlisle

By: Steven Richter

The Marquee and Marchioness of Newhaven, along with Lord Carlisle, planned a two-week itinerary traveling around Europe.

That's as far as she read word-for-word before she starts to skim the printed online article. It's a positive article in which they praise them for their efforts to promote unity with the countries. They surprise her by quoting her accurately and crediting her for being involved in issues for Newhaven's and the UK's best interest.

> "Maybe being a 'Direct Bloodline' makes her more of a UK native than some of the ones born here!"

She snickers a little, then skims a bit more...until her eyes fall on what David meant.

> "The Marchioness has been missing for a couple of days and it is rumored she is being romanced by His Majesty, King Lawrence!"

Bri's mouth falls open at the picture of her and Lawrence on the beach with their foreheads together. David smiles and finishes reading it...

> "If this is indeed true, there's a huge probability that the next 'Heir to The Throne' will grow up right here in Newhaven!"

"I-I-*Hooow*..." Bri stutters. "David..." she looks over to him, lightly shaking her head, not knowing what to say.

"Oh, Love, *no!*" He holds her face as he encourages her, "This is *really good*! If you love—."

"*This is good?*" She holds up the article.

"YES, it's good! *This isn't tabloid rubbish!*" He has a loving look on his face for her. "It's beautiful! See," he points to their foreheads resting together, "that right there says to me you have strong feelings for each other!" He hands her a tissue and she dries her eyes.

"I know I need to accept that this is how *our* life is; that you and Jack support this...I'm trying." She wipes her nose. "Honestly, there still are times, although fewer, where my mind starts to go where Katie—."

"*Don't!*" He says sternly, almost angrily. "I know you don't mean to insult me, *but you are.*" Her eyes go wide and she feels bad. "This is our tradition, Love, for almost a millennia! I've stressed, *and will keep stressing to you*, this *has to be for love* or not at all!" He taps the picture knowingly. "It looks to me like this *is* love..."

She shifts so she can look right at him. "David, I'm terribly sorry if I offended you, or insulted you. I would–I'd never–." She exhales in frustration trying to find the right words.

"Apology accepted, Macushla." He holds her cheek and lovingly tells her, "Tha gaol agam ort!"

Bri hasn't picked up much of the Scottish Gaelic because surprisingly not much is spoken around her. The phrase essentially sounds like, 'Ha g'eul ah kum orsht' and she knows what it means because David uses it a lot with her.

Her lower jaw shakes as she replies, "I love you, too!" He cups both her cheeks and kisses her, then pulls out another tissue and hands it to her. "David, I'm trying to keep the 'American glasses' off as I navigate through my relationships with you, Jack, and now Lawrence, but it's hard sometimes."

"I understand. I just *never* want you feeling like you're anything less than a lady. The three of us are perfectly aware of where you are and who you're with at any given time; this isn't cheating with sneaking around and keeping secrets. Loving Lawrence doesn't mean you stop loving Jack or me!" She kisses him this time and hugs him. He pulls her over to straddle him and they just hug each other for a few minutes.

Château de Téseau

The rest of the ride is in relaxing silence. Bri is watching the small village roll by and smiles at how it all seems like a movie set. Everything's beautifully picturesque.

They pull into the long drive of The Château, surrounded by woods. As it opens up, they pass the u-shaped stables with a partial circular drive on the left. When Bri stares at The Château, she sees the French architectural influences of *The Palace of Versailles*.

She smiles as they pull up. "I love this place!"

David's heart melts. "*I love* that you love this place." He kisses her hand. He gets out of the car then turns to help her out.

"Don't you love it?!" She's a little surprised.

"Absolutely! Only more so when you first saw it last year and loved it, plus you continue to love it!"

She laughs as they walk inside and go up to 'The Owner's Suite.' When they pass the hallway one would go down to go to 'The Honeymoon Suite,' she smiles as she remembers they stayed down there that first visit before he bought The Château. He originally was going to buy it for The Corporation, but he saw how much she loved it and decided to buy it as an investment for them with The Corporation contracted to run it.

Every couple of months David brings her here to get away, if he doesn't take her on a business trip with him somewhere else. He's a workaholic just like Jack, and she suspects Lawrence is, too; however, when it's their turn to spend time together, David and Jack focus on spending time with her, having more 'normal' working hours. On her days with David, he prefers her to work in her office at The Worthington Corporation when she can, while Jack prefers her to work at The Cottage House with him on their days together. Right now, her time is mostly spent in Kingsbury working with Peter and continuing to learn the ropes of Newhaven and UK governments.

Once inside The Owner's Suite, she walks out onto the balcony overlooking the large pond. She notices the water is so still, it looks like glass and it reflects the scenery off of it. She hears David asking for dinner to be brought up to them before he comes out and joins her. He hugs her from behind, kissing the curve of her neck.

"Enjoying the view?" He asks.

"It's wonderful," she turns to face him, "but *now* it's perfect!" She kisses him passionately and he deepens it.

"I wish I would've delayed dinner!" He smirks.

"I have a better idea." She tells him as she leads him inside.

"Better?" He scoffs. "What on *Earth* could be better?!"

She takes him over to the couch and sits him down. She straddles him, his hands sit on her hips. "How about we make-out until dinner comes?"

He smiles playfully. "I can get behind that!"

"I do need to issue a disclaimer though." She says.

He chuckles. "What would that be?"

"My hormones have been charged up and pressed down too many times to count for a couple days now, so while I'm very much in-love with you and I'm *incredibly* attracted to you——."

"I got it, Love." He playfully smirks. "It'll be fun having you frustrated and twisting for a change!"

"And you're not right now?!" She asks a little surprised.

"With you?! *Always!*" He says and she giggles. He runs a hand into her hair and brings her lips to his and kiss, igniting what she calls his 'major fiery inferno' he has for her.

Things do get pretty hot between them, but there's a knock on the door. Bri is now lying on the couch and David is on top of her. He gets up and buttons his shirt, but leaves it untucked and opens the door. Bri quickly puts herself together as the two staff members set up their table for dinner.

When they're alone again, David motions the dinner table. "Shall we?" He pulls out her chair. Bri smiles as she goes over and sits.

They talk about the things he and Jack learned in the various meetings the last couple of days. He asked how she liked Budapest and the things Lawrence showed her when they were there. When they finish dessert, there's another knock on the door; staff have come for their dishes.

Bri looks at David. "That's quick..."

"I asked them to come back for our dishes right away," he steps behind her and says next to her ear, "then we won't be disturbed later."

She smiles. "Good thinking!"

He starts to walk towards the door, but stops and turns around, "Maybe you can change into something I picked up for you that's in the closet while I take care of this?" She grins as she bites her lower lip and goes to see what David has for her.

When room service leaves again, David shuts the door and locks it. He turns and walks into the bedroom area as Bri walks out of the closet.

"*Wow*, Love!" He gets a smoldering look on his face, as he starts unbuttoning his shirt walking over to her.

"Wow, yourself!" She waits in anticipation as he finishes unbuttoning his shirt. When he reaches her, he pulls her to him...

She lays her head on his chest, tucked under his arm. She's quiet, but he knows she's awake because he can feel her eyelashes on his skin as she blinks.

"Are you alright, Love?" He asks.

"Just trying not to get my hopes up about a baby. I wish my mind didn't go to that right away!"

He shifts them so he can look at her. "How about we focus on how those fireworks were hotter than usual?!"

She lightly laughs. "They were! I think our make-out session on the couch had a lot to do with it!"

He smiles adoringly at her. "I love you, Mrs. Worthington!"

"I love you, *Mister* Worthington!" She grins.

He lightly laughs and kisses her. Then they get comfortable on their own pillows and drift off to sleep.

CHAPTER 6
Imperfectly Perfect Discussion

The next morning, Bri wakes up early, *really early*, and she can't fall back to sleep. She can't turn off thoughts of Lawrence...she's not sure how long she lays there, but she knows David is waking up when he snuggles into her, spooning her. She puts her hand on his arm and is unknowingly rubbing his arm, waking him up more.

"What's on your mind, Love?"

"Just thinking." She turns on her back and smiles, but he sees it's missing something.

He rubs his eyes. "About?"

"About my sexy handsome husband." She tries to flirt.

He half smiles. "Nice try. What else?" He yawns.

"That's not enough?!" She teases a bit.

He raises his eyebrow with a soft smile. "It's never kept you up before."

She turns on her side to face him saying, "Then you don't remember—."

"*Briii...*" His voice is a little groggy sounding.

She rolls her eyes inhaling deeply. "It's just that I have the words 'Royal Consort' going through my head like a broken record..."

David was surprised. "Why?" She shrugs. He's quick to say, "Please, Love, talk to me. We all work because we all support each other and our relationships with you. Let me help you, let me help *both of you*."

"Honestly, David, I don't really know why...with you and Jack the feelings are different than with Lawrence, who's '*The.King.*' I'm in awe of how Jack jumped so quickly into this with me, *with us*, without future knowledge from Jessica! But me with Lawrence...I can't explain it...*I have future knowledge* and I *know* there's an 'Heir to the Throne' in our future family, but..." She exhales some of her frustration.

"Bri, first of all, Jack was *already* in-love with you! Then there's the fact that the two of you had a spark that only stayed platonic because you were with me; *until* you gave yourself permission to open your heart to him."

"Because *you* wanted him to be my 'Noble Consort' *and* he wanted to be!" Bri tells him.

"Okay, let's go with that again since it worked so fantastically well last time!" David grins. "I *want* you to be 'The Royal Consort,' *if* you want to be, because *Herst* wants you to be, BUT *only if* you're in-love with each other!"

She snorts half a laugh. "I think I followed that."

He pushes the hair away from her face and looks into her eyes. "What else?"

"I don't know how to put it into words..." She replies.

"Try. Maybe we can figure it out together." He suggests. "What is it you say? 'Hum a few bars...'" She softly laughs. When there is a bit of silence, he pulls her chin with his finger so she'll look at him. "Please?"

She takes a deep, calming breath. "On our wedding day, when Lawrence and I were in the stables, I had sensed loneliness from him, but also danger."

His eyebrows come together with a bit of confusion. "Your instincts haven't steered you wrong but—."

"When I know what they mean! Sorry."

David smiles sweetly. "It's fine, Love. Go on."

"I don't know what this 'danger vibe' is, it *could* have something to do with what *he's* holding back." She exhales loudly in frustration.

"All I can tell you is Herst would *never* hurt you!"

"I do know that much!" She inserts with a small smile.

"He hasn't fully opened up to us, but Jack and I get the feeling he's been through some unspeakable and very horrific things."

Bri unknowingly nods as she listens, staring off at nothing in particular. "He hasn't given me a lot of details either, but it has to be something horrific and so awful, if we can't even begin to imagine what it all could be!"

His heart breaks for his other brother. "Rumor has it, he's different at The Palace with his parents around, but I do know his actions, right or wrong, protect his brother and sister, maybe even Genevieve. I think your instincts are right to be cautious, *especially at The Palace.*" He taps a kiss to her lips. "Bri, one thing you'll learn is the higher up one gets in positions of power, those closest to you have to be chosen with *great care.* There are many people who'll be friendly, but *almost none of them* will be a true friend."

"Because they'll sell you out in a heartbeat?! Even to let others know they 'rub elbows' with you so-to-speak." She notes and David nods. "He's at the very top, so he must be pretty lonely..." She tapers off thinking about that.

"I haven't really seen him 'in action' as 'The King' before, but Herst, Jack, and I have been friends since we were like...ten years old. He wouldn't hurt you because of that friendship, nor would he let anything happen to you because of that friendship." He smiles with a twinkle in his eye. "However, now that he's fallen in-love with you, Herst has the power, the means, and authority to *seriously protect you*...and the price someone will pay for hurting you will be costly, maybe even deadly..." He gives her a determined look. "As I've said, this *is*, and must be, *your* decision, Love!"

"I love you!" She hugs him, then pulls back to ask, "What if I'm pregnant before I'm 'The Royal Consort?!'"

"We can put a delay in the paperwork that the two years won't start until so long after the birth of our baby." He explains. "Bri, you *being* a 'Direct Bloodline' has kings lined up to have your DNA in *their* heirs."

"*So* sweet and romantic." She rolls her eyes with her sarcasm. "Hold up. You said, 'has king*s* lined up.' Right now?! *That's ridiculous!*"

"*Briii,*" he says with a 'come on now' tone, "take off the American glasses. There have been *numerous* inquiries. Remember, in our social class, it's all about the blood!"

"Ooo, I live in a vampire world!" She teases.

He snorts a laugh but continues right on. "Who's related to whom and how they can make their blood 'better' or 'purer' is important, only 'royal' is typically done through marriage. Since you're already married, there are other means for them to have a baby like in-vitro, it doesn't always mean a consort. Although a consort would give them more access—."

"*Okay,*" she cuts him off, "this could get crude..." She presses her fingers to her temple.

David softly smiles. "Basically, you could ask for anything short of the moon and many monarchs will offer it to you 'on a silver platter'...*or a gold one.*" He winks and she softly laughs. "Asking for a date further out because you're already pregnant, with an heir to a prominent duchy no less, Parliament *won't* argue and neither will the people! That's at least three generations of a solid four out of four stars, or ancestral lines, for your descendants on *any* family tree around the world."

"What?" Her eyebrows come together.

"Ha-ha! You really should read social media a little more! The people already love and admire you for taking on such a long-standing tradition. Committing yourself to this country further will make them love you *more* for your commitment in producing an heir *for the future of our country* that will run multiple generations deep!"

"No pressure..." She says with a hint of sarcasm.

He leans forward and kisses her. "Let's just let this simmer for a bit." He passionately kisses her and she rolls on top of him. He smirks up at her, "I like the subject ch—."

She kisses him. "Are you up for it?" She raises her eyebrow.

He tangles his hands in her hair and holds the back of her neck. "I'm *always* ready for this!" He pulls her head down, but she teases and ghosts his lips until he lifts his head up off the pillow and captures her lips.

"You *never* disappoint, My Love!" She smiles wide against his lips.

"It's *always* you!" He kisses her firmly.

"Ha-ha! Let's agree it was us! *Fantastically us!*" She suggests.

"How could I argue with that?" He adoringly grins.

"You're a smart man, Mister Worthington!"

"I married you, didn't I? It's the smartest decision my heart ever made!"

She smiles. "Giving into my heart because it already picked you, was *the best decision I ever made!*" He kisses her fiercely.

They eat breakfast before taking a horseback ride around the property. They race across an open field and it's neck-and-neck before they both have to slow down coming to the river that borders the property. They trot their horses side by side back to the stables enjoying their time together.

Walking out of the stables, Bri says, "That was fun!"

He gives her a knowing look as he smiles, "But you prefer Artemis?"

"*Of course!* That handsome stallion is *my horse* after all, isn't he?" She smiles a cheeky grin.

"*Yes.* He's made his decision *crystal clear* from the moment he saw you!" He wraps his arms around her. "Can't say that I blame him!" He kisses her firmly.

David takes her hand and laces their fingers as they walk back to The Château. Inside, they walk past 'The Tea Room' where Bri recognizes a gentleman and the gentleman smiles at her. The gentleman stands and excuses himself from the others and walks over to Bri and David.

The gentleman kisses her cheeks. "So good to see you, Lady Newhaven and Lord Newhaven" He extends his hand to David introducing himself, "Angus Marsh."

"How do you do, Sir?" David shakes his hand with a smile.

Bri raises her eyebrow to 'Angus' because she knows that's not the gentleman's real name but keeps quiet for the moment. She glances at McMasters who gives her a look that he's aware, too. All David sees is Bri's face to McMasters to know something was up, but he keeps quiet until he can ask them in private.

"Bri and I met in DC at a benefit for one thing or another." 'Angus' explains.

"That doesn't surprise me!" David chuckles. "Most of the people she runs into tie back to her liaison job." He asks him, "What brings you here, 'Mr. Marsh?'"

He gestures to his table. "My business associates and I felt this was a nice, centralized place for us to meet."

"It's good to have you!" David tells him and tips his chin down to the table, noticing the various ethnicities sitting around it. The people at the table either wave or tip their heads back.

Bri turns to David. "Would you give us a minute? Maybe McMasters can walk you up and 'Mr. Marsh' here can walk me to the top of the stairs when we're done?" McMasters isn't thrilled but he and David walk upstairs, after David kisses her cheek first. Bri and 'Angus' watch them until they're out of earshot.

Bri looks at him with a raised eyebrow whispering, "*Angus Marsh?*"

"Should I be worried about McMasters?" He quietly asks, matching her raised eyebrow.

"Don't worry about him," she softly dismissively waves her hand, "he's retired. I wanted a minute with you because I feel I need to ask you what you know about The King Father and The Queen Mother."

"*So, the rumors are true?*" He whispers with a faint knowing smirk. "*You're going to be named 'The Royal Consort?'*" He senses her hesitation. "*Don't worry, your secret's safe with me.*"

She quietly replies, "Things are going *that direction*. If they do, well, I'd like to be prepared as best I can." She asks, "Can you tell me anything about his parents?"

"You don't need to worry about The King Father. Ever since his 'Royal Consort' died, he's checked out of life for the most part; only sticking with his duties until he stepped down completely for his son to rule. Now The Queen Mother *is a different story*. She's known as 'The 'Devil's Master' in The

Underground for a reason." He gives her a pointed look. The Underground Secret Society is a group of criminals he handpicked to help seek justice when law enforcement's hands are tied, and sometimes *before* law enforcement gets a chance to seek justice.

Bri's face goes a little pale. "I can't picture *any* scenario where that'd be a good thing to be known for!"

"*It's not!*" They walk up the stairs. "She's big into exhorting her power by brute force and torturing, as well as trafficking anything and anyone."

"One word that goes through my mind whenever someone describes her and those before her is 'tyrant.'" Bri comments.

"Never thought of it like that, but a tyrant is exactly what she is!" He replies.

"Would you be able to get me some more information on her?" She asks. "I'm willing to pay a fee for it."

He nods, taking a card from the inside pocket of his suit coat. "That won't be necessary but here," he hands her his card, "take my number and put it into your phone right now." Bri takes out her phone and does just that. "Now text me so I have yours."

"But it'll show up as restrict—," she stops herself, "*never mind.* You have your ways." He smiles and nods.

He kisses her cheek as they say goodbye. He goes back downstairs to his table of people. She starts walking down the hallway and McMasters walks towards her, then walks with her to The Owner's Suite.

"David asked me who that was, but I said I'd let you tell him." He says.

"Thanks. I asked 'Angus,' to get me what he could on The Queen Mother. He says I don't need to worry about The King Father."

McMasters agrees. "He seems like he's in his own world; disconnected from everything and everyone."

"Interesting..." Bri makes a mental note of that for some other time and continues, "I feel very strongly she'll see me as a threat but right now, I'm more of a nuisance."

McMasters nods and warns, "It will shift sooner than you think." David hears them and opens the door.

She kisses McMasters cheek and thanks him for his loyalty *and friendship*. "It means the world to me, Oliver!" She rarely uses his first name, only in special circumstances.

"I feel guilty." He slightly tips his head towards David.

She whispers, *"Don't be! You know as well as I do that's* exactly *what he wants!"* She quietly says. "You travel everywhere with me and he needs to know that your loyalty is to me first. He has said that from the beginning!"

McMasters smiles and says to text him when they're ready to go. The hallway to The Owner's Suite is private so he usually stands at the end of it, or walks the short hall that 'T's' with it. If there aren't a lot of guests, he goes to his room across from the private hallway; he can see their door from his.

Bri walks to David with a sweet smile and he has a bit of a concerned smile. He closes the door behind her and they walk into the living room part of the suite. She sits on the couch and looks at David who has his question on his face. She pats the couch beside her.

As he sits down, she asks him, "Are you familiar with a group called, 'The Underground Secret Society?'"

"Doesn't it have something to do with 'The Black Market' or 'The Dark Web?'" He asks.

"Well, yes." She tells him, "You unknowingly met Jonathan 'Rex' Stirling."

"*Bri!*" He's shocked and horrified. "He's known as a psychopath! Easily the evilest man alive!"

"A reputation he likes to have and goes to great lengths to keep!" She explains, "He's called 'Rex' because he's considered to be *king of the criminal world*, which includes 'The Dark Web' and 'The Black Market.' In reality, if you actually looked closer at that 'evil' you'll see he's mostly killed other criminals by righting those injustices, *although...*" she thinks, "I'd think with his record, he'd make sure they were truly injustices. His group is made up of vigilante criminals seeking justice when the law ties law enforcement hands, or stops short of justice for one loophole or another." She takes a breath. "*However*, he's *not* above his own criminal activity."

"That's what I'm afraid of!" He senses something and asks with a concerned look. "Why do I feel there's more?"

"Because there is." She gives him a small smile. "I felt very strongly when he and I were talking that I needed to ask him what he knew about The Queen Mother and The King Father."

"What?!" Why would you?!—No, sorry." He squeezes her hand and takes a deep breath of his own. "I trust you; I do! And as long as you keep McMasters in the loop, I'm good." He's not comfortable with Rex Stirling being in any part of their lives but knowing Bri's 'life's journey' isn't like anyone else's, especially considering her spiritual gifts, he'll even blindly trust her.

"I appreciate that. I did tell all this to McMasters out in the hall." She casually points to the door. "To answer your question anyway," she explains, "I need to know what I can about The Queen Mother...I want to feel like I prepared the best I could because I don't like sensing evil."

He nods in understanding. "Just promise me you'll be careful." She nods a little as he hugs her from the side and kisses her temple.

She stands up so they can get ready to go. They walk into the bedroom to finish packing. They'll stop in London to pick up Jack on their way back to Newhaven.

CHAPTER 7
Imperfectly Perfect Quality Time

Bri has been working on her computer and hasn't noticed that they're landing at The London Palace until she glances out the window. When she steps off the helicopter she smiles at Jack and Lawrence when they come out of The Palace. She hugs and kisses Jack, then he gets on the helicopter to give her a moment with Lawrence.

Bri cups Lawrence's face. "This is bitter-sweet. I'm so happy to see you, but I hate leaving you behind. Are you going to be alright?"

"My day is already so much better now..." He smiles, feeling the end of a lock of her hair.

She hugs him tight and whispers, "*Remember, Ace, I've fallen hard for you!*"

"Trust me, I'll *never* forget that!" He kisses her.

Bri has tears in her eyes. "I don't want to leave you! I want you with me!"

He tangles his hands in her hair. "I'll be fine, I *promise!*" He smirks. "Besides, I don't have an heir yet, so I'm safe."

She snorts a scoff. "*Don't joke!*"

"*I'm not!*" He kisses her tenderly. "You can text me anytime and I'll respond as soon as I'm able to!" He crosses his heart with his finger.

"I love you, Ace!"

"I love you, too!" He kisses her once more before he helps her up into the helicopter. He waves to Jack before Jack shuts the door.

Bri buckles in and waves at Lawrence, then watches him walk back into The Palace as the helicopter lifts upward. The Palace gets smaller and moves behind them on their way to Newhaven. She continues to think about him, staring out the window.

Jack squeezes her hand asking, "What's wrong?"

She takes a deep breath and turns to look at them. "Lawrence not only had a tough childhood, but he's *still living it!* I wish there was something I could do for him." She wipes a tear from her cheek.

"You're doing it!" Jack tells her. "You're loving him and that's the best, most healing thing in the world for him." He reaches over to hold the other side of her head so he can kiss her temple.

The three of them play a card game to take her mind off things for a while. The flight seems to go faster, and it isn't too long before she's walking into The Manor and up to her quarters with David. She texts Lawrence before she takes a hot shower...

> Bri: "Hey there, My Handsome King! How's the thrown?" (she adds a smirking face)

She checks her phone when she gets out of the shower and sees he just sent a picture of the two thrones.

> B: "Is that dust I see collecting on them?! Doesn't anyone work around there?!"

To her pleasant surprise he texts right back.

> Lawrence: "A king can't really rule without his rightful queen...it's sad really. Those thrones do look pretty lonely and pathetic, don't you think?"

> B: (adds a pondering face) "Hate to break it to you, but I think ruling comes with the title in this country."

> L: "I can go through the motions...have been for years..."

> B: "But your heart isn't in it." (adds a sad face)

> L: "Oh, Darling, my heart has finally found its queen...now to win her over to join me!"

> B: "Sounds like you have your work cut out for you!" (she adds a kissing face)

> L: "Good thing I always get what I want!"

B: (adds an eye roll)

L: "Ooo, an eye roll by text. The King is not a fan of either version!"

B: "Good thing I'm not talking to 'The King,' or he may order my beheading!"

L: "There hasn't been a beheading in over a century! Besides, there's more fun things I think we could do to each other instead."

B: "Your Majesty!" (She adds a blushing face) "I'm trying not to go there...*yet.*"

L: "Just dancing on the line, My Darling! I do need to run, but I'll try calling later tonight."

B: "I'll talk to you then!" (She adds a kiss mark and a heart)

They talk that evening for a few minutes or so, when Bri hears a woman's voice in the background and Lawrence shushing her. It all makes Bri uncomfortable and she ends their conversation abruptly. Lawrence is left looking at his phone a bit confused.

Abby comments, "That was a rather quick exit."

"Odd, wasn't it?" Lawrence looks at her, perplexed.

"Did you say 'hullo' for me?" Abby asks him.

"I couldn't! She hung up too fast!" Lawrence answers, but stares at the wall.

Abby pushes the phone back up to him. "If she heard me laughing AND you never said it was me, where do you think her mind went if she hung up that fast?" He looks at her and she watches him realize what she's getting at.

"Oh, *NO!* No. No. No. *NO!*" He looks at his phone in a panic.

"*Calm down,* Lawrence! She'll understand." Abby tells him.

"Abby, *you* don't understand. She gave me the option of other women until we're officially together, but she never wanted to know—."

"Ah! I still stand by what I said, the girl will understand. Here..." She grabs his phone and texts Bri.

> "This is Abby. He forgot to tell you 'hello' from me when he was on the phone with you. Cheers, Luv!"

Bri sends a thumbs up to Abby's text through Lawrence's phone and then she texts Abby a smiling hugging face directly. He kisses Abby's cheek and thanks her. Lawrence leaves it at that with Bri for now.

Bri is going to be busy over the next couple of days and works from the office at The Cottage House with Jack that first morning. Bri walks into her office expecting to sit at her table under her bookshelves in the corner, but there is a writing-style desk turned outward and angled to face the doorway and Jack's desk on the other side of their office.

"You've been shopping." She mentions with a smile as he hangs up the phone. She walks around behind the desk and puts her things down.

He smiles a big smile as he stands and walks over to her. "Do you like it? If you want a different color, or a desk with a credenza—."

She puts her hand over his mouth. "Stop." She moves her hand to hug and kiss him. "I love it! It's perfect! Thank you, Amore Mio!" She sits down. "I have a desk at The Manor, at The Worthington Corporation, and in Kingsbury, now here. I like how each of them are different—oh! That reminds me!" She opens her laptop bag and pulls out a folder for Jack. "I haven't looked at this closely yet, they are Newhaven's financials. Do you mind taking a look over the weekend? I need to go into a meeting with recommendations, which I'm hoping will be from my financial genius and *very* sexy husband!"

"When you put it that way, I don't see how I could say 'no'?" He grabs her wrist of the hand with the folder and pulls her up. He still holds her wrist and kisses her as he runs his other hand down to her bum and pulls her closer.

She playfully smiles. "Thank you! And maybe," she runs her hand down the front of his chest, "I'll show you later just *how grateful.*"

He keeps his hand on her bum and tugs, "Temptress!"

She giggles. "Why *yes*! Yes, I am!" He laughs. She lightly taps a kiss to his lips.

A picture frame on the windowsill catches her eye and she picks it up; it's of the time she is singing karaoke. "I don't remember you or David taking a picture of me that night!"

She remembers the trip; it was right after the Italy honeymoon and she enjoyed every town in Newhaven they visited. She loves the people of Newhaven and had so much fun one evening with karaoke. No one knew she could sing, not even David or Jack who asked why they didn't know?! She had shrugged saying, '*It never came up.*' Now she sings in the church choir, so it's easy for them to remember. They had mentioned Lawrence plays the piano and it might be something they could enjoy together. She had forgotten about that, but she'll try to remember one of these times she is with Lawrence.

"You were in your element singing, Amore Mia! There were plenty of pictures being taken, even video. And if I had that great of a voice like yours, I'd belt it out, too!" He tells her.

She lightly laughs, shaking her head. She sets the picture back on the windowsill, "It's just karaoke." She sits back down at her desk saying, "Any drunk person can do it!"

He snorts a laugh, shaking his head. "No, smashed people *try* to sing like that and they're so intoxicated, they *think* they sound like that!"

"I wasn't drunk, so it was easy to sing better than some of those drunk people!" She smirks.

He gives her a little bit more of a serious look. "*Just take the complement!*"

"Fine." She says and focuses on her laptop and getting to work. Jack chuckles and kisses her cheek before he goes back to his own desk to work.

After dinner, David and James are shooting games of pool; Jack and Bri go back to The Cottage House. She has been quiet; she is thinking about Lawrence and how it'll all come together. She goes and takes a shower, while

Jack gets ready for bed. He is reading through the Newhaven financials and making some notes on a legal pad when she comes out in a dark red lingerie short dress for him. She's standing there waiting for him to look, watching him as he slowly turns his head, still reading to finish the line before he looks, then quickly looks again.

"*Wow!*" He says in his own sexy way.

"Like it?"

"I *love* this!" He gathers his things and tosses them on the floor.

"Well, you look incredibly sexy yourself!" She tells him as he takes off his glasses, mindlessly laying them on the nightstand; not taking his eyes off her.

He lightly laughs as he shifts to sit on the edge of the bed. He holds his finger up and gives the 'come hither.' She smiles as she walks over to him. He runs his hands down her sides.

"Where did this come from?" He asks as he admires it.

"When we visited Milan last, Valentina helped me shop for something…" she holds his jaw lightly and seductively tracing his lips with hers, "that's for the 'For Jack's Eyes Only' collection.'" She playfully grins.

He exhales, "*Jack's eyes are very pleased!*" She bites her lower lip. He carefully guides her to lay on their bed, enjoying the feel of the fabric. He looks into her eyes. "I love you, Amore Mia!"

"I love you, too! Now," her hands feeling his t-shirt covered pecs, "less talking, Carlisle!" She teases. He gives a light growl with an intense smoldering look before he kisses her passionately.

Bri is snuggled into Jack and they talk for a little bit. She fills him in on Jonathan 'Rex' Stirling and he agrees with David, that she needs to at least keep McMasters in the loop. They say 'I love you' with their goodnights and kiss before they roll over and go to sleep.

CHAPTER 8

Imperfectly Perfect Taunting of a Former BFF

A couple days later, Jack, Bri, and David are eating breakfast together at The Manor with the rest of the family. They're in the middle of various conversations when Bri's phone chimes with an unfamiliar text notification. She looks to see who it's from...it's from Katie, she has a new phone number. It was hard to believe Katie would actually text her after all this time, but she did and it includes the picture of Bri and Lawrence at the beach.

> Katie: "I do have to admit, you have great taste in men! That must help when you're whoring yourself out as breeding stock!"

Bri isn't sure how she feels about the text from Katie...she doesn't feel mad or upset...She covertly silences her phone and calmly sets it face down as she joins a conversation. She hadn't realized that her cheeks had gone a little red from embarrassment, but David and Jack noticed.

Bri finishes her breakfast and slips upstairs. Jack and David follow her up to her quarters with David where they find her deep in thought staring out the window at the rain. The guys sit in the living room and watch her for a minute. Before they can ask her anything, her phone lights up on the coffee table and David reflexively looks at it and sees it's a text, but only the number appears.

Putting two and two together, he asks with irritation, "What does Katie want now?" Jack's eyebrows go up and then his anger surfaces.

She keeps looking out the window. "Nothing new..." David walks over to her and shows her the new notification, then she looks out the window again.

He asks, "If you don't want to look, can we at least read it?"

"It'll just upset you more..." Bri plainly says, still staring out the window.

"I highly doubt our opinion of her could get worse when we're beyond loathing that woman." Jack flatly states.

Bri takes a deep breath and turns to face them. "Don't be too sure. I haven't responded, which only annoys Katie more and she gets more vicious, but I just don't want to be sucked into it." She exhales. "And I've been at a point of rarely thinking about her, then this..."

"How does she even have your number?!" Jack asks.

Bri tells them, "My phone is still taking calls for my old phone number because of my database project with US federal law enforcement agencies. We thought it would be easier than handing out my new number." Both Jack and David make comments they had forgotten about that.

There's a knock on the door and Jack goes to answer it. "Herst!" Jack hugs him and invites him in. Lawrence walks over to Bri, hugging David standing next to her.

"You're early!" She hugs him tight and he feels her noticeably relax.

"Are you alright, Darling?" He asks.

"Everything's perfect when we're all together." She replies. Lawrence looks at the guys.

"That's true!" Jack agrees.

"Then it's okay I'm early?" He asks her. "Jack and I did a little shuffling since," Jack does a throat-slice-gesture, shaking his head, "I just had to get away from The Palace for a while."

He covers quite nicely and Jack's relieved. Jack had forgotten to tell Lawrence it was a surprise trip he was planning with Bri and mouths 'thank you' to Lawrence, who covertly tips his head in a nod back to Jack.

"It's more than okay!" She happily tells him.

"Fantastic!" Lawrence says, then looks around. "Did I interrupt something? I can come back in a bit?"

Bri shakes her head. "No, no, don't do that! I'm the most relaxed with all three of you here with me."

"Prove it." David gives her a determined look, handing her the phone.

She raises her eyebrow, "Fine. You know the code, but read the texts *out loud* for all to *hear* at the same time."

She gives David a look that when he sees the photo, he understands she doesn't want Lawrence to see it and possibly feel bad. He sees there are unread messages but he scrolls up to the very first one and reads the message:

> Katie: "I have to admit, you have great taste in men! That must help when whoring yourself out as their breeding stock!"

He starts reading the next:

> Katie: "It's been a year, so we know they're fantasizing about anyone other than you!"

David glances at the other texts and sees they are gross and disgusting. "*I refuse to read these!*" He actually shivers. "I can't unsee these and the picture they've painted in my head..." he squeezes his eyes shut, "I might be sick..."

Bri goes to turn back to the window trying to hide the tears filling up her eyes...but Lawrence pulls her into a firm hug. She is finding she loves how comforting it is...she takes a deep breath and exhales slowly.

"You know that's not how you're really seen, right?" Lawrence asks.

David gives her a small, loving smile. "She knows and she also knows *her* people love her." He winks.

"Bri," Jack says in all seriousness, "you *need* to look Katie in the face and confront her once and for all!" Bri vigorously shakes her head 'no.' Jack sweetly says, "Believe it or not, it may help you to heal...without doing so, you may never really get over it."

"*Fine*," she flatly replies, "I'll videoconference her sometime!"

"I should've expected that kind of a cheeky answer from you." Jack says with plainness. David covers his chuckle by coughing into his fist.

Bri gives him a little glare. "*You're* not helping!" Then she looks at Jack with annoyance. "Tell me, how does one *get over* the *ultimate betrayal* of a best friend that couldn't even be topped by her sleeping with one of you?!"

Jack scoffs, "That would *never*—."

"Just answer the damn question, *Jackson Carlisle!*" She says sternly, but there's a bit of anger that isn't missed.

David tries to diffuse the situation, "What have Aunt Maggie and Uncle Henry heard?"

Bri peels her glare from Jack and looks at David. "Henry and Maggie don't really talk to her anymore and what little communication they have has been through texts."

Jack hands Bri her phone. "Call Ken. Maybe he knows more?"

"*Why?!*" She's surprised.

"To help us figure out what your next step should be!" Jack replies. The 'us' irritates her more.

"Ken is the family's detective friend, right?" Lawrence asks.

Bri nods as she swipes her phone out of Jack's hand in irritation. She brings up Ken's number and calls it, then puts it on speaker.

> Ken answers, "How's my favorite Scottish-American girl, er, or is it American-Scottish girl?!"
>
> Bri softly laughs. "I can't complain." She gives a little glare to Jack. "Just so you know, you're on speaker with David, Jack, Lawrence, and me. How's my favorite DCPD Detective?"
>
> He replies, "Can't complain either! Sounds like from Henry your fellas are good to you, Sweetie!"
>
> She nods. "Oh, they are! Truth be told, *too good* to me."
>
> He laughs a bit. "I'd think they'd disagree with that!"
>
> "*Yes, we would!*" Jack says.
>
> David adds, "We most certainly do!"

76

"There's no such thing as being too good to her!" Lawrence replies.

"Ha-ha! All great answers! I like their thinking!" Ken laughs.

Bri gets to the reason for the call. "I know you're busy so I'll get to the point. *We*," she glances a glare at Jack, "were wondering if Katie has been on your radar at all? *Unfortunately*, she's choosing to pop up on mine today." Then she explains the texts to him.

Ken listens to everything and sadly tells Bri, "I arrested her a few weeks back at a drug party. She has been recreational using but is on her way to full-blown addict again without some sort of intervention. She was able to go all week without using, but when it came to the weekends, she'd go all out. However, some of my informants tell me it's now becoming a struggle for her to get to Thursday some weeks."

Bri is a bit sad and disappointed. "'Recreational drug use' wouldn't completely explain her actions with me today."

"No, it wouldn't." Ken replies. "Truth be told, when you first became friends with her, there was something 'off' about her. I didn't think much of it, other than she was young and trying to find her way. I had gotten to know you through Henry and Maggie at first, then outside of them when you were the Liaison Officer. I saw her at various times and she seemed to be coming around, thought you were a good influence. That is, until the time she..." He trails off, not knowing how much the guys knew.

Bri tells him, "It's okay, Ken, the guys know about——."

Jack inserts with *a lot* of animosity, *"The ultimate betrayal!"*

Ken says, "Things seemed to get friendly again and your giant heart seemed to forgive her." There was silence. "Bri? Still there?"

Bri clears her throat. "Yes, sorry." She swallows. "It's just hitting me that I desperately *wanted* to forgive her because I *wanted* things to go back to how they were before that night...I *wanted* to pretend it never happened! I tried..." She shakes her head at herself, "but there's been this giant 'elephant in the room' that never went away..."

"Precisely!" Jack says with exasperation. Bri shoots him an angry look.

Ken asks, "Haven't you heard from her since putting her on a plane back to the US last year?!"

"*Nnnope.*" She replies. "Not until today. Frankly, as harsh and as heartless as this may sound, I didn't care if I never spoke to her, or saw her again! I haven't lost any sleep over it."

Ken softly tells her, "Not heartless, Sweetie. *Necessary.*"

Jack jumps in and asks, "Ken, now that Katie has opened all this back up, do you think it would be good for Bri to face Katie; confront her head on, so Bri can move into a more personal healing process? Maybe it can even help Katie move on, too, *with a lot of counseling.*"

"That could be a good idea." Ken answers.

Bri only says, "I'll think about it."

"Listen, I gotta run!" Ken says hurriedly. "Take care of yourselves!"

"You, too!" Bri replies. They say their goodbyes and hang up.

"Bri, are you headed into Kingsbury today?" David asks, looking at his watch.

"Yes. I have a lot to do for Newhaven and I'll drag *The King* with me." Bri says and smiles at Lawrence who smiles in agreement for the idea.

Bri walks David to the door and expects to walk him outside, but he turns and says, "I love when you see me off and coming home, but stay here this time." He tips his head to Jack and she rolls her eyes. David pointedly looks at Lawrence, "Maybe Herst wants to walk with me?"

"Sure!" Lawrence says, picking up on giving Bri and Jack a chance to talk.

She kisses him. "I love you, My Love! I'll see you later."

David nods and smiles as he wraps her in a tight embrace. "I love you, Macushla." He kisses her once more, before closing the door behind him and Lawrence.

Bri is annoyed with Jack for pushing her to confront Katie and she doesn't want to talk to him yet. She focuses on gathering her things.

Jack watches her. "If you're going to run away, at least tell me what exactly is troubling you!"

"I'm leaving before I say anything I might regret." She opens the door.

Jack quickly follows her out into the hallway and shouts her first name with a commanding tone for the first time, "*BriaLynn*! Stop!" Bri freezes as his voice echoes down the hall and Jack is able to catch up to her. "*Don't leave like this!*" He tells her and she turns to face him.

She strains not to raise her own voice at him. "Jack, I'm trying hard *not* to be furious with you right now. I just need some space."

"*You're already furious with me*!" Jack says taking her laptop bag with a little bit of resistance from her. It's when she looks at his expression, part angry and part *hurt*, she lets go of her bag. He offers his other hand to her, but she brushes past him and walks back into her quarters. Jack's jaw clenches as he follows her, exhaling slowly through his nose.

She walks into the living room and puts her things down. Then turns to face him, folding her arms. "You want to do this now, *so talk*!"

Jack sets her bag down and walks closer to her but keeping a little distance at the moment. "Look, *I'm trying to help you*. And don't stand there and try to act like you're 'over it' with Katie!" He uses air quotes. "How can you be?! You've never really dealt with it! You buried it deeper so you can pretend it never happened, but look where that's gotten you!"

She scoffs, "Oh? And what makes you an expert on how I should've dealt with things?" She points to herself. "I did what I thought was best for me!" She then points to him, "*You* didn't go through what I did! *You* didn't have a so-called best friend do to you, what she did to me! *Aaand*" the tears fall, "*you*.weren't.there!"

"YOU'RE RIGHT, BRI! *I WASN'T THERE*! If I had been, I'd be in an American prison *for murder* right now!" Her eyes go wide as the weight of that sinks in. "To me, anyone doing what she and this other guy did to *anyone*, was beyond cruel and vicious; but factor in you, *her best friend*, that just makes it *infinitely* worse! I have *no time* for this woman! *However*, I will tolerate her to

79

help you through this." He takes a step closer. "Your heart is so loving and wonderful that you *want* to forgive her so much, you can't accept that what she did is UNforgivable as far as friendship is concerned!" Jack uses this moment to get right up to her.

"Then why torture me with this now if there's no point?!" She asks.

"*Because she opened those wounds again, Bri*! Maybe this will, as you say, 'stop the bleeding' once and for all!" He takes a deep breath. "There are no descriptive words to accurately describe the horror she did to you! Why do you think Joe hasn't fully come around to her again and most likely never will? Katie hurt his sister in such an awful and UNforgivable way!"

"But if I'm trying to forgive her, you all need to forgive her, too!"

He's almost angry. "*How*?! You haven't even confronted her specifically about the events of that night! You've just pushed everything aside! If she had owned up to what she did and apologized, you wouldn't have to work so hard to forgive her...now forgetting, well, that's a different story!"

"Why does it bother you so much when it happened so long ago?!" She shoots back, folding her arms again.

"Damnit, BriaLynn, she hurt the woman I love in the worst possible way! *It's unimaginable!*" Jack retorts. "*I hate* what this woman continues to do to you! I love you!" When Bri scoffs at his reasoning, it triggers something inside him, and he grabs the back of her jaw and kisses her fiercely. When they pull their lips apart, they're a little out of breath, and Jack says again, "Don't you *ever* question my love for you again *or we will have one serious row!*"

"*Fine.* But I'm still angry with you, Jackson Carlisle!" She says and she kisses him again just as fiercely as he had kissed her.

He breaks the kiss. "You won't be angry with me anymore after I'm done with you!" He gives her his sexy smile he knows works on her.

She rolls her eyes. "You're always so confident of your sexiness!"

"You haven't complained once!" He has a cocky look. "I think my track record is *impeccable!*"

She clamps her lips down inside her mouth with her teeth, refusing to acknowledge he's right. He kisses her neck and below the ear.

"*You're* not playing fair!" She says.

He says against her neck, "Neither are you with all your sexy gorgeousness; not to mention your bloody stubbornness!"

"Mine?!" She's surprised and counters, "You're the one still kissing my neck and holding out!" She cups his face and gives him a determined look. "*How screwed up is that*?!"

He growls as he goes to kiss her, but tells her, "Stop talking, or it won't be as pleasurable as it could be for you!"

"*Liar*!" She says. "You *have* to, or——."

He kisses her. "*Shut it*!" He whispers loudly against her lips.

This time she's smiling more playfully. "*Make me*!"

He raises his eyebrow just as playful. "Temptress!" He scoops her up and takes her to the bedroom next door he uses when he stays at The Manor, dropping her on it. He joins her and ghosts her lips, "Amore Mia..."

She tells him, "I'm still mad at you!"

He looks at her so lovingly. "Are you sure?"

"Ugh...*no*!" She holds his face in her hands, looking into his eyes and says, "*My Sexy Jack*!"

"Just yours, Amore Mia, and forever will be..."

Bri lays next to Jack tracing her finger in the grooves of his muscles. She knows he's awake when she hears, "I'm sorry for pushing you." She lifts her head up to look at his face. He adds, "I'm angry at Katie for what she and that snake boyfriend of hers did to you, her snippiness at the wedding, not to mention her appalling actions in Rome. Then she's finally quiet and we're moving on with our lives, only she reaches out now, over a year later, *just to provoke you*! I get so angry and disgusted——."

Bri sweetly kisses him. "I get it. I just don't know what to do about it, never have. Now it feels like you're trying to force my hand."

His eyes close with that statement and his heart sinks. "Oh, Bri," he opens his eyes and turns to her, "I *never* wanted—."

She shakes her head interrupting, "You've already apologized and that's enough. I trust you mean it when you say you're sorry!" She faintly smirks, "*Aaand* I kind of forgave you *before* we were naked." He chuckles.

While she's in the bathroom, Jack checks his phone. He responds to a couple business texts and sets his phone down, only to have it ping again.

Bri says to him walking back to the living room in her quarters with David, "I should get going if I'm going to get to Kingsbury at a decent time."

He says as he embraces her tight, "I'm going to kiss you once more before I send you to Lawrence..." He does, squeezing her bum with one hand before releasing her. She smiles at him and they say their goodbyes for the day.

CHAPTER 9

Imperfectly Perfect & Royal History of Newhaven

Newhaven is unique because, while it's considered part of Scotland and the United Kingdom of Provinces, it's in many ways its own country. In Kingsbury, 'The Newhaven Parliament' is structured like their national government but, being an American, Bri does see similarities to the US government helping her to learn and understand faster.

As she and Lawrence ride to Kingsbury, they talk more in-depth about Newhaven history. Bri shifts more comfortably to face him.

She asks, "How much Newhaven history do you know?"

He raises his eyebrow. "Actually, I've been refreshing my knowledge and learning more specifics once we confessed our love for each other." He feels the end of a lock of her hair.

"*Oh?*" She smirks.

He chuckles. "I would think that if we're in-love with each other, then we're working towards the same goal." He winks as he kisses her hand and she sweetly smiles. "What's on your mind, My Darling?"

"Well, it's just...from what I understand about historical European duchies, earldoms, and so on, they're basically an estate and a local village on land that the estate owns as well."

"Like 'The Worthington Estate' and 'The Worthington Village.'" He says following along.

"Right." She smiles. "Everyone around here says, 'The Village,' but properly it would be 'The Worthington Village.'"

"But now as you learn the ropes of Newhaven and our national government, you find Newhaven is the exception." He replies.

"Well, I hadn't thought of it like that, but yes. *And* His Majesty still rules overall." She grins.

He laughs a little. "I don't know how to simplify what I know, so let's see..." Lawrence thinks.

"Remember, Ace, I *love* history, so worry about laying it out and not about trying to keep someone's interest."

"Ha-ha! Alright." He replies. "Well, during European medieval times duchies were a large estate, fife, county, country, or territory of its own, and they were ruled by a duke. They were only second to the king and queen, or equivalent ruler. Technically, Newhaven was a 'Grand Duchy' because of its sovereign state, along with a few others."

"Hold up. 'Sovereign state?'" She's confused. "I need to look up the definition of 'sovereign state' because I thought Newhaven runs like a sovereign state now...then again, if that were the case then it would still be a 'Grand Duchy' today."

He explains, "Back when King Andrew, The First, reigned, he was considered the most powerful king in *all* of Europe. Prior to his reign, he had consolidated two of the larger duchies with his marriage and when he succeeded The Throne, he reduced power to the 'Grand Duchies' by removing their sovereign statuses."

"Ah, he was paranoid that he would be overthrown..." Bri notes.

"And my however many 'great' grandfather, would raise King William III to be strong, powerful, *and brutal*. It would be his son, King Phillip IV, that would be the most hated king in our history; and raising his son, the first King Lawrence, to be just as brutal *and ruthless*. If someone wouldn't swear allegiance to them, they'd cut out their tongue right then to make sure the others would swear allegiance without hesitation. If someone was caught stealing, a hand would be cut off; if they were caught staring at The Queen or Royal Consort too long, their eyes would be cut out...if they raped a woman, well..., I think you know what would come next."

She gives him an 'eek' look. "If I also remember correctly, that's the two bloodiest centuries known as, 'The Age of Bloodshed.'"

"You're correct." He gives her a small smile. His thoughts go to his mother and how she wanted her reign to mark the beginning of 'The Age of Terror.'

"Unfortunately, when someone stomps on other people to get to the top, they worry about the people they've stepped on banding together to take away their power...think of the various revolutions!"

"Precisely." He agrees.

"Which is why another ancestor of yours, a different King Andrew, created Parliament to give his subjects a voice and avoided a revolution that was on the horizon with the French Revolution already underway." She states.

"You've learned quite a bit of history already!" He smiles and continues. "Newhaven is 'The Gem of the Isles' for many reasons, but like gems, when they're tucked away, they can be overlooked, or forgotten about altogether. Being in the location where it is, monarchs knew it was there, operating on its own and generating revenue for the UK, but sadly it was never really considered much more than that from those monarchs."

"So back when there were 'Grand Duchies,' a 'Grand Duke' ruled?" She asks for clarification.

"Yes, and remember, duchies were kept in the family since they began. Male heirs were important because, prior to women having rights, the laws only allowed males to own and control everything. If a male heir didn't exist, illegitimate males were accepted as long as they could be proven, although it was difficult the further back we go in history. That allowed for legitimate female heirs to inherit the duchy and they typically did for that reason. However, if a daughter inherited, her husband ruled while their family, particularly the children, would carry on the wife's maiden name, which was also the name of 'The House.'"

"Okay, that makes sense considering the times back then." She follows. "David and I have talked a lot about The Worthington Estate and Newhaven, but I never specifically asked why Newhaven was never named 'Worthington' after his ancestors were given the titles? If he said, I can't recall."

Lawrence answers, "Grand Duchies had to have royal blood ruling it. For example, a king's devoted nephew, his sister's son, John Newhaven, was given this island to rule over a millennia ago."

"Ah, and a strategic move for the king having a devoted family member protecting this border of the kingdom with the Scandinavian countries, particularly the Vikings, nearby." She notes. Lawrence studies her for a minute, which makes Bri a little nervous. "Did I say something wrong?"

"Not at all! I love how you're so *bloody brilliant*!" He smiles wide. "It definitely was a strategic move and most people miss that!"

She quietly laughs and shakes her head. She gets them back on track. "So, 'consorts' were put into place to legitimize children and increase chances of a male heir." Lawrence nods. She notes, "It's crazy to think, back then a woman was blamed for 'not producing an heir' when there's so much emphasis placed on how men were more superior than women! Of course, we now know the determining chromosome actually does come from the man." She rolls her eyes, shaking her head. She continues, "If we consider the lack of medicine back then, if an epidemic or plague swept through, it would wipe out families of all social classes. More children also helped their chances of at least one child surviving."

"I'm sure a lot of royal and noble families would've faired differently, had consorts not been an option centuries ago." He notes.

"Perhaps, but then there are other things to consider. Anyway, if a 'Newhaven' no longer rules, that means..." she puts it all together, "not even an unclaimed, illegitimate child, *a daughter*, was able to inherit?"

"Right, but this is where it gets tricky!" He tells her, "There was an illegitimate daughter married to a Carlisle."

Bri inhales a loud gasp. "Jack's ancestors?!".

He nods, then apologetically says, "He didn't tell you..."

Bri shakes her head. "No. Jack doesn't really like to talk about his biological family, let alone their family history. He says our family is all that matters to him." She softly smiles at the memory.

Lawrence gives a small smile. "Sounds like Jack."

She assures him, "I'll talk with Jack, but he won't care. He'll know we're discussing Newhaven history for my benefit and he'll be relieved he didn't have to sit through it."

He agrees. He takes a deep breath and continues to explain. "The King at the time named David's ancestors the titles' successors. They decided not to change the name of Newhaven, although, as you're aware, it was a common thing to do. There was always a kinship between The Newhaven and The Worthington Families, but the bitterness started growing between The Worthington and The Carlisle Families at that time." He tells her.

"Wow..." she's processing, "that bitterness is still apparent now!" She thinks about the stories Jack and David have told her about the hatred Jack's father has towards Peter. After the way Jack's father treated Jack through his cancer, the feelings are *definitely* mutual with Peter.

Lawrence nods. "The new Grand Duke tries to make peace with The Carlisle's since they were a prominent family back then. Eventually, The Carlisle Family found the proof to legitimize the illegitimate daughter as 'The Heir,' and also claimed to have more connections to royalty. *Unfortunately*, it was too late since The Worthington Family had already been given the titles. It would've been bad form to resend the titles without just cause *against* the new Grand Duke of Newhaven or the family. Remember, these were *legitimate male heirs* to The Worthington Family titles, who originally had an earldom. The Grand Duke went to The King and asked for The Carlisle Family to be given The Earldom and The Worthington Family would allow the family to stay on the estate they were already living on, for as long as they held those titles, which is The Newhaven Estate now belonging to The Grand Duke."

Bri is stunned. "That means Jack's family's estate is the *original* Newhaven Estate?! Wow..."

"Yes. The entire estate is taken care of through a—."

"Trust!" Bri interrupts. "The Newhaven Trust...er, wait, only the trust doesn't actually own it..."

"No, The Worthington's have it since they have the titles; the trust maintains it. It has a large manor, stables, barns, lots of acreage, complete with its own cathedral." Lawrence says. "It would take *quite a bit of money* for its upkeep which The Earl doesn't have and it would be a shame for the original Newhaven Manor to be reduced to ruins and the whole estate neglected for most tourists to see on their way into Kingsbury no less!"

Bri nods. "I remember David saying the large estates can be difficult to maintain. He told me that his ancestor did very well for himself, being a successful businessman; a trait he passed on down the line. A lasting legacy of his own because David's great-grandfather had the trait and started a business that grew into the huge conglomerate corporation it is today with businesses around the world. With the corporation, they're able to take care of The Worthington Estate. Now they don't need the rent from The Village and they keep the rent down and use the money for its improvements."

"It must be a great honor to have such a legacy to come from..." Lawrence says, staring off.

"To be the start of a better one can be the greater honor." She replies and he studies her with a sweet smile as he reaches over and squeezes her hand.

He says, "With bloodlines to royalty being necessary and when the rarity of a 'Direct Bloodline' is found, *like the beauty next to me*, it opens so many doors and avenues to play around with."

She shakes her head in confusion. "Play around? What does that mean?"

He smiles a bit. "I'm afraid to say more only because I don't want to influence your decision one way or the other. Like we agree, we have to do this for love, *if* you want to do this with me."

She softly smiles and leans over, which he leans over to meet her for a little kiss. "Thank you. But it's 'if *we* want to do this.'" She clarifies.

"Oh no! *I already know I want to do this*!" He grins showing his dimples and she giggles. "I'd set it up in an hour if I thought you would agree to it!" She purses her lips trying to hide a smile, giving him his first hint that she is really going to do this with him!

They had been sitting for a few minutes in front of the entrance of Newhaven's Civic Hall Building. It's a bigger building to house municipal offices such as The Lord Mayor, courts, police, a smaller jail, and of course offices for The Duke and Duchess of Newhaven. Bri's office is what would've been Carlotta's, but Carlotta preferred to office out of The Manor when the boys were young. She doesn't handle any of the government business, Peter and his father took care of it, so when the boys went to various boarding schools, she remained at The Manor. When James got older, he worked with Carlotta managing The Estate and now The Inn, learning from Jack all that he could about finances, and continues to learn all he can from Jack.

Carlotta happily gave Bri her office as Bri took on more of Peter's duties, except certain ones that require David because technically, *officially*, The Duchy will pass to him as Peter's heir.

When they walk into the building, The King is bowed and curtsied to, with 'Your Majesty' said a lot. He does acknowledge this, but at the same time, he still makes Bri feel like she has his full attention. Something he, David, and Jack have in common.

Lawrence has asked Bri what she thinks about the government, the changes they have already made, and what she sees for improvements. He's interested in how the textile business and her '*New Beginnings Foundation*' are doing. Plus, he's curious how she likes hearing the appeal cases. Each working royal has various objectives within their tenure, but they each have something, a purpose, they will be known for. Whether Bri realizes it or not, her main purpose and objective is starting to take shape within the criminal justice system. They're touring the courtrooms section of the building as Lawrence asks his questions and they talk as they walk. However, they talk about the appeals cases when they're back in her office.

She shuts the door before she begins and has Lawrence sit in a comfier chair. "Only not *my* overstuffed chair." She grins. "Okay, okay. I'll give my special chair up to you..." He chuckles and motions in the direction of the chair for her to take it; then he watches her sit before he does. It occurs to him...there's one at The Manor *and* The Cottage House, so he makes a mental note to get one for her for The Royal Apartment.

When they're settled, she asks, "Do you remember me telling you about my gift for seeing spirits and ghosts?"

He softly chuckles. "It's not the type of thing that's easily forgotten, Darling."

"Well, my gift seems to be expanding." She tells him.

"Clairvoyance comes to mind when you say that...like '*seeing into the future.*'" He comments.

She lightly laughs. "In this case, I'm able to see past events, but I don't have control over it. See, one of the first appeals cases I was given had to do with this fourteen-year-old kid, Jaleel Winter, sentenced to life in prison. He was raised by his elderly grandmother, who was trying to get him *to stay* on the right path. She tried to teach him not to make the same awful choices his parents made. His mother was in prison already, while his father had been paroled, but disappears from his life for long stretches; his other grandparents wanted nothing to do with him; one sibling in and out of jail herself and two family members who overdosed on...one was cocaine and the other heroin."

Lawrence sadly says, "Poor kid."

Bri nods. "One day, I was thumbing through the file and I see in a vision, his dad firing the gun that kills the clerk, then wiping it off. Somehow, I'm able to know his dad's thought process was that his son's a minor and 'they'll go easier on him.' His dad tosses the gun to his son, because he knows his son will reflexively catch it, which puts *his* fingerprints on it."

"That's awful!" He shakes his head. He dully adds, "I guess there's a club for lousy parenting!"

"It's horrifying to think how many parents would fall into that category!" She notes and he raises his eyebrows nodding. "Well, making things worse yet, the son was tried and convicted *as an adult* and spending life in prison!" Bri tells him. Lawrence exhales in frustration for the son. She goes on, "At the appeals hearing, I met with a few people including the prosecutor and barrister, as well as this kid and his grandmother. I told him to tell me what happened. He kept saying his dad tosses him the gun and wants him to take the blame since he's a minor. The prosecutor is a bit annoyed and throws out there that the only prints on the gun were the defendant's fingerprints." I look straight at this kid and say, 'You're missing a key piece, aren't you?' I'm wanting him to think about it and say it on his own."

"Good point." Lawrence notes.

"I could see him struggling to remember, so I asked him to close his eyes and picture the scene, to maybe go back to when his dad first took him to the gas, *er,* petrol station. That seemed to work because he casually runs through the steps they took. When he says his dad wiped the gun clean of his fingerprints, I looked at the prosecutor who heard that part, as did his barrister. I asked if the gun was dusted for a fingerprint *on the trigger,* which no one knew at that moment. I suggested testing that and to study the fingerprint placement. Do they line up, but then again, he could've held it normally out of another 'reflex?' Did they test for gun powder residue on the father? No one could answer the questions. After that, it was pretty easy to grant the appeal and let the prosecutor and barrister hash it out later. I just found out that this kid's case wasn't going to be retried, but dad had a warrant issued for his arrest. I'm also working to have a law passed that in a situation where a minor is involved in a crime with an adult, the adult is most culpable; there are similar ones in the US. I'm told these here are likely going to be passed soon." She holds up crossed fingers.

"I'm sure a lot of people support something like that." He replies.

She's excited. "Oh! Plus, plus, this kid joined up with The New Beginnings Foundation and I couldn't be more excited!" She has a huge smile. "He's such a *great* kid and will go places, if given a chance! *And I SO want to give him a chance!*"

"That's fantastic!" Lawrence happily says; her excitement is contagious. "What about his grandmother? Is she around for him?"

"She is in a nursing home, er, they're called 'care homes' here. She went into one a couple years into his sentence. I approved a transfer for her to be moved into a care home not far from The Textile Mill and paid for by The Foundation, so Jaleel can see her frequently. It's also a better facility for her specific needs! I'm sure all this could help keep her going for quite a while!"

"I'm sure it will!" He agrees, smiling as he watches her beam with excitement for the grandmother and grandson.

"I'm so excited when good things come out of a bad situation!" She adds. "I only wish I could erase the effects completely for Jaleel..."

Lawrence smiles lovingly. "*But,* as you believe, 'everything happens for a reason.' *Maybe* this experience will help him help others? Maybe he'll be instrumental working with your foundation or becomes the next Prime Minister!" She lightly laughs as she nods.

There's a brief knock before the door pops open. Peter sees Lawrence and apologizes. "Oh! Sorry, Herst! I'm in a hurry, but I should've waited for Bri to answer!" He's smiling and shaking Lawrence's hand. "How are you, Son?!"

"Good, Sir!" Lawrence happily replies. He loves The Worthington Family! Peter and Carlotta have always made him feel like part of the family.

Before Lawrence could ask him how he is in return, Peter says, "Bri, I was going to discuss something, but you can take this with you," he holds up a file, "and we can discuss it this evening," he looks at Lawrence again, "*or* as soon as you're able to." He smiles.

"Of course! If you don't mind, set my phone on it so I'll remember to slide it into my bag?" She asks and he does just that.

"Great! I'll let you two get back to your conversation." He says as he walks back to the door, with everyone saying a version of 'bye.' Lawrence and Bri watch the door close behind Peter.

Bri looks at Lawrence. "Peter has been preparing the Newhaven people for me being at the helm for most governmental matters, running more of the day-to-day things." Bri's desk phone rings. She goes over and smiles when she sees the number "It's David." She tells Lawrence.

"Hi, My Love!" Bri greets him. "You're on speaker."

"Hullo, Beautiful! Hullo, Brother!" David replies. "We were curious what your plans were for this evening. If you two want to be alone together, that's fine, if you plan on family or the four of us, we're okay with whatever."

Bri looks at Lawrence as she tells David, "We'll be finished here in a bit and we'll let you know."

"Fantastic! Jack wants to talk privately with you for a moment. I love you, Macushla!"

Bri smiles. "Love you more!"

She picks up the phone as Jack gets on the other end of the line.

"Hi, Gorgeous!"

"Hi, Amore Mio! What's up?" There's a long pause... "Out with it, *Mister* Carlisle, or no more sss—!"

"Whoa, whoa, *whoa!*" Jack halfway chuckles knowing where she was going with that. "*No need to get hostile and threaten that!* You couldn't even go a week without—*Oh!*" He realizes how David would fit into it and Bri's eyebrow goes up as she hears it dawn on him. He chuckles saying, "*Well played, Amore Mia.*"

"I think so!" She smiles a big cheeky grin. "*Now, out with it!*"

"I just wanted to apologize again. You have such a huge, loving heart that doesn't like to judge or hold grudges. Here I am, trying to *make you* move past something you're not ready for because *I'm holding the grudge!* It's not fair to you."

"I'm not doing a very good job of that right now, because I'm having lots of thoughts of retaliation!" She admits.

"You're human!" He says.

"*I'm human?!*" She fakes being hurt. "That's such an *awful* thing to say to the woman you *supposedly* love!" Lawrence snorts a laugh.

Jack laughs saying. "I *do* love you! Wouldn't you want me to be honest with you, or would you prefer I lie to you?!"

"Both!"

"Liar!" He smirks. "Besides, I said you were human, *not mental!*"

She giggles. "I'll give you that. Although, there are days I do feel *completely* mental!"

Both Jack and Lawrence chuckle. Jack and Bri say 'goodbye' and 'I love you' before hanging up.

CHAPTER 10

Imperfectly Perfect Improvised Dinner

On the way back to The Manor later that afternoon, Bri turns to Lawrence and asks, "What would you like to do this evening?"

He asks, "Would you have dinner with me? It's nothing fancy because my guards wouldn't have time to secure a location, but maybe I could arrange something private in my room at The Manor?"

She smiles. "I'd love that! Let me text David and Jack so they don't wait on us." He nods and calls to arrange the dinner personally with The Chef.

She types a quick text to send both at once, ending with 'I'll stay at The Manor tonight' and 'I love you.' Jack texts for both of them. They're going to meet up with friends at a pub in The Village and play some arrows, or darts as they're called in the US. She tells them she'll see Jack tomorrow and David later that night.

When they pull up to The Manor, Lawrence gets out, then he holds his hand out to Bri to help her. They walk back to his room, where they sit on the couch. His blue-green eyes were intense and it's hard for her *not* to hold his gaze. The ringing of his phone helps snap them out of it.

He turns up his nose when he sees it's his mother. "Ugh," he rolls his eyes, "it's Mother." He holds his finger up, "Give me a second?" He stands up and she nods. He steps away.

"Mother." His tone is unfeeling.

Her voice is hateful, "*Have you done your job or did you forget the purpose of why you're there!*" Her tone is blunt and mean. "*Get The Marchioness onboard with this by the time you get back, or we'll come at this from a different angle! Do.you.understand.me?*" She enunciates with anger.

He doesn't realize how good Bri's hearing is...she nervously stands, trying not to panic, and slips out the door. She walks fast to her quarters...*Their plan???* She asks herself. *There's a plan?!*

"Mother, that's——."

"NO! YOU UNGRATEFUL LITTLE TWIT! IF YOU CAN'T ACCOMPLISH THIS BY THE TIME YOU COME BACK, WE'LL *TAKE* WHAT WE NEED FROM HER!" She tells him.

"*No*. We won't." He states and there is an audible gasp on the other end. He knows better than to talk to her like that.

"*YOU MISERABLE, STUPID PRA*—," he rolls his eyes, tuning out the foul language she uses, even holding the phone away from his ear; he's heard this all *countless times* before, he could probably recite it word-for-word by this point. He hears, "I'LL MAKE YOU SORRY!"

That's code for she'll seek out Abby, but he knows she's with Seth and Genevieve touring Ireland.

She's in the middle of telling him he doesn't even have to officially make her 'The Royal Consort.' "...It won't matter if it's a bas—."

"*Stop it, Mother!* It's insulting and I won't stand—."

"*YOU* WON'T STAND FOR WHAT?!" She laughs at the ridiculousness of it. "We both know you're too weak and pathetic to do anything about it, but this heir will be *MY LEGACY*—."

"GOODNIGHT, Mother!"

"*Don't you DARE* hang up—."

He hangs up on her and he's pretty proud of himself for doing so. It's a waste of time to engage this woman and the more time he spends with Bri, the less interested he gets in pleasing his mother to keep her satisfied. He needs to talk with Seth and Abby to think of a new strategy that still protects them, even Gen, when he gets back to London.

Lawrence turns around to find Bri is gone. He chases after her and goes to her quarters. He knocks, but she doesn't answer. He calls her phone and hears it ring inside. His heart sinks because she won't answer.

He walks up to the door. "Bri, if you don't answer I'm coming in." She opens the door as he says, "You didn't have to go."

"Yes. *I did*. Hearing her talk to you like that, for her to talk about me like that—," she inhales sharply to get control of her emotions, "makes me want to vomit—," she stops herself to swallow hard. He reaches for her, but she steps back. "Let's just call it a night..."

He grabs the door and puts his foot in front of it to stop her from closing it on him. He senses there's more. "What *aren't* you saying?"

She exhales, "*You have a plan with your mother!*" She turns away from him, whispering more to herself walking away from him, "*I feel like such a fool...*"

Everything caught up to her and she tried to be strong, tried to not let Katie's texts bother her, but after what she overheard between Lawrence and his mother...maybe Jack's right and she needs to confront Katie once and for all. As she quickly wipes her tears, her mind goes to when Lawrence says he loves her, it *feels* genuine—. Her thoughts are interrupted when she feels his arms wrap around her from behind and he kisses the curve of her neck.

His mouth is close to her ear as he tells her, "I promise you; I'm *not* playing you, nor using you! I've been open with David and Jack from the beginning and I'll answer whatever you want to know, but *I swear to you*," he pulls back and turns her to look at her. "I want this for *all* the right reasons! *I love you!*" He stresses.

She gives him a little smile. "I believe you. I *couldn't* doubt that." She sees relief go across his face. "I was actually thinking when you say you love me, I *feel* it. *It feels genuine.* When someone says, 'I love you' it's words; it's only felt when someone puts action behind it." She explains. "I *feel it* from you when you're spending time with me, holding my hand, hugging me, wanting to be with me—." She stops to push down her urge to cry. "Then I overhear your mother tell you..."

"Wait. *You overheard us...*" *He* gets nauseous! "*All of it?!*"

"Up until I left." She informs him. "I have really good hearing."

"I'll say!" He's surprised. He cups her face, "Bri, it's not as bad as it may seem. She has her agenda, but I *can't* let her know I even have an agenda, nor that *my agenda* is the only one I promised David and Jack, and I swear to you now! I love you and I'll bow out of this, of us, if you ask me to; *if that's what you want?*" He holds her face again and wipes her tears with his thumbs. She shakes her head and she sees him exhale in relief.

"Lawrence," she points to her face, "some of these tears are because of everything that's happened...starting with Katie and ending with your mother..." She wipes her tears taking a deep breath.

He nods. "When you're ready, I believe we have a dinner to get to?" He says with such an adorable expression, her heart skips a beat. She smiles and threads her arm through his.

They walk back down the hallway and Bri can't help the sarcasm that comes when she says to him, "And here I thought your mother would hate me."

"Mother hates *almost* everyone! Unfortunately, the woman abhors you." He flatly tells her.

"Already?!" She's a little surprised.

"Well, yes. *She needs you!*" He tells her. "And because *you'll* be the mother to *our baby*; however, in her mind our baby will be *her legacy.*"

"Ah. So, narcissistic with a bit sociopathic, a dash psychopathic, and maybe a pinch of a few other personality disorders." She says.

Lawrence chuckles. "While that piques my curiosity, shall we have dinner delivered first?" She smiles her agreement.

He calls for the food, then he turns back to her. She looks at him and softly smiles. "Bri, I swear you won't be 'used' for anything. But to be perfectly honest, and there's no easy way to say this, my mother has insisted I use my power *as king* to force your hand. From the beginning, I went to David and Jack to use their solicitors, because I wanted to protect *you, and your body*, from the powers of The Monarchy. David reminded me about your dual citizenship a while back. My mother sees it differently and has her own agenda; an agenda *she has to think* I'm reluctantly following to keep her from finding out the truth! *Our baby*," he gestures the two of them, "will be with their mother!" He points to her.

"You realize she doesn't want you to fall in-love because it will complicate her hold on you!" She notes.

"Bri, I've already fallen in-love with you! So loving you *already* complicates things for her! I'm finding the more I love you, the less I care about keeping her 'happy,' if that's what you'd call it." He cups her cheek. "We haven't talked about your decision, but you can relax knowing David and Jack are handling the paperwork. My mother will have hers drawn up, but only the paperwork David and Jack are having drawn up will be signed! *And* it will be checked as we're signing it, just to make absolutely sure it wasn't switched at the last second!"

She studies him and he feels like she's seeing right into his soul. "No."

He looks at her confused. "No?"

"That's all secondary, Lawrence, but the truth is, you'd never force *any* woman, whether to be your Royal Consort and have your baby, or just have your baby; nor would you even demand her eggs! There's no way, under *any* circumstances, you'd ever do that to a woman, *let alone to me*!" She raises her eyebrow. "Am I wrong?"

He smiles and pulls her lips to his and kisses her fiercely. "No, you're not wrong." He rests their foreheads together. "Thank you for believing in me."

She sits on the coffee table across from him to holds his hands on his knees. "I'll *always* believe in you! I'm your biggest cheerleader, just as I am for David and Jack."

He smiles lovingly. "As we are for you!"

"Right!" She smiles and kisses him. He tries to pull her to straddle him as they kiss, but she shakes her head breaking the kiss. "Straddling you right now would be playing with fire," she runs her finger down his lips, "...extremely *hot* fire!" She's incredibly attracted to David and Jack, as well as Lawrence, but this attraction to Lawrence is something else, too, she just hasn't figured it out yet.

Before Lawrence could say anything, there is a knock on the door. He gets up and puts his finger up in a 'just a second' gesture again. He heads for the door, then turns back. "That means 'just a minute,' even 'hold that thought.' It does *not* mean you can leave. *Got it?*" Lawrence grins.

She giggles. "Could I walk over to the table?" She winks. He exhales chuckling, shaking his head. He runs his hand into his hair and scratches his head on the way to answer the door.

Lawrence answers the door and Bri goes over to the table. There are a couple of people who bring in the meal and set up the table; Bri thanks them by name. Lawrence pulls out Bri's chair for her. He smiles as he sits next to her, rather than across from her.

When they're alone again she squeezes his hand and says, "I'm sorry if I'm frustrating you with waiting."

He places his hand on top of hers, "Bri, after the time we have spent together, the phone calls, countless text messages, I'm in this! For you, with you, *waiting* doesn't scare me as long as we don't have to wait until next year to make things official."

"Don't worry! I couldn't wait another year either!" She winks at him.

He gives her a determined look with a slight smile, "I mean by the end of *this* year, Darling."

She studies him a moment, "That *maaay* be possible."

He's serious for a moment. "When my mother asks, I'll have to..." he struggles to find the words.

"'Throw her a bone' in a way?" She helps.

"That's a good way of putting it." He chuckles before he gets serious again, "I need you to *always remember*, no matter what happens, I'm on *your side*. I'm *always* on your side!" He stresses.

She smiles with a nod, then changes the topic. "How's Gen and Seth?"

"They're excited for me and for us!" He looks at her. "They also want it to work for the country. Gen thinks like you, that *our* people would benefit with a king finding love!" He smiles lovingly at her. "My mother is *still* furious with me that I wanted Seth and Gen to continue their relationship and I refuse to make Gen have *my* baby."

"*Proving* my point earlier!" She grins. "There's no way you'd ever force a woman to have your baby!" He kisses her hand. "There are, however, a lot of women out there who would walk through fire to make a baby with you, even those who'd sell your mother the baby and walk away."

"While that's true," he gives her a pointed look, "they wouldn't be the right mother for any child of mine."

"Good point." She replies.

He takes a deep breath. "I guess if the by-laws were written and Genevieve *had* to have The Heir, then it'd be more like surrogacy or in-vitro. I swear the arrangement for my marriage to Genevieve was Mother's spitefulness and her enjoyment of hurting people, *especially her children*."

"From what you've told me and what I've heard myself, I don't doubt that at all." She gives him a faint smile.

He smiles sweetly, then gets serious for a moment. "While we're on the subject of my mother...she gets people's loyalty to her one way or another. I know you have many loyalties: David, Jack, The Worthington's, The Bradshaw's, and they're loyal to you! But I need to be clear: *I need your loyalty!*"

"You have my love, Lawrence, so you have my loyalty!" She firmly tells him. "The three of you are first and foremost; our children being a part of that loyalty." He nods and smiles.

"Thank you. I believe it's what Americans call 'a dealbreaker.'" He says. Bri remembers David's comment, a version of 'it's lonely at the top.'

She looks him in the eyes. "Lawrence, I'll *never* choose to be disloyal to you! Could I do something to make you doubt it? Maybe, although I can't think of a scenario yet. All I ask is you talk to me. Communication is key in *any* relationship, especially in the ones I have with you, Jack, and David. If I don't know if I did something or should've done something, *I need to know*. I won't ever purposely set out to hurt you, I swear to you, and I'll feel horrible if I ever do!"

"The same goes for me, Darling." He smiles and gives her a sweet kiss.

When they've finished eating, he stands and pulls her up. He wraps his arms around her and kisses her. He rests their foreheads together for a moment, then lifts his head to ask, "We've talked about this before, but I was wanting to know if you'll tell me more about Katie?" He knows what happened, but he was hoping for more details.

Her eyebrows scrunch together. "I thought I told you everything?"

He replies, "It felt like you were holding back."

She thinks about that as she walks with him over to the couch. She rehashes everything, telling him what Katie and her boyfriend did to her. She realizes she did hold back some of those memories that have returned, although it's still sketchy and comes in flashes because of the drugs they gave her. She hesitates to tell him some of the specifics when she sees Jessica.

"Don't hold back, Bri. His heart will make an important connection to you, but he needs the *whole* story of what you remember, and found out later, even the flashes, to help him bond more deeply with you."

Bri would explain all the horrible things Katie and her boyfriend did, in more graphic detail than she's ever done because of the flashes of memories that are coming back. It took a while because of the emotions and the questions he asked throughout.

She tells him of the situation in Rome with Jack on their honeymoon. "That was the limit for me by that point! I just couldn't do it anymore...I couldn't pretend anymore...I told David to send her home and he did, right then and there." Lawrence snickers a bit. "Even as the memories have come back, it still feels like a dream or a different lifetime..." She trails off trying to stop the memories popping into her mind. She looks over at him and sees he is relating as well.

She holds his jaw and whispers, "*What happened to you, Lawrence? I can only feel it was something unimaginable and horrendous for you!*"

He holds her hands and stares at them as he tells her everything. "I had been abused on every level, for as long as I can remember. I'm rather good at withstanding torture by this point." He gives her a weak, half smile as he rubs his thumbs across the soft skin of her knuckles. "I was weeks from my thirteenth birthday when the abuse escalated beyond what anyone would ever conceive possible!" She keeps a straight face but her gift takes her back to that time in *his* childhood and she actually sees it. When she looks down, he thinks she is emotional but she is seeing it in a vision. He continues, "I'm almost the same age as my mother was when she 'made love,' as she puts it, with her uncle for the first time." He fidgets with her hands. "For me, I was tied up on some rack and whipped until they were so sexually excited from my slash marks and pain, they had to..." he shivers at the thought of his mother and uncle in any sexual way. He tries to spare her the worst of it and the extent of his torture.

"*Oh, Lawrence...*" She barely manages to whisper still staring at the floor; a tear drops from her eye straight to the floor. "How long did this go on?!" She saw the same images he talked about play out in her mind.

"A few years or so. It may sound weird, but I had to separate myself and go to a different place in my mind."

She feels it from him, "*To protect yourself.*"

He closes his eyes and nods, resting his forehead to her head since she was looking down. "One day, I overheard talk about being replaced and her parting gift after they were done with me for the last time was a prostitute...this will sound crazy, but that was probably the most humiliating time for me."

"Not weird, Lawrence." She lifts her head. "Being a mom, I can't even begin to wrap my mind around purposely doing something so awful and disgusting on so many levels to any child, let alone my own, *and countless times*! It's mindboggling to me! Then hearing it all happened to you, and seeing it, only makes me love you more——."

"How?!" He's surprised she loves him more. His lower jaw shakes for a few seconds as he tries to stop his emotions again. "It should make you want to run as far away from me and my family as possible!"

"Lawrence." Bri holds his face. "You not only love me, but you trust me with something you may have never fully told anyone else, not even your brother or sister!"

"They know terrible things happened, but not all the disgusting details." He replies.

"How can I *not* love you more?!" She smiles with tears. She kisses him tenderly, then hugs him and straddles him to firmly hug him.

He furrows his brow as he remembers. "Did you say, 'seeing it' a minute ago?" He asks.

She sits back, exhaling, "Yeah..." She has an apologetic face. "I wasn't sure if I should say anything? You were finally opening up, but I didn't take myself there, I promise! It just happened!"

He holds her face and kisses her, then wraps his arms firmly around her. She hugs him and she faintly whispers, "*It's not your fault, Lawrence! Do you hear me?! None of it was your fault!*"

They just hug each other for a while. "Bri, I...I've never told another soul for many reasons and one being I couldn't trust..."

Bri pulls back and looks at him with such love and compassion, for the first time in his life he realizes he's seeing, *and has been seeing,* 'unconditional love' reflected back. "Not another soul will hear it from me! Not David or Jack, but they won't ask me to break your confidence either! It's your story to tell if you want someone to know; *not mine!*" She points to the door. "'Behind bedroom doors,' remember?" She has teary eyes. "Lawrence, there's *nothing* wrong with you! That was partly her plan, *their plan,* of manipulating you, the future king. It had to be her uncle's plan from the beginning when he helped your grandfather overthrow his brother so *her uncle* could ultimately control The Monarchy!" Lawrence's eyebrows shoot up as he considers the significance of that statement. She tells him, "If you had responded differently to sex with a prostitute, or started craving what they had done to you all those years, then she would've had *more* control because you would've bonded in some sick and twisted way. Which is odd she and your father stepped down because you'd think in their minds, you wouldn't have been ready to assume the throne?" She exhales in disgust, "A true-mother is to *love and protect her children* and if it were any of my children, I'm not so sure *she'd* still be alive!"

"*You?!*" He's genuinely surprised.

"It's hard for you to imagine because I try to be quick to forgive. *However,* anyone touching my kids would be dealing with a mama bear, crossed with a lioness!" She says with determination, "Touch 'my cubs' and 'there will be hell to pay!' *No prisoners!*"

"*That* makes sense!" He agrees.

She sees there's something he's not saying. "It's a mistake to think my kindness is a weakness, *Darling,*" she teases with his accent and gets him to smile a little. She puts her forehead to his and taps on top of his heart. "This tells me you're a wonderful man with so much potential to be *a great king*!"

He shakes his head. "You haven't seen the other side of me."

"No, I haven't seen the shell you created just to survive and protect Seth and Abby." She lifts her head and looks at him. "Your secrets are safe with me. *You're* safe with me." She holds his face and smiles lovingly. "Will I frustrate you? Yes, *absolutely*! I'm feisty and I'll fight for what's right." She gives him a small grin. "You'll learn to love me for it!"

He snorts a bit of a laugh. "I'm afraid I already do, *Darling*!"

She softly giggles and continues. "As I've said before, will I make mistakes? Unfortunately, yes. Marrying an heir, having a 'Noble consort,' *and then there's you*...I'm in *a lot* of uncharted territory! Will I say or do something that might hurt your feelings? Regrettably, yes." He sees the pained look as she says that. "But I also know that applies vice versa." He nods and she says, "What I can promise, and you'll hopefully agree, is the intentions are never going to be malicious or vindictive." He does agree and she explains further, "When we have time to reflect on those mistakes, we'll feel bad and want to make up with the other one; but the sooner the better, so there's no permanent damage." He nods.

She pulls back and kisses him tenderly, but it changes to fiercely. She feels the roots of her bond with Lawrence growing, stretching deeper, and getting stronger. They hug, soaking in their love for each other.

Lawrence looks at her and gives her a sweet smile. "You're absolutely incredible! How did you become so bloody amazing, fantastic, *and brilliant*?!" He cups her cheek and kisses her slowly and meaningfully.

They decide to watch a movie, or as they say, a film. After which, he walks her back to her quarters and they say 'goodnight' at the door. He tangles a hand in her hair and wraps his other arm around her waist, as he looks into her eyes and they hold each other's gaze.

"I adore you, BriaLynn!"

"I adore you, too, Lawrence Alexander!" She grins and sees him smile. "See you in the morning?" He nods and gives her one last goodnight kiss and hug before she goes into her quarters to go to bed.

As he walks back to his room, his phone rings and with his thoughts on Bri and their evening together, he mindlessly answers the phone.

"Hullo..."

"How dare you hang up on me and then avoid my calls, you pathetic little ba—!"

"*WHAT* do you want, Mother?" He purposely interrupts.

"Do we have her for producing our heir?!"

He thinks of Bri's comment of 'throwing a bone' and that's what he has to do, but he grins when he thinks of what 'bone' to throw...

"She's agreed for it to be less than a year when she'll become 'The Royal Consort.'" He smiles to himself as she twists a bit...

His mother goes into a tirade about 'a year' that he doesn't listen to, hanging up on her again but this time without a word. When his phone rings again, it's her; he sends it to voicemail. She keeps calling, so he silences her calls. He stood up to his mother and he knows there will be repercussions he'll have to pay, but he didn't care. He'll think of Bri and the sting of whatever she uses to inflict pain on him won't be noticeable.

When he goes to bed that night, he knows he has found someone he can truly trust with his heart; and he *sleeps* for the first time in a *very* long time.

CHAPTER 11

Imperfect Retaliation, Royally Executed

A couple days later, Bri feels David stir as he gets up to get ready to go exercise. She slowly wakes herself up and says, "I'm going to go wait for Lawrence so we can have a little time this morning before he leaves."

David smiles and leans over the bed. "I think that's a *fantastic* idea!" He kisses her. "Want me to tell him?"

"That would probably be a good idea, considering I may rest on the bed while I wait. And if he comes in and starts stripping down before he realizes I'm in his room, well..."

He's smirking. "And that's a problem *beeecause*???"

She raises her eyebrows. "David, I made you wait until we were married, and then when Jack came into the picture, I made him wait until we were official; although he and I ended up waiting until you and I came back from our honeymoon. Regardless, I don't feel right not waiting because—." She's surprised at her emotions that snuck up on her and the lump in her throat cutting her off in mid-sentence. She holds her fingers to her throat trying to swallow the lump down.

David quickly puts his t-shirt over his head, then sits down next to her on the bed. He holds her cheek and rests their foreheads together; their eyes are closed for a moment...

"My apologies for not thinking that through." He looks at her. "Waiting to be official is your way of making sure the relationship is built on love. To keep inside the rules of 'behind bedroom doors,' I won't ask any questions, if I had them."

She smiles lovingly. "*You* have my heart! Jack has a special place in it, and now Lawrence. Without you, *none* of this would even be! My heart has been in great hands because, while I always knew I had more love to give, *you* unlocked it and freed my heart to love. *And* you made it possible for me to be loved so much more than I *ever* could've imagined! You're an incredible man, *David Christopher Worthington!*"

"Oh, no, Love! YOU are the most important ingredient in all this! I'm sure there are other women out there like you, but it's more like one in a billion. You love us each *individually*, and we actually *gain* so much more love when you love all three of us; *that's* the incredible part of all this! It's a cliché to say you're as beautiful inside as you are on the outside, *but it's true*! People gravitate to you because you're genuine, *and in this society*, well, that's the rarest characteristic there is!" He holds her face and smiles adoringly at her. "I know you remember what 'Macushla' means?"

"It's a kind of 'Gaelic shorthand' that means 'pulse of my heart.'" She replies.

"Good girl. It's 'chuisle mo chroí.'"

She closes her eyes and smiles. "I love it when you say that and anything else that highlights your accent."

He lightly chuckles and repeats it. "'Chuisle mo chroí.'"

She opens her eyes and looks at him with a playfulness in them. "It *has* to be said with your accent for the full effect!"

He softly laughs again. "Bri, you have my heart, too! *You're the reason* why my heart beats every day. Without you, I was empty, but since you came into my life, *life makes sense, Macushla*!" He kisses her again.

"You sweet talker!" She glances at the door. "You're probably late."

He looks at the time. "That I am." He shrugs.

"One thing." She explains while he puts his shoes on. "I told Lawrence I didn't want to know if he does or not, but I gave him the option of other women until we're official."

"*Ah*," following along, "because you have Jack and me."

"I want you to know this, and tell Jack, in case either of you see something, I *don't* want to know about." She walks over to him. "Tell Lawrence I'll be waiting. I love you, *Mister* Worthington!"

"Will do! I love you, too, Mrs. Worthington!" He kisses her quickly and leaves.

Bri throws some leisure wear on before heading to Lawrence's room. She is walking down the hallway that goes to his room when all of a sudden, she feels like she is being watched. She looks around and the halls are empty. This isn't unusual because within The Manor, security for 'The King' is light when there are no other visitors and the staff are the longtime vetted ones.

Bri goes into Lawrence's room to wait for him. She sees the couch and glances at the comfier looking bed. She crawls into the bed and dozes off to sleep. She hears the room door open and footsteps, then she feels someone crawling onto the bed with her. There's a strange cologne somehow mixed with sweat. Her eyes pop open when it registers: *this isn't Lawrence.* Just then someone grabs her, rolling her onto her back with one hand and has a knife in the other. When she screams, the side of his arm goes over her mouth. He is pushing his arm down so hard her lips are flat against her teeth, threatening to split them open.

"The Queen Mother wants me to carve a *permanent* reminder of who's in charge!" His voice is strained trying to hold her down while she struggles to free herself.

She manages to free a leg but she can't really move until he happens to shift and she hears in her mind, 'Pull up your knee as hard as you can!' She quickly does and the guard lets out a loud gasp, then holds his breath because he can't breathe from the pain. He is frozen in place, holding himself, but he furiously glares at her. She closes her eyes and pushes him as hard as she can to get him off her...There's a loud thud as his body hits the floor.

She quickly scrambles to get off the bed, jumping over him to run, but he grabs her foot, tripping her and her body makes a smacking sound when she hits the floor. He holds her ankle as he picks up the knife and struggles to get to his knees. Bri kicks at his forearm with her other foot to get him to let go of her. The guard holds the handle of the blade in his mouth and struggles with her to pin her down again, sitting at her waist and hips this time. He has had enough and holds the knife to the side of her throat above an artery.

He's angry and says through gritted teeth, "With one swift movement, you won't even be able to scream for help!"

She glares. "Kill me and what do you think The Queen Mother will do to you, *Genius?!*"

She continues to fight him and it's all he can do to hold her down with both wrists pinned to the floor. His anger grows with his frustration and more crude language pours out of his mouth.

Then he angrily tells her, "*You can't keep this up forever!*"

Bri looks him in the eye and glares with disgust. "*Neither can you!*"

"You'll tire out first, Luv! I can wait." He tells her.

"Really?! You're so out of shape, you can barely catch your breath! You better hope I don't get another chance to hurt you, because you may not get up the next time!" She snaps at him.

He is seething and looks around the room. He sees a charging cord on top of a bag right there within his reach. He uses it to tie her hands, even though she fights the best she can to prevent it. Now he's able to easily hold her wrists with one hand. He then takes his knife and hooks the tip of the blade inside her short shirt sleeve, cutting her shirt. She doesn't show him fear, although she is trying to figure out how she is going to get out of this...

"How much time do you think you have before The King shows up and catches you?!"

"The Queen Mother will take care of him!" He tells her. "*She always does.*"

"She's losing her grip on him." Bri says and he scoffs. "Why do you think she sent you here?! Although a smarter person wouldn't do this *here*, in his room, of *all* places?!"

She feels his one hand grip tighter at her tied wrists and he pushes the tip of the knife into her skin on her shoulder. She feels it break through her skin and tear through her flesh as he *yanks* down in anger. Before he can do much more for an 'M,' two sets of hands grab him, yanking him off of her and he is pushed into the other two guards entering the room.

"HOLD HIM!" Lawrence orders his men.

He turns and goes back over to Bri where McMasters had helped her up and is untying the cord to free her hands. Lawrence holds her hands to look at her wrists; they have red lines around them from the charging cord being tightly wrapped around them. He looks at the cut on her shoulder then grabs some tissues and holds them there with pressure.

He whispers, "*Did he——?*"

"*No!*" She quickly answers the question she knew he was going to ask. "It wasn't like that." She was determined not to become emotional. She rolls her eyes and whispers, "*Rape is about power and control. It took all that man had just to keep me pinned down!*" Lawrence proudly looks at her.

"Atta girl!" McMasters tells her.

Lawrence quietly says, "I need to take care of this." He whispers so only she and McMasters can hear, "*You remember when we talked about my not letting you see me in my role as 'The King?'*" Her eyebrows come together as she slowly nods. "*I'll do this right here, if you promise not to judge me too harshly.*"

She crosses her heart and whispers, "*No judgements.*" Lawrence nods with an appreciative look.

McMasters takes a protective position near Bri in case the guard somehow breaks free. They both watch Lawrence as his whole demeanor changes and he now stands before his men as 'The King.' He sees the guard's gun and sword on the chair. Bri has a thought of a sword going into a torso. She pushes that thought out of her head, scolding herself for thinking of revenge.

The man scoffs at The King. "The Queen Mother won't allow anything to happen to me! *She's the one who sent me!*"

"Well," he slides the sword out of its sheath, "we could debate that *I'm* The King and can do what *I* want, but it doesn't really matter for you." He holds the sword straight up and down in front of his face, studying it...thinking it's been a while since he's practiced his fencing skills. "You *are* aware, *as a Royal Guard,* you're not allowed to forcibly lay your hands on *any* woman without just cause?" The guard refuses to answer.

Royal Guards are held to a higher standard, even that of a higher 'gentleman's code,' only this is worse because of Bri's connection to The King.

"The Queen Mother wanted me to give this woman a permanent reminder of who's in charge. And to remind *you* to do as you're told!" He says with a sneer. "Like The King *taking* what *she* wants him to take from this woman!" He gestures Bri.

An anger comes over Lawrence. He video calls his mother but when she answers, the sound echoes in the hallway. She answers with satisfaction in her voice, not knowing yet her plan failed.

She has an evil twisted smile. "Did you get my message?"

Lawrence watches the doorway as she walks into the room hanging up her phone. Her smile slowly fades as she takes in the scene. Her eyes snap to the guard being held by Tristan and another guard.

She is livid! *"I'M SURROUNDED BY IDIOTS!"*

Lawrence matches her anger. "THIS IS UNACCEPTABLE, MOTHER!"

"NO!" She points her finger at him. "WHAT'S UNACCEPATABLE AND PATHETIC IS YOU LETTING THIS DRAG ON FOR SO LONG! IT'S JUST SEX!" She looks at Lawrence while pointing to Bri, "DO I NEED TO SHOW YOU HOW TO TAKE WHAT WE NEED AND GET THE JOB DONE?!"

Lawrence angrily tells her, "I'VE *NEVER* FORCED MYSELF ON ANY WOMAN *AND I NEVER WILL!*"

The captured guard tells Lawrence, "You wouldn't have to! You could be the ugliest guy in the universe and women would line up to shag *The King*!" He gestures Bri with his head. "But somehow, with this slag, you can't even close the deal!"

"That's the problem! You're a spineless coward!" The Queen Mother demeans Lawrence. "You can't even do your job *as a man*, let alone as The King, with a 'Direct Bloodline!' You *stupid, pathetic excuse—*."

Lawrence rolls his eyes snapping, "OH, SHUT IT, MOTHER! I've had my limit with you!" She glares at his insubordination. He gestures the guard and Bri asking, "Is this because I told you she'd become my Royal Consort *within the next year*?!" Bri hides her surprise and then sadness that this was, in a small part, her fault.

The Queen Mother says with frustration, *"You can't seem to do anything right without my help, you stupid idiot! You've already wasted too much precious time giving me my heir!"*

"IT'S NOT UP TO YOU!" He angrily yells.

"THE HELL IT'S NOT!" There is a whole new level of hatred that comes over The Queen Mother for Bri, causing chills to go down Bri's neck and spine when they lock eyes before she looks at Lawrence again. "DO YOU THINK YOU HAVE A CHOICE?! DO YOU THINK YOU HAVE WHAT IT TAKES TO GO UP AGAINST ME?! *ME!* You keep forgetting—!"

Bri is disgusted and blurts out, "And what did you think *this* guard was going to accomplish?!" Bri tsks. "He's not physically up to the task when he's out of breath just trying to hold me down! He shouldn't even be a guard being so out of shape!" In the back of his head, Lawrence agrees.

With a loathing tone, *"How DARE YOU speak to me you disgusting swine!"* The Queen Mother is fuming, offended Bri would dare interject anything in their conversation!

The guard glares at Bri, *"That B—!"*

Lawrence points the tip of the sword at his mouth. "Finish that sentence and I'll cut your tongue out!" The King warns. *"Don't speak again!"*

"If you have the nerve to really do that, I'd like to see it!" The Queen Mother dares him. For the first time, the guard realizes he wasn't as protected as he was led to believe. He was warned he wouldn't be protected when he was no longer useful to her. The Queen Mother says, "But we both know you can't do anything without me telling you what to do!"

On the one hand, Lawrence knew his mother was right because he had done everything she had ever wanted him to do to protect Seth and Abby. He feels he is at a crossroads and doesn't want to just protect them and Bri, he wants to start setting boundaries with his mother, *starting with Bri.* The more strength he feels from Bri's love and support, the more he wants to stand up to his mother and get out from under her control.

"Mother, this is how I'll deal with all crimes against Lady Newhaven." The King turns and faces the guilty guard. There is an evil smile forming across

112

The Queen Mother's face again. The guard looks to The Queen Mother to intervene, so he doesn't see it coming but he feels the blade when The King stabs him in his abdomen with the guard's own sword.

Bri silently gasps, but she stops her mouth from falling open. Her mind goes to the image she had pictured a few minutes ago of what she thought was revenge, but it wasn't revenge at all! She's stunned that she had seen a brief moment of what was *going to happen!*

McMasters didn't seem phased and of course none of the other guards were surprised. However, there were a couple guards who are not happy with The King and Lawrence makes a mental note of them; he'll dismiss them from The *King's* Guard as soon as he returns to London. He doesn't want any of his personal guards loyal to anyone, but him...*least of all his mother!*

His guards aren't used to The King making decisions like this on his own! He usually lets The Queen Mother tend to the punishments; it's 'The Queen's Dungeon' after all, and she wants it that way. He lets her run it to keep her busy because it relieves some of the attacks against Seth, Abby, the staff, and even him a bit.

The Queen Mother is momentarily proud of 'Her King!' "You're *finally* becoming The King I've worked so hard to make you into!"

"No, Mother! *I'm not!* I want everyone to know I won't tolerate any mistreatment of Bri!" He corrects her.

She lightly scoffs, "Any which way you want to word it, you finally reacted the way I've been trying to train you *for years!*"

"You don't understand." He replies.

She responds in a plain voice and an expressionless face, "Try me."

"*You can't possibly understand.* You don't have a heart." He tells her.

"*Hearts get in the way, you stupid fool!*" She snaps at him. "Something else I've tried to teach you but maybe we need to teach you a harder way on that!" She says as she turns to leave.

Lawrence angrily grabs her upper arm and forcefully walks her to the door saying, "Mother, Bri's off limits! Don't try *anything* again! *Do you hear me?!*" He lets go of her outside the door.

She starts to reply, "And just how are *you* going to stop—." He slams the door in her face and locks it.

Bri knows when the guard has died because she sees his spirit. The guard looks down over his body and then looks around. He sees Bri is looking right at him.

"You can see me?" He starts to walk over to her, getting a sly smile, "This could be a lot of fun..."

"*Don't be too sure.*" Bri tells him in a quiet whisper. Before anything else can be said, dark shadows come up through the floor and yank him downwards to where she can only assume is Hell.

"Get him out of here, Tristan." Lawrence tells him, handing him the sword. "And no mess!" Tristan nods.

As Tristan reaches for the hilt of the sword, Bri notices he has something green tattooed on his wrist...a small green something...*a snake, maybe?* She wonders to herself. McMasters goes with them to help out.

The Queen Mother had stormed off and left to go home. She is angry and calculating her next move. She sees love as a weakness and the closer Lawrence gets to Bri, she thinks the greater his weakness will be and the best way to control him will be *through her.*

With her next move, she knows she'll have to come on strong to gain total control so he'll tow *her line* again. She'll need some time to determine what this next move will be and it'll give Lawrence, even Bri, time to let their guard down again.

CHAPTER 12

Imperfectly Perfect Surprise Trip to Reñiato

Lawrence walks over to Bri sitting on the bed, but his heart freezes when he sees her expression, but her expression isn't what he thinks. Her expression is because she finds herself unexpectedly attracted to this kind of power, which scares her *about herself.*

Lawrence kneels in front of her. "I didn't mean to scare you. I'm so—."

She kisses him...*very passionately*! He's surprised, but wraps his arms around her waist and returns the passionate kiss...*and things heat up*. When they pull apart, she hugs him with her hand still in his hair at the back of his head. He holds her firmly and takes a deep breath, relaxing more into her promise she kept of 'no judgements.'

"I have an embarrassing confession." She says next to his ear.

"What's that?" He asks, pulling back to look at her face.

"I'm not sure what to think about myself, but I found myself incredibly attracted to 'The King' right now..." she confesses.

He exhales loudly saying, "Ooo, well, that's going to be a problem." He keeps a straight face.

"What?" She's confused. "*Why?*"

"Because I can't do anything with that," he tips his head at the bed, "*yet*." He winks at her.

She lightly slaps his shoulder with a small smile. "This isn't funny!"

"*Oh, I know, Darling!*" He gets up and sits on the bed next to her. "Here I was, nervous I did scare you off, even though you promised no judgements. I was thinking we would have to talk this through to make you comfortable. This is slightly better." He grins.

"*Slightly?*" She teases with a scoff, then she clears her throat. "How *do you feel* about your mother sending one of your own guards to hurt me?"

"I'm used to her doing things like this but I was hoping you were safe, at least for a while." He looks down at her hand and holds it, staring at her wedding rings. "I'm worried if I can't get her to back off, she'll scare you away completely."

"Well, I can definitely agree that might be an issue," he looks at her and she squeezes his hand with a loving smile, "*if I wasn't already in-love with you.*"

He smiles appreciatively. "I'm grateful for that!" He feels the end of her hair, "Do you have any questions about what I did, or is there anything you'd like to talk about?"

She hugs him, saying, "I meant what I said: *no* judgements."

He buries his face in her hair and inhales the wonderful smell of her shampoo, then rests his chin on her shoulder. They stay like this for some time. After a while, he doesn't know what to say, but he doesn't have to because when she pulls back and looks into his eyes...there's such a look of love there, so much compassion...his heart squeezes *so* hard for her, he can't breathe.

He can only whisper, "*I love you, Bri!*"

Her heart is doing the same thing and she can only squeak, "*I know.*" She wipes her cheeks as a couple tears skip down them.

"I'd still like to know what you're thoughts are about what happened...what I did..." He looks at her with a bit of concern.

"I'm still stunned..." She answers, then sees his face fall a little with sadness. "Lawrence, I'm stunned because when you had first pulled the sword out of its sheath, I had a brief flash of a sword going into a torso." Lawrence furrows his eyebrows a bit, listening. "I pushed it aside, scolding myself for thinking of revenge." She takes a deep breath, exhaling shakily. "Then when you executed him, what stunned me was I had *just seen it* in a vision of sorts. Yes, this man is dead...executed for something that normally would've carried a prison sentence, not a life sentence, nor a death sentence."

He goes to defend his actions, "That's for the average——." She puts her hand over his mouth again with another loving look.

She faintly smiles. "I was getting to the difference."

"Sorry." He says.

She squeezes his hand. "I'm just walking you through so you can see I have no judgements for you, only observations." He gives a little nod. "No, this wasn't a crime against just anyone, but *ultimately* a crime against *you*." He nods as he listens. "It's common knowledge *now*, but it's been basic knowledge for 'The Royal Guard' and of course, 'The King's Guard,' what your intent has been with me for a while." He nods. "A crime against 'The King' *needs* to have swift punishment and be more severe to deter as many future crimes against you as possible, *especially by The King's Guard, your top guards*. They need to know that doing her bidding is a suicide mission." He agrees with that. "A side note is that this was also a crime against the woman getting in your mother's way."

He holds her face and asks her, "Then why do I see *guilt* in your eyes?"

Her eyebrow goes up. "I only feel guilty because of the attraction."

"There's more." He states.

Her eyebrows come together as she looks away thinking about that, softly shaking her head. She looks back at him when it occurs to her, "There *is* a piece but it's not from today. Bear with me because I'm not sure how to say this." He nods. "Since meeting you at the wedding, I've felt a sense of danger with you, but *not* that you'd be dangerous towards me. *And now*, I'm scared of being attracted to that..." She sees him with a smoldering smirk and she partially laughs.

"Bri, *could it be* your drawn to the same thing most women are drawn to me for, and I'd love to say it's because of my great looks—."

"Oh no! *Nothing like that!*" She teases and he raises an eyebrow. She adds, "More like *bloody fantastic* looks!"

He softly chuckles. "*My point is*, it's what's behind the danger that would make a king dangerous."

She scrunches her eyebrows again thinking, then they shoot up as it occurs to her and she whispers, "*Power!*"

117

"Precisely. And is that a bad thing?" He genuinely asks.

"*Weeell...*" she bites her lower lip playfully smiling.

He chuckles, "Because we can't do anything about it *right now.*"

"*Precisely.*" She playfully him.

He laughs as they stand and walk out onto the balcony. He leans on the railing and looks out at the landscape.

"For the first time in my life I *really* stood up to my mother. I even hung up on her last night...*twice.*" Lawrence explains. "I knew there'd be repercussions, but I didn't think she would come after you for it!"

"For what it's worth, I'm proud of you." She has a small, loving smile for him as she stands up.

"*You are?!*" He asks, standing up. He's surprised she feels that way because his mother targeted her. However, he does feel a bit liberated doing so.

"I'm *absolutely* proud of you, Lawrence! I've heard it said better, but I believe it: 'people let others treat them however they want to be treated.' For many, it's subconscious because they don't really think about it. You can either 'reward' your mother for her behavior and actions by allowing it to continue, *or* put a stop to it." She warns, "If you go to put a stop to it, keep your guard up! Your mother knows what *used to* work when manipulating and threatening you but when it no longer works, those manipulation tactics and threats will increase as she tries to reestablish control. You just need to stay strong, hang on, and hold the course!"

"She already increased her tactics! *She targeted you!*" He turns and folds his arms as he leans his backside against the rail. "Bri, she's always held Seth and Abby over me, but she decided to raise the stakes with you and I don't know if that's a price I'm willing to have you pay for me!"

"Lawrence, *that's exactly what she wants!* That's exactly why she 'tested the waters' and used me to get to you!" She stands in front of him and puts her hands on his folded arms. "She *wants* you to back down, but if you step down *now*, then you might as well gift wrap your 'family jewels,' because you'll *never* have another chance to get your life back and be the king *you want to be!*"

"Wow! *That'sss*...blunt." He tells her.

"*But true.*" She holds his cheek. "Her next attempt will be a planned, strategic move. Don't worry about me!" She smirks at him. "I'm tougher than I look!" He softly chuckles. She adds, "Lawrence, nothing she could ever do to me will top what Katie, my supposed best friend, did to me!" He takes her hand and kisses it. "Whatever comes my way because you're trying to break free of her control, *bring it on*! I have the faith that I'll be given what I need, when I need it!"

"Bri, my mother lives to inflict pain!"

"*I know.* I kind of picked up on her sadistic side when I saw a few of your childhood memories. Besides," She smirks, "*I* have a high pain tolerance, as well."

"I'm not sure what to think about that?" He tells her with concern.

She gives him a small smile. "Let's change the subject."

He nods and takes her hands. "Let's go get ready for breakfast!"

"Sounds good, Ace!" She smiles and starts texting McMasters to walk her to her room. "I just need to go throw some clothes on and you probably want to shower." She sends the text.

"I can walk you to your quarters first and then—."

"No need. McMasters can come and get me." She reads the text she gets back from McMasters and tells Lawrence, "McMasters says he's outside your door." Lawrence walks her to the door and opens it to be sure it's McMasters for his own peace of mind. Lawrence shakes McMasters hand to thank him for his help, then he kisses Bri's cheek and watches her leave. He closes the door and goes to take a shower.

Bri walks into her quarters and sees David sitting on the couch with his laptop on the coffee table in front of him. He looks at Bri and waves with a wink and a smile before going back to his conversation and laptop. She had smiled and waved back before walking into their bedroom to get ready for the day.

She goes to bandage up her shoulder but sees it isn't bleeding anymore. She looks closer in the mirror...*It's healing*? She asks herself, noticing it looks like it's a few days old already. She figures it has to do with her gift and goes to get dressed.

She finishes putting her earrings in when David walks in and asks if she's ready to head down to breakfast. She nods and he gently grabs her arm as she walks by to stop her, the same one with the cut but it's not as painful. In fact, she feels it tingling.

He asks, "Everything alright?"

"Yes, sorry." She softly kisses him. "Good morning!"

"Nice try, but Jack and I are aware of what happen with a guard this morning." David informs her. "Want to try again?"

"*Why not flat out ask me then*?!" She folds her arms and raises her eyebrow, asking with a bit of annoyance, "Do *you* want to try again?"

"You're right." He caresses her cheek. "I'm sorry, Love. Let me try 'How are you holding up?'"

"Better." She says. Then she takes a deep breath, exhaling her slight irritation. She tells him, "Lawrence and I talked about it."

He's pleasantly surprised. "Thank you for telling me that." He hugs her tight.

She quietly says, "This helps, too."

"Glad to hear it!" He continues to hold her firmly for a minute. When he feels her take another deep breath, they pull apart. He asks, "Is Lawrence coming here or are you meeting downstairs?"

"He didn't say, but I can text him quick that we're ready and you'll escort me down." She winks and David smiles.

> Lawrence texts back: "Sounds good. I won't be too far behind. See you two there." (Adds a heart)

Lawrence was about to walk into *The Dining Room* to meet up with Bri and David, when he hears Jack call out to him. "Herst!" Lawrence stops and turns to wait for Jack to catch up. "I tracked down 'The Pink Heart Diamond Ring' for you." Jack says, showing him a screenshot of it.

 Lawrence smiles excitedly. "Is this the current bid?!"

"*That's your winning bid!*" Jack points to the screen.

"That's *brilliant*, Jack!" Lawrence hugs him. "I can't believe I finally have this rare find! Thank you so much! I'll transf—."

"No need. Since I have access to your account, it's all taken care of!" Jack pats his back. "The bid and transaction are all anonymous; behind the bid are me and Watchtower Financial."

Lawrence hugs and thanks Jack again. "*Now* I feel prepared...like this is actually going to happen! To have her has my 'Royal Consort' is right at my fingertips!" He's excited. "I need to plan the *perfect* evening!"

"Relax, Herst! She's easy to please!" Jack laughs and pats Lawrence's shoulder a couple times. "I arranged the ring to be hand delivered to Nigel at The Royal Jewelers, and for him to verify the authenticity of the ring before taking possession of it for you."

"I can't thank you enough, Jack!" Lawrence says, staring at the ring on the screen as he hands Jack his phone back.

"Loving her is all the 'thanks' I need!" Jack tells him.

"That's easy!" Lawrence happily replies.

Jack smiles. "Herst, I know you've seen some of her amazingness, but she *is* remarkable in so many ways! One of those ways is how much love is in that woman's heart, which has David and me, and I'm sure you, *gobsmacked!*" Lawrence nods in agreement. "And the more love she feels, the more her love grows and she radiates it! It makes you want to be with her, whether she's in your arms or in the same building, it just feels good to be near her!"

"It feels like my life is more at peace with her in it...I just hope I can love her as much as she deserves!" Lawrence says thoughtfully.

"A comment like that leads me to believe you will!" Jack tells him. "Look, when David and I discussed me being her Noble Consort, she was already overflowing with love and he promised she would be loved more than any woman has ever been loved. My loving her helps him to fulfill his promise, but with you loving her, I'd say his promise *is* fulfilled! She loves you and it's written all over her face! Herst, having that kind of love is an incredibly powerful feeling and, at the risk of sounding as she says, 'sappy,' loving her *is* magical!"

Lawrence takes that in and realizes that the unconditional love Bri was talking about a while back. The unconditional love everyone desires! It's the love Jack has found with Bri, that David has found with her, and love she has found with them. That love is there when he tells her his darkest secrets, that he has never told another soul and she doesn't flinch—*that's* unconditional love! For the first time in his life, he's hopeful that maybe, *just maybe*, the darkness of his past might eventually disappear with the light of *her* "*unconditional love...*" Lawrence whispers to himself, but Jack hears him.

"Yes, unconditional love!" Jack replies. "Herst, I know our childhoods were less than ideal, but I was incredibly lucky because of Peter and Carlotta. Those two raised me with unconditional love. And if I dare say, Bri may be your first at showing you unconditional love outside of your siblings, *and* those times when you were here with us?" He nods. "How did she react to the execution of your guard?"

"*She was remarkable in how she handled that*. She *understood* why I had to do it." Lawrence tells him. "Most Americans would've been outraged..."

"May I ask what happened?" Jack asks as they walk into *The Dining Room* where everyone else is.

"I'd like to know!" Peter overhears and smiles a little 'hello' to them.

"As you know, here at 'The Manor,' it's a little more relaxed when there's no visitors or new staff." They nod. Lawrence tells them, "This guard went to my room and attacked Bri, but I'm not sure as to the details."

"Bri, are you alright?" Carlotta asks with concern.

"Oh, I'm fine." She replies. "I fought back and managed to push him off me, *and off the bed*."

"Good girl!" Carlotta tells her, everyone else nods in agreement.

Bri gives her a small smile. "Unfortunately, he tripped me when I went to run away and was able to get the upper hand again. He was just starting to cut into my skin, to carve some sort of message from The Queen Mother, but that's when Lawrence and McMasters pulled him off me."

"Carve?" Peter asks.

She shrugs. "He said something about carving some sort of a reminder of who's in charge? He never said what he was going to carve and he didn't get very far. I was relieved when Lawrence and McMasters came in and pulled him off me when they did. I really don't want to know."

Lawrence adds, "I took care of things right there. I hope it sends a message that I won't tolerate anything happening to Bri." Everyone agrees.

They all eat together for a little bit, but David has a meeting he has to get to. He leans over and whispers, "*Are you sure you're alright?*" She nods with a sweet smile. He says, "I love you!"

She smiles back. "I love you, My Love!" They quickly kiss once more before he leaves. He hugs Lawrence. "Safe travels, Brother!" David sees Jack is on the phone in the entryway and they wave to each other.

Lawrence was already sitting next to Bri. She asks, "How's Abby, Gen, and Seth this morning?"

He laughs. "Abby?! Like you! Nothing stops her from being quick-witted and sassy!" He winks.

She teases. "Me?! Why I'm as innocent as a baby!" Lawrence bursts out laughing. "*Mister* Heathherst, I'm *shocked* you would have me pegged as—."

"*I believe* David described you that beautiful June day in the gardens over a year ago as a 'feisty firecracker!'" He looks pointedly at her, referring to her wedding day.

She gets close to whisper in his ear, "*I have a sneaking suspicion a firecracker is* exactly *who you want* surrendering to you *in the bedroom.*" He sees her wink at him.

This is another moment he feels exposed to her, like she can see into his very soul again...that she might actually know things about him that he doesn't

123

even know about himself! Lawrence's cousin and part of 'The King's Guard,' Tristan, stands in the doorway.

"We're ready, Your Majesty."

Lawrence stands and thanks him, then he looks at Bri. "Walk with me, Darling?" He asks. She nods and stands. He holds her hand as they walk outside and towards the helicopter. He stops and turns, taking both her hands. "Have you ever been to The London Clock Tower before?"

"Unfortunately, when Katie and I visited for the first time, we didn't have enough time to make it there." She tells him.

He smiles. "Residents of London can get admission for free, but the very top isn't open to the public and it has an even more *spectacular* view."

"Ha-ha!" She giggles. "Let me guess, 'not open to the public' doesn't pertain to His Majesty, The King?"

"*And* his beautiful date, *if* she goes with me." He smiles. "I was thinking when we're together next, so I can plan it out and most importantly, I won't take away from David or Jack's time with you?"

"I look forward to it! However, splitting my time between the three of you is my absolute limit, especially when we're going to be adding children to the family. The time spent has to be quality time with all three of you and the children, too."

He holds her face and kisses her tenderly, then rests his forehead to hers for a minute. "I'm *hating* that I have to leave."

"Does it help if I hate you have to leave, too, and go back to that *awful woman*?" She asks.

He smiles and runs his fingers across her cheek. "I love you, BriaLynn!"

She gets a big smile that makes his heart squeeze. "I love *you*, Ace!" He pulls her into an embrace and kisses her one last time.

He gets on the helicopter and Bri backs up to a safe distance. She stays where she is and waves as they lift into the air. When they fly out of sight, she walks to The Cottage and McMasters catches up to walk beside her, which she prefers over walking by herself and being followed. It also gives her a chance to thank him for being there for her.

"I just wish it never happened! You should've been safe!" He replies.

"Oliver, we both know your job is more often *reactive* to something that happens." She states.

He nods. "*Unfortunately.*"

Bri changes the subject. She asks him about how his wife is doing and if she likes living in Newhaven...

When Bri arrives at The Cottage, she sees Jack in the kitchen drinking orange juice and talking on his phone. He smiles at her and she smiles back as she walks up to him and quietly kisses his cheek. She sees some brownies Isla has made. Isla is in charge of all the cleaning staff on The Estate, including The Cottage, but chose to be the primary one on staff for The Cottage House. Bri wants it to be as close to normal as possible with her and Jack cleaning up after themselves. Isla comes through on a regular schedule for cleaning the house, mostly when Jack's there by himself.

Bri takes a bite of a brownie and silently mouths 'sssooo *goood*' to Jack and he hears her '*mmm*' as she enjoys another bite. Jack stands behind her at the counter as he finishes his call.

He hangs up and puts his hands on her hips telling her, "Amore Mia, those brownies had better not be a substitute for something *way* more fun!"

She turns her head and kisses his cheek again before going to the fridge. "Right now, my hormones are so charged up from being with Lawrence, I need something to compensate since we're waiting!" She pours herself a glass of milk.

Jack thinks for a moment about 'waiting,' then it dawns on him she's waiting with Lawrence for the same reasons she wanted David and him to wait. It makes sense, but he never really thought about it.

He smirks as he gets closer. "I *could* help you out with that!"

"I wouldn't want to do that to you, Amore Mio." She genuinely smiles. "I should just go take a cold shower!" She takes another drink of milk.

"And waste *all* that energy?! *That's absurd!*" He says and she chokes on her milk; it just about comes out her nose. He gets a smirk on his face, "Will you be able to focus on *our* fun?!"

Her eyebrow raises. "Depends on what you have in mind?!" She flirts. He scoops her up and starts to walk out of the kitchen. "But my brownie…" She reaches behind him, with a look of longing on her face for the brownie.

"I'll get you one when we're done." He carries her upstairs.

She giggles. "It had better be a *huge* one!"

"Hey now!" He pauses on the stairs. "If we do this right, you shouldn't *need* any brownie!"

She smiles as she bites her lower lip. "You're right! I momentarily lapsed into crazy thinking! Let's blame it on the racing hormones."

"Deal!" Jack chuckles as he walks up the rest of the stairs and into their bedroom.

He sets her down and sees the playful grin on her face when she says, "Let's see what you got up your sleeve, Carlisle!"

He captures her lips in a heated kiss…

Laying tucked under his arm, she has her arm draped over his chest and he lightly tickles it. She lifts her head and holds his cheek. "I love you, Amore Mio…" She kisses him.

"I love *you*, Amore Mia!" He kisses her fingers.

She watches his face turn a little solemn. "What is it?" She asks.

"I don't know why, but my mind went to a memory of my childhood when David and I went on a family holiday."

"Oh? Where to?" She asks.

"Some coastal village, but it was so...so...*normal*." He kisses her head. "Growing up, I always dreamed my father would just let me be officially adopted by The Worthington's, to be 'Jack Worthington,' but that would mean my father would have to admit some sort of defeat, or some sort of loss of a possession. He is probably boasting on how my now 'elevated status' was his doing; how he somehow brought David and I together in nursery school and 'allowed' my time with The Worthington's, which resulted in my being 'The Noble Consort' and now——." Bri's annoyance for his father shows as she sits up. "Amore Mia..." he says to her, but she doesn't hear him. When she hears, "BriaLynn," she looks and sees he's sitting up next to her.

"I love you so much and I get *so angry* when I think about how your father treated you!" She replies.

"But even your faith has you understanding it was necessary to create the very sexy man I am now, the man *you* love!" He smirks and cups her cheek, "Even Herst's childhood and background made him who he is and the man you love."

"*So*, true!" She smiles and rests her forehead to his.

"Your love brings me such happiness and joy! You're *everything* to me, Bri!" He kisses her firmly.

"For the record, I do like the last name 'Carlisle' and I'm grateful you grew up with David and James, that you were raised by Peter and Carlotta as *their son* because we both know *you are*!" She winks and he smiles with his nod. "*That childhood* is hugely responsible for creating this *very sexy* man I love." She sweetly kisses him.

"Shall we fix dinner here tonight?" He asks.

"I'd love that!" She says. "But first," she giggles and gets up before he can pull her back into bed, "I just remembered I need to get back to my brownie!" She slips his shirt on and hurries downstairs. He chuckles as he gets up to follow. She passes suitcases next to the front door and looks at Jack who's not too far behind her. "What are these for?"

"I'm taking you away for a few days." Jack happily tells her.

She excitedly asks, "Where?!"

"It's for work, but I'm thinking you'd like to join me on a trip to a small, but powerful little Mediterranean country called Reñiato?" He teases because she's fully aware of the country; Ambassador Lombardi and his wife live there. She has a huge smile and squeals as she throws her arms around his neck and hugs him.

She pulls back and asks, "Isn't it near Greece?"

"It's roughly between Greece and Italy." He replies.

She hugs and kisses him again. "I can't wait!" He chuckles. "How many times have you been to Reñiato?" She asks.

"Other than the occasional business trip, I have very faint childhood memories of the Mediterranean with Uncle Max and my mother."

"Uncle Max?" She thinks back, "I don't recall you mentioning—oh wait! He and your mom were a couple!"

He slightly nods. "It's like a wisp of a memory...I'm not sure which country it was exactly." He thinks for a moment. "I barely remember my mother's face." He reads her face and turns to walk to the kitchen holding her hand. "I've thought about asking you to call for her, but I just can't..."

She gives him an understanding look. "When you're ready, Amore Mio."

He nods and clears his throat. "I believe I owe you one of these..." He hands her a brownie.

She takes a bite. "Mmm..." With her hand in front of her mouth she says, "Why Lord Carlisle, you really are *the perfect* man!" She winks.

He chuckles and holds her jaw. "I don't know about that, but I'm definitely looking at *the perfect* woman!" She giggles, rolling her eyes and shaking her head. He kisses her temple as she takes another bite of her brownie.

Their trip to Reñiato has Jack pulling back a little, as memories of certain places come to his consciousness. Bri suggests they go do the touristy things to bring him around again and they can really see the country for the first time together. Then they'll know where to spend more time the next time they come to visit.

Jack chuckles, "You're already planning our next visit?!"

"Absolutely! This is a beautiful place, don't you think?!"

"With you, it most definitely is!" He winks.

"Besides, Ambassador Lombardi and his wife are sad they missed us and made me promise we'd visit again *soon*." She gives him a grin. "You wouldn't want me to break my promise *now would you*?" He chuckles, shaking his head.

One of her favorite places to go was The Royal Palace's extensive gardens that is open to the public. They didn't tour the palace itself because it took longer to get out of the garden maze they were in; the hedges were over seven feet tall so no one could see over them. The center had a rock garden and pond with a small waterfall.

This palace seemed grander than The London Palace, with so many gold ornamental statues and decorations outside. Although, both palaces have beautifully landscaped gardens.

"Maybe next time we can tour inside?" Bri asks.

"I think we could *easily* arrange that." Jack smiles, as they casually walk back to the awaiting car to take them back to their hotel.

"*Easily*?" She asks.

"You'll probably be 'The Royal Consort' by then so they'll want to give us the *royal* VIP tour!" She laughs and rolls her eyes, shaking her head a bit.

CHAPTER 13

Imperfectly Perfect & Royally Planned Date

When Lawrence's date night comes around, he sends *The Royal Helicopter*, with a dress and shoes for Bri. She dresses at The Manor and adds 'The Snowflake Diamond Necklace' set from David and her diamond watch from Jack to complete the look. Jack and David see her off as she climbs into the helicopter to be taken to London.

For the first time Lawrence doesn't have his mother breathing down his neck. She has been glued to him since he returned from Newhaven last week. She never had the chance to touch Abby or Seth, which means she found other ways to vent her anger, other than just him.

He never told his mother about his date, but he isn't naïve to think she doesn't know; she has spies *everywhere*. Her knowing would explain why she is leaving him alone today. He loved being able to plan this date and pull everything together, this night is even more meaningful because of that...this night is theirs.

The helicopter lands on The Royal Apartment side of The London Palace and a motorcade of security awaits in front of the entrance. Lawrence meets Bri at the helicopter. She nervously sees the press all snapping photos, but she is already smiling brightly at him. He kisses her cheek while holding her other cheek.

He looks at her so lovingly and slightly apologetically when he sees the nervousness in her eyes. "You weren't expecting the press."

"I should have! I was just too focused on you and us. *Of course*, they'd want to know what The King is up to, especially with this American, now Scottish woman." She smiles, then quickly apologizes, "Sorry. I need to remember to be more formal when we're together in public; I forget—."

"Don't worry about that." He tells her. "For the record, there's an American phrase that comes to mind that fits here: you're *way* out of my league!"

She giggles, shaking her head and discreetly gestures him, "King," and then herself, "commoner."

"No, Darling. First, you were *never* 'common.' Secondly," Lawrence holds her face, "*and seriously*, there's no room for inequality in love." He winks. She laughs but agrees. "Some monarchs have their spouse so many paces behind them, for various reasons. Typically, to show who is the actual successor of a monarchy."

"Unfortunately, to many people it looks like two people in *separate* roles, rather than side-by-side and *united* together." She notes.

"The thought behind that is they're the regnant and therefore *needs to be* set apart from everyone, even their spouse."

"That's an antiquated view, but still common! It's a view that came when marriages were arranged between countries and were used as a way of keeping the spouse's home country 'in their place.' There's the 'upper elite class view,' where they *expect* to be seen and treated differently. Your comment, 'therefore needs to be set apart,' is actually making a statement that the couple isn't unified." He studies her as he wonders where this could be going. She continues, "For the most part, The United Kingdom of Provinces' monarchy *does* make logical sense, compared to other monarchies. For example, saying, 'The Duchess' refers to a duchess and using 'The' respects her importance; however, in some countries, 'The' is used if she were divorced. Here, if she were divorced and not the heir, she loses her title altogether, which makes sense. If 'The Duchess' steps down, like whenever Carlotta would retire, she wouldn't have 'The' in front but she would still be called Duchess Carlotta or Duchess of Newhaven. That, too, makes sense, rather than calling her Lady Carlotta after they retire, which would seem disrespectful."

"There are those who fight tooth-and-nail to keep their title when they divorce." He says.

"David's ex, Ava, was one of them! Logically, it doesn't make sense to keep a title that was part of marrying the person who *is* 'The Heir.' With that said, I'd be a *little inclined* to support a spouse keeping their title in a divorce if they've been working in that role for *many* years." She takes his arm. "Perception is always at play! When two people are married, yet are *not* walking side-by-side, it's *perceived* as inequality among the ranks. It *appears* they're not really partners, not united *together* to face their challenges. Factor in if they're 'The King' and 'The Queen,' or whichever ruling titles, and the country may seem weak to their enemies."

131

"Bri, I never want you to feel you're below me," he smirks, "*unless—.*"

She quickly covers his mouth as she giggles, but keeps them on topic. "It looks better and encourages the people to stand behind their leaders when their leaders show a united front. It can simply be walking side-by-side, or," she takes his hand, "even more so walking hand-in-hand." She smiles apologetically, "Sorry, got a bit long winded."

"Don't be!" He replies. "I *never* want you to be apologetic with pointing something out, especially when I haven't even considered it for one reason or another. I *need* to know these things, even if I fight against them at first. I'd like to think once they settled into my brain that, like David, I'd see that the intelligent beauty I love is right, or at least has a point. Like now, any which way you look at it, you're right, it shows division. And I do need *My Queen* by my side to show our united front."

"If *Your* Queen is walking alongside *The* King, and she's not officially '*The Queen*,' we both know *that* would be pushing it." She notes.

He wraps his arms around her. "A *husband* needs *his wife* by his side. We don't have a traditional family, but as long as you're with me, you're by my side just as when you're with David or Jack!"

"Alright, you *maaay* have a point..." Bri has a hint of a smile.

"Enough of that for now." He holds his arm out again. "Shall we, My Beautiful Darling?"

"*Can't wait,* Ace!" She grins then she teases with his accent, "We're going to have a *smashing good time!*"

He chuckles. "As you say, '*no pressure!*'" He teases with *her* accent.

They're laughing as they get to the car, the back door being opened for them, but before she gets in, she turns and looks at Lawrence with such love, she hears his breath catch. "Alright *My King*, you can relax! We've been through this. I'm *super* easy to please, because all you need to remember is *I'm happy just being with you!* Anything beyond that is just...'icing on the cake' and whatever toppings!" She smiles big and kisses his cheek, then gets in.

Maurice, the majordomo who's in charge of *The Royal Apartment*, whispers, "I really *like her, Your Majesty!*"

Lawrence happily tells him, "And I *absolutely adore her*!" Maurice chuckles as Lawrence slides in the backseat next to Bri and Maurice closes the door.

The car is a golden cream colored 'Majestic Crowne' made specifically for The Royal Family, with larger windows allowing people to see whoever's inside more easily, but the whole car is bulletproof. The interior is soft leather with dark wood color accents. Bri smiles, waving here and there as they ride through the streets.

At one point, Lawrence holds her hand and he is surprised! "You're shaking!"

"Yes." She turns to him. "I'm just an American, who happened to be a 'Direct Bloodline' when she married 'The Heir to Newhaven,' and took Jack off the market, but now I'm being wooed by 'The King.' I can only imagine what people must be thinking, let alone saying!"

"Darling, we call tabloids 'rags' and 'rubbish' for a reason." He tells her. "It doesn't speak for the people, although that's what those rags would want you to think!"

"I don't read them!" She smirks.

"Glad to hear it! But by doing that, I think you've avoided *all* the media, haven't you?" Lawrence smiles sweetly.

"I'm sorry, but *is* there a good tabloid?" She retorts.

"Of course not! Now reputable media sources——."

"*Those are rare!*" Bri notes.

"True. Although, Newhaven has a very reputable newspaper and it goes to great lengths to report the news accurately and factually; emotions are kept out of the news reports in the first pages and saved for other sections. They even show and compare 'sources of information' from other media sources against the facts!"

Bri agrees. "It's the only one I'll actually read all the way through, if I read any at all."

Lawrence replies, "I've become a *huge* fan of that paper and I'm thinking about having a committee put together that monitors all the 'news media' in the UK using Newhaven's newspaper as a model. I would like to have guidelines and credentials established for being known as a 'news *source*,' or they're reclassified as a tabloid and lose their 'credibility' status." He smirks. "I'm also a huge fan because Newhaven's editorials are in your favor."

"They're biased." She replies.

"Of course, they are! And, *to be fair*," he waves across her at some people, as he continues to talk, "even some of the oldest rags have jumped to 'Team Bri' *and that's unheard of!*"

"Well, I think it's a great idea to hold the news media outlets to a higher standard. I wish the US held the news media to a higher standard that *respects* the First Amendment and they're not allowed to abuse it! Of course, the US Supreme Court allows for its abuse..." She notes. "All the so-called-news outlets are a joke and I consider almost all of it tabloids at this point."

"Sensationalism has seemed to destroy their credibility." He adds.

"*It absolutely has!* A lot of people think, as I do, that all news is tabloid news and distrust all of them! Which isn't fair to the scarce few who *are reputable* and try to be an accurate source of news and information. It's creating a perfect environment that will soon allow people to get away with the greatest evil the world has ever known because no one will trust any news source! It's scary and sad to think about...that one day, in the not-too-distant future, no one will care if their picture is on the front page with an 'expose article' because they know not many people will believe it anyway."

He tells her, "As you already know, it's not much different here. *However*, here, *I can do something about it*. We can respect people's right to 'free speech,' but draw lines that prevent it from being destroyed, or destroying people."

"It's also in your power to protect *credible* sources. Yes, credible sources need to be protected but those sources should be proven! They need to be revealed to the judge in a case but in a judge's chambers, off the record, for a judge to confirm it's an actual credible source. If it is, protect the source!"

"Brilliant!" He smiles. Then they hear a louder group. He smirks and gestures, "*Look at them!* Your fans *and supporters* are excited to see *you!*"

"*Oh no, Ace!* They're excited to see their *extremely* handsome King!" She tells him. "*You're the one they're excited about!*"

He chuckles. "You'll see." He kisses her hand again. "You're becoming just as popular in the UK, as you are Newhaven."

They wind and turn through a few more streets of London. Waving and smiling to those who've come out to see them. Bri is fascinated by all the fuss people are making...then again, they're showing their excitement for their country when they come out to see 'The King.' It's the same for when 'The President of the United States' goes driving through an American city.

As they pull up to The Clock Tower, he says to her, "*Pay attention*, Darling. It's *not* my name they'll be calling out the most!"

 The door opens and he gets out first, then helps her. She raises her eyebrow to him with a smirk when she hears, "Your Majesty!" But he raises his eyebrow back when there's a slew of "Lady Newhaven!" And "Lady Bri!" They're waving flags of the UK, Newhaven, and Scotland, as well as flags that were half UK and US flags.

They smile and wave before heading inside The Clock Tower. She hears someone tell the crowd it'll be *at least* a couple of hours before they come back out. Inside, Lawrence dismisses his guards. Then he pulls out a black silky blindfold and shows it to Bri.

"Will you trust me?" He smiles with a hint of playfulness.

She smiles. "Always!" Then she closes her eyes.

He steps directly in front of her and gently puts the blindfold over her eyes. They carefully step into a modernized old-fashioned elevator, with the wrought iron look of how it's always been. When the elevator stops, he guides her off and he goes to take the blindfold off, but he can't resist kissing her lip-glossed lips. He kisses her softly, intending for that to be all it was, but their passion sparks. They wrap their arms around each other and when she hears herself moan, she abruptly breaks the kiss.

"*Wow!*" She gasps, barely louder than a whisper.

He is only feeling complete seduction with her eyes still blindfolded and they're both breathing heavily, so he quickly, but carefully, takes her blindfold off. She blinks a few times for her eyes to adjust.

Lawrence tells her, "Had I known *all that* would happen because of a blindfold," he looks into her eyes, "I would've rethought it." He exhales with raised eyebrows.

She smirks and asks, "Will you keep the blindfold?" She bites her lower lip.

He has a sexy smile. "Absolutely!" He folds it up and tucks it inside his suit coat. He holds her close again. "I can honestly say, I never knew how *exciting* blindfolds could be..." he ghosts her lips, "until now."

She giggles. "Neither did I!" He doesn't catch the meaning behind that...*at first*. He pauses and looks at her with his eyebrow raised. She gives him a grin. "I've never been kissed blindfolded before!"

He grins with a bit of playfulness. "Then we'll have to do something more with that soon!" She agrees.

He leads her away from the elevator. She sees a small table for their dinner and the three-hundred-sixty-degree view of London.

"Lawrence, this is a *spectacular* view!"

She takes some pictures and he notices she doesn't send them to anyone. He asks, "You're not sending any to David and Jack?"

She hugs him. "This is a particularly special evening you planned. I want to be here, in this moment, with you, Acc. *Only you.*"

He looks at her with such love and appreciation for that. He sweetly kisses her, then rests his forehead to hers. "You never cease to amaze me, BriaLynn!"

"Oh, I'm human, you'll see soon enough." She grins.

He quietly laughs as he holds her face as he kisses her again. He gently pulls their lips apart and when he opens his eyes, he smiles when he sees her eyes are still closed for a few seconds longer.

She opens them, smiling adoringly. "I love you, Lawrence."

He's still smiling as he rests their foreheads together again. "I love you, too. I've tried to come up with some eloquent words to say to you, but all that goes through my mind is," he lifts his head, "'*marry me!*'"

She smiles. "Hnnn, right to the point."

He's smiling the happiest she's ever seen him. "My whole life, *everything* was mapped out for me, even my marriage to Gen...I started to lose hope in finding love. When you agreed to take things slow so we could get to know each other, to decide if we really wanted to do this, I didn't want to get caught up in 'us' because—."

"You didn't want to get disappointed, *or hurt*, if this didn't work out." Bri follows along.

He nods and gestures, "Over the years, I'd come up here and look around; taking in the view and how all those people have no idea the death grip my mother has had on me."

"For your power." Bri interjects.

He turns to her saying, "True. I'd look out and wish I could just break free, but eventually I'd have to leave here and go back to the drudgery of The Palace, *of my mother*. Then to hear you say that you love me for the first time, it stirred something inside me..."

"Yourself." She says and sees a little confusion on his face. "Lawrence, you found unconditional love, which is freeing your heart, your very soul, 'to become!' *To become* who you were always meant to be, who *you* want to be!"

"To become..." Lawrence says, thinking about what she's saying.

"You could be the one that changes the very fabric of your family's ruling legacy! You could be the descendant who has all the power the people *could* fear, but see you using your power to protect and rule your people *benevolently. Don't you see?!*" She holds and squeezes his hands some. "Your predecessors, *your very namesake*, thought to gain obedience was with strict rules and brute force, with swift and harsh punishments to give them ultimate power. That's a recipe to be the most hated; *to inspire a revolution!* Lawrence, you're getting into a fantastic position to lead and rule in strength and power, but with *compassion and mercy.* That compassion is what will have your people flock to you because they'll see you *honestly do care about them.*"

"Only with you by my side!" He states.

"You could do it on your own! *But yes*, it'll help that you have my love and support behind you!" She sweetly smiles and he agrees.

"We've established you're fantastically brilliant, amazing, and incredibly beautiful, oh, and *way* out my league!" She giggles, shaking her head. "Bri, there's something about you that draws people to you and I hope with all that you are, you'll help me become that king I *want* to be!" He pulls out a ring box, tosses a small pillow on the floor that was sitting off to the side and goes down on one knee. "Will you, BriaLynn, in a *very real way*, marry me?"

 When he opens the box, Bri gasps as she covers her mouth with her hands and whispering, "*Oh, good gracious, Lawrence! It's huge!*"

"If you don't like it——."

"Lawrence, it's *beautiful!*" She says looking at it. The ring has a large heart-shaped pink diamond center stone with a smaller heart-shaped white diamond on each side, all set in white gold. "I can't believe I'm saying that because it's *extremely* out of my one-karat comfort zone! I couldn't even begin to guess how many karats that is?!" She's sounding overwhelmed.

"Eleven." He states.

"*Wha*——." She gasps. "Lawrence Alexander Heathherst, you've gone and *lost* your mind! This would've cost you millions——."

"*Focus*, Darling." He chuckles, gesturing that he's still on his knee waiting for an answer. He takes the ring out of the box explaining, "I stumbled upon 'The Pink Heart Diamond' some time ago. This may seem silly, but every so often, a stone seems to call to me."

"I can see that." Bri replies.

"This has been a ring that always seemed to elude me before now." He says, "After reading the paperwork that came with it, I now know why it did."

"Why?" She's curious.

He sweetly smiles, "The registered name is, 'True-Love's Ring.'" Her breath catches. "There was *no way* I would've gotten my hands on it before now, *before you*."

She shakes her head a little, her eyes welling up with tears. "You were longing for true-love, not specifically me."

"*My heart longed for you*! I knew it the moment I laid eyes on you!" He sweetly smiles and his eyes are little teary. "When Seth found true-love in Gen, it made our mother want to drive them apart——."

"Hence, arranging *you* to marry Genevieve." Bri adds.

"Right. And as you know, Gen has been spearheading support of this, of you and me!" He states.

"Lawrence, what I want most for Gen is for her and Seth to *finally* be able to start their family!"

"When we are, *if we are*," giving her a look acknowledging she still hasn't answered yet, "legally *bound*, Gen will settle down with Seth and do just that! They were waiting for me to find you, so we could start shifting things to the way they should've been...with Gen and Seth being together and now with *you* by my side." He looks at her with so much love.

"Lawrence..." she lovingly smiles, "ask me again?"

 He happily asks, "BriaLynn, will you do me the greatest honor and marry me?'" He asks as his eyes get teary once again, sliding the ring on her right ring finger.

She has a smile to match as she enthusiastically says, "Yes!" He stands and picks her up in a hug, spinning her around; she holds his face and kisses him.

He slowly sets her down and holds her close, his cheek next to hers. They're just soaking their feelings at the moment...she hears him faintly whisper, "*Thank you...*"

She pulls back her head to look into his eyes with a smirky little grin. "Are you sure you're ready for me?"

"I'm ready for incredible!" He taps a kiss to her lips. "Fantastic!" He taps another kiss. "Brilliant!" And another.

She smiles. "Good answers!" She kisses him firmly; he deepens it and dips her back. They stop when they hear the elevator move.

"I sent everyone away, so this *should* be the food." Lawrence tells her, protectively placing her slightly behind him. Bri hears a text chime with McMasters ringtone. She glances at it.

She lays her hand on Lawrence's arm and smirks, "I guess you don't have the authority to send McMasters away." She shows him McMasters' 'thumbs up' text and he relaxes. "No one would be coming up that elevator if he didn't check it out first."

He cups her cheek, "From the beginning, I told McMasters, with my guards, he can do whatever he needs to do to protect you." He gives her a sweet smile. Her eyes are a teary and she quickly kisses him as the elevator arrives.

Lawrence helps arrange everything to be placed where he wants it, while Bri turns to walk over and look out at the bridge over the river. She pauses when she sees a ghost standing there, looking out. The ghost is emotionally devastated and has no idea Bri is even there. Bri doesn't want to use her gift just yet, so she moves over to a different window and looks out at a different part of the city.

When the set-up is complete and they're alone once again, Lawrence comes up behind her and wraps his arms around her. She points out to a huge section of green trees.

"Is that London's version of New York City's Central Park?"

He points over to a different green location. "That would be 'The King's Park,' but it's barely half the size of Central Park. That," he points back to where she was first pointing, "is the estate I'll be giving you and Jack."

"Wait." She turns in his arms. "What?!"

He gently kisses her. "Let's eat."

"Hold on!" She says as he starts to lead her to the table.

He takes her over to a beautifully set table and pulls out her chair. He pours the champagne saying, "I asked David and Jack what you liked..." He grins as he shows her the 'Tuscan Vineyards' label on it. "Jack tells me it's now *all* nonalcoholic." She smiles and nods. He raises his glass, "A toast," but it surprises him when his emotions make it too difficult to speak.

She raises her glass and helps. "To an adventure of love, family, and a legacy 'King Lawrence the Second' will make his descendants proud to follow!" She's emotional, but more so now because she sees her son she'll have with Lawrence standing behind him.

He's grateful for that toast and adds, "To us!" Then clinks his glass to hers, they both drink. "Still amazing! I never knew nonalcoholic champagne could taste so good before your wedding!" He studies his champagne flute.

She smiles, but it's clear her mind was somewhere else for a moment. "Bri? Are you alright, Darling?"

"Hmmm?" Her eyes flick from their son to him as she realizes what he asked. "Yes! Sorry." She shakes her head.

"Where did you go?" He genuinely asks.

"Oh! Uh, nowhere. Sorry." She steers the conversation in a different direction, "Okay, the estate you *think* you're giving Jack and me—"

"*My favorite castle!*" He gives her a little bit bigger smile. "It hasn't had anyone in its titles for a very long time. That's all I'm going to say for now." He reaches for her hand and wants to go back to what was on her mind, "You can tell me...where were you a minute ago?"

"I just don't know if I should say..." She has a worried look and bites her lips together inside her mouth.

"Well, now you *have to* tell me!" He tells her. "You can't say something like that and leave it there with my interest this piqued."

She laughs. "Ha-ha! I could just change the subject."

"You already tried that and it didn't work." He raises his eyebrow.

"Oh really? Is that a challenge?" She smirks back.

"Not this time." He answers and she raises *her* eyebrow. "There's only one way I can think of that *might* shift my...*focus*, shall we say. And since we aren't official yet, that won't be happening so," he gives her a dimpled smile he knows works on her, "*spill.*"

"No fair." She laughs.

"I know!" He winks.

She shakes her head smiling and then takes a deep breath. "I told you about when I was in a coma, but not everything. I was told I have children yet to be born, I even saw one of them during that time. Then I saw three of them at the wedding, but right now I see," she looks to where her son with Lawrence is and starts to say 'one,' but sees her other two appearing, "*the same three.*" She can only whisper that last part and her lower jaw shakes.

She sees Lawrence's blue-green eyes fill with happy tears. "Really?" He instinctually turns to where she's looking.

"One of them is ours." She smiles sweetly with tears skipping down her cheeks; he looks at her in awe. She carefully wipes her eyes with her napkin and takes another deep breath. She looks at her plate. "I'm *starving* and this smells *so* good!" Lawrence smiles, watching her take her first bite. "*Mmm.*"

"When did you see *your* children at the wedding?" He asks, then takes a bite of his food.

"It was when I was already the most emotional I had been during the ceremony, only it got worse when I saw all three of them at once and I had to turn my back to everyone. I'd see them again on the bridge after the ceremony, too."

"Has David or Jack seen them?"

"David's only seen and spoke with Jessica."

"Did you know this whole time one of them was ours?" He studies her as she answers.

"Not right away, but when I did figure it out, I was told by Jessica that being 'The Royal Consort' would still be my choice." She explains.

"What would've happened if this didn't work between us?" He's curious.

"Like all choices, there are consequences. If this didn't work and we didn't have a baby some other way, our child would be denied their place in our family, *and their birthright.*" She smiles as it occurs to her. "Then again, to see our child would mean this was going to work out..." she looks at him with a loving smile.

He matches her smile. "Do we have a son or a daughter?" He asks, looking around. "Would I be able to see them or this Jessica?"

"If she were here." She grins. There's a hint of mischievousness in her smile. "*And* I purposely didn't say son or daughter." She smirks as she takes a drink.

He laughs. "Do you think that's fair?! You know and we don't!"

"To be perfectly honest, as wedding *gift* I did tell David."

"So, *as a gift* when we're—." He starts to say.

"Hold up, Ace! I never told Jack. I make no promises!" She gives him a cheeky smile. "*However,* I will take it under advisement."

"Alright, Darling, but be aware," he hugs her waist closer, "I *do* like a challenge!"

"*Oh, I know!*" She says with a knowing smile; his eyebrow raises. "Ace, I've been with David and Jack and have picked up a few things along the way. Plus, I've had this same amount of time to pick up a few things about *you,* just as you have me." He nods. "I know you like a challenge *and a complete surrender.*" She winks. He softly chuckles.

They spend the rest of their meal talking about her job in DC and the people she knows. When they're finished, she asks, "What happens now, *My King?*"

"I'm still working on the next steps, but after that blindfolded kiss I can't get out of my head," he helps her up from the table, "how do you feel about legalizing things as soon as possible, rather than waiting several months?"

"The sooner the better!" She kisses and hugs him; he deepens it and dips her again. He brings her back up and rests his forehead to hers.

CHAPTER 14

Imperfectly Perfect Ghostly Encounter

As the evening continues up in The Clock Tower, Bri is facing Lawrence when she sees the heartbroken woman again, just past Lawrence's upper arm. This woman was still looking out over the river, towards London's famous Draw Bridge.

Lawrence looks the direction she is looking asking, "Are you seeing a ghost right now?"

"Yes, but she doesn't see me."

"Really? Not even with your special gift?" Lawrence looks around. "Are there others up here with us?"

Bri lightly laughs. "I haven't used my gift on a ghost yet. First," she turns to him, "are there any legends associated with this tower?"

Lawrence thinks for a moment. "There's only one I can think of...I believe her name was Lady Jane, who fell in-love with someone who worked down on the docks that are no longer there, near The Draw Bridge." He points in the direction the ghost is looking. "Her parents didn't approve, and her father offered this young man a lot of money to disappear; he agreed. This broke Lady Jane's heart and when she came up here, she jumped to her death."

"Seriously?! Who's this man she's supposed to love?" Bri asks.

"I don't remember if I ever did hear his name." He says, trying to remember.

"Jessica, would you come see me?" Bri asks for Jessica for the first time. When Jessica appears, Bri concentrates so Lawrence can see her, as well as the ghost; he is speechless as Bri and Jessica talk. "Jessica, is this Lady Jane?"

Jessica looks over at the woman. "Yes." She looks back at Bri with a smile. "When you look at her, open yourself up and you'll know."

"Really? I can just look at her and know who she, or who someone else, is?" Bri asks and Jessica nods. "*Good to know.*" She says more to herself. Then asks, "What information do you have on what happened to this poor woman?" Bri asks. "Lawrence gave me 'the legend' version."

"Ah." Jessica thinks about this 'legend.' "This is something you can do as well, Bri." She tells them, "Thomas *did* accept the money her father offered him to leave; *however*, when he told Lady Jane of the money, he also told her of his plan to runaway *together*." Lawrence was a little surprised but then again, that's how legends go. "They were to go home and gather their things, then meet at the docks where a ship taking passengers to France would be disembarking that night; her aunt and uncle lived there. Unfortunately, when Lady Jane showed up at the docks, she finds Thomas floating in bloody water. She's so distraught she came back to The Clock Tower but was pushed to her death. She has been here ever since, mourning Thomas."

"*She was pushed?!*" Bri asks.

"Yes. Lord Richard shot Thomas so Lady Jane would marry *him*, but when they were up in this tower, he became so enraged he pushed her to her death." Jessica explains.

Bri looks at Lady Jane and concentrates...she hears the sound of the faint echo of Jane's scream, then sees through Jane's eyes as she falls to her death; Bri jolts herself out of the vision when she, well Jane, hits the ground. Lawrence helps to brace her and she leans on him for a moment. She holds her hand to her chest as she catches her breath and feels her heart is racing.

Lawrence softly asks, "You saw her death, didn't you?"

"I f-felt it!" She looks from him to Jessica.

"The more empathic you become, the more visions you'll see *and feel.*" Jessica informs her.

Lawrence asks, "Visions of the past or will her visions of the future become more real?"

Jessica replies, "Both." She looks to Bri. "Visions of the past will help you understand where someone has been and then you can help them move on. Visions of the future will help you to be able to time intervening without taking someone's choice away from them. But remember, *you can't, and won't, save everyone!* There are allotted times for every mortal to die and you won't be able to intervene *to stop it* from happening but you may be able to help..."

"Help?" Bri asks.

"That's for another time." Jessica replies.

Bri looks at Lady Jane and understands more. "Lady Jane's heart is still breaking," Bri puts her hand over her own heart again, "and she doesn't know what to do. To her, Thomas just died and she's still reeling from that, but when this Lord Richard shows up, it overwhelms her even more!"

Lawrence looks at Lady Jane with compassion. "Can you help her?"

Bri looks to Jessica, who nods encouragingly at her. Bri turns to where Lady Jane stands saying, "I've never done this kind of thing before."

Lawrence supportively tells her, "You can't fail, Darling!"

She looks at him skeptically. "You seem so sure about something I've never done before."

"I know you're amazing, so that's all I need to know!" He walks over to the woman. "Let's see how this works!" He looks at her closely. "You can see her, but she's transparent, too!" He takes his hand and passes it through her. "*Incredible!*"

"Okay, Ace, I can understand the desire to pass your hand through a ghost or a spirit, but it just doesn't seem respectful."

Lawrence looks at his hand. "Oh, right!" He quickly snaps his hand back. "My apologies, Darling." He steps back over next to her.

She gives him a little smile. "Like I said, I get the desire to do it."

Lawrence asks, "You said ghost or spirit? Aren't they the same thing?"

"No. From what I've been able to figure out, spirits are aware of their surroundings and of the living. *Ghosts*," she gestures to the woman, "are unaware of us and the world going on without them; oblivious to hands passing through them." She winks at Lawrence. "She hasn't even noticed the docks aren't there anymore!"

Lawrence looks at the woman, then at Bri with a reassuring smile. "You've got this, Darling." Lawrence gestures with his hand towards the ghost.

Bri steps over and closes her eyes to concentrate, inhaling deeply and thinking about her desire to help this poor woman move on. When she exhales, she opens her eyes and waves her hand around in a circle towards Lady Jane. The woman looks over and sees Bri for the first time; startled for a moment. Then she speaks like they would in Shakespearean time and Bri waves her hand again, having her speak and understand more modern speaking.

"My name is Bri and this is Lawrence." Lawrence smiles when Jane looks at him, her eyes are red. "And you're Lady Jane?" The woman nods. "We'd like to help you?"

"My Thomas…he-he's dead…I-I don't understand…" Tears drip down Lady Jane's cheeks as she looks towards where the docks once were.

"Why don't you tell us what you do remember?" Lawrence suggests.

"My father *hates* that I love Thomas. He said Thomas was a dock worker, worse than a peasant, and that I had to marry Lord Richard, not some 'river-rat.' When I said I wouldn't, my father took a different approach. Thomas told me my father approached him and offered him a lot of money to run away and disappear. Thomas told me he took the money and wanted us to run away together. That money would help us start a new life somewhere, anywhere, *free* of my father. Then I remembered my favorite aunt and uncle, that they lived in France, and I thought we could go stay with them; she was always inviting me to come stay with her." She looks out the window towards the river again.

Bri quietly asks, "Then what happened?"

Jane gets upset at the memory. "After I gathered what I could get in my bag, I went to the docks to meet Thomas. I saw a crowd looking at something in the water, I weaved through to get a closer look. *I glanced down and saw Thomas*," she squeaks through her tears and emotions, "*being pulled out of the red, bloodied water and they laid him on the dock*. I was horrified and pushed my way back out of the crowd, *I needed to get out of there*! I was scared to find Lord Richard there! He tried to grab me but I ran. I just kept thinking maybe I was wrong about Thomas, hoping it was someone else and that he would come looking for me here…" She looks at them. "Have you seen him?"

"Jane. Concentrate." Bri tells her. "What happened when you came up here?"

"If it helps, retrace your steps." Lawrence suggests.

"Retrace?" Jane asks, shaking her head in confusion.

"Start by going back to the stairs and walk over here, thinking about what happened that night." Bri answers.

Jane follows the suggestion. By the stairs, she walks back towards them saying, "I remember walking all the way over here, but then…nothing." She exhales in frustration and tries not to cry.

"Do you remember Lord Richard coming up here?" Lawrence asks.

Her gaze drops to the floor as she thinks and shakes her head. "I'm sorry…" she's frustrated.

Bri has an idea. "Richard?" She looks around. "Richard, I need you to come talk to us." They wait and wait. Bri feels overwhelmingly he's avoiding her on purpose. Bri stomps her foot, "I command you to reveal yourself to me *immediately*!" It doesn't even take a few seconds and he appears to her; she waves her hand to Lawrence for him to see, both see the resemblance to Richard McCleary. Bri stops herself from shuddering when she remembers the incident at her and David's wedding reception.

Richard's spirit has a tinge of darkness about him, but Bri senses it's only the surface. She waves her hand towards Richard so he'll speak and understand more modern English.

Bri tells him, "Tell Lady Jane what you did to her, Richard."

Richard sneers with his nose up in the air. "It's *Lord* Richard."

"You could also be called 'murderer,' 'scoundrel,' '*a cad*.'" Bri spouts off.

He glares as he stares at her, questioning her determination. When she raises her eyebrow and folds her arms; he relents.

"She was so upset over that-that *river rat*!" He says with disgust. "She refused to see reason over that piece of filth!"

"*I remember*…" Jane whispers as her memory starts to return. "You were being callous about Thomas!"

Bri interjects, "And Richard killed him?"

"*Lord* Richard!" He looks at Bri loathing, "You disgusting—."

"I'd say your name that way *if* I thought you deserved that kind of respect!" Bri says flatly. He folds his arms and refuses to talk. She commands, "*Talk.*"

"Thomas was dealt with!" Richard can't help but answer. "He was a *nobody* and she *refused* to see that!" He looks at her in frustration, "You refused to understand we need to stay with our own kind!"

Jane goes to say something, but Lawrence steps in. "The only *nobody* here is *you*! None of your 'kind' is here, but there's plenty of it in some muck heap somewhere!"

Richard scoffs. "I refuse to be insulted by the likes of a *commoner*!" He glares his eyes to slits. "I've never seen you in any court—."

"*King* Lawrence wouldn't be in just any of those courts, society functions, or parties." Bri purposely states for shock value. They watch the color drain out of Richard's face...

"K-*King* Lawrence?!" Richard is horrified and kneels before 'The King.'

Lawrence keeps a poker face, even though he wants to laugh. He knows his ancestors' history and the first Lawrence was a prince during their time. "The *Prince* Lawrence you're thinking of, is my ancestor. I'm *King* Lawrence, *The Second.* This is The Marchioness of Newhaven." His voice takes a very authoritative tone, "You will talk to these ladies with decency and respect, or I'll ask The Marchioness to banish your spirit *straight to Hell*!" Lawrence isn't sure if Bri can do that, but by the look on Lord Richard's face, he believes she could and that's what matters.

Bri now knows what she sees in Lawrence...the danger, the power, *his demeanor*! It all came together and she's *extremely* attracted to him *when he takes control*! It scares her a little, but she pushes that out of her mind for now.

Richard respects the titles and stands up, then steps back. "My apologies to you all. The Marchioness of Newhaven?" Bri nods. "That makes you kin."

"By marriage." Bri states.

Lawrence tells Richard. "The Marchioness minimizes her importance. She is a 'Direct Bloodline' to a lot of monarchies in Europe and a couple dynasties in the Middle East, I believe." Lawrence explains. The 'Middle East' was news to her.

"*Fascinating!*" Richard whispers looking at Bri in astonishment.

King Lawrence takes a step towards him. "The Marchioness will soon be *my* Royal Consort." Richard nods in understanding. "Now, if I heard you correctly, you pushed Lady Jane to her death because you acted like a spoiled child when you didn't get your way!" To his credit, Richard seemed a bit embarrassed.

"What happened?" Bri asks.

Lady Jane looks back out the window, then leans over and looks down. "Richard wanted to take me home..." she recalls.

"You were so distraught, you fought me when I was trying to *help* you get home!" Richard argues.

"You kept telling me that I'd get over him. I don't *want* to get over him! I love him!" Jane tells him.

Richard scoffs. "You can't love someone like *that* river rat!"

Bri interrupts them and looks at Richard. "Love knows no social class! When these two came together, it was because of true-love and no amount of money; *or threats*, would come between them!"

"A gentleman protects the woman he loves," Lawrence interrupts and looks from Richard to Bri, tucking some hair behind her ear, "he *certainly* would *never* hurt her!"

Bri looks at Richard. "Before we come to mortality our spirits grow and learn. This mortal life is part of our eternal growth, we come to mortality to continue learning and growing. When we die, our spirits are still meant *to continue* to grow and learn!" She takes a deep breath. "Whether it's mortals who are stuck and not progressing forward, or ghosts and spirits who are stuck and not moving on, we're *not meant to be stuck*; we *have* to keep learning and moving forward. You *both* need to move on!" Bri turns to Jane. "I can summon Thomas if you'd like?"

She has a hopeful look on her face. "You can bring him to me?!"

Bri gives her a compassionate smile. "I can." Jane is overcome with happiness and emotions. Bri says, "Thomas please show yourself to us, to Lady Jane..." A few moments of quiet pass and Bri is overcome with a feeling that he's stuck in a sort of limbo of his own, down where the docks used to be. "Thomas, I need you to snap out of it right now and come to The Clock Tower to see Jane." A few moments later, Thomas begins to appear before them. Bri slightly waves for Lawrence to see him, too, along with making Thomas speak and understand modern English.

Jane's eyes fill with tears. "Thomas!" He turns just as she throws her arms around his neck and hugs him. Richard's face turns from sadness to the faintest of happy looks. "Thomas, where have you *been*?!" Her British accent very evident with 'been' sounding like 'bean.'

"At the docks, waiting for you, My Love!" Thomas replies. "That's where we agreed to meet!" He sees Lord Richard and remembers, "Lord Richard came to see me...at one point I saw you, but you were running away." Bri realizes it was his spirit seeing Jane run away. The dislike for Richard is thick in Thomas' voice. "I remember he figured out that Jane was coming with me and he tried to convince me to leave without you; that Jane's place was here and there would be other ladies in a distant town that I could love." He looks at Jane so adoringly, it's incredibly sweet. "*There could be no other woman*! You've stolen my heart, Jane!"

"Oh, Thomas! I *do* love you!"

"And I you!" He says back to her.

Bri smiles. "Are you able to move on together? I'm new at this, so is there some sort of light?"

They look around for it and the three of them see it. Just then, Bri and Lawrence watch a white light cover them by getting brighter and brighter, it gets so bright Lawrence and Bri have to look away, until it switches off so-to-speak and dissipates completely. Jessica, Thomas, and Jane were gone, but when her eyes adjust, Bri notices Richard and she is confused. "Why didn't you go with them?"

Bri senses the humility Richard now has; he no longer has a darkness to him. He tells her, "I took innocent blood, Lady Newhaven. My time should be spent in the emptiness of limbo, to wander...left to my thoughts..."

"To torture yourself?" Bri asks.

Richard nods. "In a manner of speaking." Bri wonders if this is a type of 'Hell' for him and any others who feel unworthy to enter into Heaven?

Lawrence is curious and asks Richard, "What happens to those who are truly evil? Those who enjoy hurting others?" He's thinking of his mother.

Bri whispers to herself, "*The guard!*" Lawrence hears her. She has a compassionate look on her face. "The executed guard was swiftly taken down to where I assume is Hell." She looks at Richard to confirm.

He nods. "Probably. I've also seen evil spirits attack the arrival of another evil spirit. They rip them apart and pull the pieces down to Hell. Other times, the very ground they stand on opens up to reveal an orange glow and that new spirit is sucked down into it. Both situations lead to different parts of Hell, but those depths are unknown. Rarely, a spirit will be ripped apart into pieces and no one knows what happens to those pieces, but I'd think it would be to the darkest places *beyond Hell.*"

"Wow..." Bri says, trying to picture that happening. "That sounds painful, if that's possible for a spirit?"

Richard's eyebrows raise a little as he considers that. "Their screams sound that way!" He shivers a bit.

"Lord Richard, if you were meant for Hell, wouldn't you be there? I mean, if you're here now, maybe you need to go into the light and face any punishment, or justice of sorts, there? Let them oversee things! Do you see a light?" She asks.

"Faintly...oh, now it's getting bigger?"

Bri smiles. "It's getting bigger because you have hope."

"Hope?" He questions.

"*Yes.* Hope of going into that light and receiving forgiveness." She's thinking of the time when she was in a coma, "I've felt those same things you do with that light! Hope, love, peace..."

"Mercy." Lawrence adds.

Bri smiles with a nod at Lawrence then looks back to Richard who is studying the light. "You're not meant to stay 'in-between' realms, or worlds, like purgatory or whatever this is called, if you think about it... Hell doesn't seem to want you, or it would've snatched you up already! I don't think you would've seen the light at all if it wasn't meant for you."

"You're probably right, but I feel I need to stay here just a little while longer." Lord Richard looks at Bri.

She kindly smiles. "If it's a peaceful feeling, then maybe it is The Spirit, so I won't convince you otherwise."

He gives her a small appreciative look. "If you need anything, just call out for me. I'll respond quicker next time." He tells her and she nods. He looks at Lawrence. "It seems you're already a much better king than some of your predecessors." He bows to The King and Lawrence tips his head down in acknowledgement.

They watch Lord Richard disappear, then Bri and Lawrence stand in silence for a moment, absorbing what they just heard and witnessed. Lawrence turns to Bri. "Thank you for sharing that with me! *That was incredible!*" He holds her hand and walks to the elevator, then pushes the elevator button.

"All I did was make it so you could see what I see." Bri states.

"You helped them and I got to witness that!" He smiles adoringly.

They enter the elevator and she wraps her arms around him, smiling as she says, "No, Ace, *WE* helped them!" She kisses him.

The doors open and they see McMasters. "Your Majesty, I've been asked to keep you both here to wait for your motorcade to arrive." Lawrence nods.

They only have to wait a few minutes before they are walking out to the motorcade. Even though it's nighttime, there is still a crowd with more people than when they first arrived. They are shouting with excitement. "Lady Newhaven!" Sprinkled with, "Your Majesty," "Lady Bri," and "Long live The King!"

He stops and pulls her into a sweet kiss, causing lots of cheering and even more so when he romantically dips her down low. She lovingly smiles up at him.

She runs her hand into his hair. "Incorrigible." She taps another kiss to his lips and he brings her back up.

"Then I'm in fantastic company!" He grins, kissing her ring, inciting more cheers, screams, and questions of her becoming 'The Royal Consort.' Lawrence and Bri don't answer, they only wave before getting into the backseat of their car.

"Abby, Seth, and Gen will be waiting for us in The Royal Apartment." Lawrence says as he texts David to gather everyone for a videoconference call and to call when they are ready.

Lawrence's phone rings for the call and he slides into the middle of the seat. He answers it and they see David and Jack; Bri can't help but smile so happily at them. They are at The Manor with a tablet they have set on a table so Peter, Carlotta, James, and Amy can join them.

"We're all here!" David excitedly says.

"Aaand," Jack gestures, "the girls are here!"

Bri smiles wide at them. "Hi, Loves!" She blows them a kiss and they excitedly smile at her.

Lawrence smiles. "It's official!" Bri lovingly smiles at Lawrence. He sees so much love in her eyes for him, he gets a little choked up. He swallows hard to push it down and says, "She's agreed to—."

"*More* insanity!" She kisses his cheek with the others laughing and congratulating them. Then she says, "Seriously, life's going to become more, um...*interesting*!"

"With a whole bunch more love and family!" Jack happily adds. She wipes her own tears, nodding. Lawrence agrees, too.

155

Lawrence wonders, "Your Graces, would you be upset if we made everything official at your Midnight Ball?"

Peter and Carlotta are excited. Peter replies, "Not at all!"

"I think that would be absolutely lovely!" Carlotta says enthusiastically. "We'll make the theme more of a 'twilight with romantic candlelight' this year!"

"Carlotta, that sounds beautiful!" Bri happily smiles.

"David, will that be enough time?" Lawrence asks, wondering if the solicitors will have enough time to finalize their paperwork, but being careful not to say anything in case the call is being secretly listened to.

"I'd think so!" David replies, being careful, too. "But I'll look into it first thing in the morning and let you know."

"Wonderful! I'll be in touch!" Lawrence tells him. They all say their goodbyes and hang up.

They motorcade pulls up to The Royal Apartment of The London Palace and are dropped off at the door. Lawrence takes her hand and walks her up to The Royal Apartment where Genevieve, Seth, and Abagail anxiously await them and the news. When Lawrence shows them the hand he is holding, they see the ring and they're ecstatic, hugging and congratulating them both.

"*Finally!*" Gen smiles excitedly.

Abby squeals, "It's about time!" She hugs Bri again. "Now the three of us will *officially* be sisters!"

Gen mischievously says, "Now, I get to spearhead Bri to become queen."

"What?! No! *Absolutely not!*" Bri panics. Although Bri knows from her sons that is coming soon enough, she doesn't want to be hurried into it! "I have the duties with Newhaven and I'm stressed with that, along with The Foundation, The Textile Mill, *and* The Wool Farm! I can't take on anything more until I get a handle on what I've already got!"

"Bri," Gen squeezes her hand a little. "Don't worry! I'll continue doing what I've been doing; this will be in title only."

"I can help!" Abby adds. "I can be your 'Queen-in-Waiting.'" She giggles.

Bri laughs asking Abby, "Is that even a real thing?!"

Abby laughs shaking her head saying, "No, just a play on 'Lady-in-Waiting.' Look, Bri, my schedule is yours. I'll talk to Gabriel if you approve of this. Lawrence said you're protective of him."

Bri gives Lawrence an eyeroll and looks back at Abby. "I'm *loyal*. Gabriel has been wonderful and so patient with me, always keeping me 'in the know' of people's titles and all the protocols, he keeps my schedule organized and me on-time! He does so much I couldn't possibly begin to list everything; *he's priceless*! I'm still trying to earn his trust in return!"

"I could talk to a different assistant, if you prefer?" Abby offers.

Bri smiles appreciatively. "I told Gabriel *he's it*! I have only one assistant and it's him. *He* can hire whoever he needs, to accomplish whatever needs to get done!"

"Will he have enough people to handle my schedule, too?" She asks.

"If not, there will be!" Bri grins and Abby giggles. "Abby, I don't know what to say..." Her throat starts to fill with a lump.

"Bri, my schedule alongside yours will help spread the workload of everything. This way it won't be an overload for anyone!" Abby explains. "Plus, I need something to do with my life!" She holds Bri's hands. "Promise me you'll think about it."

"I don't need to..." Bri wipes a tear from her cheek. "I accept!" Abby has a huge smile and hugs Bri tight.

They all talk for a while longer, but when they see Bri yawn hard for a third time, they say goodnight. Lawrence walks her to her room.

At the door, she says, "I love you, Lawrence! Goodnight."

"I love you, too, *My* Queen!" With one last kiss, he turns and leaves, shutting the door behind himself.

Bri gets ready for bed and it isn't long before she is falling asleep.

CHAPTER 15

Imperfectly Perfect Good Morning

The next morning, Bri feels her shirt covered shoulder being kissed and hears. "Good morning, My Queen!"

"*Craaap*, why do you have to be a *dreadful* morning person, too?!" She mocks his accent. "*All three of you* are '*off your trolley*' morning people?! That's just messed up!" Her annoyed tone is evident, even though she is teasing him.

He softly chuckles. "I thought we could eat breakfast together."

"Not if breakfast requires me to get out of this bed anytime soon!"

"Then it's a good thing I had breakfast brought *to you*!" He kisses her jaw line back to her ear.

"What *is it* with you men?! *Seriously*! It's like you get some twisted pleasure out of waking me up early when I don't have to be, *My King*!" She can't see him smiling as he takes the covers in his hands, then he throws them back. She turns over on her back and has her eyebrows furled. He grabs her legs and easily yanks her to him; she gasps and yells, "*LAWRENCE ALEXANDER!*"

He is now towering over her and bends down, placing one hand on each side of her on the bed. With an intense smoldering look in his eye, he tells her, "I can think of a more enjoyable way to *twist up* your cheekiness."

He takes her wrists in one hand and pins them above her head. With a more dominating look that catches her breath, he runs the backs of his fingers all the way down her arm and the side of her torso...resting between her ribcage and her hip.

He leans down and has his mouth *so* close to hers, she can feel the heat from his breath against her lips. "For now, just *eat*.the.breakfast, *Darling*!" He ghosts to her lips.

"Fine." She says with a bit of sass and an eye roll.

"Careful..." He still has his hand on her hip and slips his fingers just under the edge if her shirt. He feels a sliver of her warm soft skin. She inhales and holds her breath. He locks his gaze with her eyes. "You *will* eat without the cheekiness or the eyerolls, *or* I will push our boundaries just to watch you squirm..."

She glares, "*Then you'll be making yourself squirm, too!*" She snaps at him. She sees his jaw clenching.

"You're challenging me." He furrows his eyebrows studying her. "*Why?*"

"Because challenging you is *exactly* what you like *and want.*" She answers and watches his eyebrow raise. "You're attracted to me because I'm not like the women who throw themselves at you, or they are thrown at you by your mother. You *want me to* push back because *you want the challenge.*"

"You think so?" He asks. "I know I'm attracted to beauty and some of those women are beautiful."

"Yeah, *for sex!*" She grins. "But *none of them* were in the running for a relationship, *especially* the ones being sent to you by your mother." She purses her lips and raise her eyebrow, with a look that says, 'she's right.'

"I know I'm driven to *complete distraction* with you, and when you push back it only exacerbates the frustration. Which means," he slides his hand to her bum, "if you don't shut it and eat, I'm going to be driven to extremes *I haven't navigated before*; the intensity of this attraction on the many levels we feel, *is* dangerous." He lightly squeezes her bum. "Do you want to risk it, Darling?" He moves his hand to her waist.

She goes to sass again, but quickly realizes he's right and closes her mouth, shaking her head instead. With her racing hormones, these are part of *their unchartered waters* and if they're not careful, it'd be way too easy to get regrettably caught up in the rapids.

He helps her sit up and she gets situated, then he brings the tray over. Since the beach, she knew he was a bit broader shouldered and muscular than Jac and David, but the way he effortlessly yanked her to him and the t-shirt he had on wasn't helping to extinguish her racing hormones! Only now they're racing faster than ever with him and getting worse! He sets the tray down and crawls onto the bed to sit next to her, only he's facing her.

"Are you alright?" He asks.

"Nnnope." She takes a deep breath and holds it as she picks up her napkin and lays it in her lap.

He's surprised by her answer, then asks, "What can I do?"

"Oh, you *can't* do anything *aaand* therein lies the problem!" She tells him as she purposely avoids looking at him, picking up a piece of toast.

He raises an eyebrow and notices her avoidance of looking at him. "There isn't anything I wouldn't do for you, Darling. *Ohhh...*" He starts to smile when he begins to follow.

"Between all that you just did, causing the hormones to ramp up..." '*Paybacks?*' She asks herself. '*You bet!*' "Seeing you in your t-shirt and all those rippling muscles," she runs a finger down his arm, "has things going through my mind that would cause *ice* to ignite into flames. I've realized I'm attracted to the strength, power, and control you have, as well as the dominating control you *want* to have in *our bedroom*; do you still want to play around with these feelings, driving ourselves insane and risking everything for lust?"

He shifts and clears his throat. Her ability to see into his soul stretches his comfort level with her because he can't control how exposed he feels. However, he does find some comfort that someone knows the darkest parts of his soul and loves him anyway.

He gives her a weak smile. "How about we talk about other things?"

She smiles compassionately. "Oh, Ace, I'm not sure if such a topic exists that could help—."

"My mother." He smirks.

"*Aaand* just like that the fire is out." She's serious, but there's a hint of sarcasm. "Thank you..."

"You're welcome." He winks with his dimples showing as he bites into a strawberry. She had a picture of a beautiful baby pop into her mind with dimples, she puts it away for now and listens as he continues. "Maybe I'm paranoid, but I wouldn't put *anything* past your mother. We need to keep that you and David are..." he gives her a look and she knows he's implying they're trying to have a baby, she nods. "Even Seth, Gen, or Abby, could accidentally say something that someone overhears and it gets back to her."

She holds his cheek. "I understand."

He takes her hand and kisses it. "I love you! And I'm also in awe at *how much* I love you!"

"Why?! You make it sound like an anomaly."

"*You are*! A bloody fantastic and *brilliant* anomaly!" He grins.

"A sweet talking 'King Charming,'" she fans herself and uses a southern American accent to add, "Bless your heart, I may just swoon!" She puts the backs of her fingers to her forehead.

"You're making it difficult to go to work..." he notes.

"That's part of my charm!" She grins.

"While I'm all for exploring this further," he runs a finger down her neck, "I want to respect your request and wait. Which means, *I need to leave* and calm down my own racing hormones so I won't have trouble, um...*walking* to my office on the other side of The Palace."

She smiles. "If you must."

He kisses her cheek. "Trust me, Darling, *I must*!" He smiles with dimples as he gets up and goes to the door. "I'll see you later for lunch?"

"Absolutely!" Bri smiles wide. He winks, then he walks out of the room.

They spend a couple days together. Lawrence worked in his primary office to appease his mother; Bri worked at the desk in her bedroom in The Royal Apartment. She is getting ready to leave this morning and packing what little she had left to pack. She feels inspired to write Lawrence a quick note. Then she tucks a strip of the photo booth photos they posed for last night, inside the envelope. Yesterday, after hours, they went to the photo booth that sits near the main entrance and had a lot of fun.

 She seals the envelope and writes, 'My King Charming' on the front, with 'XOXO' under it and off to the side. She looks at it and smiles. Then she gets the idea to add lipstick to her lips and she puts a kiss on the envelope, under 'My King Charming' and next to the 'XOXO.'

 She stands up from the writing desk and turns to see she was slipped a manila envelope under the door with a symbol of two S's, one upside down, stacked in the middle of an underlined 'U.' It's the symbol for 'The Underground Secret Society.'

Bri turns it over and goes to open it, but Jessica appears. *"Don't open it right now!"* Bri freezes. "Tuck it into your bag and keep it with you *at all times*. Your things are looked through thoroughly by The Queen Mother's people and if you leave any bag unattended," pointing to the ones Bri keeps with her as she travels, "they'll be looked through, too. They *will* recognize the symbol instantly and will want to prevent you from seeing what's inside, once they see what was sent to you!"

"Really?!" Bri asks, trying not to panic.

"Lawrence is right. The Queen Mother has spies *everywhere*, so trust *no one* but Lawrence and of course McMasters." She stresses as she's walking over to Bri. *"Not even those Lawrence trusts most*, perhaps especially, are *not* to be trusted!"

Bri's heart is saddened. "Another example of Lawrence being betrayed. How will he trust *anyone* when he finds out about that?!"

"Other than Seth, Gen, and Abby, Lawrence trusts you, David, and Jack, as well as the whole Worthington family. He just needs to shift his trust to solely all of you. Unfortunately, he'll be forced to do that soon enough."

Bri nods and thanks Jessica before she disappears. Bri puts both envelopes in her bag and zips it up. When she is finished putting on her shoes, there's a knock at the door.

"It's me, Darling." She hears Lawrence say on the other side of the door.

She opens the door. "Hi, Ace!" She says with a smile and a kiss.

"Ready?" He asks.

"I am!" She puts her hands on her bags and Lawrence comes up behind her to take her tote bag.

"Did you get everything?" He asks.

"I think so." She looks around, then looks at him. "I need to ask you a question, but you can't ask me why I'm asking it!" She gives him a small, apologetic smile.

He raises his eyebrow in curiosity. "*I'll try.*"

"No. Lawrence. I need you to promise you won't."

A bit concerned and reluctant to do so, he does agree exhaling, "Okay, I won't."

"Is my luggage searched when I arrive, or before I leave?" She asks.

There is a surprised look on his face that relieves Bri. "Is that what—." He stops himself. "*Ugh.* You can't drop something like that and then ask me to leave it alone!"

"I'm sorry. I'll at least tell you that McMasters didn't raise the question and it falls into a 'Sixth Sense' category." She reads his concern and tells him, "Lawrence, think of your already short list of people you trust...if they're not Seth, Gen, Abby, a Worthington, or a Worthington by adoption or marriage, *trust.none.of.them*!"

He studies her. "How do—."

"I'm sorry I can't say more; at least not yet." She puts her hand on his arm. "Look, you're alone here at The Palace except for Abby, Seth, and Gen. *Regardless of your reasoning*, anyone can be bought or threatened to work for your mother, even on a case-by-case or job-by-job basis. *Trust no one.* Say it back to me."

"*Trust no one.*" He repeats.

"Thank you." She gives him a faint smile and he taps a kiss to her lips.

Another knock and it's McMasters, with Tristan, coming to walk with them outside. Lawrence takes her tote bag in one hand and her hand with his other hand, tucking her arm under his. Tristan reaches out for Bri's bag Lawrence is carrying for her, offering to take it. Lawrence feels Bri squeeze his hand and he squeezes it back, telling Tristan he's got it. Bri senses Tristan's frustration, but on the outside he seems unphased. *Curious*...she notes to herself.

They stop outside the helicopter and she pulls his suit coat jacket open and tucks the envelope with her note and pictures inside his pocket. "Read this sometime *after* I leave." She smiles so lovingly and happily, his heart squeezes for her.

He kisses her fiercely. "I love you, My Queen!" He taps another kiss to her lips. "I'm going to miss you!"

"And I'm going to miss you! I love you, *My* King Charming!" They kiss once more before she gets into the helicopter.

Lawrence moves away to a safe distance. He waves as they lift into the air and watches for a minute as they fly off towards Edinburgh. He reaches into his pocket as he walks towards the door of The Palace. He pulls out the envelope and opens it. He stops and reads it with a smile on his face, a bit of a lump forming in his throat.

> *When you look at these cheesy photo booth pictures, see how much fun we're having just being together! And when I'm spending time with you, I couldn't be happier!*
>
> *You are an amazing, wonderful, brilliant, handsome man, who has a place forever in my heart! I look forward to our future together, and I'll miss you terribly while we're apart!*
>
> *Loving you,*
>   *BriaLynn*

He tucks the note and photos back in the envelope, then puts them back in the inside pocket of his suit coat. He thinks to himself, '*For once in my life, something is finally going really right!*' He clears his throat and walks to his office with the purpose of keeping himself busy and to *try* and not miss her so much...but it doesn't help as well as he hoped, even with his mother overseeing his duties like she does all day, every day.

CHAPTER 16

Imperfectly Perfectly Stressful Week

The helicopter lands on top of The Worthington Corporation building. Bri makes her way to the executive floor where David's office is at one end of the floor and hers is at the other. Bri walks out of the stairwell and hears David and Mary talking in his office, so she just heads to her own office to put down her things; she'll go back down in a few minutes.

Mary heard the helicopter and figured it was Bri. When she heard the door to the stairwell close, she looked out of David's office and saw Bri walking towards her own office in the opposite direction of David's office. Mary is relieved Bri is here because it has shaped up to be a stressful week for David and *just seeing* Bri will help ease his tension a bit.

David is thumbing through the papers Mary has him signing. He didn't even hear the helicopter, but he had seen Mary look down the hall.

"Is someone here?" He asks, looking at Mary as she walks back over.

She takes the stack of papers he is handing back to her with a knowing smile. "*Mrs. Worthington.*"

David shoots up from his desk chair, which rolls back into the credenza that sits against the windows behind him, and he follows Mary out of his office. He walks down to Bri's office, walking in as she's finishing a phone conversation with Jack.

"I'll be down after I see David, so it'll be a few minutes."

She hears Jack smirk and he tells her, "I'm walking into The Worthington Corporation's lobby as we speak."

Bri giggles. "Well, then, I'll see you in a couple of minutes!"

She shakes her head, hanging up. She sees David and studies him for a moment...his face reads that he's already had a long week. She has a loving, compassionate smile for him as they walk over to each other and she hugs him tight.

He returns her hug, taking a deep breath and as he exhales, he whispers, "*I needed this...*"

She pulls her head back and looks at him. "Are you alright?"

"I'm better now that you're here..." He says, putting their foreheads together and closing his eyes; he doesn't want to talk about it at the moment.

She lifts her head. "David, I feel like I'm getting more empathic so *please*, don't shut me out." She pleads.

"I'm not. I *do* feel better hugging you! *But* I just don't want to talk about it right now. I have a raging fire I'm dealing with, which reminds me," he says looking at his watch, "I've got to go to another meeting."

"David—." She starts to say, but he kisses her and embraces her firmly.

He gently pulls their lips apart. "There's just a lot happening, and I wouldn't know where to begin with such a short amount of time. It's been a long week and the week isn't over. Plus, I swear to you, I *always* feel better just seeing you or hearing your voice, even more so holding you..." he looks at her with a look that the weight of the world on his shoulders, "*you know this.*"

She nods and holds his jaw, giving him a small smile. "I just want to help. I hate seeing you stressed like this! If you need *anything*, all you have to do is say the word and I'll drop everything—."

He kisses her. "I know and I appreciate the thought, but there's nothing you can, or could, do." He taps another kiss to her lips. "It sounds like Jack is picking you up early—."

"I am!" Jack walks in with a huge smile. "I have a meeting at The Mill about the next phase of remodeling. I thought she'd want to be there since she's around, rather than be on the phone or have another videoconference. I have to run by the house first." He smiles and kisses Bri's cheek. "Hi, Gorgeous!" He steps back and says to David, "You look like your week is about to get worse! Want to talk about it yet?"

"No. There's no time. I can only walk you two to the lift if you're ready?" David tells them and Bri nods. They walk to the elevator and he kisses Bri with a little more than a tap on her lips. "I am starting to feel better just seeing you!"

She hugs him tight. "I love you, My Love!"

He smiles sweetly. "And I love you." He taps another kiss to her lips. "I'll see you both at dinner tonight." David fist-bumps Jack and they all wave as the elevator doors close.

David walks back to his office to gather his things for his meeting in a conference room on the ground floor. Normally he would bring the meetings up to his floor for the VIP treatment, *but not this time.*

Bri and Jack walk off the elevator and Bri sees the receptionist who replaced Ms. Wilson. "Have a wonderful rest of the day, Mrs. Pennington!"

"Thank you!" She replies. "And to you, Lady Newhaven and Lord Carlisle." Jack gives her his signature smile and even though she tries to hide it, Mrs. Pennington is not immune to its 'feel good' effect and smiles wide!

Mrs. Pennington is very nice under a rigid layer of proper protocol and procedure. She was raised in an upper-middle class family by parents who supported her desire to work for a noble or royal family one day. To do so meant certain schools, strict adherence to traditions and how things are done, as well as knowing what is expected of those who work for them. She sees that Bri saw her slip, but Bri winks and does a small gesture of zipping her lips. Mrs. Pennington gains her stoic composure and nods...with a small wink of her own to Bri. Bri has mentioned to Gabriel that she really likes this woman and he logs that as a possible 'new hire' for an assistant to Bri in the future. She isn't sure about poaching David's employee, but she trusts Gabriel to respectfully handle it like it should be.

Jack and Bri are about to walk out the front doors and Bri freezes in mid stride. "McMasters! I forgot to ask Gabriel to make arrangements with McMasters and a car!"

Jack says, "I did." He kisses her cheek, pointing to the car out front.

"Thank you!" She says, as they walk up to their car.

"Since Gabriel is the true keeper of your schedule, I called to make sure you were *actually* free. Once I knew that, Gabriel arranged McMasters to pick me up first."

"Interesting..." Bri smiles as Jack kisses her hand.

"Gabriel says when you're available, or could be, or suggests a better time, things like that. We still ask you because it's still your choice if you want to do something or not." He says.

"So, when you need to know David's schedule, it's David for the actual day, but Mary the next day and out." She had figured that part out already.

"Right. Plus, Mary and Gabriel talk a lot, even to my team's assistant."

"Wait. Tessa is a *shared* assistant?" Bri asks.

"Yep. Tessa's the assistant for my team. She handles a lot of the electronic paperwork with signatures, wire transfers, and a ton of other things. She keeps tabs on all our schedules; but it's easier for us to make our own individual appointments. It's nice to have someone who keeps track of all of them, so I can call her for more than one schedule—."

"And not make a number of calls!" She smiles. "Well, I'm ashamed I didn't know that piece about Tessa being *the team's* assistant! I figured she was just your assistant." Bri looks surprised. "You know, maybe we need to be talking more and having less sss—."

Jack covers her mouth. "Don't you *dare* finish that sentence, Amore Mia!" McMasters is quietly chuckling. Jack still giving her a serious look tells her, "I'd rather hear you say we need more pillow-talk *afterwards*!"

She laughs. "But there isn't always time for that either!"

"Amore Mia, I'll tell you *anything* you want to know!"

"That's just it! Sometimes I don't know what I should've known until I'm in a situation and realize I *should've* known it!" She replies.

Bri rests her eyes but falls asleep. Jack wakes her as they pull up to The Cottage House. They go inside, walking through the kitchen and into the open living room that has a vaulted ceiling. The stairs are on the far wall, a stained light oak banister that runs up the stairs and around so people on the second floor can look down onto the living room.

Jack comes up behind her and wraps his arms around her, she smiles as she tells him, "I can picture little ones running around and up those stairs, with *at least* one of them taking after you and sliding down the banister!"

"And I can picture a sweet girl with her mother's heart having me wrapped around her finger, too." He says, kissing the curve of her neck. Bri lightly laughs.

Jack grabs what they need for their meeting, then they go out to the garage and climb in his car. McMasters will follow behind on their way to *The Textile Mill* to meet up with a couple of men David, Jack, and Lawrence have known for years. Their family owns a big contracting company with offices all over the UK and a couple in France. Jason and Kyle Wayford are brothers and give their personal touch to their clients.

When Bri and Jack arrive at The Mill, they settle into the office and start working on some things for a bit. They are so focused, it's a knock on the office door that interrupts them. Jason and Kyle walk in and are reintroduced to Bri.

"You're still as lovely as ever!" Jason kisses her hand, then Kyle.

Bri laughs. "*You're* still laying it on pretty thick, Mr. Wayford!"

"Alright you two, she's *still* taken!" Jack says, breaking them up and teasingly shooing them away from her. He wraps his arm around her. "She's *very* taken!"

"And I have my hands full with the men already in my life, then this wool project and—!"

"Hey now!" Jack tugging her closer, his other hand going to his chest. "I can't believe you think you have your hands full with *me*!"

"Can't you?" Bri bites her lower lip and smiles raising her eyebrows.

He chuckles and winks, but that's all he will engage in. He won't play a game like that any further with Kyle and Jason right there; if they weren't friends, it wouldn't have started at all. She is to be treated as The Marchioness she is, with dignity and respect in public; as David and Jack insist, and there's no doubt Lawrence also insists upon it.

They talk with Jason and Kyle about the improvements with The Mill and what was left, as well as their timeframes and budget. It isn't a long meeting and after they finish up, they say their goodbyes. Jack and Bri work on a few things that afternoon in the office. When they get ready to leave, he playfully grabs her and his hands slide down to her bum. He kisses her and she returns it, wrapping her arms around him.

"I love you, Amore Mia!"

She beams, "I love you, Amore Mio!"

He holds his hand out with the wonderful smile of his, "Shall we then, Gorgeous?" She smiles back and takes it. They walk out to the car and he tosses her the keys. "You drive!"

"Me?" She asks.

"It's sexier when you drive." He winks.

She laughs, shaking her head. "Oh, I don't know about that!" She says as they climb into the car and she drives them home.

Inside The Manor, Jack and Bri are walking into The Dining Room with a couple minutes to spare. David looks rough; she hugs and kisses him.

She sits next to him and whispers, *"You don't look too great, Love. Will you talk to me later?"*

"Long meeting, long day." David says it a bit grumpy. "Long and dreadful week. I just *don't* want to relive it!" This isn't normally like him, so she backs down and gives him some space.

That evening, Jack, James, and David play pool, at Jack's suggestion, to help David unwind. When the guys finish their game, Jack and James play another round, David goes to his quarters. When he gets to the bedroom, he pauses at the door a second when he sees Bri reading in bed.

"Feeling better?" She asks.

"No." His answer is short and he goes to get ready for bed.

She puts her tablet down and takes her glasses off, then turns off her light since she turned David's light on earlier. She gets comfortable and waits for David. He comes out of the bathroom and turns his light out. He slides into their bed, staying on his side. It's rare for this, too, they usually cuddle for a little while. But there are times, like now, when he goes right to sleep. Tonight, though, she doesn't even get a kiss. She understandingly smiles to herself and closes her eyes.

A few minutes later her eyes pop open as she feels herself being rolled onto her back and being kissed. David runs his hand up the side of her body but stops at her lower ribs. He's waiting for her to stop him, or let him continue.

She can barely see him in the darkness. She whispers, *"Can't sleep?"*

"Love, I just need the stress relief only you can give me. I promise to make it up to you, but right now——."

She kisses him as she lifts up his t-shirt, breaking their kiss to take it off. For the first time in days, he feels some of his stress ease up and he relaxes...

A little later, she taps a kiss to his lips and quietly says, "Let's get some sleep."

He nods as his heart grows more in-love with his beautiful wife than ever. "I love *you*, Mrs. Worthington!"

She lifts her head with a cheeky grin. "I know!" He has a faint smile she can barely see before she taps another kiss to his lips. "I love *you*, *Mister* Worthington! Goodnight."

He leans in with his faint smile and lightly kisses her cheek. They lay on their own pillows and go to sleep.

CHAPTER 17

Imperfectly Perfectly Unwanted Work Union

That morning, David planned on waking Bri to talk when he got back from the gym, but when he gets back, she is already in the shower. He decides to join her.

He gets in and hugs her from behind, inhaling and exhales. "You smell good." He kisses her neck. "Will you let me wash your back?"

She smiles, handing him the luffa in her hands. He's quiet as he washes her back, staring at the trail of suds and thinking. After a couple minutes, she turns around and uses the luffa on his back.

She asks, "Do you want to talk about it, yet?"

He stares at the floor as she washes his back. "I know I owe you an explanation."

"You don't *owe me* anything!" Bri hugs him from behind and kisses his shoulder. "David, I want you to talk to me when you're ready, but I don't want you to feel like you *have to* talk to me if you're not there yet." She continues to wash his back.

He places his hands on the wall. "A hotel the corporation owns in New York City has been threatening to unionize."

He hears her whisper, "*Yikes!*"

"I *never* wanted that to happen and we work hard to make sure we stay very competitive with pay, benefits, retirement, *everything*." He explains.

"Ah." Bri says, listening. He turns a little to read her face. He doesn't want to insult her, so he's trying to be delicate. Luckily, Bri senses this and helps him out. "David, unions are not looked at favorably as a whole by Americans. The worse ones have greedy executives that are only out for themselves and getting the most money for their own pockets. Plus, unions can make it worse and unfair for people who actually work, because it can be an easy paycheck for those who don't want to work." She sees his tension ease up some more.

"This particular union *did* see dollar signs. I made it clear to my employees: if they unionize, I *will* shut down the hotel. At the meeting yesterday, after you two left, I was told they had unionized by that arrogant bas—, er, Union President. He handed me signed copies of all the employees who agreed to unionize, basically challenging me on my hotel; MY *hotel*." He hits his palm against the marble wall of the shower. "My heart sinks for what they're forcing me to do to those employees; plus, all those who agreed to the union were led to believe I couldn't legally follow through with closing down the hotel." He takes a deep breath. "All those hundreds of people, *all their families*, Bri..." His jaw clenches in anger and frustration.

Bri hugs him from behind again. "I'm so sorry, David." She kisses his shoulder again; he squeezes her arms back.

"I have to go into the office this morning and release a mass email, after human resources tells all those employees they'll be out of a job in thirty days. A mass email, which will later be used as a press release, will let employees know what happened and why." He exhales. "Then staff will have to go through reservations beyond two weeks and cancel all those reservations, refund any prepayments, and give recommendations for other nearby hotels." He shuts the water off, exhaling more irritation. "The union people thought I was bluffing, but it's *my* employees who'll find out the hard way I wasn't...all those employees out of a job, with all their families suffering the consequences, too..." His mind continuously swirls around his employees and their families. "The only good to come from all of this is all our other employees will now know for future reference that *this is* what will happen; that when I say, 'no unions,' I mean it!" He hits the shower wall again with the palm of his hand. All Bri can do is hug him and he turns around to hug her back. "Sorry. I wasn't sure how to say all that yesterday when you asked because I'm so...so...."

"Mad, angry, and frustrated you *have to* follow through, but your mind is also swirling because you're heartbroken for your employees who'll now be looking for a new job and their families who could potentially suffer the most." She helps him to say and he just hugs her tighter. "It sounds like this union president somehow lied his way in, poisoned a few employees so they'd spread the toxins, despite your measures to make your employees resistant to a union." Bri notes.

"Yeah...I keep trying to figure out what I could've done differently, but I don't know? Competitive pay, benefits, retirement..." he lets out a humorless laugh, "I even ask employees to complete *anonymous* satisfaction surveys!

175

They're done through a third party to make sure they stay anonymous. Copies of those surveys are sent directly to me, department heads, as well as HR." He softly kisses her temple. "I feel like I've let everyone down...the corporation, my father, *you*!"

"Oh, no!" She pulls back shaking her head. "First of all, you've done *no* such thing, My Love! You haven't let me down *in the slightest*!" She gives him a loving smile. "I'm proud of you!"

"You are?!" He was surprised. "Why?!"

"I'm proud of you for following through with what you said you would do! If you don't, your word will mean *nothing* out in the world. You keeping your word is *crucial* for the corporation and as the future Duke of Newhaven. Yes, it's *horrible* that the people who had nothing to do with the union will lose their jobs, but it's not like you're closing the doors right this moment. Thirty days is *more* than fair as would a generous severance package to all!" She holds his hands. "Would you mind if I made a suggestion?"

"I'm never joking when I say I love your intelligence!" He kisses the inside of her wrist. "What is it?"

"I would add a condition with whatever your norm is for a formal letter, that while they are 'highly encouraged' to apply working for a Worthington owned or operated business, there's a stipulation from *ever* promoting or signing on with another union while employed with The Worthington Corporation, or however the lawyers want to word it. I'd then add a penalty to discourage them from doing it anyway in the future, but a compensation bonus too good to pass up, that any decent lawyer would tell them to sign. You've probably thought about this, but in the likelihood it was missed among the awfulness, and your mind was spinning; I'd check with lawyers on both sides of the pond to see if maybe there is a way to *prohibit* this union altogether, before shutting it down. Since The Worthington Corporation is an international company, those laws may be different and easier to work around, then again, they could be more difficult..." She bites her lower lip with an 'eek' look.

He smiles with so much love for her. "My love just keeps grow—." He chokes up and just kisses her with a fierceness that *does* make her feel loved. "Last night, you didn't hesitate when I just wanted to—."

"Stop!" She firmly states. "I think we've been doing pretty well at having open communication. You were clear you needed some stress relief and then you left it to me to decide. I understood what you were asking, and I also felt safe to say 'no,' too." She runs her finger down his chest a little way, biting her lower lip. "I'm insanely attracted to you, My Love, so the odds of me *ever* turning you down are next to none!" She taps a little kiss to his lips. "If you need something like that again, hopefully for a different reason than closing down a hotel, but any which way, *I got you*!" He chuckles a bit, slowly coming out of his mood. "*I love you, Mister* Worthington!"

"I love you so much more, *Mrs. Worthington*!"

"I know!" She grins. He cups her face and kisses her again before she gets out of the shower.

"Apologize to Jack for me for making you late. He knows as much as you did last night, and it's okay if you tell him what you know now."

"David, I'll go in with you after Jack and I are done. You shouldn't be going in by yourself." She says.

"I appreciate that, but Mary will be there to help with the paperwork, as well as sending it all back and forth with HR and Legal. We don't have a lot of time before the three of us leave for the US later this morning, I just need to get going on this right away!" He holds her face. "But having your support means the world to me!" He kisses her tenderly.

She smiles, tucking a corner of the towel she wrapped towel around herself to secure it. "I'm *always* going to be on your side, David! I love and adore you!"

"I know that now, more than ever! And I love and adore you, too!" He says.

"Good!" She grins. As she turns to walk out of the shower, she turns back. "David?" He looks at her as he shampoos his hair. "Are you able to sell the hotel to me or Jack, or whoever? This way we can reopen, but *outside* of the corporation. The corporation could maybe manage it until they buy it back?"

He slowly gets a sweet smile spreading across his face. "That's an interesting thought...I *have* to shut this down to prove a point; *however,* you might be on to something." He kisses her one more time and playfully swats her towel covered backside as she leaves.

Jack has texted numerous times, it was now 6:20.

Bri texts: "I promise I'll only be a *liiittle* bit late *and* I promise you'll understand."

Bri gets dressed and pulls her wet hair into a bun and throws some powder makeup on. Jack responded but she didn't hear the notification right away:

"It's a good thing you look bloody fantastic WITHOUT makeup! That should put you out here even closer to on time." (adds a winking face)

Bri: "Gasp! I didn't know we were filming a HORROR scene this morning!"

She's grabbing her phone which has her bankcard and her ID in the case and walks fast to meet up with Jack in front of The Manor. Jack is waiting for her outside in the car and is laughing at her text and responding. He sends it as she gets in.

As Jack drives back over to The Wool Farm, she reads his reply.

"If we're shooting ANY movie scene it wouldn't be for a horror film! (smirking emoji) It'd be a scene WAY too hot for ANY audience!"

"A skin flick...*really*?!" She looks at Jack pursing her lips with a raised eyebrow.

He stops the car. "*Pure romance*, Gorgeous!" He smirks and kisses her.

"Better! *But no*. More like romantic *comedy*," she points to her face, "without makeup." She teases.

"The comedy being how bloody gorgeous you are, but clueless to it!" He kisses her hand and starts driving again.

She rolls her eyes and softly laughs. "Anyway, David said to apologize for making me late and that I could tell you. First, full discloser, we did *not* have shower sex this morning."

Jack chuckles softly. "*Okaaay?*"

"I say that because it *would* cross your mind!" She smirks. "When I woke up this morning, my alarm hadn't gone off yet by a few minutes. I decided to

178

just shut it off and get into the shower. It wasn't long when David joined me." She looks at Jack chuckling.

He squeezes her hand. "It'd be fine if you two had, Amore Mia."

She smiles sweetly. "Well, I would've felt bad if we had and it made me late, because you asked me to meet you this morning! You don't ask for much, Amore Mio," she cups his face with a loving smile, "*and* I want to do what I say I'll do."

He smiles. "I have nothing to ask for when I already have *everything* with you!" Tears threaten to escape her eyes and she wipes the corners of her eyes with the tissue he hands her. She clears her throat and explains what happened and what will happen this morning.

"How bad is he beating himself up?" Jack wonders.

"He was feeling better when I got out of the shower, which I'm glad, but I offered to go in with him after we were done here, only he wanted to get things started before he got to New York City today."

"It's all going to be okay, Amore Mia, but I'd suggest just letting him do this. He knows he has your support and that's what he needs! To be honest, if you went with, you may feel more in the way. Let him work his own magic, then when all this is done in New York, wear something—no, wear *nothing* to bed and he'll be back to normal soon enough!" Bri laughs and shakes her head. Jack looks down the driveway. "Looks like this guy is finally showing up." He smiles and kisses her quickly before they get out of the car.

"Late? I wasn't even five minutes late?" She smirks.

"And what's your personal rule about being on time?" He lifts his eyebrow with a grin. She rolls her eyes, so he says it. "You feel if you're on time, you're already late."

"Has anyone told you I hate it when my own words are used against me?" She asks him.

"I was merely proving *your* point with your own words." He winks.

The gentleman parks next to Jack and after an hour of walking around the barn and the farm, the guy gives 'ballpark figures' for expansion. He'll work up a more accurate quote with the soonest he can start and will email it to Jack. They thank him and he leaves.

"Breakfast at 'The Manor?'" She asks Jack.

"Sounds good to me!"

They head back and walk into The Dining Room together. Bri sits next to Jack and texts David to see when he plans on being back at The Manor. He helicoptered to the corporate office in Edinburgh and he did the same coming back, so he was walking down the hall when her text came through. '*Odd...*' she thinks to herself, '*I didn't hear the helicopter...*' David walks over to hug and kiss Bri.

"That was quick!" She says to David. "I must've gotten used to the sound of a helicopter; it didn't even register when you came back."

"I got things going and will handle more on the plane with Mary's help, and more when I get to New York City."

As Peter and Carlotta have joined them, David talks about closing one of their American hotels. "You did what you had to, David, to make sure you're taken seriously by outsiders *and* by our employees. I think having them sign an agreement with a generous compensation package that encourages them to apply for other positions with us, but stressing they can't have anything to do with unions while employed with us—that's *genius*!" Peter says and everyone agrees.

"Well," David looks at Bri, "I'm married to the genius." He gives her a sweet little smile.

Peter laughs. "I should've guessed that! It sounds like Bri! Having intelligent women beside us only makes us better!" He kisses Carlotta's hand and she smiles adoringly back.

"Couldn't agree more!" Jack adds while quietly giving a 'high-five' to David behind her. Bri hears it and softly laughs.

"She gave me an idea, too." David says. "I do have to officially shut the hotel down for a two-year period, which I've had an offer to buy that building and will more than likely sell. There is a hotel on the market that overlooks Central Park and if we buy it in Bri's name, maybe we can hire some of the employees back, at least the better ones who've signed they'll never agree to unionize." He says to his father, then looks at Bri. "If you're up for being a hotel owner, I'll look into it and we can talk more about it later." David says.

"I'm definitely interested!" She smiles.

"Jack? Are you up for doing this with us?" David asks.

"Always!" Jack replies. "And Lawrence might interested, too!"

David nods. "I was thinking the same thing."

"Bri, how's The Foundation, along with Newhaven Wool & Textiles, coming along?" Carlotta asks.

"I've been so busy with Newhaven's government and Lawrence; I've only had time for personal life with Jack and David. Jack has been *almost* running it all by himself! I did work on some things yesterday afternoon." Bri explains that in more detail, with Jack filling in pieces.

"Wonderful!" Carlotta exclaims. "And you're all off to DC today?"

"They are." David answers, checking his watch. "Right now, in fact...If I'm to make it to New York City on time."

They all get up and go to The Sitting Room. They say their goodbyes to everyone at the back door. Then David, Jack, and Bri go out to the helicopter that takes them to the private airport for their flight to the US.

CHAPTER 18

Imperfectly Perfectly Complicated Family

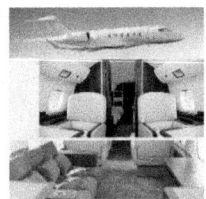 The flight to DC is smooth. Jack, David, and Bri play card games and talk about nothing in particular until Jack changes the direction of their conversation.

"So, Bri, why do you always change the subject when we want to talk about your family?" Jack asks.

"Oy..." she rolls her eyes, "I like talking about them as much as you like talking about yours, Jack. We weren't the type of family that does family get-togethers or reunions. I prefer the distance rather than the fake caring and concern."

"When I was planning the wedding, I spoke with Uncle Henry about them." David tells Jack. "Uncle Henry said in this case, the proverbial apple fell *far* from the tree!"

"Didn't your parents just get a divorce?" Jack asks.

"What can I say?" She shrugs. "I didn't like how my mother went about it, but there was no reasoning with her. Honestly, I wish them both happiness. My dad seems to be better off and happier not caught up in that rollercoaster anymore. As you both know, I've been done with the lying and manipulation *for years* now. My mother thinks she's clever and lies about so much, it puts people off. She lies about things that don't even matter, so it's hard to believe anything she says at all." She takes a deep breath. "Once I distanced myself, things made more sense! My faith that seemed to fade when she was around, started growing again because I wasn't on that out-of-control-rollercoaster-train anymore!"

Jack gives her an empathetic look. "Sometimes maintaining distance is the healthiest thing we can do for ourselves!"

She nods. "*And our family*! As I've also said before, I had no idea what love was, but I started to understand what love *wasn't*. When I had the girls, they started to teach me what love is. I mean I've felt love in my heart, but I always felt there was so much more love I could give, I just *couldn't* open up that part of my heart, at least not on my own..." She gestures to them. "When I hit rock bottom in self-esteem and self-worth, I needed a 'lifesaver' emotionally.

It felt like I was just holding onto a cement block trying not to drown in a lake. With Henry's and Maggie's help, that's when my faith grew incredibly deep roots. I'd read scriptures cover-to-cover countless times, read tons of spiritual books, and I was on a very sacred path. I'd learn that *all* connections to my mother had to be severed, so the roots of my faith could strengthen." She smiles asking, "Who *wouldn't* run and stay with people like Henry and Maggie," she looks to Jack, "or Peter and Carlotta?!" Jack nods. Bri goes on, "When I had hit that emotional rock bottom, I would also describe my mental health at the time like being at the top of a high-rise building about to *emotionally* jump."

"Hate to say it, Love, but *you did* 'emotionally jump.'" David softly says to her, giving her hand a squeeze.

Bri's curious. "Why do you think that?"

"When you convince yourself that you missed your chance at real, adoring love, you emotionally did jump." He answers.

Bri's mouth opens a little in surprise. "You think so?"

"Bri! You're the most optimistic and believer in love and romance I know! For you to believe you missed your chance at love, *you had to have jumped!*" He states.

"Perhaps..." She also tells them. "When my mother tried to help with the girls, she would tell me that the girls and I took such a toll on her health, specifically heart problems, she just couldn't do it anymore...which basically meant the girls and I were on our own."

"She doesn't know Uncle Henry *or* Aunt Maggie!" David chuckles.

"No, but she's never taken the time to get to know them either! She just got aggravated and jealous they're a part of the girls' lives as much as they are!"

"But she had her chance and turned you all away." Jack states.

"Strange, isn't it?" Bri states. "The Lord brought us to Maggie and Henry and when I needed them the most; they were there with open arms!" Bri smiles warmly at the memories. "Henry and Maggie are my parents in every way possible, because they *truly* love and accept me, flaws and all, and it's wonderful because *they didn't have to!* They built me up, inspired me," she gestures to them, "and happily handed me over to those who would pick up where they left off, while they continue to support *all of us*."

"Wait a second! Back up! Flaws?" Jack asks David. "Have you seen any so-called flaws in her, Brother?"

"Not one!" David smiles and winks at her.

Bri snorts a laugh but she continues. "There was added pressure when Jeff told me it wasn't fair to let Henry and Maggie take care of the girls when they are so much work; it was like having ten kids at once. Poor Maggie was hurt when I pulled back, but when I explained I didn't want the girls, or me, to be a burden, she was quick to quash that! I still remember her words to me, 'We take care of those we love to whatever extent they need it *and* for however long they need it!' She then tells me something else I'll never forget: 'You prevent The Lord from answering any part of your prayers through me and Henry!' Maggie would also relay this to Jeff and he would back down."

"I love Uncle Henry and Aunt Maggie even more!" Jack smiles sweetly.

"Me, too!" She weakly smiles as she wipes her tears.

David agrees. "Something you said earlier...If you can't trust someone who should love you to be truthful, especially about the little and insignificant things, then you'll *never* trust them when it really matters. Maybe that would mean their love would *feel fake*!"

"*Exactly*!" She tells them, "What's sad is to this day my mother isn't settled. She always seems to be looking for something...never really content. She keeps doing things the same way she's always done, expecting different results every time, *but it never happens, even though she tries to force them to*!"

Jack says, "It sounds like your mother is trying to fit a puzzle piece into a place that looks like it *should fit*, but it doesn't."

"That's a good analogy." She replies. "Sometimes it's like she knows it doesn't, but doesn't want to admit it, so she'll use a mallet to force it into place."

"The mallet being things like the lying and manipulation." David follows.

"I'm still surprised how innocently the girls saw through it all and I never did! Then again, that's how my mother has been my whole life; it would've been nearly impossible for me to ever see it on my own. Once I did know, I couldn't continue to expose the girls to it and focused them on Henry and Maggie to do what they do best...love unconditionally." She inhales deeply. "What's maddening is *my mother knows she needs help*! When she's convinced to seek counseling, she won't stick to getting better. She'll be on medication and think she's doing so well she doesn't need the medicine anymore. *Um, nnnooo.* The medication is why she was doing so well and that's *exactly why she needed to continue taking it!* The worst thing she could do is 'cold turkey' but she has, *more than once*...That also takes its toll on the mind and body?"

"Are you sure you weren't adopted?" Jack asks with David snickering.

"*I was!*" She grins playfully. "By Henry and Maggie!" The guys laugh in agreement. "The girls are definitely blessings; the lack of support of everyone around me when I needed help most, before Henry and Maggie, *broke me.* The girls didn't do anything wrong! They're just being like all kids their age, only as I said, with twins it's like having ten kids at once. Parenting isn't meant to be easy! It's meant to grow us, change us, making us better than we ever were or would be otherwise. With all that, I was led to an incredibly blessed life! The girls are a joy more than ever and they keep becoming more and more *fantastic!*" She playfully smiles using their accent. "But their awesomeness isn't because of me! Lord knows I've made and keep making mistakes all the time and He's helped them to maneuver around them!"

"*BriaLynn Worthington!*" David says sternly. "Their amazingness started when their mother fought like hell to raise them right and get the support she needed! 'It takes a village to raise kids' isn't just a saying, Mother says it's the truth!" Bri nods a bit. "Jeff and Olivia are able to step in and co-parent with you because of the hard work *you already put into them!*"

"Jeff did, too. I don't want to minimalize his role as 'dad.'" Bri says.

David exhales. "Bri, *you're* minimizing *your* role! You wouldn't have hit 'rock bottom' if you had the support you needed!" He sees her next comment. "No, you two weren't in-love and yes, that is a huge part because if he had, he would've *always* had your well-being at heart."

She gives a little nod with tears and squeezes his hand a little. She adds, "You know, I was the youngest of all the siblings, so I didn't understand then what I've come to understand later; my older siblings had to get away, *and stay away,*

185

because it was vital to their survival!" She also says, "I also learned 'cutting the chord' with my mother was necessary and vital *to my very survival* on various levels! But I feel cutting all ties, including with the girls, is on the horizon because I will not allow her to manipulate the girls to manipulate me!" She smiles at Jack and David. "Life is good! *Really, really good*! The Spirit led me to more love and happiness than I ever could've imagined and perhaps I wouldn't have the appreciation for it like I do now, without my past..."

David holds her left hand and looks at her rings. "I completely agree! Being honest with ourselves is sometimes the most difficult thing we ever have to do in our lifetime! From experience, it's worth it when the outcome is having you *in* our lives, Love."

"I wholeheartedly agree with all that!" Jack smiles sweetly.

Bri smiles back. "Well, everything that happened to me on my 'life's journey' has led me to being here and I know, with all my heart, *I was meant to be here*! There was no other path that would've led me here; just like each of you. *Ultimately*, I was led to all the family I'd ever need and with more love than any one person deserves, *especially me*!" She looks at them with adoring love and they're looking at her with so much affection.

Jack wipes a tear about to fall from his own eye and clears his throat. David had swallowed his lump and tells her, "I think both of us just fell in love you more..." He kisses the inside of her wrist sweetly. Jack smiles in agreement.

"I love you both *so much*!" Bri tells them. They both say they love her, too.

She excuses herself to use the restroom. When she returns, she sees her tote bag and remembers the envelope. She had thought about it on and off, but with everything going on, she forgot.

She sits on the couch and pulls the envelope out of her bag. She figures it's the information on The Queen Mother she asked Rex Stirling for and when she opens it, she finds that's exactly what it is! The top page is typed out with various information:

> BIRTH NAME: Lady Millicent Marie Luxton Devonridge
> DOB: March 13 (68)   SEX: Female
> HAIR COLOR: Black   EYE COLOR: Brown
> HEIGHT: Above Average   WEIGHT: Gaunt

HOME: Duchy of Devonridge   PARENTS: Deceased
RAISED BY: Uncle/Duke of Devonridge

MARITAL STATUS: Married to King Phillip, The King Father
CURRENT TITLE: The Queen Mother
MAIN RESIDENCE: The London Palace

AKA: The Devil's Master ('Red-Listed')

FIXATION: Power & control (to raise 'The Heir to The Throne' by
any and *all means necessary*)

That sends a chill down Bri's spine...

MOST SIGNIFICANT TRAIT: Ruthless and cunning
WEAKEST TRAIT: Mistakes fear for power and loyalty
(most people want to stay out of her way)
GREATEST THREAT: King Lawrence II
(Although The Marchioness of Newhaven is emerging)

FINANCIAL BANK: International Secured Banking Group
BALANCE: 21 million

PERSONAL BUSINESS: All Trafficking — Human, animals,
art/artifacts, etc.
ASSETS DURING TYPICAL AUCTION: easily 215+ million
AUCTION DATES: Roughly every 3 months (*by secret invitation only*)

The guys were talking and David sees her reading papers so intently, her
eyebrows are scrunched together. Bri flips the page and finds a bank
statement with a reoccurring scheduled payment highlighted; money is
withdrawn from this account and on the next set of documents she sees they
are deposited into a local 'Royal Crown Bank' account. Bri skims those
statements and notices there's a lot of 'cash withdrawals.'

She sees surveillance photos but when she goes to flip through them, the
flight attendant comes over to tell them they're about to land. Bri puts them
and the rest of the paperwork back in the envelope, so she doesn't see the
list of people on The Queen Mother's 'payroll,' the list of scheduled
payments, nor a list of those with sporadic scheduled payments. David has
been watching her at different times, and he sees her putting things back into

the envelope. He wonders if it's the information she asked Rex Stirling for on The Queen Mother.

After landing in DC, Jack and Bri gather their things. Jack takes her bags out to their awaiting car so Bri and David can have a minute alone.

David wraps his arms around her and she hugs him back. He gets close to her ear to whisper, "*Was that envelope from Rex Stirling?*"

Bri nods as she pulls back to look at him. "I'm just not sure what it all means; I didn't look at all yet."

"I can take a look when I come back from New York?" He offers.

"Sounds promising." She grins.

He lightly chuckles. "I love you, Macushla!" He tangles a hand in her hair. "You do so much for me, I could *never* repay——."

"We're *not* keeping score and we're *never* going to!" She purposely interrupts. "Because you'll find *I'm* the one in serious debt *to you*!"

"Ha-ha! How do you figure?!" He asks. "You give me so much love! You married me and——."

"No matter what you list off, nothing will top your love for me, Jack's love for me, *and now* Lawrence's love for me! I'll be forever——."

He kisses her fiercely. "It comes down to *your heart*, Macushla! Your love keeps growing for all of us——."

"Because you three love me so much, it's the only *logical effect*! My heart entrusted itself to you and you've taken such *great* care of it!" She hugs him tighter. "You will always have my heart, *Mister* Worthington!"

"And because I have your heart, I'm the one eternally indebted *to you*. You chose to marry me *and* go on this unconventional, but *incredible* journey with me! That's what tips the scales in your favor and it will *every* time! You've blessed our whole family in countless ways, Bri! My life never really started until the day I saw you in that hotel lobby! A life I wouldn't give up for anything, but I'd lay down my life for without a moment's hesitation! I love you, Mrs. Worthington!" She beams and he smiles. "And I love how you light up when I say that!"

She can only whisper, *"Because I'm happy and honored to be your wife!"*

He looks at her so lovingly. "I'm proud to have you as my wife, just as *I'm honored* to be your husband!" He squeezes her hand. "I'll see you in a couple days." She smiles and nods.

David walks her to the door of the plane, kissing her once more, and he watches her go down the stairs; he waves to Jack and he waves back. David ducks back into the plane to go to New York City to deal with the hotel he's having to shut down. He'll also find out more about the hotel that's for sale facing Central Park.

Bri happily smiles and hugs Mateo who's their driver again. Then Bri and Jack, along with McMasters, get into the car and they go to their hotel and settle in.

CHAPTER 19

Imperfectly Perfectly Cathartic

Bri spends the next day-and-a-half in meetings for the database she helped put together for the US federal law enforcement agencies. Right now, she's making sure all is going well and makes any necessary changes or improvements. She'll be going back to Newhaven with a fresh template to begin the same task there.

She has also managed to start finalizing the recipe for the essential oils going into their production of 'Heirloom Wool' at the textile mill. There is a great company that has various farms of plants, trees, and flowers, around the world. They have been hired to help with this recipe and their logo will go onto the textile products as well.

Bri has left her last meeting and is in the car headed to Katie's office. She hopes they can 'bury the hatchet' so-to-speak, once and for all, but going their separate ways. McMasters is in the front seat with Mateo.

"BFF time?" Mateo asks.

"Not exactly." Bri says in a monotoned voice.

As they drive over, she gives Mateo a quick version of the BFF situation. "Wow," he says, "I never would've seen that coming!"

"Seems no one did!" McMasters replies.

While the guys talk to each other up front, Bri is lost in thought trying to figure out what she could *possibly* say to Katie to help them move on from this so-call 'friendship.' Mateo takes her to the front door of the office building and as she gets out, she lets Mateo know they'll text when they are ready to leave. He never goes far, but he'll stick even closer at McMaster's request.

McMasters will hang back in the lobby at first. "If I show up with you, Katie may feel ganged up on and instantly become hostile. I'll come up in about five minutes or so and wait outside her door." Bri agrees as they walk up to the reception desk.

Bri smiles at the familiar receptionist. "Hi! I'm BriaLynn Worthington and I have an appointment with Ms. Barnes." As she brings up Katie's schedule, Bri remembers Jack made the appointment for her because she was dragging her feet making one. "It may be under 'Jack Carlisle.'" Bri mentions to her.

"Ah, yes, Jack Carlisle and BriaLynn Worthington. He's already up there." She explains to Bri how to get to Katie's new office and Bri thanks her.

McMasters reminds Bri, "I'll be up in about five minutes." Bri nods and turns towards the elevators.

When she walks up to Katie's office, she hears voices. She feels very strongly she needs to start recording, so she finds the recording app on her phone she uses for meetings and starts recording. Bri listens by the door, carefully trying to peek through the window here and there.

Katie has an 'I told you so smile.' "I told you that you'd come to me when you got bored with her!"

"Not at all!" Jack's facial expression shows annoyance.

"What?" She asks, trying to sound innocent. "'Plain and tiring' hasn't bored you yet?" She deviously smiles. "Or are you guys teaching her some things."

He won't go there with her. Instead, he asks, "You two were best friends once! Why did you agree to meet if you're not going to take this seriously?"

She shrugs. "I guess I was hoping you'd come without her," she gestures, "and here you are."

Jack is baffled. "*Were you ever her friend?!*"

"She was just a tool." Katie responds flatly with another shrug.

Bri thinks to herself, '*Ouch.*' But then she has a feeling come over her that it's a lie Katie has been telling herself because she doesn't want to admit the truth of who she became being on drugs...

"How do you figure?" He asks.

"She was a means to an end and when she married David and stole you, it was the end." She replies.

191

He frowns at her, "She didn't steal anything!" Katie rolls her eyes and Jack tells her, "And the end came that horrific night! All she's guilty of is being *your* best friend! Only you weren't much of a friend back, were you?!"

"It's easy to play a '*bestie*'" she says with one side of her nose turned up, "when she is so naïve."

"Naïve for trusting you? For not knowing what you and your boyfriend were going to do to her?" He takes another long drink of his water.

Katie raises her eyebrow as he drinks. "No, she's lying about that! She doesn't want to admit how much fun she had with us!"

"How would you know?! You drugged her?!" Jack asks.

Katie snorts a laugh, "We loosened her up! The drugs lowered her inhibitions and she no longer had any hang-ups!"

"She wasn't conscious enough to form a complete thought, Katie, let alone voice any kind of dispute! You set her up to be raped numerous times!" Jack tells her sternly, "No one deserves that! *Not even you*!"

She scoffs. "I've experienced these drugs *countless times* and you don't hear me complaining!"

He says flatly, "Maybe you should, so you'll stop lying to yourself! *Then again, you'd have to have self-respect to do that*!" She glares, but watches him closely as he drinks and finishes the water bottle.

She gasps with an idea to distract him. "Jack!" She moves closer to Jack on the couch as she laughs and claps with excitement, "I have the *greatest* idea! With your mad finance manager skills, along with my marketing skills, we could run *our* own company!"

His accent is heard, "*You can't be serious*!"

"It'll be great, Jack!" She excitedly smiles.

"You just finished telling me that you'll backstab your best friend and set her up to raped multiple times, *without flinching*! *No one* should go into business with you!" He leans away from her. "Besides, I could've started my own

192

company years ago, but that's not me. That's David's forte and why *he* runs The Worthington Corporation brilliantly! I work for Watchtower Financial at the job I love."

She snorts a scoff. "Yeah, says the man running a textile company!" Katie tells him.

"Bri would agree with you, but she's *so busy* she doesn't realize how much she contributes! Everything has to work 'just so' because it has to work in concert with her foundation." He explains. "*Sheee...*" he's getting dizzy and puts the palm of his hand to his head. Bri wonders what's happening and tries to look in through the window.

Katie scoots right next to him and starts to run her hand up the inside of his thigh, "We could do some great things together..." she smiles deviously, "professionally *and personally*."

He quickly grabs her hand, saying with a bit of anger, "*I'm not yours to touch!*"

"Playing 'hard to get' doesn't become you, Jack!" She states.

"I never wanted your hands on me to begin with, but I want them even *less* the more you talk and knowing what you did to Bri." He leans in and looks her right in the eyes, "I'm always *and forever* hers!" Bri's heart squeezes.

Katie feels the fury start to burn inside her and uses it to channel her energies differently... "I bet I can change your mind. In fact..." she begins to feel him up with both hands.

Jack jumps up and stumbles a couple of steps. "What *is it* with you?!" Jack's annoyance is clear, but his vision is getting blurred. "I say 'no' and you keep touching me? If a man did that to a woman, she'd cry sexual harassment! *And it is!*"

"I'm not most people, Jack, and neither are you! You'd *never* accuse me of sexual harassment!" She has a sly smile.

"What are you saying?" He's confused and not very stable, so he leans in a partial standing and partial sitting position against the front of her desk.

She stands and walks over to him with a sly grin. "I have other ways to get what I want..."

"*Nnnot* with...*mmme!*" He puts the palm of his hand to his forehead again. Jack's speech is slurring more and he's becoming disoriented. Bri hears he doesn't sound normal.

"Even with *you*." Katie gets a small evil grin on her face. "I knew I'd get my hands on you one day, Jack!" Bri gasps to herself as it hits her; Jack's been drugged. Katie starts to tell Jack, "Relax and let me——."

Bri bursts into Katie's office. "STOP TOUCHING HIM!"

Startled, Katie's head snaps in the direction of Bri. Katie yells, "GET——." Katie has the strangest sensation and tries to move her hands on Jack's chest, but she can't. She starts to get frustrated and angry.

Bri has no words forming in her head, nor does she want to hear anything Katie had to say at this point. She has unknowingly closed her hand into a fist and before she could rethink it, Bri's fist punches Katie in the face with such force, Katie is knocked backwards hitting her head *hard* against floor and she's out cold. Bri's hand is numb and she shakes it a couple times.

McMasters rushes in and sees Bri still standing. "Are you okay?" He asks as he bends down to check to make sure Katie is still alive.

"Yes, but Jack isn't." Bri replies as she quickly goes over to him. He's now sitting in a chair, barely coherent. He starts to push her hands away, thinking Bri was Katie. "Shh, Jack. It's Bri." She kisses his cheek. He's relieved to hear her voice and tries to talk, but he can't even open his mouth. She says soothingly, "I'm right here with you, Amore Mio, so is McMasters! We're going to move you to the couch and then call an ambulance to get you to the hospital." He nods and exhales in relief.

Once they have Jack laying down on the couch, McMasters says, "I'll call 9-1-1!" He puts the phone up to his ear."

Bri tells him, "Thank you." She texts Henry about what happened.

Bri: "I maaay need a lawyer."

She then quickly explains in her next text what happened. She puts her phone down and kneels beside Jack. She holds his hand and she runs her other hand through his hair.

When McMasters hangs up from the 9-1-1 operator, he asks what happened and Bri gives him a short version. She also tells him she recorded their conversation since she got to the door and she plays it for him.

"It may not hold up in court," she admits after they have listened to it, "but at least there's no doubt what happened."

"Great job!" McMasters fist bumps her.

He goes out to the hallway and deals with the crowd gathering in the hall. He is also watching for the paramedics.

When the paramedics arrive, Katie is still out cold. Ken arrives with his partner, Detective Bill Baker; Henry had called them. Ken says it's okay for Bri to go to the hospital with Jack and they'll go over things with her there.

McMasters says, "I'll have Mateo follow the ambulance." She nods.

Bri texts David on the way to the hospital.

> Bri: "Jack's fine, but he was drugged in Katie's office. I may have legal issues and I'll explain later, or you can call Uncle Henry."

Lawrence receives her text by mistake and forwards it to David with his own message.

> Lawrence: "Bri accidentally sent this to me, but I'm on my way to DC to deal with any repercussions that might happen."

> David: "Henry and Ken will do their best to take care of her, but it wouldn't hurt having you, and King Lawrence, there just in case."

> Lawrence: "I'll call you in a little while."

Lawrence calls his assistant as he gathers his things and tells her, "Make flight arrangements straight away for Washington, D.C. and reschedule everything for the week." He calls Gen and Seth; they'll take care of things as he needs them to, but their main job is to keep Abby safe. They decide to send her to The Worthington Inn right away for a few days for James and The

Worthington Family to look out for her there. Lawrence's mother tries to stop him from leaving as he rushes to get out to the helicopter.

"Where are you going?!" The Queen Mother snaps.

Lawrence continues walking to the door that will take him outside to the helicopter, but says emotionless, "To Washington, D.C., Mother."

"Why?! We have no business with the US right now!" She says louder, "*Come back here!*"

"Stop it, Mother." His voice has a bored tone.

"*You idiot!* You're 'The King' and have responsibilities HERE!" She shoots back. "YOU CAN'T JUST UP AND LEAVE!"

"Well, I *am* leaving." He replies. "There are various technological inventions that will help me stay on top of those responsibilities!" He walks out the door and hurries to the helicopter.

The Queen Mother has insisted she and Lawrence share the same assistant to save time, but she secretly wanted to keep track of him. Lawrence has known this from the beginning, only it's a battle he chose not to fight; he just withholds things from their secretary when he wants his privacy. She walks into the reception of The Royal Offices and demands her assistant to find out why he's left for DC!

When David got the text from Lawrence, he sent a 'thumbs up' to Bri. When it's short like that, she knows he is in a meeting, but she knows he will step out as quickly as he can...he always does. He calls a ten-minute break when he sees he just missed her call. He goes to call her back but listens to her voicemail first. She tells him *not* to cut things short yet, nothing seemed life threatening. She'd call back when she knew more.

Jack is in a private room and whatever they gave him to counteract the drugs seems to be working. Bri is standing next to the window in the corner to stay out of the way of medical staff; McMasters is just outside the room. The doctor sees the test results and Bri overhears him say to the staff that with the amount in his system, he's lucky someone was there to get him to the hospital, or he could've died of an overdose. Bri gasps just loud enough to be heard and everyone looks her way. The doctor's face turns apologetic.

"Don't be sorry, Doctor." Bri kindly tells him.

He has a small reluctant smile. "It could've been said differently."

Bri gives him a look with a faint smile. "I doubt there's a good way."

There is a nurse that glances at Bri and then glances again. She sees Bri's hand and has an intern doctor, Dr. Billings, look at it. He walks over to her and carefully looks at her hand.

"Can you get your ring off?" Dr. Billings asks. "It will help."

Bri looks at her pink-heart-diamond ring and struggles a little but manages to free it. She'll give it to McMasters to keep it safe for her. Dr. Billings wants to x-ray her hand, but she doesn't want to leave Jack.

"He's in good hands. I promise!" Dr. Billings tells her. She sees Jack is still sleeping and reluctantly agrees to allow her hand to be x-rayed.

Bri's x-ray shows nothing is broken, but it would be bruised for a while. Dr. Billings wraps her hand in Jack's room and gives her instructions for it. She and McMasters thank Dr. Billings and he leaves.

Bri tries calling David, but it goes right to voicemail, she hopes he's not flying to DC. She calls Henry and he helps her feel better. He also says he spoke with Ken who isn't worried for Bri legally; she was defending Jack who had been drugged with what they now know could've been a lethal dose.

When Ken and Bill arrive at the hospital, they give Bri a firm squeeze in their hugs. They ask her routine questions she knows they have to ask. She tells them she recorded the conversation between Katie and Jack, starting when she got to Katie's office door, and they want to hear it. She pulls it up and hands them her phone to listen to it.

"That's disappointing." Ken sadly says, handing Bri her phone back to her and has her email it to him at work.

"Ken, I punched her in the face!" She throws her hands up in frustration asking, "*What got into me?*!"

"Hopefully, you *finally* knocked some sense *into* her!" McMasters chimes in.

Bill agrees with him. "It could get uglier, but to what extent, I don't know."

"Uglier? She just about killed Jack! But what I don't understand is how?!" She says upset. "The 'why' was she wanted to sleep with him to prove she could, and she would, hold it over our heads for the rest of our lives."

"The 'how' is one of the things we're looking into, Sweetie." Ken says.

Just then, Bri's phone rings; it's David calling to discuss what happened and to see how Jack is doing. She convinces him to stay and finish the work that needs to be done in New York.

> She tells him, "This way, when you leave New York, you don't have to turn around and go back."

David knows Lawrence is on his way, so he agrees to stay in New York City, only Bri doesn't know Lawrence is coming. David says he'll call later and they say, 'I love you,' then they hang up for now.

CHAPTER 20

Imperfectly Perfect Royal Support

The drugs are getting flushed out of Jack's system. The doctor wants to keep Jack overnight for observation, but he isn't happy about it.

"Jack, please. I'll stay with you." Her eyes fill with tears. "You were overdosed and could've *died*!" She shakes her head. "The thought of losing you..." She puts her hand up to her mouth and pushes hard, trying to push all her emotions down.

Jack looks lovingly at her. "Amore Mia," he reaches out his arm and holds his hand open for her to take, "come here." She walks over and takes his hand and he gently pulls her to him. "I'm fine." He pats the bed and she sits, but he pulls her to lie down next to him. "I won't go down *that* easy!"

She lightly hits his chest. "NOT funny, *Jackson* Carlisle! The thought of losing you, David, or Lawrence——." She has a lump that closes up her throat and it actually hurts.

"That's why it was so surreal last year when you were shot!" He hugs her close. "*For you*, I will stay here tonight." He feels her exhale of relief.

McMasters' phone rings and as he steps out of the room to talk, he holds the door open for the nurse to come into the room. When he returns to the room, the nurse has just left.

"Bri, that was the hotel." He says. "The manager said security was doing a sweep through the hallways and saw the door to your room was ajar. When they took a look, they saw things were in disarray in an odd way." Bri's mouth falls open a little. He tells her, "I called Ken and he said he'd go check it out."

"What would anyone want from me?" Bri's face shows her disbelief. She thinks, "Well, Katie's been unconscious, so there's no way she could've been directly involved and I don't see her hiring someone..."

There is a knock at the door. McMasters opens it and Lawrence walks in. Bri smiles, but she's confused. She catches a glimpse of his guard and cousin, Tristan, as the door closes. Lawrence goes to Jack to shake his hand and halfway hugs him while he sits in his bed. He asks him how he is feeling.

"I've been better." Jack honestly tells him.

"I bet!" Lawrence replies with a small empathetic smile.

Lawrence walks over to Bri, who's smiling at him, but there's a sadness about her that he expected; he embraces her firmly. There's just something so comforting in Lawrence's hugs, Bri can't hold her emotions in anymore and she just cries...he holds her firmly.

When Bri has stopped, Lawrence says, "I wasn't sure if I should come to the hospital, but I wanted to be here as things unfolded, just in case." He kisses her head. "I'm glad I came here first, even if all I can do is hug you."

"*This* means a lot to me, Ace! I'm *really* happy to see you, but ashamed I didn't tell you myself." She says.

"Well, unknowingly you sort of did." He smiles and she lifts her head to look at him with a puzzled look. Lawrence tells her, "You accidentally sent one of David's texts to me, which I passed along to him."

"Oh! Well, thanks for sending it on, but I should've sent one directly to you. I'm sorry." She replies.

He smiles sweetly, caressing her cheek. "I think we can say we're figuring all this out as we go." She nods. "In weird situations, especially when the police are involved, it's best to start with me *after* any call for help. As we go forward with you becoming 'The Royal Consort,' your face will become more recognizable, Bri, and your movements tracked not only by the media, but also by 'Royal Watchers.'"

"I hadn't thought of being tracked." She says with an 'eek' look. Her thoughts go back to McMasters' phone call and their hotel suite.

"Bri..." He waves his hand in front of her eyes.

She smiles. "Sorry. I was thinking about the hotel suite."

"What about your hotel suite?" He asks with concern. McMasters tells him what he told her and Jack. Lawrence tells them, "I have guards that should be there by now securing the hotel." He looks at McMasters. "Why don't you reach out to them?"

There is another knock on the door and McMasters answers it. It's Ken and Bill, with Henry, Maggie, and Joe. He greets them before stepping out of the room. Bri introduces everyone to Lawrence and hugs are given, with Maggie and Henry hugging Bri for a little longer. Ken and Bill had told them what had happened on the way to the hospital.

"I told them about the recording and they want to hear it, if you're okay with that." He says and Lawrence says he does, too.

Bri looks at Jack and he nods. She puts it on speaker and plays it for all of them. They hear a hard, dull sounding 'smack' and Joe asks, "What was that?!" Bri looks at her hand. "No, way, Sis! You *punched* her!" Joe claps and laughs, "That's *freaking* awesome!"

"Knocked her out cold for quite a long time and she has a concussion." Ken explains.

Bill tells them, "Preliminary tests came back telling us that the water bottle Jack drank from contained the drug Katie used."

"She almost killed him! What if he *had* died?!" She asks. Jack reaches for her hand and squeezes. She looks at him and gives him a small smile.

McMasters comes in and Ken explains, "We searched her office and found only one of the few water bottles in her fridge were tampered with. The syringe we found had her prints on it with trace amounts of the drug in the used syringe."

Bill has Bri sit on Jack's bed. "She's being charged with attempted murder, among other things. We searched her condo," he reaches into his jacket and pulls out some polaroids, individually bagged for evidence. "We found a stash of pictures in her condo and there are some of you." She gets a sick feeling in her stomach. He hands them to her, guessing what she's thinking, "*No*, not everyone saw these. The tech was individually bagging each photo of a large shoebox full of multiple people. He was more focused on making sure they weren't sticking together than the actual photographs themselves and who was in them. I was ahead of the person logging the evidence, so I got to these before they did."

She starts to thumb through them...they begin to bring back clips of foggy memories she had suppressed all these years. She can't get through more than a few without stopping to wipe the tears. Lawrence hands her a tissue.

Maggie comes over and Lawrence watches them. "Sweetie, this can't be easy. Would you like one of us to look through them?"

Bri's jaw shakes. "*No one* should see these, Maggie, especially parents!"

Henry stands in front of Bri. "Sweetie, we hate seeing you relive what she did to you."

"That's just it. I didn't remember much!" She stands up and waves the pictures saying, "It's *frustrating*, because I know my so-called 'best friend' drugged me to let her boyfriend take advantage of me *and participated in who knows what else*?! Which, for the record, I don't *ever* want to know! Unfortunately, when I see these photos, more of my suppressed sketchy memories start to break free!" She exhales in frustration. "I was actually okay with *never reliving* any more of the disgusting details!"

Jack sits up more. "Then let me, Amore Mia." He holds out his hand.

She shakes her head. "You shouldn't see these either, Jack!"

"Bri, let *me* look at them and protect you from reliving any of *that*!" He points to the pictures, giving her a small compassionate smile as he holds out his hand again. "Please let me do this for you." She reluctantly hands him the pictures.

Lawrence steps over to her and hugs her while Jack looks at the photos. His face is showing more disgust with each picture; more heartache over what was done to the woman he loves. He has to work hard to push down his emotions by the end.

When Jack finishes, Bri goes and sits next to him. "Are they all me?"

Jack nods and pulls her into a firm hug against his chest, kissing her head. "Oh, Amore Mia. I'm so glad you might not ever remember any of that! There are no words to describe those *ghastly* and horrific things they did to you!"

Lawrence looks at Ken. "Detective, could I have a word please?"

Ken steps over near the window with Lawrence and tells him, "Please, call me Ken."

Lawrence nods and asks Ken, "Would you check with your boss and ask how necessary these pictures will be for the case? If you think it would be better if I talk to your boss, then we can arrange that. I imagine it's been too long to even be able to prosecute this specifically." Ken nods. "You and I know, the more well-known Bri gets, those photos are going to be worth a fortune! There's a price someone *is* willing to pay to get them out of evidence and into those tabloids!"

Ken knows he's right about the tabloids. He turns and steps over to the others in the room. "Listen up! First, anyone who's not willing to keep a secret about Bri's case, please step out now." Bill, Henry, Maggie, Joe, Bri, Jack, and Lawrence, look around at each other and look back to Ken. "Alright. Good. This doesn't leave this room."

"I should tell David whatever this is about. No secrets." Bri states. "Then my lips are sealed."

Ken nods. "Sounds good. Now," he gestures the pictures on Jack's lap, "those pictures are only known of by Bill and me. The tech going through the photos wouldn't know about Bri being in them unless he studied them."

"And he didn't." Bill states. "I knew what happened to Bri, so I knew who I was looking for in the pictures."

Bri gives him a little nod, then looks to Ken, "What are you saying, Ken?"

"I'm saying I want *you* to keep those." He tells her, pointing to the pictures.

Bri's mouth drops open. "No. *Absolutely not*! You could lose your job!"

"Misplacing evidence long past the statute of limitations, would be a slap on the wrist for me, and misplacing evidence happens every now and then anyhow. I can't remember a time I ever misplaced evidence, and *this* is a safe risk for me."

Bri raises her eyebrow. "That's an oxymoron." She shakes her head telling him, "I can't let you—."

"Bri, Lawrence is right! The more popular you are, the more money those will be worth." Ken points to the pictures. Bri's eyes flash panic, but the others are concerned, too. "If they get into the wrong hands, we'll be seeing those on the front page of every tabloid around the world!"

"Everyone has a currency." She remembers him saying that at various times. He and Bill nodded. She somehow feels violated all over again.

The few memories she does have of what happened when Katie's boyfriend repeatedly raped her, keep coming into her mind. Then the girls come to mind and if they, or their friends, do an internet search on Bri, she wouldn't want these photos showing up...

Lawrence asks Ken, "Considering all those other photos, how many victims did she have?!"

"We're not sure how many in total yet." Ken answers. "The problem will be identifying the victims because some of them may not have any recollection of what happened to them, so there wouldn't be a police report of any kind. We will check the rape reports filed, but we'll start with the most recent and work our way backwards."

Bri's phone lights up, it's silently ringing. "David is checking in."

"May I?" Henry asks. Bri hands him the phone and Henry answers it as he walks to the other side of the room. Bri overhears him say, "I'm going to call my office to see if John can put restraining orders together...are you coming here to DC...we'll meet the four of you at 9:00 in the morning outside the courthouse not too far from here." They hang up and Henry tells Bri, "David says to call him after we're done." She nods with a small smile, taking her phone back from Henry and he hugs her again.

McMasters offers to order food for everyone. When he goes to leave, he pauses when he hears Bri ask Ken, "Did anything come from your investigation in the hotel suite?"

"That one baffles me." He replies. "It looks like your things have been gone through, but I can't figure out what they could've wanted? The safe wasn't touched, the few valuables out in plain sight are still there! It seems their focus was on paperwork because they made a mess of your various files!"

Bri's eyes go wide for a split-second micro-expression, but she covers it well. She knows they are still looking for the envelope from The Underground Secret Society!

McMasters has the family-style food set up in the conference room a few doors down. They will go down to fix their plates and bring them back to Jack's room, with a plate for him. Bri grabs her bag to bring it with her.

Lawrence suggests, "I can have Tristan come in here and stay while we go and come back."

"No." Bri says. She looks him in the eyes and whispers sternly, "*Trust.no.one!*"

He studies her face a moment then tells everyone, "Please, leave us," he tips his head, "except Jack. We'll meet you there." He keeps his eyes locked with hers while everyone files out of the room. When they're alone with Jack, Lawrence asks, "*What's going on, Bri?*"

"*Shhh.*" She whispers. "*Lawrence, I was given an envelope that Jessica would appear to specifically warn me to safeguard it; that all my things are searched at The Palace unless I keep them with me.*"

He closes his eyes and quietly says, "And *she* told you to '*trust no one.*'" He opens his eyes and takes a deep breath. He whispers, "*What's in this envelope?*" He looks from Bri to Jack, but Jack shrugs with an 'I don't know.'

She whispers, "*Not now.*" He nods and takes her bag to carry it as they go down to the conference room.

Once everyone has their food, they sit around Jack's room eating and talking about more enjoyable things, like Lawrence officially asking Bri to be his 'Royal Consort.'

Maggie looks at her ring McMasters shows her since Bri can't wear it at the moment. "A pink heart diamond?" She tries it on and says, "This is stunning!" She looks at Lawrence, "You have *incredible* taste!"

Lawrence thanks her, but Bri tells her, "*He's* being modest. All three men have great taste and Lawrence is *truly gifted* at designing jewelry!" Lawrence gives her a sweet smile as his heart squeezes for this woman who believes in him with such enthusiasm!

After she and Maggie have wrapped up talking about Lawrence's jewelry, Bri changes direction a little asking, "How's Amy coming along with the wedding planning?! Amy makes it sound like 'a piece of cake,' but she has to be having a tremendous amount of help for that to be the case *and* work at her job with some form of sanity right now!"

Henry and Maggie have gotten to know Amy since she has been working with Bri, but more so this past year, and really like her. "She has a wedding planner app on her phone and her mom's help. I convinced her to hand some of the tasks over to me to keep me busy. The girls are so self-sufficient and getting more so by the minute, needing me even less!" She smiles with an extra twinkle in her eyes. "I'll be excited to have more grandchildren to take some of this free time off my hands!"

"It's in God's hands completely!" Bri giggles. "David and I have been 'seeing what happens' for several months now." Bri tells her. "As for Amy, I'm so glad she and I have gotten close. I'm so grateful for her!"

Henry smiles at her. "We are, too, Sweetie!"

Later that night, Jack was already sleeping and Lawrence had arranged for another bed to be brought in. Once Lawrence and Bri are ready for bed, they crawl into it. She snuggles in with him for a while, resting in peaceful silence before they close their eyes and fall asleep.

CHAPTER 21

Imperfectly Perfectly Silent

Bri wakes to the feeling of a hand running through her hair and smiles. "That feels nice, Ace." She opens her eyes and looks up at him.

Lawrence smiles a dimpled smile. "I like it when you wake up this way." He kisses her head. "A beautiful smile without the cheekiness."

"Wait for it." She smirks.

He raises his eyebrow. "I don't think I have to..."

She holds up her finger and goes to brush her teeth in the bathroom. Lawrence uses the sink right there to brush his. He crawls back into bed and waits patiently. He hears the bathroom door and watches her walk back over to the bed.

She holds his face and smiles. "I love you, Lawrence!"

"I love *you*, My Queen." She kisses him tenderly, which he deepens momentarily. "I wanted a glimpse of how our first morning will be once we're official, but I don't want to push it."

"Thank you." She taps another kiss to his lips. "I hope it's okay, but I want breakfast in here?"

"I think I can get onboard with that, *if* I can have one more kiss..." He smiles and taps his finger to his lips; she kisses him again.

David walks in and has a big smile. He swiftly comes over to her and hugs her, then hugs Lawrence while Bri goes over to snuggle in with Jack who's just waking up.

"How are you feeling?" Jack asks Bri and watches David come over to them.

"Hey, that's my line!" Bri smiles.

David chuckles. "How *are* you feeling this morning, Jack?"

"Glad to have those drugs out of my system!" He replies.

"Me, too!" Bri struggles to say with a lump in her throat and hugs him close.

He gently pushes her head back to look into her worried eyes. "Hey now, I'm fine. Alright?" She nods and he gently kisses her forehead.

She looks over and smiles at David, who claps his hands together asking, "What about breakfast?"

"I could eat a little bacon and eggs." Jack answers.

"Ooo, that and toast for me!" She smiles at David.

Jack looks at Lawrence. "Thanks for being here, Herst."

"There's *no way* I'd be able to stay in London knowing all this was going on!" Lawrence says.

Bri looks at Lawrence, then David and asks him, "Did you know he was coming when we talked about you staying in New York to finish up there?"

He sweetly smiles. "I did, or I wouldn't have let you convince me to finish up there yesterday and fly here this morning!" He smirks.

There's a hint of annoyance in her voice and a 'tsk.' "Seriously you guys! *I can take care of myself and twins*! I could manage to take care of Jack!"

David holds her face. "*I never doubted that*! We wanted someone here for you because of what happened with Katie, as well as Jack." He leans down and rests his forehead to hers.

"Alright, I'll give you that." She sweetly smiles.

"Thank you." David smiles and taps a kiss to her lips before he arranges breakfast for them once Herst tells him what he wants.

Jack sits up and swings his legs off the side so he can get up and go to the bathroom. A few minutes later he comes out of the bathroom and pats her bum on his way back to bed.

She lightly giggles. "You're *definitely* feeling better!"

"It's you." He sits on the bed and smiles sweetly at her. "I can't help but feel better being with you."

While they're waiting for breakfast, Bri sits with Jack on his bed. Bri asks David, "How did it go in New York? How are *you* holding up, My Love?" She asks, holding out her hand for his.

He smiles and takes her hand giving it a little squeeze. "The hardest thing I ever had to do, but most employees took it rather well. Security was in the room as a precaution, only they got involved to keep the peace when some of the employees got angry with the employees who joined up with the union. It was a shock to those who joined the union when they found out I was actually closing the hotel because, like you and I discussed, they didn't think I legally could. I apologized they were lied to by this union, but I wasn't going to apologize for following through with what I said I would do. I've always found that my employees want the truth, no matter how bad it may be, rather than being disrespected and lied to."

"Everyone does." Bri gives him a little smile. "I bet they appreciated that more coming directly from you, the CEO, in this situation, too."

"They did. I told them that now they know I mean what I say, no matter what an outside source wants them to believe with *their lies*." Bri stands in front of him and hugs him. He takes a deep breath as he returns her hug.

Bri sits back down next to Jack again and asks him, "Do you remember what happened yesterday?"

"I remember going to go see Katie." He replies. "I've been trying to think back and remember the details of what happened, but some of it is sketchy." He gently kisses the fingers of her bruised hand. "I only wish I had seen you punch her!"

David glances at Bri's bruised hand, realizing he'd seen her bandaged hand, but hadn't her about it asked yet. "*You punched her*?!" David is surprised and she nods. Bri grabs her phone and plays the recording for David, with Jack listening more closely this time, now that he's thinking more clearly than when he first heard it.

After the recording ends, Jack gently lifts her hand and he kisses it. "I'm sorry for the pain, but I am glad you punched her!"

She snorts an exhale with a slight smile. "*You would be!*"

"Come on, Amore Mia. It *had* to be a *huge* cathartic release for you!" Jack says. "*Wasn't it?!*"

"*Maaaybe* a little." Bri says looking at her bruised hand and knuckles.

Lawrence smirks. "I'm told Bri punched Katie so hard, she was knocked out cold for a long time."

David whistles his exhale. "*Wow*...all those pent-up emotions..." Bri is quiet.

"Like I said Amore Mia," Jack grins, "*cathartic.*" Bri scoffs but she is smiling.

The knock on the door interrupts them; it's breakfast. Bri notices David also has a pastry for her with milk. She smiles at him while Jack starts eating the food on his plate. David unfolds his napkin and winks at her.

Lawrence sees this and is curious. He leans over to David asking, "What's significant about the pastry?"

Jack replies, "Bri usually has a sweet tooth in the mornings. A lot of times that's all she wants, but every now and then she'll eat things like eggs with a breakfast meat, but still has to have a little something sweet, too."

"I'm sorry to say I ordered an array of breakfast food because I didn't know what you liked, but we were always talking about different things when we ate, I didn't paid attention to what you actually did eat." Lawrence says, then asks Bri, "Do you like omelets?"

She smiles. "I do! I tend to favor mushrooms and tomatoes with ham or sausage, bacon is iffy. I joked with the chef at The White House, Chef André, that I'm a bacon snob. Sometimes pork can have a weird taste to me and if it does, I won't eat it. André had my quirks down! He didn't have to cater to me but we had been friends for so long, he actually used it as a guide if he noticed someone he was cooking for didn't like something."

"What about The Manor? Edwin?" Jack asks. "I don't think I've seen you turn anything away on count of taste..."

Bri ponders this. "You know, come to think of it..." She looks at David, "Did you have Edwin call André?"

David explains, "I figured if anyone knew Bri's food quirks it *had* to be André. So, when he gave me his card and offered to 'guest chef,' I passed the message along to Edwin with André's card, but I also asked Edwin to call and get any information he could on Bri's likes and dislikes." He smirks.

Bri's eyes fill up with tears and she wipes the corner of her eyes. "David Worthington..." a lump swells in her throat. She swallows hard and whispers, *"you got that card the first week of our relationship!"*

"Bri, I always thought people who said they knew the moment they met, he or she was 'The One,' were lucky to be so sure *and* be right! I *felt that* when I first saw you that day in the hotel lobby, *before* meeting you the next day! It's crazy that I fought it as much as I did!" He gestures Jack, *"That's what best friends are for*! They'll tell you straight away when you're being an idiot!"

Jack lifts his glass of orange juice. "Anytime, Brother!" He looks at Bri with love, talking to David and Lawrence, *"I also knew in my heart!"* He winks at her. "And I was determined she wasn't going to get away, so one of us was going to marry her!" He grins. "Look at us now!" The guys lightly laugh.

With Lawrence's dimples showing perfectly he asks, "Now, what does 'bacon snob' mean?!"

Bri giggles. "It can't be too chewy or too crispy, *and* the taste of the bacon has to be right, too. Oh," she picks up a grape out of her fruit, "I'm a grape snob, too! Hard and crunchy," she squeezes, "or no way!" She pops the grape in her mouth. "I won't eat iceberg lettuce. I love romaine, kale, cabbage, and spinach; to*ma*toes firm, not mushy..." She teases with their accent. "Same for noodles…I think that's it for now, other than I try to limit the chemicals in the things I eat and drink."

Lawrence says, "Is that why I don't see you with a fizzy drink?"

"Yes. I don't know why, but I picture drinking cleaning chemicals out of a jug when I see a soda, or fizzy drink as you all call them." She takes a drink of milk. "I do question whether all these chemicals and dyes we consume have anything to do with Autism, ADHD, and various health problems we see more of now than prior to, let's say...1950?"

"Fascinating..." Lawrence replies as he thinks about what she said.

Bri takes her empty plate to the counter where the other plates are. She sees a newspaper and opens it, regretting it almost immediately when she sees an article about herself. It's not even the full paper, just a gossip page she mindlessly starts reading part of a random paragraph, but she stops herself...

🌸 <u>ROYAL NEWS</u> 🌸

The American Marchioness Gives BFF the 1-2-Punch!

By: Hayes Buchanan

...Seems our American Noble needs some anger management classes with her etiquette lessons, folks! She was witnessed giving a woman a knockout punch yesterday. Sources say it wasn't just any woman, but HER BEST FRIEND! She was upset when she walked in on her BFF with Lord Carlisle!

Bri looks at the author and slams the newspaper in half again. "Ugh! I should've known it was him! Why did I open it?! I hardly ever open newspapers! *Why* do we even have a copy of the paper the sleazy *Hayes Buchanan* writes for?!" She tries to push out the picture of what she imagines is him: overweight fifty or sixty-something sitting behind a desk with a cigar in his mouth, typing away at his next 'article' in a cloud of cigar smoke.

"It came with breakfast and I didn't even think about the headlines this morning. My apologies, Love." David says.

"It's not your fault, but do be advised, those *were not* 'news headlines!'" She snickers. "Jokes on Jack though."

"Oh?" Jack asks, raising an eyebrow.

"Yep. The sentences I skimmed says I punched my '*BFF*' because I walked in on the two of you and the article leads the readers to believe the two of you were having sex."

Jack chokes on his food. His nose turns up as David pats his shoulder and says with disappointment, "We need to talk later, Old Chap!"

"The first thing that always comes to mind with her is 'walking infestation'..." He shivers in revulsion. "If that were *ever* true, *don't waste your breath*! Just shoot me in the head because I'm *beyond help* at that point!" He has a sick look on his face. "*I'll even write a suicide note!*"

"Done." David says and they all laugh.

They talk about other things for a little while before they get ready for the day. When Jack is released, they all go to the courthouse together.

 Lawrence, Jack, David, and Bri meet up with the family, along with Ken and Bill, at the courthouse. The judge is thorough but doesn't waste any time moving things right along. When their restraining orders are granted, he moves on to Katie's arraignment. Katie's list of charges is staggering and her bail is steep, but her lawyer tells her not to worry about it, she'll get her out on bail.

When the hearing is over, Jack and Bri, along with everyone that is with them, leave the courtroom. It takes a bit of weaving, but they eventually make their way to the main doors of the courthouse.

Bri doesn't hear her name the few times it's called it out, but she hears Katie scream, "HEY!" It causes everyone within a certain radius to stop and look around. Katie points at Bri and angrily says, "I want that woman arrested for assault!" She quickly walks up to Bri but McMasters moves to a protective stance. Bri can see her whole left cheek, reaching up to her eye, is almost black from the deep bruising caused by Bri punching her. There is also a heart shaped mark on her cheek from where her pink-heart diamond ring from Lawrence made contact with Katie's face. Katie sneers, "That sucker punch will cost you! The press has been calling you their precious 'Royal American Sweetheart,'" her face takes on an evilness to it that makes Bri uncomfortable, but she doesn't show it, "only that will soon change to '*Royal Slut.*'"

With a burst, David is in Katie's face. "We both know who the slut is and I'm looking at her!" David is incredibly angry! The stress of work, what happened to Jack, and Bri having to deal with her again, all collides at this point in time. Katie is glaring at him and she goes to say something, but David won't let her. "Shut up! You're a miserable, pathetic, and *disgusting human being* for everything you've done to various people, but you're a special kind of filth when you did it to someone you called your best friend! Go crawl back into the hole you came out of and leave us all alone!" There were cameras and partial video taken of this incident, but David didn't care. He takes Bri's hand and laces their fingers as they walk out of the building together with Jack, Lawrence, and the rest of the family.

213

 Katie is so angry *and embarrassed* looking around at everyone staring at her and she is upset that Bri leaves without saying a word to her. Katie walks fast and mixes in with everyone going out the door. When she catches up, she reaches for Bri's arm, only it's Lawrence who grabs Katie's arm first and stops her. He had been watching Katie and kept really close to Bri when he saw Katie had her sights, once again, locked on Bri.

Lawrence puts his hand up to stop his guards and the police officers from coming over. The vultures of the press are drooling and circling the story; Lawrence is aware of this, too, and sees Bri looking around.

He leans in and whispers in Katie's ear, "*The last person that put their hands on Bri to hurt her, I* personally *executed right on the spot. I'll only say this once and keep in mind I have diplomatic immunity,*" through a stiff jaw and an authoritative tone, he enunciates, "Walk.away.*right.now.*"

Katie is still glaring as she yanks her arm away. Bri breaks things up more when she turns and walks to the car where Mateo holds the back door open; everyone with her follows her lead. Bri is also aware Katie only gets angrier when she doesn't respond to anything, but what could she possibly say that wouldn't add fuel to this, or to the gossip columns? At least accurate ones will report she didn't say anything.

The Prosecutor and Katie's defense attorney pull her to the side. The prosecutor asks Katie, "Don't you know who that is?!"

"A nobody, who married into a well-to-do family and now she thinks she's a somebody." Katie states.

"I mean *King* Lawrence...you know...of The United Kingdom of Provinces!" The prosecutor tells her.

She plainly says, "Yes, *and* he's interested in using Bri as breeding stock."

"I would show more respect if I were you." The prosecutor suggests discreetly motioning the press and paparazzi. "You could rub someone the wrong way and they could target you because of the trouble you're causing!" Katie scoffs. The prosecutor looks at the defense attorney telling him, "Good luck keeping this one out of trouble." The defense attorney takes a deep breath, nodding in agreement.

Katie thinks she knows Lawrence and groups him with the powerful ones that once they get what they want, they move on to the next woman. She smirks to herself thinking about Bri getting dumped *by a king*!

That afternoon Jack rents two convertibles for the four of them, and the girls, to take to The Bradshaw's beach house to spend the rest of the day. Jack arranges for the girls to be able to drive. They have security in front of them, behind them, and some were already at the beach house and on the beach securing it. They did a great job trying to stay back as much as possible so they could enjoy time as a family; some of the security men and women blending in on the beach to accomplish this.

That evening, Jeff and Olivia come out and enjoy some family time with all of them, too. They brought chocolate, marshmallows, and graham crackers for s'mores at their small bonfire. Bri sits next to Lawrence toasting his marshmallow. He nostalgically tells her of the few times he got to do this with The Worthington's.

"I look at my childhood and most of my happiest moments, perhaps *all* of my happiest moments are with them..." he says with a small smile. He pulls his marshmallow out of the fire and looks at Bri. "I'm so lucky to have you in my life, Bri, to be a part of *your* family and that these kinds of moments happen more often." He leans over for a tender kiss with her.

She smiles sweetly. "I love you."

"I love you." He taps another kiss to her lips, then offers her a bite of his s'more.

She takes a bite and while she chews, she threads her arms around his arm, and they watch the girls with Jack, Jeff, Olivia, and David; they're all hysterically laughing at something. Bri can't help but smile and she feels Lawrence smiling against her temple, right before he places a little kiss there. She looks at him with happiness all over her face, then she rests her head on his shoulder, still holding his arm; he rests his hand on her knee.

He whispers, "*Life is* really good *at this very moment...I wish it never had to end...*" She hugs his arm a little tighter, smiling in agreement.

In their hotel suite the next morning, they're getting ready to fly back to the UK. Jack takes Bri's hand and pulls her into their bedroom.

"I need to say something to you." Jack says sitting on the bed and he waits for her to sit next to him.

"Okay..." She says as she sits down looking a little puzzled.

He looks into her eyes. "I know on a *very small scale* what it's like being affected by those drugs and how scared you must've been. I'm sorry it happened to you, I'm *so* sorry she never really was your friend, BUT I'm *not sorry* you punched her for everything she has done to you!"

Bri gives him a surprised look, followed by a look of love for him. "Oh, Jack." She cups his cheek. "No, Amore Mio, *to you!*"

"What do you mean?" He asks.

She explains, "I had no intentions, no thoughts, as to what to say to her. Regardless, one look at where her hands were on you and you being drugged, it was easy to figure out what she was trying to do! I didn't realize my hand was even in a fist until my fist made contact with her face. *I reacted to protect you, Jack!*"

"Knocking her out took a lot of strength, Bri. There has to be more to it than just me." He tells her.

"While that may be true, it wasn't *why* I punched her." She replies. "Jack, I mourn*ed* the loss of the best friend she *never* was. I'm disappointed in her because she *can be* better, but her jealousy is consuming her right now! We have so much history outside of the horrible assault, I wonder if *she* even knows who she is underneath it all? *This woman she is...*" she looks at her bandaged hand, "well...I *pity* her. While I don't hold any ill-will towards her, I can't say I'd cry if she died tomorrow. *However,* I feel sorry for her and her life choices; the awful choices she continues to make, causing me to go around in circles because I remember and mourn a friendship that never was what I thought it was...trying to find some way to forgive myself for not seeing any of the warning signs."

"Bri, she said she was playing the part of your 'best friend' and by the sounds of it, she did a great job." Her eyebrows raise and she nods. He tells her, "Don't punish yourself for being a loving, caring, and trusting person." He cups her cheek. "I think you would regret it more if you hardened yourself."

She gives him a matching expression when she says, "You're right."

He asks her. "What can we do to help you through this?"

"You're *always* doing it! You, Lawrence, and David, being there for me, hugging me, giving me your strength to lean on..." she wipes a tear about to fall. She tearfully smiles at him as she touches his cheek. "I haven't quite figured out how on earth I ended up with three of the most amazing and wonderful men in the world?!"

"You forgot incredibly hot and sexy!" Jack teases.

She giggles. "That goes without saying! Have you seen yourselves lately?! You're all so *bloody fantastic* in your own right!" She playfully mocks his accent. They chuckle as Jack stands and pulls her up. He wraps his arms around her and he hugs her tight; he hears her take a deep relaxing breath. He gives her a sweet, tender kiss and hugs her once more.

When they walk back into the living room, Lawrence's phone rings and his whole demeanor changes to rigidness. It's obvious that it's his mother. He ducks into the bedroom to take it but forgets to shut the door. They hear the exchange of words that makes Bri proud of him for standing up to her, but she also has a sinking feeling it'll come back to bite *her*...When Bri hears him hang up, she slips into the bedroom and shuts the door to see if he is okay.

He gives her a little smile. "I'm fine, Darling." She gives him a doubting look and he walks over to her. He hugs her and says, "This isn't new to me, Bri, this is an everyday thing." He pulls back and asks, "Are we ready to go?"

"I think so, but you're forgetting something..." She smirks. Before she says anything, he pulls her into a deep, passionate kiss. "*Much* better, My King!" He taps another kiss to her lips before they go out to David and Jack, and they all go downstairs to make their way to the airport.

CHAPTER 22
Imperfect Discovery of Information

On The Royal Jet back to the UK, David and Lawrence play chess while Bri sits next to Jack on a comfortable couch. She looks at Jack and says, "Okay Carlisle, I had to spill about my family on the flight over, now it's your turn to spill more about yours." She holds his hand. "I'd like to fit more pieces of *your* puzzle together."

He rests the side of his head to the side of her head. He reminds her, "You know you can ask me anything."

She gives him a small smile. "You've told me your father didn't marry your mother for love. Your father thinks he has what women want, but his reputation as a 'gold digger' precedes him." She pauses and thinks. "You said when your brother was born, your father was ecstatic to have his heir and doted on him, but he couldn't have cared less when you came along." She cups his cheek. "You still remember your mother made up for it and her love could *almost* fill the emptiness of being unwanted by your father...until she died." She tries not to cry, "It's *despicable* for a parent to make their child truly feel unloved and disposable!"

His eyes get a little wet when her hand goes up into his hair. Her tenderness causes his feelings to come to the surface. Bri straddles him and hugs him tight. David and Lawrence have overheard this and watch them. Lawrence is a little emotional for Jack, too, being able to personally relate to terrible parents.

After a few minutes, Jack takes a deep breath and Bri sits back on his lap some. He shakily exhales, telling her with a sweet smile, "I love you. You know that, right?"

She softly giggles. "You've mentioned it a time or two!" He hugs her close and she says next to his ear, "You mean the world to me and to *our* family!" She pulls back and he wipes her tears with his thumbs.

She sits back on his lap again and he says, "Can't imagine a better family!" He gestures the four of them and they all agree.

Bri gets back on track. She asks, "I can't remember if you said when you last saw them?"

"Well, like your family, I rarely ever do, and *we all* prefer it that way!" He kisses her fingers. "My father would send for me only when it was crucial in my father's mind for us to be seen as 'a happy family,' like when he married Beverly...that was until around the time I was diagnosed with cancer—."

"And Peter got so angry with them for not even *wanting* to get tested..." Bri's irritation is evident. "I *still* can't believe Reginald had to be paid off by Peter to do it! *You're his son!*" She gets angry. "I never thought I could hate someone, but your father definitely proves that wrong and your brother is right behind him!" She has a determined look on her face.

He gives her a slight smile as he cups her face, his eyes so full of love for her. "Yes, you're very angry with them, but no, you don't hate them because it isn't in your nature! You have way too much love in your heart for any hate to reside."

She scoffs. "You act as if you *know* that, but we all have darkness within us."

"*Bri.* I do know!" Jack says with determination.

"How—?"

"After *everything* Katie did to you, that would make *anyone* else despise her, *and we do*," he gestures Lawrence and David, "*you don't!* Why?" She looks down as she thinks about what he's saying. "If you don't hate *her*, if you haven't turned your back completely on her, there's no way you can hate my father or brother, who you've never even met!" He states.

"But everything he's done is against *you!* I love and adore *you!*" Bri says. "*It's so much worse!*"

"I'm not sure about that, considering what Katie has done is against the woman *I* love and adore! *And* what she did was *far* worse than what any of my family has ever done to me! But let's move on..."

Bri gives him a skeptical look. "Alright...for now." He winks at her. She asks, "So your brother was a 'good enough' match, but there was an even better match to someone registered in London?"

"Yes. Not long after all that with my father and brother, they found the match to someone who was tested in London. They reached out to this gentleman about being my donor who happened to be in Reñiato at the time. *This stranger* dropped *everything* right away to come help me! It was at that moment I realized my father didn't care if I died...the weight of that realization would've crushed me if Carlotta and Peter weren't there every single day, making sure I knew I *was loved* and *they wanted me*!" He could barely get that last bit out.

Bri holds Jack's jaw with her bandaged hand and tells him, "And you always will be, Amore Mio!"

He gently kisses her hand, then explains more, "Peter was so disgusted by my father's actions that he threatened him to never send for me again and when I wanted to see them, *I* would reach out. The next time I would hear from them would be for money *years* later." Jack continues, "David and I were already best friends, and he *never* left my side," he can only whisper. "Whenever I had a treatment or a hospital stay, he was there. It's rare for Peter or Carlotta use their titles to persuade rules to be broken, but when visitors weren't allowed somewhere, David *always* was." David nods.

Bri smiles at David. "Like you two were there for me after I was shot."

"Yes, exactly!" Jack smiles at her. "David and I were always together, but after my illness, our relationship solidified and it easily included Herst!"

"The 'Three Musketeers.'" She smiles sweetly.

He nods. "We were, *and are*, inseparable, *even in our marriages*." He playfully grins. "David, Herst, and I, know that we will drop everything, jump over mountains if we have to, if we need each other." He taps a sweet kiss to her lips. "With Herst in this, we know that you're fully loved and supported, and at least one of us will always be around for you." She looks at Lawrence and lovingly smiles; he winks at her.

She takes a deep breath and asks Jack, "Is Beverly still around?"

"My stepmom's always traveling with 'her family's money.' She's a smart woman and knew my father was marrying her for her money; however, she was using him, too...*for a title*."

"If your father was bad at managing the family's money, then we can assume your brother isn't good with money either because your father couldn't teach your brother about something he hasn't learned himself." Bri offhandedly mentions to Jack.

"I hadn't thought of it like that...you make an interesting point." Jack says. "Peter made sure the three of us knew about money, he has a gift of seeing someone's talent and was so encouraging with all three of our talents!"

"Even with Bri he saw her talent and has her working with Newhaven's government!" David adds.

Lawrence grins. "And the UKs government soon."

"No, Ace, *that's you*! You're 'The King.'" She replies.

He laughs and shakes his head. "I could argue that's why I need you by my side, but we'll talk about that later."

Jack is lightly chuckling and Bri looks at him expectantly. He tells her, "There really isn't much left. My brother would see that I would go to Columbia in New York City, which, after Harvard, David would come up and we'd get our Master's degrees in finance. Lawrence went to Oxbridge, something about having prettier girls." Jack teases.

He scoffs a laugh. "If only I had a choice!"

"None of us are as smart as 'Ms. Summa Cum Laude' here!" Jack beams proudly of her.

Bri rolls her eyes. "I didn't go to an Ivy League, so we're at most equal, but I'd tend to think your degrees are better!"

"Oh, Darling, graduating Summa is a *huge* fete no matter what college you go to!" Lawrence smiles.

"No, it wasn't easy! *But* I'd be lucky to do half as well at any of the Ivy Leagues you three went to!" She replies.

Jack laughs lightly, shaking his head. He continues, "I went to work for Watchtower Financial; however, David was determined to work in a position he was *qualified for* with his schooling at The Worthington Corporation, which Peter supported."

"I wanted to work with my future employees and *earn* their respect." David adds. "I wanted to show them that I did belong there because of hard work, not nepotism."

Jack agrees. "*Most* were very receptive to what David was doing. Those who weren't at first, were quick to see how serious he was about working hard alongside them, and the rest eventually came around or left." Jack shifts a little and Bri goes to move. "Where are you going?" He holds her hips.

Bri smiles. "I thought maybe this was getting uncomfortable for you."

"This is probably one of the more comfortable ways to talk, Amore Mia." He tells her. She smiles and gets comfortable again. Jack thinks out loud a moment, "Now, where were we? Ah, right. My brother tried to match my success with some 'quicker way,' making risky investments and using the estate as collateral."

"Which is when they'd come to you for money." Bri recalls.

"Yes." Jack replies.

"But The Newhaven Estate isn't theirs to begin with." Bri notes.

Jack explains, "They'd need twenty-three million to save the furnishings, the paintings, antiques, and such. I'd give it to them, expecting *nothing* in return."

"Which is what you got in return." She rolls her eyes at the thought.

He chuckles lightly. "But when you don't expect anything, you can't be let down so much when nothing happens. I have offered to teach my brother, but his pride wouldn't allow him to learn anything from his younger brother."

"Not surprising." She states.

"No, but you're interested and you're learning. You already know a lot about the financial world!" Jack tells her and cups her cheek. "Amore Mia, you *more* than make up for *anything* I might've lacked in my life." She smiles lovingly.

Lawrence raises his glass. "Here, here." She smiles adoringly at Lawrence.

Bri tells Jack, "Well, you wouldn't be who you are today if you stayed in that neglectful environment, especially without your mother to love and care for you." She smiles with so much love, he melts. She says, "I'm so grateful Peter and Carlotta rescued that little boy who had no one after his mother died! I wish I could take the pain and heartache away—."

"You do!" Jack happily insists. "Bri, your love has melted all the heartache away! Like you, I wouldn't change anything because it led me to David, Peter, Carlotta, James, *Herst*, and being a part of The Worthington Family! And now, it brought me to the greatest love of my life!" He kisses her firmly.

"I love you, Amore Mio!"

He rests his forehead to hers. "I love you, too, Amore Mia!" They soak in those feelings of love between them.

Lawrence observes this and his mind goes to The Clock Tower...that kiss when she was blindfolded...it sparked something inside him that he fears may be tied to his dark past, but he shakes it off. He is grateful to be part of *this* family and he *can't wait* for it to become official!

The guys settle in and play a card game while Bri goes to the bedroom to lay down, but only tosses and turns. She gets up and is about to go join the guys, when she sees her bag and remembers the envelope from The Underground Secret Society is inside it. She pulls it out and sits on the bed with it. She reads through the top page again and also the bank statements. Then she looks at the photos and doesn't recognize anyone, except The Queen Mother in various ones. She wonders if she still has a small magnifying glass in her bag. She starts digging and the guys hear the noises of her emptying the contents of her bag and an 'ah-ha' when she finds it. They come into the bedroom and see her scrutinizing a photo.

David asks, "Is that the information from a certain secretive someone?"

She nods. "Come. Sit." She pats the bed and they sit down with her.

 Lawrence sees the symbol on the envelope and stares at it. "I've seen this before, but I can't remember where...it feels like it was such a long time ago..."

"It's the symbol for The Underground Secret Society." She replies.

Lawrence stares, shaking his head, saying, "That doesn't sound familiar..."

She opens the envelope and explains the paperwork, then she lets them look through it all. "I flipped through these photos, but given they were probably looking for this envelope in our hotel suite, I think everything in this envelope should be scrutinized by all of you. You would see something I wouldn't!"

As the guys read through the papers and examine the photos, Bri looks at Lawrence and sees he hasn't moved, but his facial expression is livid. Bri puts her hand on his arm.

He looks at her with his livid expression, handing her the picture as he tells her, "I understand more about the warning to 'trust no one'..."

She scrunches her eyebrows together as she takes the picture and looks at it. It's a photo of The Queen Mother at some place that looks like an opening to a mine, but it would have to be her location for wherever she stores things, *or people*, for her auctions. There are a few people around them, but in the center, next to The Queen Mother, is his 'trusted' cousin, Tristan, with a gun in his hand pointed at what looks like a dead body at their feet. She turns it over...she isn't sure what she was expecting to be there, but it's blank.

Lawrence looks at the rest of the pictures, still angry but wanting to see who else is in his mother's pocket. Bri comes across 'The Queen Mother's Payroll List' and her eyebrows furrow as she looks at it.

"What's that?" David asks, looking over her shoulder.

"It's a list of people who are on The Queen Mother's payroll and ones that are paid sporadically, yet often."

Lawrence asks, "May I see it?"

"Sure." She hands it to him. "I won't be able to recognize any of the names, except maybe Tristan's."

He takes the paper and looks at it. "Seems like my suspicions of some of these people are correct, I just never suspected Tristan!" Jack and David pick up the papers and pictures to put back in the envelope. Then Lawrence hands them the sheets he was looking at so they can put them into the envelope as well. He looks at Bri, "Please keep all that tucked away. I'll want to see it again." He takes a deep breath and says as he exhales, "I need a drink." He goes out to the main cabin to get one.

Bri looks at David and Jack saying, "I'm worried about him."

They nod with David saying, "I am, too. It can't be easy finding out someone close to you has betrayed you." He gives Bri a sad look. "Something you can relate to..."

"*Sadly...*" Bri reluctantly says. She walks out to Lawrence and sits next to him on the couch.

"*I should've seen it!*" Lawrence kicks himself.

"*How?!*" Jack and David ask at the same time.

David adds, "He's family—."

"But he's *her* family, too! *First!*" Lawrence says and clenches his jaw staring down at nothing in particular.

Bri quietly says to him, "Whatever you do, *be smart about this!* I know you're angry and you have every right to be, but a knee-jerk reaction may not be the best way."

"I know. I feel I don't want him to know that I know, at least not right now." He replies, staring at his glass before he takes another drink.

"For what it's worth, I think *that's* a smart move." She hugs his arm.

Lawrence is quiet the rest of the flight, but he does let Bri snuggle in with him and rest her head on his shoulder. When the plane lands, Lawrence and Bri gather their things; David and Jack will head to Newhaven, while Bri spends a few days with Lawrence. Bri says her goodbyes with hugs and kisses to Jack and David before she leaves the plane with Lawrence.

CHAPTER 23

Imperfectly Perfect Timing

One evening a few days later, James and Amy join Peter, Carlotta, Jack, David, and Bri, outside on the patio. Bri and Amy hug each other, then sit and talk about the wedding plans.

"Sometimes I wish we could just do what you and David did and keep the ceremony small, but my family wouldn't be very happy. My mother has loved planning all this with Maggie and me, having the time of her life!" Amy beams. "She just *loves* Maggie and is excited to see you again, and of course, meet everyone else!" She grins.

David chuckles a little, "It was easier for me since I had it all mapped out while Bri was in the hospital. Once she said yes, it was a hectic few days, but mother*s* are a *huge* asset!" He smiles and winks at Carlotta.

Carlotta laughs. "And *I* had the time of my life, too!" Everyone lightly laughs. "Let me arrange for a wedding planner to help you going forward? They will make the day of the wedding go that much smoother and it'll be less stressful for you!"

Amy happily replies, *"That would be wonderful!* Thank you!" She hugs Carlotta.

Peter stands up and steps next to Carlotta. They squeeze each other's hand and give each other a little nod. They look at everyone who are looking at them, waiting for them to say something.

Peter begins, "As you know, your mother and I have talked about retiring while we still have time to travel and enjoy various places around the world." He smiles at Bri. "Since our Bri here has been doing a *fantastic* job in Kingsbury, and now has agreed to be 'The Royal Consort,' Carlotta and I think this would be the perfect time to step down and hand over Newhaven to her and David." Peter explains. Bri freezes...

"We want to be grandparents and take the girls with us, if they want to go, and enjoy new grandbabies whenever they get here!" Carlotta adds with a loving smile of excitement to both Bri and Amy; Bri's mouth has dropped open a bit.

Peter smiles and nods at Carlotta, then looks at Bri and David. "So? Are you two ready to take the reins?"

David smiles as he stands, looking around saying, "I think we are—."

Bri jumps up. "*Have you lost your mind, David Christopher Worthington*?! I'm not ready! *How could I possibly be ready*?! I can't jump into this! What about the people—*Newhaven*?!" She is panicked. "Oh my gosh," she looks and gestures Jack, "then there's Newhaven Heirloom Wool, The Textile Mill, *and* The Foundation! Then, if there are duties coming with—." David kisses her, wrapping his arms around her and doesn't stop kissing her until he feels her relax a bit in his arms...then he gently pulls their lips apart.

He smiles with love in his eyes. "You're overthinking this, Love."

"*Nnnooo...*" she scrunches her eyebrows together, "*pretty sure you're* UNDER-thinking this, David! This.is.*huge!*"

Gabriel steps in. "With all due respect, Bri, you *are* ready! You've been more than ready from the moment you started formulating how to use your wedding dress to help the economy of The Duchy!"

She looks at Peter and Carlotta with a frightened look. Carlotta supportively says, "Bri, you think like a great businesswoman! Take Jack for example: you know his strengths and want his help with Newhaven's financials!" Bri's heart is racing. She looks to David and Jack, who are looking at her with so much adoration, she could melt right there.

Peter adds, "Bri, you've already assumed the role for quite some time in Kingsbury, and David has been juggling certain duties on top of being CEO for a while now, and both of you're doing *splendidly*! All Carlotta and I have been doing is supporting you two, that won't change! All this does is gives you both the actual titles."

"It's not like we're retiring and walking away from everyone and everything either, Sweetie." Carlotta tells her.

"For what it's worth Bri," James adds, "we're a family and we have each other's backs. No one here wants anyone to feel overwhelmed. We'll step in for whatever is necessary, if it means headlines read: 'The Three Worthington Brothers Make an Appearance' or 'The Former Duke Accompanies The

Duchess,'" then he smirks, "and we all know Lord Carlisle will accompany The Duchess anywhere!"

"Apparently right off a cliff!" He playfully smiles implying the waterfall before their honeymoon, and he convinced her to jump again for their anniversary, wanting to start a tradition.

Bri giggles. "I think you have that backwards, Amore Mio!"

He shrugs as he laughs. "I seem to also remember taking a bullet and then there's Mt. Vesuvius!"

"*And* some pretty heavy-duty drugs more recently." She sweetly smiles.

"I shudder to think what she would've done if you hadn't been there, *or* if she had drugged *you* again?!" He shakes his head at the thought.

Bri has a 'eek' look on her face. "Let's not go there..." She looks at Gabriel. "Abby said she wanted me to talk with you about running her schedule, too."

"I can definitely reach out to her, too, but wouldn't she be helping Queen Genevieve?" He asks.

Bri looks around. "I guess you all deserve the full picture and the whole reason for my freaking out." She takes a deep breath. "I need this to stay between us and I *don't* want added pressure," she looks to David, then Jack, and around at all of them as they agree. "Genevieve has been leading a campaign to support me as 'The Royal Consort' *but* once I accepted Lawrence's proposal, she told me she's going to change direction and lead a campaign for me to become 'The Queen.'" There are gasps and Bri looks at David and Jack. "I wanted to discuss this between us first, but I was trying to absorb it myself. Then with everything going on, I forgot about it. Oh. That's why Abby offered me her schedule." She inhales deeply and blows out her exhale. "Abby said she needed to do something with her time that mattered instead of wasting her time on nothing significant." She's overcome with all her mixed emotions; her lower jaw shakes as she pushes it all down.

David goes to step over to her again, but Peter puts his hand up in a stopping gesture to David, mouthing, 'Let me.' David gives him a small nod and sits back down. Peter walks over to Bri and holds her hand and lifts her chin for her to look at him.

Peter tells her, "I swear to you, *we all swear to you*, no one will fail!" They all agree. "*You* will *not* fail!" He has her sit and he sits next to her. "Bri, as Gabriel said, you *are* ready! And you're ready for whatever comes your way with being 'The Royal Consort' and what might come next!" He sweetly smiles. "It'll be better, too, if you're a duchess when Herst makes you 'The Royal Consort.'" Peter adds.

"You really think so?" She asks.

"Yes." He chuckles. "While 'The Marchioness' would've been fine, being The Duchess and of a significant duchy will be even better. Not to mention David as The Duke will have him in a better position as well."

Jack steps in front of Bri and squats down. "Bri, we've been on the same page since day one with The Wool Farm, The Textile Mill, and your foundation. We've worked through different ideas *and* disagreements. You nailed the project you had in DC, you're working on Newhaven's law enforcement database, and now The Royal Police wants your expertise! You're amazing and *more than ready* to officially take this on, *before* you and David have a baby." Everyone agrees with that good point. Jack stands back up and pulls her up to hug her, hugging her firmly.

"Love, Gen won't step away from anything either and you now have Abby's schedule." David says.

"Gen said that to me, too." Bri admits.

Amy adds. "And I'll do whatever I can, even dragging James with me!"

James smiles adoringly at Amy. "I'd *willingly* go anywhere with you, My Love!"

Bri looks at all of them. "You're all so wonderful!" David hugs her close. Bri asks Peter, "When would all this happen?"

"At the end of the week." Peter answers.

Bri laughs, then abruptly stops. "Oh my gosh, you're *not* kidding!"

Peter replies, "Everything will be official Friday and then Saturday we'll have a ball announcing both of you to Newhaven and our country as the new 'Duke and Duchess of Newhaven.'"

Carlotta adds, "We want to have this all done before The Midnight Ball!"

Peter has a fatherly smile on his face when he says to Bri, "You *are* ready, Duchess Bri!" He winks at her and looks to David, "And you've been ready *for years*, Son!"

"Not quite..." David tells Peter, then turns to Bri. "We had to find this amazing, fantastically brilliant woman first!" He says to her, "With you, this doesn't seem insurmountable anymore."

"Son, you'll have priority use of the family helicopter to go back and forth with, which will save you travel time between Edinburgh and home or Kingsbury." Peter turns to Bri. "Richard will now be David's driver as Paul has already requested to be your permanent driver. I believe McMasters is in agreement if you are." Bri nods. "The next few days or so will be more hectic as we pull all this together."

Bri looks to David and Jack, taking another deep breath. Jack smiles sweetly, as he tells her, "I'll take the jump with you anytime, anywhere!" Jack hugs her tight and she lightly laughs, relaxing into his embrace.

Peter wasn't kidding! Bri *barely* saw David that week. She was working with Jack on things with The Foundation, Newhaven Wool and The Mill, as well as working on her duties in Kingsbury. Jack had to be in Edinburgh today, so she decides to have a change of scenery and works in her office at The Worthington Corporation Business Complex. She hasn't even seen much of David today either; he has barely had time for two words, let alone two minutes.

Bri stops by his office for a couple minutes. "Love, I'm sorry," David says apologetically, "but I have to get over to the other side of the complex and across the street for a lunch appointment with Father and another gentleman——." She thinks she has covered her disappointment, but he caught the split second it was there. He tries to let it go, *just this once*...she already nodded her head and had a little smile for him as she walks out; he knows she understands but maybe that's why he can't let it go...

When David passes Mary's empty desk, he sees she has gone to lunch. Before he hits the elevator button, he checks his watch and thinks, *I could bring her...it wouldn't be much alone time, but they'd be together on their walk over and she'll be happy to have that time with him...he also misses her.*

He catches a glimpse of her as she came out of her office to leave, probably to grab lunch somewhere. She doesn't see him as she digs through her bag and turns back to her office; it looks like she's looking for something. He quickly walks to her office and sees her by the chair closest to the door, digging in her bag deeper. Before he says anything about lunch, he drops his things to her floor, startling her.

She jumps and turns her head with her hand to her chest. "Dav—." He kisses her passionately. He pivots with her, kicking the door shut, as he pushes her up against the wall. She whispers in a panic, "*David, we can't do this here!*"

He sees the worried look on her face. "This whole floor is empty, even Mary is out to lunch." He locks the door. "I miss you, too, Macushla! I don't have a lot of time if—." He stops in mid-sentence when he sees the playfulness in her eyes...

After they've straightened their clothes, she hugs him again. "That was fun!" She taps a kiss to his lips. "I love you!"

He caresses her cheek as he looks at her beautiful face. "It isn't much, but we'd be together if you want to come to lunch with me?"

"How about I come and order something to go, make small talk until it's ready, then slip out for you guys to talk business?" He smiles in agreement as he helps her with her coat. He takes her hand and laces their fingers together. Bri looks at her watch and leans in as they walk, "David! You're *always* incredible, but *daaang!* You're only going to be a couple minutes late!"

"I do aim to please." He grins with a wink.

She lightly laughs. "You *definitely* do please!"

He kisses the back of her hand and smiles. "Thank you for that, by the way."

"Are you *kidding*?! That was *hot!* I'm tempted to ask Mary to keep you that swamped on a regular basis!" She bites her lower lip with a smile.

"*Really*?!" He asks.

"No!" She giggles. "Seriously, I couldn't stand it if you were always *this* swamped! You three are workaholics as it is, but I like that when it's our time together, you each take a step back for a few days and at the very least work more 'normal hours.'" They walk in comfortable silence.

She stops him in front of the restaurant. "I love and adore you, *Mister* Worthington!"

"The feelings are *very* mutual, Mrs. Worthington!" He taps a quick kiss to her lips before he opens the door to the restaurant.

Inside, Peter is already there and he is happy to see Bri, kissing her on the cheek before introducing her. "Donald Hughes, this is my *wonderful* daughter-in-law, Lady Newhaven."

Mr. Hughes shakes her hand as he slightly bows as an acknowledgement of her soon-to-be-duchess' status. David shakes his hand then motions for Bri to sit between him and his father; Peter pulling out her chair for her. "I hope you gentlemen don't mind me crashing your lunch for a little bit. I'm *famished* and walked with David to grab something to go?"

Mr. Hughes happily says, "I don't mind at all, but I *must* insist that you join us!" She looks at David who smiles.

Peter asks, "If you're available for lunch, then I'll insist you do, too!" He gives her a genuine smile, but she also feels that this must be an important man for her to get to know because of her position as 'The Duchess.'

"Well, then, I'd love, too!" Bri smiles.

"*Splendid!*" Mr. Hughes says and waves their waitress over.

Their lunch was filled with talk about Peter and Carlotta stepping down, the direction of Newhaven, not to mention they ate great food. When they leave, the men were going to circle the block to drop her off at the office, but she insists on walking and not having them go in the opposite direction just for her. David doesn't argue too much because McMasters will walk with her.

Mr. Hughes takes her hand and pats the back of it. "So wonderful to meet you and I look forward to working with you!"

Bri has learned that Donald Hughes is their elected member of the UK Parliament, particularly The House of Lords. She happily tells him, "Likewise!"

Peter kisses her cheek. "Thanks for brightening up our lunch, Sweetie.'" Bri caught '*Sweetie*' and even though he's called her that before, something about it this time makes her feel like she truly was his daughter.

Peter climbs in the car and David pulls Bri into a kiss. "Thank you for *everything*." He winks. "I'll come by to take you home with me later. Jack has a late meeting with a client and a couple of others from his team."

She remembers Jack saying that and nods. "Sounds great. I love you!"

"I love you, too!" He quickly taps a kiss to her lips before he gets in the car.

She hustles with McMasters to cross the street behind the small crowd and the two talk along the way back to the office. That afternoon, Bri gets a lot of things done. She doesn't realize it's time to go home for the day until David shows up at her office door.

"David, this is sweet, but you didn't have to come up just to go back down again. A text would've worked." Bri tells him.

"Love, I'll *always* want to walk out of the office with my beautiful wife whenever she's here! *No* exceptions!" He handsomely smiles.

"Yeah, *if* you're up here! But if you're in The Lobby—."

He lightly places his fingers on her lips. "As I said the week we first met, I take great pride having you on my arm!" Bri's smile is so full of love, he just pulls her into his arms and hugs her. "I'm sorry I haven't been around much. I figured you'd spent the extra time with Jack."

"Oh, I did! But don't forget, I love all of you!" She smiles sweetly through her semi-watery eyes.

He smiles. "I would *never* forget that!" Then he says with a knowing look, "I'd like to go on record that your tears *prove* I'm right!"

She lifts her eyebrow. "About what?"

234

"I said you are the only person I know who could love Jack and I so fully, *so completely*, that you'd actually have lots of love left over to love Herst completely, too!"

She snickers a little as she gathers her things. "I refuse to admit anything and have it go to your head."

He chuckles as he says, "You have my heart, too, Bri, and *you* always will! Just as I imagine you have Jack's, and now Herst's heart, too! Your very own collection of hearts..." he grins, "a soon-to-be 'Queen of Hearts.'" He kisses the inside of her wrist. He raises his eyebrow with another smirk, waiting for her to admit he's right.

"I still refuse to say anything and plead 'The Fifth Amendment.'"

"Ah, but you're not in America, Love!"

"Lucky for me, I have *dual* citizenship! Besides, there are laws here, too, that protect against self-incrimination." She replies.

He chuckles. "*You're impossible!*"

"Take me home, *Mister* Worthington! Or should I say, take me home, *Your Grace?*" She playfully smiles.

"Anything you wish, *Your Grace!*" He takes her hand and laces their fingers together.

He holds her hand pretty much all the way home to The Worthington Estate. Bri tells him on their drive she just wants to spend the evening with her handsome men having dinner, a game of pool, and maybe a movie.

David's onboard. "I'm absolutely yours the rest of the night!" She texts Jack who says her plan sounds *'fantastic'* to him!

They had a lot of laughs throughout the night and were having so much fun playing pool, or billiards, they never watched a movie, but played more games. Bri says goodnight to Jack who'll work a couple hours in the morning, his boss has a proposal for him. Then he'll spend the rest of the day with her. She kisses him goodnight before she slips upstairs to her quarters with David.

Bri is getting out of the shower when David is at the door unbuttoning his shirt. He drops her towel then takes his shirt off and puts it on her. "Ooo, nice and warm..." she smells the cologne in his shirt, "mmm, smells *so* good!" She goes to step around him but he stops her and whispers into her ear, "*Only this.*" He kisses just below her ear and sees her goosebumps before he kisses down her neck. He steps away smiling to himself.

Bri is smiling to herself as she gets ready for bed. She reads while she waits for David, getting so deep into her book, she only notices David had crawled onto the bed when he slips the bookmark into the book and closes it on her.

"I owe you a little more consideration." He cups her face.

"David!" She tells him, "I *swear* today in the office goes down in the books as incredibly hot!"

"Well, if you're not interested..." he teases as he lays down beside her.

"You don't fool me one bit, *Mister* Worthington!" She tickles him.

He struggles but manages to get her into a bear hug that locks her arms to her side. He pulls her on top of him. "Do I get a reward if I let you go?"

She fakes a shocked look. "My kisses aren't enough of an award?!"

He chuckles. "*Always*, but I'm at a better advantage to negotiate!"

She flicks up her eyebrow. "How about I make it worth your time in a *very* fun way?"

"Now you're talking!" He releases her and she kisses him deeply...

CHAPTER 24

Imperfectly Perfect Bet

Friday morning, David goes to his office in Edinburgh for various meetings. Bri goes to The Cottage House and hears Jack's phone ring walking into their living room. When she walks into the office, he is talking on the phone but they smile at each other.

It isn't a long conversation and he stands up as he hangs up, then walks over to her. "Good morning, Gorgeous!"

"Good morning, Handsome!"

He playfully asks, "Don't you mean 'Sexy'?" She bites her lower lip with a smile. "Right." He grins. "I'll work on my title a little later." He kisses her and she wraps her arms around his neck as he dips her back.

When he brings her back up, she fans herself. "You're off to a *brilliant* start!" She teases with his accent and he chuckles. "Is something up this morning already?" She looks at the diamond watch he had bought for her in Italy; he happens to have the matching men's watch on. She surprises herself when occasionally, she *really* likes something expensive she is given, like this watch. It's actually one of her favorite pieces.

He was lost in thought for a moment. When he sees her looking at him expectantly for an answer, he snaps out of it. "Oh! Uh, no. Not really. That call was my boss."

"Oh?" She asks curiously.

"He wants me to start slowly handpicking whatever clients I want to keep and start handing the rest of them off to my team, especially the busier we get with our businesses and the foundation."

She replies, "And you need to make adjustments, so you can free up your time to help me—."

He shakes his head telling her, "Bri, I *will never* say I'm in this, but only to a point, because *nothing* will top partnering with you *in anything*!" He sees her eyes get a little teary at the sentiment. "Yes, I love the company I work for and yes, I love the people I work with, even my clients. I have a few clients that will only work with me and will probably seek me out to work for them on my own if I leave, like David and The Worthington Corporation, even Herst. My boss knows this and these are also some of their top clients. He also knows I'm not interested in starting my own financial business; never have been. He thought this would be a win-win. I'm interested in his offer because I can stay current and up to date with the financial business, which will only improve *our businesses*, well, your businesses."

"No, Jack, you had it right. *OUR* businesses...I just get the final say." She teases with that last part and winks with her smile.

He chuckles and kisses her rings. "I figure as the wool and textile production grows; I'd shift to working more with the businesses. That is, if you're okay with this strategy."

"Jack, I want you to be happy. I'll support whatever *you want*, and we can coordinate what we need to, especially now that we have a *great* farm manager with Hugo." She holds his cheek. "I can even see us having everything fully operational and having the right people hired, so that you can work with your handpicked clients indefinitely!"

He is surprised. "*Seriously?!*"

"Yes!" She giggles. "*If* that's what you want!" She sees him relax and starts to become more excited about that prospect. "Like you said, if it helps *our* businesses and the foundation, even Newhaven, in the long run, it's just more wins! I'm so grateful you went on this venture with me and, well, maybe again with Lawrence's jewelry!"

"Oh, Amore Mia...I love that this business can have a lasting legacy!" He holds her face and kisses her fiercely. "Does Herst know about you wanting to go into business with his jewelry line?"

"I haven't really discussed it, but he has so much!" She says. "Why? Is it like other monarchies where they can't go into business?"

"Those other monarchies are different. Here, we're *ruled* by the monarchy so The King can do whatever he likes; *however*, Herst is smart and knows he shouldn't go overboard as king either. He'd be more inclined to agree to doing something with his jewelry if the profits went to charity, like The Royal Charity Fund, or yours."

"I'll keep that in mind whenever I do talk to him about it, but probably not *our* foundation because it might be considered a 'conflict of interest.'" She hugs him. "I love you, Amore Mio!" Then kisses him with a love and fierceness that he feels deep to his center. He holds her tight and continues to kiss her for a bit longer. When they pull apart, she smiles and he taps another kiss to her lips. She hugs him and takes a deep breath. "This new work arrangement with Watchtower Financial, how will this work exactly? Will you have set days you'll go into Edinburgh?"

"I'm going to have my main office here. Cullen, whom you've met," Bri nods remembering, "will take on more of my responsibilities, with the understanding that he'll be named Junior Team Leader. He'll help me if I need to juggle anything and basically be in a better position to take on the team later whenever I do fully step down as the team's leader. Between you and me, my goal is to hand over the reins and be a silent member of the team with baby number two, but for sure by number three."

"Sexier already, Amore Mio!" She grins and hugs him a little firmer. "All I ask is we continue to communicate. And thank you."

"You don't have to thank me, Amore Mia, I *want* to do this!"

She looks at him and smiles. "*Thank you* for running this by *me* first." Jack was a little surprised. "It's usually David, *then me*."

His heart squeezes. "Shamefully, having this discussion with you before I spoke with David is because of timing, but I promise——."

She puts her hand over his mouth. "Don't promise. Just try to let me know." He nods. She shifts the conversation. "*I'm sorry* I didn't talk with any of you about Gen's campaign for me to be queen. I was going to talk to you and David, but David had a bad week. I sort of forgot about it until Peter and Carlotta were announcing their retirement and well..."

"Bri, it's okay." Jack tells her. "That discussion called for it. But, since *you* brought it up, *how do you feel about becoming queen?*"

"Honestly, I don't know...I mean, Gen and Seth have put their own family on hold for *way* too long! And I *completely* understand wanting a chance to start a family with the man she loves on *their terms*, not The Queen Mother's!" Jack agrees.

Jack's phone rings and he kisses her hand before he goes to answer it. While he talks, she stares out the window; The Manor isn't too far away. He watches her as he talks and when he hangs up, he walks back over to her asking, "What else, Amore Mia?"

"Hmm?" She turns her head to him.

"What else is on your mind?" He asks.

"Oh..." She exhales. "I was just thinking you and I are in such a great flow, as well as me and David, it's amazing how Lawrence—."

"Fits in like he's been here from the beginning?" Jack finishes for her with a loving look.

She smiles sweetly and nods. "Then I think about the business and how it's really starting to come together, but that's mostly you—." Jack bursts out laughing. Bri's eyebrows come together and she has a hint of irritation in her voice when she asks, "*What's so funny?*"

"Bri! YOU'VE done the most work! I've worked *with* you and being 'The Duchess of Newhaven' won't change *a thing*! You'll be just as focused because this has been *your project* from the beginning!"

"*Our* project!" She corrects him.

"Now, maybe, but when it was first starting, it was yours. *I* was lucky enough to be trusted to help you with it!" He winks with his pearly whites showing in a smile. She quietly laughs, shaking her head. He tucks some hair behind her ear. "What else?"

"With these businesses, Lawrence, *all of us*, it's finally feeling like I'm just getting my footing solidly in place underneath me, like everything is starting to flow like it should, but I'm about to find out I'm standing on quicksand..." She takes a deep shaky breath.

"I can see why this would feel overwhelming, but you're *not* on quicksand!" He holds her jaw and looks at her. "Bri, not only do you have so many people in your corner, but Newhaven can also run itself eighty-five to ninety percent of the time! Five percent is management and the last percentages are appeals cases and let's face it, you have to be *bloody brilliant* there!"

She lightly laughs. "How would you know?!"

"*I know you*!" He confidently states and quickly kisses her before she can refute his statement. "Bri..." he rests their foreheads together, "David, Herst, and I are *your* greatest fans! You know I've been your fan since you told David off at our first Black-Tie Party together! But I first saw how bloody fantastic you were when you held your own in the stables! I was hooked! I think you'll be an amazing duchess, princess, and soon-to-be-queen!"

She scoffs. "*Be serious!*"

"*I AM*! Your intelligence and big heart are a great combination to do such real and lasting good for Newhaven *and* this country! You don't read the articles people write about you, the soon-to-be *American* Duchess, but *we* read the more reputable ones. You're becoming more and more popular! *Your* people *will be* beside themselves *when* you become 'The Queen!'"

"Back up! You said, '*princess*' before?!"

"Bri, we both know Herst wants you to be queen. The logical step from his position is to elevate your title as close to his as possible; preparing everyone for what he *will* do, but I can only speculate now."

Bri says more to herself, "Like a princess?"

"Like a princess *and* 'The Duchess.' Remember, a duchess typically outranks princess in the hierarchy. I don't know if Peter discussed it with Herst, but it had to have played a part in Peter and Carlotta's decision to retire. *Thus*, freeing up the titles to be given to you and David, in preparation for however Herst decides to elevate you," he smiles, "and, of course, whatever you'll allow." She wraps her arms around him and hugs him firmly.

"According to you, he'll do what he wants." Bri reluctantly says.

"Ah, but I stress *to a point*, Bri." Jack says. "He loves you and he wants *you* to be happy, as David and I do."

"*And I already am*!" She stresses and exhales a bit of frustration. "Which is part of why I feel like I might drown or suffocate in that quicksand; I don't want to fail any of you!"

Jack chuckles. "*Won't happen*! I *guarantee* it! In fact, I'll even do a friendly bet to prove I know you can do this, *and* you'll excel at it!"

Her jaw shakes and as she wipes her eyes of the tears about to fall. She's barely audible, "*How can you be so convinced of that?!*"

"Like I said, *I know you*!" He lovingly smiles. "*One*, you're a perfectionist in your work; *two*, you won't *let* yourself fail, you're a fighter!" He winks. "*Three*, there are *tons* of people in your corner willing to help; and *most* important, *number four*, I'm.never.wrong!" She lifts her eyebrow. "*About you*! I'm never wrong about you!"

"How do you know I won't sabotage this on purpose just to prove you wrong?" She tries to hide her smile, but she doesn't do it very well.

He points to her face saying, "That cheekiness right there, for one thing. Then refer back to my first two points: you're a perfectionist and you won't *let* yourself fail!" He wraps his arms around her and holds her firmly, kissing her so passionately, her knees get weak and he has to help hold her up. He gently pulls their lips apart and he watches her face, her eyes are slow to open.

"And..." she's slow to form a coherent sentence, "and what is it you want *if* you win?"

"Oh, I *will* win, Amore Mia!" He's so confident, he's a bit cocky.

"Careful...confidence on you is sexy, but cocky is bordering arrogance and it's unbecoming on *anyone*." She states. "Do you want me—."

"*Always*!" He grins. "When I win, you'll let *me* name our baby!" He has so much love in his eyes for her at that moment, she doesn't realize she's holding her breath.

When she has the sensation to breathe again, she clears her throat. "If you lose, there's nothing I want—."

"*I won't lose*, so you don't need to worry about that!" He looks intensely into her eyes asking, "Do we have a deal?"

"Do you have a name in mind already?!" She asks.

Jack laughs with excitement. "Not at all! That's what will be so fun!" He walks with her out of the office and towards the stairs.

"Promise not to name them Bessie or Norman? In America, Bessie is a common name for a milk cow and Norman's a name some people hear and think, 'psychotic killer!' Then there's names for killer toys and animals—."

"Hold on! How about," he takes her hand and begins to head towards the stairs, "we pick out names of ones you and I *both* like—."

"And you pick from those?" She finishes his sentence.

"Yes." He lightly laughs seeing the relief on her face. "You don't have to look so relieved!"

"Oh?" She raises her eyebrow. "What name comes to mind right away for a boy?"

"We're not having a boy." He knowingly smiles.

"How do you know?" She curiously asks.

"*Hoping.*" He grins.

She lightly laughs. "Alright then, a girl's name?"

"So, I *am* right!" He happily grins and she softly laughs, shaking her head. He replies, "Victoria. Alexandra. Isabella. Christina. Lydia. Maxima..."

"Okay, okay, okay. Those are all actually pretty good."

He smiles his signature smile. "Do we have a deal?" When he doesn't hear her respond, he stops at the bottom of the stairs and smiles.

"No one knows you're naming our child until it's all said and done?"

He pulls her close and whispers, "*It'll be our little secret for as long as you'd like! No one else ever has to know!*" He kisses her neck and hears her breath get shaky. He smiles against her skin. "*Do we have a deal,* Amore Mia?"

She takes her shoes off as he continues to kiss her neck, then she pulls back and takes her shirt off. She tosses it at him, then runs up the stairs saying, "Guess you're going to have to come find out!"

He tosses her shirt over his shoulder and takes his own shirt off, tossing it as he chases after her!

Jack props himself up on his arm next to her in bed. He looks at her with so much love, kissing her fingertips. She smiles adoringly at him. "I love you more than words can describe, Jack! You make me feel like I can do anything! Like I could *actually* fly!"

He holds her hand on his heart. "You know I like to enjoy life and stay positive, so I need you to take me seriously when I say something Americans might say is 'cheesy.'"

Bri smiles sweetly. "Okay."

"You're not just the 'love of my life,' BriaLynn, you make me whole because you were the missing piece of my puzzle!" He tells her. "I didn't know how big of a hole was in my heart with what happened in my life, before I met you. It says a lot about how wonderful Peter and Carlotta are because they were there for me, the whole family was *and is*! The more I'm with you, the more that previous time in my life with my father and my brother seems...I don't know..."

She gives a little smile. "Feels like a different lifetime?"

"Yes! That's exactly what it feels like! Even life when my mother was alive feels like a different lifetime as well!"

"That's what my life feels like prior to coming here the very first time! Then again, living this life seems so surreal to me!"

"How's that?" He teases, "Going from 'Firecracker' to 'Noble Firecracker,' and soon—."

"*Not quite*! But sort of..."

"Bri, *you're* surreal! An absolutely *amazing* woman who I'm proud to call my wife! Let come what may, Amore Mia, we make a *great* team! You make a great team with each of us, and the four of us make a brilliant team! Herst *AND* you will be incredible rulers of our fantastic country!" He looks at her with adoration.

"With yours and David's immense support! Besides, why do you sound so certain of it?! I've done absolutely *nothing* to prove I'd even be a good 'Royal Consort!'" She states.

"You most certainly have!" Jack replies. "First, and always foremost, David, Herst, and I, love and adore you! We know that people see how you genuinely care about others and that's *huge*!"

"That matters *how* exactly?" She asks. "A lot of people genuinely care about others. There are better people than me out there, those who devote their *entire lives* to helping others! I'm—."

"Bri! You're an anomaly when it comes to the Upper-Class Society!"

"Jack, I don't consider myself 'upper-class,'" she uses air quotes, "I just married into it." She sasses back.

He matches her sass, "Sorry to burst your bubble, *Duchess*, but marrying into it *automatically makes you one*!" He gives her a handsome grin and Bri scoffs. "With David and my money combined, makes you one of the richest *people* in the world, easily the richest woman in the world. When we factor Herst into this—."

"*Thank you* for that..." she interrupts, her sarcasm evident in her voice. "That's nauseating to think about and freaks me out! I don't want to combine money; I don't want to be on *any* list like that! You did, however, point out that the target on my back will get bigger and let's not even think about being queen and that bullseye!" She takes a deep breath. "Then again, maybe the only way to prevent that target from getting astronomical, means there's *no way* I should become queen!"

"OR it *could mean* criminals won't bother because there'll be a massive amount of security around you." He comments.

"Around *me*, yes. But lots of ransoms demands are made by kidnapping someone *close* to the target. That means you, David, all the Worthington's, and the Bradshaw's, not to mention Lawrence—." She has a horrified look, "*...the girls and our future kids!*"

245

Jack pulls her into a hug. "Security around them is already in place."

"The girls, too?! I told David they needed normal—."

"Bri, their protection is unseen; David was adamant about that! Originally, it was just following behind, watching who came and went into their house or school, keeping an eye on their friends and now boyfriends. Only now, some of their security blends in with the staff and parents."

"How come I didn't know about this?!" She's annoyed.

"McMasters came to David and me because he didn't want to alarm you and we didn't either. He thought as long as they didn't know about the security, then maybe we could do this—."

"But without me knowing about it?!" Bri snaps sitting up.

Jack slowly nods as he sees Bri's face is going from annoyance to anger. He exhales and lays back, running a hand through his hair. "These are your children! Of course you'd want to know everything that affects them, both directly and indirectly..." he sits up and looks at her with an apologetic face. "I'm sorry. We should've told you."

"*Someone* should've told me! *McMasters should've come to me first!* I would've been fine with indirect security measures; I would've even suggested someone could go undercover as a 'teacher's assistant' or 'teacher's aide' or *whatever!* Unfortunately, in this day in age, there's even security on school campuses! We could've used that to our advantage and done something through them." She inhales a deep breath, holds it a few seconds, and exhales. She softly says, "I just don't want them to lose friends or have special treatment because of all this. Being a teenager is hard enough to navigate and find out who your friends are *in normal circumstances!*"

"I get that. We *all* get that! I swear we did discuss all that!" He holds her neck and puts their foreheads together. "I love you, Amore Mia! *We* love you and the girls and just want to protect them!"

She exhales saying, "I know. Which is why I'm not furious." She looks into his eyes. "I love you, too, Amore Mio!" He kisses her firmly as he tangles a hand in her hair at the back of her head.

CHAPTER 25

Imperfectly Perfect Relaxing Afternoon

Later that afternoon, Peter, Carlotta, James, Jack, and Bri, are in The Sitting Room of The Manor and Jack is telling Bri the hilarious story where he, David, Herst, and a bunch of friends thoroughly planned out an elaborate prank on their meanest professor.

"This professor's car was a convertible and his 'pride and joy.' So much so, he always wore slippers when he was in it, as well as gloves, a hat, and goggles whenever he drove it. He wiped it down every single time he parked it; if it was raining, he'd cover it." Jack explains. "We knew if we were going to really get him, we had to play a prank with his car, but we weren't heartless; we didn't want to use his actual car. Besides, we weren't looking to break any *major* laws either. It took us a long time to find the perfect salvaged car where the back half of the frame was in really good, if not pristine, condition."

"The back half?" Bri asks.

"When we set up this prank up, we needed him without his car, and we happened to know this professor's car was going to be serviced very soon. We also knew once that appointment happened, this prank had to be set up fast and luckily there were *a lot of chaps* who hated this professor, even the guys at the salvage yard!"

Bri's mouth drops, then she notes with a bit of disbelief, "*If Lawrence's parents would've found out...*"

"The ones in this room, in addition to the actual prank, are the only ones who know he was involved. All of us protected him and made sure he was innocent!" Jack tells her. Then he continues, "When this professor saw 'his car' that morning, the shocked look on his face was *bloody fantastic!* From inside his classroom, it looked as if *a* car smashed through his wall from the outside because of the huge pile of bricks surrounding a smashed front third of the unrecognizable car. When he ran to his window to get a better look at the smashed car through the wall of his classroom, his mouth slowly dropped open as it registers what he thinks is *his* precious car!"

Bri is laughing. "How did you manage all that? *And at school!*"

"With the help of the salvage yard, but the rest of that answer, well, we all swore to take to our graves!"

"Ha-ha! Fair enough. How angry was this guy?" She asks.

Jack is laughing so hard, his cheeks hurt and he is in tears! He's holding his stomach, which also hurts and he's out of breath as he tries to say, "Once it registered that it was 'his car,' he screamed so loud and high-pitched, he sounded like a little girl! He climbed out the window and looked at this car from various directions, screaming even more!"

David came home and heard them all laughing hysterically and followed the laughing to where they all were. "What's so funny?" He leans down, holding his tie against his chest, to kiss Bri, before taking a seat next to her.

"Hi, Handsome!" She has been laughing, but he sees some sparkles in her eyes for him.

Jack explains, "I was regaling our girl and the rest of the family about the time we pranked Professor Cooper!" He gets David caught up.

David is now laughing and adds, "We started to worry he'd drop dead of a heart attack or an aneurysm right then and there!"

"So how did he find out it was all a prank?!" Bri asks, wiping her eyes.

"That was a bonus we never intended!" David laughs.

"He's handed a message from the mechanic that the repairs were finished and it also had the amount of his bill!" Jack tells them and Bri covers her mouth in surprise.

David says, "He stomps down the hall and calls the mechanic. He's so livid, we could hear him yelling and demanding to know how his car was stolen?! That it was smashed *through* the wall of the school and he was going to take them to court for the damages and full value of the car!"

"Oh no," Bri gasps, "those poor mechanics!"

Jack slightly nods. "Well, whatever they said had the professor flying out of the school, running all the way to this shop, which was a good distance away!"

"We knew heads would roll if he ever found out who did it, so we swore ourselves to secrecy!" David smirks.

"Not even to take credit for such a *brilliant* prank?!" She asks.

"*No way*! Otherwise, he would've made sure we had his class the following term just to torment us and get even!" David laughs.

Carlotta scoffs, hiding a smile. "Oh, you two *really*! Professor Cooper wasn't as *beastly* as students made him out to be!"

Peter teases her, "*Says his favorite student*!"

"Wait." Bri asks, "If you were the favorite, how did Jack and David get on his bad—," she looks at them, then shakes her head and giggles, "never mind...your mother's a lady and Professor Cooper *a proper gentleman*." She says the last part with their accent.

Jack and David reminisce about some other things, before Peter, Carlotta, and James leave for various reasons. Jack's phone rings and he walks away to take the call. Bri turns and smiles lovingly at David.

He leans back and over to her. "I could watch you smile at me like that all day." He caresses her cheek.

"Awe, you sweet talker..." She pulls him close with a hand on his jaw and kisses him.

He smiles. "You've been absolutely wonderful through all this."

"Well, it's only fair when you consider the thousands of phone calls and texts each week from me just getting Newhaven Wool and Textiles started! Now it's down to what? Fifty?" She smiles and winks.

"Ah no, Love, I don't think of it like that! I love you and I always have a better day just talking to you, even if it can only be by text. Besides, it's not *quite that much*..." He grins, she playfully slaps his thigh. He tells her, "You do text me more than you call, but I'm like you, I prefer texts, although I love hearing your voice when I'm able to." He kisses her with such love and hugs her close.

"*I* could kiss you like that *all day*!" She sweetly smiles. He chuckles and kisses her once more.

"Now, there *is* some order of business I'd like to discuss with you, Mrs. Worthington." He watches her because she beams when he calls her that.

She purses her lips with a smile. "Anything, *Mister* Worthington!"

"With all your land—."

"*Our land*! We're a family!"

He chuckles. "We *could* have something built if you'd like to move into something new and design something for *our whole family*."

Bri is confused. "Wait." She shakes her head a little as she turns to face him more. "You *love* The Manor—." He goes to say something, but she stops him. "Please, let me finish." She smiles with a loving smile; he can't help but smile back at her the same way and nod. She puts her hand to her chest. "I love The Manor, too, and I've grown to think of it as *our* home. I don't want anywhere else to be called *our home*!" He's touched by that and she tells him, "If we ever had to leave, I'd be heartbroken! This is not only our first home, but we met in the stables, we had a couple of 'rows' here and our walls finally came down out in the gardens. *We fell in-love here*!" She stresses. "I wouldn't *and couldn't* leave here! Besides, wouldn't it be a 'job requirement' of sorts for 'The Duke and Duchess' to reside *here* at 'The Worthington Manor' since 'The Newhaven Manor' is otherwise occupied?"

"You're making a dream of mine come true." He begins to explain. "Ava wanted to live in the townhouse in Edinburgh and be in the high society papers. It began to frustrate me because she wasn't interested in the work being 'The Duchess of Newhaven' required."

"I'm starting to think that's what the socialites from this generation think, that having a significant title is just that, a title, lots of money and the press on the side!" Bri adds.

He agrees. "My dream of a partner with the woman I love faded away, and virtually died by the time I was divorcing Ava. It surprised me when that dream started to creep back in right around the time I would see you in the hotel lobby that day before we actually met. After the stables, that dream began to have you in it, which scared me and I fought it, yet I just couldn't run away from you either."

Bri smiles and cups his cheek. "David, I'm so unbelievably sorry that woman was *ever* in your life! I truly mean it when I say this to you: I'm happy and grateful *I* get to love you!"

"Me, too, *Macushla!*" He rests his forehead to hers. "Let me take you to dinner before it gets more difficult to do so on a whim in the future."

"I'd love that!" She smiles and he gives her a little more than a tap of a kiss.

When they get back from dinner, David and Bri stay outside and get into the backseat of his convertible he drove into town. McMasters bids them goodnight for the evening. Since buying the property next to The Estate, they are able to close the main road and put up a guard station down there; only residents, employees, and guests on their guest list can have access after 8:00 at night.

As they stare up at the countless stars, they're both snuggled together under a blanket. He sits angled in the backseat so she can lean back against his chest. They gaze up marveling at the infinite, the eternal vastness the starry sky brings with it.

He holds her close to keep them both warm. He whispers next to her ear, *"I love you, Macushla..."*

She slightly turns her head. "I love you, My Love!" He kisses her cheek while her hand cups his cheek.

After a while, David asks, "Shall we go inside, Mrs. Worthington?"

"I suppose..." She exhales. "I'd hate for us to catch a cold, *or worse*, be on life support *before* your parents actually have time to enjoy their retirement! *Your mother would pull the plug on us herself!*"

He snorts into a laugh replying, "Isn't that the truth!"

"Then again, we don't have your heir yet..." She notes. David chuckles. She sits up and turns to look at him. "What am I going to do with the handsome men in my life?!"

"Hopefully keep us around!" He replies.

"Hmmm..." she taps her finger on her chin, teasing him like she's thinking about it. "How about..." she holds his face, "forever?" He sits up to capture her lips and kisses her with such affection, she gets a lump in her throat.

"Good!" He says. "Because that's how long I plan on being with you! Only I'd tell you, 'You're *never* getting rid of me!'" They laugh, climbing out of the car. As they walk towards The Manor, he asks, "Are you ready for tomorrow evening?"

"No." Then she stops. She looks at him and asks, "I haven't had to do anything! It's weird, not even a dress!" They start walking again. "Is it a dress handed down?"

"No." He chuckles, but that's all he says.

"Um..." she sounds worried, "could you give me a bit more than that?"

"No." He holds the door open.

"David——." She's cut off from finishing that sentence with another kiss. She goes to pull apart, but he holds her firmly until she relaxes in his arms. He loosens his hold on her just a bit. "Sometimes *I hate it* when you do that!" She says mostly smiling, but there is a hint of annoyance.

"That's why I try to hold the kiss until you relax into my arms." He gives her a knowing smile. "Once you relax, your frustration with me usually does, too. Then we can move past it."

She runs her finger down his lips. "Here's another tip." He raises an eyebrow. "Your sexy smile!"

He halfway laughs, "*If only!*" He looks at her. "When you're frustrated, a kiss is the *only* way." He tugs her closer and kisses her again.

"Mmm...while I love kissing you, I still need you to say more about the dress." She insists as they walk in the front door.

"No." David says once again, handing the keys to his convertible to Robert to put the car into the garage.

Bri stops in her tracks. "Why?" She asks a question that leads to more than a 'yes' or 'no' answer.

David has a reluctant look. "Love, if you insist on this, I *will* tell you but I prefer we leave this in the category of 'trust me.' If it helps, Mother has been fussing over the details for you."

Bri studies him a minute and says, "I do love you, *Mister* Worthington, and adore you *immensely*, so I'll go with 'trust'...*for now*." She smirks, then takes his hand and they walk to their quarters; David lacing his fingers with hers. "Just don't let me down!" She teases.

"Have I yet?" He smirks.

She giggles. "Good point!"

"I love you, too, Bri." He stops her. "Thank you."

"For trusting you?" She asks, then she smiles wide. "*Always!*"

"*That* and thank you for being *my* partner in this and taking on being 'The Duchess of Newhaven' and well, taking on running Newhaven." He taps a kiss to her lips. "Since marrying you, running The Duchy has seemed less like an obligation to a title and more like a partnership."

"It didn't seem *completely* official today when we signed some forms and 'King Lawrence' officiated the noble coronation in front of Newhaven's Parliament." She notes. "Then again, maybe it's because he had to turn around and leave Kingsbury right after?"

"Maybe with The Midnight Ball and the unveiling of the updated 'Worthington Family's Coat of Arms,' things will feel more official for you."

"Maybe..." She shrugs. She doesn't see how a coat of arms would help, but she'll keep an open mind. She tells him, "That partnership you mentioned is the reason for my hesitation for saying 'yes' to being queen. I've partnered with you and Jack, but partnering with 'King Lawrence' is on a *much bigger scale* and the amount of time I have on any given day *won't increase*...I don't want to let any of you down and I feel that's where all this could be headed. I told Jack that I feel like at any moment I'm going to find myself standing on quicksand."

"Oh, Macushla." He holds the back of her jaw. "Time increases when you have Abby and Amy donating their schedules to help you accomplish the tasks at hand, plus Gen will be continuing in her duties."

They step inside their quarters and she faces him with an appreciative smile. "I do appreciate you believing in me, which will help me come around." She looks into his dark blue eyes with a playful look. He knows what she's thinking, and he has his own playful look spreading across his face. He scoops her up and she giggles saying, "To the bedroom, *Mister* Worthington!"

Hearing her laugh always makes him feel really good...

CHAPTER 26
Imperfectly Perfect Noble Preparation

It's Saturday and The Coronation Ball is that evening. They made everything official at noon yesterday, with the small noble coronation officiated by King Lawrence. Not too many people were invited to attend the noble coronation held in front of Newhaven's Parliament; it would have been too crowded. Tonight, everyone celebrates the new Duke and Duchess of Newhaven.

Bri has been using the same designers for her wedding dresses for other dresses she has needed over the last year or so. Carlotta reached out to the designer who made Bri's reception dress to make Bri's coronation gown. Carlotta has been working with them on the details of the dress because there are specifications to tradition she needs to ensure are there; plus, adhere to specifications since Bri is a 'Direct Bloodline.'

Bri's dress for the coronation was the required navy-blue color with the colors of The Worthington's new tartan, which had been traditionally updated with Bri's ancestral tartan colors around the time she and David were married. The designer used this updated tartan as a loose belt around her waist, while The Worthington Family, particularly the men, all wear kilts made of the new tartan. Carlotta and the designer were fussing around with her dress once more to make sure all is still perfect for tonight's celebration.

 They help Bri into the dress and she steps in front of the full-length mirror. She takes the time to really look at the dress because yesterday there wasn't a mirror for her to stand in front of to see it on herself. The dark navy-blue dress has a V-neck, that's fitted from her shoulders, down over her hips, then it's free flowing from her mid-thigh to the floor. There is a cape attached to the hem at her shoulders and edged with a gold color. The tartan sash is tied around her waist and has a loose knot above her left hip. The two ends hang down the length of the dress, with a coat of arms brooch to be pinned to the knot itself. Bri had a good look at it all for the first time, right before Carlotta pins the brooch directly to the knot again.

 'The Royal Coat of Arms Pin' is made with a thin layer of sapphires and rubies as the quadrant background colors, with silver and gold symbols on a gold shield. In the top left section, the lion has a very tiny emerald for an eye. There is a griffin in the upper-right, a winged unicorn in the lower-left, and the Heathherst 'H' in the

lower right. Around the edge of the gold shield is a stretched-out Triquetra and a gold king's crown on top.

Carlotta gives her a loving smile when she sees Bri staring at the brooch before she pins it on the knot on her tartan belt. "Even though you're The Duchess of Newhaven and would have a different pin, Lawrence is lining himself up with you because he wants your becoming 'The Royal Consort,' *to pave the way to becoming 'The Queen.'* The symbols you use, he wants to keep using them with your future titles. Eventually, *if* you choose to become queen, he'll combine your symbolism with The Monarchy's symbolism. If you had a separate coat of arms, then he would combine yours with his, but we didn't do that yet because David and Jack said you would want to keep using the family's coat of arms."

"They would be right!" She replies. "If it was a necessary part of tradition, I would've had a separate one, but I didn't *need* one." She smiles, then asks, "What's all involved for updating or changing a coat of arms?"

"Some countries have it where not only does the family have a coat of arms, like 'The Worthington Family Coat of Arms,' but each son has their own coat of arms that they base off the family's and individualize it. The eldest son being heir, would inherit his father's personal one to use and all the sons may use their mother's family's coat of arms if they want. They can get messy with all kinds of symbols, plus all the decorations around them. Here in The United Kingdom of Provinces, prominent families keep an updated coat of arms and all family members use it with a simple monogram, usually on a very small shield at the bottom of the coat of arms, to differentiate between family members themselves."

"Makes sense." Bri inserts. "It's official when someone receives correspondence, but they can know specifically *who* it's from."

Carlotta agrees and continues. "A family's coat of arms doesn't really change much and ours hasn't for many generations because The Worthington's line above all noble families who aren't royal. Any coat of arms in noble families would only be changed to add certain symbolism that would show the elevation to their family's status."

Carlotta had The Worthington Family Coat of Arms freshened up, taking out the dated filigree around it, along with the other decorative additions around the shield. She has also researched the symbolism from the various ancestral coats of arms of Bri's ancestry.

"With all of your ancestral coats of arms, there was *a lot* of symbolism that had been used to designate royalty. While the Worthington's haven't held a royal title in quite some time, it's also been awhile since there's been a 'Direct Bloodline.' Here you are, a 'Direct Bloodline' *and* you'll have a royal title." She smiles with a mother's love. Carlotta puts her fingertips under Bri's chin. "I know it can sound heartless when we talk of things like this, but I want you to know, I couldn't love you or enjoy you more for a daughter than I already do!" She pulls her into a hug, saying, "*You blessed girl!* I love you, Sweetie!"

"Oh, Carlotta! I love you, too! Your genuine motives were clear when you were working to set me up with David the weekend we all met. You *certainly* didn't know the full extent of my genealogy then!"

"I just want my children to be happy and all of them *finally* are now that James has found love with Amy!" She softly laughs, "I will even have two more sons with Lawrence and Seth, as well as three more daughters with Amy, Abby, and Genevieve. You've blessed our family in more ways than any of us could've ever imagined!"

"James and Amy are wonderful and it does my heart good to see them both happy and more so with each other!" Bri sits and touches up her makeup. "The credit goes to you and Peter." Bri looks at Carlotta in the mirror. "You took Jack in when nobody *wanted* him and made sure he knew you two *did* want him *and love him* as your son! You made Lawrence feel loved and free to be himself when he was able to spend time with all of you!" She stands up. "You may not think you did much, but those two, along with David and James, wouldn't be half the men they are without you and Peter!"

"You give *me* too much credit, especially with Lawrence." She says.

"*No, I don't!*" Bri lovingly expresses. "One thing I was told in my coma is the 'pure love of a true mother' is a powerful thing! It's a powerful gift to give someone like Jack! You're the very definition of a 'true mother!'" She states. "*Take Lawrence!* The King, the man he is, has never forgotten those times he has spent with your family and he is grateful to be permanently part of it all now! I can only pray to be half the mother you and Maggie are!"

Carlotta dries her eyes. "I always prayed for more children, and when Jack came along Peter and I knew we needed him in our family just as much as he needed us! If we couldn't adopt him, then we did everything we could to make sure he stayed a part of *our* family!"

Bri smiles through her tears. "You did an amazing job because he knows that *and* feels it!"

Carlotta smiles back. "When Lawrence would be with us, I figured maybe we could help plant a seed or few so he wouldn't grow up to be the mean and vicious ruler they were grooming him to be." She smiles at the memories. "He never wanted to leave."

"*Can you blame him*?!" Bri giggles and stands up. "He found unconditional love and acceptance with two of the most amazing and wonderful parents any kid would be lucky to call their parents!" They both hug once more, then dry their eyes. Bri changes the subject back to something less emotional. "What kinds of things did you see on my ancestors' coats of arms?"

"What you would expect with lions, crowns, suns, flowers. Then dragons, griffins, leopards, unicorns, and of course there's fleur-de-lis, columns, lightning bolts, the infinity symbol...*Oh*! And considering your logo for your 'New Beginnings Foundation,' I notice there was a beehive with bees!"

"Really?!" Bri's surprised. "It's not like they're ferocious looking like griffins or dragons?!"

"No, but as you know they represent hard work, industry, productivity, duty, diligence, prosperity, much like this family," she touches Bri's upper arm, "*much like you*!"

"I did pick the bee for the hard work that someone has to give to come out of the muck and mire of hard times, to bloom in their life like a lotus flower on a murky pond...adding their unique beauty to the pond water of the world!" Bri explains.

Carlotta tells her, "Your life, this story, is *uniquely yours*. You're a *beautiful person* in a world that can be dark and bleak." She gives her a smile and squeezes Bri's hand.

There's a light knock on the dressing room door. Carlotta answers it and finds Lawrence and Genevieve. She greets them with big hugs before stepping out of the room.

"Genevieve!" Bri happily says, hugging her.

Genevieve sets a box on the vanity. When she turns back to Bri, she sees Bri smiling so lovingly at Lawrence; she smiles at the two of them looking into each other's eyes, it's obvious they're in-love.

"Bri, as you know, Seth and I were in school together and are, what do Americans call it? 'Something Sweethearts?'"

Bri smiles. "'High School Sweethearts.'"

"Yes! When our parents arranged the marriage with Lawrence, I was devastated. Oh, not because—."

"You were in-love with Seth and the unfairness of the arranged marriage involved *all three of you!*" Bri gives her a kind smile.

Gen nods. "Because we were *forced* into the marriage, it wouldn't work like yours does with David and Jack, and soon Lawrence."

"I get that, too! David was always stressing it had to be for love *and* it had to be my choice." She smiles at Lawrence who is nodding in agreement. "But you're it, Ace!" She winks at him and he caresses her cheek.

Gen tells her, "Lawrence has been so wonderful and encouraging with my relationship with Seth." She smiles at him. "He's such a wonderful man who deserves to love and *be* loved by someone special," she looks at Bri, "and I'm so happy and excited he has found it!" She walks over to the vanity where she set a box down. "Bri, you and I are very distant cousins!"

"Really?!" Bri's surprised.

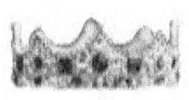 "We're connected together in our ancestry through The Duchy of Somershire." She opens the box she brought says, "This is *The Somershire Gold & Sapphire Crown.*" She lifts it out of the box and shows Bri.

"This is beautiful!" Bri says as she looks closer at it.

Gen explains, "Carlotta hires great genealogists and the ones at The Palace just did their diligence in verifying its authentication. Anyway, when they were verifying everything, they made this interesting discovery! While the lands and titles are still being passed down in Somershire, this secondary crown ended up with The Crown Jewels. It was never passed along with its titles and lands that are still active today. It was to be passed down as a gift from a mother to her daughter, the youngest daughter if there was more than one, until one daughter married into the royal family however long ago. What's fascinating is that as they traced the lineage from that daughter, and following the tradition, *it could've led to you*!"

Bri is confused. "*What*?! That's incredible!" Bri hands the crown back to Gen. "Unfortunately, I think the crown would've been sold before it ever got to me. I have some greedy not-too-distant family members that would've saw dollar signs over tradition."

Lawrence steps into the conversation. "Well, if we apply the saying you like, 'everything happens for a reason,' then having it kept with the crown jewels was so that it *could* be given to you!" He cups her cheek. "The one who will protect the tradition." She smiles sweetly and nods.

 "I know you're wearing The Newhaven Tiara and Necklace Set, but I thought maybe Amy would like to wear a crown for the occasion, in honor of you, since she's joining the family very soon." Gen laughs. "Carlotta already has small tiaras on Emmie and Natty."

Bri replies. "I think Amy should wear this, but I don't have time to—."

Gen happily says, "I'll take care of it! If I do it in front of the press, no one will question protocol with The Queen!" She winks with her grin.

"I'm grateful to have a connection to you!" She hugs Gen. "Thank you!"

"I'm going to go and let you two have a minute." She says to them as she walks out.

Lawrence pulls out a gold bracelet from his pocket and shows it to Bri. She takes it, looks it over, and sees it's a beautiful, intricate pattern of gold hearts with scrollwork and loops that interlink one heart to the next. There are tiny, shaved diamonds pieces scattered to give the gold a sparkly look.

Lawrence can't read her face. "Do you like it?"

"I *love* it! You made it for me and that makes it priceless!" She replies.

Bri says, "This is something I could wear for a special occasion, or just casually; it's perfect!" She taps a lingering kiss to his lips, then puts it on.

Bri has such an adoring look on her face for him, he feels it into his very core. Lawrence isn't just captivated by her beauty and genuineness, but how deeply she loves and appreciates things, even the seemingly insignificant.

He smiles adoringly at her. "One last gift..." Lawrence pulls out a little flat velvet box and opens it, revealing a small, beautiful gold brooch. Bri sees the significance of this gift; the symbolism Carlotta was talking to her about.

"I've been working on this 'Royal Consort' brooch. It looks just like the one passed from consort to consort, but I've added personal touches to this one to make it just yours." He gives her a little nervous smile.

 It has two solid gold lions holding up a gold circle shield, a gold crown on top, a heraldic lion on its own shield on the bottom of the main shield, at the very bottom there's the name 'Heathherst' carved on a gold ribbon. Inside the gold circle shield is a sapphire-blue triquetra outline with a heart outline going through each loop; a monogram of a ruby-red 'L' and a ruby-red 'B,' with a heart as part of the B and it sits behind the letter 'L.'

"This is used by 'The King' to officially show 'The King's Court' who he intends to make his 'Royal Consort.'"

"Lawrence, this is beautiful! I love the monogram on top the Triquetra heart!" Bri says.

"Bri," he sits her down and kneels in front of her, "this makes it official in the eyes of The King's Court. Once you put this on, the paperwork signing is only a formality."

She looks at him with a bit of a perplexed look. "Lawrence, I thought we established we were in-love with each other already, and this was official up in The Clock Tower?" She holds up her right hand and the ring he gave her.

"This," he points to the ring, "was for you and me." Lawrence has a little teary smile. "I guess this just feels too good to be true. If you backed out now, it'd be more private; however, this," he gestures the brooch, "would be *way more public*."

"I'm sorry life has been so awful for you for way too long." She holds his cheek with her left hand and holds up her right ring finger again. "This means you are now, and forever will be, *stuck with me!*" He lightly chuckles as he pulls her into a firm kiss. She pulls back just enough to look him in the eyes. "I love you, Lawrence!" She kisses him once more before she sits up, lost in thought...

He pulls her chin to him. "What?"

"There's just a part of your life I haven't really been a part of and I would like to observe you at The Palace being 'The King' before we're official."

He scoffs. "I don't want you to! That's *not* my best side." Lawrence never wants her to be there while his mother is hovering. "I tend to do what Mother wants and act like she wants 'The King' to act, it's just all so 'second nature' at this point to keep her satisfied and reduce the fallout. If I take the brunt of it, Seth and Abby will be alright; she's never really bothered with Gen that I know of, probably because Gen's never really tried to establish herself as '*The Queen.*' As far as Mother is concerned, Gen hasn't challenged her." He gives her a sweet smile. "I want you to be by my side *and rule with me*, but I'm not sure how to get rid of Mother and have her think it was her idea."

"Um...I'm not sure about that either, but an idea or solution may come later." Bri says. "Until then, *My King*, just trust I love you!" He nods and kisses her deeply. The passion is getting intense between them, so she pulls back. "Wow!" She puts her fingertips on her lips. "This is getting too...WOW!" She can't even finish her thought.

He smirks. "Good thing we'll be in a room full of people!"

Bri laughs a little and then there is a knock at the door. "That must be David and Jack."

Lawrence stands up. "That means we need to head down to the ball. I'll answer the door while you put this on?" He places the brooch in her hand.

 She smiles and agrees. He answers the door and Bri looks closer and sees how the 'L' and 'B' are obvious, but she sees a 'D' in the top loop of the 'B' and an upside down 'J' forms using the stem, or the spine, of the 'L' and 'B.' She smiles and attaches the pin to the front of her right shoulder, since her other brooch is on the knot of the tartan on her left hip.

"Jack! David!" Lawrence says, moving aside for them to come into the room.

All three men have on kilt tuxedos for the evening. David and Jack in the same family tartan matching the tartan around her waist, but what surprises Bri is she didn't notice before that Lawrence matches, too.

He sees her looking at that. "To honor the woman I love, and two of my fine brothers!"

David walks over to Bri with an adoring look. "There are never any words to describe your exquisite beauty, Love!" He kisses her cheek with so much love, Bri smiles as she fights back the tears and lump in her throat. He smiles at her then sees the crown pin and points to it saying, "This is fantastic!"

Lawrence tells them, "There's the 'L' and 'B,' but if you look closely, there's a 'D' and a 'J' in the monogram as well." David and Jack both look and smile.

Jack says, "*That's brilliant*, Herst!" David agrees.

Jack holds her arms out to take her in. "Wow, Gorgeous!" He looks her up and down. "You...look...*ravishing*!" He kisses her hand.

Bri tells them, "Well, you three look *incredibly* handsome!"

The three look at each other with Jack asking, "We do, don't we brothers!"

Bri laughs and holds up her phone for a picture; they stand together and smile for her. Then they take ones of her with each of them.

She grabs her clutch. "Okay you three, let's get to the ball before they send out a search party!"

David holds his hand out for her to take and Jack opens the door for all of them. David can feel her shaking and assures her, "It's going to be great! You'll see!" She gives David a nervous smile, then looks to Jack and Lawrence who agree.

In a monotoned voice she tells them, "I guess this is the moment of truth...people will be giving their opinions for tomorrow's papers."

"No, Love. Don't refer to the media vultures as 'people.'" Bri tries to stifle the urge to crack up laughing; it's difficult, but she manages to laugh quietly. Exactly what David wanted to do; make her smile.

"Your smile infinitely multiplies your beauty!" Jack says.

The main doors to The Ballroom are closed and they wait patiently for the announcement of the three of them. Lawrence is talking with Gen, then the doors open for King Lawrence and Queen Genevieve. They go into The Grand Ballroom before David and Bri so The Duke and Duchess of Newhaven can officially be presented to The King and The Queen.

Bri asks, "Does this crown pin really tell everyone Lawrence chose me as his 'Royal Consort.'"

Jack answers, "Yes. It definitely means he's officially chosen you, but the decision is *still* yours...."

"*Always will be*!" David adds.

Bri studies him and lifts her eyebrow. "But it's frowned upon, right."

David answers, "Technically, if 'The King' chose someone, that's final. Herst wouldn't want to force someone, although he does have the power to do so. However, your dual citizenship hinders that outcome, which is why The Queen Mother backed down. That's why there was this..." He holds up her right hand with her pink diamond heart ring. "He wanted the real deal!" Bri softly smiles at the ring as the memory of that night, up in The Clock Tower, when Lawrence gave it to her. She looks at David who winks at her with his beautiful smile.

Jack whispers to her, "*Relax! You're amazing! You've got this and we've got you!*" David agrees and Bri takes a deep breath.

Bri sees the spirit of a beautiful woman. It's one of a few spirits, or ghosts, she has seen, but never spoken with. The woman smiles sweetly at Bri, only, before Bri can do or say anything, the room on the other side of the doors goes quiet and the three need to get into position. Bri glances back over and the woman's spirit is gone. One day, she'll hopefully be able to talk to these spirits and ghosts, hear their stories and maybe help them move on.

CHAPTER 27

Imperfectly Perfect Noble Coronation Ball

When the doors open, they hear someone speak and Bri's heart is pounding so loudly in her ears, she can't hear anything. Bri has her arm wrapped around David's arm, but she holds Jack's hand with her other hand; both men squeeze a little to show their support, before Jack let's go and they begin to walk through the open doorway.

Bri is surprised by all the cheers and applause. They walk into the ballroom and acknowledge people by smiling and nodding. When her crown pin is noticed, the whispering chatter begins.

The three of them walk to King Lawrence and Queen Genevieve. They stand up as the three come up to the stage, then bow and curtsy to Their Majesties who acknowledge them. The Queen genuinely smiles at them, as The King addresses the room full of people.

> "Good evening, Ladies and Gentlemen. On behalf of The Royal Family and The Worthington Family, thank you all for coming. Queen Genevieve and I are in full support of the new Duke and Duchess of Newhaven, David and BriaLynn Worthington." He gestures to, "Peter and Carlotta Worthington have fulfilled these roles with honor and dignity, and we give them our deepest gratitude for all they've accomplished in their years of service to Newhaven and The Crown."

Peter bows and shakes The King's hand he is offering to him and says, "Thank you, Your Majesty. The honor was ours." Lawrence steps over as Carlotta curtsies and *he* kisses *her* on the cheek.

 "As many of you know, Duchess BriaLynn, is a 'Direct Bloodline' with ancestral connections to many of the European monarchies that *have* existed and to ones that still do exist. The Worthington Family Coat of Arms has been in the process of being updated over the past year to reflect the marriage of The Heir of Newhaven to a 'Direct Bloodline.'" He looks at David, Jack, James, Carlotta, and Peter. "I hope you don't mind, but in the spirit of Bri accepting my proposal to become my 'Royal Consort,'" there's excited

cheering and applause, Lawrence winks at Bri, "I have added a couple things." He gestures to the unveiling. "In upper-left square

there's a lion passant with a scepter on top of the shield with a rampant lion for their 'special badge of honor' for their family's continued service to The Crown. In the upper right, The Newhaven Government Seal is above the symbol for Newhaven Heirloom Wool & Textiles. I had a chevron added with The Newhaven Government Seal for their exemplary service."

While it is seen on various coats of arms in the UK, a chevron is something only The King can bestow upon it, whether an updated coat of arms keeps it, or other royal symbolism, it's still up to The King. There's a couple of lions on the coat of arms not only for the bravery and magnanimity of The Worthington Family, but for the royal connection they once again have with a 'Direct Bloodline' in their family.

He explains, "For the new Duchess and 'Direct Bloodline,' they added the bee above The Worthington Estate shield as a tribute to her and the work she's already done, and continues to do, within the government, *along* with Newhaven Heirloom Wool & Textiles."

There's applause for Bri, which Lawrence patiently waits for it to subside before continuing.

"A Pegasus holds up the shield with the royal unicorn. The unicorn represents virtue and strength with a crown around its neck to show their noble duty to The Crown. The Pegasus symbolizes inspiration and faith, which is something our new Duchess holds near and dear to her heart." He looks lovingly at Bri. He addresses the guests again. "There is an eagle with its head bowed at the top of a flagpole for the brave American who's taken on her duties superbly."

Peter and Carlotta thank him before they step forward to look at the coat of arms more closely. Followed by David, Bri, Jack, James, and Amy. A few minutes later, they step down and back into the places they were, except Bri. He takes her hand and tucks her arm under his.

Lawrence continues to speak to the guests. "The Duchess didn't want a separate coat of arms, so I hope she forgives me when I tell her that I enlisted the help of The Duke and Lord Carlisle to come up with a shield that represents The Duchess." He explains. "We came up with this one..." He gestures to the next shield that is revealed. "Keep in mind we're still working on it." She sweetly smiles. "We tried to keep it similar to The Worthington's, but at the  bottom we put our monogram of the Triquetra with a heart through its loops." He looks out to the guests, "This monogram was carefully crafted to not only have hers and my initials, the 'L' and a 'B,' but a closer look and you'll see a 'D' and a 'J' in the calligraphy, too." He kisses the back of her hand he is holding, then says to her, "A symbol of *her* unique life story."

She smiles adoringly. "*Our* unique *love* story."

He cups her cheek with his free hand and smiles back just as adoringly. "*And I do love you, My Darling.*" There are 'aws' and more excitement from the guests. He turns and addresses the guests once again.

"Changes are going to be made to The Royal Coat of Arms in preparation for The Duchess becoming The Royal Consort, one of them is to add this Triquetra," he points to their monogrammed Triquetra heart, "because our families will forever be linked together, through Duchess Bri. This symbolism Bri loves because it represents: friendship, integrity, and loyalty; and held together with love represented by the heart going through each section of the Triquetra." He smiles at her for a moment. "Symbolism that if you haven't seen it yet, you'll hopefully soon see this amazing woman represents all of them!"

He looks at Bri. "The last symbol is the most obvious. The phoenix. I think this is a great representation of you, along with the Triquetra heart."

"It's *wonderful*, L—er, *Your Majesty*." She says. He takes the hand he holds and kisses the back of it again. Bri looks at it again saying, "A phoenix...I think of a rebirth, a new life I *never* expected," she looks at David and Jack, then back at Lawrence, "creating our family within an amazing family!" She gestures Peter, Carlotta, James, and Amy, then she looks at Lawrence with love, "And it keeps giving me the unexpected." She kisses his cheek, holding his other cheek, and hugs him...they hear awes and light claps of approval. She looks at the two coats of arms closely for another couple minutes.

"What do you think?" He asks.

"I think these are wonderful, Ace!" She looks at him and grins, "But you know I'm okay with simply the monogrammed Triquetra heart, right?" She winks and taps a kiss to his lips before she and Lawrence walk back over and she steps down to David and Jack. She hugs them both, thanking them for their input in her coat of arms.

"Now, Duchess, I'll let Lord Carlisle and The Duke explain how combining shields works. For now, I say, let the celebration of the new Duke and Duchess of Newhaven *commence!*"

Everyone claps and cheers as they spread out around the room and some gather around the dance floor. David takes Bri to the dance floor where they dance a very formal waltz steps but, about three-fourths of the way through the dance, David hugs her close with one arm around her waist and he tucks their hands under his chin. He lightly kisses near her ear, with smiles from some of the people watching.

David whispers in her ear, "*I told you they would love all of this, and more so, because of you!*"

She whispers back, "*Nothing is official until official opinions are out tomorrow.*"

She can barely hear David chuckle over the music, but she can feel his body move. He quietly says near her ear, "Oh, Love, you're about to see *how right I am!*" He twirls her and brings her back in close. He kisses her as the song winds down.

There is another slow song purposely played so David can put Bri's hand in Jack's hand. David pats his best friend's back in a partial hug, both genuinely happy and it was beautifully noticeable to people coming and going from the dance floor.

Jack guides Bri through their ballroom dance before he, too, brings her in close to him. She tells him how nervous she is about people's reactions. Jack replies, "The only bad thing they could say is you're the woman who has stolen *three* men's hearts."

"Pity..." she feigns disappointment, "here I thought they were *freely* given." She teases.

270

"Ooo..." He laughs. "*Touché*, Amore Mia!"

She lightly giggles. "I love you, Amore Mio!" She puts their foreheads together. "It's crazy, but I can't imagine life without any one of you *three!*" She lifts her head and studies his face. "David *is* right."

"He usually is." Jack grins. "What's he right about this time?"

"That I love you two so much, my heart overflows to have more than enough to give Lawrence." She gives him a loving smile.

Jack smiles just as lovingly at her. "He's also right that you're one in a million who could love us *individually* and *so* completely, *we* overflow in our love for you! You're everything to me, Bri! And that's the same with David *and* Herst!" She looks over to Lawrence, who is dancing with someone familiar, which she assumes is one of his 'party regular' girls. She looks back to Jack as he says, "I love you, Amore Mia!" He dips her as he kisses her with the last notes of the song playing.

Bri and Jack make their way to David. They are stopped by people telling them of their support and many people, along with the three familiar reporters from DC, see how much love there is between them.

"I had my reservations at first, but anyone with their eyes open can see the love and why this works!" Marie says. "It's beautiful!" Bri thanks her and hugs her.

Bri and David mingle together for some time. They pass through a cool breeze from outside and Bri asks, "Can we step out for a moment? We can stay right by the doors so people know we haven't left."

David smiles. "We can step out for a few minutes, Love. McMasters won't lead a search party without checking out here first." He winks, holding her hand as they walk outside.

They find a place that has a heater close by. "Not too close to it; I need to cool down." She says, fanning herself with her hand.

David feels her forehead and cheeks. "You do look and feel flushed, Love." She nods. He stands back up. "Let me go grab you some water."

She gives a little smile. "Thanks."

271

"I'll be right back!" He tells her and she watches him go back inside.

Bri overhears laughing and some women talking. She looks around and sees they're sitting next to a heater in the light pouring out the windows from the ballroom. She tries not to listen, but they're so loud, she can't help but hear the conversation.

She hears one of them ask, "So you're here with The King?"

A woman playfully corrects her, "The King is here with The Queen." The ladies laugh a little. "I've traveled to so many various parties and engagements lately, I feel like I'm living out of my suitcases."

The woman has light-brown hair with blond highlights and is wearing a shimmering dark green velvet dress. She was extremely beautiful and in much better taste than other women Bri has witnessed gossiping at these parties.

"Didn't he announce his choice for 'Royal Consort' this evening?" A different one asks.

"He did! But what's so odd with this American is she won't shag him until she is *actually* his royal consort." Her friends gasp.

One gasps, "Can she even do that?!"

"Is she crazy?!" A different friend asks.

The light-brown haired woman scoffs with confusion, "*Apparently.*"

"So, you're filling in until...?" The first friend wonders.

The second friend inserts, "'Filling-in' makes it sound like our Eleanor is second-rate."

"Eleanor, my apologies if that's how it sounds. I'm just confused and—."

"Oh, it's alright, *Luv*! I understand. I'm confused, too! I was hoping he'd pick me when I had his mother's support. Then this woman shows up, a 'Direct Bloodline' no less, and screws *everything* up. The Queen Mother isn't too happy with her either—."

"That is one woman you don't want to be on the bad side of!" Someone notes.

"No, you don't!" Eleanor agrees. "She thinks an heir is long overdue and she wants The King to have a baby already!" She tells them. "In fact, we've been tracking my ovulation and she told me I had to come because I'm prime for—." She stops her sentence when she sees David walking outside with two glasses of water.

The ladies watch him walk over and sit next to Bri. Bri acts as if she never overheard anything. The ladies at least had the decency to look horrified before they change the subject as they stand up and walk back inside.

David feels the tension and when they're alone, he quietly asks, "What was that about?"

Bri matter-of-factly answers, "'Eleanor' is the only name I caught, happens to be ovulating and The Queen Mother sent her *here* for Lawrence to knock up tonight."

David chokes on his water and wipes his mouth with a napkin. He follows Bri's gaze as she looks inside watching Lawrence talk with some dignitaries.

He is surprised. "She's here for that?!"

Bri turns to him, her face still expressionless, "I'm trying not to make too much of it. If her being here *is* his mother's doing, *I know* that's not a good thing!" She shrugs. "It is what it is, I guess...." She takes another drink of the water he brought her and she sees his annoyed expression. "David," she puts her hand on his knee, "I discussed this with him; however, I was clear I didn't want him to answer because he could regret either way he answered about discreetly seeing the ladies he already sees. I want him to be free and clear because I have you and Jack, *and trust me*, there have been times Lawrence and I really had to force ourselves to stop—."

"Because the hormones and feelings can't be shut off like a switch?" He knowingly smiles, talking about their experience the day before they got married.

"Right. I gave Jack the 'okay' for this, too, because he would've had to hold out longer while you and I were *finally* on our honeymoon."

David states, "He would've honored you and your relationship."

Bri agrees with his true statement. "Right." Bri stares back inside. "I think Lawrence would, too, but he's a man under that kingly handsomeness, not to mention the pressure he's under with his mother..." She takes a deep breath. "I just didn't want to know...but now that we're 'committed' to this, I would expect he would start 'tapering off' the closer we get, but maybe it's too much to ask? *However*, if he gets another woman pregnant, right or wrong, it'll feel like a betrayal!" She looks at him. "Take my mind off this." She stands and holds out her hand. He smiles taking her hand as he stands up. She goes to walk back inside, but he pulls her back into a kiss. She smiles against his lips, "You're off to a great start, Your Grace!" She giggles and he kisses her again. "Let's go in and enjoy more of this wonderful evening!"

"Anything you desire, *Your Grace!*" David kisses the back of her hand and they walk back inside.

"Oh no, My Love! It's 'Mrs. Worthington' to you and," she leans in close to his ear, "I *desire* you!" She winks with a grin.

He chuckles. "We can take care of those *desires* a little later, *Mrs. Worthington.*" He gives her a mischievous smile and she giggles.

All four of them mingle and dance with certain guests. Since her wedding reception, Bri isn't keen on dancing with anyone anymore just to be polite and David never really danced with many, but Jack follows suit. Lawrence was already limited, but his mother was still throwing beautiful women at him because she thinks he's failed again by not having an heir yet. She wants him to just take what she wants him to; *he is 'The King' after all!*

Lawrence dances closely with Bri and whispers next to her ear, "*The Midnight Ball can't come fast enough! The thoughts trying to go through my mind with you...*"

"Trust me, I'm having them about you, too!" Bri quietly says as she pulls back to look at him. "The thoughts that have gotten stronger since seeing you on the beach...*Wow...*" She whispers and adds, "*Then the blindfold kiss...*" She inhales and holds her breath, she feels his arm grip her waist a little tighter, she snaps out of it and clears her throat. "And now we need to think of something less..."

He whispers, "*Don't push them too deep, maybe we can revisit those right after The Midnight Ball...*"

She smiles. "Can't wait!" He hugs her a little tighter. She looks out into the crowd and happens to see Eleanor.

"Bri?" He pulls his head back to look at her when she doesn't respond. He sees her staring off. "What is it?" She looks at him and he watches her try to cover her concern with a smile as she shakes her head. "*Briii...*" He pleads with her. "We've gotten to know each other pretty well this last year and I think I can tell sometimes when something's troubling you." The music ends and Bri is relieved she can avoid the conversation. She starts to pull away, but he says, "*Oh, no!* You're not getting away that easily. We'll dance all night if we have to, until you tell——."

A woman interrupts, snaking an arm around Lawrence's arm. "He isn't all yours, *yet*, Dear. I want my dance, Baby..."

Bri slaps on a smile. "You're right!" Bri doesn't recall seeing her outside earlier at Eleanor's table. She wonders how many of these 'party regulars' Lawrence has? Then again, she doesn't want to know that answer.

Lawrence goes to step away but is held back by the woman's arms. Lawrence takes the woman's hands and tries to untangle himself with her. When he glances up, Bri had already slipped away. *Damnit.* He thinks to himself.

"Stacy. *Enough.*" He scolds her.

"*But——.*" She whispers, trying to get his attention by cupping his cheek. "*I was hoping we could have some fun tonight——.*"

"No. *We can't.*" He sternly states. He sees Stacy's face. "I'm sorry to be so blunt, but I just want one woman in my life *and in my bed.* I won't hurt her like that, *no matter what my mother may have told you!*"

He does walk her off the dance floor as the gentleman he is, then tasks Tristan with taking her to her room. He knows Tristan will report back to his mother and he smiles to himself at the thought of frustrating his mother. He goes to find Bri, but he isn't able to because of the people wanting to talk to him.

By the end of the night, when The King and The Queen go to retire for the evening, Bri is cordial. "Thank you so much for everything, Your Majesties!" They all hug and say 'goodnight.'

Lawrence steps her to the side. *"Please talk to me."*

"Lawrence, it's fine, *really*. I didn't know how many women show up to these things *for you*." She stresses, "I never wanted to know...Ugh! Then I overheard Eleanor and her friends a little bit ago—."

"Eleanor's here?!" He's genuinely surprised and it helps. "I didn't—I don't— I had no id—." She puts her hand on his mouth.

With a loving little smile she says, "Don't say anything else and it can *almost* go back to how it was, where I wouldn't know either way. Please..." she asks and stares into his eyes until he nods. She removes her hand, "Thank you." She kisses him firmly. "There *is* a side note," Bri leans in really close to whisper, *"apparently she and your mother have been tracking her ovulation and she's...well...ready."* He jerks back with a horrifying surprise. "I tell you this so you won't walk into a setup, but to caution you, Lawrence..." she takes a deep breath, "right or wrong, if you get her pregnant, I honestly don't know if I could be this calm...*and* I don't think I could do this, *any part of this*, with that kind of betrayal." She quietly stresses, "Someone else having your baby isn't part of *our* plans."

Lawrence cups her cheek with a loving look. *"Hear me* when I say this: I only want *you* as our child's mother, my children are your children. Period." Her eyes are teary. "Thank you for telling me about Eleanor, because she won't be stepping one toe in my room to even discuss that she and I are done! We'll have that discussion in the hall. I wouldn't put it past my mother to have *her* drug me..." He kisses her and hugs her tight.

She hugs him back and says next to his ear, "I love you, Ace!" He hears she has a lump in her throat.

He smiles and has so many wonderful emotions for her. "I.love.you! *No one else*, My Queen!" He kisses her fiercely, then he hugs her and whispers, *"I only want* your *babies!"* He feels her cheek move on his cheek as she smiles. She kisses him again before they say goodnight.

Lawrence, Genevieve, and Seth head upstairs while Bri, David, and Jack say goodnight to their guests. Lawrence has his 'dates,' but he's always known Eleanor has been collaborating with his mother. When Eleanor comes knocking on his door and knowing what he knows about her ovulating, *she's not coming in*!

"I'm not interested, Eleanor. I've been telling you that for some time as you follow me on business trips and various parties. You're wasting your time. Please, go home and stop following me. I don't want to put you on a list."

"What do you mean? We always have lots of fun together." She smiles as she bites her lower lip.

"We have had fun, in spite of you conspiring with my mother—." He starts to say.

"Wait. What?! How did—." She's surprised until she remembers Bri on the patio, but she doesn't have a chance to ask about her and second guesses that when he explains what he means.

"All this time, I knew my mother sent you!" He wants to spare her feelings a little. "It wasn't hard to enjoy spending time with you, Eleanor." That did make her feel a *little* better. He says, "But now I want Bri, and only Bri."

Eleanor glares. "You bloody ba—."

She goes to slap him and he catches her wrist. "Stop right there!" She sees a dangerous look in his eyes she's never seen before, she freezes. "I've *tolerated* this arrangement, but I'm losing patience. Tell my mother once Bri said she loved me, I only wanted her. *That's it.*" He drops her wrist and steps back, shutting the door and locking it to make sure she, nor anyone else, would barge in.

He gets ready for bed and works on the plans for the day Bri becomes 'The Royal Consort.' He wants to surprise her with a small wedding-like ceremony to show her how serious he is about them; to make it special for them.

As David, Bri, and Jack walk to David and Bri's quarters, Bri pauses and braces herself with Jack's arm to take off her shoes. "Why do shoes have to make your feet hurt so much? Will my feet ever be like your guys' and not bother me?" She asks, grimacing as she painfully stretches them before placing her feet on the cold floor; the coldness has her stretching out her aching toes.

They quietly laugh. "Not as long as you wear these kinds of shoes with barely any cushion in them." Jack says pointing to the shoes in her hands. He scoops her up and happily carries her the rest of the way. "We need to get you some custom-made shoes and really great inserts for your other shoes."

"Those sound expensive." She quietly says, then yawns.

"You'll love them and wear them all the time. It's worth every penny for your well-being." Jack says and David agrees. David adds a reminder to his calendar to talk to Gabriel about the shoe inserts Monday morning.

David walks ahead of them a few steps to open the door to their quarters. Jack takes Bri to her bedroom with David and she's about to fall asleep. The three of them take off her jewelry and her dress before she lays down and she's asleep before they finish covering her up. David and Jack half hug, then Jack heads across their living room to the attached room he stays in when he stays at The Manor.

After a few hours of sleep, Bri wakes to use the restroom and brushes her teeth, then she sees David's shirt and slips it on. She goes back to bed and sees David sleeping so content she snuggles in behind him. She kisses his shoulder sweetly all the way to his neck. She feels her fingers being kissed.

She whispers, "*Sorry to wake you. I couldn't help it; I just love you so much!*" David tries to roll to his back to kiss her properly, but she teases and won't let him.

He chuckles a little. "I'll be right back." He gets up and goes to the restroom.

When he comes back to bed, he goes to spoon her, whispering into her ear, "*I love you, too, Macushla!*" He makes it known he has other things on his mind, but only if she wants to...

Later that morning, Bri is waking up and sitting up in bed, rubbing her eyes. She hears the guys talking in the other room and is about to get up when she sees David had laid a few articles on the bed for her. The guys hear her scoff and come in to see her.

"You don't believe them?" Jack asks as he sits at the foot of the bed to talk.

David sits on his side of the bed. "It's even *more* favorable than we thought!"

Bri picks up the article from the local newspaper. They tend to be pretty straightforward with some bias in 'non-news articles,' which comes from the pride of their island and nobles. She reads the first and last paragraphs of an article, skipping the middle for now.

NEWHAVEN NEWS
CHRONICLES

Duke & Duchess of Newhaven Officially Retire

By: Steven Richter

Peter and Carlotta Worthington, former Duke and Duchess of Newhaven, have handed over the reins of our beloved duchy to their son and daughter-in-law...

...The King also announced that he has chosen BriaLynn, The Duchess of Newhaven to be his *Royal Consort*, with full support of The Queen, as well as The Duke and *her* Noble Consort, Lord Carlisle. There have been significant changes and looks like more changes are on the horizon. But if they look as good as the ones that have already taken place here in Newhaven, we're in great hands!

"Yeah, but it's not the actual 'Newhaven people' let alone the Scots, or the other provinces of the UK for that matter!"

They laugh, then David says, "You'll see, Love!" He kisses her head as she thumbs through the other newspaper headlines.

Eventually, Bri would see that David and Jack were right. Everywhere they went, people were excited she was chosen, making her love the people that much more. As they traveled, people were excited to see them. All three, or each couple, got support; however, the most excitement came when Lawrence was with her or all of them. Although they have to laugh, because if Bri wasn't with them right away, they were almost always asked where she was or if she was coming. Now they joke that she is no longer joining them on their travels, but they're tagging along to go places *with her*. The woman has a way of making them look good, without outshining them.

David had arranged to spend a couple days with Bri at The Château. She is been tired a lot lately and he wants to give her a chance to recharge before The Midnight Ball. After she returns from a honeymoon with Lawrence, it's James and Amy's wedding that comes next, then straight on into the holidays. It'll be more nonstop for her with the holidays and more appearances with The King as 'The Royal Consort.' This is because they want to generate more excitement for her to become 'The Queen.'

CHAPTER 28
Imperfectly Perfect Quality Time

Bri is back from her time with David at The Château in France and is now enjoying her time with Jack one afternoon. She suggests playing 'The Flirting Game,' which is won by whoever can hold out the longest when they shamelessly flirt with each other. Jack happily 'lost' the game.

They're about to leave their bedroom when he holds out his hand and she lovingly smiles as she takes it. He gently pulls Bri to him and she holds his jaw, sweetly kissing him.

He handsomely smiles. "You have *no* idea what you do to me!"

She gives him a playful look with a knowing smile. "*Don't I?*" He studies her, then it hits him: getting him to join in the flirting game *was* part of her strategic seduction plan!

He exhales, "Ffff..." He laughs, "You won the second I joined the game!"

"*This time.* Normally, I just have fun flirting with you; however, today I was *going* to win." She grins. "Are you mad?!" She bites her lower lip.

"Are you kidding?! You're brilliantly wicked mind has always been *incredibly* sexy!" He kisses her. "Sei bellissima." He kisses her again. "Potrei guardarti tutto il giorno." Another kiss. "Sei tutto per me. Non posso vivere senza di te." He kisses her a little longer.

"I'm going to cry at the translation, aren't I?" She asks.

"You'll love it!" He smiles adoringly.

"That's a 'yes.'" She tells him and he chuckles. She takes a deep breath, "Alright, what's the translation?"

He caresses her face. "You're beautiful! I could look at you all day. You're *everything* to me. I can't live without you."

She hugs him tight. "I couldn't live without you either, Jack!"

"Ah, Amore Mia, one of the nice things about all this with Herst, David, and I, you'll *always* have one of us!"

"*Not* comforting! Besides, *eventually*, there will be *only one* of us left!" She wipes a tear. She pushes down the lump in her throat. The thought of losing any of them makes her heart want to bleed. "Happy thoughts and I pray we're all too old and senile before one of us outlives the other three!"

"Agreed!" He kisses her temple, then they walk down to their office to work.

The next evening, David and Bri walk to The Billiards Room to meet up with Jack after discussing some Newhaven business. He kisses the back of her hand when they come to the door, which he opens and has her go in first. Jack isn't quite there yet, so while they wait, he kisses her firmly with an arm around her waist and the other tangled in her hair. They're resting their foreheads together when the door opens and Jack walks in with a big smile for them.

"Alright you handsome men! Rack 'em up and let's see what you've got!" She gestures the table.

"What's the prize?" Jack asks with a mischievous look.

"Whatever do you mean?" She playfully grins, teasing, "You already have me, so what else could there *possibly* be?!" She gives them a saucy wink.

They both laugh and agree. "While that *IS* the best prize of all," Jack adds, "we'd like a little something to work towards." He gives her his best smile.

"Ooo, so not fair!" She glares pointing her finger at his smile he knows works on her. "Seriously, though, I have nothing to offer and you both already give me so much..." her eyes get wet which catches her off guard. "There's nothing—." A lump in her throat cuts her off; she gets frustrated.

Jack tells her, "Like you said, Amore Mia, we have you and that's priceless! How about the winner gets more like 'a wish granted?'"

"What *kind* of wish?" She asks with a skeptical, but playful look.

David runs a finger down her neck and along her collarbone. "Like a romantic one."

"Sounds fun!" She smiles.

She walks over to the table and they play...pretty soon Jack is the one to beat. David bows out gracefully as Bri and Jack play the final game. Bri is finally tied with Jack, but there's a chance it could be over. Jack strikes the cue ball and it's the easiest shot of the three balls left, with the ball going into a corner pocket. Jack lines up his next shot to bounce off the bank perpendicular to it. Bri walks up to him and puts her hand on his bum and squeezes just enough to distract him, causing him to miss his shot.

David bursts out laughing, clapping a few times. "*Nicely played*, Love!"

"*Paybacks*, Gorgeous..." Jack laughs. "But yes, *well played*." He bows, rolling his free hand and arm towards her and the table.

Bri takes a deep breath. Deciding on the other ball rather than the one Jack tried, she maps out in her head how she will hit the cue ball for the angles needed. If all goes well, it will also move the other ball a little and hopefully setting it up for a better shot. Bri walks up to the table to line up her shot, purposely sticking out her backside. It's a *little* more than needed, but she's hoping this will distract Jack *just long enough* so he won't try anything and she can get the ball to sink into the corner pocket. She calls it out as she takes her shot. Still holding her breath, she watches the shot go smoother than planned. When she sinks the last one into the middle pocket, it finishes the game.

"Well, played, Amore Mia!" Jack kisses her and she deepens it.

"Just so there are no hard feelings, Amore Mio, my 'wish' is to give each of you a wish instead." She kisses Jack again.

"Never hard feelings over a friendly game, Amore Mia." Jack tells her and pulls her into an embrace. "*Especially with the most gorgeous woman in the world!*"

She laughs. "I think you're biased!"

"*Of course!*" He grins. "But that doesn't make it any less true!"

"I think it does." She replies.

David's phone rings and interrupts them. He looks at his phone and sees it's Lawrence calling him; Bri's phone is upstairs on her desk. Lawrence tells

David he's going to arrive by helicopter in the morning. When David hangs up, he smiles at Bri, sliding his phone back into his pocket.

"There's a helicopter arriving for you tomorrow, Love." He tells her.

"Lawrence?!" She asks excitedly. David and Jack laugh.

David tells her, "If you don't know the answer, then you'll have to wait and find out! *Or bring your phone with you next time.*" He winks. "Want to play again?"

"Sure!" Jack answers.

"I'm going to go get ready for bed." She goes and kisses both of them before she heads to The Cottage.

Outside the next morning, the helicopter is landing and Bri arrives just as it shuts down. She has a huge, excited smile on her face throwing her arms around Lawrence as he catches her and swings her around. She holds his face and kisses him; he slowly lets her slide down.

"I've *missed* you!" She tells him.

He smiles. "I've missed you more!"

"Are you passing through or something?" She asks, scrunching her eyebrows together looking at the helicopter.

"I was hoping to take you with me to a charity event that Abby and Gen are putting on tonight. I told Gen and Seth to go together, regardless if you could be my date because—."

She kisses him firmly. "I'd love to!"

"*Fantastic!* I brought you a dress and shoes." He tells her.

"Lawrence, I'll go *anywhere* with you!" She has such a beautiful and genuine smile on her face. The day she officially becomes *The Royal Consort* is fast approaching, but not fast enough...

"This will be our first public appearance together now that people know I've chosen you..." he hesitates when he hears her taking a deep breath as she nods, sensing her reservation. "Too much?"

She explains, "Lawrence, the only thing giving me 'second thoughts' is if I'd bring your approval ratings down. I *never* want to be respons—."

"*That's never going to happen!*" He states. "Actually, since we went public that you're my choice as 'The Royal Consort,' my approval ratings have gone up." Bri snorts a laugh. "*I'm bloody serious!*"

"I'm an American." She states.

"Are you?" He raises his eyebrow in a bit of a challenge.

"That's what I'm reminded of in the various media outlets!" She replies.

"Perhaps it's time *you* thought of it differently." Lawrence suggests.

"What do mean?" She asks.

"Well, Mother didn't like a comment that was said a while back, something like '*finally, The Monarchy will be what it should be!*' And another was saying something like, 'It's about time there's love in The Monarchy!' And my favorite," he pulls out a newspaper clipping and reads part of it to her:

> *...Ever since she married into The Worthington Family, The Duchess has had Newhaven's well-being at heart. She has worked hard with Lord Carlisle to bring back Newhaven's Heirloom Wool, opening a textile mill in an old mill that was long ago abandoned when Newhaven's wool was no longer in mass production. She started 'The New Beginnings Foundation' to help get people back on their feet and she plans on opening more housing located next to The Textile Mill this coming Spring.*
>
> *Since learning from her father-in-law about running The Duchy, The Duchess has helped to improve Newhaven even more and she personally hears all the appeals cases. She has also been working on inmates with the least dangerous offenses and drug offenses, not including dealers, to be under house arrest. Why?*
>
> *The Duchess explains, "This way, they are still confined and monitored with ankle monitors, but they can go to work and provide for themselves rather than the taxpayers paying. The only thing is they have to go to*

counseling and show consistent improvement. Guards at the prisons didn't lose their jobs. They're now tracking their assigned prisoners and no longer a referee of an occasional 'contact sport.' Most inmates, if not all of them, would tell you they'd prefer 'house arrest' to a prison cell, and will fall in line and follow the rules, rather than risk losing the opportunity and have to go back to a prison cell."

The Duchess has also been focusing on helping those who really want to do better; and isn't that what's best for all of us? She feels, "When healthier people are coming back into society, the less taxpayers also have to pay in government assistance; then a lot of times there are children and that's a crucial piece to consider!" The Duchess had all this in mind when she formed her foundation and is building the wool and textile businesses to help those on the island truly have 'a new beginning.'

His Majesty has finally begun the steps of a promising reign! Partnering with The Duchess of Newhaven and of course The Duke, Lord Carlisle, and The Worthington's, has to be his most brilliant move to-date!'"

Lawrence looks up and sees that Bri's mouth had fallen open a little. He hands her the article. "For your journal or scrapbook, whichever you'd like." She takes it and he hugs her again. When he pulls back, he asks, "Are you alright, Darling?"

"Yeah-Yes," she shakes her head, "just surprised..."

"I'm not!" He laughs. "The most wonderful and intelligent woman I've ever had the pleasure of knowing, *loves me*! *And* she's helping me get on track for a promising reign!" He kisses her again, hugging her even tighter. He holds her firmly and says, *"I'll gratefully never be the same!"*

Bri and Lawrence spend the day together, part of it with Jack and David as Jack and Bri show David and Lawrence around The Newhaven Heirloom Wool Farm and The Newhaven Textile Mill, explaining their current plans and future ones. They eat lunch together and discuss more of all that, as well as The Duchy.

Back at The Estate, Bri starts asking Lawrence more about the various coats of arms. He explains symbols like the lion and the unicorn are strictly a royal symbol in The United Kingdom of Provinces, yet crowned lions are rare all over, even more so are winged lions.

Lawrence also explains to her, "The Worthington Family Coat of Arms also includes the Scottish Thistle, which is traditional on Scottish Coats of Arms, and they're in the 'grass' below the shield." He points.

She smiles sweetly. "Wow, Ace! Sounds like you know your stuff!"

He lightly laughs. "I've been deep in this stuff since I have to sign off on these things. It's good to know what they represent, especially the ones pertaining to royalty. You wouldn't believe people actually try to slip something royal past me!"

"I don't mean any disrespect when I ask this," she hesitates to say, "I've seen animals on some of these coats of arms and they look so...oh, I don't know..." she thinks how to say it nicely, but David helps.

"Ghastly?" David asks.

"Yes! I saw one creature that looked like it was stabbing itself with one or two swords! I had to look it up to know it was a lion! There are other animals that are also unrecognizable!" She notes.

Lawrence tells her, "We do allow animals to be updated and as long as that's all it is, my staff can approve those pretty easily without involving me much."

She sees there is a flower with the Scottish Thistle. "What are the flowers for if thistles pay tribute to Scotland?"

Jack softly laughs. "The rose represents grace and beauty," he gestures the coat of arms, "but it's for your gorgeousness on here!" He smiles lovingly.

Bri laughs and shakes her head. *"Don't clutter the shield."*

"We were thinking the Triquetra heart and monogram on a shield with a phoenix for your official seal." David says.

She stares at the various phoenix choices. "Why would I need a seal?"

"A seal would be used for sealing envelopes, to being put on the airplane you're flying in that isn't The Royal Jet. It'll also be used for your helicopter." Lawrence starts to explain.

"I like the phoenix with the Triquetra heart and monogram for my coat of arms, too. If that's poss...*waaait* a second, *my* helicopter?!" Her surprise evident. "Are you *crazy*?! What will the public think?!"

David steps closer. "Bri, we're personally paying for it so you'll be comfortable using it for anything!"

She questions, "This doesn't look good when the world is calling for people to reduce their carbon—."

"It's the top of the line, with state-of-the-art technology, including the latest in environmentally friendly technology, too!" Jack excitedly tells her. "This one is cleaner than any other transportation out there! We figured environmentalists would have something to say, so we hoped to relax some of those concerns when we release that we're *personally* buying a specific helicopter and its specifications in that regard."

"As for your shield, we can simplify it by not using the phoenix." Lawrence tells her.

She shakes her head. "Too much to keep track of, unless it's absolutely necessary. Just the monogrammed Triquetra heart on a shield, the same border of the stretched-out Triquetra, held by the phoenix."

Jack says, "I like the one that is protective with its wings curved into the shield and it has its head tipped back in a warning."

David adds, "I think it'd look pretty fantastic as a double phoenix, too, after you're officially 'The Royal Consort!'"

Lawrence tucks it all aside for now. It's too soon to get ready for the party, so Lawrence and Bri go for a walk in the gardens, then get ready when they come back.

CHAPTER 29
Imperfectly Perfect Royal Date

Bri is ready for the charity event and comes down The Grand Staircase with Lawrence seeing her first. "Wow! That dress looks *sensational*, Darling!" He holds his hand out as she gets closer and she takes it.

"Thank you!" She beams. "All three of you have *brilliant* taste!" She teases with his accent.

"You're breathtaking, Gorgeous!" Jack smiles his wonderful smile and kisses her cheek.

David smiles holding her arms out. "Stunning!" He kisses her cheek, too, holding it there a few seconds longer.

Carlotta comes down the stairs and her mouth drops. "You both look *absolutely wonderful together*!"

Bri's dress is a lacey mauve V-neck, short sleeve evening gown hugging her body to her hips. She's wearing her diamond cluster necklace set and her full diamond watch, all from Jack. Her long dark brown hair is half up with large curls in the back.

"As you said, Darling, we have good taste! Plus, it also helps that we know what we like *on you*!" Lawrence sweetly smiles. "And you're *almost* perfect."

She raises her eyebrow. "Oh?"

He waves McMasters over with a box. He opens the box and Bri gasps when she sees a diamond tiara. "Lawrence!" She whispers as her hands go up to her mouth, looking at it as he pulls it out of the box.

 "I call this, 'The Diamond Heart Tiara.'" He smiles, but there's a hint of shyness. "Fit for My Queen, *The Queen of My Heart*."

She looks at David remembering his reference to her having a collection of hearts with his, Lawrence's, and Jack's hearts; thus, being a future 'Queen of Hearts.' He remembers, too, and winks at her. She looks back to Lawrence wondering, "Isn't it a bit early to wear this big of a diamond tiara?"

Carlotta smiles sweetly at her, "You're The Duchess of Newhaven now, but had you still been The Marchioness, then you're right; it would've been too soon to wear this."

 The main row has larger heart-shaped diamonds evenly spaced apart with the middle one being bigger, and they taper down in size as they go back. There is another row of diamonds below the main row, a third of the size of the row of the main big ones, running along the base with a little bit smaller diamonds in between those. There are loops and swirls of tiny diamonds weaving around the tiara. Then on the top of each large heart-diamond is a heart of teeny tiny diamonds and a pear-shaped diamond at the very top of the heart, pointed downward.

"This is *beautiful*...your talent never ceases to amaze me, Ace! How did you come up with something like this?!" She asks.

He caresses her cheek. "It helps to have the inspiration of the love I have for you." He takes the tiara and helps place it on her head.

"I'm glad my hair is at least halfway up already!" Bri notes.

"That matters?" Lawrence asks.

"With a bigger diadem or tiara, like this one, I could probably get away with my hair all the way down." Bri starts to explain to him.

Carlotta helps. "A lesson she learned is that *typically* tiaras look best with hair neatly pulled into an updo." She holds up a small box and rattles the hairpins inside. "As she said, her hair is already halfway pulled back, so it should only take a couple minutes to secure it into place." Carlotta works quickly, but carefully, securing the tiara in Bri's hair. As she does so, Carlotta says, "This crown is exquisite, Lawrence!"

"Thank you. I had some pieces that I had started and stopped over the years. I pulled them altogether and I've been staring at them for days, weeks even. When I saw one that looked like a heart, this tiara started to take shape in my head and I drew it out. Nigel helped to set some of the stones into place so I could have it done in time for tonight. Our first night together, as an *official couple*." He kisses her right hand.

290

"I love this tiara, Lawrence!" She smiles at him as Carlotta secures it.

Carlotta steps back and says with a smile, "Stunning!" She gestures them both, "You both look wonderful!" Bri hugs her and everyone else before she and Lawrence go out to in The Royal Helicopter.

On the flight over, the nerves in her stomach get increasingly more intense. Lawrence is so excited and she does her best to cover it and focuses on enjoying her time with him.

His motorcade is waiting when their helicopter lands. "We're heading to an old castle in Somershire."

Bri excitedly smiles. "Sounds wonderful!"

It doesn't take long before they are pulling up in front of the castle. Bri gets out and she hears people calling out to her. She smiles and waves as Lawrence takes her other hand and they walk into the castle.

She quietly says to him, "I guess word is officially out."

"Darling, word will forever get out when it comes to you, true or not, or the 'not-so-much' truth." He kisses her hand.

"The 'not-so-much' is what makes me sick. A little truth with lies and people take it as *all* truth! That's worse than flat out lies!"

Lawrence plainly says, "This is where we can '*thank*' the various media outlets."

"People don't see, or they're not humble enough to consider, that their opinions are what others have told them, without verifying 'facts' or listening to other pieces of an issue or problem." She says.

He replies, "You said one word that is key: listening. You have one extreme side accusing the other extreme side of being close-minded but fail to see that's *exactly* how they are! They say they support that everyone has a right to choose the way they think, believe, and live, then get offended if any of those things goes against what they think, believe, or how they choose to live their own lives."

"Well said." She agrees. "I'd only add I'm all for people exercising their rights as long as they don't infringe or step on other people's rights. For example, protesting an injustice is one thing," she waves to some people shouting their names as she talks, "but vandalism, hurting others, or whatever, violates other people's rights and that's *worse!*" She glances at him and looks again because he is staring at her. She quietly asks, "What? Did I say something wrong?"

"*No!* Not at all! Your *fascinating!* I can't wait for you to become queen and we can do some wonderful things togeth—."

"Whoa, whoa, slow down there, Ace!" She stops him. "I'm not even 'The Royal Consort' yet! One step at a time and no giant leaps of any kind!" Bri teases a little. "Besides, why do we have to wait until I become queen to do some wonderful things together?"

He chuckles. "Excellent point, Darling." He doesn't say anything more and they pose for some pictures.

She hears a growing number of, "Long live The King and future Queen!" Bri pauses, about to stop in her tracks as it sinks in, but Lawrence moves her right along.

He says just loud enough for her to hear, "Keep smiling, Darling! Remember, I said Abby and Gen are putting on this event and what you just heard sounds a lot like Gen's doing with Abby's full support." He covertly tips his head in the direction of the fans. "They really do love you, Darling!"

"*They don't even know me!*" She whispers.

"Of all the articles out there, I seem to recall a few you've actually endorsed and they give a pretty good picture of you. Right off the top of my head I can think of the in-depth article on 'Newhaven Heirloom Wool and Textiles' for 'The Business Daily News.'"

"That article featured Jack more than me, *as it should have!* David says he has the 'Midas Touch' when it comes to finance and we're definitely on track for that! He's a genius in his own right, just like you and David!"

"I'll agree with Jack and David—."

She scolds in a whisper with a smile on her face, "*Lawrence Alexander Heathherst! You* will *become The King you were always meant to be!*"

He gets close to her ear. "*With you by my side, I will be!*"

She smiles with a twinkle in her eye. "I already am!"

"*You know exactly what I mean!*" He gives her a determined look with a smile.

They are outside *The Grand Ballroom* where they are announced together for the first time. "His Majesty, King Lawrence, and Her Grace, The Duchess of Newhaven!" Lawrence can feel her shaking walking into the room, even though she is smiling beautifully.

Queen Genevieve comes up to Bri and gives her a huge hug, along with Abby. Seth is with them and says to her, "We're so *thrilled* you're here with our brother!"

"Thanks, Seth! I'm glad to have the three of you in our family, too!" Bri smiles and he kisses her cheek.

The evening is spent dining, then mingling and dancing. Abby's date, Lord George Stanton, a former prosecutor and now in the private sector, asks Bri for a dance. She does because it's proper to dance with the men at her table. Lawrence watches as he talks with guests, he's not comfortable with her dancing with men outside of family.

Lawrence goes up to them when the song ends. "May I have this dance, Your Grace?" Lawrence asks. Lord Stanton thanks Bri for the dance, bows to The King, then goes to find Abby. Lawrence wraps Bri in his arms and whispers, "*Aside from those in our family, why is it I'm not liking you dancing with any other man?*"

She snorts quietly and giggles, but her smile drops when she sees Lawrence's face. "*You're serious?!*"

He gives her a determined look, holding her a little firmer, and in a deep whisper he says next to her ear, "*Very.*" Her breath catches at the low sexy tone she hears in his voice.

She clears her throat. "It'll pass..."

He chuckles. "Oh, Darling, you have no idea how wrong you are! It's only gotten worse this past year!"

She gives him a skeptical look. "Lawrence, 'The Midnight Ball' will be here before we know it, then you'll settle down."

"*Not bloody likely!*" His hand is on her low waist, still modestly placed given their relationship, but any lower and it wouldn't be. "It could get worse!"

Trying not to become alarmed she calmly says to him, "Please tell me now if you are the crazy *insanely* jealous type. If you are, then we need to have a lengthy discussion about trust and—." He captures her lips in a very passionate, heated kiss that makes her forget everything...even where she is. When he pulls their lips apart, it's slow and gentle, her lips still hot and tingly from the passion between them.

He whispers, "*Breathe.*" She hadn't realized she was still holding her breath; she inhales.

Her thoughts start to form and she begins to wonder if she's right, that he likes control in the bedroom...with all the terrible things in his childhood, she can't believe it's anything extreme...maybe more like an intense sort of power play with an alpha-male...perhaps it could be therapeutic, a way to take back, or undo, *a little bit* of the damage from his childhood. Lawrence is studying her and watches her reaction as he runs his lips across her knuckles.

She can barely whisper, "*Stooop...*"

He playfully matches her whisper, "*Whyyy?*"

"*Please.*" She has a hint of desperation in her eyes and he stops. She clears her throat a little. "Lawrence, that was working *way* too well." She then says apologetically, "I'm sorry—."

"For what? I needed to stop for *both* our sakes." He sweetly kisses her cheek and they dance snuggled in close. She pulls back a moment and he smiles, holding her gaze with his incredible blue-green eyes. He asks, "What's going on in that beautiful head of yours?"

"I was just wondering if *I* could get away with kissing His Majesty..." she playfully smiles.

"His Majesty will allow *only* you..." he smirks.

She leans in and whispers with a smile, "*A marvelous answer*, Your Majesty!" She gives him a sweet kiss before she puts their foreheads together. There were lots of photos taken of this scene and those pictures will be in tomorrow's editions of various media outlets.

The evening wraps up and Bri asks if Lawrence minds flying back to The Palace. "Not at all, but is there a problem?"

"Lawrence, once everything is official and we're essentially married, being here will be fine because I'll be in bed right next to you...then a sense of home will be wherever you are. Until then, my bedroom at The Palace has been a consistent place for me the few times I have visited. I'd feel more settled and comfortable—gosh I hope this makes sense."

He pulls his phone out to make the arrangements. "It makes perfect sense, Darling." He makes a call.

While everything is being organized, she hugs him. "Thank you, Lawrence."

"Bri, I'd do *anything* for you, and *this* is such a very simple request."

"Well, I think we'd need to ask those who are actually changing the plans and carrying them out, if they think my request is 'simple' or not!" She softly giggles and he agrees.

By the time they reach The Royal Apartment, her luggage is already in her room. She thanks everyone and says goodnight to Lawrence. She gets ready for bed and reads for a while before she falls asleep.

CHAPTER 30

Imperfectly Perfect & Naked Truth

The next morning, after Bri eats breakfast alone, she walks around The Royal Apartment. She winds her way around and is on the second floor, technically third floor from the American way of counting floors. The hallway is lit up by the sunlight shining through the stained-glass windows and she gets caught up in the beauty of it. The door to Lawrence's study is ajar and Bri opens it up all the way and walks in, only to duck back out again and run. The image of the backside of an almost naked woman and Lawrence's hands on her arms, were *more* than what she needed to get out of there...she's grateful this woman blocked Lawrence's view of her.

She ran fast and barely hears the echo of Lawrence asking, "Who's there?"

He thinks it might be Bri and runs after her to the anger of the woman he leaves behind, which is heard out in the hallway. He looks around for Bri, but she is nowhere to be seen and no footsteps can be heard either, which is odd...*Which way did she go?* He asks himself.

Embarrassment carried her feet away...down the stairs and out the main door of The Apartment. She has slowed to walking as fast as she could to, well, *anywhere* with lots of people. Unfortunately, she gets all turned around.

She texts McMasters: "I'm sorry, I got lost..." (adds a sad emoji)

McMasters: "I'll come to you, just tell me what's around you."

Bri describes her surroundings and he knows exactly where she is at; he tells her to stay put. He isn't happy she was somewhere without him, but he waits for an explanation before getting upset. It doesn't take him long to get to her and she looks shaken.

"Are you okay?" He asks.

"Oh, yeah, I'll be fine. My head is spinning right now." She answers.

"It'll be alright, just take some deep breaths." He says, assuming she is upset because she got lost.

"I need to stop the replaying of something in my head that I just saw! Let's go do something, *anything*! I really *need* to take my mind off it."

"Are you sure you're okay?" He asks again.

"Yes, I'm sure. Just shaken from something I never wanted to see. I just had to get out of there and I ran—I'm sorry for not grabbing you." She tells him.

"I can understand your state of mind wasn't processing like it should, but *try* not to do it again." He says and she nods again, apologetically. "How about an official London Palace Tour?" He asks with a slight smile and adds, "You love history."

"Perfect!" She walks beside him, and he guides the way to where the next tour group has barely started.

 They tour quite a bit of The Palace and at one point, Bri is looking at a plaque, reading about the insignia and various badges of *The Royal Guard*. She starts to hear lots of whispering, then she hears a man clear his throat behind her. Bri glances around and sees people looking at her... Then she feels The King's presence.

She turns around and simply says with a curtsy, "Your Majesty."

"We need to talk, Your Grace." He says with determination.

"Nnnooo, we *really* don't. It's fine. We're fine." Bri stumbles through. "I really want to finish this tour—."

"This *isn't* a request." His tone is stern. She folds her arms and raises her eyebrow. He gives her a look implying the very public display.

"Is that 'The American Duchess?'" A woman whispers.

Another whispers back, *"I think it is!"*

Lawrence turns to them saying with a smooth sounding voice, "The Duchess and I have some things we need to discuss. Would you all please excuse us?" And he gives a dimpled smile to the ladies.

Bri quietly takes a deep breath and smiles through her reluctance, stepping towards him. The people around them say goodbye as they leave, Bri waves and smiles. She quietly follows him and for the first time Bri feels *very* vulnerable. Lawrence pauses to step in line with her, but they walk in silence...

Lawrence's main office is closer, but he takes Bri all the way back to The Royal Apartment to keep his mother from eavesdropping. He can sense Bri tensing up and tries to step closer, but she moves away. She's still not sure how to register what's going on. The Apartment door is opened for them and he gestures Bri to walk in first. Once inside and the door closes, Bri turns on her heel to Lawrence.

"Look, Lawrence, I'm sorry I walked in." She begins. "The door was partially open, and I was curious about the room—."

"*Stop talking!*" Lawrence spouts off without thinking how that would sound.

Her mouth almost falls open in shock for a *brief* moment at his tone, then she recovers. "*Excuse me?!*" She snaps.

"I don't know where to start!" His frustration shows. "You run out of the room, you disappear, and you don't take my calls or answer my texts! *That's unacceptable, BriaLynn!*"

"I wasn't ready to talk to you yet! I'm *still* trying to process why you would do *that* while I'm here! That's distasteful and disrespectful when I said I never wanted to know! Not to mention, I stupidly *assumed* when you told me you didn't want anyone else," she points upstairs, "well, what I just saw makes it look like you LIED to me!"

He looks at her with a slight arrogant look. "*How much did you actually see?*"

"*Are you kidding me?!* That's the best you can come up with?!" She scoffs in disgust. "I didn't actually stand around to watch the show!" She pushes past him to go up the stairs, but he grabs hold of her upper arm to stop her.

"I know for a fact, you didn't see anything, because *nothing* happened." He tells her.

She glares at him and jerks her arm free. "Because you were interrupted!"

"Doesn't matter! These lips," he points to his mouth, "*never* touched her."

298

She lifts her eyebrow in a skeptical look. "Lawrence, there was a naked woman in front of you" She states. "It's a bit hard to believe *nothing would've happened* because if I recall the seared image in my brain, *your hands* were definitely on her!"

"My hands were only on her arms to keep her away from me!" He starts to explain and her face still has a skeptical look. "The fact that my mother has been pushing her on me for some time now, is a turn off!"

"Wait. *That was Eleanor?!*" Bri asks.

He scrunches his eyebrows this time, confused. "No! I told you I would send her away *and I did!* That night, in fact!"

Her eyebrows furrow. "Yeeeah, your credibility is in question at the moment. She could've come back! *How would I know?*" She asks rhetorically as she turns and goes up the stairs.

He vehemently states, "I'VE *NEVER* LIED TO YOU!" His frustration is growing. He takes a deep breath and exhales walking up the stairs and gets around her to face her. "Bri, when I fell for you, my desire has *only been* for you. Yes, I've had other women, but I can honestly say the last time was *before* I took you to The Clock Tower! It's everything I can do *not* to seduce you! It's getting harder and harder every moment I'm alone with you!"

She gives him an angry confused look. "*Do you seriously think you'd be able to seduce me right now?!* I just saw you with a naked woman!"

He reaches for her, but she pulls away again stepping up another stair. He continues, "I heard someone come into the office, but I couldn't get up fast enough; although, I figured it had to be you. When I got out into the hallway it was like you vanished into thin air!"

"And yet, you were still able to find me." She glares with annoyance.

He smirks. "I *am* 'The King,' Bri."

She fakes a shocked look and scoffs, "Really?! I had *absolutely* no idea!"

He exhales. "Bri, I would have to answer to David and Jack; *we answer to each other*. Those times when you said it was my choice," he looks into her eyes, "it started to feel like cheating and I lost interest. David spoke with me that night of The Noble Coronation Ball. We talked about how he had his share of meaningless sex; Jack did, too! They both swear the intimacy with you, *making love*, is worth the wait!" Bri folds her arms, not sure what to say.

Lawrence is at a loss of what else to do, so he quickly holds her face and kisses her fiercely. She goes to break the kiss and he slides a hand behind her head and wraps the other around her waist, holding her firmly. She grips his lapels trying to push him away, but not that hard; the kissing only gets more heated. Lawrence reaches down and lifts her up like she's weightless, her legs wrapping around his waist as he pushes her up against the closest wall. She runs her hands into his hair at the back of his head and she fists her hands, holding his hair firmly—.

She breaks the kiss gasping. "Oh my gosh," she inhales and holds her breath an extra second, "this is SO white hot, Lawrence! We can't! This is literally 'playing with fire' and—."

"We want to keep this special, meaningful?" He finishes her sentence, trying to catch his breath, too, and looking at her with such desire, but struggling to push it down.

She rests her forehead to his as she puts her feet on the floor, then looks into his eyes. "What I did see, flashes on a continuous 'instant replay,' making me nauseous. It pains me to wait until we're official, but if we give in when we're this close..."

"Darling, first of all," he tucks some hair behind her ear, "I love you! And I *want* to honor your request." He kisses her again, but not too much. Then he takes her hand and leads her up to the private rooftop garden.

She quietly, but lovingly says to him, "I'm in love with you, Lawrence Alexander Heathherst..." She chokes up. He hugs her, lifting her feet off the ground an inch or two. When he sets her down, she sees how emotional he is. She holds his jaw and adoringly looks at him. "I.love.*you.*"

He locks his lips to hers and kisses her fiercely, but only for a couple seconds. He pulls their lips apart and he sweetly smiles when he sees her eyes are still closed, then he watches her open them.

He smiles. "I haven't loved *anyone* like I love you, *My Queen!*"

She smiles. "I can't say it was instant; however, when you were so sweet and kind to me, indulging me with Artemis, you were definitely in my small circle of people at that point! But once I did fall in-love with you, I fell *hard* for you. I have so many strong emotions of love for you, it's overwhelming at times."

He smirks. "Well, there had to be something special about a woman who tamed that wild stallion!"

Bri laughs. "And he was the easy one!"

Lawrence bursts out laughing, "You're saying *I'm* difficult?!"

She purses her lips to hide a grin. "Oh, My King, I choose *not* to answer that right now." She looks down his body and back up saying, "I would need further research to have an expert diagnosis."

He quietly laughs, nodding, and walks over to the railing to look out over London. She walks over and leans on the railing next to him. "Bri, I've purposely kept you away from this place because of my mother and who I am around her just to keep the peace. I know the rumors and I'm not proud of it, but it protects Seth and Abby."

Still leaning on the railing, she takes his hand and says, "All you can do is grab onto love and let *it* make you stronger, because love is *already* changing you, Lawrence."

He nods, then kisses her hand. "I want to show you, to prove to you, there is some good in me before you see me as 'The King.'" He gives her a slight vulnerable look.

She shakes her head. "That would be 'The Queen Mother's King.' *Not you.*"

"Thank you for that," he gives her an appreciative look, "and please remember that."

She nods, then asks, "Do you have a place to escape? A place to clear your head and gain perspective?"

He picks up the pendant on her thin gold necklace. "Nigel's workshop and designing various pieces." He takes her hand and they go back inside, then they start walking down the stairs back to the main part of The Palace.

"Ooo, am I about to get an in-depth look into the world of 'King Lawrence's Jewelry Creations?!'" She has a huge, hopeful smile.

He softly chuckles. "*You are!*"

"I'm so excited!" She tells him with matching excitement.

He smiles with his dimples. "We can take the passageways I usually take to avoid, well, *everyone!*"

When they make a third turn inside the passageways, she quietly says, "Even the passageways are spotless?! How does *that* work?!"

"We have excellent people working here?" He softly replies.

"Well, yes, *that's obvious!*" She grins. "Seriously though, these aren't 'secret passageways' if everyone knows about them!"

"Keep whispering and people will definitely be intrigued to *look* for them!" He winks. They walk a little further and he stops at a door. He cracks it open and looks around. Then he explains, "Most people know a lot of castles and palaces, *even manors*, have secret passageways to give the kings, queens, dukes, duchesses, and family, a way to escape, but it's also to slip out of all the craziness and breathe. Not many people know where to get into them, and only a couple of the senior staff know of the secret passageways to take care of them. Not even all of 'The Royal Guard' knows where they are and only a few of 'The King's Guard' knows of them."

"Now that makes sense." She says as he opens the door, looks around again, then motions for her to go first.

She steps into a room and looks around. She sees a workspace along the wall with two stools spaced out. There's a large magnifying glass, small tools, and a small safe nearby, but at the other end from where she is standing is a large vault you could walk into, similar to a bank vault. Lawrence takes her inside this large vault where there are loose gems of various shapes and sizes of diamonds, sapphires, rubies, emeralds, and various semi-precious stones. Empty settings for rings, earrings, necklaces, and so on, of gold, silver, white gold, and such. One section in particular seems to be Lawrence's with many completed pieces, along with ones that are in process, and then lots of sketches. She sees an 'L' in the corner like the monogram he used on the brooch he gave her.

Lawrence holds up a few necklaces to show her. "Lawrence, these are stunning! Did you design these?!" She asks.

"The ones on this wall are mine and I have a case out in the store."

She smiles. "You have so much talent!"

"It means a lot you feel that way." He smiles at her with a little shyness that comes from revealing something so personal.

She touches his cheek. "Thank you for sharing this with me!"

He holds up his finger for her to wait a moment as he steps out of the vault. She hears voices, then he comes back inside with a velvet box in his hands.

"I started making this for you when I realized I was in-love with you. I paused to design the tiara, but this is something I'm hoping you like as much as I hope you will..." he runs his hand on top of the box.

She lovingly asks, "Will you let me see it?!"

He gives her a shy smile and opens it to reveal a channeled heart-shaped diamond necklace. She gasps as she touches the necklace. The biggest heart is the center stone and it's bigger than her pink heart diamond on her ring; then the heart diamonds on the necklace tapered down to the smallest diamond hearts in the back. He watches her mouth open like she wants to say something, but no words come out.

"Well?" He smiles. "Use your words, Bri, I'm dying of suspense!"

"I can't find a better word than 'amazing' and my brain is frozen with 'wow' at the moment!"

He softly chuckles, "*I'll accept that*!" He takes the necklace out and puts it on her, while she switches out her earrings with the matching ones.

She steps out and finds a mirror. "I absolutely love this set! I never, in a million years, would've thought I would want to wear so many diamonds on a daily basis, and this is *the second time* I will eat those words!"

He's curious. "What was the first?"

She holds up her wrist. "Jack bought me this in Italy on our honeymoon. It matches his, but his doesn't have nearly as many diamonds like this one to be more *manly.*" She teases a little. Then she tells him, "A different one back with my luggage is a two-tone diamond watch from David. It's simpler and I love that one, too!" She lays her hand on the necklace. "This necklace set is *perfect!* It's the right size to wear with just about anything for almost *any* reason, or no reason at all!" He lightly laughs. She wraps her arms around his neck. "Thank you for making this for me. I'm really liking the heart-shaped jewelry." She holds up her right hand with the pink-heart diamond ring, then she hugs him.

He holds her firmly in an embrace and exhales. When Bri pulls back to look at him, she scrunches her eyebrows together when she sees his questioning look. He says, "I'm wondering what I can do to help you, *and us,* move past the incident in the study. I'm sorry you had to see that at all—." Although it sounded like he said, 'at toll.'

She had covered his mouth with her hand and gives him a determined look, but with love in her eyes. "*I have absolutely no idea what you're talking about.*"

She sees the relived look on his face and he replies, "I love you."

"I love you!" She kisses him again before they walk around and talk about more of his pieces.

CHAPTER 31

Imperfectly Perfect Spiritual Visit

A couple days later, Bri wakes up one morning and she checks the time on her phone. She knows David and Jack are probably exercising. She sees there's a text from Jack.

> Jack: "Good morning, Gorgeous! Hope you have a wonderful day! I love you!"

> Bri: "Good morning, My Sexy Jack! Hope you have a great day, too! I love you, Amore Mio!"

She lays there for a few minutes, thinking of Lawrence. She can't shake that there's something 'looming' and it makes her nervous as her feelings for Lawrence are getting more *intense*. She gets ready for the day and when it's still gnawing on her, she decides to call out to Jessica.

"Jessica? Can you hear me?" She looks around. "Jess—oh!"

Standing before Bri is a lovely woman in a white dress that seems to glow, and she radiates warmth and love. David walks in and without thinking Bri slightly waves her hand; David pauses in mid stride when he sees Jessica. Bri looks from David, then back to Jessica who is smiling at her.

"You're getting pretty good at that!" Jessica says.

"I guess I didn't overthink how to do it this time..." Bri looks at her hand as David and Jessica exchange hellos.

David caught her comment and asks, "Didn't over think what *this* time?" Bri smiles and quickly explains The Clock Tower with Lady Jane, Thomas, and Lord Richard. "*That's fantastic!* Wait, Lord Richard *didn't* crossover?"

"No..." she takes a deep breath with a touch of sadness.

"Ultimately," Jessica explains, "it's up to each of us what we'll do. We'll *never* be forced to choose the light, but the darkness will *always* claim its own; one way or another."

"Lord Richard would've been claimed if he was dark, or evil; like the guard Lawrence executed." Bri states and Jessica nods. Bri taps into her empathic side and feels, "Lord Richard is punishing himself and trying to reconcile his life before he can accept the love and forgiveness that is in the light." Bri surprises herself with what she knows.

"That makes sense." David says.

"*All* your skills seem to be improving." Jessica smiles at Bri. "What else do you feel about Lord Richard?"

"Well..." Bri thinks about it, "Lord Richard also said he saw the light, but said he took an innocent life and he felt he couldn't go into the light yet. I'm glad it's 'yet' and it's better than feeling he never can." Bri says to them and they agree. "I do know murder is a great sin on both sides, so it's interesting he said 'yet'...like he senses there is forgiveness but he isn't ready to accept it because he's not quite finished punishing himself."

"You'll find you can have answers to anything you wish, Bri, but you need to use that information with caution. You'll feel when you can or can't share." She looks at David and tells him, "It's important you three support her in that because there could be times you won't know everything she does and if you, Jack, or Lawrence, can't handle that, then she needs to be aware of that so she can navigate around it." Jessica states and David nods understandingly.

Bri looks at Jessica. "Why do I feel like there's something crucial about Lawrence I'm missing, or is coming?"

Jessica explains. "When you were in the coma, there was a lot said to you, but you left with only a teensy fraction of it. We didn't want you to feel overwhelmed and you'd be given more information as you need it." She smiles in kindness.

"Like after David proposed that morning." Bri notes.

"Right." Jessica replies. "There is just a bit more you need to know of what was said about Lawrence."

 Jessica smiles as she opens her hands. They see light in Jessica's hands and David watches it flow to Bri's forehead.

Bri feels her consciousness open and the memories start to play out in her mind as David curiously observes Bri.

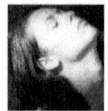 Bri looks at Jessica. "Wow! I've been drawn to the Triquetra and heart combination, with David, Jack, and Lawrence, each representing a loop on the Triquetra, and the heart represents all their love——."

"No, in this situation, the heart represents *you!*" Jessica smiles.

"Wife and mother!" Her son with David steps over to her.

And so does her son with Lawrence, saying, "And queen." Bri's hands go up to her mouth.

Jessica smiles over at them, but David can only see Jessica. He studies her and comments, "You see our son again, don't you?" She nods and she waves her hand for him to see *both* sons. David smiles with so much love at both of them, then looks at Bri in awe. "This is remarkable!" With tears in his eyes, he puts his hand on his chest, over his heart and says to the young men, "The love I feel for both of you is *incredible!*"

David reaches out to touch his son, but he quickly steps back and says, "Only our mother is able to touch us."

Her son with Lawrence adds, "It's because she has 'the pure love of a mother.'" He looks from David to his mother with a son's love for his mother.

Bri steps over to her son with Lawrence. "It had occurred to me a while ago *who* you reminded me of!" She says, reaching out and touching his cheek. "*Your* father is Lawrence!"

David grins. "He *definitely* looks like Herst!"

"Ha-ha! Just like *your* son looks like you!" Bri waves her arm a bit towards their son. "Right down to those incredible dark blue eyes!" She looks to Lawrence's son. "And your dimples are just like *your* father's!"

Her son with Lawrence takes her hand in his. "Mum, it will get more difficult for you, but your bond is getting deeper the closer you get with father." He squeezes her hand to plea, "Keep in mind that the pain and abuse he has been put through *all his life* runs deep, too. *However*, pure love, *your love* for him *is* more powerful and you're already starting to figure out how you'll break through it!"

She studies him for a minute. And she doesn't realize she is projecting her thoughts *to* him...'*Intimacy will be...*'

Lawrence's son says, "Intense."

"Lawrence's mother will be a challenge..." She says more to herself.

"'Challenge' regarding Millicent is an understatement!" Lawrence's son plainly states. He affectionately touches his mother's cheek and smiles. "Mother*hood* generates a general bond, but a true mother's love is what grows and *nurtures* children in positive ways. *Love* between two people, like," he motions between her and David, "you two, as well as you and Uncle Jack, is a real bonding *power*! The love you and father are growing is bonding you both together *and changing him*! Keep this close to your heart, Mum: Father will *always* choose you *every single time*, even in situations that look like he is against you!" She gives him a confused look and he adds, "Mum, there will come moments when father's bond with you will be tested by The Queen Mother! What will soon happen will scare you at first, but it'll deepen that bond and solidify you and father, *and* our family."

Bri has a confused look, feeling nervous. "*Okay...*"

Jessica steps in. "Bri, I'm to tell you that you'll be given the strength to endure and inspiration on what to do." She kindly smiles. "Keep doing what you're doing. Love Lawrence, David, and Jack. There will be a moment in the very near future where you'll have a choice to stand up to The King and The Queen Mother, or shrink away. *Make your stand!* As he takes in what happened and what you said, *he will be on your side*!"

"Make my stand? *You're kidding, right?!*" Bri humorlessly laughs.

"Bri?" David asks.

Bri is still looking at Jessica as she says, "I love Lawrence, but there's this wall he has up to keep me separate from his world as 'The King.'" She uses air quotes. "So how on earth am I to forge this *significant bond* with him that will shatter whatever hold his mother has over him *and not die in the process?!*"

Jessica and Bri's sons say together, "*With your faith!*"

David steps closer to Bri and turns her to face him. "Maybe you need put yourself *in* his world!"

She scoffs, "*How?*! I'm not interested in pushing him so far they throw me in The Royal Dungeons!"

"That's where you should start, Mum!" Her son with Lawrence says.

"You don't know your grandmother that well, but the woman has people who'll kill me and they'd be protected by her for doing her dirty work!" Bri tells him.

"Mum, I *do* know my grandmother, *quite well actually.*" He replies.

She gives him that. "I suppose you're at a better advantage than we are."

"More than you know!" He answers, she raises her eyebrow. "Sometimes you're not given the full picture, but rely on your faith and your sensitivity to The Spirit. Trust it! Trust in the love *all of us* have for you!"

Jessica has an apologetic look. "We need to go."

With teary eyes, Bri asks, "Why is it so hard?" She touches her sons' cheeks, then holds their hands. "I love you both *so* much, I only wish I could've seen your sister as well."

"Oh, she's the most special one of all!" Her son with Lawrence happily smiles with his dimples. "And that's all we can say, but you will—."

"Find out." Both David and Bri laugh as they say it.

David steps over to Lawrence's son. "Even though your father is Herst, I still feel a strong connection with you."

"*You should*, Uncle David!" He says with an excited dimpled smile. "You gave our family an *extraordinary* gift! By loving Mum and giving her the gifts of love with Uncle Jack and my father, she has so much more love to give! That's the love that gives us the most *extraordinary mother*! We have great dads and the best uncles, and aunts, too, along with grandfathers, grandmothers, and extended family; all because of *you* and you opening Mum's heart!" David's own tears drip down his cheeks as he kisses Bri's temple. Bri is choked up herself as she hugs them both and blows them a kiss as they fade away. She and David hold each other while Jessica stays a little longer.

"We're told 'The Royal Dungeons' is the place to start. Remember, you'll have added strength and peace when you need them." Jessica waves as she disappears.

Bri and David continue to hold each other and he can barely whisper, *"Bri...that was amazing...thank you for sharing it with me!"*

"Thank you for supporting me, or I wouldn't be able to share this with you." She kisses him.

"I love you, Macushla!" He rests their foreheads together.

She quietly says, "If I do this with Lawrence, if I push back, probably harder than I ever had to with you—."

"It'll be alright!" He steps back and holds her hands, giving them a squeeze. "Even if he gets angry, as reality sets in, they said he *won't waiver* in his love for you, Bri! I had that thought, too, but I believe it even more now after talking with the three of them!"

She inhales deeply and exhales saying, "I wish I could be so sure."

"Look," David explains, "I don't know everything that happened to Herst when he was a kid, maybe you know and I won't ask you to break that confidence if he did; *however*, I do know he protects Seth and Abby fiercely."

Bri quietly says, "He's already shown how far he'll go to protect me..."

David lifts her chin. "I can't say I'd do anything differently, Bri." He caresses her cheek. "The guard *did* know better and he also knew Royal Guards are held to a higher code of conduct than other law enforcement officers, as well as gentlemen; a 'King's Guard' is held to a higher standard than that. He gambled Lawrence wouldn't do anything because The Queen Mother was behind it and he lost. I hope you don't feel sorry for this man—."

She gives him a little smile. "I only feel sorry that he didn't make better choices at any point before, or during, this sequence of events..."

He studies her for a moment. *"Briii, what aren't you saying?"*

"It's more what I'm still putting together...If I'm to push Lawrence further than I ever have with you, could more people get hurt in the process? Or worse?!" She asks.

"Possibly, but we'll increase security. In the end, the loyal ones to The Queen Mother, make their own executions imminent." He adds, "'Everything happens for a reason.'" He winks.

"Like you already increased security with the girls?" She gives him a stern knowing look.

His mouth drops open a little when he realizes, *"I forgot to tell you."*

She raises her eyebrow as she folds her arms. "The better response would be you forgot to discuss it with me *beforehand."*

He goes to apologize, but she holds up her hand and tells him, *"Don't do it again* with *any* of our children, or we won't move past it so easily." He nods and she asks, "Can I ask you about 'The Royal Consort' paperwork?"

"Sure!" He replies.

"Lawrence says his mother is drawing up the paperwork with their solicitors, but he came to you to use yours?" She clarifies.

"Oh, he did! The paperwork is pretty much completed. I want to read through it and then Jack is going to read through it, just in case we missed something." David lovingly smiles. "Love, we discussed *from the beginning* that you wouldn't want *any of your children* raised alone, and you'd *never* leave a child behind to be raised in The Palace by a nanny, *or otherwise."* He implies The Queen Mother.

"David, I need something ironclad so *that woman* will never *ever,* legally get her hands on *any* of my babies." She pleads with teary eyes.

"We know, Love, even Herst. We also know that, God forbid, in the event of your death, you'll want *all* your babies raised with their siblings and based more here in New——." She kisses this man with everything she has!

"Thank you!" She's relieved. "I'm so blessed and incredibly grateful for you, David! There aren't enough words to describe how much I love you!" She looks at him with love in her eyes. "My heart is bursting and falling for you once again, all at the same time!"

He holds her in his arms, her head on the front part of his shoulder but its tipped back to look up at him. He tips his chin down a bit to look at her better. "I feel those same feelings all the time with you! Even my worse days melt away with you!"

She scoffs, "You can't say that! You just had *an entire bad week...*"

"Bri, that was the ultimate worst of dreadful weeks! A typical bad day literally melts away when I'm with you, or talk to you, even get a simple 'I love you' text can make my day!" She kisses him. He says against her lips, "If we have some really hot sex, would it make you late for anything important?" He asks with a playful look.

"*Nnnope!*" Bri playfully replies back with happiness.

David and Bri head down to breakfast. She says good morning to everyone but gives Jack a 'good morning' kiss before she takes her seat between Jack and David. Bri is thinking about The Midnight Ball and Halloween.

"I've been meaning to ask, what started 'The Midnight Ball?'" She asks.

David smiles. "Mother had wanted James, Jack, and me, to see that our dancing lessons had a payoff and organized a ball for us. She was thinking 'Fall Ball' and Halloween, although costume parties can be difficult, especially dealing with teenagers. One year, there were costumes that were, well...weren't only grotesque, but some in very poor form! Mother and Father were never going to have one again...until we wore her down," he grins at Carlotta, who laughs a little as she and Peter reminisce with them.

Jack continues, "We came up with a 'Masquerade Ball' theme, only Mother came up with 'a mask will be provided to all guests' rule. All guests came dressed for a masquerade ball and would be able to choose a mask at the door. And, to ensure it actually ended at a decent hour, she officially called it, 'The Midnight Masquerade Ball.'"

"That's ingenious!" Bri laughs, looking at Carlotta who winks at her. They talk for a bit longer and when they are done eating, Bri stands up saying, "I should take a trip into town and see how my dress is coming along."

"It's ready to go." David tells her

"Oh? And how would you know?" Bri asks with a raised eyebrow.

He wipes his mouth with his napkin and stands up replying, "I may have made a few changes for the evening, at Herst's request."

"You're up to something!" Bri's voice is accusatory, although she fails at hiding her smile. "Can *I* make a request?"

"Of course!" He replies.

"Yours and Jack's tuxes usually do but will—."

"Will Herst's match your dress?" He asks and she nods. "*Absolutely*!" He points to his lips for her to kiss him. She smiles and holds his jaw to give him a passionate kiss. "Mmm...now that's a kiss!" He says, smiling, and taps another kiss to her lips, then leaves for work.

Bri's phone rings and it's Amy's ringtone. She steps out into the hallway to talk to her.

"Hi, Amy! It's good to hear from you but isn't it *super* early there?!"

"Bri, I can't sleep! I have a HUGE favor to ask you!" Amy says nervously.

"Amy Nicole Walker! You know you can ask me *anything* and I'll happily try to accomplish the impossible for you!"

Amy's nodding to herself, then rattles off, "The Skyward Lounge where we're supposed to have the ceremony and a light reception is being threatened by that wretched senator woman who wants it for her daughter's wedding *that same day*! She's insisting our ceremony and reception be bumped to the ballroom so they can have the rooftop. They even offered to pay twice the price to do so!" She panics. "Bri, would you be able to do anything! My family can't afford to pay twice the price when they don't even know how much it really costs to begin with!"

"Amy, don't give it another thought. I've got this! I've never been a fan of this woman and I no longer have to finesse things to keep her happy *or keep her quiet!*"

Amy is relieved. "You're the best, Bri."

"Only because I have you on my team!" Bri laughs a little and then Amy does, too, as she relaxes a bit more. "Let me worry about this *for you*, alright."

"Alright." Amy takes a deep breath because she does trust Bri to handle it! They say goodbye for now.

Bri looks in the dining room for Jack but he isn't there. She texts him right away, knowing he's around somewhere. She wants to talk to him about changing their business days, and nights, around a bit.

Bri: "Need to talk to you about something important! Call me, please!"

He calls her right then.

She answers her phone, "Hi, Handsome!" She hears him smile.

"Hi, Gorgeous!"

"I need to buzz to DC tomorrow. You don't need to come with if you have appointments, but you can." She explains, "Amy said there's a senator woman who's trying to bribe the hotel to let them have The Sky Lounge for *her daughter's wedding*, when it's already booked for James and Amy's wedding."

Jack whistles and says, "Wow, that's harsh. Wait a second...wouldn't invitations for *any* wedding need to be sent out already being this close to the big day?!"

"Yes!" Bri tells him, "This senator is the minority whip and those who have been in this position usually have a little bit of power and influence, but she has managed to alienate herself from just about anyone and everyone. By this point, most can barely give her the respect to tell her the time of day. She's about to fully accomplish alienation with the most significant men and women of her own party because she's so focused on the wrong things, it's seen as a huge waste of everyone's time and taxpayers' money. A lot of politicians have had to distance themselves from her if they ever hope to have a chance at being re-elected in their own states."

Jack asks, "Is she that short pudgy woman?"

"With tiny glasses on a beaded chain?" Bri adds.

"Yes!" He laughs.

"That's her! She gets reporters to say she's 'the most powerful woman in DC,' and it only makes her more of a joke!"

Senator Sonja Watson is a peacock. She is a short, pudgy woman with her eyes and cheeks standing out from too much makeup. Bri does admit the woman dresses very nice with a brooch that does make her look polished. Sadly, when she applies fresh lipstick, it's often on her teeth.

Jack asks, "What's the plan?"

"Well, she's so stuck on herself and being the center of attention, I'm not sure yet." Bri thinks out loud. "One of the things I need to do is get this woman to show up at the hotel at the same time I'll be there...then see where it goes."

"I have an idea." He tells her. "Don't have McMasters arrange the bare minimum! I'll have him arrange the full security detail McMasters can arrange as The Duchess and soon-to-be Royal Consort, because that woman is the type to make a show with hers."

"*Right!* To make sure she's *seen* as important." Bri says.

"*Precisely.* Only she won't have nearly the circus you'll arrive with!"

Bri rolls her eyes a little. "If you're trying to convince me to ditch security as soon as I'm done, it's working!"

"*Of course not!* "Jack quickly replies. "David would have my head, not to mention Herst would have the rest of me 'drawn and quartered!'

But I'd save them the hassle and jump in front of a double-decker bus!"

She lightly giggles. "Wait. Isn't 'drawn and quartered' part of the punishment for treason?"

"Don't you think something happening to you, The Duchess of Newhaven and soon-to-be-Royal Consort, would be considered 'treasonous?!'" He retorts with a grin. "When this senator sees your entourage and that *you're* 'the real deal,' I'd love to see the look on her face!" He snickers a little.

The Senator likes to make sure everyone knows who she is to inflate her ego and delusion of 'power.' For most of those who preceded her it did, but only to a point. Those who didn't follow politics wouldn't know many politicians in the first place, let alone her position in the senate. She has been desperate to regain this self-perceived power and good standing with her peers, because the time is soon coming when she can be booted out. Unfortunately, she's gone about 'regaining her importance' in the worst possible way and coming across as desperate. It makes sense she would want her daughter's wedding to be at the 'Regal Summit.'

 The Skyward Lounge of The Regal Summit Hotel for a wedding ceremony and The Grand Ballroom are the most sought-after venues in the DC, Maryland, and Virginia area. Amy was able to secure them when she and James first became engaged, because Bri has used the location numerous times over the years working in DC, as does Amy's new boss. They have gotten to know a lot of the managing staff so if Amy's venue is being threatened, it's more likely coming from above them.

Bri realizes, "It may require paying everything in full, though, and I'm not sure if Amy's parents are ready to pay—."

Jack laughs a little. "Well then pay for it, Bri!" She scoffs a little and he tells her, "You have a bank account you barely use—*Use it!*"

Bri says, "You make it sound like I can't just swipe a card and go like some fast-food drive-thru!"

He tells her, "There's *plenty* in your account to do so. You started with four million over a year ago; David and I each put in two million. You don't use much, *and* money is added regularly. Don't worry about the cost; you could pay for the wedding a few times over!"

Bri softly says, "You're such a *wonderful* man!" He hears her choke up.

Jack teases, "You forgot to mention sexy again."

Bri giggles. "Did I?! I never forget to envision that!"

Jack laughs. "I like that answer!"

"Good!" She replies.

"Don't worry about the days; I'll be okay with whatever works for you." He says.

"Thank you for letting me juggle some days, but this will also line up better for The Midnight Ball and spending time with Lawrence. I'll talk to you later! I love you, Amore Mio!"

"I love you, too, Amore Mia!"

CHAPTER 32
Imperfectly Imperfect Change of Plans

The helicopter arrives at The London Palace, where Bri and McMasters are greeted by Royal Guards and escorted inside. They walk in the direction of Lawrence's office, but about halfway there he is coming around a corner to meet up with her. He sees her light up for him and his heart squeezes for her, but outwardly he's stiff; his mother has been particularly nasty today.

"*My* King!" She beams as she gets closer to him.

Lawrence manages a small, sweet smile as he pulls her into his arms and taps a kiss to her lips. She notices he isn't himself, but she hasn't had a chance to study him or ask questions yet. She hears him take a deep breath as he hugs her tight, exhaling and whispering more to himself, "*My Queen.*" She hugs him firmer and it almost sounds like he grimaces. He pulls back and rests his forehead to hers. He doesn't want her to see the bruises on his back from the cane-like stick his mother uses. The staff watch, holding their breath on how he will treat her because The King is in a *very* ill-tempered mood.

"What are you doing here?" He sharply asks.

"I believe the correct response is: 'What a surprise! I'm *so happy* to see you! What brings you my way earlier than expected?'" She tries to tease him, then sees his irritated expression. "*Okaaay.* Well, we need to talk."

He rolls his eyes in annoyance thinking it was about being *The Royal Consort.* "You've changed your mind?"

"What?" Her eyebrows come together in confusion "Oh!" She realizes what he meant. "*Absolutely not!*" His relief shows. "It's not bad, just important."

His tone, thick in agitation, asks, "Are you needing to skip out on our time, so this is more of a kiss off before you leave?"

"I haven't even thought about it like that. I guess I should check in with Gabriel to see what he has planned out because I need to help Amy with something for her wedding. I can buzz to DC quick, but I can make it a day trip or less."

He harshly says, "Then you're here *why*, exactly?"

"Okay, *ouch!*" She is trying hard not to get irritated herself. "I wanted to talk to you in person and not over the phone. I'm hoping to juggle some days around which might work out better for us for The Midnight Ball."

"KING LAWRENCE!" The screeching comes from around the corner and down the hallway he just came from. Bri jumps a little and she sees Lawrence cringe. "YOU HAVE A JOB TO GET BACK TO, YOU PATHETIC EXCUSE OF A KING!"

He clenches his jaw as he looks at his watch and starts walking with her next to him. "It's been a long day already and I need to wrap some things up." He comes across like he's being imposed upon. "If you text me what Gabriel tells you, I'll see what I can do to rearrange my schedule." He tells her as they get to the reception area of The Royal Offices.

"You don't have to rearrange your schedule. I can literally do this within a workday." Bri says.

He's a little snippy. "I don't have time to argue! Just let me know what Gabriel schedules!"

"I could text..." she reads the woman's name on the front of his assistant's desk, "Ms. Dunn. Then—."

In a thick, snobby, pretentious tone, Ms. Dunn states, "I don't *text*, Ma'am."

This woman reminds Bri of a stereotypical librarian. The version with mostly gray hair in a super tight bun, but deeper scowling wrinkles, lighter brown eyes. Her lips are pencil thin and have deep, vertical wrinkles around her mouth from always frowning. Bri literally had the thought that this woman's face would actually crack if she were to smile.

"Um...right...okay, well..." Bri is at a loss for how to win this woman over at the moment.

"Ms. Dunn's mine *and my mother's* executive secretary." He tells her with a pointed look.

"Ah." Bri says impassively.

"Plus, if you text *me*, then I'll know right away and there's less of a chance of me *missing something*." He says with another pointed look, meaning if his mother, or the secretary, didn't find it important, he won't be told and it *won't* be added to his calendar.

"And there's that..." She faintly smiles.

They hear a few swear words coming from The Queen Mother's office, then, "Go take care of those whining idiots before *I* have to deal with them!" She yells out of her office to Lawrence.

"I need to get into a meeting." Lawrence tells Bri. He looks to his guards, "Take her wherever she wishes to go." The Dungeons flashes through Bri's mind, but before she can say anything, he adds, "I'll wrap this up, then meet up with you later."

The Queen Mother orders, "GET TO THAT MEETING, YOU GIT!"

He barely kisses her cheek before he leaves. She thinks he is a bit too irritable for her to want to deal with today anyway. She is sad watching him walk away, hunched down a bit, like someone who has been beaten down...

As Bri goes to leave, Ms. Dunn says, "I'll be getting with Gabriel and start making the transition."

Bri is a bit perplexed. "*Transition*? What transition?"

Ms. Dunn 'tsks' in annoyance. "Once your officially 'The Royal Consort,' The Queen wants *me* to handle your schedule as well."

Bri is confused. "The Queen? Why would Queen Genevieve—."

Ms. Dunn now has a disgusted look for Bri. "*Queen Millicent,* The Queen Mother."

Bri firmly states, "That *won't* be necessary. I have Gabriel."

"I'm afraid you *won't* have a choice!" Ms. Dunn *tells* her, getting downright disrespectful.

"Obviously, *you* don't know me very well because there is *no way* anyone will replace Gabriel! Now, I do need to brush up on my protocol because I don't remember executive assistants being above nobility, let alone royalty or the monarchy, then how The Queen Mother fits into all that is another piece." Bri lets that sit with Ms. Dunn, then she turns on her heel and leaves.

Ms. Dunn takes in the subtle reminder, slightly embarrassed, but irritated also that Bri said 'no' to The Queen Mother. Protocol doesn't have the title of 'The Queen Mother' at much of an advantage. She can't force Bri, The Duchess, to do anything without The King enforcing it for her.

Out in the hall, Bri looks around and sees signs for various things. When she sees a sign for 'The Royal Dungeons' with an arrow; she asks the guards. "Would you take us to The Royal Dungeons?"

The guards remember The King said she could go anywhere. So, with McMasters is by her side, they reluctantly take her to The Dungeons, 'The Queen Mother's Dungeons.' As Bri and McMasters follow along, she texts Gabriel.

> Bri: "I was just told by The Queen Mother's Secretary that she will be transitioning to take over for you. DON'T BELIEVE IT! There's NO WAY that woman, or anyone else for that matter, will take over for you! If you ever leave, I'll miss you dearly, but it'll be YOUR DECISION to move on!"

> Gabriel: "Generally speaking, sometimes that happens to keep The King's and The Queen's schedules in sync. They must be preparing for you to be The Queen; however, in this case, Ms. Dunn would realize how much work is involved, that I have two other people working with me, and may try to say we all report to her, which would be a possibility if you need to keep the peace."

> Bri: "No! ABSOLUTELY NOT! When Lawrence is done with his meeting, I'll tell him about my feelings on this matter! You report to me and your assistants report to you, or me in your absence that day!"

> Gabriel: "Will do! Oh, I can arrange your flight to DC whenever you'd like."

> Bri: "Let's aim for right away in the morning, but I'll confirm in a little while. With Lawrence's foul mood, I might still go today."

> Gabriel: "Just let me know what you decide."

Bri finishes her texts with Gabriel just before they get to The Dungeons. Bri asks one of the guards walking with her and McMasters, "How often does The King visit down here?"

"He doesn't." The guard simply answers.

"What?!" Bri is surprised and has a bit of an appalled expression.

"If you don't mind me asking, Your Grace, do you have any idea what your about to see?" The guard asks.

"Not really. I hear the word 'dungeon' and I think dark, damp, and dreary, with rats and mice; but I try to replace them with slightly better images of jails or prisons."

Another guard says more matter-of-factly, "Your first images are closer to the truth."

"Wha—*Whyyy*?!" Her mouth drops.

"The Dungeons are known as 'The Queen Mother's Dungeons' and they're *very much* her dungeons!"

Bri gets a sick feeling. "She oversees The Dungeons and decides how people are punished?"

"Yes, Ma'am." He answers.

When the door is opened for her, the smell alone makes her throw up in the nearest trash bin. When she is able, she stands up and straightens her clothes. Someone hands her a small glass of water. She thanks them and uses it to rinse her mouth out. She digs in her purse for her breath mints and pops one in before she takes a deep breath before the door is opened again. She steps through the door and the mint helps a little with the awful smell. The floors are damp and the walls have condensation on them. The more steps she takes, the more horrible it feels as she starts to see people, even ghosts and spirits, and a heavy feeling the despair. The people are cold, sick, with a look of living a miserable existence on their faces. The Dungeon's Keeper approaches and Bri senses something dark about him...in her mind she is curious about the thick darkness she senses. He introduces himself proudly as 'The Keeper,' shaking her hand.

Bri asks, "Has it always been like this?"

"*This* is how The Queen Mother wants it." He gestures proudly around with his arms. "Real punishments for these *offenders to The Crown*!"

"But does that mean decades of these conditions?!" Bri asks more in shock.

"Centuries really, Ma'am." He states with satisfaction, not catching her disgust at the appalling conditions.

Bri walks along the corridor a few steps. "How many die each year?" She closes her eyes, waiting for an answer.

"I've stopped keeping track like that, Ma'am. It's too difficult. May I call you Bri?" He requests.

Bri is looking around as she offhandedly answers, "No." She pauses to look at him. "It's interesting it got too difficult to keep track...Why do you suppose that is?"

He clears his throat to recover. "The flu itself can wipeout a whole row in a short period of time, Your Grace."

"And is there a warm, dry place for the sick? An infirmary of sorts?"

"Down here?!" The Keeper laughs. "Ma'am this place is meant to punish criminals! It's not for someone to serve a sentence in comfort, just to be sent back out into society to commit more serious crimes against The Crown!"

With his laughing response, she steers the conversation from a different angle. "How many souls are down here right now?!"

"Seventy-three. I think the most ever squeezed in here was something like two-hundred fifty-eight." He tells her.

Her mouth falls open. "What happened to warrant that many?!"

His tone is in defense of The Queen Mother, which doesn't surprise her at this point. "The Queen Mother has to rule with an iron fist! That number was composed of a large group of 'rebels' against Her Majesty, *Queen Millicent*, at the time. They had handcuffed themselves to the front gate of The Palace,

323

calling her disrespectful names and accusing her of being a bully of a tyrant and not caring about her people!"

"What happened to them?" She touches the cold bars of a cell and she senses the answer before he confirms it.

"These prats were surprised when she ordered their execution. Can you believe that?!" He laughs in scoff. "She was protecting The Crown and The Palace from these stupid gits!"

"From doing what? It's not like these so-called 'rebels' were actually *breaking down the gate and storming into The Palace.*" Bri retorts.

"With all due respect, Ma'am, it might start out relatively harmless, but it can quickly turn into a revolution, bringing down *the entire* Monarchy!" He defensively replies.

She gives him a 'come on now' look as she states, "What she did was *exactly* what gets the public angry and *ignites* a revolution!" Bri keeps her composure even though she is surrounded by spirits of former inmates and empathically channeling their strong emotions. She is also getting a strong feeling he is either a sociopath or a psychopath, but she would need more time to determine which one. She sees he has taken them to... "Are these The Torture Chambers?" She asks, looking around at the ghosts inside these cells.

The atmosphere feels heavier and more somber. She sees a few of these ghosts reenacting their torturous deaths. One reenactment in particular keeps her attention. They have a hood over their head with their arms tied above their head and their shirt is ripped in back. She watches as this person is whipped and notices they never make a noise with the pain...she has to peel her eyes away from what she is seeing because it starts to feel like some sort of premonition...

She takes a deep breath as she looks around the rest of the chambers. Even though she is starting to feel overwhelmed by the spirits, ghosts, and premonition, she *refuses* to cry or shed one tear; she is determined to hold her resolve. If he is a psychopath, he has been faking any feelings of concern for the inmates but will have more difficulty hiding his excitement with any talk of torture.

"What causes a prisoner to be brought *in here*?" She asks, motioning around the room.

"Usually, we bring them in here when they're being insubordinate, or hurting other prisoners, things like that." He replies.

She offhandedly states based on the inspired feelings she feels, "Wouldn't it be hard to follow the rules when they keep changing and there is a punishment *for everything*?"

"Ma'am?" He is unsure and nervous about how to answer.

"Well, Mister...?" She asks.

"Gillery."

"Well, Mister Gillery," she explains, "the problem with corporal punishments and torture chambers is that it's so easy to cross a line into abuse and use it as an excuse to release one's anger and frustrations on a prisoner, turned victim, for the smallest things? *Or worse*, take pleasure in their pain or death?" There were many spirits whose 'ears perk up' in intrigue.

He smugly replies, "I only take satisfaction when they *finally* learn the lesson!"

Bri has a disgusted look on her face and exhales it away. She knows taking pleasure in 'teaching lessons' is sadistic, a characteristic for psychopathy, although the power derived from it would attract sociopaths...

Bri continues. "Down here, in this room, it has been *way* too easy to cross the line into abuse and assault."

She hears no rebuttal, but she sees a couple of spirits in particular take on a special loathing for Mister Gillery. He becomes nervous and now wants to hurry her out of The Dungeons. He needs to call to talk to The Queen Mother and let her know *they might have a problem*.

"Ma'am, is there something you specifically needed?" He asks with a fake smile and clenching jaw.

"No. I've never visited any dungeons before." Bri wonders, "Have there been any prisoners who were released?"

"Not many. I'm not sure I should answer any more questions without The Queen Mother's approval." He worries.

A guard tells him, "The King said she could go anywhere she wanted to go."

Bri sees a back door swing open with a van waiting outside. She acts like she doesn't care, but Mr. Gillery is suspicious. He doesn't want her to know that this van transports certain prisoners out to The Queen Mother's family estate in Devonridge. Bri sees a desk by the back door and walks past it to make Mr. Gillery nervous, then up the next corridor. She walks the way to the door they first came in. Bri and McMasters leave The Dungeons and thankfully, more Royal Guards are right outside The Dungeons.

One whispers, *"Good thing you're coming out now before The Queen Mother goes in for her daily visit."*

"Daily?" Bri asks.

He nods. "Your Grace," he gestures Mr. Gillery and the others, "they're only doing what The Queen Mother wants them to do!"

"I picked up on that, but they seem to enjoy torturing others and *they* own their personal feelings. I think I might be sick again..." They take her to the bathroom but she's able to overcome it. She takes a paper towel and dampens it with cold water, then presses it into her neck. She does this for a few minutes before she has the guards take her to the main hallway, then she and McMasters will go to The Royal Apartment with a few of them. With Lawrence not being in the best of moods today, she'll talk to him at another time about the conditions in The Dungeons. Her phone chimes a text notification.

Lawrence: "SEE ME NOW!"

Her heart sinks.

Lawrence texts again: "THAT'S NOT A REQUEST DUCHESS!"

That text annoys her and she refuses to respond, but she does tell McMasters she needs to go to Lawrence's office.

CHAPTER 33

Imperfectly Perfect Royal Confrontation

McMasters is outside the main door of the office suite, which is also Ms. Dunn's office. Bri walks in and Ms. Dunn is already whispering into the phone, then hangs up with The Queen Mother.

"He says to go in." She has a smug, faint smile on her face.

Bri fights the urge to throw up again. She walks to the office Ms. Dunn pointed to and she knocks before she opens the door.

Lawrence's annoyance is clear! As she opens the door he yells, "COME!" He jumps to his feet. Lawrence's face shows his anger. "LEAVE US!" He says to the few people in the room and everyone scurries out, with the last one shutting the door and leaving Bri alone with Lawrence.

Bri tries to remain calm; Lawrence has never been this way *with* her. She senses his mother is behind this and now braces for whatever this woman has fired '*Her King*' up about...then she faintly hears the words:

> *"You have a choice: stand up to Lawrence and his mother, or shrink back..."*

Lawrence's voice is eerily calm, but there's no mistaking the anger in it. "*Did you*, or did you not, visit The Dungeons?"

She stands firm in the words she had just heard and remembers. She goes to explain their deplorable conditions. "Lawrence, do you know—."

"*YES OR NO!*" He cuts her off.

"Yes, but—."

"You had NO business *being down there!*" Lawrence shouts.

Bri's temper is starting to flare. "*You said I could go anywhere!*"

He furiously scoffs, "OH, *BE REASONABLE!*"

"That's the problem!" She gestures herself, "*I am*! No wonder no one *reasonable* is allowed down there! Those awful conditions are deplorable, Lawrence Heathherst! I can't believe you—."

"You will *not* address The King so formerly, *Duchess*!" He walks around from behind his desk. "As for *my* prisoners, how else will these prisoners learn?! Things can't be like American prisons, all warm and cozy?!"

She points in the direction of The Dungeons, "*Those conditions aren't fit—*."

"STOP TALKING!" He yells and she glares. "THINGS *HAVE* TO BE THIS WAY!" He yells. She goes to say something again, but he won't let her. "*DON'T SPEAK!*" Frustrating her. She's not listening to him rant and marches over to an adjacent door as he yells at her; she yanks the door open.

A startled Queen Mother stumbles out of her office and into Lawrence's office, "Wha..." she catches herself and turns to glare at Bri, "What's the meaning of this?!"

Bri gets a surge of courage and ignores The Queen Mother, turning back to face 'The King.' "*Why is it* she doesn't want anyone to see how these prisoners are treated or that they even exist?! Could it be that you'd have all kinds of human rights violat—."

WHACK! The Queen Mother backhands Bri across the face; Bri's hand goes to her face but she doesn't flinch any other way. The Queen Mother steps next to The King, stopping him from intervening. She glares at Bri and with loathing in her voice, "How *DARE YOU* speak so freely to me and *YOUR* King, *you sniveling little ingrate?!*"

"OH NO!" Bri gestures Lawrence with her arm, "That is NOT *my king!*" She points to The Queen Mother. "This is *your* pathetic attempt at keeping a grip on power." Bri sees the hint of fear in The Queen Mother's eyes.

The Queen Mother looks at Lawrence. "Take care of this NOW, you stupid fool!" She seethes with anger adding, "Or *she* will walk all over you!"

"Like you?!" Bri folds her arms and raises her eyebrow.

Lawrence tells her again, "*As I told you, it isn't like American prisons! The Dungeons are for punishment!*"

"TORTURE, YOU MEAN!" Bri's anger is now evident.

The Queen Mother inhales a huge gasp. She looks from Bri back to Lawrence still seething, "YOU'RE GOING TO LET HER SPEAK TO US LIKE THAT?!"

Bri's starts to understand more. "*You think these are forgotten souls no one will miss!*" Remembering the white van by a back door of The Dungeons, "If—."

The Queen Mother interrupts with a hatred tone, "*Remember.your.place!* AMERICANS CAN'T UNDERSTAND OUR ROYAL WAYS!"

Lawrence adds, "*You know crimes against The Monarchy have to be dealt with more harshly! You have to understand—.*"

Bri channels herself from when she stood up to David at the first Black-Tie Party. She ignores his mother and talks directly to Lawrence. He sees the angry look on her face with a hint of mocking smile, unnerving him a bit.

"Understand what?! The ways of an arrogant king or a conniving *witch*?!" She points her finger angrily into Lawrence's chest enunciating, "You've *let her* bury your head in the sand, *Your Majesty!*" He cringes at the tone she uses for that. She goes on, "These are NOT royal ways, *nor humane ways*, and it has *nothing* to do with being an American and *everything* to do with being a *decent human being*; the very basis of a great person, let alone a great king!" She looks at The Queen Mother as she says to him, "I'm questioning whether this woman is actually human!" She pivots to walk to the door.

She hears his mother yelling at Lawrence, "*STOP HER!*"

"DON'T WALK AWAY FROM ME, DUCHESS!" He yells after her as she opens the door. "I HAVEN'T DISMISSED YOU! *DO YOU HEAR ME?!*"

She sees people staring into the office from the hallway. She knows there has to be countless others in the various corridors. She hears the words in her mind, '*This is the moment.*' She turns on her heels and he sees the look on her face; *now he's worried!* She purposely leaves the door open so *everyone* listening can hear what comes next.

She's walking right up to him, glaring at him in a way that continues to unnerve him. He tells her, "DON'T LOOK AT ME LIKE THAT! YOU'LL RESPECT THE KING, DAMNIT!"

She slaps him incredibly *hard* across the face, saying, "THEN ACT LIKE IT!" Gasps flow throughout the hallways in The Palace.

She sees his fury as he grabs her throat and shoves her up against the wall. His hand is at her throat and he's firmly squeezing, pinning her there. Bri sees in his eyes that this excites him. What surprises Bri more is how she's attracted to this, too, and *he* sees it in *her* eyes, only adding more to their passionate chemistry, but he's still furious about being slapped across the face *and* in front of his mother!

He enunciates through gritted teeth, "DON'T.*EVER*.SLAP.ME.AGAIN!"

She glares as he adds a hint of pressure on her neck. She struggles a little to say, "Or you'll what? *Kill me*?!"

He yells in frustration with her challenge to him. *"BEING KING ISN'T SOME GAME!"*

"THEN CUT THE DAMN STRINGS ALREADY, *YOUR MAJESTY!*" He cringes again at how she says that and he loosens his grip. She uses this moment to forcefully push him away. "BE THE KING *YOU* REALLY ARE AND NOT THIS…" she waves her hand up and down motioning him, "THIS *PATHETIC KING* SHE BRINGS OUT IN YOU! BE THE KING YOUR PEOPLE NEED YOU TO BE, THE KING *I* NEED YOU TO BE, THE KING *OUR FAMILY* NEEDS YOU TO BE!" She takes her ring off. "STEP UP OR DON'T COME FOR ME AND HAVE A NICE LIFE!" She slams the ring into his chest and he catches it in his hand. He stares at it, listening to her footsteps get further away. His heart begins to sink under the weight of what just happened…

Bri steps into the hallway with McMasters and a whole lot of frozen people in the halls. McMasters knows Bri well enough by now that it wasn't easy to say all that because she loves him, but that it needed to be said *because she loves him*! Bri sees Jessica and she wants Bri to follow her, which she manages to do even with her mind spinning and her heart racing.

Lawrence is still stunned, but now he feels like something is melting away…it's his mother's death grip on him. She's in a tirade but Lawrence doesn't hear a word of it at first, which makes it worse. He's angry, only he's realizing his anger is with his mother *and himself*. This time he grabs *her* by the throat, slamming her against the wall and he squeezes her throat hard to shut her up. For the first time his voice booms and echoes in those hallways when he yells, "ENOUGH, MOTHER! Clean out your office and have *your* assistant separate our schedules! I'll be hiring my own assistant." He coldly states, "FROM HERE ON OUT, *MOTHER*, I'LL BE RULING WITHOUT YOU!" She goes to argue but he stops her with one statement: *"DON'T MAKE ME TAKE YOUR TITLE AWAY!"*

Then he sees it! For the first time he sees the fear in her eyes as her nightmare starts to come true: she has lost control over him, over The Monarchy; the power she covets! In a desperate attempt to stop this from unraveling, The Queen Mother struggles to tell him, "I'm your mother and I have devoted people in this place! You *can't* rule without me! *They won't let you!"*

"You won't have all of them if your title is taken away!" With a humorless laugh he lets go of her and watches her rub her throat. "I can't do any worse than what you've been doing and having me do!"

"You'll let everyone walk all over you!" She points to the door where Bri left through. "Because of that pathetic excuse—." He steps closer and she defensively steps back.

He has never let himself admit it before because she is his mother, but he finally lets it in: *he despises this woman*! "Watch it, *Mother*! That's the woman I love!"

"Oh, please! You don't know what love is! *I made sure of that*! I didn't want you weaker than you already are!" She had disposed of any woman he started to care about *before* it became love, only with Bri being a 'Direct Bloodline,' and Lawrence needing that heir, well, things got complicated.

"YOU don't get it! *You* soulless, wretched old woman! You *wasted* your life away and now have *nothing* to show for *your* pathetic existence! You're trying to use me, to be who *you never could be*! Tell me, if you couldn't be that person yourself, what made you think you could *raise someone* to be that person?! And you say *I'm* pathetic?!" If looks could kill, his mother's glare would've incinerated him. He walks over and stands by the door between their offices, his hand on the doorknob and with angry determination he clearly enunciates, *"Get.Out."*

Before his mother walks through it, she stops in front of him and warns, "You best remember quickly who you're dealing with because it's better to keep me *by* your side! If we shift to enemies, you don't have the resolve, *nor the stomach*, to come out on top!" She pats his cheek. "I do, you piece of—!" She gasps when Lawrence's hand grips her upper arm and jerks her close.

He says in a low voice that send chills through her body, which she isn't one to get affected this way, "If I were you, I'd be worried about the man you raised torturing and is no longer tethered to *your* leash!"

He sees a flash of fear go across her eyes! She exhales in an angry huff as she turns and stomps off through the door with Lawrence slamming it shut behind her heels. He faces his desk from the side of the room thinking he needed to find Bri, but how?! And how in the world is he going to apologize for all this?! His heart sinks...*for what he did?* He tries to call her, but understandably she sends it right to voicemail...

Bri follows Jessica, and McMasters is following Bri as he calls Gabriel to schedule her flight to DC right away. Jessica leads them through the secret passageways, even some secret stairs within them. There was a hidden section of The King's Library, a hidden closet of sorts, where Jessica has her take a specific black, leather-bound book.

"Important reading." Jessica tells her.

"This looks like a journal?" Bri is concerned about privacy, "I can't—."

"It's alright. *I promise.*" Jessica assures her. Bri nods and puts it in her bag.

There were all kinds of things in this closet and she'd like to come back some day. Jessica leads them through the secret passageways as much as possible when Bri hears the helicopter.

Bri's phone is ringing as they make their way to the helicopter. She sees it's Lawrence calling her. She purposely sends it to voicemail; she doesn't want to talk to him yet.

Seth had heard what happened and grabbed Abby on his way to find Lawrence. They walk into Lawrence's office and he's listening to the sound of Bri's helicopter flying away. His hands ball into fists and he clenches his jaw, angry with himself. He looks at Seth and Abby, with Seth asking about what he has heard.

"Is it true?! The whole Palace is buzzing about the beautiful Duchess standing up to The King AND The Queen Mother!" Seth asks in amazement. "Would've *loved* to have seen that!"

"You and everyone else! Of course, those in the hallways heard everything...*daaamn*, Seth." He slams the palm of his hand into his desk hard enough to make a loud noise. "I'm going to go down as the most foolish puppet king there ever was, but what bothers me most is putting yours and Abby's lives at a greater risk, maybe even Gen's, *and I could very well lose Bri over this!*"

"You won't go down that way! Not with that *fantastic* Duchess!" Seth replies.

"Don't worry about Seth and me! We were just talking with Gen the other day that we're tired of being pawns in this sick and twisted game Mother plays all the time with us!" Abby tells him. "Mother won't kill Bri, at least not before she has 'her heir.'"

Seth looks at Lawrence's desk and points, "Her ring?!" Seth lets out a swear word or few.

Abby is in shock and gets protective of her sister-friend. "What *did* you do, Lawrence Alexander Heathherst?!"

"*The worst thing I've ever done!*" He picks up the ring and stares at it. "I screamed and yelled *at her*...I held her against the wall by the throat—."

Seth is stunned! "*You what?!* You've *never* touched a woman—."

"*I know!* It was right after she slapped me!" He rubs his cheek. "If my day wasn't already horrible—gah! There's *no* excuse!" He has a few 'choice words' for himself.

Seth puts his hand on his brother's shoulder and says, "One of the many things I remember David and Jack saying about her is she's not only the most loving woman *on the planet*, but she's also the most forgiving. *And I'd wager* she's quickest to forgive those she loves."

"This *isn't* easily forgivable, Seth..." Lawrence replies.

Abby thoughtfully asks, "What exactly did she say when she gave you the ring back?!"

334

He quietly answers, "To step up or don't come after her."

"Lawrence! *Don't you see?*! She knew exactly who she was dealing with! Lawrence, you stepped up! You threw Mother out to rule on your own! Now *go after Bri*!" Seth says. "We'll cover here for as long as you need!"

Lawrence replies, "I'm not sure what to do. She sent my call to voicemail and if she needs time, I don't want to make it worse by pushing her."

Seth reluctantly says, "By the sound of it, *you couldn't make it worse...*"

Abby chimes in, "Unless you let her leave your life for good!"

Seth sits on the corner of the desk. "Call Jack or David and see what they say. She had a face-off with David when they first met." He snaps his fingers as he remembers, "He also says that was the same night *his walls* came down and now I'm thinking you had a similar experience!"

Lawrence nods and decides to call Jack, he can't face David right now who has every right to be *royally* angry with him. Lawrence doesn't know it yet; but since Jack knows where Bri is, he's the one to talk to anyway. When Jack answers, he notices Lawrence's voice isn't normal.

Jack asks, "Is everything's okay?"

"No..." Lawrence replies and explains his despicable behavior. "Jack, I need to fix this, but she won't take my calls, *not* that I blame her. I need your help...*will you help me?*"

"She needs to calm down a bit. She's hurt and needs some space. I do know she's on her way to DC. She needs to help Amy out with something important for her wedding."

Lawrence asks with a slight panic, "So, I have to wait until she comes back?!"

"No, no. Her flight to DC should be enough time for her anger and the rawness of the hurt to subside." Jack tells him.

"Seriously? She could make me pay for this for some time *and I'd pay it*!" Lawrence throws out there.

Jack snorts a laugh. "A lot of women would! But as you're fully aware, she isn't like that!"

Lawrence faintly smiles. "*No, she's not...*"

"Herst, the woman loves and she does it brilliantly well, even when she helps us to grow up. I'll call to see about the pilots slowing down and you see about speeding up your jet! Hopefully it'll be enough for you to beat her there."

"On my way!" Lawrence says.

Lawrence hangs up and says to Seth and Abby, "Bri said when she first arrived that this trip could be done in a day."

"Great! You can go to the airport straight away!" Seth says as he and Abby push him out the door.

Lawrence says walking out, "I have a favor to ask of you."

"Anything!" Abby replies.

"I told Mother I was no longer using *her* assistant."

Seth happily asks, "Hire a new one?"

Lawrence smiles. "Please! Maybe Gabriel, Bri's assistant, would have some ideas or could assist?"

"We'll take care of it! Just worry about Bri and we'll take care of everything here!" Abby says.

Lawrence thanks them and quickly hugs them before he rushes out to meet The Royal Helicopter that is arriving.

CHAPTER 34
Imperfectly Perfect & Royally Messy

Lawrence isn't able to get too far ahead of Bri without her becoming suspicious with her flight's time taking *too* long. She has been back and forth enough by now to know how long the longest flight time would take in a headwind. Lawrence is able to get ahead just enough to be waiting on the tarmac with the motorcade, as her plane pulls up to them.

Bri gathers up her things as the flight attendant, Linda, opens the door. Out her window Bri sees the motorcade and texts Amy:

> Bri: "Girl, seriously?! I don't need a full escort for royalty!"

> Amy: "You're funny!"

Bri sends her a picture as she throws her purse and bag over her shoulder.

> Bri: "No joke."

> Amy: "???"

When Bri steps off the plane she pauses at the top of the stairs and looks around...then she sees the *royal* reason waiting for her. She forces herself to inhale, but holds her breath as she texts Amy.

> Bri: "NVM. Now I see the 'kingly' reason why." (adds an annoyed face)

> Amy: "Sorry. I thought you were joking with me."

> Bri: "I'm upset with him, not you. You're fine. Ttyl."

> Amy: (sends a 'thumbs up')

Bri descends the stairs and sees Mateo coming up with his arms out happily greeting her, "Bri!"

She slaps a smile on her face but it's sincere. "Mateo!" She hugs him, happy to see him.

Lawrence is bothered a little by this and she catches it out of the corner of her eye. She doesn't care to make him feel better yet, so she lets Lawrence twist a bit.

"Amy asked me to be your driver, but I guess——." He throws his thumb over his shoulder to the motorcade.

"*You* are definitely *my* driver! *Always!*" She states. "I'm on my way to sort out a mess Senator Watson has caused Amy and her fiancé, James!" She looks at Lawrence. "*I don't have the patience to deal with anything else.*" He quietly nods.

Bri follows Mateo and Lawrence follows her to the car Mateo is driving, hoping she will let him come along. She slides into the backseat, but she does slide all the way over for Lawrence, which he is grateful for. While she isn't ready to talk to him, she loves this man who dropped everything to follow her to DC to try to make things right and he deserves credit for that!

Bri's phone rings and she sees it's The President. He wants them to stop by The White House; he said they won't take too much time. When they pull up to The White House, The President and First Lady are outside waiting for their arrival.

Bri flatly says, "Put your game-face on." He does, which he's used to doing.

King Lawrence gets out of the car first, with a smile, then they hear the members of the press and public making lots of noise. He gives Bri his hand, which she takes, and helps her out of the car. She hugs their hosts and reintroduces them to King Lawrence before the four of them head inside. Bri can sense Lawrence wants to hold her hand, but he was expecting her not to let him. Instead, Bri reaches for his hand and holds it firm herself. This catches Lawrence by surprise and chokes him up a little...even though she was upset *with* him, she wasn't giving up *on him*.

After the meeting at The White House, Bri heads over to The Regal Summit Hotel with Lawrence to get everything squared away. She isn't sure how he did it, but Jack got Senator Watson and the press there before Bri. Her face is priceless and is caught in pictures that Jack will get a kick out of, especially when the senator realizes she won't be getting her way with the hotel accommodating her daughter's wedding. Bri wasn't going to let James and Amy's wedding be turned upside down because this woman wants what she wants and aims to get it by bribing and making demands, regardless of who it hurts.

Bri took Jack's advice to pay for everything. David gets a call from The Royal Crown Bank of a charge on Bri's account; she's never had anything remotely that big before and they wanted to make sure it wasn't a fraudulent charge. David couldn't believe it! Bri went to DC without saying a word! He remembers McMasters saying she just got lost in The Palace taking off by herself! *How could she be so careless*?! It scares him to think of something happening to her and he lets his fear get the better of him.

The Newhaven News Chronicle has an article in their evening edition covering her trip to DC. Unfortunately, David only reads the headline and it aggravates him more, causing him to fold it back in half again and slam it down on the table. If only he had read just a few sentences...

The Duchess of Newhaven in Washington, D.C.

By: Francis Chapman

His Majesty, King Lawrence, and Her Grace, The Duchess of Newhaven, met with The President of the United States and The First Lady at The White House today. The King and The Duchess then made a stop at The Regal Summit Hotel where The Duchess' brother-in-law, Lord James Worthington, will marry Ms. Amy Walker, a D.C. local, in a few weeks.

Sources tell us that U.S. Senator Sonja Watson's daughter wants to get married that same Saturday and they have their sights on the popular rooftop lounge for her wedding venue. Unfortunately for them, it's been booked for the Walker-Worthington Wedding. No one knows exactly what was said in a meeting with The Duchess, The Hotel Manager, and of course, Senator Watson, but the Senator was *not* happy when she left the hotel.

With the wedding venue still set for the Walker–Worthington Wedding, we know The King and The Worthington Family will return to DC in the very near future for the event.

Bri quickly texts Amy on her way out of the hotel:

> "ALL is as you planned! The Sky Lounge and The Grand Ballroom are still YOUR venues! Wedding is paid for, our gift."

Bri calls Henry's office on their way back to the airport and Theresa, his assistant, tells her she'll try to keep him there and keep her visit a surprise if she can. Bri's phone chimes with Amy's tone.

> Amy: "You're the best! Thank you! Thank you! Thank you! My parents already paid. (adds a winking face) Seriously though, you didn't have to pay for the wedding as a gift!

> Bri: "You're so welcome and I'm glad I could help! It was Jack's idea to pay to help ensure your venue wouldn't be at risk again. See you soon, Soon-To-Be-Sister!"

In ten minutes, Bri's walking into the building with Lawrence beside her, but she doesn't give him an opportunity to hold her hand this time.

She walks up to the reception desk and then hears from behind her a loud, "*HELLOOO*, Beautiful!"

Bri recognizes the voice and a huge smile spreads across her face as she turns around. "Hey, Good Lookin'!" She hugs Sam and he lifts her, spinning her around before he sets her back down. Bri and Sam stand beside each other, with his arm around her waist. "What are you doing here?!" She happily asks.

"Me?! I was going to ask you the same thing, Sis!" Sam laughs. Lawrence relaxes as he realizes who this is in relation to her and David. Lawrence can't believe how grown-up Sam looks!

"Would you believe me if I said to see you?!" She asks with a grin.

He snorts a laugh. "No!"

Lawrence interrupts, "Sam, it's good to see you again!" He genuinely tells him, shaking his hand and patting his upper arm.

"Likewise!" Sam smiles wide. He looks over at the reception desk, but the receptionist isn't there. "Where's Dad?"

"In a meeting." Bri answers, looking at her watch. "I was hoping to see him as we passed through town."

"He's not in a meeting anymore!" Sam says and points behind her.

"Ha-ha! How's my girl?!" Henry has his arms out wide with a huge smile on his face and he hugs her tight. "Did I hear right? You're just passing through?" Joe is right behind Henry.

She continues to hug him. "Yeah, I wanted to help Amy personally with something that popped up with the wedding and it couldn't wait, but I have to get back." She hugs Joe.

"You're still staying with us for a couple days after the wedding, right?" Henry asks.

"Absolutely!" Bri replies.

He holds her chin as a father would to study her face and to let her know *he knows* something is bothering her. "I think we may need to talk sooner?"

She sweetly smiles. "I do miss sitting in your study with you and talking as we watch the girls swim in the pool through the patio doors."

"Me, too." He senses she's not wanting to talk. "Promise to call me later and *I guess* we can let you pass through town."

"More like breeze through!" Joe teases.

Henry does a double take with Lawrence. "Oh! Your—."

"Always 'Herst' or 'Lawrence.' *Please.*" He looks at Bri. "I've been marveling at all the people who enjoy seeing Bri!"

Henry looks from him to Bri. "She's *definitely* a special one! Have you been to Capitol Hill with her yet?"

Lawrence's eyebrow raises as he looks at Bri. "I haven't had the pleasure."

Henry smiles proudly at Bri. "That's where I *really* marvel!"

"Seriously?" Bri laughs. "That's the biggest group of people who know how to fake charm people."

Joe tells her, "And yet, with you *that's when they're the most genuine!*" She teasingly glares at him.

She takes a deep breath. "We should get going so we can get back at a decent time." They say 'goodbye' and they all walk outside.

They wave as Lawrence and Bri climb into the car. Mateo and McMasters get in the car and they make their way to the airport to fly back to London. Sitting in the back seat Bri is quiet; she wants to stay mad at Lawrence for a little longer, only her heart just wants to love him. Thankfully, her heart was winning the battle.

On the tarmac, Bri goes around and thanks everyone. She hugs Mateo and says, "This isn't goodbye!"

He grins, "Until next time, *Your Grace*! Stay cool!" He fist bumps her, then he shakes Lawrence's hand and they say goodbye.

When she and Lawrence are walking up the stairs, she tells Lawrence, "If it helps, Mateo is *happily* married with kids."

He pauses for a moment as it sinks in; she doesn't want him to be jealous of Mateo. He quietly answers, "It does."

Bri finishes going up the stairs and sees she missed a couple calls from David. She calls him back, but when he answers, there's no greeting and he's short with her.

> "I got a call from the bank that your account had an unusual amount debited."

> She replies, "It's the place James—."

> David couldn't keep his anger in check. "*AND* you flew to DC without telling me, Bri! What the h—."

> "*Hey!*" Bri interrupts. "J—." Bri hears a growl of frustration from David before it's cut off when David hangs up on her.

Being hung up on doesn't sit well with her. She gets settled in and as soon as they're airborne, she pulls up an email to draft to David; however, she decides to discuss things in person instead so there are no more misunderstandings. She reads her email from Jack explaining some of the remodeling at The Mill. He wants her to think about the email and they will talk when she gets back. She responds saying she needs to stop by David's office when she comes back into town, but not to tell David. She says he is really upset about not knowing she was going to DC, and she hopes he's not upset she paid for the rest of the wedding. Jack's response email won't come through for a little bit. A wave of exhaustion hits her and she can't keep her eyes open. She gets up to go lay down.

"Bri, you *need* to talk to me!" Lawrence pleads, but she *needs* to sleep. "I think I've been patient long enough."

"I just had a wave of exhaustion hit me and I can't keep my eyes open, *Your Majesty.*" He cringes. She tells him, "I think we said enough today, even the whole Palace heard and by now, the world." She starts to walk back to where there is a bedroom. She stops and looks back, "If I promise we can talk, just not when I'm this tired; would it help?" He's a little disappointed and she senses she needs to add, "If I were done with you and us, there is no way I would've let you come with me today. And I would've had a call into Jack by now chewing him out for arranging this." She gives him a look that she knows he had Jack's help.

He stands and nods, giving her a faint smile as he walks over to her. He takes a deep breath, exhaling slowly as he places a hand on the wall on either side of her; she's nervous at the intense look in his eyes. He captures her gaze and continues to look at her so intensely, but there's so much love *and remorse*, it breaks her resolve. She holds his face and pulls him into a kiss, kissing him fiercely, deeply. He pins her to the wall with his body as he kisses her just as fiercely, then more so.

She can't control the tears and breaks the kiss. She says sternly, "*You really hurt me AND you lied to me.*"

He pauses to look her in the eyes, his pain is even more evident. "I know I hurt you and I wish that 'I'm sorry' would fix it—."

"It's a start."

"Then from the bottom of my heart, My Queen, I'm so *very* sorry." He holds her gaze.

"Me, too." Her lower jaw shakes a little. "I'm deeply sorry for breaking any rules, for disresp—."

"No, Bri. You have absolutely *nothing* to be sorry for!" His heart sinks more as he grasps...he *had* lied to her. "Oh, Darling..." he holds her face, "I told you that you could tell me anything and at the first moment you try, I wouldn't let you...I let you down in another way!" He sees her yawn so hard she shakes. He gives her a hint of a smile. "First, let's get you some rest and it'll give me a chance to, um…cool down." He pulls at his collar.

"Well, when you cool down *and if you can handle it*, you can come lay next to me, on *top* of the covers *with* the door open." She offers.

He smiles. "Give me a few minutes to finish up something for Seth who is managing things for me with Abby, then I'll be in." He leans in and kisses her cheek. She smiles before she goes back to the bedroom.

When the plane starts to descend, Lawrence places a hand on her shoulder to wake her. Bri smiles slightly and lays there a moment to wake up. She crawls out of bed and makes her way to the table and her laptop. Before she shuts it down, she sees the email from Jack. In it, Jack says he doubts David even cares about the money at all, but Jack replaced the amount in her account anyways. He agrees it's a misunderstanding of sorts, that he'll fly to The Palace in the morning to fly back with her to Edinburgh, and he ends with, "I love you!" She shuts her laptop down and packs it up. The landing is a little rough, even for someone who likes to fly. She has to grab a bag to throw up in and apologizes to the flight attendant.

"Are you alright, Darling?" Lawrence asks as he hands her a tissue.

"I think so." Taking the tissue and wiping her mouth; apologizing again to the flight attendant.

She assures Bri that there's no need to be sorry. "It happens to the best of us!"

They go from the airplane to the helicopter, but Lawrence pauses. "Maybe I should call for a car?"

"It's fine. Really, Your Majesty." She climbs in before he can object to the formality. "This will be faster."

The helicopter is landing on The Royal Apartment side of The London Palace. She is yawning like crazy again and says goodnight to Lawrence before going into the bedroom she uses when she stays there. Bri takes a shower and crawls into bed. She checks her phone; David is still 'radio silent.' She quickly wipes her cheek and pushes away the urge to cry.

Lawrence knocks, his voice is a bit more muffled than usual. She goes and answers the door. "We're not talking tonight either, Lawrence. *Especially when you've been drinking.*" She says 'goodnight,' then shuts the door and locks it.

He lightly hits his head on the door and she hears him whisper to himself, "*Impossible...*"

He goes back to his bedroom for the rest of the night. He decides he has had enough to drink and just goes to bed where he sleeps hard all night.

CHAPTER 35

Imperfectly Perfectly Paying a Price...Royally

In the middle of the night, Bri wakes up to a pillowcase going over her head. She starts to scream but a hand goes over mouth to stop her.

Someone whispers gruffly in her ear, *"We're told to tell you, if you don't come quietly, The King's punishment will be THE MOST SEVERE!"* She panics for Lawrence and doesn't make another sound.

McMasters woke up to a noise; he's half-awake as he listens for whatever it was, but when he doesn't hear anything, he figures it was a part of a dream and lays back down. However, he can't fall back asleep.

They bind Bri's hands, then her feet. She hears another man whisper, *"Hurry up...let's get this over with!"*

She is still fighting them and one of them knocks over a vase that crashes to the floor. McMasters bolts upright and without thinking about it, he rushes to Bri's door. He lightly taps with the knuckle of his forefinger just loud enough that if she's awake she will hear him, but not too loud to wake her.

"Bri? Is everything okay?" He softly asks.

She hears the gruff voice whisper in her ear again, *"Get rid of him or we will; PERMANENTLY!"*

She tries to alert him without getting him killed...she uses his first name since she doesn't use it all that often. "I'm fine, Oliver. I accidentally bumped into a table."

"Do you need help cleaning up?" He offers, hoping she lets him in so he can check things out and see her for himself.

"No, I'm fine." She tries to imply she isn't alone, "If I was more awake, I'd joke about how many people it takes to clean up whatever this thing is that broke?" Unfortunately, he doesn't get it.

"Well, if you're okay, I'll leave you to it." He says. "Goodnight."

"Goodnight, Oliver." Her voice getting shaky as her only connection to help is walking away from her door.

McMasters walks back to his room. He senses something doesn't feel right and it's gnawing at him. He paces the bedroom floor...

The men waited to hear McMasters' door close before they throw Bri over a shoulder as the gruff voice informs her, "*Someone wants to* personally *teach you a lesson!*"

She is carried for some distance and even though she can't see, she can soon tell by the stench she's in The Dungeons. When she can't take much more jostling, they set her bare feet down on the cold, damp stone floor. Her forearms are grabbed, right above the rope that ties her wrists together and her arms are raised above her head. Her mind flashes to her vision earlier when she toured The Dungeons of a person's arms being raised above their head. Bri glances down and notices a small gap at the opening of the pillowcase, or whatever it is over her head, where she catches a glimpse of a green snake tattoo on a man's right wrist. It's familiar and she tries to remember where she has seen it before...

She snaps back into reality when someone else hoists her up, just high enough to force her to stand up on her toes. They tear the back part of her pajama shirt open and she recalls the rest of her vision, realizing it was a premonition of herself! Then her mind jumps to a vision of a young Lawrence's shirt being torn open and being whipped. Anytime he yelled out, his mother's smile got wider as she watched, *and participated,* with a small hand whip that broke his flesh! It changes to a scene Bri can sense is more recent and she sees they're in The Queen Mother's office. Lawrence is held by half a dozen hood covered men and The Queen Mother is whipping him with a cane like stick; Bri notices he doesn't make a sound! Then she's shown that he grimaced when she arrived and hugged him! She feels warm tears start to run down her cool cheeks.

Her body shakes uncontrollably because she realizes those are the favorite 'tools' of The Queen Mother's lessons and they could be used on her tonight. She feels a sudden blanket of calmness come over her and her shaking stops. Then she feels a surge of strength so she *can endure——.*

'CRACK!' The loud sound echoes in the room and down the corridors of The Dungeons.

Bri feels a very painful stinging sensation across her back. She inhales her breath and holds it, refusing to give any of them the satisfaction of hearing her cry out in pain. She is gripping part of the rope her fingers can hang onto. Then another 'CRACK!' and a third; eventually she loses count after six.

Her back has gone numb for some time, then she hears a familiar voice plainly say, "That's adequate." Bri hears The Queen Mother's footsteps come up to her and she sees a woman's shoes in the small opening. The Queen Mother is right up to Bri's pillowcase covered face and adds, *"For now."* Bri closes her eyes as the numbness wears off and more pain sets in.

She hears a man inhaling and says as he exhales, "She smells good, Auntie! Let me have her before *him.*" He inhales again, feeling her hourglass curves.

"All in good time, Tristan, My Pet." The Queen Mother tells him. Bri's mouth drops when she hears 'Tristan.' Bri's mind flashes to the green tattoo on his wrist she couldn't make out that one day a guard tried to carve 'a reminder' in her upper arm from The Queen Mother; Lawrence had executed the guard right then. "I'd let you have her first, but we need his blood with hers to get control of The Throne back. We can't risk you doing such a great job that you get her pregnant!" The Queen Mother continues to talk to her lackeys about her; Bri wanted to vomit at the thought. "This little American slag thinks she can motivate *my son* to become a different king than the one *I* want him to be!" She turns to Bri's covered face and says, "I've worked too long and too hard to get him *this far*, I'll be damned if you're going to ruin it all now! Ruling with an iron fist may not be in his genetic makeup, but it's been a *long* hard-fought road and he *won't* just dismiss me like he did! ME! *I'm The Queen*! AND YOU..." she whips off the pillowcase, pulling strands of Bri's hair with it, "YOU DISGUSTING SWINE! You think you can get rid of me?!" She sneers, "To rule this country yourselves?!" She scoffs, *"Oh, please*! This country would be destroyed *in weeks*!"

Another familiar voice Bri hears says, "There's only one rightful queen, *Your Majesty*!" It's The Keeper, Mr. Gillery, flattering her.

Bri's head is hanging down again when she sees another 'snake wrist' as it rests on her waist. "Halt!" She tells him and Bri hears a smile go across The Queen Mother's face. "Tristan wasn't allowed and you're not either...*yet...*"

"I just want to feel..." he says and she feels his hands travel her body. Bri lifts her head enough to see Gavan, another guard of Lawrence's has his hands on her body. She sees another man who is familiar in that he has been part

348

of The Royal Guard; Bri feels his name is 'Lucas' and that he's another favorite of The Queen Mother. Her heart sinks for Lawrence...he's surrounded by so many traitors!

The Queen Mother ignores the hands traveling around Bri's body and conceitedly says to her, "You really should've done your homework, *Deary*." Saying the endearment through gritted teeth. "*I* run The Palace and those who don't obey are taught a lesson, most learn quickly. This..." she presses her fingers into Bri's open wounds on her back and she silently hisses, "is only a start to what I'm capable of!" She gets close to Bri's ear, "Once you're The Royal Consort, *I'll own you*, even your eggs!" She steps back, licking Bri's blood off her fingers, "My Pet," Tristan comes over and sucks some of Bri's blood from her fingers, "has generously volunteered to make an heir with you. *Our* family pedigree with yours would create quite 'The Spare!'" She and Tristan evilly grin at her.

Bri is confused because her pedigree with Lawrence's should be enough...unless she wants to cut out the 'Heathherst' somehow...but that doesn't make sense either because she has seen their son? *Whatever*. She thinks to herself and lets it go because she really didn't care at the moment. She is more interested in getting out of this predicament.

The Queen Mother caresses Bri's face, making Bri even more uncomfortable, creeped out. The Queen Mother looks at Tristan and turns his chin to her. "I'll take care of you in a bit, My Pet." Bri pushes down another urge to vomit with the thought of what that could mean; however, considering what she already knows of Lawrence's past, she has a harder time covering the disgusted look about to form on her face.

Bri feels Tristan's hands at her waist and runs his fingers just inside her waistband from her hips to the front, to untie the strings of her pajama bottoms. The Queen Mother with her smug smile, The Keeper with his evil grin, and the others eagerly anticipate as they watch Bri squirm. Bri remembers she has power over spirits and is inspired to stop him.

She looks him straight in the eye and with determination she tells him, "Remove your hands and *never* touch me with sexual intent again!"

The Queen Mother says with her nose turned up at Bri, "*Cute*, but *I* control him, *not you*."

Bri raises her eyebrow. "Are you sure about that?" Bri tips her chin to gesture Tristan and everyone looks at him, then down at his hands.

Tristan wasn't paying attention to what they were saying because he was fighting against not being able to touch Bri's pants. They hear him say in frustration, "I can't put my hands on her! It's like an invisible barrier!" He looks at his hands asking, "What's going on?!"

The Queen Mother exhales in frustration. *"Can't you do anything right?!"* She snaps. "Keep!"

Bri watches Mr. Gillery walk up to her and she tells all of them, "None of you will touch my body in *any* sexual way!" She is not sure if that kind of a blanket statement would work so she tries being specific; she's about to find out...Mr. Gillery can't touch her either but she isn't sure about whether it worked with the others.

The Queen Mother is clearly angry Bri is somehow able to intervene. She quickly steps over to a table, wrapping her hand in a firm grip around something. She angrily spins back around and shouts, "YOU INSOLENT LITTLE—!" Bri doesn't hear anything else, but feels the pain when The Queen Mother swings a club of sorts that strikes Bri in the abdomen. "HOW MUCH MORE OF A LESSON DO YOU NEED YOU *STUPID* FOOL?!"

Another blow, with a greater force, hits her abdomen again; just missing her ribs. She can't think, *she can't breathe*! She has been holding her breath and now closes her eyes as her body absorbs the blows and she tries to get a handle on the pain. Bri can't focus to make The Queen Mother stop all this.

The Queen Mother gets in Bri's face once again. She yanks her hair to jerk her head back and, with controlled anger, tells her, "When you essentially become *MY Royal Consort*," she touches Bri's lower abdomen in a very unnerving way and Bri grimaces, "'The Heir' will be mine and *MY legacy*. Lawrence has always been too weak to stop me!" Bri manages to remember her conversation with David and Lawrence about all that and keeps calm. "I'll even let other rulers from all over the world have access to you in any way *I choose*!"

Bri scoffs, "NO YOU WON'T!"

"*I WON'T?!*" The Queen Mother scowls.

"You'll realize that 'The Heir' wouldn't want their mother passed around like that; nor would the people of UK want that for 'The Royal Consort' and the mother of the next king or queen! That would weaken the strength in The Monarchy and that could cause a revol—."

"WHO SAID ANYTHING ABOUT *YOU* BEING *MY HEIR'S* MOTHER?" The Queen Mother snaps.

Bri was in pain and just wanted to get out of there. She knew it's also their choice to keep her there, so with the same determination she used before to command their spirits, she tells The Queen Mother, "You *will* send me back to my room right now, *safely!*"

"Take her back to her room!" The Queen Mother says, shocked that the words rolled right out of her mouth.

"You can't be serious?!" The Keeper is bewildered. The Queen Mother shoots him an enraged look at being questioned. "Sorry, Your Majesty."

"Just get her out of here!" She shouts in irritation, then randomly stabs a man in frustration who happens to be a guard in The Dungeons.

In the back of her head, The Queen Mother is curious about what was happening with Bri...*how did it happened?* But she'll eventually dismiss this as being tired. The men don't forget and swear to never speak of it because they don't think anyone will believe them anyway.

While a couple of them remove the stabbed guard, others lower Bri down and Tristan throws her over his shoulder but she struggles to exhale because of the pain. Bri's hair at the back of her head is pulled to lift her head up again. The Queen Mother gets in her face, "A word of this to anyone and I'll make you regret going up against me."

Bri snorts in disbelief. "I thought that's what this was supposed to do; make me regret my actions earlier...*but I don't*. I'll send you to Hell first before that *ever* happens!"

The Queen Mother grabs the front of Bri's neck with her other hand and squeezes hard. "You have *no idea* who you're dealing with!"

Bri looks her in the eyes and pushes out through the pressure on her throat. "NO! *YOU* have no idea who *YOU'RE* dealing with!" Bri summons the energy to snap, "You won't kill me! YOU.*NEED*.ME!" They both know she's right. The Queen Mother goes to say something but Bri glares, "*Don't say anything else to me and have them take me to my room!*"

The Queen Mother has to comply. "Take her back to her room!"

The Queen Mother exhales raging, realizing that maybe Bri is a bigger threat than she thought! She needs to prepare to leave right away, because with Bri's defiance right to her face, The Queen Mother can be sure Bri will tell Lawrence *everything*...including anyone involved! *However*, she doesn't think Lawrence will believe Bri about Tristan, not after these many years of Tristan's 'devotion' to Lawrence.

When her abductors reach Bri's room, she has passed out from the pain. By the time she does wake, a couple hours later, they are long gone. She fumbles on the nightstand for her phone and is about to panic that maybe they took it with them, when her hand stumbles across it. She is relieved and makes a note to memorize a phone number or few before The Queen Mother's next attack. She sees the time and remembers Jack is going to be there early in the morning to fly back with her; she passes out again.

A few hours later, Jack texts he's on his way. When she doesn't respond after a couple of texting attempts and no answer to his calls, he calls McMasters:

> "Have you spoken with Bri this morning? I've texted her but she hasn't responded, so I tried calling and no answer. I'm starting to get worried!"

> McMasters' heart sinks as he recalls last night and cusses under his breath before he replies, "Something hasn't felt right since the middle of the night! Let me go check on her again and I'll call you right back!"

> Jack's confused. "Again?"

Unfortunately, McMasters had already hung up before he answered Jack to run down to Bri's room. He knocks on the door, but no answer. He knocks again, only louder. He listens for footsteps or any noises, but it's quiet. He looks the door over, the solid wood door won't 'break open' quick enough. He runs back to his room and grabs his tools to pick the lock. He comes back to her door and knocks loudly once more, pounding like a law enforcement officer this time; those knocks are designed to 'wake the dead!' She stirs a little but there's still only silence. McMasters bends down and in less than a minute, he successfully picks the lock.

He opens the door, talking to Bri as he does. "Bri, it's Oliver! I'm coming in!" He hears rustling on the bed as his voice starts to pierce Bri's subconscious. It's then he starts to piece earlier that morning together when she used his first name...his stomach twists.

The room is dark with the drapes closed. It's getting lighter outside, so he walks over to the window and opens the drapes. He turns around and gasps when he sees the blood scattered around on the sheets. He rushes over to her as he hears a chime for a text notification.

Jack: "We're about to land."

McMasters thinks fast. He needs to get Bri out of here, but he also needs to investigate what happened...

McMasters: "Have the pilot come down on The Royal Apartment side and stay there! We're coming out!"

Jack thinks it's strange but he relays the message to the pilots.

Jack: (Sends a 'thumbs up')

McMasters looks more closely at Bri and sees she is twisted up in the sheet. She is on her side with her shirt partially up and exposing a little of her bruised abdomen. He lifts it a little bit more and figures it has to be her whole abdomen that's bruised. He tries to lift the back of her shirt, but she's so twisted up in the sheet, he can only see a couple of inches, but it was enough to see part of a slash mark with blood. He determines she must have slashes all over her back considering all the blood he sees. He carefully slides his arm under her neck, then the other under her knees; she partially wakes and cries out a bit feeling the piercing pain. She inhales and holds her breath as McMasters lifts her up and off the bed.

Rushing out of the room he tells her, "Hang on Bri! I'm taking you out to the helicopter where Jack's waiting!"

She struggles through the pain to say, "*Okay.*"

Maurice is beginning his day a little early and sees McMasters carrying Bri. He rushes over. "What can I do?"

"You can help me by guarding her room. *No one goes in*! I need to get her to the helicopter and Lord Carlisle, but I'll be back to investigate!" McMasters says. Maurice nods and holds the various doors open as McMasters hurries out to the awaiting helicopter and Jack. Maurice turns quickly to go to Bri's room and stand guard for McMasters.

Bri wakes up a little when she hears the helicopter. Jack pops his head out when he sees them, then he sees the blood on the sheets. He's horrified! "*What the hell happened?!*"

McMasters replies, "I don't know, but I'm sure going to find out! Get her to a hospital!"

Jack helps McMasters inside so he can gently sit Bri down, the pain intensifies but Bri holds her breath to hide it. Jack sees Bri's eyes halfway open, "Bri, you gotta talk to us! Where's Herst—."

She shakes her head. "It wasn't him...dungeons..." she was in a lot of pain and couldn't form sentences. She manages to look Jack in the eyes, "Jack, Edin—," she inhales sharply and struggles to say, "hosp..."

McMasters asks Jack, "Did she say 'dungeons?'"

Jack nods. "Does that mean anything to you?"

"It might. I'm going to investigate! Take care of her and I'll let you know what I find out!" McMasters says.

"I've got her, just go do your thing, but get Lawrence involved right away!" Jack tells him.

"You can count on it!" McMasters reaches down to his ankle for his back-up piece. "Jack, take this! I don't know what happened and that's worse! I'd feel better if you had a way to protect yourselves if something more happens! Do you know how to use this?!" Jack nods, taking the gun and reflexively checks the safety before he tucks it in his messenger bag. McMasters says, "Text me when you arrive and keep me posted?"

"Will do!" Jack tells him.

McMasters shuts the door to the helicopter and pats the pilot's window with his hand a couple of times to tell the pilots they can go. He backs away to a safe distance and watches them lift into the air and fly off towards Edinburgh.

The Queen Mother is secretly peering out a window on her way to stay at Devonridge Hall until things cool down. She's watching this with an evil grin on her face thinking, '*Next time, she won't be so lucky to get off so easy!*'

McMasters quickly walks back to The Apartment to start his investigation, remembering his newly hired partner, Ryan Mitchell, was flying in tomorrow. Even though he is probably sleeping, McMasters calls Mitchell to see about him coming right away; Mitchell agrees. McMasters will have Gabriel call him to make those arrangements.

Bri wakes again, this time she is closer to fully awake. Jack asks, "What happened, Bri?" He pushes the hair out of her face.

She tries to explain but the pain makes it difficult. She tries to show him her ripped pajama top, but she hisses through gritted teeth when she feels her shirt and the sheet have started to dry *into* her wounds.

"Oh, Bri, that looks *incredibly* painful!" He takes his phone. "Since we're going to Edinburgh, we need to call David and have him meet—."

"NO! Don't tell David!" She pushes out then struggles to say, "*He's already upset with me and I haven't had a chance to talk with him about the DC misunderstanding. If he continues to ice me out and doesn't come, it'll hurt that much more—.*" She puts her hand to her mouth, pressing it tight against her lips to stop herself from sobbing.

"I *swear* that wouldn't happen." He quietly says, trying to sooth her.

She shakes her head. "I don't want to risk it. *I can't!* It's been hard enough not talking with him and being 'ghosted,' I just can't take anything more at the moment. I promise I'll go straight to his office when we're done at the hospital and will tell him everything! That's why I wanted to go to the hospital in Edinburgh and not Kingsbury. Wait. *Lawrence!*"

Jack is confused. "Lawrence?"

"I promise he's *not* responsible for this!" She tells him.

"I never thought he was, Amore Mia. He loves you and he should've been able to protect you." He tells her. *"That's what doesn't make sense!"*

"He needs to know his mother is behind this...she planned this in the middle of the night and by secret passageways, *so he couldn't intervene! This was part of her punishment for him, too!"*

Back at The Manor, David is about to head to work for the day. He sees Bri's texts and missed calls before she went to bed last night, but she hasn't left anymore voicemails...'*At least I won't have to delete them without listening to them this morning. How will I get her to understand her safety is of the utmost concern?! Now that she's The Duchess of Newhaven and the next 'Royal Consort,' she's even more at risk!*' He slams his helicopter door a little harder than he meant to with his frustration. '*I should've talked with her about leaving The Royal Apartment without McMasters and getting lost the other day!*' He thinks to himself.

CHAPTER 36
Imperfectly Perfect & Royal Fallout

The pilots receive approval to land the helicopter at the hospital knowing The Duchess of Newhaven needs emergency medical attention. A doctor and nurses are waiting on standby with a gurney. They watch the helicopter land and rush out to it. When the doctor goes to peel back the sheet, Jack says to keep it there. They move quickly to get her inside.

They on-call doctor has sworn his team to secrecy. They hide her on a floor they use for overflow, which is completely vacant right now. Jack asks for additional security on their floor, as well as the other floors, including inside the elevators.

A male nurse steps forward and says, "*I'm on it!*" Then rushes out to take care of it.

Jack looks at the woman next to him. "If you'll write down everyone's name, all," he counts and adds one more for the nurse that left, "six of you, there will be significant bonuses given if this stays out of the papers while she's here." Jack says to the doctor, "She has slashes on her back that her shirt and the sheet have dried into; if they were to be yanked off—."

"It would be cruel." The doctor gives him an empathetic look. "We'll take good care of her, Sir. I promise." Jack nods with a small appreciative smile.

The medical team works on Bri by drawing blood, hooking up an IV, and so on. Jack stands aside, watching all this going on and seeing her in pain. The room clears as nurses come and go with their tasks. Then the doctor and a nurse set up to start working on the now soaked sheet and shirt out of her wounds. Bri tucks her bent arm against her side with her hand in a fist and up to her mouth. Jack takes a picture as a nurse rushes in with papers in her hand and whispers to the doctor.

Jack asks, "Is everything alright?"

The doctor takes the results from the nurse and looks it over. He kindly smiles at Jack and says to Bri, "Your Grace, a little good news for you to hold onto. Your hCG levels in your blood test show that you're early, but you're *definitely* pregnant!"

Bri lifts her head and looks at the nurse confused, asking with a hoarse voice and wet eyes, "*What?!*" Her thought go back to the blows to her abdomen and she's scared.

"Call the OB." The doctor tells the nurse, then looks back to Bri. The doctor tells her, "With this new information, we need to change pain meds for you."

Bri's head shoots up again. "No! *No* pain meds!"

"But Your Grace——."

"No! *Please* doctor. We both know there is so much development in this first trimester! Of all things, *a heart right now*! So, no!" She shakes her head. "No pain meds!"

"Your Grace." He says compassionately, looking from her to Jack.

"Please, call me Bri." She takes a deep breath. "I'm not a fan of pain, *trust me*, but my baby is too important. Especially if they survive the blows to my abdomen." Jack's face went from shock to a mixture of white, sadness, and anger towards the guilty party. Bri reaches for the doctor's forearm. "*It'll be okay.*" She assures him in a quiet, but determined voice.

"Bri, if you took blows to the abdomen, the added stress——." The doctor starts to say.

"If it gets to be too much, I know that can't be good for the baby either and I'll let you know. *I promise you*!" She assures him.

"Very well. We're going to be in close quarters for a while. My friends call me, Sean." He looks at Jack. "Please call me, Sean, too." Gesturing his nurse, "This is Carrie."

"I'm Jack."

"Jack, would you please pull that chair up from over there," he tips his head, "and then you can hold Bri's hand." Watching Jack, Sean explains, "I feel a topical numbing agent wouldn't touch the pain because of the shirt and sheet being in the way. However, as we start to clear them away, we will start adding the cream and get you some relief as soon as possible."

"I understand." She quietly replies.

Once Jack is settled in the chair next to her, the doctor and nurse begin their work. Bri tucks her and Jack's hands in and presses their hands against her mouth, as she tries to hold in her screams of pain while the doctor and the nurse tend her wounds; Jack can also feel her shake here and there with the intensity of the pain. He goes back and forth watching them work on her back and watching her face, her tears running in a stream down to the pillow. He kisses her head so lovingly, so affectionately, that when he runs his hand into her hair and rests his forehead to her temple, she loses it and just cries.

"Stop! Stop, stop, stop a minute!" Jack stands up and then lays with her on the bed, sliding an arm carefully under her neck with his other arm coming up and around her upper shoulders to hold her close. He kisses her head as she tries to get as comfortable as she can.

The OB comes in when Jack is doing this and talks with the doctor. He then comes over to Bri and squats down so Bri can see him better. "Doctor Carver says you don't want anything for the pain because of the baby?" The doctor and nurse begin their work again.

Bri shakes her head to the OB. "It's too early and there's so much growth— OW!" She cries out in pain.

They had hoped she was distracted a little bit by the conversation with the OB. She has been holding most of it in, so when she cries out, they know it must be that much more painful for her. Bri buries her face in Jack's chest and silently cries.

The OB looks at Jack, "If the pain won't let her sleep, she'll need to reconsider because she'll need her sleep to help her heal. I'll add a prescription to her discharge paperwork."

Jack nods. "Thanks, Doctor."

By the time they finished bandaging her up, Bri was asleep. They were able to put some topical cream with antiseptic on her wounds to give her a bit of relief as they went along stitching up the deeper gashes. Jack had been running his fingers in her hair, which always relaxes her and it does so now; that, with her exhaustion, she is able to sleep.

He whispers to the nurse. "*She's exhausted.*"

The nurse agrees, then tells him, "I'm going to step out, but I'll be right outside. Press this," she holds up the remote device, "to call me and I'll come back straight away." She puts it next to his hip so he can reach it. "Otherwise, I'll be back in a little bit to check on her."

"I appreciate that." Jack says.

"I wish there was more we could do for her." The nurse puts her hand on Bri's head in a caring way.

"You and the doctor got the cream on her wounds to relieve her pain and bandaged her up as quickly as you could! *That's huge*, Carrie!" Jack states. She nods and she softly pats his arm before she quietly slips out of the room.

Jack was hoping he put his phone in the pocket he could reach, but it wasn't there. His eyes go to the table next to him and he sees it there. With the bed guardrail and the table where it was, his arm doesn't bend at that angle and he has to wait for the nurse....

It's less than fifteen minutes when the nurse comes back and hands Jack his phone. She checks Bri's vitals and makes her notes, then leaves again. Jack sees a text from McMasters with an update.

When McMasters got to Bri's room, he sent Maurice to wake up The King and then went into the bedroom to start investigating. It's not even three minutes later when Lawrence is running into Bri's room. Maurice woke him and when he said something happened to The Duchess, he shot up and ran to her room. He saw she wasn't there and McMasters explained Jack was already flying back to Edinburgh with her. Not knowing what happened, McMasters wanted to get her out of there as soon as possible and to the hospital. McMasters tells Lawrence he will need his help to investigate effectively without any hassles; Lawrence understands and they get to work.

McMasters sends an update to Jack: "With Lawrence's help, we figured out they snuck into her room through passageways, which they took her through those passageways all the way to The Dungeons. We found a barely noticeable trail of blood leading right to The Torture Chambers...the scene of the crime. It looks like they had her hanging with her arms above her head to whip her with various things, one being an actual whip. Another one being a medieval handheld whip that has a number of straps on it; Lawrence says it's his mother's weapon of choice because of the metal balls at the end. We've bagged these things for evidence and will send it to the FBI in DC for testing."

Jack attaches the photo of Bri's back and the one he quickly took of her abdomen: "This is some of what they did to her!"

McMasters gets Jack's text and picture. "*Daaamn...*" he whispers and Lawrence hears him. McMasters hands him his phone.

McMasters sees anger come over Lawrence, only it's a protective anger like nothing he's ever seen on *anyone's* face before. "They DARE to team up with *that woman*! I'll have *each* of their heads for this!"

McMasters has been preparing for Bri to become The Royal Consort by recruiting the now Retired Secret Service Special Agent Ryan Mitchell, thinking he'd be a great fit with his quick wit and snarky comebacks; he should hit it off with Bri. Between the two of them, Bri will have at least one of them with her at all times.

McMasters got to thinking, "Sir? Is there anyone in your Royal Guard you trust implicitly?"

Lawrence angrily answers, "AFTER ALL THIS?! I trust *none of them*!" He looks at McMasters. "You've gotten to know them! *Are there any?*"

McMasters kindly smiles. "*A few.*" He looks at his watch. "I hired Retired Secret Service Agent Ryan Mitchell for Bri's security and he's right downstairs. Let me grab him and bring him into this conversation." Lawrence nods, then starts to pace.

McMasters goes and gets Mitchell. On their way back to Bri's room where Lawrence is, he brings Mitchell up to speed. A few minutes later, McMasters is introducing the two men; Lawrence giving him the same permission McMasters has to skip formalities in private.

Mitchell speaks to them. "Look, I know we need to get to the bottom of things, but safety first. McMasters, you probably have an idea of who's actually loyal to The King and we need to get them here and profiled in an interview." McMasters nods.

Lawrence nervously shifts stating, "And I *need* to get to Bri!"

Mitchell says with compassion, "I understand the need to rush to her side, but we *can't* let this get worse for either of you. This was a 'weak spot' The Queen Mother will continue to exploit if we don't get your security cleaned up and reinforced as soon as possible!"

McMasters says to Lawrence. "Let me call Jack and see how things are." He presses a few buttons and puts the phone to his ear. Jack answers in a whisper and he quickly explains how secure they are. They hang up and McMasters tells Mitchell and Lawrence, "Jack secured the overflow floor, which they're the only ones on that floor. Security is posted there and then he has more security spread out on the other floors *and* on the elevators. He even offered bonuses to those directly involved to keep the story out of the media while Bri is being treated there."

Mitchell whistles. "That's great thinking! With them secure, we need to get those interviews going. It shouldn't take long, then we can get you to her!"

"I appreciate that." Lawrence isn't excited about waiting, but he trusts McMasters and if McMasters trusts Mitchell, then he will, too!

McMasters flips through sheets of phone numbers highlighting the members of The Royal Guard he trusts and makes the necessary phone calls. Lawrence looks through those pages to see who McMasters highlighted and right away he notices two don't make the cut: Tristan and Gavan. This man already knew they weren't to be trusted?! *'Damn!'* He thinks to himself. *'I'm going to have to lean on McMasters more often to know who is actually trustworthy!'* He looks for 'Lucas Brownwood,' the 'Grand Marshall' of The Royal Guard, and Lawrence's 'inside man' with his mother...he finds Lucas' name and sees he isn't highlighted either! Lawrence cusses to himself, *and at himself.*

Mitchell clears his throat. "While McMasters is doing that, I can assume all the evidence is collected in her room?"

"Yes. Even The Secret Passageways and on through to The Torture Chambers." McMasters replies as he calls the next number on his list.

Mitchell nods. "We should look into the locks being changed throughout The Apartment and have selected guards posted in the passageways as well." He suggests to Lawrence, who agrees.

Lawrence texts Jack wanting to check on Bri and talk with her if she was up for it. Jack sent a text with a photo of Bri sleeping.

Jack: "She's exhausted from being so strong."

Lawrence: "Give her my love and I'll check in later."

Jack: "I'll have her read this text. (adds a winking face)."

Lawrence: (adds a 'thumbs up')

When they're done, Jack texts Gabriel.

Jack: "Would you have a full set of clothes brought over to the Edinburgh Hospital for Bri?" He includes Nurse Carrie's info.

Gabriel: "Sure thing! Is Bri alright?"

Jack: "She will be, but Bri doesn't want anyone to say anything to David; she wants to tell him."

Gabriel: (a zipped-lip face).

Jack doesn't know that Gabriel heard from McMasters and helped arrange Mitchell's flight to London as quickly as possible. Gabriel only knew that Mitchell needed to get to London right away to help McMasters with something urgent. Gabriel hasn't said anything to David yet.

It's been a while, but Bri slowly wakes up and lays there, relaxing for a bit as Jack runs his fingers through her hair. He only knows she is awake when she squeaks, *"Thank you for being here with me, Amore Mio."* She lifts her head and gives him a weak smile.

"There's nowhere else I'd rather be, just like David, *if he knew.*" He hugs her.

"I—..." He hears her hold her breath as she tries to get up. Jack helps her and points to the change of clothes that were slipped into the room while she was sleeping. "I need to get to David. Nothing makes sense when I'm fighting with him, or you, even Lawrence...but," she strains an exhale as she goes to put her bra on, "with David, it's just a misunderstanding and I *knnnow*," she struggles hooking her bra, Jack gently helps her, "once he understands that it'll be okay—*it has to be*!" She winces some more as she gets dressed. "He just needs to talk to me." She looks at Jack with sad, teary, but hopeful eyes asking, "Right?"

"Yes! Let's get you discharged and over there, only *after* Uncle Jack feeds the baby by feeding their gorgeous mama!" He says.

She gives him a little smile. "I could eat a little something, I suppose."

After she is discharged, Jack holds her hand as they walk to the cafeteria. People saw them but Bri kept her head down so no one knew for sure if it was her or not. Jack was hoping Bri would've eaten more, but it was almost three o'clock. He called Mary to make sure David was still in the office. She said he is preparing for an appointment there at three, so after four o'clock would be better. Jack asked her not to say anything, Mary said the conversation never happened.

Jack tells her, "Good girl!" And he hears Mary snort a little laugh, then they say goodbye.

Bri looks at Jack. "Want to go for a walk with me? I just need to catch my breath, so not a lot of talking."

"Amore Mia, I'm here for you. If you need a walk to get fresh air and clear your head," he takes her hand, "then that's what we'll do." He gently squeezes her hand as she wipes a tear in the corner of her eye as she nods.

They walk for a long time and Jack never says a word, not until she does. "I'm officially lost..." she says as she looks around.

Jack chuckles a little. "I'm not. Are you wanting to start walking towards David's office?"

Bri takes a deep breath. "It's probably time..." She looks around and senses the direction; she points as she asks, "Is it that way?"

"It is!" Jack answers and leads them a little ways before Bri recognizes where they are. She has always had a good sense of direction, if she knows the general layout from a map point of view in her head.

Bri begins to tell Jack what happened that caused the assault. Jack was at a loss as to what to say, proud of her for not backing down but also scared knowing she could've died...then again, she should be safe from at least that much until Lawrence's heir is born.

"I *guarantee* my days are numbered in that woman's mind!" She tells him. "I'm not to be 'her heir's' mother. Not *exactly* sure what that means, although I think it means once I give birth, I'm dead; or it could mean she plans to use my eggs with a surrogate. There was also talk about her allowing other monarchs to use me in any way *she* chooses."

He's alarmed but he tries to calm her and himself saying, "One problem at a time and let's not think about her right at this moment. Let's get you to David." She nods.

When Jack walks her inside The Worthington Corporation Lobby and he escorts her to the elevator. She asks, "What time is it?"

"A few minutes after four." He answers. He holds her jaw and assures her, "It'll be okay."

"I hope so, because I have this sinking feeling and this thought, '*it's only going to get worse,*' continually going through my mind." She shakes it off and slaps on a smile.

She taps a kiss to his lips before she gets in the elevator. She nervously waves to him as the doors close and he waves back. Jack goes out to the car where Paul waits for him. He had texted Paul while walking with Bri asking Paul to come pick him up and Bri would ride home with David. They need time together, *especially* when she has *fantastic news* to tell him!

The elevator doors open and Bri sees Mary getting her things together to leave. "I'm so glad you're here!" She quietly says to Bri with a small, kind smile. "He's been in a *foul mood* for the last couple days."

"Sorry. It's a misunderstanding and it'll be fine." Bri reassures her, although Bri is silently praying it will be.

Mary smiles and tells her David is in his office. She says goodnight and leaves in the elevator. Bri watches the doors shut then takes a deep breath as she walks to David's office door.

She watches him type on his laptop for a moment before saying, "You won't take my calls or answer any texts, but we have to talk, My Love." She walks in, but he doesn't look up. He stops typing and stands up, slamming his laptop closed; she jumps a little. He notices but forces himself not to care and gathers his things together. "David, *please talk to me.*" Bri pleas with him.

He angrily puts his coat on saying, "*I didn't know you were going to go to DC!*"

Bri's heart sinks as she follows him to the elevator, only the pain she is in slows her down a little, making it hard to keep up. "David, stop! I'm—."

"SHUT IT!" He yells and she is shocked into silence. There is the 'ding' of the elevator and as the doors open, he turns his head to the side and looks at the floor. "I'm just so *FURIOUS* with you!" He steps in the elevator and pushes the button for the lobby. "You take off on a whim, *not even thinking of your safety* and get lost in The Palace; only to get another 'whim' of yours—!" He exhales in frustration. The doors start to close and he snaps at her again, "You can't just leave town, let alone the country, BriaLynn! You don't realize how dangerous it can be *all by yourself,* because you're more popular than you want to admit to yourself!"

She stands there staring at the closed doors...dumbfounded that he thought she went to DC by herself, *and without McMasters?*! Then it hits her...*He just left*! Her mind starts spinning. '*He wouldn't leave without me, would he?*' She goes to the elevator and pushes the button to call the elevator back up. She reminds herself, '*He said he'd always leave with* me when we're here together, no exceptions! He has to be waiting in the lobby!*'

When she gets to the lobby she looks around and nothing. She looks out the front window in time to see the back of David's car as it pulls away from the curb and slips out of sight. She freezes again, but this time it's like all the air is sucked out of her lungs and she can't breathe. She stands like that for a few minutes before a familiar guard walks over.

"We can call a car for you, Your Grace." George offers.

Bri is coming out of her shock and quietly replies, "I don't have my phone or purse." She last had them in her bedroom at The Palace.

George gives her a little smile. He takes out his phone saying, "I can call Lord Carlisle for you..."

Jack answers, "Hullo?"

"Lord Carlisle, this is George from The Worthington Corp—."

"*George! Is everything alright?!*" Jack recognizes him and starts to panic about Bri.

"I'm not sure what happened, but it seems Mr. Worthington left without Mrs. Worthington. Since Paul took you home—."

"A helicopter will be there in less than twenty minutes! *Please* don't let her out of your sight until the helicopter is airborne with her on it?!" Jack asks him. "McMasters is still in London."

George looks at Bri. "I won't let her out of my sight, Sir." Jack thanks him and makes the helicopter arrangements for Bri.

George keeps an eye on her as he tells the other security guards that he needs to stay with Mrs. Worthington until she is airborne. He comes back over to her and they walk to the elevator to go up to the rooftop. When they are in the elevator, George looks at her with thoughtfulness.

"Is there anything I can do?" He asks.

Bri looks at him with a kind smile. "Thank you, but you're already going 'above and beyond' when you should be on your way home to your family."

"I have a later shift tonight, so we're good there, but I'd be here anyways because my family would understand helping a friend." He smiles and she smiles back in acknowledgment. After a few minutes he asks, "May I say something?"

"I think being my friend gives you a 'yes' for an answer." She winks.

He lightly chuckles. "You two don't seem to hold onto fights, so whatever this is and comparing to past observations, it's safe to say this will pass."

"It will." She exhales with a faint smile. "I was just hoping to move past it before David left."

They watch the helicopter coming in. When it lands, she thanks George for keeping her company and he pats her hand. Bri climbs inside the helicopter and she thanks the pilot for coming so quickly. She tries to fight back the tears, but *that moment* when the car drove off and she was completely alone...*that stung the worst of anything else that happened to her*! She works hard not to cry on the way to The Estate.

CHAPTER 37

Imperfectly Perfectly Let Down

David had never left Bri behind before, going out of his way to walk out with her...he said he'd always walk out with her, *no exceptions*. That is, until he just did and it hasn't hit him...*yet*...

On the ride home, his heart starts to get the better of him.

David texts Bri: "We can talk after dinner."

He said what had been on his mind and now he doesn't want to fight anymore. He looks at his phone, waiting for her response, only he doesn't know she doesn't have her phone because she left it at The Palace. He gets a little annoyed when she doesn't respond. '*I finally get to a point where I'll hear her out and she won't even respond to my text?!*' He continues to wait for her to answer, even to show she's read it, but nothing. When there continues to be no response from her, David starts to feel humbled thinking he deserved it for his behavior with her these last couple of days.

He is grabbing his things when he hears a helicopter in the not-too-far-off distance and his heart sinks as he realizes *he was her ride home*! He walks inside The Manor, kicking himself, as he sets his stuff down. He walks into the dining room and sees his parents are already seated, along with Jack and James. Jack stands up so fast, his chair crashes to the floor behind him. He's looking at David with the angriest look David has ever seen directed at him before!

"*What the hell did you do, David?!*" He doesn't give David a chance to answer. "You ghosted her all this time that she has to go to *your* office to talk to you and straighten things out, but instead you leave her stranded?!" Jack says, trying to control the volume of his voice, but struggling. Everyone else watches and listens, surprised by Jack's anger when he's normally 'happy-go-lucky' and laid back; *he's usually the peacemaker*! "What you're upset about is over *your* misunderstanding!"

David's confused. "I texted her that we could talk after dinner, so we could straighten things out then."

Carlotta asks, "Is everything okay?"

"Besides leaving Bri stranded?! SHE DOESN'T EVEN HAVE HER PHONE!" Jack yells at David, answering Carlotta. David feels even worse. "George from your security had to call me *for her*!"

Carlotta and Peter are still in shock, but Peter has a bit of anger in his own voice, "David, you should've——."

"*I was a bloody Bastard*!" David interrupts talking to Jack. "Alright?!" Jack could see David is kicking himself.

"*David*! Language!" Carlotta scolds.

"No, Mother," Jack puts his hand up in a gentle stop gesture, "in this case it isn't strong enough!" David is still in the archway as Jack walks over. "She went to DC to stop a politician from stealing part of James and Amy's wedding venue." Carlotta whispers a little 'oh no.' Peter continues to listen with an angry look on his face.

David tells him, "I can see wanting to help, but she can't just come and go as she pleases without telling——wait. *You knew* she went to DC *beforehand?*"

Jack grabs David's shirt and pushes him hard up against the wall, with Peter and James jumping up to try to intervene. "She would've told you that, had you given her *two minutes* to explain! HELL, *ONE* MINUTE WOULD'VE SUFFICED! That's what the money out of her account paid for, to ensure the wedding is *locked* in. When she said you were upset with her for going to DC, I transferred the money back into her account just to make sure we were good there." Jack lets go of David's shirt.

"I don't care about the money for the wedding! I told James and Amy that I wanted to pay for it as a wedding gift." David states.

"Bri has had the roughest two days since almost dying last year and the worst of it isn't over for another," his arms fly up some, "*however many days.*"

"What do you mean? The last time we discussed anything she was going to visit The Dungeons when she visited Lawrence next."

"You knew she was going to visit The Dungeons?!" Jack is bewildered. "*Why in the world would you encourage that?!*"

"Jessica and——." David stops himself from saying 'Bri sons,' clearing his throat, "Jessica told her that would be the best place to start when she was trying to understand that part of Herst's life."

"Bri made me promise not to say anything because she wanted to work things out with you herself. She wanted to be able to fix *one* thing...but *that* was before she went to your office!" He pulls out his phone to find the photo of her back, saying, "She made a point to make sure the hospital she went to is the one by your office because she was *determined* to see you right after! I believe she said something to the effect of, 'nothing is right with the world' when she's fighting with one of us. We were at the hospital *all* day. It was almost three o'clock when we left the cafeteria after feeding her and th–*then* we went for a walk." He caught himself before giving *that* secret away.

David gives him a scrutinizing look, catching the word stumble. He goes to call Jack on it, but Jack is a step ahead and sends the picture to David in a text. David's phone chimes with the text and he opens it up.

David's face goes from horrified to fury in about two seconds flat. "*What the hell happened?!*"

Jack loses his cool completely and punches David, causing him to stumble back through the archway into the main entry hall. David manages to catch himself on the large round table in the center.

Jack shakes out his hurting hand. "*You son of a*—I told her..." his voice cuts off and his jaw shakes. "UGH!" He exhales and swallows hard. "She even felt things were going to get worse as she stepped into the lift to go up to see you! I told her it would be fine, *but it wasn't!* You made it worse!"

"I know..." David agrees, with his hand on his jaw and moving it around.

"Going to The Dungeons cost a verbal price from *The King* with The Queen Mother right there. Bri gave Lawrence an ultimatum and he must have met the terms because last night, well, the wee hours of this morning really, Bri paid a physical punishment..." Jack points to David's phone and the picture.

Peter holds his hand out for the phone to see for himself, David hands him his phone; Jack hands James his phone so he can see. Peter and James both swear under their breath, then Peter passes David's phone to Carlotta and she gasps in shock, horrified by what she sees.

All of a sudden David says, "The Queen Mother?"

"Oh, David, *really!*" Carlotta says. "She's The Queen *Mother*. She has no power, except whatever Lawrence permits and he would *not* permit this! I'd think she would be stripped of her title, *at the very least*, if she's behind—."

"Exactly, Mother!" Jack answers. "The ultimatum Bri challenged Herst with must've also challenged her hold on Herst."

"By the look of this," Peter points to the picture, "I'd say The Queen Mother lost that hold on him." He asks Jack, "Is there anything we can do?"

"Right now, we need to keep the wounds cleaned out, because it's crucial we prevent infection." Jack reads David face and explains a bit more. "Look, the DC trip came *after* this ultimatum. She told *The King* to grow up and start acting like a king, but then again," he pointedly looks at David, "Herst isn't the only one who needs to grow up some more, is he?!" Jack hears the helicopter coming in and tells everyone, "I need to go meet up with Bri." He hurries out of the room.

"Hold up!" David jogs a little to catch up. "*Jack!*"

Jack stops to face David and compassion comes over him for his best friend. "The only other thing I can think of to tell you is that Bri is the strongest person *we've ever known!* Stronger than you, me, and Herst, *combined!* More than I ever knew was possible for one human being!"

"*What specifically happened?*" David asks.

"*Damnit*, David! *She wanted to tell you!* She was *so* nervous coming to you because she needed that mess straightened out first! She was scared you'd reject her once more by phone or text, and she couldn't take another rejection from you!" He takes a deep breath. "She told me she had a feeling all this would get worse, but I *stupidly* put her on the lift to go up to you *after* I *stupidly* told her it would be okay! It *should've* been okay! YOU UNBELIEVABLE BAS—!" He stops himself when he glances at Carlotta. "The pain she *suffered through*, pain so bad," he looks down, overwhelmed with his emotions, "sh-she shook, holding back what had to have been screams, while they were pulling out the shirt and sheet they had to soak first because they started to dry into her wounds; then they cleaned and bandaged them all up. She was exhausted after all that and fell asleep as they were finishing with her. I love you, Brother, but right now there isn't a harsh, descriptive enough word for

372

you and I need to leave before I physically hurt you again!" Jack goes through the sitting room, to the back door. As he opens it, he turns to David and sees everyone else has followed them. "You'll be sorrier than you know right now." David scrunches his eyebrows as he tries to guess what he means.

Carlotta asks Jack, "Can we bring her anything?"

"I filled the prescription she probably won't use for the pain, because...well, she wants to manage without it." David has been sensing he's holding something back. Jack tells him, "The doctor convinced her to have some at home in case she can't sleep. *David*, had you read the articles like you usually do, you would've realized your mistake and you probably would've also read there was a *showdown*." Jack leaves it at that. He looks around and says, "Goodnight." He wants to get out of there before David corners him on what he's not saying.

"Give her our love." Peter tells him and Jack waves to them over his shoulder, in response.

They watch him walk out to the helicopter and he helps Bri off; they see her movements are strained. Bri glances and sees the family watching and continues her brave face, even though they're too far away for them to see it. She wraps her arm around Jack's arm and they walk down the trail they use to go back and forth to The Cottage House. When David can't see them anymore, he goes up to his room...he's angry and frustrated...it all takes its toll on him.

By the time he gets into his room, he starts throwing things, smashing them on the floor in anger and frustration with himself, but also with what happened to her. After a couple minutes of that, he remembers what Jack said about the articles. He thinks back to the newspaper article that he never read past its headline. He searches for it online and finds it. He reads the first line and it reports she was in DC *with Herst*! He starts to wonder, '*How do I even begin to apologize for this*?!'

Inside The Cottage House, Bri lays on the couch and on her front. Jack can barely hear her quietly crying as he walks over to her. She whispers, "*Please, don't*." She squeaks, "*Don't* say anything to try to make me feel better..."

Jack's phone is on the coffee table when Lawrence's text chimes. Jack reads it out loud that Lawrence is about to get on the helicopter and he would see her in the morning.

Her voice is soft, "Ask him to stay here tonight, if that's alright with you?"

"That's what the second master bedroom is for, Amore Mia. Mainly for David or Herst to use when they stay here." He gently smiles before he texts Lawrence back. Lawrence responds and Jack reads to her that he'll be there!

Flashes of what happened come to her mind and she closes her eyes tight. Jack sits and runs his fingers through her hair and all he can think to say is, "Everything *will* be alright!"

"*You don't know that!*" She starts to cry. "I told you *not* to say anything to try to make me feel better!" She sobs, turning her head away. "*Just go away!*"

"I'm sorry, Amore Mia. My heart hurts for you..." He tells her. Jack gets a text that Bri recognizes as David's chime; She is annoyed. She doesn't want to talk to him and she doesn't want Jack to either.

She snaps, "Shouldn't he be in bed, sleeping like a baby by now?!"

"He's worried about you, Bri?" He says as he looks at the text.

She scoffs, "Why? Did he think I'd stay there all night?!" Then it hits her and she turns her head back to look at him, glaring as she pushes herself up. She angrily yells, "*YOU TOLD HIM?!*"

"I did, but—."

She struggles with the pain to stand up, but she yells, "*YOU PROMISED!*"

"*I promised* that I'd let you tell him after the hospital visit, *but he wouldn't listen to you!* I never promised not to tell him in the event he was an unbelievable Bas—." Jack catches himself. Like Carlotta, Bri is a lady and doesn't really like to hear much of the bad language either; rarely using it herself, usually using it when she is *really* upset. "He's also aware that I knew you went to DC; I can't remember if I mentioned Herst or not. I refuse to apologize for telling him, Bri! You did *nothing* wrong and he needed to know that so he'd *finally* see reason!" Bri is emotionless, staring into the dark fireplace. "He said he texted you something about talking after dinner, but I told him you left your phone at The Palace."

She nods as she continues to stare into the fireplace. She closes her eyes to push out the images coming into her mind again. Jack sits on the coffee table and gently pulls down on her arm for her to sit in front of him on the couch; she does.

He asks, "What is it?!"

She shakes her head. "Just images of what happened popping into my mind."

Tears leak down her face as she holds back what she can and tries not to cry, but one look at Jack and she loses it! She bends forward, resting her forehead to his chest, and cries. She feels his hands in her hair and he kisses her head, making her sob.

When she quiets down, she sits back up. He grabs a blanket and has Bri stand, then he lays down on his back. He gets comfortable and he wants her to lie on top of him.

"No, Jack. That won't be comfortable for you!"

He sweetly smiles. "I promise if it's uncomfortable, I'll tell you."

Bri hesitantly lays down. He puts the blanket on her and carefully hugs her just below the waist and at the back of her head.

She plainly asks, "You want to lie to me and tell me how comfortable you are right now?"

"Amore Mia, I'm *exactly* where I want to be! I've *always* loved laying like this on the couch with you! Having you lie like this when we're watching the telly together is comforting somehow. Of all the craziness in our life, *in your life*, you can find a way to relax into the simplicities with me! *I love that!* I love you! And having you lay like this now so I can comfort you in some small way, means the world to me!"

"Jack, this is NOT 'some a small way' *and it means the world to me*! You *are* 'my calm *in* the storms of life.' Remember?" She asks and he only nods. He is choked up thinking back to the waterfall last year, before they left for their honeymoon. She adds, "*Well, it's been storming like a freaking hurricane right now and I'm ready for it to be over!*"

He kisses the top of her head and begins lightly running his fingers up and down her arm to relax her. She hears his heartbeat in his chest and she also finds comfort with that, too. She's quiet, soaking in the sensation of Jack's fingers going up and down her arm while listening to his heartbeat; he hears her take a deep breath...

She faintly says, "He left me..."

"I know and I'm sorry that happened..."

"'*No exceptions,*' he'd tell me, but he left me anyway because he was angry with me..." she doesn't expect an answer.

Jack kisses her head again. "He was scared for your safety, Amore Mia. He let that *fear* show as anger."

"Well, it's been a bad couple of days..." she takes another deep breath, "but I felt the *worst* when David left me there..." Her voice is froggy. "For a brief moment I felt *all* alone...then I remembered you and Lawrence, so the feeling vanished just as quickly. But for that teeny, tiny moment in time, it was the most horrible feeling in the world...worse than the assault on my body!"

Jack has tears when he thinks of the pain she was in, but it was when David left her behind that was the worst part for her?! Jack hugs her.

"When David came home without you, he called himself a 'bloody bastard.' I told him that wasn't harsh enough! I told him you had a row with Herst, but at the hospital you were in so much pain you shook and cried. I also said you're this *incredible* woman—," he chokes up and he swallows hard to push it down, "refusing pain meds but I didn't say why. I told him you're the strongest person I've ever known; *we've ever known!*" He kisses her head. "Oh! *And* somewhere in the midst of all that I *maaay* have punched him."

She takes that in a moment, then she kisses his chest over his heart. "I think a smidgen of that was from the anger and frustration of what was done to me because I think all this," she points to her back, "took its toll on you, too." Jack kisses her hand. She lifts her head and raises her eyebrow with a faint smirk and asks, "Was it cathartic for you?"

He slightly shakes his head. "No. But then again, he's always been my best friend and brother."

"True." She agrees. "David is nothing like Katie!"

"Will he be forgiven then." He asks.

"I already have." She squeaks.

"Of course you have." He exhales.

She lays her head back down and says, "I just need to let go of the hurt..."

He flips through the channels and waits for Lawrence's text of his arrival. When the text finally comes, Jack texts back that Bri had fallen asleep on the couch with him and he doesn't want to wake her. He says the door is open for him and to come right inside. Lawrence sends a 'thumbs up.'

A little bit later, Lawrence walks in and smiles compassionately at them. Bri's things are set by the stairs and Lawrence goes over to shake Jack's hand and kisses Bri's head.

He whispers, "*See you both in the morning.*" Jack nods. Lawrence sets Bri's phone on the coffee table noting, "It's all charged for her." He goes upstairs while his *mostly* new 'King's Guard,' along with McMasters, strengthens security in and around the house and farm, as well as The Manor, The Inn, and he purposely has Tristan adding security to The Grounds and various entry points.

Jack falls asleep, and thankfully it's not as restless of a night for Bri as he thought it might be...

CHAPTER 38

Imperfectly Perfect Mending on Various Levels

While Jack and Bri both sleep in, Lawrence slips out to go up to The Manor to exercise with David. Later, a text from David wakes Bri, and she realizes Lawrence left her phone on the coffee table for her when he got there. She sees Lawrence coming up to and in the door as he comes back from exercising. She slowly lifts up her head and gives him a little smile. He smiles back when he sees her.

He walks over to her and sits on the coffee table. He whispers, *"Good morning, Darling."* He taps a kiss to her lips, then rests his forehead to hers. "I'm *so* sorry."

She pulls back and tells him, "Lawrence, *you* didn't do this and I don't blame you!" She cups his cheek and gives him a loving look. "Go take your shower and we'll talk after."

He sweetly grins, "Yes, Ma'am!" He kisses her forehead and heads upstairs.

She watches him, then she hears another reminder chime of David's text and looks at her phone again. She is debating whether to look at David's text as she lays her head back down on Jack's chest. She thinks about David...he hurt her, deeper than the actual wounds on her back, but *she knows* David loves her...

With his eyes still closed, Jack tells her, "Read the message, BriaLynn. You know he's worked *all night* on his apology and has barely slept, *if* he slept."

Lawrence is upstairs and pauses, looking down into the living room. "David has been punishing himself this morning in his workout. He feels horrible and what he did isn't anywhere close to half as bad as what *I'm* guilty of." He gives her a faint, apologetic smile before he goes to his room; her heart squeezes for him.

Bri kisses Jack's chest and sits up. Then Jack gets up and he lightly drapes the blanket on her before going upstairs to give her a minute alone. She picks up her phone and goes to David's text.

"Macushla, my inexcusable actions spoke WAY too loudly...I'm SO sorry! Please, forgive me for my dreadful behavior and awful actions.

378

I hope you can feel how much I love you. I'll do everything in my power to show you how terribly sorry I am, when you're willing to forgive me. You're the love of my life, and your love for me is all that matters in this life and in eternity.

Bri texts back: "You assume 'when' and not 'if' I'll forgive you?"

Bri sends her text, then glances up to see David walking up to their front door. He stops to read it and types his response back. Jack and Lawrence are coming down the stairs when they see David, so they let him in. Bri shakes her head and David freezes. Jack walks closer to her and David realizes she is shaking her head at Jack because he is carrying a box of bandages and antiseptic.

"*No, Jack...*" she can barely whisper, her lower jaw shaking. "*Please...*"

He gives her a compassionate look. "I don't *want* to, Amore Mia, but doctor's orders. We have to prevent infection or that could affect—." He stops but looks pointedly into her eyes; Bri nods in understanding, he's worrying about the baby.

Lawrence asks, "What doesn't she want to do?"

Jack tucks a strand of hair behind her ear. "I need to clean and redress the wounds to prevent infection, *and since Bri isn't The Royal Consort yet*, David will need to—."

Bri glares at Jack. "*You've gone and lost your mind!*" She stands and steps around the coffee table. "You're certifiably *insane?!*" With her hands holding the blanket closed, she turns and points to David with a blanket covered finger and steps over to him angrily saying, "YOU *LEFT* ME! *You* said you'd *always* walk out of the office *with* me—NO *EXCEPTIONS*! *You* LIED! YOU *LEFT ME BEHIND*! No ride home, no phone, no McMasters!" She looks to Jack who came over to them and points her finger right on his chest, "And *you* want me to find comfort in the arms of the man who abandoned me, *after* I confided in you last night *that was the worst feeling out of ALL that's happened to me?*! I'd rather do this myself!" Jack reaches for her and she pulls away. She uses her blanketed hands to cover her face and works to push down the urge to cry.

Jack softly tells her, "If you choose to do that, then I *insist* on pain meds, unless you have another idea?"

"*YOU!*" Bri snaps. "Then again, I seem to get slapped with hurt any direction I turn!"

"Hey! *That's not fair!*" Jack gently scolds her.

"You're right. I'm sorry..." She looks at him with pain in her eyes.

"It's forgiven, Amore Mia." He caresses her cheek. "It'll be easier, *and faster*, for me to just do it and less painful for you overall."

David walks over to her, but her eyes fill with tears again and all she can do is look down and whisper, "*You left me!*"

His heart is breaking the most right now. "I don't know how to express how *sorry* I am, Love! Did you read my last text before I came inside?" Her eyebrows come together and she shakes her head. He reads her the text:

> "We love each other, so forgiveness isn't a question of 'if' but you make it clear it's 'always,' so it's merely *when*." He emphasizes as he reads it to her.

She angrily grabs his phone and whips it hard into the kitchen, hitting the ceramic flooring and breaking it into various pieces. "I'm trying really hard not to say *horrible* things to you right now, David! So, 'when' is *not* now!"

"*Say them*, Bri!" David encourages her. "I can take it! I deserve them! *All of them!* We *will* get through this, *if* we get it all out there so we can deal with it!"

"No! I refuse—."

"Refuse?!" He pushes a little more to get her to say what she needs to say. "You *want* to hold onto this hurt and the pain?! To *not* move forward?!" He scoffs, "That's not like you!"

"*YOU DID!*" Her words have a bite to them. "That's why you left me there, isn't it?! I knew there was a misunderstanding and *I* wanted to clear it up *in person* but *you* wouldn't let me!" She angrily points at him. "*You* didn't take my calls, *you never* texted back! YOU.froze.*ME*.out!"

He exhales and shoots back, "Because *I* was scared, Bri! I was hurt you just up and left the country, *or so I thought!* I was scared you went alone and unprotected, like when you got lost the other day in The Palace! Scared I'd get a call from Uncle Henry or Ken telling me you were hurt, *or worse!*"

"Getting lost in The Palace is a separate issue with Lawrence and I *won't* discuss it with you!" She firmly states. "*And you can't use that against me!*"

"I'm—." He starts to say.

"I was hurt when you froze me out! Then to add insult to injury, YOU left me alone in your office building! I *never* felt more alone *in my life!*" She points at him again. "*You* did that! And you're talking to someone who enjoys her alone time! Are *you* happy?!" She sees him shake his head a bit, but he's quietly listening. "When you went down the elevator without me, I was only stunned and I *physically* couldn't move...my mind went to what you said in the past, that you'd always leave with me, *no exceptions...*" She says with his accent and rolling her eyes in disgust. His heart squeezes as it sinks in *how severely* he hurt her; even Jack's and Lawrence's eyes get teary. Bri turns away from David or she would melt at his teary eyes. She continues, "I finally came to my senses and push the elevator button when I remember 'we leave together' could *technically* mean you were still waiting in the lobby, even if you were angry with me, only when I got down there and looked around, I see your car pulling away, leaving me behind..." Tears run down her cheeks as those feelings hit her again. She senses he was coming over to comfort her, but she puts her hand up in a 'stop' gesture, shaking her head. He grabs the box of tissues, pulling one out and hands it to her, which she does take and wipes her eyes and nose.

Bri is quiet and when she doesn't continue, he asks, "There's more...it's at the center of this..." Lawrence is curious what else it could be; so is Jack. She closes her eyes, not wanting to feel it, but he sees this 'tell' and adds, "*Don't* push it away, Bri. Cards on the table, Love! We *can't* move forward until you tell me *everything.*" Lawrence is fascinated! He's never seen how fighting can actually be done in a loving way.

"For the first time since we met, you not only broke your word to me," she takes a deep breath, exhaling slowly, "for a brief moment, I felt utterly and completely alone. *It was the worst feeling!*" David's emotions just about overcome him; his jaw is shaking as he forces his emotions down. "The world was dark and empty...then that feeling disappears when I think about Jack and Lawrence. I knew I wasn't really alone, but at that dark moment...*that* was the deepest cut out of all of this!" She points to her back telling him, "And there are some of these that needed stitches!"

Without giving her a chance to stop him from getting closer, he holds her face and says with teary eyes, "If I could change that moment I would." He wipes her eyes with his thumbs. "I thought about you and the urge to not want to fight with you kept growing the *entire* ride home! That's *why* I wanted to talk after dinner, but I didn't know you didn't have your phone. It wasn't until I was getting out of the car at The Manor and I heard the helicopter in the distance that it hit me: *I* was your ride home."

"Really?!" She asks.

"I swear to you, Love, it wasn't intentional!" He replies.

"Well, I guess that counts for something." Bri softly says.

He gives her a bit of a grateful smile and continues, "When I got inside..." he looks to Jack.

"I told her already." Jack tells him.

David gives him a reluctant look, "You were right." He looks back at Bri, "*And* being sloshed wasn't harsh enough! After hearing all the specifics Jack should've punched me more!"

Bri's voice is flat, "A few times..."

David holds the back of her jaw. "I'm *so very sorry*, BriaLynn. *Please.* Let me be here for you now." He looks into her eyes. "Then you can go back to hating me again."

When she closes her eyes, tears escape down her cheeks. "I don't hate you, David. I could *never* hate you! I just want to love you!" She gestures to all of them and makes eye contact with Lawrence, "I want to love all three of you, *not fight!*" Lawrence gives her a hint of a nod.

David and Jack were in t-shirts and lounging pants. Jack looks at David, "You almost never wear anything but a button up shirt out of the house! Of all days to be proud of you for being *normal*..." Jack lightly teases as he gets up and walks over to the stairs, "she needs a button-up shirt."

"Hold up, Jack!" Lawrence stops him. "She can use mine." He undoes his tie and unbuttons his shirt; he has a t-shirt on underneath.

"While t-shirts under a dress shirt make the dress shirt look nicer, especially a white t-shirt under a white dress shirt makes it look crispier, *whiter*, I'm *kiiinda* disappointed right now..." Bri softly teases. Lawrence lightly chuckles, as does Jack and David. Lawrence hands the shirt to Jack who is closest to him, then he turns around to give Bri privacy.

She takes off the blanket and David gets a look at the bandages on her back. He says some swear words under his breath, then kisses the side of her head before he goes to the couch. Jack has Bri put Lawrence's shirt on backwards.

"Bri?!" Jack gasps, getting a good look at her abdomen for the first time helping her with Lawrence's shirt.

David sits up to see what Jack is reacting to. "*Oh, Love...*" he holds his hands out for her to take and he brings her closer to stand between his legs for a closer look. He lightly touches the outer edges of it. "*Why* did they have to do this, too?!" He sucks in his breath and holds it so he doesn't get emotional, but she catches it.

She holds his face and looks down into his teary eyes. She gives him a small smile and sees if he'll catch, "We'll be okay."

Lawrence still has his back turned. "What is it?"

"Her whole stomach area is all black and blue...well, *more black* than blue." Jack answers, looking at Bri.

"If there was anything more to it, the doctors would've said so after seeing the x-rays." She replies.

"Can I see?" Lawrence asks. Jack and David look at Bri.

"Doesn't bother me." David grins.

Jack agrees. "You have bottoms on and his shirt covers your, um, 'top.'" He winks. Bri carefully turns Lawrence's shirt around and leaves a few buttons unbuttoned at the bottom. She tells Lawrence, "You can turn around."

Lawrence walks over and sits next to David and Bri opens the shirt to show him just her bruised abdomen. "*This looks...*" he angrily exhales and quietly asks, "Was this checked for internal bleeding?!"

Jack walks behind the couch and says, "It was and *thoroughly*." He remembers the OB also wanted to personally do the ultrasound and check the baby out.

"What aren't you saying?" David says, looking at Bri and then back at Jack. "You've been saying things in such a way or stopping yourself from finishing altogether. Why's he being..." he looks back to Bri, remembering her *'we'll be okay'* comment and now understands! He says in a surprised whisper, "*You're pregnant!*" Bri gives him a small smile. "BRI!" He pulls her to stand in front of him again and he carefully kisses her lower abdomen. She's not as excited as he expected her to be. Then again, these are not typical circumstances either, so he helps her. "You *really* need to think about that, Love! *You're pregnant! We're going to have a baby!*"

She looks down at his hand on her lower abdomen. She can barely whisper, "*I'm scared...*"

"Ah, no, Love." He motions her black and blue lower abdomen. "If he's still in there after all this, we all know our son gets his strength from his incredible mum!" She stares at his hand again, as the feeling of being pregnant *finally* sinks in. She looks at David with happy tears. "*Macushla...*" he whispers and nods because of the lump in his throat.

She holds his face and whispers, "*We're having a baby...*"

David stands up. "We're having a baby!" He holds her jaw and kisses her firmly. Resting his forehead to hers, "*Our family is having a baby!*"

Standing up, Lawrence has a huge smile across his face. "I can't think of *anything better* than that to come out of all that you went through." He holds her cheek furthest away from him and kisses the cheek closest to him.

Jack had walked over and she looks at him. He rests his forehead to hers a moment. "Why don't you let Herst help you get comfortable on the couch with David. I'll text Gabriel to make an appointment with an OB here in Kingsbury so we can start establishing yours and the baby's care." Bri nods.

Bri had pulled her arms in and turned the shirt backwards again. She slowly lies down on top of David. Lawrence carefully helps her get situated and comfortable. He unbuttons the shirt as Jack comes over to remove the bandages and treat her wounds.

Lawrence gasps as he sees the full picture of her back in person. *"Briii..."* he whispers, his face showing 'enraged' at those responsible. "I *need* to know *exactly* what happened that night!"

With Bri laying on David, Jack begins to work on cleaning the wounds. She lifts her head off his chest and looks at Lawrence. "Your mother had her lackeys abduct me from my room..." she lays her head back down on David's chest, hissing from pain, then says, "I woke up to a pillowcase, or whatever it was, going over my head. I tried to scream but they told me if I wasn't quiet *your* punishment would be *most severe*! I wouldn't let that happen and kept my mouth shut! My hands and feet were tied, then I was thrown over someone's shoulder and taken away to The Dungeons. I knew where I was by the stench of it. They hung me up by my arms, pulling me up high enough that I was up just on my toes."

Lawrence holds her hand, as David kisses Bri's head. "Keep going, Darling?!"

Bri lifts her head and looks at Lawrence. He holds her gaze and she sees so much emotion. "I promise I'll explain more," she looks over her shoulder, "but let's get this over with first...please." He nods with compassion.

Jack had taken the peroxide and started dabbing her wounds. Bri slides her free hand under David's shoulder, then up to hold the top of his shoulder from behind. David holds tighter where he can, as Bri tries so hard not to cry out; he feels her shake as she holds it in and he kisses her head every now and then. The few times she screams she muffles them using David's shoulder. It's hard for the three of them because they feel so helpless and want to make her pain go away.

When he's about to add ointment, Jack asks her, "Bri, did you still want me to use the tea tree oil?"

"Yes. It'll help with any infection." She weakly answers. "Put it on right before the ointment, then after you've added the ointment let it all sit for a few minutes before bandaging them up again."

Jack does exactly as she says. When he's done with the ointment, he wipes off his hands and thinks about how she didn't scream as high-pitched as she did yesterday, a small sign of improvement.

Jack has to ask, "Was all this because of the confrontation you had with The Queen Mother and Herst?!"

She inhales deeply and slowly exhales as she nods. "I was being taught——."

"*Being taught a lesson*?!" Lawrence says through a clenched jaw. Flashes of his childhood 'lessons' come to his mind.

"The Queen Mother loves corporal punishment because she loves inflicting pain! She's sadistic and she gets off on it!" She can still feel The Queen Mother's fingers pressing into one of the wounds on her back but she doesn't tell them that, nor that she licked Bri's blood off her fingers and had Tristan do the same thing.

Jack starts to dress certain wounds. Bri reflexively grips Lawrence's hand tighter with the pain when painful memories of *his past* come to her mind again. Only this time she's given *complete* visions of Lawrence's 'lessons' and grips Lawrence's hand tighter yet. He grimaces a bit at her strength.

"*Oh, Lawrence*! I can see you when you were younger!" She says.

"See what?" He asks, not understanding what she means at first.

"I see you when you were youn—gah!" Bri reacts, but it's not to her own pain—*it's Lawrence's*!

Jack had automatically held up his hands to make sure he wasn't hurting her. She is reacting to a vision of a red-hot poker burning a younger Lawrence's skin as it's placed against the skin on the side of his ribcage by a man Bri doesn't recognize, but she feels it's his great uncle. She sees his mother is really enjoying Lawrence's pain.

"*What the...*" Jack whispers watching Bri's skin turn red and blister on the side of her ribcage, the same side and place as young Lawrence in the vision.

Lawrence leans over and sees what Jack is looking at. He looks at Bri's face, her eyes are closed as she is still seeing a vision. He leans in to kiss her upper arm. "I'm so sorry you're seeing *and feeling* any of it! What can I do?!"

She shakes her head. "You can't..."

She holds her breath as she's transported to various places to witness various times Lawrence was tortured; they were so much worse than what she just went through and corresponding marks and bruising appear on her body.

The guys freeze when she screams so hard, their ears ring; then cries Lawrence's name. David has his cheek on her head, holding her as tight as he dared to. Lawrence holds her hand in his hands and resting his cheek on her arm. Her cries turn into uncontrollable sobs for Lawrence; their eyes were teary for her, but David and Jack have tears for their brother as well...

When her crying eases, she faintly asks, "How could a mother...?!"

Jack quietly says, "I'm going to get some *water——*." His voice cracks.

Jack goes to the kitchen to get ahold of his emotions. He doesn't want Bri to see him cry; he wants to be strong for her. His heart also breaks because even though he didn't see those visions, it's more than enough to know Herst was tortured *far beyond* anyone's imagination their entire childhood and they never had a clue *how* bad it was for him!

Bri squeezes Lawrence's hand a couple times and hears her quietly say, "I *really* love you, Lawrence. What she did was *not* okay for anyone to do, but for a mother to do to her child is *despicable!*" She kisses the hand she is holding.

He can't hold back his emotions any longer and the tears start to streak down his cheeks. He smiles tenderly. "Your love *more than* makes up for it!"

"You give my love for you way too much credit for all the torture you endured for so long and," she gives him a knowing look, "for what you're still going through!" She rests her forehead to his.

"I get to have a family with three of the best people I know and their extended family!" He tells her, "I can't think of anything better!" He glances at David who gives a compassionate smile and a small nod.

Bri's exhaustion catches up to her and she closes her eyes. As she drifts off to sleep, she hears, '*The Queen Mother will have to die.*' Lawrence feels Bri's hand loosen its grip when she falls asleep. He stands up and lays a blanket on her.

Lawrence pats David's shoulder. "I'm going to go check on Jack."

David whispers, "*Thanks and Herst...*" Lawrence had turned towards the kitchen, but looks down at David who tells him, "The Worthington's *are* your family and the best part now is we're making our own family with the woman we love!"

Lawrence nods, looking from David to the now sleeping Bri and smiles with so much love he can't speak. He clears his throat and quickly goes to the kitchen, hoping to catch his breath.

CHAPTER 39

Imperfectly Perfectly Healed with Love

When Lawrence walks into the kitchen, Jack drops to the floor to covertly wipe his eyes. Lawrence sees this and looks around the kitchen for some tissues.

"Help yourself to whatever." Jack says to Lawrence as he starts to pick up the pieces of David's phone.

Lawrence hands him a tissue and takes one to wipe his own eyes. Then he squats down to help Jack pick up the pieces of the phone. Lawrence asks, "Does she normally throw things?"

"No..." Jack replies. "I don't think she would've if she were simply mad. I think it was just everything coming together. She was hurt deeply when David left without her, *after* she had already been hurt physically..." He exhales slowly to control his emotions. "That amazing woman is stronger than all three of us put together!"

Lawrence sweetly smiles. "*And she is a force!*" Jack agrees. Lawrence tells him, "Unfortunately, she was hurt *before* the physical *by me*, when she stood up to me *and my mother*. She was right to stand up to me!" He stands up to put the pieces of the phone on the counter. "I *was* my mother's puppet!" Jack comes over next to him and adds the rest of the pieces of the phone to the pile on the counter. "I just wish standing up to my mother was a price she never had to pay."

"Can I ask you something?" Jack asks.

"You're curious about my 'so-called-lessons?'" Lawrence walks to a cabinet for a drinking glass.

"Yes." Jack replies. "Was it both your parents? You don't mention your father much. I mean for as awful as those lessons were, how did you're father *not* know?!" Lawrence looks from Jack to his glass as he pours some juice.

"There's been only one parent..." he replies, then takes a drink. "My father wasn't around much. He took care of his duties and responsibilities for the country, but he had his affairs on the side. He left us for my mother to raise, so he wouldn't necessarily have known. These '*lessons*' were to teach me

389

cruelty and its power from the fear inflicted on others." He takes another drink. "Eventually, my mother and I came to an understanding: I didn't care what she did to me, so long as she left Seth and Abby alone. She would test it and if I didn't obey, she would retaliate, usually against Abby. However, my mother crossed a line with Bri, and I'll kill her myself for what she has done to her. But first, we need to deal with *all* the others who were involved in hurting her the other night! If we start from the top down, they'll band together, but if we start from the bottom up, my mother won't protect them. They have to be in her 'inner-circle' for her to care and those are few."

Jack gets a glass down for himself. "Herst," he stands next to Lawrence, "we had an idea something bad was happening...but we had *no idea* it was to any extreme!" He pours himself some juice.

"*How would you?* Being with you and David, and the times with the family, it was all an escape for me! I didn't want anyone to know because those escapes would stop coming if Peter and Carlotta ever found out; *if anyone found out!*" Lawrence tells him. "I needed them, you, and David!" Jack nods in understanding. "During those lessons, I'd go to a place to disassociate myself. Sometimes I'd dream of various scenarios of killing my mother, but I can't seem to come up with any kind that seem to satisfy 'justice' for what she has done this time!" He stares at the countertop. "There's no 'poetic justice' because all the scenarios that come to mind don't seem *anticlimactic* somehow..."

Bri had gotten up to use the restroom and David comes to the kitchen. He hears the end of the 'anticlimactic' comment. "I'm assuming you're talking about Herst's mother?" They nod. David asks Lawrence, "What happened in that standoff in your office to cause this much hatred towards a woman who'll give you an heir? *With a 'Direct Bloodline' no less!*"

Lawrence digs in his pocket, "Bri basically told me to cut the puppet strings..." he puts her ring on the counter, "or don't bother coming after her." He smiles as he leans over the counter on his elbows and slides the ring partially on his forefinger. "Right before that, I had yelled at her that *I* was king, so she responded by telling me to grow up and act like one! *She was right!*" David and Jack softly chuckle picturing her doing that. "Sadly," Lawrence adds, "she does all this right in front of my mother *and* people hear it as it echoes throughout the halls of The Palace."

"Which makes your mother frantic to keep what power and control she does have by controlling——." David stops himself.

"By controlling me, *The King*." Lawrence finishes the sentence. "You're absolutely right!" He also says, "I knew what I had to do to protect Abby and Seth."

Jack sees how Lawrence is looking at the ring and adds, "Your mother may be desperate," he smiles, "but it's a lost cause for her now that you have Bri." Lawrence nods with a loving smile at the thought of Bri.

"What are we going to do?" David asks.

"We need to flush out and deal with all those involved," Larence replies, "with McMasters' and Mitchell's help."

Jack wonders, "Do you think Bri will see killing—."

"They're being *executed* for the crimes committed against me, but ultimately *The King*." Bri had walked into the kitchen. "He needs to come on strong, with significant strength to show how powerful *he is* by executing those involved. Which will show his people that The Queen Mother is no longer in charge!" They see her eyes go to an empty place between them. With a slight wave of her hand, they're able to see Jessica, too.

David looks at Jessica, struggling not to yell. "*She was told to start with The Dungeons!* Why on earth would—!" Bri had walked over to him and now reaches up to touch David's cheek. He closes his eyes as he puts his hand on top of hers.

"Look at me." Bri says and when he looks at her, she gently reminds him, "Remember, David, back when I was in a coma, *I chose* to come back; however, I knew choosing to come back *came with a price*. Only now I'm seeing you three are *also* paying a price for that..."

"You seriously think a price to pay was a price like *this*!" He points to her wounds. "To lure you to The Dungeons and later you end up—."

"First of all, *I* accepted the *unknown* price, David, whatever that might have been, to come back, or I would've died." Bri sees the fear flick across his face as he remembers that time. "Secondly, don't forget: Jessica *isn't* in charge! She is a 'Messenger,' or a 'Guide.' Sometimes she may have the full picture, but other times, like this one, I don't think even *they* had all the pieces." He knows

391

she's implying his son and Lawrence's son. "What I'm sensing is they *couldn't* have had the full picture!"

David looks puzzled. "Why not?!"

Bri gives Jessica a kind smile. "To ensure I was told to start there. Had any of you known, you would've, at the very least, hesitated; at most, you would've interfered with the plan of Who really is in charge! The Lord foresaw *the choices* The Queen Mother and her lackeys made and prepared for them! David, do you remember in that same conversation I was also told I would be given comfort and strength?" He slowly nods as he recalls the morning visit of Jessica and Bri's sons with David and Lawrence. "I remember right before I was whipped with whatever they used, I was trembling uncontrollably with fear and the tears started to pour down my cheeks," each guy inhales and holds their breath to stop their anger from boiling over, "but then I felt a calmness come over me like a blanket, followed by a strength. *That strength* helped me *not* give The Queen Mother, or her henchmen, the sadistic satisfaction of hearing me scream in pain, *not even a little.*"

"Bri, I..." Lawrence is so angry his words escape him.

Bri gets closer to him. "This *needed* to happen! *I see that now!*" She holds his hands. "One reason being to give you the surge *you needed* to take on your mother without thinking twice!" Bri tells him and she sees him clenching his jaw, as he nods. "Lawrence, I can get through this with the three of you, plus McMasters and this Mitchell because I trust and have faith in, '*everything* happens for a reason' *and* I know that the answers aren't always instantly ascertained." She takes a deep breath. "What McMasters and I saw on our tour of The Dungeons got to me." Seeing Jessica fade, Jack and David decide to go back into the living room to give Lawrence and Bri a minute.

Lawrence gives her a hint of a smile and caresses her cheek. "Oh, My Darling..." Lawrence looks lovingly at Bri. "My behavior was *ghastly* and *inexcusable!*"

"It was!" She states. "*But* I'd rather label that time as 'a turning point' in *our* relationship, in *our* lives, *aaand* King Lawrence's reign and rule!" She smiles with a twinkle in her eyes as she says, "That the *real* King Lawrence is here to stay!"

His watery eyes glisten with his smile. "I love you, My Queen!" He kisses the hand he is holding. "Bri," he takes a deep breath, "the whole thing was like an 'out of body experience.' The entire day started awful and it felt like it would never end!"

It comes to Bri and she surprisingly says, "You were whipped *that morning* with the cane in her office..."

He nods as he sees her compassionate look for him. "I shouldn't have said what I said to you! I knew you were right, but when I watched you walk out of my office and possibly out of my life, my mind went blank. My mother was ranting again and *I had had enough*. I told her I didn't need her anymore." His face is apologetic. "You should've been safe, *at least until the papers were signed*. However, when she finds out the signed, binding paperwork isn't what she designed, *I had hoped* it would buy us more time to figure out a way to protect you and your children..."

"How?" She sweetly smiles. "Lock me up, with *our* children, until, well, *when?* You can't keep us locked up forever!"

"I was thinking one of us would always be with you, or I'd secretly have to have a tracking device on you." He playfully grins. "Or maybe my mother."

"Ha-ha! *That* would have to be strategically inserted where she would never see it, *or feel it*, like...under the armpit, towards the back? Out of the way of deodorant and be missed by clothes going on or coming off. Oh! But then there would be the obstacle of getting her unconscious to do it, only at that point, why not lock her up or execute her right then and there?"

Lawrence's eyebrow goes up as he mischievously smiles saying, "Anyone else saying that and I would question their sanity!"

Bri snorts into a laugh. "What can I say? I can think like a criminal *and* law enforcement." She points to her head. "The things I could come up with and plan out for 'war games' and such would *blow your mind!*" She gestures with wide eyes and her hands 'exploding.' She leans in and gives him a small, lingering kiss.

"Not long enough." He tells her and goes to kiss her again, but she only pecks him this time and he softly laughs.

"Lawrence, I need you to know that what I'm about to say, I *swear* I don't blame you for anything that night." She holds his face and he nods with a little concern. "I just *can't* go back to The Palace until I'm actually sleeping next to you!"

He closes his eyes and says, "And if you had been with me, you wouldn't have been hurt that night."

"Lawrence," she squeezes his hand and reminds him, "we wanted to do this right, *for love*, and build it solidly. Had we been in the same room without me *officially* 'The Royal Consort,' we would've been playing with *serious fire!*" She smirks. "And we've already been dangerously there *without being horizontal.*" Her hands are at his waist. "We both know she wanted to teach me this 'lesson' and she would've found another way if he had to. Besides, if we broke that rule before I'm officially 'The Royal Consort,' then our *entire relationship* would be tainted—."

"And forever corrupted." He simply states, giving a faint smile. "The way my mother would've wanted it!"

"Lawrence, there's another reason this lesson happened...it was for us." She takes a deep breath to keep her emotions in check. "The visions that I saw, there aren't enough words to describe what I saw *and felt*, which is only a fraction of what you've had to go through *your entire life!*" She wraps her arms around his neck. He hugs her with one arm at her lower waist and his other hand holding the back of her head. She whispers in his ear, "*YOU are the strongest person I know! I love you so much, Lawrence! The roots of my love for you grew deeper and stronger than I ever could've imagined seeing those visions!*"

"Mine, too, watching you experience them *and you're still with me!* I'm so grateful for you!" He says.

He goes to pull his head back to look into her eyes, but she hugs him tighter and shakes her head. "Don't let go!" She pleas with him. "*Not just yet...*" She is feeling peace in his arms right now.

He inhales at her neck and relaxes as he exhales. "We can stay like this for as long as you need."

After a few minutes she pulls back. "Thank you," she rests her forehead to his, "I needed that."

Lawrence takes her hands and he rubs his thumbs across her fingers and notices her empty right ring finger. He takes out her ring that he had put back in his pocket. "Promise me," he holds it up, "you'll never take this off again!" Bri sweetly smiles. "I mean it, Bri. *Never* again!"

She studies him...she finds herself *very* attracted to this side of him. She looks at the ring and sees part of an engraved word. She takes the ring to look closer and reads:

"*You have my heart; guard it well!*"

She inhales a soft gasp, then she looks up at him with so much love, his heart skips a beat. "Lawrence, I love you! I'd *never* betray you, *or* the love we have!"

"I know." He gives her a loving smile and he slides it on her finger; she kisses him firmly. Then he says to her, "Thank you for letting me put this back on."

She looks at it with a sweet smile. "I was feeling *kinda* naked without it." Lawrence chuckles. She adds, "This is *MUCH* better!"

"OH no, Darling! This," he taps the ring on her finger, "is better but 'much better' would be this here and *you*, very much The Royal Consort...*and naked!*" He flirts, carefully wrapping his other arm around her lower waist again.

She flirts back, "Perhaps that can be arranged *right after* the 'Midnight Ball!'" He kisses her passionately and when their lips pull apart, Lawrence sees her eyes are still closed as she whispers, "*I love you, Ace.*" She smiles as she opens her eyes.

He puts his forehead to hers and says, "I love you more than I ever thought my heart was capable of! Your love is this amazing gift!" He looks at her. "I'm just so sor—." Her hand goes over his mouth.

"Lawrence, you've already apologized and I'd go through this as many times as needed, as long as it didn't hurt the baby, or anyone else we love."

"How can you say that?!" He's baffled. "*You* were hurt emotionally, *then* physically, and I know from experience that yesterday was *much worse* for the *raw pain!*" He kisses her forehead, empathizing with his own experiences with his mother. "I want to fix this and there's only one way I can. However, it could put *you* in even more serious danger, especially if my mother wants a war."

"She gives him a compassionate look. "My life is already in jeopardy; but it'll increase ten-fold when I give you all details and names behind my assault!" She tells him, "Lawrence, remember where my faith lies and consider this assault was necessary."

He gets a skeptical look. "How's you being hurt *necessary*?!"

"As long as something good comes from this!" She gives a little smile, but then she becomes more serious. "You already know what you have to do, because it started that day I challenged you."

He quietly thinks out loud, answering her. "I'm going to have to make a more *public* stand..."

She takes his hands in hers. "And I'll support you in whatever, or however, you decide to do it."

He lifts his eyebrow as if to challenge that statement. "Even if it entails *My* Queen becoming *The Queen*?"

"Wow!" She laughs. "Testing my loyalty so soon!" He studies her. "If it's necessary to the cause—."

"Oh-ho! Now I'm *a cause*?!" He teases.

She lifts her eyebrow, giving him a cheeky response, "At times!" He chuckles. "Seriously though, 'The Cause' I'm supporting is *you* becoming *The King* you truly are! King Lawrence no longer suppressed under his mother's control! The King *your child* will honor, respect, and be proud to follow in *that* legacy!"

Lawrence's jaw shakes and he struggles to say, "You, *believing* in *me* and having *so* much *faith* in me...*how*?" He is bewildered. "After all that I said to you?!"

She smiles so lovingly at him. "That wasn't really you, was it?! That's *not* who I have faith in! I have faith in this man, *and king*, in front of me. That's who I support, and so does our family, as will *your people*."

Bri hears a familiar voice behind her, "The King always needs his queen." She turns and sees her son with Lawrence. "Father *needs you*, his queen, to be *The Queen*, Mum."

She softly laughs. "I think *you're* biased." She wipes the corners of her eyes before the tears drop from them.

"Of course, I am! That doesn't make it any *less* true!" He is quick to reply.

She snorts a laugh, shaking her head. "You sound like your Uncle Jack!"

Lawrence is listening to her side of the conversation. "Darling, your gift is great, but it's bloody fantastic when I can see who you're talking to as well!"

She teases. "You're hearing what you would hear if I were talking on the phone."

His voice is monotoned as he teases back, "Apples and oranges, Darling."

Bri looks from Lawrence to their son, who mischievously smiles at her. "It's only fair, Mum."

She laughs, "Now, you sound like your father!"

She looks over at Lawrence. He is confused, then inhales a gasp with a bit of shock as he puts it together!

He whispers, "Bri?!"

She smiles lovingly as she asks him. "Remember when I said I have three children that haven't been born to me yet?"

"Two boys and a girl; one son being David's." He says as he stares at the empty space where Bri is talking to someone.

She smiles and cups his cheek. When he looks at her and she tells him, "The other son is yours, Lawrence."

Lawrence is choked up, "*Our son?*" He says more to himself and in awe. "*We have a son?*"

"Oh, you *definitely* do!" She replies. "Your son looks so much like you, I still can't believe how I missed it at first! The green-blue eyes, but my darker brown hair..." she smiles and turns to look lovingly at their son and back to Lawrence, "*the dimples...*" She asks, "Do you want to meet him?" He nods and Bri circles her two fingers around.

He inhales and holds his breath, taking in his son standing before him. He walks closer to his son. "*This is astonishing!* What's your name?"

She says to Lawrence. "No names."

Lawrence is surprised. "We can't know his name," he turns to his son, "er, your name?"

Their son smiles. "*Technically*, I haven't been named yet."

Lawrence chuckles as he agrees with that logic. "Definitely seeing some resemblance to his beautiful mother's sense of humor!" Lawrence smirks and she playfully grins.

She tells him, "In his smile with dimples and overall good looks, Ace, that's *all you* and it's *bloody fantastic!*" She teases back with his accent, while Lawrence and their son laugh. "See!" She gestures both of their smiles and dimples. "The stunning proof is right there!"

"Bri, I thought the experience in The Clock Tower was incredible, but *this?!*" He pauses a second, then asks, "Why did you tell our son he was being biased?"

"*Great...*" She rolls her eyes. "This is the part where I'm going to be outnumbered two-to-one!"

"Oh, I don't know," their son says, "Uncle Jack and Uncle David could make it four-to-one." He gestures the direction of his uncles in the other room, who are actually coming towards the kitchen.

"I don't actually need to be outnumbered." She tells him.

Jack and David had heard 'outnumbered' as they walked into the kitchen. Jack asks, "Outnumbered?"

She tsks. "Yes..."

Lawrence smiles a knowing smile. "*Four*-to-one."

"Who's here?" David winks at her.

Jack has a playful look. "Can we see them, too?"

Bri looks at Lawrence's son and she repeats to him what he said to her a couple minutes ago. "It's only fair?" He happily agrees. Bri circles her two fingers. "Jack, this is—."

"Herst's son! *Of course!*" He smiles wide. "You're the spitting image of your father!" Jack says and reaches out to touch him.

David stops him and shakes his head. "Only his mother can touch him." Jack looks at him confused and David adds, "I originally tried with my son."

Jack chuckles, then asks Bri, "Why?—Ah, part of the gifts?"

Lawrence's son walks over to his mother and says, "As my brother said once before, it's because of the love of a true mother, the purest love there is," he places a hand on her cheek, "that our mother can touch us..." He turns to Jack and David. "Now, Uncles, Father and I are trying to convince my beautiful mother he needs *His Queen*, by his side as *The* Queen, *but,*" he looks at her, "*she's being stubborn.*"

"I don't have to be queen to support whatever he decides to do, *however* he decides to do it!" She replies.

Lawrence's son gestures his mother repeating, "*Stubborn...*"

The men around her are laughing. David walks up to Bri and beside his nephew. "Love, think of it like a game of chess."

Bri flatly states, "*I don't know how to play chess.*"

Lawrence raises his eyebrow. "You do know the concept, Sassy."

"She does have some idea! And if she learns, she'll play like she does any game she masters, *wickedly!*" Jack smiles and winks. Bri smiles and shakes her head.

Bri tells them, "What *little I know* is every piece inevitably protects the queen, while some are sacrificed, some are used to lure the opponent's pieces away from their queen."

David looks at Bri with determination, "Yes, the game works around protecting the queen, BUT one particularly important fact to keep in mind, Love: *she IS the game*! Without her, it's 'game over.' This isn't coming from tradition, Love, this is coming from in here." He taps on her heart. "*Everyone* will do better with you by his side, even, *and especially*, the three men who love you most! Keep in mind what I've said before," he holds her face, "none of us are loved any less because of the others; it's the opposite. I have a feeling we can apply that to you taking on being queen! You'll make an even better Duchess and business owner!"

Bri is somewhat surprised. "How do you figure?!"

"*Bri*, we say you *magnify* love but just as importantly, *love magnifies you* in return! We watch as things are thrown your way and you tackle them! No, you won't have time to *personally* do everything, but you know Gabriel is already positioning you to slide right into this role so it'll feel more seamless to you and everyone involved." David explains.

Lawrence adds, "With The Queen Mother and her assistant out of the equation, Gabriel and his assistants are juggling all the schedules, even mine and Gens, until my new assistant is hired. Gabriel will oversee their training as well." Jack nods.

Lawrence's son says to her as Lawrence walks over to them, "Mum, The King needs you to officially be The Queen, but so does the country!" He looks to his father and says, "My mother is a strength and Uncle David is right, she *is* the whole game." Bri notices it looks like he could say more but doesn't.

"Bri," Lawrence says, tangling a hand in her hair, "I need you *officially* by my side and *officially* my partner within The Monarchy."

"Lawrence, I am, and forever will be, on your side! It's your people I worry about! Genevieve's a wonderful queen and I understand why she wants to step down, I just don't know if the public is really ready to switch to an American, now Scottish-American Duchess."

Lawrence's son explains differently. "Mum, you love the Triquetra with a heart going through the three loops." Bri nods. "Think of the Triquetra representing Uncle David, Uncle Jack, and my father, with you" he points to her, "being the heart of everything, *the queen of this Triquetra chessboard*." He winks. "With that symbol being a part of your monogram and coat of arms, it'll also be representative of *you* years to come. While the heart goes through those loops representing Uncle Jack, Uncle David, and my father, they also stand for who you are! *Wife*, mother, and *beloved queen*!" Lawrence's son tells her. "You're looking at your roles individually but being queen would encompass *every* role!"

Bri's smile fades a little at Lawrence's son as she recalls something. "The last time we talked, your brother mentioned bonding." Her son has a little smile and points beside him as her son with David appears.

Bri has a smile that goes to horrified. She touches her lower abdomen shaking her head, "*I don't understand?*"

David's son waves his hands a little assuring her, "Your fine! *I'm* fine!" He's excited. "I'll be joining you soon enough!"

The guys see her face show relief as she takes a deep breath, then she smiles a bit exhaling slowly. "You're *really* excited about this!" She looks at her hands that are on her abdomen.

Her son with David chuckles, "Are you kidding?! As you already know, we come into mortality to progress on our eternal path!"

She slowly nods. "Right—."

"Bri?" David is confused. "Are you talking with our son right now?!" His eyebrows come together. "But how can that be..."

She looks to Jack, Lawrence, and David, circling her fingers for them to see David's son and she explains to David, "No one knows exactly when the spirit joins up with the baby. *My theory was* when the heart starts beating, but now I wonder if it's when movements happen? That's right in the second trimester."

David's son tells her as he touches her cheek, "While my body is very much alive, you'll know when my spirit joins up with it because a mother knows. There is a general bond naturally created between a mother and child but as we talked about before, true and pure love, *your love, is* the real bonding power."

Lawrence's son says, "The Queen Mother will test Mum's bond with Father."

"I think I can keep loving Lawrence," she takes his hand, "*and*, we *all* can work on continuing to make what we have unshakable *and* unbreakable." She points with her hand at David and Jack, too.

Lawrence's son walks over to her, looking into her eyes and projecting the rest of his thoughts for only her to hear. *'The scars that are no longer on father's back are important; father doesn't fully understand why Grandpa wanted them covered up, but, when the time is right, he needs to.'* Bri nods with David, Lawrence, and Jack looking confused.

David's son says they need to go. "One more thing, Mum. You do have the power within you to heal yourself...*with love.*" He points his finger at Lawrence, Jack, and David.

Jack, clearly frustrated, says, "*I wish we knew about that sooner!*"

"Jack..." Bri says softly.

"Bri! You were in so much pain, *you shook*! There were many times you cried out, which meant that pain was the most unbearable. If you were set up to have this happen, then why not set you up sooner to heal yourself?!" His frustration escaping.

"Uncle Jack," David's son says to him, "it's hard for you to see anyone you love hurt and in pain, but more so to see Mum that way." He nods. "The power to heal herself has been within her, but the love to activate it comes from you three!" David's son compassionately and lovingly smiles to his mother, "Dad said it already, her love magnifies each of you and your combined love magnifies her even more...even to be healed! But that wasn't going to happen with even one relationship fractured, let alone two, with those serious wounds. You needed to fix those relationships *before* you could heal Mum with this many severe wounds!" He gives her a sweet smile.

"So smaller wounds, one of us could heal her?" Jack asks.

David's son nods. He hugs his mother and kisses her cheek, as does Lawrence's son. They all say their goodbyes and watch them fade away. Bri looks at Lawrence and Jack. She turns to David and he tangles his hands in her hair.

"Love, this is always amazing to experience, but more so now that you're pregnant!" He carefully hugs her. "Do you know when you're due?"

"Not officially, but I'm thinking July." She answers. "The timeframe of conception could be during one of our visits to—."

"The Château!" David smiles wide and she nods.

Jack smiles and walks over. "Personally, I can't wait to have this little guy join our family!" He carefully puts his hand on her lower abdomen because she's still badly bruised. "He's an *extraordinary* young man! *Both of them are!*" He kisses her. "I just wish you both found out you were pregnant under better circumstances.

"Oh, My Loves," she looks at all three while staying in David's arms. She reaches for a hand of Lawrence's and one of Jack's. "Life will throw obstacles at us all the time! I *have* to believe that everything that happens to us, happens for a reason, or my faith is built on nothing!"

"What also matters is *how* we handle what comes our way..." Jack says, deep in thought leaning his backside against the counter, rubbing his thumb back and forth across Bri's hand; his eyes fixated on the floor in front of him.

"Right." Bri agrees and squeezes Jack's hand, even Lawrence's. Jack's eyes dart to her and he smiles; he kisses her hand. Tears flow down her cheeks and she feels so much love from all three. "Thank you all for being here! I love you more than I could ever put into words, but I feel it so strongly right n—." She stops abruptly. Bri feels a tingling sensation inside that radiates to her front and her back. Lawrence and Jack go to step back to look at her better but says with a panic, "No! *Don't move!* Keep doing what you're doing! I think it's working!"

"What's working?" David asks.

"Healing!" She thinks out loud, "It's coming from all of your love!" Bri tells them with relief, "The pain is disappearing!"

Lawrence and Jack stand closer to her and hug her on top of David's arms already hugging her. They just focus on how much they love her... After a few minutes she tells them the tingling has stopped, with Jack and Lawrence taking a small step back.

Jack quickly, but carefully, takes her bandages off to look at her back. He stares in awe. "*Bloody fantastic!*"

403

Lawrence looks and whispers, "*Amazing...*" to himself.

Bri turns for David to see. "Like they said, Bri," he lightly feels her back, "*this is incredible!*"

"I can't see, but I can feel your hand on my back and it *feels* normal, no pain!" Bri says with a whole lot of relief in her voice. She looks at them. "The love of you three *healed me...*" she whispers as she chokes up. She hugs David and he fiercely hugs her back.

She turns to Lawrence. "Thank you!" He tangles his hands in her hair and holds her neck. She smiles saying, "I love you!"

"I love *you*, My Queen!" He says and taps another kiss to her lips.

She turns to Jack. He has his hand out and when she takes it, he pulls her closer and just hugs her, holding her tight.

CHAPTER 40
Imperfectly Perfect & Royal Bonding

In the living room, Bri sees the laptop screen on the coffee table on her way over to her overstuffed chair. David sees her looking at the screen and explains, "While you were in the kitchen, we were curious about any news on your face-off with *The King* and The Queen Mother."

Bri raises her eyebrow with a skeptical look. "And you know what curiosity did to the cat?"

"I expected a cheeky comment." David gives her a look. "*The cat was nosy*! We were just adding to *our* big picture."

"Mmm-hmmm...that excuse doesn't work for Lawrence when he's part of that '*big picture*.'"

Bri sits and gets comfortable when there is a knock on the door. They could see Gabriel and someone holding a bouquet of red roses right behind him. Jack answers the door, helping the woman by taking the flowers and sets them on a shelf, an 'I'm so sorry' note facing outward so Bri could see it. David tips the woman and Jack shows her out while David talks with Gabriel, who brought him a new phone.

Jack curiously looks at the laptop for a couple minutes. Then he walks over to Lawrence who is staring out the window. Jack throws his thumb over his shoulder saying, "If any of that on the internet is true, Bri sure did take a stand!"

Lawrence has remorse in his eyes. "Yeah...I can't believe I yelled at her in a way I should never talk to anyone, let alone—."

"The woman you love." David finishes walking over to them after Gabriel leaves. Lawrence just nods his head, still looking out the window. David sees Bri sitting in her chair reading an email and he thinks about how beautiful she looks.

She glances at David and looks again asking, "What?" She looks down at herself in Lawrence's shirt trying to figure out what he was looking at.

He walks over to her. "You're even more beautiful at this moment!" He gives her a sweet smile as he sits on the ottoman in front of her.

"If you say it's because 'I'm glowing' that could quite possibly be the cheesiest line you've ever said to me." She smiles with pursed lips.

David says, "While *that's true*, you *are* glowing, I was thinking about you, sitting here, and what you went through the last few days..." he tucks a loose strand of hair behind her ear. He lays his hand on one of her knees; her legs are stretched out on the ottoman beside him. "You have so much strength, Bri, it matches your intelligence, which only adds to your beauty. What's frustrating is you don't see it!"

She says with conviction, "David, there *is* beauty in strength! There are also *a lot* of women out there like me—*no*, there are a lot of women *SO much better than me* because they work harder, make more sacrifices, go through *harder* things, all for the love for their family, friends; *some of them for perfect strangers!*"

David states with certainty, "I'll admit there are very few in our world, my mother and Aunt Maggie being two of them, who are an exception to the severely privileged women. Those women are empty because they've never *had* to be tough, life was made *way too easy for them*, usually by their parents. There's nothing wrong with nannies, they are a great *asset* if they're—."

"An extension of parents actually doing the parenting." She adds following along.

"Yes! Nannies supporting family rules and helping parents come and go for work and 'shuffling kids' to school, appointments, and various activities, as needed *to help*." David says.

Bri tells him. *"However,* after school or work, parents should be involved in family life!"

"Right!" Lawrence chimes in. "Many nannies are left to raise the kids; unfortunately, parents interfere and undermine the nannies who are trying to give structure and raise them with morals and values. That lack of structure, of not knowing what's really important, leaves a void in those kids that they may never fill, or they'll *try* to fill it in every wrong way possible."

"Or focus on the wrong things, like a pedigree, or marrying an heir." Bri adds and they nod.

David says to her, "You bring *real* to our lives in so many ways!"

She snorts a laugh. "A *real* 'firecracker,' you mean!" Lawrence and Jack laugh.

David grins. "It's *'feisty firecracker!'*" He winks, then gets a little more serious taking her hands and kissing them. "I *hate* screwing up with you, Love! I shouldn't have left you! *Twice!*" He says with anger towards himself in his voice. "The second time made it so much worse!"

"I don't want to count that as two times, because you could've just taken the elevator without me, but waited in the lobby." She tells him. "You should be able to catch yourself, or choose not to be in the elevator with me to have a couple minutes of space!"

"No, Love, I should never have left you standing there!" He cups her face as he says, "No matter how mad or angry you think I am or will be, I *love* you and I *never* want you to *ever* feel all alone even for a split second." The tears fill her eyes as she feels that loneliness again. "Oh, Love..." he says, sliding into the overstuffed chair with her and hugging her close; she brings her legs up and across his lap. He tells her, "I just want to love you, too!" He rests their foreheads together. "*Please* forgive me. I promise I'll make it up to you!"

"David, what did you text me in response to exactly that?" She asks.

"Something along the lines that we love each other," he runs his fingers up her cheek, "so it's only a matter of 'when.'" He answers.

"*Sssooo*, you've had your answer." She grins and adds, "*Mister* Worthington, I'll *always* forgive you because I trust you'll never do anything that's *un*forgivable." She taps a tender kiss to his lips. "I love you and could never hold anything over you for the rest of your life; that's an *awful* way for *both of us* to live!" She looks at Lawrence and Jack, "I think we can agree that we'll all screw up with each other over the years," they agree, "but I think we can also agree it'll never be malicious or mean-spirited." The three shake their heads quickly that it would never be that way. "David, you said you didn't realize you left me stranded until *after* you got to The Manor and heard the helicopter." She says.

"Right." David answers.

Jack kicking himself a little, says, "Proving you didn't leave her stranded *on purpose*! I'm sorry I was so hard on you, Brother."

David smiles compassionately at Jack. "Nah, you were right! It wasn't harsh enough!" He looks at Bri still talking to Jack. "I deserved everything I got!"

She hugs David and whispers so only he hears, "*How can I not forgive the man who holds my heart?*"

He takes a deep breath and exhales. "Yes, there are many fantastic, wonderful, beautiful women out there, but there's only one who could love *all three of us* and fill us with that love, *all at the same time.*"

She smiles. "It's easy!" The three men scoff and she giggles. She turns her head and glances at Lawrence and Jack, then her eyes see his new phone on the ottoman and she is embarrassed. "*Oh, David...*"

He looks to where she is looking and grins, "It was worth it!"

She is confused. "How can you say that?!"

"Because even though it sounded like you wanted to push me away, you helped me see how *deeply hurt* you were." He explains. "Love, I agree that our world isn't quite right when we're 'misaligned' and fighting."

She shakes her head agreeing, "*No, it's not!*" She looks at Jack and Lawrence, "It's not with any of you!"

"I asked Gabriel if he would run into town and buy a new one for me. It's actually the newest model, which is a few upgrades from my last. I'd say it turned out better!" He winks with his smile.

 "Not sure about 'better.'" She remembers the flowers and looks at the huge bouquet of red roses in a vase, with a card displaying, '*I'm so sorry.*' "They're beautiful, David..." she trails off.

"I was expecting a *slightly different* response than that, Love." David softly laughs.

She exhales, "I just wish I wasn't a 'rose murderer!'" The guys crack up laughing, which she lightly laughs as she says, "*I'm serious!* The only way they last are when the fabulous staff take care of them! I'm *awful* at keeping even one rose alive for more than a couple days, then there's *all* these...what? Eighteen?" She exhales, "I'm not only a 'serial rose killer,' but a 'mass rose murderer,' too!" The guys laugh some more.

David has an idea. "Then I'll enlist Jack's and Herst's help to make sure you have a fresh batch every single day and you'll never know."

"Ah, so all three of you would agree *to lie to me* every single day?" Bri teases.

"Would it be a lie if the flowers were disposed of *before* they died?" David teases back.

"Perhaps not..." Bri concedes. "But that seems like a bigger shame, I suppose...I guess I'll have to keep appreciating them when they come, for however long they last." She sits a little more comfortably with David in her chair with her. "Let's talk about the other night." Jack and Lawrence get comfortable, as well. "*Wait.* Sorry. Backup. I do need to say something about the DC trip." Bri looks at David. "I promise I'll make sure all three of you know when—."

"Just a second, Love." David gives her a faint appreciative smile. "What I didn't consider, is that Jack *did* know you were in DC, *and* you were with Herst. *Shamefully* I didn't think about that."

"Well, going forward, it shouldn't matter." Bri starts to explain.

"Bri, if you have to worry about telling *all of us* everywhere you go, you can't live in the moment with whoever you're with." He holds her cheek. "That's not fair to you *or* the one you're with. Gabriel's the keeper of your schedule and he knows of all your trips and that should've been good, too. But I panicked after hearing you got lost when you were by yourself in The Palace." He looks to Jack and Lawrence. "What do you think?"

"Sounds good." Jack says.

Lawrence concurs, "I think so."

"I appreciate that, *I do*! But honestly, what's the harm of a quick 'going to DC' text to those of you who aren't traveling with me?" She asks. "I doubt either one of you will care if I pause time for a minute to say to the other two

'I'm headed out of town at the last minute,' or ask one of you, even Gabriel, to pass along the information."

"True." David agrees.

"David, I *promise* I'll always take McMasters! As Duchess and then..." she looks at Lawrence, "*elevating...*" she playfully smiles, "McMasters will tighten everything up! In fact, he's already started with this Mitchell! Besides, if I *ever* left town without him or Mitchell, I honestly think that man would *fire me!*" They all burst into laughter!

David holds her face tenderly. "As you would say, 'Fair enough.' A quick text is good, even in mid-flight, but we'll—*I'll* trust you're not completely by yourself anywhere."

"Thank you, My Love." She smiles, then looks to Lawrence. "Now, your assistant said that, um...*day*, prior to The Dungeons tour, *she* would be taking over Gabriel's job as my assistant and there's *no way*—."

"I fired her as my assistant at the same time I essentially fired my mother." He tells her. "Seth and Abby were more than happy to work on a replacement while I was gone and enlisted Gabriel's help."

Bri explains, "I also bring it up to be clear: I'm loyal to those who are loyal to me and Gabriel has *more* than earned my loyalty! Same goes for McMasters, Mateo in DC, and *especially Amy!*"

"Point taken, Darling." Lawrence admits.

"Enough about that. Clean slate?" She looks to David and Lawrence, who agree. "Now, the subject of why I went to DC....Amy needed help with a horrible senator woman!" She explains in more detail what happened at the hotel with her.

"Wow..." David says.

"I also explained why bumping the wedding I was attending would be bad press, bad for business, and bad for one board member wanting to sell his shares to retire. I reminded the hotel manager that he did know Amy and he worked with us all these years. I also mentioned Amy was marrying a Worthington who's brother is The Duke of Newhaven and our in-laws, the former Duke and Duchess of Newhaven, have been part of the noble and royal courts for decades with some of those people attending this wedding...*aaand* these were the same Worthington's who own The Worthington Corporation."

Jack teases her, "Wow, Bri...name dropping isn't usually your style."

"No. It's not. But this wasn't for me, was it?" Bri raises her eyebrow with a determined look and a faint smile.

"Good point!" Jack chuckles.

"Oh! In the middle of that, *before the 'name dropping,'* this senator scrambles and reminds the Hotel Manager of her offer to pay double. That's also why I 'name dropped.' I wanted him to see reason, like bad press leading to loss of revenue, rather than her dollar signs. I could see him having a hard time letting all that money go, so when I said my date was The King of The United Kingdom of Provinces, he finally tells the senator they can't accommodate her daughter's wedding that same day. She was *not* happy and mentioned the invitations were going out that day. I said the invitations for this wedding went out over *two months ago*! That's what good and proper hostesses do! They don't expect everyone to scramble and cater to them at the last minute, while ruining someone else's wedding in the process! She was mad and embarrassed, glaring at me before she stormed out of the hotel. Since Jack and I talked about this before I left, I paid for the rest of the wedding to ensure it was locked in..."

"If they signed a contract, which good business practice says they did," David explains, "any of the extra money would've been given to James and Amy anyway to prevent a lawsuit, let alone that bad press. Not to mention that by the end of it, they probably would've lost *more* than double...*a lot more* than they would've made on *both* weddings; *I would've made sure of that*!" There's a bit of anger in his voice with that.

Bri gives an 'eek.' "I should've come to you or brought you with..." she says to David.

"Why? Because I'm in the hotel business?" He teases. "Bri, as you said, you know the staff because you've worked with them. I would've told you to lean on that and you did! You had Herst in the wings, which is a great 'plan B' to have!"

She adoringly looks at Lawrence. "My 'ace in the hole.'"

"Forever." He smiles back.

"Well, I was so happy and relieved to text Amy that everything was still as she planned it to be. Oh, as far as her parents are concerned, they already paid for the whole wedding. I'm telling you all this just in case you're in some bazaar conversation about it." The men nod.

Bri's stomach growls really loud and the men smile. Lawrence suggests, "Let's get to The Manor so *the five of us* can eat!"

They all stand up and make their way to The Manor.

CHAPTER 41

Imperfectly Perfect & Royally Defenseless

After Lawrence, David, Jack, and Bri eat dinner, they walk upstairs to David and Bri's quarters. Bri sits in her comfy chair and Jack leans against the back of the couch where David and Lawrence are sitting.

Jack asks, "David, what did you mean when you said it was good Bri 'took a stand'?" Lawrence is curious, too.

"Jessica came to visit Bri one morning. She said there would come a time for Bri to make a stand with Herst, which was also the same time Bri was encouraged to start in The Dungeons. What happened when you toured The Dungeons, Love?" David asks her.

Lawrence sits on the ottoman. He leans forward and takes Bri's hands in his. "*Please* tell me what I wouldn't let you tell me that day."

She takes a deep breath. "I was going to tell you it wasn't even fit for rats to live there! In fact, I never saw one! However, the very first thing I noticed when the door was opened was the revolting stench. It was so overwhelming I had to throw up before I could continue. It was cold, wet, filthy, unsanitary, with too many forgotten people in the cells. The only empty one was..."

"Was?" Lawrence asks, then he realizes, "The Torture Chambers."

She nods and continues, "I saw someone in a vision being hoisted up by their arms and their shirt torn open...I would later realize it was a premonition about me." The guys are startled. She cups Lawrence's cheek, "I would even flash back to one of you when you were younger, but only visual that time." He closes his eyes wishing she hadn't. "There were a lot of lost spirits down there. I became uneasy and I just had to get out of there. At one point, I asked a royal guard if The King had ever been down there and they said 'no.'"

"That would be correct. I'm ashamed to say that it never made my list of things to do. It was always my mother who took care of it and preferred it that way..." There is reluctance in Lawrence's voice, "I stayed away and out of her business. I was trying to keep Abby and Seth safe, so I had to pick my battles." Bri nods in understanding.

413

"I acted like I didn't care, but there was a white van that pulled up to the back door. It looked like they were getting ready to transport some prisoners." Bri tells them.

"Transport? *Where?!*" Lawrence wonders.

"I assume to wherever your mother does her auctions. The information in the envelope we've all read said that your mother is trafficking all kinds of things, *humans* being part of that!" She states.

Lawrence quietly whispers, "*Daaamn...!*"

Bri closes her eyes as images of her abduction and assault come into her mind's eye; she can still feel The Queen Mother's fingers going into a wound on her back. David sees this first and asks, "Tell us everything that happened that night."

"If I do, you need to know she threatened to make me regret it if I told anyone. This puts you three in more danger than me because she can use you to get to me. *And she will go after those I love* since I've already challenged her! She has to assume *I've defiantly already told you.*"

"Bri," Lawrence says, "we're all in danger as long as that woman walks this earth." David and Jack agree, even Bri.

Jack encourages her, "Tell us, Amore Mia."

Bri begins, "In the middle of the night..." and she proceeds to tell them.

Lawrence asks, "Was the pillowcase over your head the whole time?! Did you recognize or see anyone?!" He's wanting names.

"That's just it! They must rely on people being too scared to talk because those around me talked normally, even using their names! But the only woman was your mother and she's the one who whipped the hood off my head."

"I would've thought she'd keep her hands clean *because it was you...*" He gets up and paces.

"Oh, Ace, she was directly involved *because it was me!*" Bri tells him.

Lawrence stops. "Bri..." he walks over to her and squats down, "you *need* to come back with me," he sees the fear in her eyes, "but with Jack and David, so you won't be alone at night." She exhales in relief. "Only I should go back first and—."

"Lawrence," Bri looks at him in all seriousness, "do you trust those *closest* to you, especially in The King's Guard?!"

He cups her cheek, "McMasters asked me the same question that morning."

"*And you said?*" She urges him.

"I was raw with my emotions after what just happened to you, I said I trusted none of them! I've taken his lead with who to trust! He and Mitchell are working to sift through the entire Royal Guard and Palace staff; flushing out those who are not only untrustworthy, but those who were directly and indirectly involved with your assault."

David warily asks, "Bri, who *did* you see besides The Queen Mother?"

"At first, there was a gap at the bottom of the pillowcase and I could see a man's hands at my waist at various times, until your mother whipped off the pillowcase." She quickly wipes the tear from her cheek. She looks at Lawrence and raises her eyebrow asking, "Did you know your mother uses 'My Pet' to refer to someone?"

"*No.*" Lawrence turns up his nose at the thought and studies her. "I'm not sure I want t—." He's horrified as it comes to him! "Tristan?!" Bri nods. "That's what my uncle would call her!"

"The only others I recognized were Gavan and Mr. Gillery, The Keeper of The Dungeons. I felt the name of one of them is Lucas." She says, watching Lawrence about to stand up but she stops him. "Talk to me, Lawrence."

He hesitates but he reluctantly says, "I was wondering if he was involved."

"Do you know who I mean? I don't have a last name and 'Lucas' is somewhat of a common name." She says.

He agrees. "The 'Lucas' I'm referring to is The Grand Marshall of The Royal Guard. If you see the 'Lucas' you're referring to let me know and then we'll know for sure."

She nods. "What scares me the most is that a lot of these men could be anywhere, *be anyone...*"

"Instead of being protected by loyal and trustworthy guards, *I'm surrounded by traitors!*" He exhales loudly.

She takes Lawrence's hand and holds it close. "I need to know your safe. If that means—."

"Bri, *I need you safe!*" Lawrence says.

"Here me out." She tells him and looks at David and Jack, "All of you!" They all nod. She looks back to Lawrence. "Mitchell could stay with me and McMasters can go back with you, or vice versa! The two of you can work together to do what you need to do to take back control of The Palace." She squeezes his hands and says, "You can even have both guys and I'll never leave The Manor until one or both of them return!" She gets him to smile. "Please. *For me?*"

He rests his forehead to hers. "I'd do anything you ask of me."

"I promise, I'll respect that and this is one of those times I'm actually pleading with you." She looks at him.

"Alright." He hugs her. "I'll see what McMasters and Mitchell recommend?"

"I'll go with you." David says as he stands and leaves with Lawrence to go talk to McMasters and Mitchell.

Jack stares at Bri and she lovingly smiles at him. "I can't thank you enough for being by my side since you showed up in the helicopter yesterday morning!" She wipes a tear.

He tells her, "*You* amaze me!" She goes to roll her eyes, but he quickly tells her, "*Don't* roll your eyes! You've been so bloody strong through all this!"

"I cried like a baby, in your arms—your *very fantastic* arms—." She playfully smiles a bit watching him sit down in front of her.

He lightly chuckles, cupping her face. "You went through something so painful, without *anything* for the pain!"

"*Jack!*" She whispers as a lump fills her throat. "*I h-had you!*" She struggles to say. "I made it through," her lower jaw shakes, "because I was in *your* arms..." she holds his face, "a man I love *tremendously!*"

"*And I love you tremendously*, Amore Mia! I'll *always* be here for you!" Jack says with conviction.

"You can't promise always...using words like always, never, ever, and such, in various statements can imply perfection that no one can achieve." She kisses him.

"How about as long as I li—."

"No! Stop. I *never* want to think about the other part of that!" She says. "I'd command all of you to live forever if I could!"

Jack looks at her with love. "We don't want to live without you either!"

She laughs a little. "Well, lucky for you I couldn't command you to live forever anyway!"

"Why's that?" He's curious.

"Simply stated: I'm not God."

"True." He asks, "And not simply stated?"

She lightly laughs. "What was said to me is I have power over *spirits*, so I can only conclude that I don't have any kind of power over physical bodies, like raising the dead. Besides, spirits are already eternal, immortal, and already living forever!" She winks and he softly chuckles. She takes a deep breath in, hugging him close, and slowly exhales. "It's been a hard couple of days, Jack..."

"But there's some good news to hang onto..." he smiles with so much love.

She puts their hands on her lower abdomen with a loving smile, "*The best news!*" She looks down at their hands.

"I've been thinking," he says and she lifts her head to look at him again, "and *I think* I have an idea."

She snorts a little laugh. "What's that?"

"Since I have more flexibility in my schedule, clients, and days than David or Herst, I feel I could travel with you more. The flight to The Palace is not quite an hour and I *easily* spend a couple of hours at my desk every day. You typically travel on the fourth day from Newhaven to The Palace, then four days after that, you would fly back to Newhaven. Then there's a week before you would travel again. I can travel with you, whenever you're traveling alone."

"I think that's a wonderful idea, Jack!"

"You do?!" He's pleasantly surprised there wasn't any push back from her.

"Yes! It's *brilliant*!" She teases with his accent. "I love the thought of having you travel with me when I would otherwise be traveling by myself; I feel safer already!"

"Good!" He kisses her.

Bri looks at Jack with love. "I've only seen *our daughter* on our wedding day."

Jack smiles adoringly, "I was hoping..."

Her heart squeezes. "Oh Jack, she looks so much like you! That girl will have her daddy and two uncles wrapped around her finger so tight it'll turn blue! The first time since the wedding both boys came to visit and she wasn't there. The boys said—." Bri's throat fills with a lump again and she looks down to swallow hard.

"Let me guess. If she's our daughter, she has to be pretty amazing!" He grins and Bri nods as she looks back up.

"The boys said she's the most special one of them all! They said she's the sweetest, kindest, and most like..." her smiles freezes as she remembers what they said next.

"If they said, 'the most like you,' she already has me wrapped around her finger!" He beams. Bri wipes her eyes. Jack hugs Bri. "A baby with you, is great news, and a girl is bloody *fantastic*!"

She giggles. "I have a feeling you'd say that even if we were having a boy!"

"Of course, but it's still true! I'd be thrilled if we had a boy, I'm thrilled we're having a girl! Emmie and Natty are brilliant and gorgeous, just like their mother! Another daughter would be in *great* company with them!"

CHAPTER 42

Imperfectly Perfect Royal Conundrum

Jack and Bri walk downstairs to where everyone has gathered in The Sitting Room. They pass a guard who makes her uneasy, but he's in uniform making it difficult for her to place if he's from that night...then again, she's been asking that question a lot of anyone she doesn't personally know; she shakes it off.

Carlotta hurries over and carefully hugs Bri as soon as she comes into the room. Carlotta steps back and asks, "How are you holding up, Sweetie?!"

"I'm fine now!" Bri smiles.

Carlotta has a skeptical look on her face. "Bri, we knew it had to be severe for Jack to be *that* furious with David last night and then we saw the picture!"

"Oh, it *was* bad." Bri states. "We discovered that one of my 'gifts' allows me to heal myself with the help of David, Lawrence, and Jack!" Bri turns her back to them, "I don't have a mark on my back now." She points. Carlotta looks and gasps.

Peter respectfully looks and whispers, *"Well, I'll be..."*

"It's a miracle!" Carlotta says and really hugs Bri.

Lawrence comes over to Bri and gestures to McMasters and Mitchell. "McMasters will come with me and Mitchell will stay here, but Mitchell will assist McMasters from here with what he can." Bri is introduced to Mitchell.

"Can we rethink this?!" Bri asks. "Can both McMasters and Mitchell go with you? *I'm really nervous for you!* For *anyone* who's connected with me, but this feels like you're going right into 'the snake pit' in 'the lion's den!'"

Lawrence replies, "Bri, *your* security is important, *now more than ever!*"

"I'll stay here and never leave until McMasters or Mitchell return!" She says. "Ooo, better yet, I could stay at The Inn! Easier to keep unwanted visitors away!"

McMasters jumps in, "That's not a bad idea and it's something to keep in mind if something like that becomes necessary! For now, I like having Mitchell here in my absence for you, but to also keep an eye on everything and on *everyone's* safety."

"Okay, you do have a point there." She admits.

"You already know The Queen Mother as an enemy is a very serious threat!" McMasters states. "Bri, you know as well as I do that the best way to seek revenge on someone is to save them for last as they hurt those closest to you. I need you to give Mitchell the same consideration you give me to keep you safe." Bri nods.

Lawrence slips in, "In a game of chess, you protect the queen."

"Or the game is over." She stares off at nothing important, thinking of The Queen Mother's psychological behavior and the actions The Queen Mother could take against her.

She sees the guard that made her feel uneasy and it hits her: he *was* there that night! *This is Lucas!* The guard passes her and no one realizes anything's amiss until they see Bri do a side kick, striking her foot into his abdomen. He bends in half, holding his arms across his stomach, and falls to his knees; everyone is staring at them. Lawrence is the first one to them and stands between them reaching down to pick up Lucas, bringing him to his feet with Mitchell's help.

Mitchell says to Bri, looking at the guard, "Can we assume Lucas was there during your assault?"

"Yes." She answers. She looks at Lawrence and was going to ask if this was the same Lucas, but the answer is written in fury all over his face.

McMasters comes over and grabs Lucas in Lawrence's place saying, "We'll take care of him!"

Lawrence remembers a dagger on a shelf and no one notices that he went to get it because Lucas is angrily fighting against being taken away. Mitchell twists his arm a little harder to force him to walk.

"Halt!" The King tells them. Lucas has a smug smile on his face thinking Lawrence is going to help him. Mitchell and McMasters stop, with The King stepping around to get in front of Lucas, stabbing him in the side at an upward angle to puncture his lung. The King angrily says through gritted teeth, "*I trusted you*! And you have the audacity to think I'm going to be loyal to you when *you* betrayed *me*?!" He yanks the dagger back out. "You're getting off easy compared to what you helped facilitate against The Duchess!" Everyone's mouth had dropped a bit. No one saw this coming, not even Tristan who had just come in to see what was going on. Lawrence purposely hands the bloody dagger to Tristan knowing he'd run to The Queen Mother. Lawrence tells him, "Clean this up and make sure it's put back on the shelf!" Lawrence points to the shelf. Tristan takes it, covering his anger that his friend is dead; The Queen Mother won't be happy about this either! Lawrence goes to Bri and holds her upper arms asking, "Are you alright, Darling?" She nods and steps closer to hug him; he hugs her firmly.

Bri hears her son with Lawrence before she sees him, "You need to go back with Father, but both of you should go *after* the honeymoon." Bri takes a deep breath as her eyes find him. "Right now, everyone is on heightened alert, especially The Queen Mother! She expects Father to retaliate and she plans on him not having a good plan. Although," he thinks about Lucas, "she wasn't expecting this blow to her small, trusted inner circle."

Lawrence hears Bri quietly ask, "Is she still at The Palace?"

McMasters overhears and answers, "She fled not too long after you were flown out that morning with Jack."

Her son with Lawrence reiterates, "Mum, you *need* to go back to The Palace with him to show a united front, but you *both* shouldn't go just yet——."

"What is it?" Lawrence unknowingly interrupts his son when he sees Bri trying to hide her reaction to something being said that no one else hears.

Lawrence's son also says, "After the ball, McMasters, with assistance from Mitchell, will have sifted through all the guards and the staff arresting those responsible or connected to your assault, except the few that are secretly known."

She whispers so only Lawrence can hear. "Our son is telling me I need to return with you as a united front, but *we* shouldn't return until *after* our honeymoon."

"Mum, will you let Father see me?" Their son asks. "He needs to hear this."

Bri smiles at Lawrence and whispers. "He wants *you* to see him, too." Lawrence nods and Bri circles only one finger this time. Lawrence is able to control his emotions better when he sees his son again.

"Mum, I won't lie to you, there will be difficult moments and *very* horrible times ahead. You taught us, well, *will* teach us, *and Father...*" he looks at Lawrence.

The feeling of Luke 12:48 comes over her and she says, "Whomsoever much is given, of him shall be much required..." Everyone hears her. She says, "I know choosing to come back came with a price, but I didn't know how much of a price I would have to pay by the time all this, or my mortal life, is over."

Their son lightly touches her face, "For us, you'll say it a little differently, but it's more significant when you factor in our lives. You say: 'When one has a privileged life," he looks at his father, but Bri repeats *and* finishes.

"When one has a much-privileged life; one has a much-privileged *responsibility to others!*" Bri finishes and he smiles. Peter and Carlotta overhear this and it reminds Peter of a poem.

"Mum, you need to find time to meditate, to find the place within you where your powers reside. Right now, you have power over spirits, but they must *decide* to do something for themselves. Then, once they've committed to their choice, usually by acting upon it, or going to act upon it, you can intervene. But as your powers grow, you can figure out a way to stop some of them *before* there's even a choice for them to make, as you've already navigated. You will be given visions to act upon, to change the course of events, and hopefully change the outcome."

"Where does her power reside?" Lawrence asks. "Love?"

Bri actually answers. "Well, love controls them but my powers are connected to my faith and emotions. I understand our 'free will' is a gift of love from God, our Heavenly Father. Because He loves us, He gives us the freedom to make our own choices; right or wrong, good or bad. Which means I need to have faith in my abilities He has given me, because He has also given me the power that comes with them. I'm also empathic and getting more so, which means my emotions are affected by other people's emotions."

"What you need to know, Mum, is McMasters, with Mitchell's help, is restructuring The Royal Guard so *you'll* have the staff's loyalty."

"Wait. Loyalty *to me*?" Bri clarifies.

"After taking a stand with Father and he siding with you, there are many gathering behind Queen Genevieve's mission for you to become queen!" He grins. Lawrence and Bri chuckle. Their son continues, "Now, when it comes to The Royal Guard, some may not seem loyal because they don't trust father, but they trust The Queen Mother even less! McMasters and Mitchell will help them come around to support him *because of you*!" He holds his mother's hand. "You need to tell him, Mum." Bri's eyebrows scrunch together.

"Tell me what?" Lawrence asks. Bri shrugs and shakes her head.

"*Everything* about that night including what was said!" Her son says.

"That I'm not to be 'her heir's' mother, so either after I give birth she'll have me killed, or she'll use a surrogate and I'm already dead." She sees Lawrence clench his jaw. She says, "She thinks she will be able to allow any ruler to have access to me in any way *she decides*." She looks at her son, "Do I tell him about my blood on The Queen Mother's fingers?"

"*Yes*!" Lawrence strongly whispers.

She looks at him with sad eyes whispering, "*Lawrence, I think you'll wish you didn't know. It's disgusting.*"

"*Nothing* will surprise me at this point." He replies.

She softly says with her nose turned up, "She pressed her fingers into a wound on my back to get blood on her fingers, which she would lick off." Lawrence is unphased. "She called Tristan over and...*shared*. Then told him she would 'take care of him later' which I didn't let my thoughts 'go there' with what that could mean!"

Still unphased, Lawrence pulls her into a hug. "I guess now I see why he's so loyal to her and the worst traitor to me."

Their son tells them, "I need to go." He touches his mother's cheek. "I can't wait to be born into this family!" He looks at Lawrence. "Relax! You'll be a *great* father *and* uncle!" He hugs his mother and Bri is overcome with love and emotions. "Goodbye for now!" He steps back and fades away.

He whispers, "*I wish we knew his name?*"

"*All I can figure is that the names are meaningful when they're decided. If we know beforehand, it* kiiinda *takes away from their meaningfulness.*"

"*That makes sense.*" He whispers in understanding.

Bri sees David smiling next to his parents and she smiles back at him saying, "Oh, Love, we need to tell them or you'll burst."

"Tell us what?" Carlotta clasps her hands together hoping it was baby news.

David walks over to her and wraps an arm around her waist and looks at his parents, "We're going to have a baby!"

Carlotta and Peter are so excited! They jump up and go over to them. Carlotta exclaims, "This is *absolutely* wonderful!" They all hug.

Peter holds Bri's hands. "Have you ever read any William Ross Wallace poetry?"

"Doesn't sound familiar." She says as she thinks about the name and the little poetry she knows. "I may have heard it, but I just haven't stored the name with the poem." She points to her head.

He lightly chuckles. "I'm sure you've heard the phrase, '*The hand that rocks the cradle is the hand that rules the world.*"

"*I have!*" Bri answers with a smile of recognition.

"When you spoke of having 'a privileged life means having a great privileged responsibility to others,' that poem, well the title and meaning, came to mind." Peter explains. "Bri, your greatest legacy will be your children! Emmie and Natty are absolutely delightful and incredibly brilliant; they're truly a joy to be around! Seeing three of our now five sons adore you," he's including Lawrence and Seth, "and how they get overcome with emotions in their love for you...well, a gift we all have in this family is *you*! We're so proud of you, for all you've accomplished in such a short amount of time, and for what you're trying to accomplish. It'll be your children who'll carry on your *wonderful* legacy!" He kisses her cheek.

He hugs him. "Thank you."

David asks, "McMasters, since they're to stay here, how long would you suggest before going back to The Palace?"

Bri answers, "Lawrence's son was saying after the honeymoon, *and* for me to go back with him." Everyone was talking at the same time, but all were saying roughly the same thing: they didn't think it was a good idea. "Well, he thought it would show a united front." They reluctantly agreed.

"I'll have the guards go on a rotation with the others I have coming up from London." McMasters steps out and Bri is sick to her stomach at the thought of Tristan or Gavan staying, but they can't move on yet.

Jack steps over to Bri and tells everyone, "Bri and I talked, and since my schedule is the most flexible, I can travel at various times with Bri when David or Herst can't, so she'll never travel without one of us."

"*That's brilliant!*" David says and Lawrence agrees.

McMasters comes in as Peter and Carlotta leave to go to The Inn and welcome some guests. He walks over and says to Lawrence, "I have Mitchell making some calls to get more guards up here."

Gavan comes up to them. "Here's a list."

 Bri sees the same green snake tattoo Tristan has, only now she sees it's a snake wrapped around a black flame of sorts, or maybe barbed wire. Lawrence takes the list and thanks him. Gavan looks at Bri and he thinks she is too scared to look at him and keeping her mouth shut. Tristan thinks the same thing, or they both would've ended up like Lucas, *or worse*.

"Your Grace." Gavan bows, then turns and leaves smirking to himself and Tristan, not realizing Lawrence was watching the whole thing. Tristan follows Gavan out.

"Bri?" Lawrence says to her.

Her eyes flick to him first, then she turns her head. She wonders, "Is his green snake tattoo on the inside of his wrist like Tristan's tattoo?"

"I'm not sure. Why?" He asks.

"I suspect it's a mark The Queen Mother uses for something." She takes the list of names Gavan gave Lawrence and they go over to McMasters. "This list should be retitled as, *'Those Most Loyal to The Queen Mother.'*" Bri looks to Mitchell, "Would you make sure no one is listening to this conversation?" He nods. "Thank you." She turns back to McMasters and Lawrence, with David and Jack listening. "I've seen the green snake tattoo, coiled around something black on Tristan's wrist and I also saw one on Gavan's wrist. I'm thinking this green snake tattoo is to show some sort of exclusive membership or something with The Queen Mother."

"How deep does this go? How many guards and staff would have this tattoo?" David asks.

"It's hard to say until our investigation is done and we have everyone involved, but you'd think if it were just anyone loyal to her, we would've noticed the tattoo before now?" Lawrence looks at Bri with a sadness; he has to ask, "Did any of them force themselves on you?"

She shakes her head. "Your mother was clear that once the paperwork is signed and she has control over me, my body, *and my eggs*...that she'll let other royal families have access to me in any way *she* wants them to have, along with having a baby with Tristan and have an heir of some sorts with him." Bri tells him, visibly shaking at that thought. "She wasn't bothered that their hands were on me, but I told them that none of them could touch me with sexual intent and thankfully it seemed to have worked."

"I'll kill him!" Lawrence whispers through gritted teeth.

Bri tells him, "No. You won't!"

"Like Hell——." Lawrence goes to argue.

"*Lawrence Alexander Heathherst!*" She whispers sternly. "*I need you to think, NOT react! This gives US the advantage because he doesn't know YOU know!*"

He gives her a smile as he pulls her into a hug. He holds her firm, taking a deep breath and he exhales, "What do you suggest?"

"Depends on how good of a 'poker face' you have..." she pulls back. "I keep thinking of the saying, 'keep your friends close, but your enemies closer.' If you can keep up the same interactions you've always had so Tristan, nor

Gavan, will catch on I've told you," she looks to David, Jack, and McMasters, "or any of you *for everyone's safety*," she looks back to Lawrence, "until the time comes to reveal our hand." She smirks. "Think of it as justice on *our* terms."

Lawrence's jaw was clenching but it softens as he soaks in what she's saying. He quietly says, "I'm glad you're here to be my strength."

"We give each other strength..." She smiles and hugs him again.

He takes a small step back. "What's the plan?"

"Check his list." She replies. "If these have checked out already, then the screening process doesn't work. With Gavan, I'd say the process at the very least needs to be reviewed!"

"Well, he and Tristan weren't interviewed," McMasters tells them, looking at a list on his phone. Lawrence's codes passed them off."

He looks at Lawrence who is shaking his head. "I won't trust anyone you haven't cleared!"

"Mitchell and I will go over our list again, even comparing it to this one, and make sure if we didn't interview any of them personally, *we will*!" Lawrence agrees.

Bri looks at Lawrence with compassion and squeezes his hand. "Lawrence don't beat yourself up. Your mother is evil and people learn to be useful and do her bidding; or get out of the way and *hope* she'll leave them alone!"

He can relate. "Like I've been doing letting her control me, so I could protect Seth and Abby."

"That's different—." Bri starts to defend him.

"*It's really not*. Like you said, it's all about survival with that woman!" He says. She hears in her mind, '*The Queen Mother must die*.'

McMasters steps in. "We can even look to assign Tristan and Gavan to something different. We could use their interviews as a discussion of where they want to be, then go from there."

"They can't be reassigned if Mother wants them in their current posts." Lawrence tells them. "But you can talk with them and see; make it seem like a positive change." McMasters nods in understanding.

Jack says, "It's getting late. Lawrence and I will go to The Cottage for the night and Bri," he looks at her with a loving smile, "you may not have told David you were pregnant like you would've wanted to, but you two should have some time together, *just the two of you*, and enjoy the wonderful news."

Bri smiles at Jack. "I love you, Amore Mio!"

He channels her saying, "I've sort of picked up on that." She giggles little. "You both need to reconnect," he cups her cheek, "*for all our sakes.*"

"Jack, I'd be unsettled if we weren't on solid terms either." She states.

"To a large degree, yes, even with Herst; but not entirely. Our relationships are stemmed off of your relationship with David. You both have had an incredibly strong magnetic pull towards each other since the beginning. You and I are bonded and that bond is *incredible*! I feel if, God forbid, anything happened to David, we'd be solid; but I hope to *never* test that theory."

"*Right!*" She wholeheartedly agrees. Then things click more in her mind to what he fully means. "*That's why I froze when he left!* That's why, for a brief moment, the world was empty."

"*Precisely.*" Jack kisses her fiercely before 'I love you' and 'goodnight' are said to each other.

She pulls Lawrence aside. "I love you, Ace!"

"I love you, My Queen!" He smiles adoringly at her. He pulls her in for a sweet kiss and he hugs her firmly.

David and Bri walk Jack and Lawrence to the back door right there and wave as they leave. When Jack and Lawrence get to The Cottage House that evening, they'll play some billiards before turning in for the night. David takes Bri's hand, lacing his fingers with hers and they walk up to their quarters together.

David holds the door open and Bri steps into the small entryway in the corner of their living room. She sees the table against the wall, under a mirror, and sees it's completely bare. She looks around and sees a few other things are missing. She couldn't tell anyone what was specifically missing, it was a few fancy figurines and knickknacks you'd expect to see around an old manor house, but things were definitely missing.

"Is it just me or does this seem...*bare*?" She points at the empty table.

"I was upset with myself when I realized I left you alone and angry for what happened to you! I wanted to be with you but if I went to The Cottage House, I was afraid it'd cause you more grief..." He cups her cheek. "I watched you walk from the helicopter and down the path until I couldn't see you anymore. When I came up here, well..." he trails off, almost ashamed, "I took it out on the decor." Bri wraps her arms around his neck and rests their foreheads together. "I need you to promise me something, Macushla."

With love in her eyes for him, she asks, "What's that?"

"No matter what happens, you *never* keep me in the dark again! I know I didn't give you a chance, but before that, when Jack found out he would've had the reflex to call me." Bri looks down at his chest when her memory flashes to Jack wanting to do just that. He takes a finger to her chin and lifts up for her to look at him again, her eyes are teary. "No tears, Love. All I'm saying is let him call me."

She nods and wipes the tears. "I'm s——." He places his fingertips on her lips.

"Don't apologize either. This is all on me. While I hope to gain wisdom from my, we'll say 'mental state,'" she snickers a little, "but if I didn't gain enough, I need to know I will be informed, or I won't let you out of my sight. The Queen Mother already hurt you with the help of *who knows how many*?! And I'm trusting Herst, McMasters, and Mitchell, to deal with them and make it safer for you!"

Bri has a small, compassionate smile on her face. "The misunderstanding should've been put aside on *both* our parts." He nods. "David, my only defense is that I didn't want that part to be forgotten about and left to gnaw at your feelings towards me."

He holds her face. "I can understand that, but this specific topic would've been inadvertently dealt with at the same time."

Her jaw shakes and she closes her eyes. "You're right..." she looks at him, "I was just wanting to fix this, because it seemed so simple to do. I needed *something* to go right."

"Ah, Love, like I said, this is on me! This should've been a simple fix even before you came to my office. I could've read any number of articles and realized you weren't alone." He hugs her close. "Promise me, or *we* won't move past this so easily." She smiles because she had used the same words when he hired extra security for Emmie and Natty without telling her.

"I promise." She replies and taps a little kiss to his lips.

They stay hugging for a few minutes. She takes a deep breath...she was feeling a deeper peace in her soul because now they were back on track.

David is still hugging her close when he says to her, "As long as The Queen Mother is out there, you're in serious danger."

"David," she lifts her head to look at him, "as long as she's out there, you, Jack, Lawrence, *everyone I care about*, are in even *bigger* danger...until I have Lawrence's heir, then we all are!"

"You really think she'll use us to get to you, don't you?" He asks.

"She definitely has psychopathic tendencies. She'll want to inflict as much pain and torture as she possibly can on an enemy. If I were her, the best way to do that is to torture and kill everyone my enemy holds dear in their life and make that enemy live with it for the rest of their life! Also, if I were her, I would kill anyone new coming into their life as well, to prevent them from gaining any strength in any number; unless there was something to seriously blackmail this new person with and use that to evil's advantage!"

He exhales a whistle. "*Brilliant...*" he quietly says, "horrifying, but definitely *wickedly brilliant!*"

She sadly responds, "Yeah, but you wouldn't be the one left to live alone..."

"With your gift, neither would you." He gives a faint smile.

"*That wouldn't be the same thing!*" She tells him.

"No, I guess it wouldn't. But it would be better than not having your gift at all!" David rests his forehead to hers. "Bri, I don't want to scare you more, but things *are* going to get a whole lot worse with this woman, before they get better..."

"I know. They'll be at their absolute worse when I'm pregnant with Lawrence's baby." She states.

He hugs her a little tighter. "McMasters knows I'll do whatever is necessary to keep you, including all our children, safe. If it means we shut The Inn down and move in there, along with the girls and those we care about, then so be it!"

"It won't be enough." She states.

He pulls back and looks at her. "We can try!"

"*Oh, absolutely*! I'm not going to let her take me, or anyone else, down without a fight!" She replies. "We just can't underestimate evil! She has *perfected her craft* all these years and when she hits again, *she'll hit hard* because she'll want to knock me down and keep me down; too emotional to retaliate. She wants the upper hand again and will do what she has to do to get it, then keep it until the day she dies!"

He has an apologetic look, "I'd say I was sorry for bringing you into all this, but as you keep reminding us..."

"'Everything happens for a reason.'" She gives him a loving smile and nods. "And if we consider the complexities of a Divine plan, there are a number of reasons."

"One reason..." he tangles his hands in her hair, "to show me how beautiful love is!" He kisses her sweetly.

She suggests, "Let's get ready for bed and snuggle in, maybe watch something on the *telly*." She lightly teases with his accent to make him smile.

He chuckles a little and taps another kiss to her lips. He playfully swats her bum as she walks away. She looks over her shoulder, biting her lower lip, and winks. He laughs and shakes his head as he follows her into their bedroom.

He's waiting on the edge of their bed and after a few minutes he asks, "Are you coming to bed, Mrs. Worthington?"

"Yes, *Mister* Worthington!" Bri answers and he softly laughs.

She turns out the bathroom light before stepping into the bedroom. She is wearing black silk lingerie and she watches David's eyes look her down and back up again as a lustful look spreads across his face.

"You look...WOW!" He tells her as she walks over to him. He stands and holds out his hand, which she takes. "Oh, Macushla..." he pulls her close and wraps her in his arms. He kisses her neck. *"This is a wonderful surprise,"* he whispers in her ear as his hands feel the silky material.

She smiles. "Hnnn, I thought you might like it..."

He smiles against her neck. "Oh, Love, I love this, but I have a feeling I'm going to love it more when I toss it on the floor in a minute..." He scoops her up.

With a squeal of laughter, she says to him, "I think we're about to have some fun, *Mister* Worthington!"

"You can count on it, *Mrs. Worthington!*" She giggles and kisses him as he carries her over to their bed.

CHAPTER 43

Imperfectly Perfect Titles & Royal Surprises

It's the day of The Midnight Ball and David gives Lawrence the finalized paperwork one last time. David hasn't looked at this printed set yet, but he will after Lawrence announces the new titles he has in mind. Lawrence had blanks for all titles and had their solicitors put them in right before they printed this set out. David has Lawrence look them all over to make sure everything says what he wants and how he wants it.

After Lawrence reads through them, he says he doesn't want to change anything. "It's all good to go!"

The family gathers in The Study that afternoon. Prior to the official announcement that comes, Lawrence wants to explain the titles to everyone that he has given to Bri, as well as David and Jack, and indirectly the family.

"David, I know you said you didn't want to be elevated because of your position as CEO and of course being The Duke of Newhaven. I decided to *compromise*." He grins.

"Is there a compromise?" David is a bit confused. He looks at his parents trying to figure out how in the world there could be a compromise? Peter and Carlotta shake their heads with an 'I don't know' shrug.

"Yes." He laughs a little. "While there weren't added responsibilities of a title, I want to reestablish something with The Duchy itself."

"What do you mean?" David asks. Bri's ears perk up remembering a conversation she had with Lawrence not too long ago.

Lawrence sees her reaction and smiles at her. "Do you remember what we talked about with Newhaven's history?"

"I do!" She replies.

Lawrence explains to the others. "Bri and I discussed how my many distant grandfather ordered the removal of 'sovereign' from all the duchies to reduce their power after he overthrew his own brother."

James laughs as he teases, "That's in the history books!" Everyone else snickers a bit.

"*Well*, in all my recent research of the UK and Newhaven history, I noticed that one was missed." Lawrence tells them. He gives James a look as he tells him, "I don't think *that's* in the history books!"

"*Or* I *maaay* have been out sick that day!" James jokes back.

Lawrence chuckles. "Anyway, the one missed was Newhaven, which means it has always been, and technically *still is*, a sovereign duchy." The family is surprised and looking around at each other knowing what this means. Lawrence says, "I'm restoring the titles of The Duchy to The *Grand* Duke and The *Grand* Duchess of Newhaven."

"Wow, Herst..." David says with surprise, "I don't know what to say?!"

"There's nothing *to* say. This is how it's always been, it just needed to be rectified." Lawrence tells him. "I've changed up how you'll be addressed. Originally, it was 'His Grand Ducal Highness,' or HGDH; however, considering Bri's title which I'll get to, I want you to be addressed as 'His Highness' or 'Your Highness.'"

David, still stunned, says, "I'm still speechless..."

Lawrence smiles before he turns to Jack. "Now, as for Jack..." Jack looks at him with a raised eyebrow. Lawrence says, "I have a special estate in mind, the one that's always been my favorite and I think Bri will like it as well."

"Wait. Are you talking about the one you had me take a look at the financials for?" Jack asks.

"That's the one!" Lawrence grins.

Jack has a playful smile. "*Bri will love it!*"

Lawrence laughs and turns to Bri for a moment and smiles. "The top of The Clock Tower you noticed a large green area in the distance and asked if it was a park."

She laughs a little. "You briefly mentioned it, but we never discussed it."

ASHBOURNE

"Well, that was The Ashbourne Estate." He looks from Bri and back to Jack. The family has happy and excited gasps. "I want you two to oversee this duchy and its estate, making Jack, The Duke of Ashbourne, and Bri," he smiles at her, "The Duchess of Ashbourne."

Jack's mouth drops, then he says, "Herst, I don't need a whole estate, let alone Ashbourne! What in the world am I going to do with it?!"

"I'm counting on your 'golden touch' making it magnificent and fantastic once again! Mr. Woodsley does a wonderful job overseeing it, but for Ashbourne Castle to be restored to its former glory, perhaps a better glory, it needs you," he looks at Bri, "*both of you.*"

Carlotta has a big smile on her face. "Oh, Jack, you'll have something to pass down to your children!"

Jack replies, "Mother, I don't need—."

"Of course you don't, but this just feels right!" She looks at him like the proud mother she is of him. Jack smiles sweetly back at her.

Lawrence looks at Bri telling everyone, "Bri needs a place that's in London that *isn't* The Palace." Lawrence holds Bri's cheek. "As I said, The Estate has been taken very good care of, but needs some improvements that I think you and Jack would enjoy overseeing those, as well as the renovations to The Royal Quarters."

"I thought this estate is for your heir, Herst?!" Jack asks.

"When we walked through Ashbourne Estate, I said it has been kept for *an heir.*" He grins. "My child will be 'The Heir to The Throne' and have either The Duchy of Oxbridge or Yorkfordshire. There's also Luxton, which Abby was offered when she came of age, but turned it down to keep our mother out of her life. However, when we were talking about it one day, she thought it would be a great fit for an heir once mother passes on."

Jack is also at a loss for words. "Herst, this wasn't necessary. I was happy to support Bri, David, *and you*, in your roles. I was happy to escort The Duchess and now The *Grand* Duchess to wherever."

"I know, Jack." Lawrence replies. "You're such a wonderful person, a bloody fantastic brother, I wanted to do this for you *aaand* it's also a *little* selfish on my part. I'm hoping Ashbourne will get the TLC it needs and deserves; I just don't have the time to devote to it."

Jack hugs Lawrence. "Thank you, Brother."

Lawrence then goes and sits next to Bri and holds her hands. "Now, as you know I've done a lot of research," she nods, "and I've thought long and hard about how to do this. You see, I wanted to title you 'Princess' but I needed to place you above your children, if you continued to turn down being queen." He gives her a small wink. "It had to be something royal, majestic, regal," he holds her hand over his heart, "*queenly*. However, knowing you, having something too grand could make you very uncomfortable." Bri nods a bit. "Luckily, I have some flexibility with Newhaven's sovereign status reinstated and you being a 'Direct Bloodline.' I could've made your title 'Princess of Newhaven.' However, 'Grand Duchess' is a higher rank than a 'princess' or even a 'duchess.'" He smiles lovingly.

"Then what in the world exceeds 'Grand Duchess,' but not queen?" She asks Lawrence.

"I toyed with using the word 'Imperial.'" He smirks.

"*Imperial?* This isn't Russia, Ace!" She teases.

"Oh, Darling, as I said, I've done my homework!" He smirks. "The word 'imperial' holds it all: majestic, regal, royal, queenly, even sovereign!" He smiles, happy with himself.

"*Aaand*, I'm not an empress or anything like that!" She tells him with a sweet smile. "Plus, Gen still needs to outrank me since she's actually 'The Queen.'" She raises her eyebrow.

"Darling, 'imperial' can be used several ways. In The United Kingdom of Provinces history, 'Princess Imperial' has actually been used a few times with The Royal Consort. It's a title as close to 'queen' as one can get, without *being* queen. I'm not sure the reasoning for the others, but my father only named his Royal Consort 'Princess' which may have to do with my mother not wanting another woman anywhere near her territory and she would want any of her heirs to 'outrank' 'The Royal Consort' so being a duchess of any duchy would have been *out of the question*."

Bri agrees. "If she wouldn't feel so threatened by people, maybe she wouldn't be so nasty..." Bri stares off, getting lost in that thought.

Lawrence brings her back to the task at hand. "Bri, please let me do this. The paperwork is all done and ready to be signed."

She playfully lifts an eyebrow. "Do which one? Princess of Newhaven or Princess Imperial?" She smirks. She sees a loving and pleading little smile on his face and she caves. "Alright, Ace. I'll let you have this win!" She smiles back and taps a kiss to his lips.

He smiles big. "Thank you, Darling! Now, I'm that much closer to my goal!" He winks and she laughs, shaking her head. He tells her, "Your full title will be Her Royal Majesty, BriaLynn, The Princess Imperial, The Grand Duchess of Newhaven, The Duchess of Ashbourne, The Royal Consort, and Privy Counsellor to The King. However, to be styled as 'Her Royal Majesty, BriaLynn, The Princess Imperial.'"

"I'm confused...*Royal Majesty*?" Bri asks. "That sounds like one's addressing a monarch! That can't be right?!"

"As I said, *My Queen*, I've been doing a lot of research. 'Imperial' is most often related to Russian Tzars. I researched that, as well as styles of HM and HRH. This wasn't something I picked out of nowhere, I can assure you. Royal Consorts of The King or The Queen, have had the style of 'Royal Majesty.' I want to use 'royal' and 'majesty' because right now you'll be The King's Royal Consort, making you 'royal' as well as all *your* children, but 'majesty' because," he holds her face, "you'll *never* walk behind me, but *only* by my side."

"I'm not queen, Ace! That seems disrespectful to the people *and Queen Genevieve*!" Bri notes.

"Bri, don't you think we need to show a united front right from the start!" He holds her hands with a smirky smile.

She glares a little. "*I really don't like it when any of you use my words against me!*"

"*I'm not!* I'm using them *for me*!" He winks and she giggles. He then speaks to David and Jack, "Yours and Jack's heirs will be titled with prince or princess, with the distinction of Newhaven or Ashbourne, along with my heir at birth with our country as their distinction." He turns and faces Bri. "I would like to bestow upon Emmie and Natty the courtesy titles of 'Lady' under the Ashbourne dukedom. Is this alright with you, Darling?"

Bri turns with a mother's loving smile to her daughters, Emmie and Natty, while saying to Lawrence, "I'd support it, but it's *entirely* up to them!" She speaks to them and says, "If you agree to this, I only ask that you not use your title for everyday use at school."

Emmie smiles. "We don't want our friends to be jealous, but we don't want people trying to be our friends just to meet you, *or any of you for that matter*!"

"Agreed!" Natty chimes in.

Lawrence smiles at them. "What do you say?"

Emmie and Natty look at Jack and he smiles wide telling them, "I'd be honored to have you beautiful ladies titled under Ashbourne!"

Emmie and Natty look at each other and nod, then look at Lawrence and Emmie says, "*We'd* be honored!"

Peter happily says, "Wonderful!" The family agrees and they all hug the girls. Then Peter turns and asks Lawrence, "Now, Herst, when do you plan to announce all this?"

"As soon as," he looks at Bri, "*Her Royal Majesty* approves the press release." He tells Bri. "We'll have to release that you're already pregnant to make sure there's no question this first baby will be 'The Heir to Newhaven.'" He says. "Plus, it'll make sense that the 'two-year timeframe' won't begin until late Fall of *next year*, giving you time to recuperate after having this baby. I don't want to add more pressure to what you may already feel, but hear me out." She nods with a hint of a confused look. "When you become queen, the same rule applies to you being a 'Direct Bloodline' as it did when you married David." She furrows her eyebrows and starts to shake her head, but before she can say anything he tells her, "Hold on! I'm just, as you all say, laying all the cards on the table. It should help that I'll name David as *your* Royal Consort when you're coronated as The Queen, which will in turn," Peter's mouth drops open as he puts it together in his head, "make David's child temporarily the first 'Heir to The Throne.'"

"What?! *Seriously*?!" Bri puts her fingertips to her forehead. "This is going to give me a headache."

He gently puts his hand on her abdomen, "They'll be 'The Heir Apparent' *until* our child is born." Lawrence explains. "Our child will officially be 'The Crown Prince.'"

Bri looks at David who chuckles saying, "I *seriously* didn't see that coming! I'm ashamed to say I hadn't even thought about Bri needing a 'Royal Consort' when she became queen!"

Jack jumps in. "Well, I didn't either, but I wholeheartedly approve!" He pats David's shoulder.

"As do I!" David winks and laughs, as does everyone else. David takes Bri aside and says, "Love, I'm ready, whenever you are, to announce your pregnancy. I understand wanting to wait for the first trimester to be over, but is it necessary considering we've already *seen* him?" He tucks a strand of hair behind her ear.

"True..." she thinks about it. She takes a deep breath and exhales, "Alright then." She looks at Lawrence. "Let's do this!"

Lawrence looks at her sweetly. "If you want to change your mind, I swear to you as me, *and* as The King—."

She covers his mouth and he sees tears in her eyes as she smiles. "*Not.a.chance, Ace*! My heart is *way* too involved now!" She holds up the hand with The Pink Heart Diamond Ring he gave her. "*You* had your chance, but you're stuck with me forever!"

He snorts a laugh. "As you say, 'good answer,' Darling!" She giggles and Jack and David laugh, too. Lawrence kisses her firmly.

David lovingly kisses Bri's cheek, holding it there a few extra seconds. "Now, I think we all can give you and Lawrence a little bit of time together." They all nod and head out of the room; Lawrence and Bri going down to The Sitting Room.

Bri looks over at Lawrence and he smiles at her. It's a smile she has learned is only for her. He is handed a tablet from Gavan and she ignores him. Lawrence reads it as she ponders on their relationship...a relationship that may not have started like a typical relationship, but they're becoming extremely close. He looks at her and sees she's staring at him. He winks with a smile, then leans in and kisses her.

He hands the tablet to her. "The press release is set to go, pending your approval."

> PRESS RELEASE: Their Majesties, King Lawrence and Queen Genevieve, would like to make a few announcements today. First, it has been discovered that The Duchy of Newhaven never officially lost its status as a sovereign duchy. The King has reinstated the titles of The Grand Duke and The Grand Duchess of Newhaven effective immediately.
>
> Second, and most importantly, Their Majesties are happy to express their sincerest joy and excitement to Their Highnesses, The Grand Duke and The Grand Duchess of Newhaven on the upcoming birth of their baby, "The Heir to Newhaven," this coming summer.
>
> Third, His Majesty would like to announce that in honor of The Grand Duchess of Newhaven becoming 'The Royal Consort,' he has bestowed The Ashbourne Estate to Lord Jackson Carlisle, now The Duke of Ashbourne. This also adds the title of The Duchess of Ashbourne to The Grand Duchess of Newhaven's titles.
>
> Lastly, His Majesty would like to announce the full title and style of his Royal Consort:
>
>> Her Royal Majesty, BriaLynn, The Princess Imperial, The Grand Duchess of Newhaven, The Duchess of Ashbourne, The Royal Consort, and Privy Counsellor to The King.
>>
>> She will be styled as: Her Royal Majesty, BriaLynn, The Princess Imperial.

Bri rereads her title before handing the tablet back to Lawrence. "That's...*wow*..."

He is concerned. "What's wrong?"

"It's just all so surreal!" She comments.

"If you need to change——." Lawrence starts to say and she shakes her head.

"I appreciate you doing all you can to ease me into this." She has a hint of reluctance. "But on some level, there's really no easy to ease someone into all this and you just have to 'rip the bandage off' so-to-speak."

"I just don't want you to feel pressured." He softly says.

"I am but not by you...like I said, there's no way to ease one into this. Do what you need to and let's move this conversation on, before my nerves do get the better of me and I pull out of *all* this!" She lightly teases.

"Let me respond quick to go ahead and release this..." he says as he types; she looks out to the gardens. "There. Done." She turns back to him, but he puts up a finger for the 'one sec' gesture. He hands his tablet off to Gavan and walks out of the room with him. When he comes back into the room, he has a vase of flowers.

"Rainbow roses!" She happily smiles and he puts them on the center large table. "They're *beautiful*, thank you!" She hugs and kisses him. "But you do remember the conversation about how I murder roses?"

He softly chuckles, "I'd call it 'rose-slaughter,' since you don't intend for them to die." She snorts a laugh at his play on 'manslaughter.' He leads her to the piano. "But I'll risk it every single time just to see your face light up like it does!"

He sits at the piano and she excitedly remembers, "That's right! One day, a while back, Jack offhandedly mentioned you play piano!"

"*I do.*" He says as he scoots over to give her room to sit next to him.

"What brought that up?" He asks.

"Jack has framed a picture of me singing karaoke on our first tour around Newhaven after our honeymoons."

"You sing?" He asks.

She changes the focus a bit. "Will you play something for me?"

He studies her as he thinks of his own melody he has played around with and starts to play it. He has played these notes over the years; however, he has never played it for another soul...now his fingers are taken over by his heart. He didn't just play the melody; it was a full song. When he finishes, the song touched her deeply she has to wipe the tears from her eyes. She kisses him sweetly and then rests their foreheads together.

Bri asks, "What song was that? It was so moving!"

"I haven't named it yet." He simply states.

"You composed it?!" She smiles so proud of him.

He turns his body to her and she turns to him, giving each other a soft smile. "I've played around with the melody for years, never for anyone; and this was the first time the whole song came to me."

She goes to say something more, but all they do is stare into each other's eyes. He cups her cheek, pulling her lips closer as he leans in. He ghosts them with his lips; feeling each other's warm breath. Lawrence then kisses her with his whole heart, nothing holding him back; Bri feels it and she breaks the kiss as it becomes too intense. He gives her an intense seductive look that has her stand, but before she can walk away, he stands and grabs her, easily sitting her on the piano keys; the sound of which was not 'music to the ears.'

"I want you, Bri." He says and captures her lips in another heated kiss.

It takes every bit of strength she has to break their kiss again. She can only whisper, "*Lawrence, this is hard...we're so close to being official...*" He nods and goes to say something but sees Jack and David standing in the doorway, smirking.

"Mother asked if we'd send Bri to the dressing room." David says, playfully smiling at her. She steps to the side and clears her throat.

"It's a bit early to get ready, isn't it?" She asks, looking at her watch.

Lawrence answers. "It's part of the evening's plans, *before* The Midnight Ball."

"Oh?" She asks. "What's that?"

Lawrence grins. "You'll have to go get ready so you can find out..."

Bri taps a kiss on Lawrence's cheek. "I love you."

He looks at her adoringly. "I love you." He kisses the back of her hand. She turns to leave, lovingly smiling at Jack and David as she walks past them.

Jack exhales a whistle as he and David walk over to Lawrence. Jack says, "*Bloody hell that was hot*!" Lawrence rubs the back of his neck and nods.

David gives him an understanding look. "It may be hard to resist, but we swear it's worth it because *love* makes it worth the wait! The amount of love in that woman's heart is *never ending*! Jack and I have never experienced true, adoring love before Bri." He leans in so only Lawrence and Jack can hear, "I would've given up being The Heir to Newhaven if she didn't have any bloodlines at all!"

Lawrence has a surprised look on his face; he knows how seriously David takes his duties and responsibilities. Lawrence pats David's shoulder then they go and get ready for a small, private ceremony Lawrence has arranged for Bri and himself, with everyone's help.

CHAPTER 44

Imperfectly Perfect & Royally Perfect

Bri is putting the final touches on her makeup and hair, with the help of Nicole and Antionette this evening. She sees the time and starts to rush a bit. They pull Bri's dress out of the garment bag and Bri's mouth drops open as she sees a dress that is similar to her wedding dress.

"This is beautiful, but it isn't the dress——." Panic starts to come over her.

Nicole holds up a card and hands it to Bri. She opens the envelope and reads:

Change in plans, Macushla! ~ Love, David

The short-sleeve dress is a sparkly deep-red satin, with scrolling gold stencil-like accents and sequins. It has a gold wrap look at her shoulders. The satin dress is fitted at the top and down through her hips, then flows out from the lower thigh to the floor. The dress opens from the left hip and goes down to the center and a little to the right, to show The Worthington Family's new tartan.

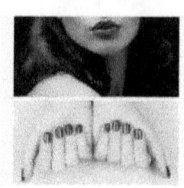

Antionette excitedly says, "I have the perfect dark-red lip gloss and matching nail polish for this, Bri!"

She shows Bri and they quickly do her nails. While Antionette dries her nails, Nicole puts the matching lip gloss on Bri's lips. She puckers her lips for them in the mirror and they giggle.

"This *is* perfect! Thank you!" Bri tells them.

Nicole puts on and secures The Diamond Heart Tiara on Bri's head, then steps back to look at Bri. "You look beautiful!"

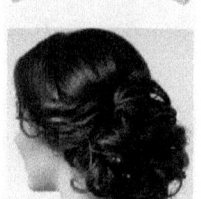

Antoinette takes a look. "You look wonderful, Bri! But you're missing a couple of pieces!" She grins.

Bri says with a skeptical look with her smile. "Let me guess, *King Lawrence* has something to be added?"

"We were told to tell you these are a gift from *Lawrence* to the woman he loves." Nicole says.

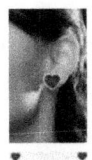

Antoinette smiles excitedly for their friend and opens the flat velvet box. Inside is a necklace of ruby hearts, haloed with tiny diamonds with matching heart earrings. They help her put them on before stepping back again to see the completed look.

Nicole tells Bri, "You look exquisite!"

"Bri," Antionette smiles, "you look like 'The Queen of Hearts!'"

Bri's eyebrows come together as she turns and looks at herself in the full-length mirror. She lightly gasps...the dress and tiara alone seem to suggest that, but with the necklace set makes it obvious.

There's a knock on the door and Bri knows it's Jack. Nicole answers it and lets him in. She and Antionette step out to let Bri have a few minutes alone with him.

Jack comes over, looking her up and down. He can only whisper, "*Wow...*" He takes her hands and kisses them before he holds them out for a better look. He says with amazement, "You look *absolutely, gorgeously stunning!*"

"Thank you." She giggles. She looks down at herself. "This dress is similar to my ceremonial wedding dress."

"David and I asked the same designer to work with Lawrence using that same dress for inspiration. Your wedding dress is still our favorite!" He grins.

"*Oh really?*" She raises her eyebrow.

"Bri, it was perfect! However, *this* dress is perfect for today! *YOU'RE* perfect!" Jack says, cupping her neck just below her jaw and kisses her cheek. "You look *royally* perfect!"

"No pressure..." She says plainly.

"There shouldn't be any pressure!" He firmly states. "You love each other *and* you want this, *right?*" He asks, knowing the answer.

"I *do* love him!" She happily agrees.

"So, tonight it'll all be official and you two can move forward together, and we can all move forward as a family; preparing for our joyful addition this coming summer!"

She smiles saying, "Sounds wonderful!" Then she looks up at Jack with so much love. "I love you, Amore Mio!"

"I love *you*, Amore Mia!" He kisses the back of her hand, then wraps her arm around his. "Shall we?" She nods with a little teary smile and they walk to The Grand Ballroom together, only there is a slight detour first.

David and Lawrence are talking when David sees them approach. He sends Lawrence in the doors they're standing in front of so Lawrence doesn't see her yet. David turns to Bri and his eyes brighten as a huge smile spreads across his face.

His hand goes up to his chest and he takes a deep breath. "You look...*breathtaking!*" He says in awe of her. He holds his hands out for hers and looks her up and down, "Once again, all descriptive words are wrapped up into a description of you!" David kisses Bri's cheek with so much love her breath catches! "You're absolutely *stunning*, Macushla! You look like 'The Queen of Hearts!'"

Bri is surprised to hear that reference again. "That's what Antionette said to me right before Jack came to get me!"

Jack handsomely smiles. "I enthusiastically agree!"

David pats Jack's shoulder as they take their proper places on each side of Bri. The doors open so they can lead her into a small room that had been set up beautifully for a mini wedding ceremony.

"What's this?" She whispers, looking around as they walk inside and down the aisle.

Family and really close friends are standing and the doors close behind them, shutting out the press and any other onlookers. Lawrence stood up front with The Bishop and Bri smiles at him, then focuses on Lawrence.

Lawrence stands with his one hand holding the wrist of the other behind him. He sees her in full view and he freezes. Lawrence forgets to breathe for several seconds as he is overcome with emotions. The closer Bri gets, the more tears he gets in his eyes, and by the time she reaches him and The Bishop, Lawrence wipes his cheeks. He remembers her wedding to David and how emotional she, David, and Jack were; he now knows how they feel.

Jack, Bri, and David, stop in front of The Bishop who says to everyone, "Please be seated." Then The Bishop says to Bri, "*Your Highness.*" Bri then remembers that Lawrence's press release went out and she is officially 'The Grand Duchess' at that moment. The Bishop is smiling with twinkles in his eyes. "These wonderful men thought it would be beneficial to your unique relationships if we didn't have just a signing ceremony of sorts, but a small wedding to honor this special 29th day of October." Bri tearily and adoringly smiles at Lawrence. He looks at her with so much love, Bri has to hold her breath to help push down her emotions that are about to erupt.

The Bishop gestures to, "The Grand Duke of Newhaven and The Duke of Ashbourne escorted you down here as a sign that they support this, by all purposes, marriage to The King, and for you to become The Royal Consort, *and by all purposes*, his wife." The Bishop speaks to the guests. "From this point forward, His Majesty has agreed to take the formality out of the ceremony. This ceremony," he motions with his arms at them, "is about joining Lawrence and BriaLynn in their love." He looks at David and speaks to him and Jack, "Please place BriaLynn's hand in Lawrence's before both of you take your seats." Jack and David kiss Bri's cheek, before David places her hand in Lawrence's and goes with Jack to their seats.

The Bishop says, "Lawrence has asked to say a few words before more traditional vows." She smiles when The Bishop hands her a tissue from one of the packages he has tucked away in the pocket of his suit coat.

Lawrence holds both her hands and lovingly looks at her. "I wish I could be as eloquent as David or Jack are, but this does come from my heart nonetheless." She gives him a little encouraging nod, as tears already start to fill her eyes. "BriaLynn, I stand before you not as 'The King' but as a man in love with you. *You* are the force I needed to take control of my own life. You're the first woman to say you're in-love with me *and truly mean it*. Here's

448

only a small portion of *why* I love you; if I tried to list them all, we'd be here *all* night!" There's soft laughter around them; Bri keeps looking at him with love. Lawrence explains. "I love you because you feel I'm worth your time, effort, and devotion!"

She whispers, "*Because you are!*"

He gives her a small smile. "I love you because of your genuine nature. I love how your caring and nurturing side has a way of healing wounds I never dreamed *could be healed*. I love you because you have a strength to bear the *unimaginable*; yet, you also know how to be soft like a lady. I love you because of your solid stance in your faith in God and in Jesus Christ! I love how that unshakeable faith keeps you moving forward; your trust and the strength in Them is inspiring!" The Bishop is nodding in agreement. "I love that you'd never force those beliefs on others because you know that would do more harm than good; *however*, you have a special way of bringing people of all beliefs into your circle *spiritually*. I love you because of your patience, kindness, and understanding with others, *and perhaps especially with me*! I love you because that love and kindness is a real strength for you! I love you because that force within you can challenge people to rise up and be the person they were meant to be! I love you because you encourage people to begin where they're at and that their past is to be learned from, *but it needs to be left in their past*, or they can't move forward; *not really.*" She is faintly shaking her head 'no.' "I love you because you want to celebrate how far a person has come in their life, never judging them, only encouraging them wherever they're going! I love you because of how you're looking at me right now——." His emotions overcome him and a lump in his throat cuts off his sentence.

She tearily smiles. "*Because I love you!*"

His lower jaw shakes as he nods and he looks down a moment to suppress some of the more overwhelming feelings; she gently squeezes his hands. He takes a deep breath and shakily exhales slowly...

He continues. "I love you because my heart has found its home with you." He hears Bri's breath catch and he just about loses his hold on his emotions completely. Lawrence takes another deep breath and holds it a moment before he goes on. "I promise to show you I love you by *remaining* faithful and true to you!" He stresses 'remaining' in such a way, Bri understands he is telling her he *hasn't* been with anyone else. "I promise to adore you, our relationship, our whole unique family!" She smiles and more tears escape her eyes. "I may not be the 'fun uncle' like Jack naturally will be," he tips his head towards Jack, "but I can promise to love *all* our family's children as my own and will protect them all just as fiercely; just as I promise to protect you at *all* costs!" He kisses the back of her hand. "I love you and will support you in every aspect of your business and foundation, as well as your duties in Newhaven and now Ashbourne. I *wholeheartedly* support Genevieve's quest and will support you *when* you become queen!" Bri laughs a little and looks to Genevieve who nods and winks at her with a huge smile. "I promise to *always* love you and honor you as '*My Queen*'" He holds both her hands firmly. "My love runs deep for you and gets deeper every single day! With everything that I am as a man and as a king, I am and will forever be, *in-love with you*! I love you, *My Queen*! You're 'The Queen of *My* Heart!'"

Bri realizes he *deliberately* has her looking like 'The Queen of Hearts.' She wipes her tears; she is on her fourth or fifth tissue by this point. Lawrence takes another tissue from The Bishop and dries his eyes, along with their guests who are drying their eyes or wiping their cheeks.

After a couple minutes, Bri and Lawrence are once again holding hands and The Bishop addresses Bri. "I don't mean to put you on the spot—."

"No, no! I'd like to say a few words!" Bri says. Then she looks to Lawrence. "Lawrence..." she takes a deep breath to calm her nerves, "as you know I've fallen in-love with you and I didn't do it blindly. We agreed to take our time and I walked right into it, knowing full well there would be some great challenges on the horizon."

"And yet you're *still* here!" He quietly says, as a tear skips down his cheek.

Bri smiles with love as she wipes his tear with her thumb. "Yes, Ace. And *forever* will be!" She wipes her own tears. Unknown to most, The King Father slips in and sits in the very back. Bri holds Lawrence's hands again and continues. "Every child deserves a mother and a father who loves them, wants the best for them, and wants to keep them safe; to feel loved and protected. While I can't go back in time and help younger Lawrence, I can make my own promises to the man standing before me! I promise *you*..." she could barely whisper 'you' and swallows hard. She inhales and exhales, then tries again. "I promise you that I love you *for you*! I promise my love grew for you when you opened up to me about your past!" Lawrence's father catches this. "I promise my love for you grows immeasurably as you keep your promises and vows to me, just as I'm sure your love for me will grow—." She inhales sharply as a lump closes off her throat.

He brings her hand up to his mouth. "Every single day!" He kisses the back of it.

Bri's lower jaw shakes as her resolve not to cry is getting weaker, until it dissolves completely. She presses the tissue in her hand to her mouth, until she gains control again...then she sees the spirit of her son with Lawrence standing next to his father, flanked right behind him are his brother and sister. Bri loses it and turns away from the guests. Lawrence recalls what she had said about her wedding to David and Jack...how she became even more emotional during a particular moving part of the ceremony, when she saw her three children's spirits.

Lawrence whispers, "*You see them, don't you?*"

All she can do is nod, but she feels she can give him this gift, too. She slightly waves her finger, allowing Lawrence to see what she does. He looks to the side of him and gets more emotional when he sees *all three of them*! While no one sees anything but two people who love each other getting emotional during the ceremony, Jack and David caught what was happening and figured they saw his son there.

The Bishop steps forward and says only loud enough for Bri and Lawrence to hear. "*See who?*"

Lawrence smiles so lovingly at Bri and answers just as quietly to The Bishop, "Her children that are yet to be born, rather *our family's children* yet to be born to us." The Bishop stands in silence absorbing what he had heard.

Bri adds quietly, "I have a gift of seeing spirits and ghosts."

The Bishop barely whispers, "*That's remarkable!*"

Bri looks at David and Jack. She smiles as she discretely moves her finger for them to see their children's spirits. For the first time, Jack and David see Jack's daughter and Jack is overcome himself. Bri winks at him and he puts his hand over his heart and mouths 'Thank you.' She smiles and gives him a little wink back.

The Bishop clears his throat as he comes back to his senses. He kindly smiles and says to Bri and Lawrence so everyone could hear, "Shall we continue?" The couple nods.

"Now the vows. Lawrence, hold her hands and repeat after me. 'I, Lawrence, give thee, BriaLynn, my abiding love and take her to be my wife...'" Lawrence chokes up and kisses her hand again as he swallows hard, "and Royal Consort, to have and to hold from this day forward, for better, for worse, for richer, for poorer, in sickness and in health, to love, honor, and cherish, now and forever.'"

"Bri, these are a little different; repeat after me. 'I, BriaLynn, give thee, Lawrence, my abiding love as your wife and Royal Consort; to take you as my husband, to have and to hold from this day forward, for better, for worse, for richer, for poorer, in sickness and in health, to love, honor, and cherish, now and forever.'"

The Bishop looks to Lawrence. "The rings?" Lawrence pulls out a velvet bag and pours the rings on The Bishop's Bible. He blesses them and holds the rings out to Lawrence, "Take her ring and put it on her finger as you repeat after me." Bri notices the rings are exactly alike and both have the stretched-out Triquetra, but also a Triquetra with a heart symbol on them; she gets more emotional.

Lawrence takes Bri's ring and repeats after The Bishop. "With this ring, I join my life to yours. This ring is unending, just like my love and devotion to you *always* will be. This ring is a gift for you to wear as a visible sign of my enduring love for you." He pushes the ring onto her finger, next to 'The Pink Heart Diamond Ring' he gave her.

"Bri," he says as Bri takes Lawrence's ring, "repeat after me. 'With this ring, I join my life to yours. This ring is unending, just like my love and devotion to you *always* will be. This ring is a gift for you to wear as a visible sign of *my* enduring love for you." She pushes the ring onto his finger.

"Lawrence..." The Bishop winks with a huge smile on his face and he takes a step back. Lawrence's face is wet with tears, just as Bri's face is, but he didn't care. He holds the back of her jaw and kisses her fiercely. Her hands go up to hold his forearms and she returns the kiss just as fiercely. They pull apart and rest their foreheads together. She lifts her head and looks at him, but he speaks first, "I love you, My Queen!" He kisses her again.

"I love *you*, My King!" They kiss once, he embraces her in a firm hug. She looks at his lips and there's no color from her lip gloss. She touches her lips, "It's a stain? That's amazing!"

The Bishop steps forward again. "Lawrence, Bri, would you turn to your guests?" They turn and face their guests as The Bishop says to everyone, "Ladies and Gentlemen, Lawrence and BriaLynn's love is now and forever unified together!"

Lawrence pulls Bri into another kiss and without thinking, he dips her back, only a little because of her tiara, but deepens the kiss. There are cheers and clapping among the guests. He brings her back up joyfully saying, "I love you, BriaLynn!"

"I love you, Lawrence!" She kisses him once more before they turn and go down to greet their guests.

They hug and thank everyone; with David and Jack she hugs and kisses them both. She happens to see The King Father slip out and when he turns to shut the door quietly, they make eye contact. He gives her a small smile and a nod before the door closes all the way. This intrigues her and that she's not feeling anything evil with him...maybe the evilness in this family is one-sided? Like only his mother?

"Are you alright, Darling?" Lawrence asks.

She snaps out of it and with a big smile of excitement she says, "*Absolutely!*"

He chuckles and feels her excitement; he feels the same about her. "Do you have any questions, or are you ready to move on to signing the paperwork?"

"I'm sure I'd have a million questions, if my mind wasn't already spinning." She says.

He tells her, "Tonight, you're mine..." he puts a hand on her bum and tugs her closer, "*except* for the dances you dance with David, Jack, and *very few others*, you only dance with me..." He gives her a smoldering look and she lightly giggles. The doors open and she sees a small table in a room across the hall. The press was in the hall and pouring into the room with Genevieve, Seth, Abby, Jack, and David making their way there, too, along with Peter, Carlotta, James, Amy, Maggie, and Henry. The Queen Mother and The King Father are already there but out of view at the moment.

Lawrence feels Bri shaking and looks at her with compassion. "*If this was too much,*" he sadly whispers, "*I'm sorry.*"

"No, don't be! Just let me catch my breath and hopefully breathe in some courage." She whispers back with a little smile.

"What can I do?" He sweetly asks as he hugs her close.

"You're doing it." She says and he feels her relax a little as she exhales, so he hugs her more firmly. After maybe two minutes, she takes another deep breath in and exhales. "Lawrence, please understand this has nothing to do with my decision, it's everything to do with—."

"With the very public display and press?" He finishes her sentence. When she pulls back, he's smirking. She stares at Lawrence's dimpled smile, brown hair, and amazing blue-green eyes. He asks, "Darling, are you ready?"

Bri faintly smiles, "Just another moment or two..." she says and hugs him again. After those few minutes, she takes one more deep breath and exhales saying, "Let's go, Ace!"

CHAPTER 45
Imperfectly Perfect & The Royal Consort

Lawrence holds Bri's hand as they walk into the room and over to the table for the official paperwork signing. She can feel The Queen Mother's eyes piercing through her, but Bri refuses to even glance her way. She thinks Lawrence is going to leave her with David and Jack, but he firmly holds her hand and brings her to the podium with him.

"Good evening." He pauses as the room quiets down. "Thank you all for coming." Bri watches as *King Lawrence* takes control of the room. "As you all know, part of my obligation as 'The King' is to have a 'Royal Consort.' The Grand Duchess of Newhaven's ancestral background is deeply rooted in our country, from coast to coast in any direction, with a little more in and around the beautiful city of Edinburgh. Her ancestral roots stretch down throughout all of Europe in such a way that *all of her ancestral connections* go back far enough that she, herself, is a rare 'Direct Bloodline.'"

There's lots of whispering...

"The Grand Duchess of Newhaven's professional background in Washington, D.C. gives her some unique skills. I'm hoping to tap into her intelligence to help our country going forward, starting with our criminal justice system to do much like she has done in Washington, D.C., and is now doing in Newhaven."

"Queen Genevieve..." he holds his free arm out in her direction for her to join them. Bri goes to step back, but Lawrence doesn't let go of her hand, "will continue in her duties, just as she always has and doing brilliantly!"

There's happy applause for her. Genevieve smiles at Lawrence and they kiss each other's cheek as the family, *and friends*, they are. Genevieve then steps to Bri's other side for a show of support and unity.

Lawrence looks at Bri. "The Grand Duchess and I will need to 'produce an heir in two years,' but it'll be two years from *next* October. This will ensure her health after the joyful delivery of the baby she and The Grand Duke of Newhaven will have next summer!"

There's lots of excited cheers and applause, even Lawrence claps for them after he hugs Bri and shakes David's hand, hugging each other with their other arms. When the cheers and claps fade, The King continues.

> "I have always been in full support of Queen Genevieve and my brother, Prince Seth. They are not aware of this, but I'm bequeathing The Duchy of Brexton with The Brexton Estate to them and their future family."

More cheers and applause come from the people in the room. Bri and Lawrence hug Seth and Gen, along with Jack and David. The applause continues as Lawrence, with a huge smile on his face, leads Bri to the table for them to officially sign the paperwork. She sees The Bishop and he smiles; she looks at David and then the paperwork and back to David, who discreetly nods. She smiles gratefully at him as Lawrence pulls out her chair.

As he pushes in her chair, he whispers in her ear, *"David's solicitors, remember?"* She nods with a faint smile.

Lawrence asked Carlotta and Peter to keep the paperwork close and they did. They covertly, with Mitchell's help, switched out the paperwork that was already there, right before the doors opened for the press and guests to gather. They haven't taken their eyes off of it, but Lawrence will glance through it as the paperwork is signed.

Lawrence hands Bri the pen and she is walked through all the places she needs to sign, and how she needs to sign them; Lawrence glancing at certain places to make sure his mother didn't somehow find out and switch anything...thankfully she doesn't...this is the first important secret he has been able to keep from her.

When Bri is done signing, Lawrence helps her up, then leans into her ear and whispers, *"Stay with me, Darling."* Tapping a kiss to her cheek and switches places with her.

Bri waits for Lawrence as he signs everything. It occurs to her that making it binding legally also has an added layer of super glue since he is 'The King.' She tries to push back the unnecessary nervousness and reservations that come...there's no reason to have them, they're doing this out of love.

Lawrence stands and looks at David, who is walking over to them. "And for the last signatures needed," Lawrence hands David the pen, "Your Highness."

David smiles at both of them and takes the pen. "Thank you, Your Majesty." Lawrence motions to the chair as he steps over to Bri.

David is directed to where he needs to sign and he also checks to make sure it's the same paperwork it's supposed to be; it is. When he's finished, he stands with applause and cheering filling the small room, pouring out into the hallway. Bri catches sight of one of the spirit women she has seen every now and then, only this time the woman is emotional and disappears into the crowd.

David holds Bri's cheek and leans in whispering, "*Almost done.*" She sweetly smiles and hugs him.

Jack comes up and for a moment. They hug and he kisses her cheek. "*You're doing fantastic!*" He whispers in her ear.

Jack and David take a step back so Bri can join Lawrence as he addresses the crowd once again:

> "I would like to officially present to you: *Her Royal Majesty*, BriaLynn, The Princess Imperial, The Grand Duchess of Newhaven, The Duchess of Ashbourne, The Royal Consort, and Privy Counsellor to The King." He kisses her hand.

Bri is overwhelmed by the cheers, whistles, and applause, that come their way. Lawrence takes her hand and says, "We'll pose for a couple pictures, but we're going to have official photos taken in the next room." Bri works fast to dry her eyes.

Lawrence steps over to an empty area with Bri for some photos to be taken of them. He holds her close and they pose for various people for a minute then add Jack and David for their family photo, and the extended family for a group picture. Lawrence and Bri go to the next room to have their official portraits taken. They've been smiling so much, their cheeks hurt. When they're done posing, he asks for a minute alone with Bri and everyone clears the room.

"I just wanted to get formalities out of the way *and now*," he sweetly smiles, "we can focus on us, our family, and our extended family and friends."

"To be honest, it would be overwhelming no matter what, so getting through it sooner, rather than later, was probably for the best." She is surprised at what she said and how it might have sounded to him. "I'm sorry, I don't mean you, it's just, um..." She tries to explain.

He gives her an understanding look. "I know what you mean, Darling." He rests his forehead to hers for a long moment.

She lifts her head and stares into his beautiful blue green eyes. "My King..."

He softly laughs, *"My Queen..."* tapping a tender kiss to her lips.

"I want to spend as much time together as we can tonight." He says, staring back into her eyes.

"You want to be *bored* all night?!" She teases and he laughs.

He quietly says next to her ear, *"Oh, no, Darling!* You see, if you're bored *all* night, then I'll be doing something *very* wrong."

Her eyebrows flick up. She runs the palm of her hands up his upper arms, his shoulders, and around his neck, staring deeply into his eyes. Her touch is sweet, she nuzzles him cheek-to-cheek before she tips her head back for him to kiss her and he does...slowly at first, then passionately...She cups his neck, just below his jaw and moans into the kiss, but stops herself abruptly when she remembers where they are, her cheeks are a little red.

Lawrence holds her close as he softly chuckles. "I agree! You're a bloody fantastic kisser!"

"I *haaate* to say this, Ace, but we do need to get in there, they *are* expecting us. *However,*" she lifts an eyebrow as she smirks, "maybe we *could* sneak off a little while later..."

He matches her playful smile as he tugs her closer. "I'd like to, but since this was planned to be *our special day,* I'm not sure *how* to attempt that..." He inhales and exhales disappointedly.

"Then one more kiss before we go, Ace?" She smiles.

"My pleasure..." he looks at her seductively and kisses her very passionately, making it count.

"*All three of you* are fantastic kissers and if it carries over to the bedroom, don't make plans for anything in the morning...I may not be able to walk!" She gives a saucy wink, stepping away, and turns back. "Are you coming, Ace!" He chuckles and catches up to her, offering her his arm.

They are outside the main doors of The Grand Ballroom where The Midnight Ball has already started. He moves their arms so he can hold her hand and tucks her arm under his. He looks at her and smiles, she smiles back and he studies her beautiful features.

"What is it?" She asks, nervously touching her face, then looks down at herself trying to figure it out.

"Nothing! Just admiring the beauty before my eyes, 'The Queen of *My Heart*'..." He says, caressing her face with his fingertips. Before he can say anything more, King Lawrence's new assistant, Spencer Brewer, approaches.

"Your Majesty," he bows about forty-five degrees, "Your Royal Majesty," he kisses the back of her hand as he slightly bows to her. "We're ready whenever you two are."

Bri goes to let go and step behind Lawrence, but he doesn't let her. She gives him a confused look, as does Mr. Brewer who asks, "Sir?"

Lawrence looks at Bri, but talks to him, "Mr. Brewer, let it be known that The Princess Imperial will *never* walk behind me, but *always* beside me when she is with me."

Bri whispers, "*Lawrence, we're not walking a hallway together or a sidewalk.*"

He turns to her. "You are, in every way, my equal, but in reality, you're so far above me!" He squeezes her hand he is holding. "While the stuffy old bats may argue the rules, *I won't back down* from this! *Please don't ask me to.*" He pleads with a look on his face to match; she melts and concedes.

"Splendid!" Mr. Brewer replies. "Consider it done, Sir."

"Wonderful! Now, Bri, meet the man who is training with Gabriel to be my new assistant." Lawrence introduces them.

"Pleasure to meet you, Mr. Brewer!" Bri happily smiles because she gets a wonderful feeling of authenticity and dedication to 'King and Country' from this Spencer Brewer.

"The pleasure is all mine, Your Royal Majesty! I just about died right then and there when Gabriel said I was going to be appointed to this position if I wanted it!" He says with genuine excitement.

"That explains it!" Bri says.

"Ma'am?" He asks with a bit of a confused look.

"Why I already like you!" She smiles wide and he happily does, too. "If Gabriel hired you, you're golden with me!"

"*Thank you, Ma'am*! I hope I don't disappoint you, or His Majesty!"

"*Oh, no*! You'll do great!" She smiles at Lawrence, wrapping an arm around his waist and speaks to Mr. Brewer. "I know this because if you have *any* trouble with him, just let me know!" Lawrence chuckles and she looks at Mr. Brewer. "You'll have my number if you don't already! The King will never know what I know!" She looks at Lawrence with a teasing mischievous grin.

"Making him loyal to you first? Ooo, *absolutely brilliant* chess move, My Queen!" Lawrence kisses the rings on her right hand as she softly laughs.

She tells Lawrence, "Team up with him like I have Gabriel, and he'll be able to keep you in line himself." She smirks, Mr. Brewer snickers and clears his throat trying to cover it. Bri winks at him and looks back to Lawrence. "Besides, Ace, life will be so much easier if you do! I told Gabriel I only want one assistant, he's my 'chief of staff' so-to-speak, but he can have his own however many assistants *he* needs!"

Lawrence has a bit of a surprised look. "I hadn't thought of it like that! *That would be simpler*!"

"And easier to maintain loyalty, between the two of you of course." Bri gives Lawrence a look he understands to mean Spencer's loyalty will be with him and *not* his mother!

Lawrence softly laughs. "I'll tell Gabriel and Mr. Brewer I want the same thing." Lawrence explains, "I asked Gabriel to be in charge of overseeing my assistant. I mean no disrespect, Mr. Brewer, and I have the *utmost* confidence in you. These arrangements were made before anyone was ever interviewed.”

“I understand, Sir. I know I need to prove myself in my abilities.” Mr. Brewer smiles. “It would be nice for you to work with minimal disruptions of various assistants, so we’ll definitely keep that in mind!”

 Lawrence nods and turns to Bri; she is staring at a window. He squeezes her hand a little to get her attention. She looks at him with a loving smile.

“Are you alright, Darling?” He asks.

“*I’m wonderful!*” Bri replies. “I just see a woman’s spirit I’ve seen before. She’s staring out the window, deep in thought, but there’s a sadness to her today…”

“What could she be looking at when it’s pitch-black outside?” He wonders.

“I’m not sure, but her face seems to be glowing like it’s in sunlight…” Bri stares at her, “There’s something familiar about her and now I’m wondering if she might be Jack’s mom…I’ve never seen pictures of her and Jack says he isn’t ready for me to call her so I can’t be sure it’s her.” She looks back at Lawrence, “This is all for a different day! *Right now*, we have a party to go to!” She happily says to him.

He smiles a wonderful smile back at her. “Well then, *My Queen*…shall we?” He takes her hand and tucks her arm under his again.

“Let’s make some headlines!” She gives him another cheeky wink and smile.

He chuckles and tells Mr. Brewer, “We’re ready.”

Mr. Brewer nods, then steps away to talk into a walkie-talkie.

CHAPTER 46
Imperfectly Perfect Royal Ball

Then the music stops, and all gets quiet on the other side of the door... Lawrence and Bri patiently wait for the doors to the ballroom to open. Mr. Brewer steps back and gives the two of them room to stand ready.

Lawrence leans into her ear. "I *will* convince you to be My Queen!"

She laughs and teases. "I thought I was!" She gives him a determined look with a smile behind pursed lips. "Keep dreaming, Ace, *keep dreaming...*"

"His Majesty, King Lawrence, and Her Royal Majesty, BriaLynn, The Princess Imperial."

They both have big smiles on their faces as they begin to walk through the doors. Lawrence quickly whispers, *"Bri, no one says 'no' to The King."* They continue to smile and nod as they pass by people, making their way to the dance floor.

"I didn't." She says and he raises an eyebrow. She matches his raised eyebrow saying, "I *encouraged* you to *keep dreaming!*"

He tightens his grip at her waist, giving her a sultry and more determined look. She sees him studying her, then he leans in and whispers in a low, monotoned voice, *"You're challenging me..."*

"AB*solutely!*" She says with a playful look.

"That can be a dangerous thing to do." He replies.

"Perhaps for *anyone else*, but not me..." she leans into his ear, *"and* we'll see if my theory is correct tonight!"

"And what *theory* might that be?" He emphasizes.

As they take their positions, she looks at him with a look she hasn't given him before; *very seductive.* "My theory is what I said to you before, that you love a challenge..." she leans in and whispers with her hot breath on his ear, *"in the bedroom."*

She feels his hand start to slide lower, but abruptly stops at her lower waist. The music starts with a waltz. She's always been able to keep up with a dance partner, even if they change or forget a step. However, with Lawrence it's different. Something about their chemistry has them dancing so smoothly, their dancing is effortless. Guests end up gathering around the edge of the dance floor and watch them fluidly glide around.

The music ends and the guests who have been watching applaud. Bri goes to step back so they can leave the dance floor and mingle with their guests, but Lawrence takes her hand and pulls her back to him.

"Whoa, whoa, whoa. Where do you think you're going?" He starts dancing another dance with her. "You need to explain that *theory*!" He kisses the hand he is holding, then he tucks their hands into his chest.

"It's just a theory..." She simply replies.

"Oh, but there's more, Darling." He tells her. "You think I like a challenge but I'd say you're wrong."

She raises her eyebrow. "Is that because *The King always gets his way*!" She says with his accent.

"Ooo, The Princess Imperial is now *mocking* The King!" He holds her closer, making her think she is onto something with her theory.

She fakes shock with her hand to her chest and says with feistiness, "*Am I?* I had no idea! Here I thought you were Lawrence."

 He leans in and they are both smiling as they kiss each other once more. He lifts his head and looks intensely into her eyes and it gets harder for Bri to breathe under his intense stare. She breaks it when she hugs him close. They dance cheek-to-cheek until the song ends.

She steps back and curtsies. "*Your Majesty.*" Then she walks away, trying to smile while keeping her hormones in check.

Bri sees David first. He sees her flushed and when he holds one cheek and kisses the other, he whispers, "*Is everything okay?*"

She smiles and quickly nods fanning herself. "Just flushed from dancing…"

David chuckles. "Herst couldn't be more tightly wound, Love!" She sees his eyes flick behind her and she knows Lawrence is there. David looks at her and says, "You may want to go easy on him tonight."

"What fun would that be?!" She smirks.

She sees a server and weaves through the crowd to grab a glass of their nonalcoholic champagne. Lawrence pats David's shoulder as he passes by him, following Bri. Lawrence comes up behind Bri as she takes a drink and he takes a glass from the tray for himself, kissing her shoulder.

Before she turns around, he whispers in her ear, *"I'm not sure if feisty, sassy, or snarky, are a good thing right now."*

"Depends." She turns to face him. "I think you're more frustrated when you don't get your way…" she leans close to his ear and his arm reflexively wraps around her waist, she runs her hand into his hair and he feels her hot breath on his ear again that much more when she is even closer, "also part of the fun of anticipation…" She hears him hold his breath, and he holds her waist firmer as she whispers things for only him to hear.

He struggles to whisper, *"Darling, driving me mad with desire now that we're finally official may not be the best idea."* She feels his hand slide down to her lower waist.

"Oh no, I think it's a great idea!" She happily grins. "In fact, I'm going to go dance with Jack with this next song and let all this simmer." She taps a very light kiss to his lips before she slips back into the crowd again to find Jack.

David comes up next to Herst who's pulling at his collar a little. David chuckles into a bit of a laugh after watching all that. "Bri is *absolutely* a lady and should be treated as such, *but make no mistake*, Herst, she *certainly* knows how to play a very private *and very sexy game*! I've said this before and I'll remind you again," he points in Bri's direction, *"it will all be worth it!"*

"Even if she makes it hard to breathe at times?!" Lawrence asks.

David quietly chuckles watching Lawrence slam down the rest of his champagne. "If you don't figure her out tonight, you will soon enough."

Lawrence studies her as they watch Jack and Bri dance around the dance floor. He notices how good they look out there. He snaps out of it some when they're approached by some important people who want to speak to The King.

David puts his finger up to the guests and politely asks, "One moment, please." One guest nods sharply once. David speaks to Lawrence barely above a whisper to be heard over the music, "The inside advice I can give you while respecting 'The Behind Closed Doors Rule' is to covertly, *and shamelessly*, flirt like she is and watch her *thrive* in it!" David pats his brother's shoulder. He thanks the people for waiting before he goes to talk to more of their guests.

In between groups of people, Lawrence finds his heart is being pulled to Bri. He has had women in his life, but none of them ever had 'power' over him like this! Dominique had a power over him with sex that he couldn't break, but she had married and moved to southern France less than a year ago, so that part of his life has been over with. He feels his connection to Bri is proving to have an even stronger hold on him...then again, his heart knows he is safe with her because she would *never* want to control him.

Jack had finished his dance and Bri is now dancing with James, while David is dancing with Amy. Jack comes up to Lawrence and leans in to say, "Looks like you're deep in thought, *King Lawrence!*" Jack surprised Lawrence who jumped a little. "Apologies, Brother."

Lawrence shakes his head as if it was no big deal. He goes on to ask, "Does Bri have this power over you, too?"

Jack looks at him for a moment, then follows his stare out to Bri. "Herst, that's not *power!*" Jack smiles. "It's your heart *knowing* where it wants to be!" Lawrence nods in agreement. "David and I feel the same way!"

They're interrupted by the Prime Minister and his wife when they walk up and all four engage in a lengthy conversation; others join in, including David. The topic shifts to Newhaven's Judicial System.

The Prime Minister's wife, Kelly, asks David in a snobby upper-class tone, "Just how is Newhaven adjusting to these...*changes?*" She is referring to how each district was set up like the rest of the country where the sheriff was the judge of non-major felonies and down through the lesser crimes. However, now it's a different sheriff hearing cases from a different district that is not their own, not even sharing borders. "I would think it'd be a complete disaster by now!" She gives a snooty laugh.

"*On the contrary!*" To everyone's surprise, they turn and see Bri standing there with Jack. She tells them, "Most of the complaints were of sheriffs favoring their own deputies, so when we shifted things around, that complaint doesn't hold much weight anymore."

"I'm sure *that* didn't go over well either." Kelly laughs but abruptly stops when no one else is laughing with her, not even her husband.

"Change typically doesn't 'go over well,' Mrs. Lowery. *However*, I've said, and *firmly* believe, that if everything is done legally, where reports are written correctly, and evidence can be presented accurately *and* honestly, it shouldn't matter if the sheriff hearing the case is from the same district or not. Should it?" She asks with a pointed look and a raised eyebrow.

"Interesting point, Your Royal Majesty."

She looks and sees Lawrence's Father, The King Father, tucked in the crowd that opens up for him and Bri to converse more easily. She slightly curtsies to him. Lawrence's jaw clenches as he shifts to wrap an arm around Bri with a more stiff, protective stance.

The King Father asks Bri, "Tell me, was the desired outcome reached?" Lawrence is studying his father closely, unsure of his father's meaning, nor his intentions by joining in the conversation.

"Our first priority was to cut down the complaints of people's accusations of favoritism, which, if we're being honest can happen anywhere, even the US." There were nods of agreement. "But now, we can focus on other complaints and see which ones really have merit. And if we're being truthful again, there's always going to be some legitimate ones; humans uphold the judicial system, not computerized robots."

"And what do you think of our prison system?" He simply asks.

With that question there is a knot twisting in the pit of her stomach and Lawrence goes to change the subject, but Bri squeezes his waist. They wonder if The Queen Mother has said something to him, or if maybe he was in on her attack.

"Well, Sir, I've only visited one *dungeon* in his country and no prisons yet, so I wouldn't want to insult the good people of the UK and make any comparisons using that as an example. This means I can only speak of the American prisons at this point in time, but there may be similarities here that you," she gestures their little crowd, "and some of you, would be able to compare knowing the prisons here as I'm sure some of you have dealt with for various issues over the years." The King Father and the others agree. "From the US standpoint, one of the biggest issues is overcrowding, which began after a 'war on drugs' was declared."

"You don't think they should've waged a war on drugs?" The King Father is genuinely curious about her thoughts.

"Not so much as 'waged war' because, let's face it, that 'war' was lost the moment it was declared." She replies. He nods absorbing that statement. "The laws arrest people who use, deal, and then the cartels are a whole different beast for a different day. As for using, throwing them in jail and/or *demanding* rehab isn't the answer."

"It's not?!" The Prime Minister asks with a bit of disgust.

Bri hears his wife, "Foolish woman. You can't be buying this nonsense, Your Majesties?!" Everyone looks to The King for his reaction.

To everyone's shock, it's The King Father who responds. "*Mrs. Lowry*! First, remember who you're talking to and talking about; second, I find this fascinating and I think the rumors to her intelligence are accurate and I, for one, would like to hear more." Inside, Bri is surprised, but she keeps her composure outwardly. Lawrence is still leery but his hold on Bri relaxes a bit. The King Father says, "Now, either *be quiet*, or kindly leave!" The woman backs down and takes a small step back.

Bri doesn't lose her matter-of-fact tone. "As I was saying," she looks at The King Father, "if someone forced you into rehab and you have no desire to quit at that point in your life, would you quit or would it be a waste of the taxpayers' money?" Mrs. Lowry's face actually looks a little defeated at this point. "Let me be clear: I'm all for providing rehab, counseling, and whatever services to anyone who *wants* to break free of that life—."

"Because *wanting to quit* is the key." Lawrence interjects as he listens to what she's saying.

"*Exactly.*" She winks and he gives her a hint of a smile. Jack and David notice Bri's charm is working on The King Father, but Lawrence still only sees red. Bri continues, "Americans have a right to drink themselves into an oblivion if they choose, but the law limits them to what they can do when they're intoxicated. For instance, they can't drive or operate equipment while inebriated. The laws prohibit driving and operating machinery while under the influence of illegal drugs, but also legal ones that would impair driving. To me, the answer is somewhere in helping users who not only want to get clean, but also find different avenues to deal with stress. Everyone has to have their own cathartic way of dealing with stress: most cathartic ways would be good like exercising, running, yoga, reading, music, and so on; and some are unhealthy like drugs, alcohol, but even sex can be addiction, and *any* addiction isn't healthy."

"Good points." The King Father simply states as he listens. He gives her a small smile. "Much like the goals for your foundation."

She is *briefly* surprised he knows about her work; however, it makes more sense he does. "I feel there has to be a way to provide counseling, rehab, and various services, while providing relocation and jobs with housing, to help get them back on their feet. Sure, governments can provide 'low income' anything, but whether it's the old adage, 'pull yourself up by your own bootstraps' or whatever; no adage is going to work unless people know there *has to be* hard work behind a significant change! There are lessons to be learned and applied, which may be difficult to learn, let alone apply! They'll also need to *commit* to *doing* some *extremely hard work*! Learning from our mistakes is humbling and many can't let go of their pride to truly move forward. I like the saying: 'You can feed someone a fish dinner, or you can teach them—."

"*How to fish!*" The King Father happily finishes.

Bri smiles and nods back. "The Newhaven Textile Mill hires people trying to get back on their feet; they work alongside a mentor, have a room in one of our housing buildings that isn't fancy, but it's not squalor conditions like halfway housing in the US has a reputation for. However, there is a housekeeping service run by law enforcement to help keep everyone open and honest."

Lawrence hears all of this and her intelligence gets more and more *remarkable*! He is so proud of her! "Sounds like you've thought about almost everything, Darling." He smiles adoringly at her.

Mrs. Lowry snorts, "Sounds like a lot of wasted taxpayer money for people bouncing in and out!"

"I figured a two-year commitment—."

"Good luck with that!" She laughs at the ridiculousness she thinks it is. "Criminals have no intentions on making an honest living, or they wouldn't *be in prison*!"

"It's that kind of close-mindedness that keeps them down!" Lawrence is quick to defend and is seriously thinking of a new Prime Minister with a more respectful wife! "There's a very small percentage in prison who really are innocent, just as there are *people* who would jump at an opportunity like Newhaven is providing for anyone wanting a fresh start," he looks at Bri, "a new beginning for a better life!"

Bri nods and continues. "Before you *rudely* interrupted me, Mrs. Lowery, I was about to explain the two years." Bri takes a small deep breath to stay calm and unemotional. "The two years considers that they really want to get and stay clean, but there is a higher chance for relapse in the first year. A two-year commitment means they would have time for a relapse and have a chance for a 'do-over' so-to-speak."

Mrs. Lowery asks with thick snobbery, "Why would anyone *want* to be hooked on drugs?"

Bri's face gives the woman a blank expression. "*Gee*, I don't know? Who would get hooked on prescription meds and wash them down with *a variety of spirits*?" She mocks her snobby accent. The woman's mouth gaped open then snaps shut as she sees everyone looking at her. She glares at Bri for exposing a well-kept secret almost everyone knew about. Bri stares with her eyebrow raised. "Prove me wrong! Open your clutch!"

Mrs. Lowry starts to reply, "I don't have to dignify that—."

The King Father grabs her clutch because he's curious to see for himself what's inside; he wants to know how accurate Bri is. "*Interesting...*"

Lawrence is looking over his father's shoulder, his curiosity getting the better of him. Lawrence asks Mrs. Lowery, "Since when do pharmaceuticals come in unlabeled, clear packets," he pulls out a couple bags holding them between two of his fingers adding, *"and in variety packs?"*

Mrs. Lowery snatches the bags of pills back with one hand and her clutch with the other, telling her husband, *"I've never been so insulted in all my life! We're leaving!"* She stomps off with her husband following her.

Bri's yawn catches her off guard and she apologizes to everyone. "This pregnancy has me so exhausted!"

"Would you excuse us please?" Lawrence says as he steps over with her to David. "I need to speak to a few people yet tonight. David, would you mind—."

Bri looks him straight in the eye. *"Your Majesty*, I can stay for a little while yet." She holds his gaze.

"Fine. David?" Lawrence asks. "Would you take this *Firecracker* and dance with her?"

David smiles, running a hand down her arm to her hand and takes it in his, "It would be my pleasure!"

They excuse themselves and David takes her to the dance floor. Lawrence hears comments of how impressed people were by Bri. Lawrence smiles in proudness and continues to mingle with various people he needs to make a point to talk to.

David wraps Bri in his arms and holds her close. She gets lost in dancing with him, as it should be no matter which one she is dancing with.

Closer to the end she whispers, *"You look so very GQ sexy this evening, My Love!"* He chuckles and she kisses his neck.

David smiles shaking his head. "I think the truly sexy one here is *you!*" He looks at her and adds, "I love you, Macushla!"

"I love *you*, My Love!" She kisses him sweetly. "I should dance another dance with Jack and Lawrence; if I can make it, I'll leave with Lawrence."

"Let me go get one of them; wait here." David says and kisses her cheek before he winds his way to whoever he sees first...

The King Father comes up to Bri. "May I have this dance, Your Royal Majesty?" He bows to her. Bri places her hand in his and they do an easier waltz together. "Princess——."

"Please. We're family." She smiles compassionately sensing things aren't as they seem with him. "Call me, Bri." The look in his eyes is of deep sadness and her heart twists in empathy...*for his regret?*

"I don't know how much my son has confided in you and I wouldn't ask you to talk about it..." He takes a nervous breath. "I was wondering if you thought there was a chance for me to——."

"Father." Lawrence interrupts coldly.

His father nods and kisses Bri's cheek and whispers, "*Another time, maybe?*"

Bri smiles and nods a little, it looks like a polite nod so Lawrence doesn't even know he said anything other than a version of 'Thank you.' She sadly watches him disappear. Lawrence wraps his arm around her, but he feels her stiffening up.

She looks at him, but before she can say anything, he simply says, "*No, Bri. Let it go.*" She sees him clench his jaw.

She whispers, "*He asked me to dance. What was I supposed to say?!*"

He answers in a loud whisper. "*NO!*"

She is a bit taken back. "I can't say 'no' to *The King Father*, Lawrence."

"*Yes, you can, Bri!* You *have more power than he does!*" He whispers back. They smile as they argue quietly.

"*Lawrence Alexander Heathherst,*" she angrily whispers, "*this has nothing to do with 'power!' I refuse to be disrespectful——.*"

"*For me!*" He angrily whispers, but those close to them hear him and Bri goes to step back, but he holds her firmer. He looks apologetically into her eyes and he says, "I'm sorry, Darling, that was uncalled for."

She has a small smile. "The tone was, but perhaps not the words." He sees her smile now has a touch of reluctance. Then she turns and looks the direction his father left. "Lawrence, I feel there's something...ugh, I can't explain it."

"Look, right here and now," he nuzzles close to her again, whispering, "*I just want to think about us...*" he kisses down her neck... "*and you...*" he runs his lips back up her neck giving her goosebumps. When he whispers right into her ear, his hot breath makes her shiver again, "*Finally, naked in my arms...*"

She quietly whispers back, "*How long are you going to torture me?*"

She can feel his arm hug her waist and he smiles against her neck. "*A little longer.*" He whispers before placing a kiss just below her ear.

"I love you, Ace..." She pulls back with teary eyes.

He smiles compassionately back at her. "I love you, My Queen." He tucks some hair behind her ear. "More than I could ever express in words..."

She pulls him into another kiss. He deepens it...then he rests his forehead to hers. Another yawn catches her off guard. Jack and David walk up when the song ends and offer to take her upstairs.

"Thank you, Jack." Lawrence says. Bri goes to argue, but Lawrence tells her, "I'll be up shortly."

She studies him and senses there's something more. She softly, but sternly, says so only he, Jack, and David hear, "To keep the mood right, *stay away from your father!*" He is surprised when he hears that and sees her seriousness. "I mean it, Lawrence Alexander! Or the fireworks *will be cancelled because of a raging storm!*" She threatens, and he nods, but he has every intention of telling his father to stay away from Bri! He will just have to be more covert about it. He kisses her temple before they all part ways.

David takes her hand and turns to her. "I think it's time we taught you the secret way out of here, if Jack hasn't already." He looks at Jack.

Her eyebrows scrunch together. "He hasn't." She lightly teases, "You two have been holding out on me!" She looks from Jack to David and grins.

"*Never!*" David teases back. "Just an oversight."

They both walk with Bri to a corner where David opens a stone wall door and they slip through. "You realize *that's* the coolest door of all time, right?! Whoever made that door was a *genius!* No seams and right next to a door used mostly by staff!" She is trying not to whisper too loudly, as she inspects the door more closely.

David chuckles and gently tugs on her hand so they can walk down the corridor. "Well, this just takes us to the main hall."

"Seriously?! A great door like that shouldn't be *wasted!* It should lead to a secret room! Ooo! A secret room in *between rooms*—or floors!" She excitedly suggests and they're laughing. She turns and sees a lit hallway. "Are the lights always on?"

"During parties, yes, so the family can come and go, like when our beautiful pregnant *princess* needs to rest." David winks and she grins.

Jack laughs lightly, then points to the top of the wall. "If you look closely, you'll see small windows up there where a stone would go."

"Ah, so during the day and a brighter moon there would be natural light."

"Brains and beauty are *always* a sexy combination!" David smirks.

She teases with a matching look, "Careful, *Mister* Worthington, or all this flattery might go to my head!"

"Good!" He opens the door and she sees the main staircase. "It's very true!" Jack closes the door and then takes her other hand and they go to the elevator. They're taking her to their new quarters on the top floor.

She didn't see the button he pushed, but when she steps off and looks around, she says, "We're not on the right floor..."

"I hope you forgive me, but I wanted to surprise you." David smiles.

"You may have succeeded, but I *thiiink* I need to see more to be sure..." she encourages them.

"I haven't been up here after it was finished." Jack tells her. "But what I saw prior was fantastic! And knowing David, it's been updated and now fit for the gorgeous royal living with us!" He winks at Bri.

David smiles and walks around showing Bri and Jack. "There are two quarters, on opposite sides of the floor."

"Ah, so The Noble Consort would be on the same floor." Bri comments.

"Right." He points down the hallway, "That's the one closest to our quarters now and the other is way fancier. I thought you'd like to keep the similarity with our quarters—."

"I would!" She smiles in agreement.

"Good! Because I've already had the fancier one prepared to be His Majesty's and Her Royal Majesty's quarters. I have another quarters being worked on for Jack when he stays here." He grins, happily walking into 'The Royal Quarters' with them.

"Why so fancy?" She asks, looking around the room.

"This is actually the room for The Grand Duke and The Grand Duchess. However," David explains, "it was closed off when it was assumed Newhaven lost its sovereign status with all the other duchies. We opened it back up because Mother thought it would be nice for The King to stay in with The Royal Consort when he visits, *and* it would be easier for you to have us all together on the same floor every so often. Although, with The Princess Imperial living here is reason enough for opening this all back up, it's even more appropriate given we are a sovereign duchy once again, er still."

"Well, it is more convenient to have everyone on one floor." She smiles.

"Plus, there are bedrooms to accommodate a handful of children and even a few nannies! Emmie and Natty have their rooms already picked out and Mother is working with them to decorate them and make them their own. There's a common living room, too, with a hidden small refrigerator, microwave, sink, counter, and a couple cabinets."

"David! I love this!" Bri happily smiles. "Can I see our—."

"*If you'll permit me*, I'd like to wait until you get back. It's *almost* perfect, plus, I don't want to stay in it until *we* can first stay in it together."

"That's a fantastic idea!" She kisses him tenderly and smiles. "It reminds me of the night before our wedding when you insisted I stay at The Manor." He kisses her again, before taking her back to her quarters with Lawrence. As she looks around this time, she notes, "This seems so fresh and light, yet the gold and blue make it so royal!"

"Well, we can change quarters—."

"No! *Not a chance!* My nostalgia for our quarters wouldn't let me!" She says.

"Well, lucky for you, everything from down there will be brought up here." He has a grin. "If I secretly got you in the new quarters, you might not have caught the switch right away."

"I'm glad!" She tells him. "Thank you for bringing me up here and for doing all of this for *our family!*" She gestures the floor.

"Of course!" David smiles. "Jack and I are heading to The Inn with James. The guys are having one last party before James' wedding and he asked if we'd help keep an eye on things." Bri nods.

Jack steps closer and holds her face. "I love you, Amore Mia!"

She smiles sweetly. "*I love you*, Amore Mio!" He quickly kisses and hugs her, then steps back.

David sits down on the coffee table. He caresses her face with a soft smile on his face. "I'm going to say something to you that I don't want a cheeky answer...in fact, I don't want you to answer at all."

She exhales, "*Fine.*" He gives her a 'come on now' look. "Alright, I promise." She kisses the palm of his hand that is caressing her face.

He takes her hand and looks at her so lovingly. "Bri, can you blame Herst for wanting you by his side as 'The Queen?' You are brilliant, intelligent, clever, insightful, and you keep us on our toes! Life with you is *never* dull! We feel more successful with you in our corner, but more so with you *by our side.* Before I met you, I had the weight of Newhaven looming over me on top of already being CEO! I meant what I said before, with you this doesn't feel so overwhelming, because we're *partners*, side-by-side. Aren't you the one who says love is empowering?" He kisses her hand, then rubs his thumb across it.

"True." She admits.

"Think about that, alright?" He asks and she nods. He gives her a small smile, "Well, I'm leaving before everyone leaves for The Inn without us."

"Right. The pre-bachelor party..." She hugs David. "I love you, My Love!"

"I love you, Macushla!" He kisses her once more. She lays on the couch as he tells her, "We'll let Lawrence know we've come back down and Mitchell is out in the common living room."

She exhales in relief as he covers her with a blanket. They kiss once more before David leaves. Her eyelids are heavy and she closes them, dozing off for a while.

CHAPTER 47

Imperfectly & Royally Perfect Night

Bri had dozed off and wakes to light tapping on the door. She is groggy and struggles to say, "*Just a second...*" She sits up and carefully rubs around her eyes, thinking she should have washed her face. She walks to the door expecting Lawrence, but she needs to be sure. "Who is it?"

"Lawrence." He says with a super sexy low voice.

"I'm not ready!" She looks down at her dress. "I need to go change."

"It's okay." He tells her. "Just let me in, Darling." She opens the door with a smile. Lawrence steps inside and grabs her in a passionate kiss.

When they pull apart, she tastes her lips. "What is that? Scotch? Brandy?"

He captures her lips again, pushing her up against the wall. Her hands slap the wall to brace herself. He gives her a smoldering look as he pins her there. He holds eye contact as he untucks his shirt, saying, "I can assure you, Darling, I'm not drunk!" He gets a playful look. "Now," he takes off his cufflinks, "I know you like my smile, especially with the dimples..." he slips the cufflinks in his pocket, "*and my theory is...*" he runs his finger down her neck and he hears her hold her breath, "you'll find me irresistible when I take off my shirt again..." she bites a little bit of her lower lip as she recalls the first time seeing his bare chest was at the beach.

She feels his smoldering look melting every ounce of her resolve. He grips his shirt and yanks it open, popping all the buttons off his shirt. He hears her exhaling, as he slightly bends to take her hands and placing them on his bare chest and he slides his other hand around the back of her neck, lightly pulling her hair to tip her head back.

He leans in and ghosts her lips with his. "If you're not wanting to do this tonight, tell me now, My Queen..."

She can barely think to breath, but manages to say, "I just want to put something special on for you."

He still has his hand tangled in her hair and runs his finger down her lips, chin, and neck... "Not necessary...it'll just get in the way." He runs his lips along hers. "I do need to issue a word of warning..." he then lightly runs his lips along her jaw back to her ear, "I want you so much right now, my desire for you *will* take over, so slow and sweet won't happen *unless* you say so right now..." She raises her eyebrow and she is about to say something snarky, but he rests his forefinger to her lips. "*Oh, no!*" He taps. "Outside the bedroom you can challenge me all you like..." he slides his hand around to her bum, "*but...*" he tugs and she exhales with more desire in her eyes, "...in here, *you're mine...*" She leans in for a kiss, but he pulls back with a grin, "Not yet." He takes a step back. "You're wearing *far* too many clothes..." She raises her eyebrow again and he holds her gaze as much as he can as he helps her take off her dress.

Lawrence scoops her up and they stare into each other's eyes as he takes her over to the bed. He lays her down and takes off his shirt, then crawls up on the bed and straddles her. He puts her wrists together and takes his tie from neck, but when she figures out what he is about to do, she gets scared and jerks her hands away. He realizes she is thinking of her assault. He caresses her face and with the desire in his eyes, there is added compassion for her. He takes her hands and kisses the outside of her wrists.

He whispers, "*I need you to trust me, Darling...*"

She hesitates a little, but if her theory is right then the powerplay he needs in the bedroom will require her to surrender to him...*completely*. She slowly puts her wrists back together for him to wrap his tie around. He only ties them snug, not tight, so if she really wanted to free them, she could.

He lifts them to the headboard and tells her with a low voice, "Hold on and don't let go until I tell you to." He pulls back and looks her in the eyes as he runs the back of his fingers down her arm; she strains to exhale. She watches his lips get closer to hers until he passionately kisses her...

Lawrence holds her firmly in a hug as she relaxes, tucked under his arm. He goes to relax his hold, but Bri says with a breathy whisper, "*Just hold me tight for a little longer?*"

"As long as you need..." He kisses her forehead.

There was this deep connection forming with Lawrence that she didn't quite understand and he feels it, too. He lightly kisses her face a few times before kissing her passionately again. "*You're* incredible!"

She looks up at him laughing. "Ha-ha! *Me?!* My hands were *actually tied!*"

"If you weren't appreciating my efforts, then it wouldn't have been so fun!" He grins handsomely.

She smirks. "I doubt too many men have the stamina you do!"

"Stamina is huge, but what keeps me going is you, *My Queen!*"

"Let's just agree this was fantastic!" She captures his lips this time. They kiss for a couple minutes before it becomes more. She laughs, "See! Stamina is *incredibly sexy!*"

"Shhh..." He covers her lips with his.

That morning, she partially wakes to a freshly showered Lawrence snuggling in with her. It was barely morning, still dark enough to fall back asleep. When she does wake for the day, Lawrence is sleeping on his front.

She sits up and straddles his back, massaging her hands around his back and feeling his toned ridges. She looks up and watches the side of his mouth curve up into a smile. She kisses around his back so tenderly, he feels her love for him to his core.

She leans down. "Good morning, My Sexy King!" She kisses his shoulder, then kisses up to his ear. She whispers, "*I love you so much, Lawrence, my heart is* overflowing *with love* for you!" It surprises him how much it touches his heart to hear her say that.

She lays down on his back, running her hands under him, up the front of his shoulders and around the top to hug him. He takes a deep breath, exhaling slowly so he can talk.

"He wasn't there for us, Bri! The thought of him taking advantage of your compassionate heart..." He trails off and then struggles to say through his emotions, "*He let* my mother do *horrible things* to us *and for what?!*"

She softly asks, "He never said or did *anything about it?*"

"No, not really..." he swallows. "When I stabbed my great-uncle, he kept it quiet and covered it all up. We were to 'never speak of it again.' When I was getting my uniform fitted for the wedding to Genevieve, he saw my back and asked about it. He at least had the decency to be appalled when I told him some of what happened to me."

"Do you think maybe he never knew?" She asks.

"*I think he buried his head in the sand!*" He says with annoyance towards his father.

"Yeah, I know what that part is like." Thinking about her own parents. She has their son come to mind and recalls him saying Lawrence's scars are significant. "What happened *after* you told him? Did he do anything?" She was also curious because of how his father seemed last night...she could feel his regret, his remorsefulness...

"He sent me to California, to undergo plastic surgery. When I got back, I found out that my wedding was also to be my coronation; my parents were stepping down."

"Wow! *Wait.*" It just occurs to her. "I thought to step down a monarch actually had to abdicate the throne?"

Lawrence turns, as Bri slides over next to him. He explains, "Some monarchies have the 'until death' rule, but what we have is a little different. One could definitely rule until they died, which most of my ancestors did. What has been rarely done in this family's long line of monarchs, if ever, is stepping down like what Newhaven has done for a few generations now. Newhaven's transition seems to go much more smoothly when the retiring Duke and Duchess step down with The Heir and wife stepping into those roles and duties; the previous ones still around to help with the transition. My father wanted to exercise that for the first time; 'to admit defeat,' but that's all he said. It wasn't much of an apology?"

"No, Lawrence, it wasn't." She gives him a small, understanding smile. She comments, "I *never* would've thought The Queen Mother would agree to step down! I would've figured she was going to stay in that role until her last dying breath!" She rolls her eyes. Lawrence snorts a little chuckle and nods.

"She wasn't regnant, so she didn't have a choice. Especially, if Father signed the paperwork before Mother ever found out." He says.

She looks at him. "Didn't you wonder *why* your father did that? He had an easy *twenty* to thirty years before someone would think of retiring, *if at all!* Back up a second, you mentioned he said something about 'admitting defeat.' *What do you suppose he meant by that?*"

He scoffs. "That I didn't amount to the 'King Lawrence' they'd hoped I'd be. Doesn't really matter I guess..."

"Doesn't it?!" She replies.

"Bri, can we just drop this? *Please.*"

"*If* you let me throw something out there for you to think about..."

"Will I like it?" He suspiciously asks.

"No." She honestly tells him, but her face has so much genuine love he struggles to hold his determination not to let her say anything more.

"Nnn–ugh." He exhales with a bit of frustration. "I can't deny you anything...*fine*, but we drop this right after?"

"For a while, at least." She gives him a beautiful smile. "*At least* until after our honeymoon, *maybe* longer, but that's all I can promise."

He gives her a faint smile. "What words of wisdom do you have for me?"

"Part of my power is that I can empathize deeply, which is why I can see visions—."

"Like *my* so-called 'lessons' you could see *and feel* that day on the couch?!"

"Yes. When your father came and asked me to dance, I could sense *a lot* of remorse, sadness with regret...Lawrence, I *wish* I had more answers for you. As a parent, there are things that happen when we raise our kids that our kids one day learn wasn't the full picture at all, because they were looking at things through the limited view of a child's, *or a teenager's*, perception."

"True, but I'm not a child anymore." He says.

"Right." She replies. "*But* your memories, and your understanding of those memories, are from your limited childhood view. Plus, you don't know what you don't know, so you won't have an adult perspective until you talk with your father."

"That's *never* going to happen!" He says a little snippy.

She gives him a little smile and drops that piece. "Ace, all we can do is never allow anyone to hurt our family." She says.

He studies her face for a good minute before asking, "Why won't you at least *think about* becoming my queen?"

"*Think about?* That I already do almost all the time! But no. *You* want me to jump in *head-first* without any kind of plan! You *just* made me 'Princess Imperial' and I'm addressed with "Your Royal Majesty!' That's *pretty darn close* already!"

"*I don't want close, Bri!* I want you to officially be *THE* Queen! A lot of women would give anything to be in y—."

"*DON'T* finish that sentence, Lawrence Alexander Heathherst! I'm not like all those stuck up—." She's cut off when he kisses her. She breaks it, "UGH," and gets up, wrapping the sheet around herself. "Did David and Jack talk to you about that!"

"About what?" He innocently asks.

She turns to him and studies him for a moment. "Kissing me to stop me from finishing a sentence! They do it a lot *and it gets aggravating!*"

"It must work, or they wouldn't keep doing it!" He smirks.

She glares. "It can be infuriating!"

"Only because we stopped too soon!"

"No." She tells him. "We're not done with what I was saying and you're changing the direction of the conversation!"

"Look!" He stands up. "He goes around playing 'Great King Philip' and for what?! *I* know better! My brother and sister *know* better!"

"So, what you're saying is there's no finding out *the whole story* before you write him off? Don't you owe it to—."

"*Careful*, you're sounding like you're giving orders to The King."

"Oh, my apologies, *Your Majesty*!" She says it the way that makes him cringe.

"*Don't say it like that*!" He tells her. She rolls her eyes and he sees it. "Why do you *always* roll your eyes?!"

"I'm an eye roller, but I don't *always* roll my eyes! However, you've managed to bring it out, *splendidly*!" She mocks his accent. "You say you want me as your equal, but then take it back with a warning of giving you, *The King*, orders! How hypocritical is that?! You say you want me to be The Queen, only to take it back when I challenge the so-called 'K—.'"

"You're right." He apologetically says. "I *am* contradicting myself. In my defense, you're the only one who *can* challenge me, even if I don't like what I hear. If you become 'The Queen'—." Her eyes go wide as she holds her breath. "Seriously, why are you fighting this?! Even *our son* wants it!"

"I'm upset because it feels like you're pushing me to get what *you want*! Like some spoiled rich kid!" She snaps back. "The more you push, the more I *will* push back, digging my heels in if I have to! *I don't want to be this way*!" He has a surprised look. "But if I were to agree to become queen, wouldn't you want me to do it because I want to do it out of my love for you and not because you pushed me into it?"

His mouth had dropped open...then he quietly agrees, "You're right again."

"Look Lawrence, I think you'll become one of the really great kings, but we *have to* get you past this demanding what you want because you're 'The King' *rubbish*! There's a time and place for that stance, but it'll *never* be with me!"

"Oh, I think there will be times it will be with you!" He gives her a determined look that actually makes her take a step back.

He sees her trying to think, so he uses it to take a step forward, she steps back again. When he takes a third step, she has her backside to the back of the couch, and he's standing face-to-face with her. She goes to say something, but he kisses her so passionately her mind goes completely blank. It takes her ten to fifteen *solid seconds* before her arms wrap around him, holding him so tightly, there was a need driving her to be as close to him as possible. He holds the back of her head, kissing her more fiercely.

He kisses her jaw line, back to her ear and whispers, *"Your feistiness makes me want to..."* She gasps in his ear when she hears the rest of that sentence. He runs his hands down her arms, taking her hands in his, wrapping them behind her, and ghosting her lips as he smiles.

She says with exasperation, "You're torturing me *and you're smiling about it?*!"

"It's not what you think, Darling..." She hears him straining to control himself. "I love you! I'm enjoying this, us, and *finally* being intimately together. I want to enjoy some of them by taking my time with you...maybe we should wait until we get to our getaway..."

*"Careful...*that could cause me to retaliate by making *you* wait!" She warns.

"How do you figure?" He kisses her shoulder.

"I can up my game and hold out longer than you; however, with these hormones, I may have to go to The Inn!"

"Oh, I don't think so!" He says with an authority that surprises her.

"Then work your magic!" She tells him and he sees she's only teasing about The Inn.

"I only serve My Queen..." he retorts. When he sees a pinch of anger in her eyes and he says, "What I mean is my *magic,* as you say, is *only* for you, *My Queen,* The Queen of *My* Heart!"

She gives him a look with her challenge to him, *"Prove it!"*

He gives her a determined look, studying her a second before he takes on her challenge...

"That was..." she holds his cheek as he kisses her cheek, wrapping his arms firmly around her.

"*Amazing!*" He finishes her thought. "I'm not complaining, I'm only curious, why do you like being held so tight afterwards?"

She looks into his eyes and softly says, "It's only with you." She gives a shy little smile. "I can't really explain it...I feel so much, so many things from you and for you...being held tight in your arms is comforting...soothing..."

He swallows hard as the weight of what she said pierces his heart. He can barely whisper, "*I love you so much, Bri.*" He lifts her chin. "I want to look into your beautiful face when I apologize to you."

She raises her eyebrow with a little smirk. "For what? Have you changed your mind about me officially becoming 'The Queen?'"

"*Never!*" He holds her closer yet and says directly in her ear and he feels her shiver. "And I *will* get what I want, Bri." He kisses just below her ear, but she feels him smile against her neck. "I *always* do!"

"Do you plan to force my hand?" She quietly asks.

"No." He states, then adds, "I plan on weakening your determination!" He kisses her before she can say anything.

She looks up at him and her eyes have tears, his heart sinks. "I'll do it if you insist, because I love y—." She chokes up. "*I'm* not saying 'no' to be difficult, Lawrence. It's just that, right now..."

"I'll take it! A 'not yet' is a lot better than a 'no,' or a 'never.'" He tells her and she gives him a small, grateful smile. He adds, "I agree to discussing this later, but I can't guarantee waiting until after this baby is born before we discuss it again."

"Thank you for your honesty." She tells him.

"One more important thing." He gets a determined, sexy alpha-male look. "*For the record*, you going to David or Jack would *not* be okay with me! *Ever.* I'm so in-love with you that if you would've done that, I would have felt..."

"Betrayed?"

"That's not entirely fair—." He starts to say.

485

"Oh, Lawrence, yes, it's fair! And I swear I wasn't actually going to. I like to keep those 'fun times' with the one I'm with! I hope that made sense?" He nods. "I feel these pregnancy hormones are revving things up, so it may prove to be a juggling act..."

"I can understand that and, since you like to keep a line drawn with the one you're with, I'll trust you'll do your best with the hormones." He gives her a playful smile. "Keep in mind there are *a lot* of secret passageways I can use if you need me!"

She lightly giggles. "I love you, Lawrence!"

"I love you, too!" He kisses her. "Let's get ready! Our 'honeymoon' awaits!" He takes a couple steps and turns back to her. "We have a long flight ahead of us, so I asked if your things could be packed yesterday." He tips his head to the suitcases.

"How? I mean with everything that's happened?" She asks.

"McMasters wants me to assure you that the private island is small and easier to protect."

"A small island?"

"A resort owns it." He smiles saying, "Courtesy of David making the arrangements for us, with McMasters' and Mitchell's help!"

"You think you're going to keep this all quiet?" She wonders about the press.

"I'm doing my best!" He answers. "I want *you* all to myself!"

She lovingly smiles. "I'm *always* game for spending time with you!"

"Even when you're mad at me?" Lawrence asks.

She looks like she is thinking, tapping her chin with her finger. "*Weeell...*" He kisses her so fiercely; he has to catch her when her knees give out. She giggles and looks up at him. "Lawrence, just because I'm mad, hurt, or whatever, doesn't mean my love stops."

That also touches his heart and he rests his forehead to hers. He closes his eyes, focusing on getting control over his feelings. They eventually go and get ready for the day. Since this is Bri's first time out as The Princess Imperial, she's not sure what to wear.

Lawrence comes up behind her and says, "Remember, it's a long flight and you should wear what's comfortable. You don't have to worry about being hounded by photographers."

They will have breakfast with the family before they leave.

CHAPTER 48

Imperfectly Perfect & Royally Paradise

It was indeed a long flight, but The Royal Jet cuts a lot of time down. They flew into an airport, which Bri didn't know was in Hawaii, but she could see it was paradise! They took a helicopter to an exclusive island and Lawrence points to it out the helicopter window.

"This is it?!" She asks with a big smile.

"It is!" He is thrilled she is excited. "It's a bungalow, well, kind of a multi-level or multi-sectional bungalow. "Do you like it?" He asks. She sees it all sits on what seems like shallow water, but the depth of it, with the clearness of the water, would be deceiving.

"This is fantastic!" She looks down. "Wait. *Is that a pool?*" She giggles. "This all sits on the ocean, you crazy man!"

"You said you had a deathly fear of water you couldn't touch the bottom in. The saltwater swimming pool has a glass bottom to feel like you're in the ocean but have the safety of a pool." He explains.

She lovingly looks at him with just a hint of tears. "I just fell in-love with you once again! You not only remembered my stupid fear, but you planned around it!" She shifts and kisses him fiercely. When they pull apart, she adds, "The bonus with the water being that clear is we can hopefully see the sharks before they see us!"

He chuckles. "Let's just hope we don't see any!" She smiles as she nods in agreement.

When they land, the helipad is on a building that has accommodations for the staff and their security detail to stay. It isn't far from the bungalow and McMasters and Mitchell have tried to make their stay as private as possible. They ride in a Jeep for about ten minutes before they pull up to the main bungalow section.

 They walk inside and Bri sees a vase of rainbow roses. "Lawrence, I'd ask you to stop spoiling me with these if I didn't love them so much!" She smiles and smells them. He tends to always have a fresh vase of them in her bedroom at The Palace.

"I have another gift that can't wait!" He says and she scrunches her eyebrows together. "You're going to need to close your eyes..." She sweetly smiles as she closes them. He sees a woman holding something black outside and he waves her inside. He has her stand right in front of Bri. "Now, open!"

 Bri's eyes open and an excited look comes across her face when she sees a tiny baby black Schnauzer with a pink bow. "Oh my gosh, Lawrence! She has to be the sweetest puppy ever!" She looks at Lawrence. "Does this cute baby have a name?!"

He chuckles. "That's for you to decide, Darling! I wanted her to be as small as possible, so she can travel easily with you!"

Bri giggles. "She's travel sized?!"

He laughs saying, "Precisely!"

The woman hands the puppy to Bri. "And extra cute so no one will mind taking care of her when needed." She realizes she spoke to them casually, which is a royalty no-no without permission, and has a panicked look.

Bri puts her hand on the top of the woman's forearm and glances at her name tag. "Terry, I appreciate your insight, because there will be lots of times she would have to be left in the care of others. I'm thinking The Manor may be difficult with her smallness and its bigness to get outside in time; we may have to rethink things." She thanks Terry once again. Terry smiles and slightly curtsies before leaving. Bri looks at Lawrence. "This puppy is wonderful, Lawrence! Where did you get—*wait a second*...how did you know? I don't recall a conversation about dogs, let alone breeds because I don't remember your favorite?"

"Well, while McMasters and Mitchell were busy at The Palace reorganizing and cleaning things out, they came across my mother's stash of files. They found a file my mother had started on you," Bri rolls her eyes, "that looked like it was started when your bloodline was discovered." Lawrence laughs humorlessly. "McMasters thinks it's clever she found out your favorite breed

489

of dog is mini-Schnauzers. I had asked something like 'Is that even true?' McMasters confirmed it, but said you actually would love the smaller, 'toy sized' one the next time you'd ever have another dog. I tucked it away up here," he points to his head, "and remembered it when I wanted to make this trip memorable."

"Lawrence this trip is already *unforgettable* just in the fact this is a private island *and* I get you *all* to myself!" She tells him and he chuckles. "The roses and now her, are just the fabulous 'sprinkles on top!'" Bri nuzzles the puppy and kisses her soft furry head.

"McMasters suggested a carrier after remembering something you once said about crate training when you two had a discussion on K9 units."

"Other people may have more successful ways but for me I've had good luck crate training. He was talking about a K9 officer he knew that did the same thing with crates. This sweet girl would only need a mini-sized pet carrier to do the same thing as the crate. Plus, we can use it to keep track of her!"

"She's so small, I thought even the small crate looked too big so we did settle on a pet carrier." He looks at Bri and asks, "What *is* her name going to be?" He smiles petting the puppy's soft head with his finger.

Bri holds her up and looks at her face. "What *should* we call you? Something associated with black like Ebony, Starlight, or Twilight?" She says to the puppy, but says, "None of those seem right..." She holds the puppy close again and looks at Lawrence. "Do you have your phone handy?"

"I do." He pulls it out.

"Would you look up flowers native to...wherever we are?" She asks as she looks around for a clue.

He chuckles as he realizes he never told her. He tells her as he types, "Flowers native to *Hawaii?*"

"Aaahhh, I was hoping so!" She has a big smile and sparkles in her eyes. "After all this, I'd be surprised if you didn't remember we talked about Hawaii when you remembered so many other details about me, *and us!*" She taps a kiss to his lips.

He smiles and then reads the list. He gets to one and says, "Jasmine..."

"Hmm...Jazz or Jazzy for short..." she ponders it. "*Maaybe...*"

"Let's try some more Hawaiian sounding girl names..." He says. "How about Nani for beautiful? Better yet, how about Kala?!"

"What does Kala mean?"

He smiles with a twinkle in his eye. "Princess."

"While I'd never name anything, human or animal, straight up 'princess,' I do like 'Kala,' but I want to wait a little bit to see her personality."

"I think that's a good idea." Lawrence says, petting the puppy's head.

Bri walks around as everyone busies themselves and Lawrence answers questions. When they're alone again, he finds her on a mattress in a cabana on one section of the dock looking out onto the ocean. He goes up to the opposite side, setting a pet carrier on the bed and crawls in next to Bri; the puppy is curled up in her lap.

"Hi, Beautiful! This does look like the *perfect* spot." He sits next to her and kisses her.

Bri leans over and opens the pet carrier. She sees a little bed and pillow, a little food dish and a mini water bottle attached to the door. The puppy sees the door open and goes in on her own.

"Kennel Up!" Bri tells her. "Good girl!" The puppy curls up on her bed and exhales deeply, she's content. "You like your bed?" She feels it and it's made of super soft material. "I would, too!"

Bri pets her before she closes the door. Lawrence pulls the door to make sure it's secure before he sets it down next to the bed for now. Then he smiles as he gets closer to her and kisses her passionately, slowly laying down with her. She feels his hands moving around her body and she breaks the kiss.

"Lawrence! We're out in the open!" She whispers loudly, looking around.

"No one's even here to see us!" He gestures.

"That's what you think! You said McMasters made this as private *as possible*, but not completely; he *can't*! Plus, who's inside?" She points to the bungalow.

"All there is to see is ocean and waaay out there are security boats perfectly spaced apart."

She has sass, "*Riiight*! You know, there's these little inventions called, oh I don't know, *binoculars*! Then there are these special lenses invented for cameras the paparazzi use!"

"Do you think McMasters would tolerate the guards looking inward when they need to watch the perimeter? Besides," he gets a smoldering smirk on his face and rolls on top of her, "I'll cover you!" She laughs as he barely touches her lips with his. He can see the worried look on her face, so gets up and pulls the darker screens down and unfolds a sheet. "Better?"

"Much!" She giggles some more as he crawls back up to her.

They kiss each other more passionately than ever and when he puts her arms above her head, he tells her, "Nothing to hold onto, so you'll have to keep them there..."

"What if I don't want to keep my hands to myself?!" She raises her eyebrow.

He grins. "That's *exactly* why I want you to!"

She also knows it's a way for him to know he's in control. He ghosts her lips with his again, purposely breathing more on her lips. He traces his finger on her lips before kissing them again.

They lay in each other's arms; Bri's head is on Lawrence's chest. She feels Lawrence kiss her head. "I love you, My Queen."

She lifts her head. "That's good because I love you, Ace!" She smiles and kisses him, then lays her head back down and watches the ocean.

She had fallen asleep and wakes up seeing the kennel on the bed. She watches the puppy sleep, but when Bri moves to rub her eyes and wake up, the puppy's head pops up and watches her. Lawrence comes back with smoothies for them and a refill in the puppy's water bottle. She sits up on the edge of the bed with her hand on the handle of the carrier.

"Where are you going, Darling?" He asks her.

"To take her to potty. Training her means anytime she wakes up, after playtime, or after she eats, she goes potty...although now I'm realizing how difficult taking her outside is going to be..."

Smiling sweetly at her, he explains, "Bri, I had considered that before getting her for you. We'll take her to the entrance, but one of the guards will always take her. Our staff and yours in Newhaven are willing to take a break with her; David and Jack made sure of that for me. As of right now, she just went a few minutes ago." He informs her. "I just went back quick for the water and the smoothies were ready, so I brought them, too."

"Thank you." She smiles sweetly. "Although, it doesn't seem fair." Bri notes. "They're security, not dog walkers!"

"True! Here, on the island, I doubt they mind a little distraction from boring." He winks. "She's so tiny, Bri, her exercise will be more than taken care of being played with and running around The Cottage House, your quarters at The Manor, or The Royal Apartment." He pulls her out of the kennel and holds her next to his face. "See this cute face?"

She giggles saying, "I see two!"

He lightly laughs. "Well, this sweet one will have no problem with volunteers taking her for whatever reason."

She smiles and takes the puppy who's becoming more relaxed with them. Lawrence plays tug-of-war with one of her toys with her, while he and Bri drink their smoothies. Then they walk together with the puppy to the bungalow's entrance where Mitchell is waiting.

"Ah! So, you're volunteering, huh?" She raises her eyebrow. "Self-proclaimed 'Mister Chocolate Beefcake' is taking care of a pint-sized girly dog?"

"Hey now," he teases taking the puppy, "this little '*half pint* girly dog' looks good with my manly muscles!" He flexes a little and Bri laughs, shaking her head. "She and I are becoming best buddies." He looks at her. "Aren't we cutie?" The puppy licks his nose. "Honestly, she's so tiny and if she stays super small, all we'd have to do is tuck her in the pocket of our shirt if something happens! That's something we could have her trained to do, just in case."

"I think it's a great idea!" Bri tells him. "Oh, one 'love tap' of a kiss is okay, but I loathe licking." He nods and heads out as Bri thanks him. She and Lawrence go back inside.

"Do you two always joke like that?" He asks as they walk back outside.

"It's part of our banter." She senses something and stops him, "Hey..." she feels what it is and steps closer taking his hand in hers. "Is he a good-looking guy? Yes. Is he better looking than you, David, or Jack? *NO way*! I love you, Ace! Mitchell's personality with mine makes it a lot of fun to joke around, BUT when it's time to be professional that man has a switch and he can snap into serious mode quicker than McMasters!" She has a sweet smile on her face and tells him, "If you ask me to, I'll stop with the banter, but I'm asking you not to do that to me and trust me." He's taken back by that and studies her as she continues. "It's refreshing to joke around and cut down the seriousness at times, *like now*, when we can all relax a little. It's just banter, I swear! Not only do I have you, Jack, and David, Mitchell has a gorgeous wife and an adorable little girl at home!"

"Is she okay with the banter?" He wonders.

"As far as I know she is, but that's a good point. I'd like to think if she wasn't, he'd shut it down, too, but I'll ask Mitchell to be sure. It's never actual flirting, just banter. Another way to look at this, Ace, is *no one* holds a candle to all this!" She points to his body with her finger.

He chuckles, as he wraps her in his arms. "Thank you."

She looks at him confused. "For what?"

"For being willing to give up something harmless for my insecurities." He smiles sweetly.

She gives him a compassionate look. "If I wasn't willing to give it up, then it wouldn't really be harmless, would it?"

"Good point." He tells her.

She hugs him and he returns it. She whispers, *"Hug me tighter."*

494

He does, kissing her neck and inhaling the smell of her shampoo. "I love you, BriaLynn."

"I love you, Lawrence." She hugs him a little firmer and just soaks in being in his arms.

When Mitchell brings the puppy back, Lawrence invites him to stay a bit while they feed her. He wants to get to know him a little more, too. He finds that the banter Mitchell and Bri have is easy to join in on, making Lawrence more comfortable overall.

When the puppy is done eating, Bri asks Mitchell to take her for the evening. Mitchell happily agrees since the puppy really is becoming his little buddy. They say goodnight and Lawrence leads Bri out to the cabana to watch the sunset together.

CHAPTER 49

Imperfectly Perfect Ghostly Confrontation

The next morning, Lawrence came out of the shower and Bri wasn't in bed. He smiles when he sees her sitting outside on the edge of a dock. He throws on some comfortable clothes on and goes out to her. He takes her blanket and sits behind her then wraps the blanket around them, petting the puppy before wrapping her up with them.

Bri leans back against him and savors the moment. They watch the sun fully come up and he softly says, "This is definitely one of those perfect moments."

"Mmmhmm..." she smiles, reaching back and cupping his cheek as he kisses her cheek, "*it most certainly is!*"

"What would you like to do today?" He asks. "We can fly to Oahu, or see the active volcano, even swim with dolphins!" He points, "There's a reef right over there where we could snorkel."

"All the above! *Minus the snorkeling!*" She gives an 'eek' look.

He chuckles at her expression but he understands. "Too deep." He thinks about it. "Well, what about swimming with the dolphins? Isn't that going to be too deep?"

"Possibly. It depends on where they do it." She replies. "Just space some things out, add a hike or two in there, and we're good to go!" He kisses her head, then they get up to go inside for breakfast.

Afterwards, Lawrence arranges all their excursions, spreading them out over their time there. Then he sits next to Bri on the couch, playing with the puppy. He asks her, "Have you picked a name yet?" He picks up the puppy and puts her in his lap. "We can't keep calling her 'puppy' too much longer or she'll think *that's* her name."

She smiles with a winkle in her eye at him. "I think having you wrapped around her paw in record time earns her the right to be named Kala for 'princess.' However, there's no way to shorten Kala because I refuse to call her 'Ka' since she isn't a crow! Nor 'la' because that's the sound of a musical note...then again, people could mispronounce 'Kala' altogether, expecting the 'a' to be a long sound."

Lawrence is laughing. "Alright. 'Kala' it is!" He pets her soft head some more. "*Buuut*, why not spell it with an 'h' in the middle?"

"H?" She thinks about it out loud, "Kah-la? *Ooo*, I like that idea! *Kah*la, it is!"

The rest of their time goes fast and Lawrence wants to take her home to The Royal Apartment for a few days before James and Amy's wedding. Bri and Lawrence have grown closer with a very deep and strong bond between them; it's what Jessica, along with Bri's two sons said would happen. Lawrence is very commanding and intense in the bedroom, but extremely attentive, loving, and cuddly afterwards, even outside the bedroom.

He's found he likes to sit behind her and have her relax back into him; she likes it, too. They're sitting on the bed of the cabana and she's leaning back against him, watching the water. He kisses the curve of her neck.

"When do you want to leave?" He asks.

She whistles an exhale; Kahla pops her head up and Bri pets her. "That's a loaded answer. One answer would be '*never!*'"

"I like that one." He hugs her.

"Then I think about missing Jack and David, so we can't do forever."

"Understandable." He replies. "I'd like to settle in and make The Royal Apartment *our home*, as best we can before the wedding."

She is confused. "The wedding isn't quite that soon!"

"How our days line up will be around that time." He tells her and she gives him an 'ah' look.

"Well, I'd need about a half hour to get ready? Would that work?" She asks.

"Sounds fantastic!" He smiles.

She turns her head sideways and tips her head back. As she reaches up, she looks at him seductively. "I'm a sucker for you and your dimpled smile!" Then passionately kisses him.

"I thought you wanted to leave in a half hour?" He happily and lovingly smiles.

She horizontally runs her finger across his lips saying, "Building up the anticipation." He growls a little moan. She adds, "We have a long flight..." She taps a small kiss to his lips before they get up.

Bri looks for an outfit wondering what to wear. She doesn't want to over dress or under dress, but she feels a little blah and her pregnancy hormones scream comfort today. She opts for soft white pants, but dressy looking. Then puts on a deep, amethyst purple color blouse with matching wedge shoes. She adds a multi-strand pearl necklace with teeny tiny diamonds mixed in between, courtesy of Lawrence; her diamond earrings David gave her on  their honeymoon in Paris; and her diamond watch from Jack. On the front of her left shoulder she adds 'The Heart of Adoration' because of the legend behind it: a king gave it to the woman he loved and adored. The amethyst was in a gold setting, with a gold crown on top, lined with tiny round diamonds.

Lawrence sees her and smiles. "This whole outfit is lovely and you seem to be glowing brighter than usual." He touches the brooch and Bri tells him the legend. "That's *definitely* fitting for us!" He tangles his hands in her hair at the back of her neck. "This King absolutely loves and adores you!" He kisses her fiercely before they leave and head to the airport, making their way back to The London Palace.

Lawrence sees Bri getting more and more fidgety as they get closer to London. "It'll be okay!" He tells her.

"How can you say that?!" Bri asks. "That woman was actually there when I officially became 'The Royal Consort!'"

"And she didn't stay!" He tells her. "I made sure of that! I figured my father was the lesser of two evils at this point and I let him stay." He holds her face. "You forget Seth, Genevieve, and Abby, live there, too. I'll do everything I can to protect you," he sweeps his fingers across her cheek and makes that last part sound really sappy, "*my one true love!*" He grins.

Bri rolls her eyes as she lightly laughs. "Alright, I'll put myself in your hands." She smirks. "*Although*, I love the feeling of being in your arms more!"

He chuckles a little, but there is sweetness to his, "*Believe me, I'm aware...*" he holds her cheek and wraps his other arm around his waist. "I can't begin to tell you what you mean to me...you truly are 'The Queen of My Heart!'" He kisses her sweetly.

They arrive on the tarmac and Lawrence's helicopter is ready to take them to The Palace. He asks the pilots to fly around, for a full aerial view of The London Palace and The Palace Grounds.

Bri is overwhelmed. "Lawrence! I knew The Palace was huge, but from this view it could fit a medium-sized city inside!"

As he holds her hand, he feels her shaking. He sees her eyes are closed for a long moment and that's when he realizes it's not so much the title of 'The Queen' that overwhelms her, but the enormity of *being queen*.

He asks the pilots, "Gentlemen, would you focus on The Royal Apartment side." They acknowledge.

She thinks about the layout of what she does remember of the castle and asks as she points, "The Apartment is on that corner, right?" He nods. The separate private entrance to this section is to avoid the huge public ones in various places, although Lawrence uses the one by his office every now and again. "How many floors? Four, plus a basement?"

Lawrence leans over her and points. "The main floor has the offices for The Royal Guards, including McMasters, and Mitchell if needed. The floors above them and the main entrance, up to the top and around the tower to the other side," the helicopter rounds the corner, "is *our* apartment. The Courtyard in back will have a playground..." he points, "and there's the rooftop garden. We have plenty of room for David and Jack to have their own dedicated bedrooms; as well as plenty of room for a nanny, or nannies if you prefer one for each baby..."

"Well, we'll take that one step at a time. For now, I want my baby with me." She states, putting her hand on her lower abdomen. He caresses her cheek. She sees him thinking hard about something and sweetly asks, "Are *you* okay, Ace?"

"*More* than okay!" He smiles and kisses her hand.

When they land, Bri thanks the pilots and they nod, giving them a two-finger salute with a smile. The King tells them, "Thank you for obliging us."

They smiles and say, "You're welcome, Your Majesty!" When Lawrence and Bri are far enough away, the pilots take off again.

Lawrence watches Bri as she watches the helicopter fly away. When she turns and looks at him, her smile is wide and bright making his heart skip a beat! He holds the hair out of her face by tangling his hands in her hair. She tips her head back so he knows she wants him to kiss her. He smiles lovingly back at her as he closes the space between their lips and pauses realizing they're being watched.

"Public displays are usually frowned upon." He grins.

"Really?" She asks. "By whom?!"

He pulls back a little, thinking hard. "I guess that's what I've heard..."

"Good thing I have a good rapport with The King, or this could be a problem!" She teases.

"You have his heart, so you get anything you wish." He tells her, then captures her lips.

When their lips connect, their passion envelopes them! She slides her hands around his waist and pulls him close; he wraps one of his arms around her upper arms and one around her waist, hugging her close. She moans into their kiss, hugging him tighter. They pull back and put their foreheads together. Then he cups her face again to have her look at him.

"I'm so in love you, BriaLynn, it seems like a dream." He taps but holds a lingering kiss to her lips. He pulls back with a big smile, his dimples on display, her breath catches.

"You keep smiling at me like that, Ace, and I may not be able to keep my hands off you before we get somewhere private! And my hormones have me either exhausted or..." she slides her hands from his back, around to his midsection in front.

He takes her hands and holds them close. "We can take care of that, once we're inside The Royal Chambers. For now, keep smiling because we're not only being watched, but photographed and recorded as well." She nods with her continued smile.

He holds her hand and they walk to The Royal Apartment's Main Entrance. They wave to some and stand together for some pictures for the crowd that's gathered. They walk inside the front door and he watches her reaction to The Royal Apartment.

"You really like this place, but..." he says as he is figuring her out more, "it's the history you love!"

She smiles. "I appreciate all this history, I can even appreciate the history of The Dungeons..."

Bri looks around this 'receiving room' and sees a man sitting in a chair smoking a pipe and a woman at the fireplace warming her hands. Lawrence looks over where she's looking but doesn't see anyone.

"Ghosts?" He asks. McMasters and Mitchell hear this and look at each other for answers but can only give each other an 'I don't know' look.

Bri tells Lawrence, "A man sitting and smoking a pipe...I'd say he 'looks important' if that makes sense." The man sitting snaps his head to look at Bri, startling her and she jerks back a little. "*Okaaay*, he's *definitely* a spirit."

The male spirit glares at her. "I *am* important, you piece of filth!" His loftiness and imagined self-importance make the side of her nose go up in revulsion.

Bri sternly tells him, "*There's no need for your rudeness!*"

The man, in a poor choice plaid suit, stands up. Bri notices he has a darkness about him. He is a later middle-aged man, who has a family resemblance to Lawrence's mother... "*Nnno!*" She thinks to herself, but whispers it out loud.

"What?" Lawrence asks. "Who is it? What are they saying?"

Bri shakes her head a little. "I'm not certain but—."

501

"You twit!" He says. Bri is able to use her power and 'reads' who this is just before he confirms it. "I'm The Duke of Devonridge! And you *will* address me as such!"

"Or you'll what?!" Bri laughs at the ridiculousness of it. "*You're dead!*"

An evil grin goes across his face. "I guess he hasn't told you." His smugness is thick. "*He killed me!*" The Duke points to Lawrence, then to himself, "He came into my room in the middle of the night and stabbed me in *cold blood!*"

Bri flatly says, "I'm aware of what happened."

The Duke's eyes dart from Lawrence to her and he's angry she doesn't have more of a shocked or repulsed reaction towards Lawrence. "HE KILLED ME! WHY AREN'T YOU APPALLED?!" His face is getting red with fury.

"What's going on, Bri?" Lawrence asks. She gives him a 'one-minute' gesture with her finger.

Bri looks back to The Duke. "*Why should I be?*" She defiantly asks. "I think he performed a community service. I say give the man a medal!"

The Duke glares at Bri and unleashes a long tirade of language that's insulting, but some of them, because she is an American, are 'lost in translation' and they make her want to laugh. Then he goes too far with his swear words...

"THAT'S QUITE ENOUGH!" Bri sternly yells over his tirade. The Duke clamps his mouth down. Lawrence, McMasters, and Mitchell jump, then look closely and watch her as she raises her finger to someone no one else can see. "I'M STILL A LADY!" Knowing he is hung up on titles, she firmly states, "*I outrank you!*"

He scoffs saying, "A pheasant doesn't outrank a duke!"

Lawrence says, "Let me see them. Maybe I can help?"

The Duke gets a devilish look. "*Yes*, let him see me, so he can face the man *he murdered!*" He rattles off more swear word towards Lawrence.

"Like hell I will!" Bri snaps and her anger overcomes her. "No one protected him against *you* when you were alive, but *I* will protect him now!" She sees he is about to go off again and she cuts him off. "*Watch your language!* Or so help me, *I won't warn you again—.*"

"*Or you'll what?!*" The Duke mocks her from before. "*I'm dead!*" He gets right up in Lawrence's face, but Lawrence can't see him. Lawrence does sense something and sees Bri looking at the space in front of him.

"Bri?" Lawrence asks. "Is my uncle in front of me?"

Bri looks at Lawrence. "Yes, but I'm *not* going to let you see him because he's *demanding* it! Since this man won't be respectful and I can barely stomach his behavior," she looks to The Duke but tells Lawrence, "I refuse to reward *his* bad behavior!"

"How dare you!" The Duke is livid. "I COMMAND YOU—."

Her hand goes up in a 'stop' gesture. "*STOP! Now, YOU listen carefully!*" Bri's finger goes up again and she's assertive with her voice, being precise with her words. "*You* don't command *anything*, or *anyone, anymore!* Get this through your head! *You're.dead!*"

"Get this through your pea-sized brain, you twit; it's because I'm dead *you can't stop me!*" He bites back.

He goes to say something, but Bri swiftly clamps her fingers together telling him, "*I command YOU to stop talking and keep your mouth shut!*" Panic goes to The Duke's face as his hands go to his jaw and throat. He literally cannot open his mouth. "I tried to warn you that *because YOU'RE dead*, you have no control!" Her eyebrow flicks up as she says, "But *I DO!*" His uncle glares. She states, "*I command you* to leave us and everyone I care about alone, only returning *if* I ever call for you! Do *you* understand *me?!*" Bri says with a determined look on her face. The man is angry, but he can only nod. "Good! Or I could just banish you to whatever Hell you're avoiding!" She sees a flicker of horror in his eyes to know she was on to something. "Now, away with you!" Bri tells him and waves her hand in an 'away with you' movement and he disappears.

Bri glances over at the fireplace and the ghost woman is unfazed, still staring at the fire, which Bri now sees is a 'ghostly fire.' *Cool.* She thinks to herself. Mitchell and McMasters are stunned at what they witnessed.

"Is he gone?" Lawrence asks, turning her to face him and she nods. "Darling, are *you* okay?" She nods and tries to smile with confidence, but it doesn't work because, even though he only heard and saw her side of the interaction with his uncle, he knows enough. "Bri," he lifts her chin, "you're not telling me everything." She closes her eyelids and holds them shut which he's learned, as have David and Jack, that this is a 'tell' of hers. "*Please*, Darling."

"He's pompously angry and hasn't humbled himself. I didn't let you see him for a couple reasons. First, I could actually protect you from that; *and I did!* Second, it would've reinforced his belief he still calls the shots!" She holds his jaw and gives him a loving look. "He doesn't call the shots anymore! Not now, *not ever again*. Okay?" He nods and she gives him a little smile. "Thank you." She goes to kiss him, but he pulls back a little for a second.

"For what? I should be thanking you for trusting me about this whole situation when it looks unfavorable towards me." He hugs her. "I love you."

"And I love you!" She kisses him again. "And no, it doesn't look unfavorable towards you!" She lowers her voice so only he hears, "An adult man doing the things he and your mother did to you when you were barely a teenager, trust me, the first thought is, 'what an evil monster *that man* is!' I meant what I said, you performed a community service to protect your brother and sister, not to mention however many innocent kids after?!" He hugs her with so much love.

"Well," Lawrence says, taking her hand and climbing up the stairs, "I never thought about this place being haunted..."

"Which may be for the best!"

He chuckles. "Why's that?"

"You grew up here! I think any child believing their house is this haunted," she motions The Palace's grandeur, "*may not nurture the best of childhoods!*"

Lawrence snorts a laugh. "Probably not!"

CHAPTER 50

Imperfectly Perfect Mini Royal Tour

When they get up to The Royal Apartment, Mitchell and McMasters walk the whole place, all the floors, and tell them everything is secure.

"How can you be so sure?" Bri innocently asks.

"Bri," Lawrence puts his hands on her upper arms, "McMasters and Mitchell have put in added security features all over the place."

McMasters steps over. "Bri, we handpicked the men and women to even guard the passageways, but the ones into this apartment have new locks *and keys*. Mitchell and I have a set," they drop a set in his hands, "and now Lawrence has a set."

Lawrence puts them in Bri's hands. "Do what you will with them."

She puts them back in his hands and closes his fingers over them. "Lawrence, I don't blame you *at all* for what happened! I don't want the passageways locked all the time! What's the point of having them if we can't use them?!" She grins with a wink and Lawrence chuckles in agreement.

Mitchell suggests, "We can just have whoever's in charge that night lock the ones into The Apartment or block off corridors to The Apartment, then unlock them the next morning?"

Bri tells them, "I'll let you all decide how best to do that!"

"Sounds good." McMasters says. "We'll come up with something."

Mitchell and McMasters say their goodbyes and leave, locking the door behind them. Lawrence looks back at Bri and melts...she has a compassionate, loving look and he sees it on the only woman he has ever fallen in-love with!

"How can you look at me like *that*?" He struggles to finish his sentence with a lump forming in his throat.

Bri walks the few steps over to him. "What do you mean? What do you see when I'm looking at you?"

"*Love.*" He whispers.

"*So maybe* you can conclude that I'm looking at you with love *because* I *do love you?*" She lightly teases as she hugs him.

He just hugs her closer. "I guess I'm in awe...after that day in my office—my hand at your..." he's ashamed to say it.

She kindly says. "Lawrence, I know that wasn't really you, but I also knew the man who loved me was in there!"

"You're the most extraordinary woman on the planet! *Do you know that?!*"

"Not on the planet, but it's been suggested by two other *really* wonderful and handsome men." She grins.

"They sound like they're pretty good guys to have on your team." He lightly teases back.

"They are! It's an exclusive membership!" She teases some more.

"Exclusive?" He raises his eyebrow.

"*You should know*! You're the only other member!" She giggles a little.

He rests the side of his head against hers. "I'm nervous about doing all this on my own...it's *all* on me!"

"Lawrence," she lovingly smiles, "*you have been doing it*, only now you're able to do it *your own way*!"

Bri feels their son's words, 'Father *needs you* as The Queen.' She remembers what David said about how it felt with the weight of becoming The Duke of Newhaven looming over him, added to the responsibilities and duties he already had being the CEO of The Worthington Corporation...he said when he married her, he no longer felt alone because she is his partner and it didn't feel so daunting anymore." Her heart squeezes because she understands this is similar to what Lawrence is feeling now...

She changes the subject so she can ponder that on her own for a bit. "Will you tell me some of the history of The Palace, or The Royal Apartment?"

He smiles, "I'd love to, but I think you'd love having a private tour of The Palace which I will arrange with the most knowledgeable person on *our* staff."

"That sounds *fantastic!*" She jumps a little from excitement and he loves seeing her excited!

"I *will* offer a *mini* tour of The Royal Apartment." Lawrence begins with The Grand Staircase at the main entrance of The Royal Apartment.

She says, "The stained glass is *so* beautiful, it's stunning!"

He talks about the images on the stained glass being significant points of the country's history up to the time The London Palace was built. They walk and talk of the various rooms of The Royal Apartment. They walk to the staff's section of The Royal Apartment, near the kitchen, where Bri sees a simple bedroom that looks like it's frozen in the 1920s. Just a twin bed, a plain dresser with a mirror that was completely bare, a bedside table with only a small lamp and a clock, along with an armoire to hang any clothes. There's a tiny bathroom just big enough for a shower, toilet, and sink. She looks around and it looks like there are several similar rooms like this one.

"What are these rooms?" Bri asks.

"The servants' bedrooms when they're on duty." He blurts out.

Bri catches a couple of staff who stop when they hear that. "Oy, Ace, we need to change some wording in your vocabulary..."

He looks at her with a slightly confused look. "What do you mean?"

"*Well,*" she squeezes the bridge of her nose with her fingers, "do you actually own anyone here?"

"*Absolutely not!*" He says, redeeming himself to her and the staff that had overheard his comment.

"Glad to hear that kind of genuine response! Lawrence, it's just that you use 'servant' and the word *implies* ownership, that they're beneath you; *or* their single mission in life is to serve you!" She sees the wheels turning as he processes this against what he remembers saying. "Now, why use 'servant' to describe your 'house *staff*' when they serve their country and *they* may say fellow countrymen; *they* might even say they serve The Crown. No matter how *they* personally describe their wonderful service in their post, they are *staff members* and they——."

"They are *not owned*, nor live to serve me personally. Ugh, *daft* habit being around my mother all these years." He actually seems pained by it. He changes his answer. "This room is for our wonderful staff when they're on duty overnight. They're also welcome to stay the night after late-night parties, or starting an earlier shift."

She happily smiles. "*So* much better, Ace! *Now*, we need to update these rooms into the twenty-first century!"

"Done!" He smiles. The staff even smile when they hear that, then they get back to work.

The last stop was The Royal Chambers. They walk into a bright room with large windows and large glass doors to a balcony, and a living room area with a hearth, or giant fireplace that has a large screen tv above it. There is a cream-colored couch with darker royal-blue throw pillows facing the fireplace, a matching loveseat to the right of the couch. Bri smiles when she sees an overstuffed cream-colored chair to the left of the couch; it's paired off with an armchair that's turned around and angled to look out the large windows with a small table in between them. The coffee table and accent tables have creamy marble tops sitting on wrought-iron frames and legs.

There is the same color of marble as the tabletops that is also in the flooring throughout the room, except where the bed sits has columns for bedposts. There are two steps up onto a platform the bed is on with darker royal-blue carpeting; all of which extends to the bathroom door on one side and over to the windows on the other side with a tall armoire dresser that has a cabinet on top and two drawers on the bottom.

Bri looks up and sees there are various light fixtures, but the focal point is a giant crystal and gold chandelier hanging from the center of the ceiling to complete the extravagant royal look. Yet...*somehow* it fits his personality.

She walks over to the windows and doors to the balcony. "That view! It's incredible!" She walks out onto the balcony and takes in the view.

He comes up behind her, wrapping his arms around her. "It was fun showing you around!"

She turns in his arms. "It was!"

He smiles lovingly saying, "I finally feel like I have someone on *my* side!"

Through teary eyes she says, "*You do*! And you still have Jack and David, as well as Seth, Genevieve, and Abby; not to mention the whole Worthington Family!" She walks back inside and over to the fireplace that stands as tall as her shoulder. "I didn't deserve David, but his gift of Jack *and now you*!" Her lower jaw barely shakes as she shakes her head. "It's crazy because *I don't deserve all of this love*!"

"Yes, you do! And they're more deserving of you than I'll ever be of your love for me!" He exhales and sits down on the couch.

"Oh, Lawrence..." she walks over and straddles him. "You have so much greatness inside you and you'll do so much good as king now that your mother won't be interfering!" She teases. "How else would you keep the support of Seth, Genevieve, and Abby being king?"

He faintly laughs and agrees, "True."

"You have a wonderful heart, Lawrence! I wouldn't be here if you didn't!" She tells him.

He's a bit agitated. "How can you say that, let alone think it after what I said to you that day?!"

"*I have absolutely no idea what you're talking about*!" She says with determination.

He gives her an appreciative smile back. "Thank you for that."

"Ace, it's the old argument of nature versus nurture. This fantastic man *wasn't nurtured* into his amazingness by your mother!"

He bursts out a little laughter. "*No*!"

"Somewhere you have the genes, as well as your brother and sister, and you three were able to be there for one another as you raised yourselves and each other." She says.

"So, you believe it's nature, not nurture?" He asks.

"I think it's both." She expounds, "Every person is different, with their own unique part of a DNA sequence. Most parents try their best to raise well-rounded children who can take care of themselves, and to be positive, contributing members of society in adulthood. Children respond differently to different parenting styles because of their genes. Take a family of two parents with four children: three children are successful and living their best life. However, one seems to struggle...*fighting against everything*, making their life harder than necessary. There are families where the kids turn out wonderful and kind-hearted, in spite of the parents seriously lacking in their parenting abilities." She sees he's staring, "What's wrong?"

"Nothing! You're brilliance makes you that much *more* incredibly beautiful!" He gives her a smoldering grin.

She gives him a seductive look and places his hand on her throat. He takes it as the submission to him it's supposed to be. He sits up and tangles his other hand in her hair, capturing her lips with his...

Lawrence is called to his official office for a little while and Bri works on a few things for Newhaven. They meet in their dining room for dinner. She notices Lawrence barely eats anything. He sits twisting his wedding band on his finger, then takes it on and off playing with it. He's learning more about how his mother 'ruled' *for him* now that a few of his staff feel a little less threatened by her. Plus, after Bri faced his uncle, Lawrence has been thinking a lot about what happened in his childhood; trying to make sense of it on top of everything else. Bri is surprised when he abruptly leaves.

Bri had watched him leave and when she looks back to where he was sitting, her eyes see that he had left his wedding band on the table. She takes it and texts McMasters if he or Mitchell will take her to Nigel, The Crown Jeweler.

Nigel was about to close up but he waited for her. He is happy to see her when she walks in and they talk for a couple minutes before she asks, "Nigel, would you be able to engrave Lawrence's wedding band for me?"

He looks at it. "Of course, *Your Royal Majesty!*" He happily smiles. "What would you like it to say?"

"'Forever Together' and 'Forever Family.' If you can squeeze comfortably 'Ohana' in there, that would be great." She explains.

"I'll see what I can do." Nigel tells her, "Just give me a few minutes." Bri nods and thanks him. She wanders around the store while she waits.

Lawrence had gone to their bedroom and poured himself a drink. He was sitting in the angled chair he always sits in when he drinks, staring at the London city lights. He spins the drink in his glass, he hasn't had any yet. He zones out, losing track of time, but snaps out of it when he hears the door to the bedroom open.

Bri walks in. "Okay, Ace. You've been in here long enough."

He looks at his watch and jumps up. "My apologies, Darling. I didn't realize how late it was getting."

She walks over and looks at the drink as he sets it down on the table. She gives him a compassionate look, "Ghosts of the past can be a pretty powerful thing."

"They are, but I'm finding they're *slowly* getting weaker..." He holds her cheeks. "Any other time," he tips his head towards the glass, "that'd be at least my second—."

"But tonight?" She curiously asks.

"Not even a drop has touched these lips." He grins.

Her eyebrows shoot up and she studies him. "*Why?*"

He looks back at the glass. "I'm not sure..." He looks back at her. "I suspect it's because of you."

"*Me?*" She's surprised and starts shaking her head. "Lawrence, just because I don't drink doesn't mean you, David, or Jack can't! I would never force—."

"*I know*, Darling! That's not why. It's one of the things that intrigues me about you. You're so strong in your faith, you let it guide your footsteps, you kneel in prayer at night, you like to meditate in the quiet or on your walks, you somehow find beauty in things most people wouldn't even look at twice!"

511

He moves his hands to the back of her jaw and neck. "Your faith brings you such strength, making you a force...helping you to stand your ground, like when you're going up against a *ghastly* king."

"You were *acting ghastly*, but this..." she places a hand on his chest, over his heart, "*this* is wonderful and incredible; *this* is who you are!"

He gives a small scoff. "*You're* bloody extraordinary! You have a way about you that draws people in! However, with all that, you never once demanded, or forced, any of us to change because of those beliefs!"

"If someone would try to force anyone to stop drinking, doing drugs, believe in the same 'Higher Power,' or whatever it may be, they would throw up walls and fight against it. Personally, if someone got in my face demanding I believe what they believed, I'd purposely do the opposite just to prove they couldn't tell me what to do, nor force me to do anything!" She tells him.

"Is that the idea behind telling me I could keep seeing women until we were official?'" He asks.

"*Sort of.*" She admits. "I felt that since you were already used to being with whomever, if I came in and 'put a stop to it,' then it could make you desire it, er–*them*, that much more. *However*, it's much more than that. We were taking our time to do this relationship right and you were already respecting my wishes to wait. I felt it was unfair to expect you to 'go without' when I have my relationships with David and Jack; I didn't want to be a hypocrite." She gives him a slight smile.

He gives her an intense look as he considers what she said. "How do you do it?" He asks as he wraps his arms around her.

"Do what?" She asks in almost a whisper, lost in his gaze.

He marvels. "How do you stay so grounded in your faith and beliefs, in a world that contradicts them all the time?!"

"Simple. While the world *is* constantly changing, *I know* God and The Lord *never do*. For example, They speak softly through The Spirit, which is why I like the quiet; the world is loud, mean, and cruel, which is why I don't like saturating myself with the media...it's why I try to have compassion and empathy even with the darkest of souls..." her gaze drifts down to his chest.

He barely says, "*Like my mother...*"

"And your father. Although, for your mother, only to answer *how* she became so cruel and heartless. *Not* that it excuses any of it away and makes it all better by any means!" She states.

"How does one make sense of something that doesn't make sense?!" He adds with a little shrug.

"Lawrence, there's something I'm remembering, but I'm not sure you're going to want to hear it." He raises his eyebrow in curiosity and studies her. She takes a deep breath and tells him, "Jessica would tell me that I would bond with you in a way *like no one else*, but it won't take away from the bonds I have with David and Jack." He holds her hands as she continues, "That our love will help you heal from the effects of your childhood." She gives him a compassionate look. "You have some deep wounds that will take a while to heal." She kisses his hand. She has '*things aren't always as they seem*' come into her mind and she thinks of The King Father.

Lawrence sees this and asks, "What else? I haven't heard anything I didn't mind hearing."

She tells him, "Somehow, some way, I'm to help *your family heal* and, in the process, help you with your—."

"*Don't go there!*" He tells her, turning away from her. He's a bit frustrated, "I thought we weren't going to talk about him for a while!"

"I'm not, well, not specifically." Her tears blur her vision. "I'm sorry your father wasn't there for you, Seth, or Abby. I'm *so sorry* your mother did all those horrible things to you. Mothers are to love, protect, and *guide* her children *to do the right things*." She walks in front of him to face him again and he does look at her. She says, "My son with David would tell me it has something to do with a true mother's love, the love he says I have and it's the purest love of all. It's the love that can help heal not only *your* deepest wounds, but Jack's, too." She pauses and adds, "I still have no idea how I'm supposed to help all of you heal? However, if I am then I have faith that the answers will come to me when the time comes."

"Bri, I can see helping Abby, Seth, and me, to heal, but what our parents did to us falls under the category of 'unforgiveable.'"

She puts her hand on his cheek, "I'm grateful you, Seth, and Abby, all had each other to help you through those awful times!"

"*You're my family*! You, along with Jack, David," he puts a hand on her lower abdomen, "this wonderful baby!" He sweetly smiles. She puts her hands on his hands and sees her thumb with his wedding band on it. "My ring!" He's confused and looks at his empty finger asking, "*How...?*"

She takes it off her thumb and tells him, "You left it on the table in the dining room before you came up here." She hands it to him. "I snuck out with McMasters and asked Nigel to engrave it."

His eyebrows come together as he takes it and looks at it closely. In between the Triquetra heart symbols, he reads: "Forever Together...Forever Family," and he gets a little choked up with, "*Ohana.*"

She takes the ring and puts it on his finger. "You're forever a part of *this* family! *Our family*! Now," she kisses his ring, "and forever. And I expect *you* to never take this off again!" She smiles with loving tears.

He tangles his hands in her hair and says, "*I am blessed* and I don't have near the amount of the faith you do!"

"But you can if you want to! It's there to be written on your heart," she says, tapping on his heart, "but only when *you're* ready."

"I'd say I'm well on my way! I love you and that's clearly written on my heart!" Lawrence smiles and he kisses her passionately...

CHAPTER 51
Imperfectly Perfect Bonding Moment

Bri wakes up in the early morning hours a little disoriented. She is trying not to wake Lawrence as she fumbles for her phone to use its flashlight. When she can't find it, she sits up to block as much light as she can from Lawrence's face when she turns on the lamp. She waits for her eyes to adjust and notices Lawrence waking up.

"I'm so sorry! I tried to shield you from as much light as I could." She quietly explains. "I'm not sure of my bearings yet and I need the bathroom but I can't find my phone to use its flashlight."

"It's fine, Darling." He rubs his eyes and he sits up, watching her walk to the bathroom; he patiently waits for her to return.

When she comes back to bed, she sees the details of the *kingly* bed for the first time! The four bedpost columns were granite and there is gold etching on the carvings at the top of each of the columns. The wall above the cream color headboard is a darker royal-blue velvet, same as the carpet, with a gold coat of arms. Cream sheets with gold trim and a thick blue comforter with accent pillows of the other colors.

"This has been The Royal Chambers since The Palace was originally built." He says, seeing Bri looking closely at everything. "My mother has had her own quarters, something far away from my father. When he had a consort, she stayed in here with him."

"Ah, like me." She grins.

"I don't have any other place *here*. Now, I have my room at The Manor." He says. "But the only one I will share a bed with is *you*, My Queen."

"Great answer!" She smiles into a passionate kiss...

Lawrence comes out of the bathroom and since Bri had fallen asleep, he turns off the light on her nightstand and goes downstairs for his workout.

When Bri wakes later that morning, she thinks she hears the shower and listens a moment to confirm it. She glances at her nightstand and sees her water bottle is now there, along with her phone and her tablet. She smiles as she grabs the water bottle and takes a drink. She's tipping the bottle back and she sees movement in the corner of her eye. She turns to see Lawrence with a towel around his waist walking over to her. He sits next to her on the bed and smiles lovingly at her.

He sweetly asks, "Forgive me?"

She's confused. "*For what?*"

"For leaving you at the dining room table last night and selfishly sitting up here feeling sorry for myself, dwelling over the past." He caresses her face. "*Wasting our time together...*"

"Two things: first, I'll *always* forgive you because I trust you, David, and Jack won't do anything unforgiveable; second, looking like that, I would agree to just about *anything*, because I probably wouldn't hear much of what you actually say over all that!" She points to him moving her finger up and down, biting her lower lip.

He laughs and puts his hand to his chest. "So, my heartfelt apol—."

She puts her hand over his mouth. "Like right now," pointing to her ear with her free hand, "all I hear," she points to him, "is *all* this," then raises her voice a bit more than normal for effect, "*very loudly.*"

He leans into kiss her and she playfully scoots away, but he quickly takes hold of her ankles and easily yanks her down to him, making her gasp.

He leans in to kiss her and she says against his lips, "*Daaamn*, that's sexy!"

He moans a growl as he kisses back to her ear. She was right about him liking the power in the bedroom, but she's finding she likes it, too...as long as she can win every once in a while.

He smiles at her with so much love. "I've never been so deeply in-love and last night I realized the love we have requires me bearing my soul to you."

"Lawrence, true love does come from vulnerability on *both sides*. It's giving someone the power and the knowledge to hurt you, *to destroy you*, but trusting

516

in their love for you that they would *never* fathom ever doing so. Lawrence, when I said I don't care about your past it wasn't because I don't care about you; it's that it has no place in the present or future. I'll listen to whatever you share with me because I want to know what you've been through, how far you've come, and support you wherever you're going."

"I know. And it's 'wherever *we're* going!'" He adds.

She smiles, holding his face. "Stop talking, Ace!"

He smiles wide. "Gladly!" He kisses her as he pins her wrists above her head with one hand...

He so gently and lovingly kisses her face, then her lips. She hugs him tight as she kisses him once more. He lays next to her, holding her close, then they fall asleep for a little while.

When Bri wakes up, she snuggles into Lawrence's chest and thinks about the last day, mindlessly rubbing her thumb back and forth over his chest. He wakes to it and squeezes her in a little hug.

He kisses her head. "How long have you been up?"

"I'm not sure. It doesn't feel like very long." She answers.

They lay in comfortable silence for a bit until Lawrence breaks it. "My parents were rarely together, and my mother was always with my great-uncle who, as you know, was The Duke of Devonridge." Bri slightly nods. He clears his throat a little. "I go for long stretches without thinking about him or what they did to me."

"How I wish I could hug little Lawrence and protect him. I'd want to sneak into your uncle's room and do some crude surgical cuts." She feels his body move as he silently chuckles a bit.

"I told my father I killed my uncle that night when I caught my uncle sneaking out of Seth's room. His statement to me was: 'I'll clean up this mess, but we're *never* to speak of this again!'" He lifts his head to look at her. "Bri, I know there are the girls, plus there's a baby on the way and more babies to come; but I *swear* to you, I'm not like my uncle—."

"Whoa! Hold on there, Ace!" She says as she rests up on her elbow and part of his chest. She looks down into his eyes with determination, "That *never* crossed my mind!" She sees the relief in his eyes. "I swear *to you*!" He cups her face and kisses her *fiercely*. He fell in-love with her so much more in this moment, which he didn't think was possible. "Lawrence, for your piece of mind you should know the statistics are on your side." She says.

"Really?" He wonders.

"Yes. Statistics show a high percentage of those sexually abused *never* become abusers. Which could be partly why I never considered it, but a huge reason is because you're so protective of Seth and Abby." She straddles him, but pulls him up to hug him tight for a few minutes.

He says next to her ear, only his voice cracks as he says, "I *don't* deserve you!" He is able to push down his emotions until she says three words...

"*You've got me!*" She whispers firmly. The tears drip from his eyes and she holds him tight, running her hand through his hair. She tenderly says, "Lawrence, I promise, *nothing* in your past will make me love you less. In fact, I love you more for trusting me." She pulls back to look at him and her heart squeezes seeing his tears. "Lawrence, as David discovered, titles don't go on my 'pro' list, but I also know it comes with the man I love. So, they're not on a 'con' list either; they're just there. They also don't stand in my way when I know I'm right, even if it means 'The Marquee of Newhaven' could've had me thrown out of The Black-Tie Ball that weekend he, Jack, and I first met; or 'The King' could've had me beheaded for standing up to him and The Queen Mother!"

He laughs. "Thank goodness I'm not the first King Lawrence!"

"*No kidding!*" She touches her neck and lightly teases, "I'd never wear another beautiful necklace of yours again!" He gives a small burst of laughter. He takes a deep breath, rubbing his face and exhaling. He stares at her as she says, "I think you should stay at the Bradshaw's with David, Jack, and I, after James and Amy's wedding. No titles, just David, Jack, me, *and hopefully*, Lawrence. What do you think?"

He gives her a bit of a worried look. "What scares me is not being able to say 'no' to you."

"*Aaand* that's bad...*why now?*" She teases.

He smiles and his dimples are extra handsome. Her stomach growls and she taps a kiss to his lips before moving to sit on the edge of the bed. She reaches for her bag he had put next to the nightstand when he brought up her water, phone, and tablet this morning for her. She reaches into her bag and pulls out a snack. He leans over and takes the snack bag out of her hand.

He kisses her shoulder and says, "How about you let Uncle Lawrence go down and have some real food brought up? I can't believe I've been so wrapped up in myself again that I've forgotten about you *and the baby!*"

"Ace..." she squeezes his hand, "you haven't forgotten about us and you're not self-absorbed." She touches her lower abdomen. "*And we're not complaining.*" She turns her head and taps a kiss to his lips. "We're bonding. Eating can wait." Her stomach growls again.

"Your stomach growling tells me otherwise!" He winks and smiles at her. He gets up and quickly throws on some clothes. He dashes out the door barefoot and runs downstairs to the kitchen.

They're about to say, 'Your Majesty,' but he waves that off. "The Princess Imperial needs to eat and we lost track of time. Would you please, please, *please*, send some breakfast up to my, er, our chambers as soon as possible?"

"*Of course!* Right away, Sir!" The Head Chef, Julian, says with a smile. He's pleasantly surprised at how nice The King is this morning when normally he's just 'to the point' with them.

"Thank you, everyone!" Lawrence says and hurries back to Bri without telling them anything specific to make. The Chef will make up a few things he knows she likes from a conversation with Chef Edwin at The Worthington Estate.

Bri had jumped into the shower after texting David and Jack 'Good morning!' The response texts come through and Lawrence sees the notification but not what the text says when he walks in to tell her breakfast is on the way. Bri comes out as he sets her phone back down on the counter. He's a little embarrassed as she walks up to him with a slight knowing smile on her face. She opens her phone right there in front of him, telling him her code, and shows him the texts. They were saying good morning and asking how she is feeling, plus they were wondering if she has had a tour of The Palace yet.

He turns and hugs her. "I'm sorry."

"Thank you, but it's okay." She says and he lifts an eyebrow. "Lawrence, I have *nothing* to hide from you, Jack, or David. What would make all this fall apart are secrets, or for someone to feel left out, or jilted! We need to keep aware of *everyone's* feelings..." he nods. She kisses his shoulder. "Just remember, they support us being together and want this to work. How do you think I would feel if you said anything bad or unsupportive of either one of them?"

"Devastated, sad, disappointed..."

"Right, *and* I'd feel that way if they said anything bad or unsupportive about you or of us! None of our relationships would survive if just one of you were unsupportive!" She says. "Love makes a person veer away from doing things that would hurt the person they love."

Lawrence lets that all sink in and stares at the floor for a long moment before asking, "Why couldn't we have met long ago?"

She lightly laughs. "Because I wasn't who I am now, just like you aren't who you are now! Most of us aren't the same, *and we shouldn't be*, if we learn valuable lessons along the way! We're meant to change with those valuable lessons, *preferably for the better*! We're meant to grow, learn, and develop; to become a little better than we were yesterday! Basically, we weren't ready then to meet each other, because we had lessons and changing to do beforehand, things we wouldn't have learned any other way." She bites her lips together. "Sorry, getting carried away!"

"*Don't be*! You're *always* fascinating!" He smiles.

"You fascinate and intrigue me, too!" She grins.

"Ha-ha! I'm dull and boring compared to you!" He points out.

"*No, you're not*! The passion you have for me alone *proves* that! And this..." she points to his heart, then lays her hand over it, "the fact that, after everything you've gone through, after all that horrible woman did to you to make you 'her king,' *none of it* cemented into your foundation. *Most importantly*, you're making changes right now at your first *real* opportunity to be 'The King' *you* want to be! Which means I'm right about you being a kind-hearted, loving, giving, and compassionate man!"

And there it is. Once again, she sees *him*. It's a little scary because she sees all that, along with seeing such great qualities and potential in him that he hopes he can measure up to it. He cups her face and kisses her tenderly.

"Can I ask you a question about past relationships?" She asks.

"Sure." He shifts nervously.

"Did you have many?" She quickly adds, "If you would rather not answer, it's okay."

"It's just that I have had women pass through my life, but not many I'd say were relationships because my mother pushes her choices on me and always scares the others away she didn't approve of...it always felt like she wanted me to suffer for the rest of my life for killing her uncle." He takes a deep breath and exhales. "My mother's idea of a perfect woman is one who came from 'good stock' and never challenged her. Gen never challenged my mother to fully be '*The Queen*' because Gen just wanted to be with Seth."

Bri changes direction a bit. "Let's play my favorite game!" She grins. "We flirt shamelessly, but the first one to who can't hold out and initiates sex, loses."

He is slightly puzzled. "I fail to see how that's losing?!"

"Funny." She softly laughs. "That's been asked before."

He is curious. "Do you play it regularly?"

"Like I said, it's my favorite..." puts her hands under his shirt and runs them up to his chest.

She sees a playful look in his eyes. "Something like this..." then he runs his finger from the middle curve of her collarbone down the middle to the tip of the 'V' of her shirt. He notices her breath catches and the goosebumps on her skin. He leans in and kisses down her neck then back up to her ear.

"You're a fast learner!" She lightly giggles.

He smiles against her skin as he continues kissing her neck, then abruptly stops. He looks into her eyes with an eyebrow raised and a dimpled smirk, then he gets up.

521

"We should have breakfast delivered soon and we have our tour." He says.

"Oh?" She asks as she starts to quickly get ready. "You stopped our game rather swiftly! Was it boredom or—?"

He grabs her bum and tugs her close. "Remember, Darling, *I* have the control in the bedroom."

"That's *if* I let you have that control." She raises her eyebrow in a challenge.

"*We'll see...*" He notes. "One word, Darling..."

"What's that?" She asks.

"Stamina." He playfully grins.

She studies him and she's starting to think she may have *a huge challenge* on her hands with him because with Lawrence it really is about having complete control. "*Stamina can go one of two ways, Ace!*" He glares a little because she most certainly has the determination to hold out! Which makes seducing her that much hotter to him!! They're about to sit down at the small table when she says, "*Wait!* Kahla!"

"I asked Mitchell to take her while you were in the bathroom." He says.

"Thank you." She kisses him sweetly. "Now, it's still going to be fun either way, so I'm just curious if I'm going to have to share you on our tour or—."

"This is a private tour, but we will be around the public at various times."

She smiles excitedly. "I can't wait to spend time with you and learning more about this enormous place! Although, it will make it challenging for the 'flirting game.'" He chuckles and kisses her once more.

CHAPTER 52

Imperfectly Perfect Royal Palace Tour

Their tour will start at The Main Entrance of The London Palace and Lawrence holds Bri's hand as they walk there, surrounded by The King's Guard, including McMasters and Mitchell. Vistors to The Palace that they pass along the way wave and snap pictures on their phones and cameras; a few ask for a picture with them.

The London Palace is beautiful and no lavishness, luxury, or expense were spared centuries ago building it, nor since for its upkeep. The foyer is extravagant with a skylight that cuts up through the floors, shining light on the ornate carvings and columns with gold etchings, and colorful murals in the trim everywhere. The red carpeted stairs split at the first landing with ninety-degree turns, one staircase to the left and one to the right, going up to the second floor.

They arrive at The Main Entrance as a different tour is about to leave. One American teenage young woman lights up asking, "Your Royal Majesty, are you two going to take a tour with us today?"

Bri happily smiles and looks at Lawrence as she answers the young woman, "His Majesty has arranged a private tour so I can ask lots of questions without slowing another group down. I'm so excited to learn more of The Palace's history!" Those around them who heard her response were pleasantly surprised an American was this excited about their history.

The young woman smiles. "I don't think there would be too many of us that would complain when on a tour with the two of you!"

Bri softly laughs. "My love of history, and the questions I'll ask, may get to be a bit much for someone who wasn't planning on a really long tour."

Their guide shows up and Lawrence talks with him a minute while Bri has her picture taken with this young woman and signs a couple of autographs for various others. The young woman walks away, happily showing her parents who were watching their interaction. Bri glances over and sees her mother mouth, 'thank you' and Bri smiles back with a little nod.

"Ready?" Lawrence asks.

Bri excitedly says, "*I am!*"

Lawrence makes the introductions between Bri and Stewart Langstone before they begin their tour. The guards give them a little more room as they keep people further back, but McMasters and Mitchell are still close. Bri could see there were many people watching them and it didn't bother her. What bothers her is the eerie feeling of being watched, but she refuses to let anything related to The Queen Mother ruin her day in any way with Lawrence! She pushes thoughts of people lurking and her people watching through security cameras out of her mind.

Surprisingly, they're moving right along. Bri is hanging on to every historical story and enjoying all the 'fun facts' Stewart gives her. When they get to the second floor, she looks around and sees there are arches over the doors, except at the far ends. There was a fireplace in the middle at both ends and a large door on each side of both fireplaces. There were mahogany columns, one on either side of the fireplaces. There is a large famous painting framed in gold above each fireplace, with a gold sconce on each side of the paintings.

They walk over to the nearest fireplace and go into the room through the large door. The room they walk into is somewhat dark, but it's an impressive room from what she can see with some daylight coming in through the stained-glass windows.

"This marble floor looks like it actually has gold sand swirled in it!" She walks around the room. "Is that..." she looks closer, "red *silk* on the wall?"

"It is!" Stewart replies. "Most people don't realize silk has been used for over 6,000 years."

"I would've guessed two or three thousand." She replies and they lightly laugh. She asks, "What room is this?"

 She can't see Lawrence, but she hears, "Wait for it..." He's feeling for the light switch and the lights pop on. He starts walking over opening his arms saying, "The Throne Room, Your Royal Majesty." He stops next to the platform and bows, rolling his arm out towards them.

"Oh my gosh, Lawrence, those gold lions are HUGE!" She is stunned. They are a bit bigger than life-sized lions, and they sit at the front corners of the platform the thrones sit on.

"These," he stands next to one of them, "are *almost* solid gold."

He looks at Stewart who explains to Bri, "They had to pour the gold into molds, then attach the pieces with a soldering-type of process. They did all that right in this room because it was easier to bring the heavy pieces in here, rather than two large statues that would weigh even more. The statues are pure gold, except for the fasteners that are used to secure it to the floor."

"That makes sense." She says, then looks at the floor and asks, "What's supporting this massive weight below?"

"Do you remember those bigger columns in The Royal Art Gallery?" Stewart asks her.

She nods. "You said those are solid rock, right?"

"Right!" Stewart smiles. "Granite."

Bri starts looking around again. She looks up and sees a crystal chandelier. She moves out from under it for a better view, "Is that solid gold, too?!"

"It is," Stewart answers, "and it was made by a company that's still making crystal chandeliers today!"

"That's incredible! It would be older than the US!" She says still looking it over. She continues taking everything in and notes, "It's amazing how much gold is in The Palace, but the amount that is just in this room...it's unreal! The walls are covered with dark-red silk, but the decorations are in gold or, like the mirrors and artwork, they're framed in gold!"

She stares at the platform with the thrones. It's covered in red carpet, the two front corners each have one of those pure gold lions, big and tall enough that there's no need for a railing but there is a railing going down the center to keep hands *off* the statues.

Behind the thrones is a red silk curtain and Bri remembers reading that centuries ago, The Heathherst Family Coat of Arms was carved in gold and hangs in the center between the two thrones. "Hold on..." she steps forward and stares for a moment, then points to a familiar double phoenix with a shield, "Is this *ours*?" She asks with confusion in her voice.

"It is! I had perfected your seal and sent it on to my father. When he had seen it, he stopped by my office. Being The Heathherst Family Patriarch, he has to approve these kinds of things. Oddly, he suggested we create a new *family* coat of arms using your seal..." He thinks back to that conversation with a puzzled look.

Bri watches him and wonders, "Lawrence, what did he say *exactly*?"

He dismissively shrugs a little. "He thought a new coat of arms for a fresh start would be good for everyone; he even suggested changing our last name..." He tells her as he stares at the seal. When he looks at her, he sees she's about to say something and says, "Drop this. Please."

She smiles sweetly and shakes her head. "Nothing about him." She crosses her heart and he smiles in acknowledgement. "I was just going to ask why, if that represents us, do you have the queen's crown already on it?"

He smiles using his dimples. "Wishful thinking..."

She smiles, shaking her head. "Which throne is yours, Your Majesty?" Lawrence motions to the right. "May I?"

"Of course!" He watches her as she nestles into his throne. "Well?" Lawrence asks, leaning against the golden lion on that side. "How does it feel?"

"Kingly..." She shifts, then looks and notices Stewart had stepped out and Lawrence is walking over to her. "A bit stiff *and rigid*, though..." She snickers.

He leans over the chair with his hands on the arms of it. "Then maybe you're in the wrong one," he gestures the other one, "try the other one..."

Not thinking she goes and sits on the other throne and Lawrence sits next to her and says, "*Perfect!*"

"Perfect?" She asks.

"My Queen is on *her* throne, and *always* seated to my right!" He smiles handsomely.

Then it clicks. "Oh no!" She shoots straight up out of the throne like it is on fire, shaking her head saying, "Nnnoo, No, no, no!"

He quickly stands and grabs ger hand. "Yes, yes, *yes!*" He pulls her to him.

He points to the back of his throne. She sees at the top, is the double-phoenix seal on a gold crest, with 'Heathherst' on a red ribbon at the bottom of it.

"I was thinking of having a heart-shaped throne made with this crest on the back of it." He smirks.

"Don't you *dare* or I will *never* sit in it!" She insists. "*Please* don't *ever* do that!"

He chuckles. "Alright, I promise I won't have that throne made." He wraps his arms around her and hugs her, then dips her back. "I'm going to kiss My Queen in this room and hope she will one day agree to be *The* Queen and my rightful partner in here."

"Sealing your wish with a kiss?" She smiles with a twinkle in her eye.

He kisses her so meaningfully; she feels it to the very core of her soul. He gently pulls their lips apart and he watches her as it takes a couple seconds before she inhales and opens her eyes.

He *almost* misses the one word she whispers. "*Okay.*"

"Okay?" He asks with his eyebrows scrunched together bringing her back up. "Wait. Your—you mean?" He's almost scared to think she's agreeing to be 'The Queen!' She smiles and nods. He kisses her and holds her tight. He rests their foreheads together and whispers, "*Say it.*"

"I'll be '*The* Queen!'" She says.

He picks her up and swings her around. She holds his cheeks and kisses him as he does. He gently sets her down.

He looks at her and tells her, "I promise not to plan your coronation for tomorrow—."

She laughs. "*Nor this year!*" She subconsciously lays a hand on her lower abdomen; he glances down at her hand and smiles.

"Deal." Then he teases, "*New Year's it is!*"

"Ha-ha! That wouldn't be much better!" She wraps her arms around his waist. "But next year—."

"Will be a *momentous* year!" He smiles and puts his hand on the baby.

She puts her other hand on top of his. "Yes, it will!" She holds her hand out and asks, "Shall we?" He chuckles.

He holds up a finger and runs to go turn off the lights, then he meets up with her at the door. He takes her hand again and kisses the back of it before they walk out into the hallway and continue with their tour.

After their tour, Lawrence takes only McMasters and Mitchell with them as they walk in what feels like a labyrinth of Palace halls, managing to pick up a small tray of meat, cheese, crackers, and fruit, along the way. They walk some more until they get to a cross section in a secluded part of The Palace, where a grand piano sits. Lawrence wants to play for her again and he hopes she will sing for him.

As they snack, he plays some beautiful pieces. Some she recognizes, like the one he wrote and played for her at The Manor, and some she didn't...but they were all moving. Then she hears a hymn she recognizes and she gets lost in the music...she doesn't know when she started singing out loud because she had started singing the words in her head. The song ends, and they sit there as the sounds of the echoes fade through the hallways.

"I only learned the music; I never knew there were words to that one. Will you sing another when we come back here sometime?" He asks.

"I'd sing anytime for you, especially when you play so beautifully!" She sweetly kisses him. They stand and pick up the plate to take with them. She comments, "It's pretty isolated back here and the acoustics are fabulous!"

"It's a place to play by myself," he looks at her lovingly, "or now with My Queen." He smiles.

"As I've told Jack and David, flattery will get you just about anywhere!"

"I'm curious, why did you finally agree to it?" He is referring to her agreeing to be queen.

"Not only have your son *and* David's son been flat out telling me, but I've been hearing their voices in my head at various times saying you needed your queen to be *The Queen*. Then, in The Throne Room, when you kissed me, I felt it to my very core...I *felt* what our son was saying...what David's son was saying, even what David meant..." She rests her forehead to his and takes a deep breath. "I know you want a date..."

"Darling, right now I'll take what I can get in the *right* direction." He lifts his head and holds her jaw, kissing her deeply. He takes her hand and tucks it between his body and arm walking down the hallway. He asks, "What did David say?"

She lightly laughs. "He essentially asked, 'Can you really blame him for wanting you to be The Queen?' Then he told me how he felt before he met me; how he felt overwhelmed by the daunting task of becoming the next duke when Ava essentially wanted the title and his money, but *none* of the responsibility that came with the title."

"*And with you*, David feels he can accomplish the impossible?" He asks.

She nods. "He feels like he has a partner with me, someone who'll work beside him."

"He's right." He stops walking and faces her. "I feel like with you *officially* by my side, I can rule in a monarchy I can be proud of, rather than continuing to rule *and fail* in a broken one."

Bri holds his hands and asks, "Lawrence, why do you think your mother puts you down?"

"Other than to be a vicious vindictive—?" He stops himself.

"Your mother said and did the things she said and did because she needs *you* to believe you are those awful things so you'll think you need her! She needs you to believe you can't do the job without her, because if you knew you were better off without her, she would lose all the power she had over you, *which she did!*"

"I realized that after you stormed out of my office that day." He tells her as they start to walk again. Then they see a middle-aged woman and an older man walking towards them.

"Your Majesty, Your Royal Majesty, would you mind if we asked you two a question?" A thinner woman with reddish-brown hair hesitates to inquire.

"Not at all!" Lawrence says with a smile to put them at ease.

"You play so beautifully, Sir, and we enjoy hearing the various melodies you play from time to time, but there was one, a hymn I believe, and a beautiful voice. Was that you, Your Royal Majesty?"

Bri's cheeks redden, but Lawrence proudly tells them, "*It was!*" He looks at her adoringly.

"Lovely, *absolutely* lovely, Your Royal Majesty!" The older gentleman happily says to her.

The woman clears her throat and goes to say more, but Bri asks, "I'm afraid you have the advantage, Ms.?"

"Oh, my apologies!" She makes sure her name badge is more visible. "Mrs. Ellen Conway, Ma'am."

"Mrs. Conway..." Bri encourages her to continue.

"We have a Christmas concert we're preparing for and want to highlight one person for the last song. This year, me and," she gestures herself, then the gentleman, "Mr. Wilfred Rigsby head up the committee. Could we, um, interest you in singing? You could pick the song, and maybe a certain *King* would accompany you? If His Majesty wants to, but no one has to know we even asked if either of you don't want to!"

"I...I don't know what the protocol is?!" Bri tells her, turning to look at Lawrence for his lead.

"I don't think there is one for this." Lawrence tells her. "Even if there was one against it, I'd throw it out because I think you should do it!" He smiles big with his dimples.

"What if I think you should do it with me?!" She raises her eyebrow.

"Well played!"

"I know!" She playfully replies.

He chuckles, then turns and looks at them. "Mrs. Conway, Mr. Rigsby, we both would be delighted to! However, on the program, please have it read 'By Royal Request' for security reasons."

"Right. Yes. Of course!" Mrs. Conway happily agrees. "Thank you, Your Majesty! Thank you!" She clasps her hands together. "Thank you, Your Royal Majesty! Thank you so much!" She is so excited and slightly bows to both of them before stepping back.

Mr. Rigsby smiles at Mrs. Conway, then turns to Bri and Lawrence and bows to them before he and Mrs. Conway walk back the way they came. Bri and Lawrence walk to The Royal Apartment.

 Lawrence stops her in front of The Royal Apartment's main doorway. She looks and sees the great shiny double-wooden door with a gold lion's head knocker in the center of the bottom panel on each door. The doors are framed by an arch like all the other Palace doors and one wouldn't necessarily know it's the door to The Royal Apartment, except this doorway has a bronze coat of arms shield above the doors.

Lawrence holds her hands. "This is my attempt at being *close* to spontaneous." He opens the door and has Bri step inside first. She looks up the stairs right there and sees it's lit up with heart-shaped tealight candles.

She gasps. *"It's so beautiful, Lawrence!"*

His heart is elated that she likes it! "I don't know why I was so nervous? I guess I thought you'd think it was *too* sappy."

Bri lightly giggles and points to herself saying, *"Hopeless romantic!* I may tease you that something's sappy, but as long as it's genuine, it's *all* good!" He smiles and nods as he gestures up the stairs. She takes his hand and goes up the stairs with him, following the candles to The Royal Chambers.

In The Royal Chambers, the room is full of candlelight. A light rose petal path that goes from the door to the little bay-like area by the windows where the small table has been set for a romantic dinner overlooking the city of London.

"Gold silverware?" She asks. "I thought you elites were born with silver spoons in your mouths but it must be gold for royals?! This really does explain a lot, Ace!" She teases and he laughs.

Lawrence makes a call to let the staff know they're ready to be served. He pulls out her chair for her to sit and then he sits next to her not across.

"This way we can see the city and talk while we eat."

They talk about the girls and some about him, but he keeps steering the conversation back to her. He feels they've talked enough about him lately and he wants to learn more about her.

After dinner, Lawrence stands and pulls her up to hug her close. The staff come in for the last time and clear everything away. They thank them and send their 'compliments to The Chef' and kitchen staff, along with a huge 'thanks' to all the staff for their help with setting everything up. Lawrence shuts the door and comes back to Bri as he unties his tie and leaves it draped around his neck.

He wraps her in his arms again. He kisses her, running his hands just under her shirt enough to feel the soft skin on the sides of her waist and around to her lower back.

"*So soft!*" He whispers.

He leads her to the bed and has her lie down. He crawls onto the bed and kisses her lower abdomen, then runs his hand across her soft belly. She hears him whisper something to the baby, but it's too soft for her to make out. He goes up and kisses the side of her neck.

He whispers, "*Do you trust me?*" He lifts his head to look into her eyes.

"*Yyyeeesss...*" She replies with a questioning look.

He gives her a smoldering, 'bedroom eyes' look; but it's a little different this time. He whispers into her ear and her breath catches. Bri gives a little nod, her confusion changing to curiosity. He reaches over to the drawer of his nightstand and pulls out the black blindfold he used up in The Clock Tower; she smiles when she sees it, then he blindfolds her. She unknowingly bites her lower lip, reminding him of their kiss up in The Clock Tower. He smiles and passionately kisses her, melting their lips together...

Lawrence takes off the blindfold and Bri's eyes take a moment to adjust. When they do, she sees a smiling, handsome man. "Come here, My Darling." She looks at him and he cups her cheek pulling her lips to his for a kiss.

"I can't really explain it," she says, "but I feel so many things with this deep love for you—I don't have one word for it...but I feel it strongly, *intensely!*"

He replies quietly, squeezing her a little tighter, "*Me, too, Darling.*"

He taps another kiss to her lips and she lays her head on his chest. They lay like this for a little bit, then they roll onto their own pillows and fall asleep for the night.

CHAPTER 53

Imperfectly Perfect Royal Jewelry

Bri slept hard through the night and when she woke up the next morning, the sun was bright. She looks at her phone and sees it's almost nine o'clock. She figures Lawrence isn't in bed and when she rolls over, she's right *but there is a note*:

> *Good morning, My Queen,*
>
> *Please let me know when you're awake. I had to take care of a few things this morning but wanted you and the baby to get as much sleep as you both needed.*
>
> *All my love,*
> *L*

She smiles and grabs her phone to text:

> Bri: "Good morning to you, My Sexy King!"

He smiles when he reads that.

> Lawrence: "We can argue about who's sexier later. (adds a smirking face) Clothes are laid out for you, no jewelry except your rings and maybe a watch if you'd like. See you in a bit! (adds a heart)"

"Odd..." She says to herself.

Bri gets up and sees a royal-blue dress and smiles. She goes into the bathroom and gets ready. When she hears knocking on the door, she puts a robe on over her slip and goes to answer it. She finds a man and a young woman with her breakfast Lawrence had sent up for her.

"Oh, thank you!" She puts her hand on her lower abdomen and motions for them to come in with the other hand. "We're famished!"

They both smile walking in and the man asks, "Where would you like it, Your Royal Majesty?"

"On the table by the window, if that's okay?" Bri asks.

"Lovely choice, Your Royal Majesty!" He smiles.

The man pulls her chair out and asks if there's anything else she needs? Bri sits and says there isn't. The man points to a phone Bri hadn't noticed and says palace extensions are all there, including The King's Personal Assistant, Spencer Brewer, and The King's direct line.

"Thank you, Mr. Bixley!" Bri says and he's surprised. She softly giggles and points to herself where a name badge would be, he looks at his and laughs a little. She turns to the young woman and reads her name badge, "Thank you, too, Ms. Kemp." The young woman of Asian descent doesn't look much more than eighteen years old.

"Miss Sarah Kemp was hired by The Queen Mother a few weeks ago," he looks pointedly at Bri in a way that has Bri taking it as Sarah Kemp shouldn't be trusted, "to be your Lady-in-Waiting and she's learning about the different roles of The Palace."

"Isn't a Lady-in-Waiting like a personal assistant?" Bri asks.

Miss Kemp's face lights up. "That *and so much more*! I'd see to your every whim, Your Royal Majesty!"

"I don't have much for whims and the ones I do have, the men in my life like to see to themselves; usually getting away, even if it's locked away from the world." Bri sweetly smiles, gesturing to the room. "Besides, Gabriel's my assistant and he's *phenomenal*!" Bri says and takes another bite of her food.

Miss Kemp starts to ask, "What about fashion, hair, makeup—."

"Miss Kemp, we should let Her Royal Majesty eat in peace." Mr. Bixley tells her and she shyly nods.

She curtsies before turning and walking to the door. Mr. Bixley discretely pats the top of Bri's shoulder and looks down, giving her a quick nod before he follows Miss Kemp out of The Royal Chambers.

When Bri finishes her breakfast, she hears talking in the hallway. It sounds like Lawrence; it is. She hears enough to know he is with The Chef. They come into The Royal Chambers and Lawrence introduces him to Bri.

Lawrence explains, "Chef Julian said he wanted to talk with you about any cravings you might be having."

They talk for a little while about nutrition and any allergies, which she doesn't have any *exactly*, but her system is picky. She doesn't do much for greasy foods, sauces, or rich tasting desserts. "I do like pizza or the occasional grilled cheese sandwich."

"She intrigued me at our first dinner." Lawrence remembers. "I just happened to see her scraping the sauce off her asparagus."

"Yeeeah, I like asparagus and most veggies sautéed, but not a fan of sauces on them. I love plain and grilled chicken. Nothing too fancy with food that's beyond simple seasonings. I'm weird."

"What about spaghetti or Alfredo?" Chef Julian asks.

"Those sauces are usually fine as long as someone doesn't go crazy and just sticks with the classics." She smiles apologetically. "I'm sorry if I'm making your job more difficult."

"Are you kidding?" He smiles. "This is actually easier on some levels; even lighter and healthier for most of it. I may have to cook some things up and have you try them before dinner parties and State Dinners." He suggests.

Bri looks relieved. "I'd be happy to do that! You can also call The Manor and speak to Edwin, The Head Chef there."

He smiles. "Please forgive me, but I already did. I just wanted to talk to you a little bit myself. I'm hoping this will make things smoother for you overall!" She appreciates that.

When the three of them are finished talking, they walk Chef Julian to the door of The Royal Chambers; he bows to both of them before he leaves. Bri turns to Lawrence with a playful look as she walks back into their room. He watches her with intrigue. She stops and turns to face him, dropping her robe. She bites her lower lip with a bit of a smile as she sees his eyes taking her in. He walks up to her with desire in his eyes.

"You're trying to distract me..." He rests his hands on her waist.

"*Ooorrr*," she raises an eyebrow, "we could say this is a *preview* of what you *could* see later tonight...then again, *you think* you have all the control in the bedroom..." She challenges him.

"Really?" He runs a hand down to her bum and tugs her close. "If I do, then I *definitely* won't be missing this show!"

"Then you have your work cut out for you while we're out and about today!" She lightly brushes her lips against his. "You *could* have a starring role with your fine body tonight!" She runs a finger down his lips. "I'd *hate* to have to find an understudy for your part."

He responds with determination, "That is *never* going to happen!"

"Oh! I *know*! You always play your part splendidly! With raving reviews and maddening desire for an encore!" She says against his lips, "No one could even come close enough to be named your understudy!"

His expression is still determined. "*No one*——." She kisses him.

When they pull their lips apart, she matches his determined look saying, "*Same goes for you*!"

He kisses down her neck and holds her tight against him. He lightly runs his lips up her neck, making sure she can feel the trail of his hot breath. Her moan tells him they need to stop, or they'll be late for what he has planned and that's *not* an option today.

"This is painful..." He taps a kiss to her lips, then grabs her dress right there and helps her step into it, kissing her lower abdomen and the baby. He steps behind her and zips her up. "It's a struggle to resist you!" He wraps his arms around her from behind, putting his hands over the baby, her hands automatically lay on top of his. He says next to her ear, "I *can't wait* for this little one to come!" He kisses her neck. "He's going to grow into such an amazing man because of his *amazing* parents!"

"Because of our incredible family shaping him, and all our children." She smiles and nuzzles his cheek. "What did you whisper to the baby last night?"

"Can't my nephew and I have a little secret?"

"*Not* from his mother!" She says with such conviction, his eyebrow raises as he studies her and decides not to mess around with that right now.

"I said he was going to have the best mum and family in the world!" He squeezes her a little tighter. "And I won't let *anyone* take that away from him!"

"*Lawrence...*" she whispers and tears fill her eyes, "*I love you so much, my heart overflows for you!*"

"Prove it, My Queen!" He smirks.

She giggles, turning to face him. "How?!"

"Let me drape some beautiful diamonds, rubies, or sapphires from your beautiful neck." He smiles so lovingly.

She playfully tells him, "You said 'no jewelry.'" She throws her thumb over her shoulder towards the closet. "*And* I have ones I can't wear often enough as it is! *However,*" she grins, "I wear my favorite set more than any others *and it's from you!*"

"Which—." He realizes she is referring to the channeled heart-diamond necklace set and shyly smiles a bit.

"Lawrence, if someone in the past would've told me that one day, I would love wearing a full diamond necklace, with hearts all the way around it no less; *and* it tends to be my 'go-to accessory,' I would've laughed them off!"

He kisses her hand. "Please?" He purposely adds his dimpled smile.

"*Ooo,*" she glares with a light giggle, "*you never play fair with the dimples!*"

"It's fair to me!" He winks and she rolls her eyes nodding and smiling. He adds, "If we don't find anything, then at the very least I want to leave with inspiration!"

"Alright...*for you.*" She says and grabs her things. He takes her hand and they go see Nigel at the jewelry store.

When they walk inside The Royal Jewelry Store, Bri starts to look at some of the jewelry in the cases she hasn't seen yet. Lawrence walks over to her after he had talked to Nigel about a set for Bri's dress for James and Amy's wedding. Lawrence has been working to match the right colors to a unique piece he hopes she'll love. He found them and Nigel helped him finish it.

They watch her looking around and when she goes to a particular case, he watches her closely. "Anything you like?" He is very interested in her thoughts about his designs!

She gives him a skeptical look. "This feels like a trick question."

"How's that?" He asks with a bit of a laugh.

"Because I answered that once and they ended up buying all the pieces I liked, which made me uncomfortable..."

"Because you were just answering a question."

"Right!" She replies. "So I'm *not* doing that again!" She squints her eyes a bit and studies him.

He chuckles. "I'm curious because these in this case," he puts his hand to his chest, "are *my* personal designs."

She steps back and looks around, realizing she first saw this case from a different angle when he brought her here before through The Secret Passageways and they came in through the back of the store.

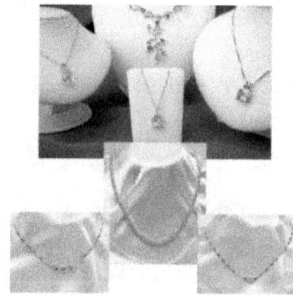

"You've changed things around! I don't remember these being in here before?!" She says peering back over the glass. "Your work is always stunning!" She always seems to light up looking at his pieces and he knows she's being genuine, making his self-confidence with his jewelry go up. "It looks like you're simplifying your pieces...I like that thicker, twisted gold strand in the front middle!"

"I am simplifying!" He smiles at her. "It seems My Queen has been influencing every part of my life!" He wraps his arms around her. "Will you try a couple of them on?"

"Alright," she smiles, "for you and your *exquisite* pieces!" She stops to say, *"But there's one condition!"*

"We won't take them *all* with us?" He finishes her thought, crossing his heart with his finger. "Just the set for the wedding and the set for today." She gives a small smile with a slight nod.

He has her try on a diamond and sapphire necklace with matching earrings and a bracelet that are in the case. He smiles lovingly and she takes those off as he hands her a few other pieces to try on and a few she looks at. He takes some pictures of the various pieces she tries on. He notices she takes a little longer on a cameo with a blue background with a silver setting.

"You'd look gorgeous in that, too!" He smiles.

"I've always loved cameos, but I'm not a huge fan of some of the peachy-orange colors that are commonly used for the background. *I love this on the darker blue!*" She tells him.

He makes a mental note of that and he moves to the counter and points, "This is the set I'm hoping you'll permit me to give you." Nigel turns it so she can see it better.

She sees a diamond necklace with a pendant of a champagne-colored square diamond, bordered by small square diamonds, and turned forty-five-degrees for a diamond-look. Larger than the small square-shaped diamonds are the pear-shaped diamonds that channel up and around to complete the necklace. Smaller versions of the pendant are used for the earrings. Lawrence takes the necklace and puts it on her.

While she is putting on the earrings, Nigel brings over 'The Diamond-Heart Tiara.' She puts it on and secures it in place, then looks at herself in one of the mirrors Nigel has on the counters. She smiles at Lawrence through the mirror.

He says, "My sincerest apologies if it feels like I'm being too demanding."

Bri is still smiling at him sweetly. "Ace, I've felt that there was a reason for all this when I had dropped my robe and you put *that* on hold!" She freezes for a moment and blushes when she realizes where they're at. She looks around to see if there is anyone else in the shop besides Nigel.

Both Nigel and Lawrence laugh lightly. "We're the only ones here, Darling."

She steers the conversation around. "*As I was saying*, I figured whatever you have planned must be important."

He says with a serious tone, "It is."

"Well, *My King*, it just so happens 'The Diamond-Heart Tiara' *is also a favorite*. I just haven't gone anywhere to wear *it* more either." She winks. "This is the first time I'm wearing it during the day."

"Bri, you're a royal now and you'll wear it more often, along with diamonds, sapphires, rubies, and emeralds. It'll be more for official functions and evening parties." Lawrence tells her.

She rolls her eyes. "Those would call for 'The Crown Jewels,' wouldn't they?"

"If all you wore were 'The Crown Jewels' you wouldn't wear them very often because they would be kept here." He gestures the direction of the vaulted room The Crown Jewels are kept in; only seen in their displays through a large, thick, bullet-proof security window.

She has a mischievous smile spread across her face. "You're right! *Much* safer! Let's stick with The Crown Jewels from now on!"

"Nice try, Beautiful!" He kisses her lips, smiling with his dimples again. He points to the champagne-colored diamond necklace on her neck, "*This* is one of *my* favorite necklaces! I made this some time ago; it's my very first *completed* design. It was the first time someone told me I had talent at anything." He tips his head towards Nigel.

"*You do!*" Nigel encourages him.

"Well, my mother demanded he crush my talent." Lawrence tells Bri.

Bri looks at Nigel with an appreciative smile. "Thank you so much for *not* doing that."

He tips his head to her with a smile. "We were secret friends, but mostly avoided each other outside of this place."

"I suppose it was safest that way. If The Queen Mother didn't see you two were friends, then she couldn't use you to threaten Lawrence with, or vice versa." Bri notes.

"You're more right than you realize, Bri." Lawrence says. "With my parents being known for their cruelness both verbally and physically; my mother would've dealt with this herself." He leaves it at that, but Bri reads him and thinks about the visions of the cruelness that were heaped upon Lawrence, *mercilessly* by The Queen Mother. She can still feel the burning sensation of her own flesh being burned in one of those visions!

She hugs him and says, "You're part of a family who loves you and would rather die than hurt you!"

Nigel whispers to Lawrence but loud enough for Bri to hear him, "*She's definitely a keeper, Lawrence!*" Nigel smiles in a fatherly way.

Lawrence smiles and agrees, "And her love is like a lifesaver to a drowning man!"

Bri smiles and they hold each other's gaze for a long moment. She lightly clears her throat and points to the necklace. "I love this!" She says. "*The whole set is beautiful!*" She looks in the mirror again. "It would be amazing to see this jewelry sold around the world! Like in a Worthington hotel, but not in the UK because of this place... *Ooo!* New York City would be *fantastic!*" She teases with their accent.

Lawrence kisses Bri fiercely! Nigel watches a man who's like a son to him, finally find love and he couldn't be happier! Nigel grabs a velvet box he had ready for them and hands it to Lawrence.

"Ah, yes. This is for your dress for the wedding." Lawrence opens it and watches her smile wide.

"It's perfect! It will stand out beautifully with the dark fuchsia pink dress Amy wants me to wear!" She beams.

"I'm sorry, Darling. I missed somewhere along the line when you said you were going to be a bridesmaid." Lawrence says.

She shakes her head. "You didn't miss anything." She squeezes his hand a bit. "Amy has her sisters as bridesmaids, but she wanted my dress to match

542

one of her other colors. She picked a pink color she always thought looked good on me." Bri explains. She points to the pearl of the same shade as her dress. "That's the color..."

Lawrence's necklace has a mixture of pearls and diamonds with a bow pendant that starts to the right of center when it's worn and is a couple inches long. A five-karat pink diamond is in the center of the bow, with the bow consisting of white and pink diamonds set in white gold. The rest of the necklace has a number of strands of various shades of pink pearls as well as white ones, along with shades of pink and white diamonds; the smaller diamonds and pearls are the same average size.

Bri's phone rings and she sees, "It's Jack."

"Do you need to take that?" He asks.

"I should. Jack or David wouldn't call unless they needed an answer to something right away." Bri explains with an apologetic look.

"It's fine, Darling. I can wrap this up while you talk." Lawrence smiles encouragingly. He knows Jack and David are already here, so Jack could be trying to wrap something up with work quick.

"Are you sure?" She worries.

He smiles. "Yes. I promise." Bri smiles and kisses his cheek before stepping away from the counter and brings the phone up to her ear.

Jack and Bri have a goal of being fully staffed and operational in April and they want to launch the first of the textiles not too long after the first Spring shearing of the sheep's wool. April 16th is the date for 'The Black & White with a Splash of Gold Ball.' He and Bri talk over a few critical things.

Before they hang up, Bri mentions what she'd like to do with Lawrence's jewelry pieces. Jack asks if he has a logo or brand. "Hold on a sec, Jack." She turns to Lawrence, "Ace, I haven't seen any of your pieces branded..." she notes, looking at the backs of some pieces.

"No...I hadn't thought of anything like that, just my 'L' that I used in our monogram as well."

 Bri grabs a piece of paper from her purse and draws something...then shows Lawrence. "This just popped into my head." The piece of paper has his 'L' inside a diamond outline, and a crown on top of the diamond. "It could work without the crown or a different one, gray or gold, too. If we use contrasting colors, it'll stand out more."

Bri suggests the name, 'Crown Lux Royale.' Lawrence does a 'so-so' for the name. She tells Jack and Lawrence, "We'll think more on the name." She suggests to Jack about his business questions, "Why don't I look at the email you just sent and we can talk later, Amore Mio?" He agrees.

He asks her to send him a picture of the logo and tells her he agrees that New York City may be the best place to launch a separate store because of the store in The London Palace. Plus, Jack knows the hotel David's been in negotiations with to buy, also has store space in it and that could be the perfect place to launch. They say, 'I love you' and hang up.

Lawrence hugs and kisses her. "Thank you!"

"Thank *you* for the jewelry I get to show off!" She smiles big. "Lawrence, you are *brilliant* in your own right! You're amazingly talented and I would love for the jewelry you've made over the years to be available to everyone. I'm guessing there's a lot?"

"Ha-ha!" Nigel bursts out laugh. "A whole store full and then some! In a store where every day people can come and go at their leisure, I'm sure he'd have people buying all kinds of his work. *Aaand* it helps that a king designed and made them, too."

"Profits going to The Crown's Royal Charity Fund, or The New Beginnings Foundation, otherwise the public may be upset I'd use 'The Crown' to sell products for my personal profit." He throws out there.

"Oh my gosh, I forgot about making money! I was just excited to get these pieces out there for people to appreciate your talent and enjoy wearing your various pieces; not sitting on some shelf collecting dust! However, I don't think it's a good idea for The New Beginnings Foundation to be a main recipient either." She states and then looks at Lawrence with so much love and excitement for him. "Tell me now if you're against this because with Jack's help, we'll make a success out of this for any charity!"

She gets a text from Jack and shows Lawrence what Jack came up with for his logo. "That's a fantastic start!" Lawrence smiles as he looks closer.

"I like the arrangement of the colors." Bri talks as she types a text back to Jack saying the same thing.

He takes the phone and adds to her text about the profits and charity. He hands her phone back and then says, "I have an idea. Let me do a simple piece for your fundraiser in April! A simple design for the occasion and we can donate *those* proceeds to your 'New Beginnings Foundation.' What do you think?"

She practically leaps into a hug, wrapping her arms around his neck; he spins her around once. "Thank you for being so *fantastically brilliant* and thank you for letting me show off your work and thank you for loving——." He kisses her quiet and Nigel quietly chuckles. This time he kisses her until she relaxes in his arms.

"*Thank you* for your love and support. Having you believing in me in so many ways, *means the world to me*, Bri!" He tells her.

She smiles lovingly. "I *do* believe in you! With all of my heart!" He kisses her once more before they leave the jewelry store, saying goodbye to Nigel.

CHAPTER 54

Imperfectly Perfect Royal Judge, Jury, & Public Execution

Lawrence holds Bri's hand as they walk through The London Palace and people are noticing her in her royal-blue dress with The Diamond-Heart Tiara and The Champagne Diamond Necklace Set; he matches her dress color with his tie and square in his front pocket. He also has a gold pin on his lapel of the new Triquetra Heart Monogram Crest. They look like the regal and royal couple they are. There is a lot of excitement and camera flashes going off as people notice them.

They arrive at an outside door that is near the hallway to go to The Dungeons. Lawrence stops and holds her hands with a serious look on his face. Bri sees this and glances around saying, "Lawrence, you're making me nervous."

He sees her look at the sign for The Dungeons. "I don't mean to do that, Darling. What comes next *is* serious and this is another look into my world and punishing those who commit a crime against The Royal Family." He caresses her cheek with the backs of his fingers. "To punish all those who would dare be involved in hurting you."

Her eyebrows furrow together. "What do you mean?"

"While McMasters, with the help of Mitchell, have replaced and restructured The Royal Guard, along with The King's Guard, *except three*." He's referring to Tristan, Gavan, and of course, The Queen Mother. "They also investigated who abducted and abused you that night. I wanted to know not only who did the actual crime, but I wanted to know who knew about it and went along with it, even if it was simply keeping quiet about what was going to happen, what was happening, or what did happen."

"And what did you find out?" She asks.

He takes her hand and holds it firmly. "Come with me."

He takes her outside with him after putting a coat on her. It's a beautiful sunny day, but the air is crisp since it's early November. They walk in comfortable silence for a little ways, until she can hear voices of a crowd in the distance. The crowd slowly starts to come into view and it's a crowd of onlookers that includes various members of the media and the press. Opposite the crowd and next to The Palace wall is where a smaller group of people and Royal Guards stood.

Bri gets an uneasy feeling. "Lawrence, what's going on?"

 "Centuries ago, this place was named 'The Killing Wall' because public executions took place here." He points to a rectangular indentation out from in front of the seating area. "That's where The Gallows once were." The first handful of rows for seating are the original stone seating. "As you know, most of our justice system is handled within our judicial system. *However*, you're also fully aware that direct crimes against The Crown and other royalty have long been reserved for 'The *King's* Justice.'"

She slows down, putting it all together. He barely hears her whisper, "*No...*"

He stands in front of her, blocking everyone's view of her face, especially cameras. He quietly and calmly asks, "Remember when we discussed I needed to make a stand?"

She looks at him and softly says, "*Yes.*"

"*This is it*, Bri, and I need your support." He tells her.

She reminds him, "I said I'd support you and be by your side, regardless if I'm 'The Queen,' *and I meant it.*"

"Good, because I need you! But you'll need to be strong, even if it means leaning on me, squeezing my hand, whatever it may be to stay strong; but *don't* break down out here in front of the public, or you could be seen as too weak to be 'The Queen.' Alright?" He asks.

She takes a deep, calming breath and nods. "Just what are you going to do?"

He hesitates. "I want *everyone* to see you're protected by me. If they manage to hurt you in *any* way, they better expect to be hunted down and punished, *even executed.*" He was expecting her to argue but instead, all she does is takes his hand and holds it, giving him a little nod. He whispers, "*Thank you!*" She gives him a faint smile before they walk in resolute silence.

When they get closer to everyone, they are announced to the audience:

"His Majesty, The King, and Her Royal Majesty, The Princess Imperial."

At the podium, Bri looks and sees Genevieve, Seth, Abby, then David and Jack, only giving slight nods to each other and nothing more.

"Thank you, Ladies and Gentlemen." Lawrence begins. "An investigation has been underway into Her Royal Majesty's abduction and brutal physical assault. To pull this off involved careful planning and included a number of my guards and staff. Her Royal Majesty's bodyguard, retired United States FBI Supervisory Special Agent Oliver McMasters, wanted to personally look into it. I agreed and put him in charge of the investigation and I also asked him to 'clean house' with The Royal Guard, including The King's Guard, and *all* Palace staff."

"McMasters had already recruited retired United States Secret Service Special Agent Aaron Mitchell to join the protection detail for The Princess Imperial. Fortunately, Mitchell came onboard a little early to help with the investigation and protection of Her Royal Majesty. Together, McMasters and Mitchell investigated the crime, sifted through all of the guards, and the entire staff. They dismissed anyone not loyal to The Crown, but innocent to the crime against The Princess Imperial."

"These two men worked tirelessly in a short amount of time and achieved the impossible. After conducting their investigation and weeding out guards and staff, they combed through our military, special forces, and law enforcement personnel, interviewing lots of exemplary men and women. They would also vet them and all the newly hired Palace staff.

For their extraordinary job, I have officially named McMasters as The Royal Guard's Grand Marshall and put Mitchell in charge of The Princess Imperial's detail."

There is applause from the crowd as McMasters and Mitchell step forward and bow to The King and The Princess Imperial. She smiles and mouths, 'Thank you!' And 'Congratulations!' Bri feels Tristan's irritation at being 'overlooked' for The Grand Marshall post and she is impressed upon that The Queen Mother is also upset when she heard this news from Tristan. Lawrence would tell Tristan he wanted him close and that there wasn't anyone else who could fill his shoes.

Lawrence continues talking to the crowd.

> "I would like Grand Marshall McMasters to brief The Princess Imperial on his findings."

He looks at McMasters and gestures for him to come up to the podium. McMasters steps up and they shake hands as they pass each other. McMasters centers himself, then slightly turns to Bri.

> "Your Royal Majesty, an investigation was conducted into your abduction and assault. We've found there were eight there that night, not counting the one that was killed that night. We were only able to apprehend five and arrest twenty-three others who knew about it and either assisted in keeping a lookout, sought information into the investigation to pass along to the guilty, or in other various ways purposely tried to impede the investigation." He turns and looks at Lawrence. "Your Majesty, these twenty-eight are here and await your sentencing. However, there is one matter you would like to take care of first..." He steps back.

Lawrence steps up to the podium again and turns to Bri.

> "Your Royal Majesty, we need you to identify one of the last three people involved in this violent crime against you. Please look at them and see if you can identify anyone from that night. We're hoping it's one of the three yet to be apprehended."

There were five men lined up for her to see if the guilty person was there, like a police line-up of sorts. They asked Gavan at the last minute 'to help' and he thinks he's doing them a favor. She walks by the first three and stops in front of Gavan, looking at the fifth one, but then she turns and stares emotionlessly at Gavan. When he realizes she's *actually* going to name him, he glares at her and goes to step back, but he bumps into McMasters who now handcuffs him; the other four men step back to give them room.

Bri leans into Gavan's ear whispering, "'*Keep your friends close, but your enemies closer.*'" She pulls back and looks him straight in the eye, continuing to whisper, "*If you really thought you were in the clear this whole time, THAT WAS THE PLAN! The King was ready to kill you right then and there when I told him the names of ALL those I knew were involved! I'M the one who wanted The King to feed you, and Tristan, false information that you'd take back and whisper to The Queen Mother.*"

He is still glaring when he angrily tells her, "The Queen Mother *will* retaliate!"

"Of course she will!" She replies plainly. "It's expected! Just as we expect her 'pet' to continue whispering into her ear, even after you're gone, but it's with the information *we* want her to know."

Gavan's eyes go wide as he inhales to warn Tristan, but McMasters is ready. When Gavan opens his mouth and inhales to call out to warn Tristan, McMasters had a rolled-up bandana ready and he quickly puts it into Gavan's mouth and ties it tight behind his head. Lawrence stands back up to the podium, speaking in his official 'kingly tone.'

"For the twenty-three who knew of the assault and indirectly assisted in it being carried out, including impeding the investigation or your silence, you are hereby sentenced to ten lashings with one of the same instruments that was used on Her Royal Majesty." Bri silently gasps as the crowd of people gasp out loud. Lawrence continues, "For four of the six who were directly involved with the assault, you are hereby sentenced to death by a firing squad.

Alastair Gillery, *former* Keeper of The Dungeons, you were *and are* held to a higher standard of conduct because of your position. For your appalling actions and atrocious behavior towards The Princess Imperial, *and your King*, you are hereby sentenced to death by being run through with the blade of your own sword. You will stay tied to the post until you are pronounced dead. *And lastly*, Gavan Luxton, a member of my personal guard, *you* are hereby stripped of your position within The Royal Guard *and* The King's Guard because of *your inexcusable* actions and *vile* behavior towards The Princess Imperial, *and your King*. *You* are hereby sentenced to death by being run through with the blade of *your own sword* and you will remain tied to the post until you are pronounced dead. All those being executed will then have a 'kill shot' administered before their bodies are removed and taken out to an undisclosed location to be buried in an unmarked grave." Before Lawrence steps away from the podium, he says, "Grand Marshall McMasters, you are hereby ordered to carry out all sentencings."

"Yes, Your Majesty." McMasters solemnly answers him with a quick nod.

Lawrence steps over to Bri, as McMasters walks over to The Killing Wall, communicating to his guards through their microphones and earpieces. The King's Guard will be carrying out the punishments, but do so with black hoods to cover their faces to keep them anonymous; their individual identity didn't need to be known because this is The King's punishment and the guards are following *his* orders. The twenty-three sentenced to lashings were turned to face the wall and handcuffed to it. There's also a place for them to hold onto and they are spaced apart so that the ten lashings can be administered to each one *at the same time*. That's to spare Bri, as well as the onlookers, of having to watch ten individual punishments.

Lawrence holds Bri's hand, tucking her arm up under his. She looks up at him and he looks at her, straight faced, but he squeezes her hand and arm a little more to show he's got her; she gives his hand a little squeeze back. She was holding onto the railing in front of her and as she lets go of the metal bar, she feels how stiff and sore her fingers are from tightly gripping it. David and Jack come up to the other side of her and David takes that hand in his.

David leans over a little bit and whispers, "*They'll never know if you're watching or not! Just stay strong if you watch, otherwise, pick a spot near them and stare at that.*"

Bri whispers, "*Thank you...*"

She laces their fingers and holds his hand firmly. David steps closer to her so their hands couldn't be easily seen, helping her look stoic as they watch the lashings; Jack was right next to David. With the first sound of a lashing, she jumps a little, but she focused on having the strength Lawrence asked of her and she felt it from the three of them.

When the punishment had been administered to all twenty-three people, they're taken down but are sat down on a bench and purposely left there to witness the rest of the punishments. The King's Guard move on to the next punishment to be carried out. Four different hooded guards take the four to be executed by a firing squad to the 'firing wall.' They're sat in wooden chairs being handcuffed with their arms behind the back of their chairs, then hoods are put over their heads. Four other hooded guards step into position out in front of the condemned men, next to their rifles. When the first four hooded guards are safely behind them, the second set of four hooded guards pick up their rifles. McMasters yells out the commands loudly so they can be carried out simultaneously...

"READYYY...AAAIM...FIRE!"

All four shots go off at *almost* the exact same time with all four shots hitting their mark...the heart. As each one dies, only seconds apart, Bri watches the spirit rise up from their body and orbs of dark spiritual matter drag the spirits away as these spirits scream in fear! She doesn't process what she had just seen because she notices one of the hooded men was smaller than the rest...Bri starts to wonder if this is a woman? *Interesting*...she thinks to herself; she has never really thought about a woman guard before, but why not?!

This *person* walks over to Mr. Gillery where words were exchanged and Bri sees the former Keeper's head sharply move forward, then slumps with his body. It takes a second for it to register, '*The hooded guard just stabbed Mr. Gillery with a sword!*' It'll take time for The Keeper to die, it was purposely done this way, and they move on to the last execution. Bri is able to see this one without any obstruction to her view. There's another hooded guard, who says a few words to Gavan before swiftly driving the blade of a sword into his side at an upward angle. Gavan's agony before death has begun... McMasters sends the twenty-three prisoners with lashings to an infirmary they have set and medical staff are on standby for their arrival.

It's a somber mood, but as she looks at the small crowd of people and media; no one seems appalled. She's a little surprised, then again, this is a different culture. It's similar to the US in many ways here, but there are definitely *huge* differences. Bri looks at Lawrence as he handsomely stands firm. Lawrence looks at Bri and is impressed by her composure. He turns and looks into her eyes and sees they have a sadness in them, but there's something else he can't quite figure out.

Lawrence leans down and whispers, "We need to stay here just a little longer." He squeezes her hand, hugging her arm close and she squeezes his hand back.

The two of them, with Jack and David, giving stoic nods as people leave. A picture is taken for the various evening editions of Bri standing next to Lawrence, both solemn in their stance. One evening's headline: '*Our King's American-Brit: One of a Kind or Perhaps...Queen of a Royal Flush.*' The next picture is of all four of them, standing together looking very much like leaders, but also as a strong family.

Abby, Genevieve, and Seth, come up to them. Abby tells her, "I'm so glad you're here to support him! People weren't sure in the past if The Monarchy should have the right to execute, but when word spread of your *ghastly attack* with photos, it seems most of them joined the support calling for severe punishments and executions! Lawrence told us," she gestures the three of them, "of the pain you were in and you wouldn't take pain medication because you were pregnant! Well, that secret got out and you'd be hard-pressed to find one person in this country that doesn't support this! All the talk now is the identity of the missing now *two* people?" Seth said his money is on their mother.

"*Pretty safe bet!*" Bri thinks to herself, but accidentally whispered it out loud.

She gives an apologetic small smile to them, but they give her understanding expressions. Just then everyone jumps at the sound of a gunshot, then another...until there were four...a hooded person had shot a 'kill shot' into all four, *now five*, as they did the same with The Keeper as well; Gavan wasn't dead yet. Bri looks over just as The Keeper's spirit is *attacked* by darker spiritual matter stretching his spirit as he screams in terrified horror and agony until his spirit is actually 'ripped apart.' Then she watches as they all disappear, taking the pieces of his spirit beneath the surface of the ground with them. It was very disturbing *and unnerving* to watch! She's able to push it aside for now.

Lawrence squeezes her hand and she jumps a little. "Are you alright?"

Bri barely whispers, "*No.*" He's about to ask, but she adds, "*I'll explain later.*"

Lawrence turns to David and Jack, leaning in a bit to whisper as he asks, "*Will you take Bri back to The Royal Apartment?*" They nod.

"No, Lawrence." She softly, but firmly, tells him, "We came here together; *we leave together.*" She tells him and looks at David and Jack, "*Plus two.*"

She jumps when the last shot rang out...Gavan was dead. She notices his spirit isn't quite as dark as the others, but she braced herself for the dark spiritual matter to come for his spirit, only it doesn't. Instead, the ground opens, giving an orangish glow to the bottom half of Gavan's spirit; his spirit is sucked down into it with Gavan's scream echoes.

Jack figures it out and leans way over to quietly ask, "You're seeing what's happening to their spirits, aren't you?!" David watches for her response and she nods; he holds her hand more firmly.

After a decent walk, they get back to The Royal Apartment. Bri is in a zone and she excuses herself to go upstairs and lie down for a while. Up in The Royal Chambers, she takes Kahla out of her pet carrier and snuggles her to her chest. Unfortunately, as Bri relaxes, everything hits her and she runs to the bathroom and throws up. She faintly hears Lawrence's voice out in the room, it sounds like he's on the phone.

"I'm checking on her now..."

Lawrence comes up to the bathroom door to ask her how she is holding up, but he hears her throwing up again. He lightly knocks and steps inside the bathroom. He walks over to her and holds her hair back until she's done. He gets a cold washcloth as Bri lays on the cold marble floor. Lawrence had already taken his suit coat off downstairs and loosened his tie. He sits on the floor and puts the cold washcloth across her forehead. He sees Kahla poke her head around Bri and he picks her up. He nuzzles Kahla for a moment, then lets the puppy curl up next to Bri and she pets Kahla's soft black fur.

Lawrence runs his hand in her hair. "Would you like me to have Jack or David——." She shakes her head as she slowly sits up; Lawrence jumps up to help her.

He takes the puppy while Bri brushes her teeth a couple times and gurgles some mouthwash. She sits on the edge of the tub next to Lawrence and dries her mouth.

He puts his hand on her thigh. "Talk to me so I can help you through this."

"Lawrence," she puts her hand on his, "I said I would support you in whatever you needed to do to make your stand. What bothers me isn't their execution so much as it's an overall sadness that they made such horrible choices, made a complete mess of their lives, and for what?! For their spirits to be dragged off, ripped apart, or sucked down to some part of Hell." She inhales and holds her breath.

"*Whaaat?*" He's surprised. "You saw *all that?!*"

"Dark orbs, well, evil matter I guess you'd call it, hauled down to Hell the spirits of those executed...except The Keeper's and Gavan's spirits...Mr. Gillery's had his spirit ripped apart by these orbs of dark spiritual matter...Gavan had the earth open up beneath his feet and he was sucked down to where I can only assume is some place in Hell. All of these sprits were very scared! *I can still hear the fear in their terrified screaming.*"

"That should've been *my* burden, not yours." He softly says.

"I'll be fine. I'm already feeling better with you here. I may seem heartless when it comes to death, but I've always looked at it differently. The body is a shell; our loved ones shouldn't be camped out at their graves because they've hopefully moved on into the light of love, mercy, and forgiveness. Our mortality is only one *necessary* step on an eternal journey." She squeezes his hand a little. "Mortal time isn't the same as eternal time. One day in eternity is thought to roughly be one thousand years here on earth. In that scenario, we're born into mortality, live our lives, and die, *all* in a small fraction of the same eternal day."

"If more people looked at death the way you do, maybe the pain of losing a loved one wouldn't be so bad?" He wonders.

"I don't know. I've never lost anyone I was close to. I mourned the loss of the best friend Katie never was, but I'd be insulting people if I said I could relate and understand mourning a loved one who's actually died." She says. "What a person mourns is the sudden loss of a relationship they can *never* get back in this life with the person who has died." She looks at him and shakes her head telling him, "I can't even begin to fathom the thought of something happening to you, David, or Jack! I never really thought about where dark and evil spirits go; however, after witnessing what I saw today, my understanding of 'Hell' was *very* generalized."

"I haven't lost anyone I've been close to either. There wouldn't be *any* loss with my mother and probably not much, if any, with my father." He says.

"For what it's worth, I *strongly feel* there's a piece of that puzzle missing with him." She gives him a gentle smile. Before he could balk at that, she asks, "How did all this work with you being judge, jury, *and* executioner, even if that part was by proxy?!"

He puts up his finger for 'just a sec' and puts a fluffy towel in the tub and puts Kahla on it. When he does that, Bri goes to the sink and cools her neck down with the washcloth. She turns to lean her backside against the sink as Lawrence comes back over to her.

"Simple answer, Bri..." he steps right up against her, "I'm King." He holds the back of her jaw and around to the back of her neck, lifting her head with his thumbs under her jaw. "Bri, use your beautiful brain full of knowledge and think back to the history you know...*how is a king essentially above the law?*" He can see her take in what he said and she thinks about it against what she already knows about ruling monarchies.

"Oy..." she rolls her eyes at herself, "*basically*, kings *are the law*. They can't prosecute themselves..."

"Well, true, but there's something else. Everyone essentially works 'at the leisure of The King.'" She nods in agreement with him. He further says, "Yes, Parliament is represented by the people and they get to move the country in the direction they want, well, they *should be* moving in the direction their voters want to go."

"Right...so if 'The King's leisure' changes, you can fire and replace whomever you want." She adds.

"As far as Mother was concerned, being king is all the answer anyone would get. We both know it's more complicated than simply that!"

She agrees. "Your mother's way is the way to get overthrown by the people in a revolution!"

He smiles at her, still holding her face. "I didn't plan on this being how I was going to make my stand, but the more I found out about your assault, the amount of people involved, those loyal to my mother, *and* what my mother has been doing *in my name*!" He takes a deep breath. "Well, the angrier I got... If my mother does one more thing to you, I don't know if I can stop myself from killing her with my bare hands."

"Let's hope it doesn't come to that!" She says. "However, there is more on the horizon..."

He nods as he takes a deep breath and smiles sweetly. "I want *everyone* here *and* around the world to know that hurting you, whether laying a finger on you or not speaking up, and everything in between, will result in a *severe* punishment! If that means a punishment of death, *I won't hesitate!*" He has a kingly tone when he *tells* her, "*I won't——.*" She kisses him, which catches him off guard, but he swiftly returns the kiss, firmly embracing her.

"Now, about using your bare hands..." She says. "Lawrence, self-defense, even justice, is one thing, but revenge is entirely another."

"Bri! She's done so much——." He starts to say but she covers his mouth.

"And here's where I once again refer back to 'everything happens for a reason.' Lawrence, do you remember what I said happened right before I was whipped?" She asks.

"*You were shaking!*" He says with a hint of exasperation.

"*Then* what did I say happened?" She asks and watches him think, but she answers, "I had a calmness come over me and I was given a strength to endure that I didn't make a sound! None of them, including your mother, got the satisfaction of hearing me cry out in pain! *Not once!*"

He exhales. "*Then why make you go through it in the first place?!*"

She gives him a small, loving smile. "Lawrence, The Lord knows what's going to happen and He can help us prepare for whatever comes our way, if we have faith *and listen* to the Spirit. He helped me by giving the strength to bear what your mother did to me." She feels his next question and adds, "Bad things happen because everyone has their own agency; they have to be left to make their own choices. *However*, they will be held accountable, if not in this life, then on the other side of this one! Nothing prevented what happened to me because that night stood against them in this life and, by the looks of it, on the other side as well. Every single one of those people today had *multiple* times to change the course of their life. Some by secretly getting word to you, then their punishment——."

"*They wouldn't have been punished!*" Lawrence says with frustration. "Had we known soon enough, we could've had some sort of trap set!" He takes a deep breath. "Bri, you also need to consider that those who were executed would've been executed by my mother as soon as their usefulness was done."

She agrees and then says, "What happened today was 'Royal Justice' because they knew what they were doing was wrong and what would happen if you caught them! As you said earlier, The Royal Guards are held to a higher standard *and* they thought they'd get away with it because of your mother. You, seeking out your mother to kill her personally because of everything she has ever done to you, *which I completely understand why*," she holds his hands, "is revenge."

"That's just it! It's about YOU! All these years I took everything she ever dished out because I was keeping Seth and Abby safe! She crossed the line with you! If I have to kill her to protect you and our—." She surprises herself when she kisses him fiercely. Something about Lawrence's protectiveness of her was *very* sexy at that moment, now add the power behind his being king and, well...the kiss becomes incredibly passionate!

She gently pulls their lips apart and catches her breath some before saying, "You just got *so much sexier*, Ace...if that's even possible!" She goes to lead him out, but he pulls her back and sits her on the counter.

"*Here.*" He commands in a sexy tone and has a slight smirk on his face, "Remember, when it comes to this..." he kisses back to her ear, "*you.are.mine.*" He feels her shiver and hears her smile. He says kissing down her neck, "Say it, Bri! Tell me you're mine."

She refuses, "No." He gives a low growl. She thinks to herself, '*Let the power play begin...*' and then she feels his hands at her hips begin to move to her waist as he runs his lips down her jawbone.

He barely touches her lips, "I *always* get what I want, Bri..."

She pulls back just enough he can't easily kiss her. "Not with me you won't!"

He tangles his hand in her hair at the back of her head, then lightly pulls her hair so she'll tip her head back. "Keep this up and I'll make you writhe in desperation, but I won't hear you..." he very lightly kisses her lips. She raises her eyebrow to him in defiance. He traces her lips with his fingertip. "All you have to do is say you're mine."

She says with a determined, but playful look, "*You're* mine."

He gives her a faint growl as he picks her up, her legs wrapping around his waist, saying, "I warned you, My Queen!"

"What?" She plays innocent. "I said the two words you told me to!"

"You knew exactly what I meant." He takes her to their bed.

He isn't rough but his moves are deliberate. He takes his time to prove a very maddening point...he *will* get what he wants, especially in the bedroom...

Bri lays with her head on his chest, he's running his fingers in her hair and kisses the top of her head. "I *am* yours, Bri." He goes to move her so he can look into her eyes, but she stops him.

"No, no! Hold me tight a little longer...please..." she softly asks. He lightly squeezes a little harder to let her know he would. She kisses his chest before she says, "Lawrence, I feel like a hypocrite when I say I'm yours because I have David and Jack pop into my head."

"*I know that*, Darling! But when you're with me, you're with me; just like when you're with David or with Jack."

She lifts her head and looks at him with a playful grin, "And with you, I'm *definitely* with you!" She leans in and sweetly kisses him. He holds the back of her head as they kiss again. She looks into his eyes and she's about to say something but his phone rings. She smirks, "Ignore it."

"Ignore what?" He grins with his dimples, rolling them over saying, "I have more homework to do!" She giggles as he pulls the sheet up and over them.

CHAPTER 55
Imperfectly Perfect & Royally Intrigued

Bri wakes up from a nap and sees Kahla is sleeping on her pet bed Lawrence had put on the bed for her. He knows Bri worries about smothering Kahla since she is so little; this bed has sides to help protect her a bit. Bri pets her for a couple minutes before getting up.

Bri sits up and checks her phone. She returns texts to David and Jack who are checking in and want to know how she is doing. She says she is just waking up and asks them to give her some time. They say they are with McMasters and Mitchell throughout the day. They send their love and tell her to rest and to let them know if she needs anything.

Bri reaches for her bag for some crackers and finds the black leather-bound book Jessica had her find that day she toured The Dungeons for the first time...*and the confrontation with The King that came afterwards*. She gets comfortable and snacks on her crackers as she begins to read what she quickly realizes is a woman's diary. Kahla comes over and curls up next to Bri while she reads.

Meanwhile, Lawrence is working away in his official office when the phone rings. He picks it up.

"Yes."

"It's about time you acted like a real king!"

He couldn't have more disdain for this woman.

"Mother."

That's about all he could stomach to say to her. He knew she and Tristan were the last two to be punished, but he was trying to come up with a plan to bring her to her knees. He was hoping one of the twenty-eight would've given up his mother, but they knew her repercussions would be far worse. And her punishments are more severe than anything The King would ever inflict upon them; even death would be swift coming from The King. No, they wouldn't risk it, not even for their very lives. He knows his mother isn't above hurting children and she would take it out on their families. He *knows* she'll try to hurt Bri again; it's only a matter of time...and it'll only get worse for everyone until she gets what she wants from Bri...his heir; then she'll kill Bri when she is no longer useful to her.

"Son, I'm proud of you and how much you've embraced your teachings! You even did it without any emotions!"

He knows she is trying to provoke him, so he jabs a little back.

"Just doing what needed to be done to protect *my family*." He can feel his mother's glare and he exhales with a hint of annoyance. "*What* do you want Mother?"

"Just to tell you that you're finally becoming a *real* king! The King I've been shaping you to be all these *years*!"

"You wanted a son who would be unfeeling and callous, that has *never* been me, Mother, and it *never* will be!"

She snaps, "Hate to break it to you, *Son*, but that's exactly what it took to issue those orders!"

"*Love* is what it took!" He tells her and she scoffs. "I did it to punish those who hurt Bri, so *others* would think twice before doing anything to her in the future! Unlike you, I found *no* pleasure in it!"

She exhales in disgust. "Love has made you even more of a *pathetic twit than I thought*! She could have been raped, but she wasn't!"

He clenches his jaw, pausing for a second, before he continues working at his desk.

As he writes something down, he notes, "Interesting...how would you know that, Mother? We managed to catch all but two, so this isn't finished. What goes around, *always* comes around! Gavan found that out!"

"As long as you blindly love, you'll never be man enough, let alone king enough to come after m—," she inhales a gasp, "*WHAT ABOUT GAVAN*?!"

He wants to say something but his mouth won't open to answer that question; however, when he decides to end the conversation, he's able to speak again.

"Well, if there's nothing *important* you want to discuss, *Mother*..." He hangs up before anything more can be said.

He takes satisfaction with that because she *hates it* when someone hangs up first, it always has to be her who ends any conversation!

Bri is pouring over the words of the diary. She began reading not knowing who the author was, but eventually determines it to be The King Father's Royal Consort. The two of them fell in-love long before his marriage to Millicent, The Queen Mother. This Royal Consort was a commoner and his family wouldn't allow a commoner to marry 'The Crown Prince.'

King Phillip was just as mean and cruel as Queen Millicent, but when he was with His Royal Consort, he was a loving and caring man. They never really fought, but when they did, it was usually about his cruelty as 'The King.' It only got worse when pressure mounted for him to have an heir. Phillip would refer to Millicent as a 'gorgon,' or more often 'The Dragon Queen.' Bri couldn't remember exactly what 'gorgon' meant, but she knew it referred to the myth of Medusa, the woman with snakes for hair; that if someone looked at Medusa they would turn into stone. Bri thinks Medusa is an accurate description to describe The Queen Mother. The Royal Consort teased Phillip suggesting he and Millicent should keep the lights off.

Bri can't help but snicker at that! She continues to read and she chokes on the sip of water she had in her mouth when she reads the first line of an entry: "*I told Phillip I was pregnant...*" She dries herself off and reads the short full entry.

"*I told Phillip I was pregnant and he was thrilled! I've never seen him so happy and excited; he had tears and all he could do was kiss me and tell me he loves me! I'm thrilled too...to have a baby with the man I love more than anything in this world, it's a dream come true...but Millicent could prove to be a nightmare. She's the type of mother who would eat her own young! What would she do to my child?!*"

Bri giggles at the '*would eat her own young.*' She looks down at Kahla, who lifts her head to look at Bri. "I want to meet this woman! She sounds *a lot* like Abby!" Bri gasps, whispering, "Could she be her mother?" It would make

562

sense given The Queen Mother seems to have her sights laser focused on punishing her to keep Lawrence in line." Bri turns her head to the side. "Wishful thinking? You're probably right...if she'd 'eat her own young,' Seth and Abby would've died in infancy." She looks back down at Kahla, "*That* makes more sense." She smiles at Kahla and pets her as she reads on.

The journal isn't daily or weekly, not even consistently monthly, but it was a good snapshot into this Royal Consort's life as she periodically 'checked in' with an entry. It isn't long before Bri reads:

> "*I gave birth to our son, Lawrence Alexander Heathherst.*"

Bri's mouth falls open.

> "*He's such a beautiful baby! He has his father's eyes and my dimples.*"

'*That's where Lawrence gets his dimples*?!' She thinks to herself with a slight smile and continues to read as she absorbs everything.

> "*I've never been so happy and Phillip's the sweetest man I've ever seen with a baby!*"

Bri is frozen...when she is finally able to form sentences again all she can think is: '*Lawrence never knew*?! *He needs to know!*"

When Bri finally comes to her senses, she sees there is only a little bit left and she finishes reading it. She gets up, texts McMasters and Mitchell that she needs to go somewhere in The Palace in about ten minutes, but just with one of them. She didn't want to risk David or Jack showing up to go with her. She gets dressed and heads downstairs.

Mitchell has Kahla taken outside and Bri picks up her bag to bring with her. Bri is trying to think of a way to call for Jessica, then all of a sudden, she appears next to her.

Bri thinks, '*Thank goodness she can read my mind!*'

Jessica lightly laughs. "It isn't 'mind reading,' but more '*thought–projecting*' and '*thought–receiving*.'"

Bri projects to her that she needs more journals and Jessica leads her to them through The Secret Passageways. She is talking out loud because only Bri can hear her.

When they get to the secret room, Bri projects to Jessica asking, '*Who knows of this room?*'

Jessica replies, "Just you, McMasters, and now Mitchell."

When Bri looks at the other journals, there are only a few of them, and Jessica tells her she can read all of them, but the one she just read and the last one are the most significant. As Bri puts the journals in her bag, Mitchell gives her a look; Bri holds up her finger and he gives her a minute.

When Bri closes her bag, she gets close to Mitchell and whispers, *"Can you just trust me if I promise you'll soon understand? Until then, will you pretend you never saw this place?"*

"What place?" He whispers with a smirk, then fist bumps her.

"Thanks!" She smiles with relief and he takes her bag to carry it for her as they follow Jessica a different way to The Royal Apartment.

Inside The Royal Apartment, Mitchell has Kahla taken for another trip outside, then he'll feed her and bring her back later. When Mitchell is out the door, she quietly asks Jessica, "What's The Royal Consort's name?"

Jessica gives her a little smile. "Vivian Brown."

"Are there any restrictions on spirits I can summon to me?" Bri asks.

"Not at all! You may call for *anyone*, at *any* time." She answers. "There's no limit, which is why there are rules surrounding 'free will' and choices."

Bri nods. "Thank you for your help!" And they say goodbye.

Bri goes to The Royal Chambers and puts her bag down, then she sits on the couch. If she was going to do this, she has to do it now before any of the guys come back to The Apartment. She clears her throat and closes her eyes, taking a deep breath to center herself for a minute.

"Vivian Brown? Will you come see me please?" It takes a few seconds and Bri focuses on a figure appearing beside her on the couch. When she comes into full view, Bri softly gasps, *"I've seen you!"* She's confused. "But mostly at The Manor...I was starting to wonder if you were Jack's mom."

This woman is one of a few spirits Bri has been seeing on and off over the last year or so. Vivian had a glowing beauty about her. Brown hair, lighter brown eyes, and a wonderful smile much like Lawrence's; *and* she can see how much Abby looks like her!

"You were still finding your footing with a new life, in a new country, and figuring out how you felt about my son. Plus, I never knew what to say because this has been a secret for so long and purposely kept from everyone, *especially my children.*"

"I can understand about timing." Bri replies and adds, "It's *remarkable* how much Abby looks like you!"

Vivian's eyes are teary as she thinks about Abby. "My sweet baby girl..."

Bri smiles. "Abby has a way of making you laugh! I'm *so* glad she and I have become really good friends!"

"I am, too! She'll need you...you'll need each other soon enough!" She says. Bri goes to ask, but Vivian sweetly puts her hand up. "That's all I can say. I don't know many details, just that the worst isn't over and if you remember anything during that time, remember to remain calm and you'll know what to do..." Bri nods with a faint, appreciative smile.

"Well, let's talk about something else..." Bri suggests. "I have so many questions to ask, but let's start with the obvious: how come no one knows you're their mother?"

Vivian stands and walks over to the fireplace. "You haven't read all my journals yet, have you?"

Bri shakes her head. "I just deduced that since Abby looks so much like you, she *has to be* your daughter!" Bri smiles saying, "I assume Seth is as well, since *all three of them* look like siblings. Plus, Millicent doesn't treat Seth any differently than Abby or Lawrence."

Vivian nods as she walks around. "Phillip and I met within the walls of The Palace. We were just getting past the age where boys and girls don't like each other. Since my parents worked here, I would go to school here with Phillip. They wanted a classroom environment for Phillip and his sister. Phillip and I eventually became the best of friends and we'd run up and down these halls." She is smiling nostalgically at the fond memories she has. "Phillip would tease me that I knew The Palace better than he did! I guess he was right if he never found my journals!" She lightly laughs. "I kept them hidden in that secret room and would write the entries while I was in there, so if anything ever happened to me, Millicent wouldn't be able to destroy them."

"I wondered why the dates were so sporadic." Bri says and Vivian nods.

Vivian tells Bri more of her story. "Love sort of *snuck up on me* because I didn't like who Phillip was when he was around others, but I also knew that's how it *had* to be." She walks over and sits back down on the couch. "Most of the time I was okay with that because he was so loving and wonderful *to me*. We knew I could never be queen, so he proposed for me to be His Royal Consort. When I was officially his Royal Consort, he was getting pressure to have an heir, but Millicent physically repulsed him. He never experienced that. He thought he could at least be with her a few times to make an heir, but he just couldn't do it."

Bri snorts a little laugh, "Not even with the lights off?!"

Vivian laughs. "I forgot about that!" She thinks back... "He'd tell me when I was pregnant with Lawrence that he's more than happy to have all his babies with me!" Happiness spreads across Vivian's face and Bri's heart squeezes for her mother-in-law. "Isn't that the sweetest thing you've ever heard?!"

Bri smiles at her excitement and agrees. "*It most certainly is*! I'm glad my first *real* glimpse of The King Father is through your eyes!"

"*My* Phillip is much like his sons, but King Phillip...well, he was definitely paired right with Queen Millicent..." Vivian actually shakes with revulsion.

"What happened?" Bri asks.

Vivian stands again and walks to the windows and looks out. "Millicent waited until Abigail was done nursing and wanted me dead to get me out of the way as their mother."

"*What?!*" Bri asks, horrified.

"Maybe she was afraid I'd undermine her or maybe she was afraid I would tell of the things I found out? Who knows?" She turns to Bri and says, "I walked into the music room once to practice the piano and found Millicent and..." she shakes with disgust again.

"*With* her uncle?" Bri helps.

Vivian barely nods, walking back over to Bri. "She confronted me and I swore I would *never* speak of it, *mostly because I never wanted to picture it again!* She said I better not because I was just about done with my usefulness. She says, 'Three is a good enough number for those ghastly creatures!' I'm laughing to myself because I hadn't told Phillip yet, but I had just found out I was pregnant and there would be another 'ghastly creature' to frustrate her!"

"*Oh no!*" Bri's hands come up to her mouth as she understands.

Vivian has teary eyes and nods at Bri's understanding. "She ended up having me poisoned before I could tell Phillip about the baby..."

Bri's curious, "How do you know someone else poisoned you?"

Vivian shrugs. "I figured she wouldn't want to get her hands dirty."

"That's just it! Poison is a common method for women killers because they consider it less messy and, with certain kinds of poison, it could easily be slipped into food or a drink and no one can taste it. Then again, you'd think it'd show up in an autopsy?" She thinks about that.

"She'd find a way around anything incriminating!" Vivian says and warns, "She *is* evil, Bri, *because* she *chooses* to be evil!"

Bri considers what Vivian says, "Then that would make her *almost* pure evil." Bri tells her.

"*Almost?*" Vivian asks for clarification.

"I think she had a type of love for her uncle." Bri answers. "One of the unique things about psychopaths is they don't *feel* emotions, they can't feel empathy, except maybe fear. She somehow has this messed up view of love since she was a child, probably since her uncle started abusing her. Most people who have been molested as a child grow up hating their abusers; some may become hypersensitive to protect their own children from situations that could put them in jeopardy. It's rare for a child to develop such an emotional bond with their abuser, like a version of 'Stockholm's Syndrome' maybe."

Vivian quietly says, "I couldn't protect my children from her..."

Bri looks at her with compassion. "Vivian, if *King Phillip* couldn't protect them, then how would you have been able to?"

"I hadn't thought of it that way." Vivian says with a weak smile.

"My guess is she has something over him—."

"She threatened Abby's and Seth's lives." Vivian tells her. "*To her*, they weren't necessary to keep around." There is anger in Vivian's tone.

"*That* would do it!" Bri throws out there. "Their lives are expendable to her..." Bri starts thinking out loud, "So that must be why she hasn't retaliated?"

"Retaliated? For what?" Vivian asks.

Bri looks at her. "For Lawrence cleaning house after the assault on me that included Gavan, and soon Tristan. We're just not sure how to show that hand yet." Bri looks at her. "Are you able to find her and listen in on her?"

"I *could* but she's protected by darkness..." Vivian physically shakes.

"Oh my gosh, Vivian," Bri gives her an apologetic look, "I'm *so sorry* I asked."

She gives her daughter-in-law a kind smile. "You didn't know. This whole palace is usually thick with evil, but it travels with her."

"Ah, which is why I would see you at The Manor."

"I don't have enough light by myself to break through that amount of thick darkness, not without connecting to someone else's light already inside." She tells Bri. "It shouldn't be a surprise The Manor is more welcoming." Bri smiles thinking of The Worthington Family and nods in understanding. Vivian touches her cheek. "I'm so happy Lawrence has you!"

"Me, too." Bri smiles. "I can see now how you've had a significant influence on his heart!" She tells her.

Vivian is confused and shakes her head, "He was five years old when I died...*much too young to remember...*"

"Too young to have easy recall memories, but one is never too young, or too old, to be influenced by a true mother's love. How else can you explain the influence of love Lawrence was able to spread to Seth and Abby? And they also grew in your love; even the short time you had with them, your love still had an influence on them! *It sure wasn't that miserable shrew!*"

"Bri?" A man's voice calls out. Bri turns around and sees Lawrence looking around. Bri's mouth has fallen open. He asks, "Is Jessica here?"

Bri's head snaps back to Vivian, but she isn't there. Bri looks around the room herself, but there's no one. She whispers to herself, but Lawrence hears, "*She's gone...*"

"If I scared her off, I'm sorry. Can you call her back?" He innocently asks.

"It wasn't Jessica." Bri hesitantly replies. "You wouldn't have scared her off."

He's a little surprised. "I guess I hadn't thought about others, but that makes sense. If you get them back, maybe I can apologize——."

"I don't want her to think she *has to* come back because my understanding is my power *summons* them to me, they don't really have a choice. I don't want anyone to feel that way if I can help it, unless it's necessary." She explains. "I ask them to come to me out of kindness and respect. This woman left for a reason and I'll talk to her about that the next time I see her." They wrap their arms around each other in a hug.

"Can I at least assume the '*miserable shrew*' you're referring to is my mother?"

"I was *definitely* referring to Millicent!" She refuses to refer to Millicent as his mother any longer!

"That's the only part I heard. What else has she done?" He plainly asks.

Normally, she wouldn't panic because she would just tell him; however, her mind and heart start racing because she wants to look into a couple things *before* she tells him. Bri didn't think it would hurt, maybe even make him laugh a little to say, "I guess you could say it goes way back to when the 'miserable shrew' was also referred to as 'The Dragon Queen.'"

He laughs and claps, "That's fantastic!" He loves the nickname. "Fitting, too!" After he's done laughing and it gets a little quieter, he watches her sit on the couch, thinking about something. "Bri? What is it?" He asks her.

She pats the couch cushion next to her. "Come." He does and she says, "There *is* more, but I need you to trust me and give me some time to look into a few things. I'm not asking for a lot of time, say a day or two...*maybe* a little more? One way or another, I *promise* I will tell you *everything!*"

She has such a pleading in her eyes, he says, "You know there's nothing I'll deny you, My Darling." He kisses her hand. "I do trust you! *Completely!* Only...to tell me I *will know,* just not right now, well, it's difficult because like anyone else, I want to know *right now.*" He smiles apologetically. "I can't *easily* give you two days, but I will and I'll give you more time if you need it, only I *hope* it's less than that!"

"Lawrence, if I was sneaking around and flat out lying, I think *that* would be insulting to you." She says and he agrees. "This way is better because you know there's a *temporary reason* for the secrecy," she squeezes his hand, "but it won't be kept from you indefinitely. I hope all that makes sense?"

He softly smiles. "It does." He taps a kiss to her lips. "I'm going to take a shower." Bri nods and watches him walk that way.

When Bri hears the shower running, Vivian comes back on her own. Bri says in a loud whisper to her, "Lawrence *needs to know* you're his real mother; the three of them have a right to know! If I were to wait too long to tell him, he could end up *hating me.*"

"Bri, there is no way he would *ever* hate you. My son *adores* you! The only way he'll accept this positively is *with* you! Phillip should probably tell him, but he can't because of the threat Millicent has over Seth and Abby."

"Is that why Millicent never went as far as killing them when she would threaten it with Lawrence?" Bri asks.

"Yes." She replies. "Your bodyguard already had his suspicions about Millicent not being Lawrence's mother and actually has test results on his desk to prove it."

Bri is surprised. "McMasters?" Vivian nods. Then again, Bri isn't really surprised; he is good at his job! "Will you meet me at his office in a few minutes?"

Vivian softly laughs. "I can come with you, Luv."

"Right!" Bri smiles, rolling her eyes and laughing at herself.

Bri goes downstairs and finds Mitchell in the living room with Kahla and she asks him to take her to McMasters office.

"Sure thing!" He says and puts Kahla in her pet carrier.

A few minutes later, Bri and Mitchell are walking into McMasters office and she sees David and Jack are there. She hugs and kisses them. They ask her how she's doing.

"I'm fine." She smiles at them apologetically. "I hate to ask this and it'll make sense soon enough, but would you two step outside the office a minute with Mitchell?" When they do, they close the door behind them. She looks at McMasters. "You have an envelope on your desk for..." she leans in and whispers to him, *"I'm assuming a DNA test?"*

"How did——?" He asks.

"No one *living* told me." She implies and he raises his eyebrows with an 'oh, right' expression. He sifts through his mail. She asks him, "I'm assuming this was a hunch?" He nods, handing her an unopened envelope. She waves the envelope a bit and asks, "I'd love to know how you got the samples?!" She has a slight, devious look and he chuckles.

He tells her, "She left abruptly and managed to leave behind her toothbrush and hairbrush. I switched out Lawrence's toothbrush the same day with the exact same one and color. Then I sent them to DC for testing under the names of 'Jane Doe' for one and 'John Doe, Jr.' for the other."

"That's incredible!" Bri tells him.

He points to the envelope. "I haven't opened it yet."

She leans in and whispers, "*Keep trusting your hunches.*" His eyebrows shoot up. "Keep this between us for now." He nods and she clears her throat. "Now...where would I find the official 'family tree' in this place?"

Before he can answer, Vivian answers, "The Main Library."

"The Main Library." Bri tells him and adds, "My '*Sixth Sense*' again." She winks and he smiles.

When they step out of his office, she brings all of them with her to The Main Library. David, Jack, and Mitchell wander around The Main Library. The Librarian was immensely helpful answering Bri's questions.

Bri tells her, "I was just curious what this looked like because it's all everyone seems to talk about and my being a 'Direct Bloodline.'" Bri looks the parchment over and notices teeny tiny stars under the names; many had one or two, but fewer had three and even less actually had four. Then Bri sees four by her name with 'DB' and realizes it's about bloodlines; David and Jack both have three. Bri has an idea. "If David has three and I have four, the baby will have three-and-a-half?" She didn't know she had put her hand over her lower abdomen. The Librarian smiles and points to an empty space all prepared for the one she is pregnant with and it shows, "Wait, *four*?!"

"Being a 'Direct Bloodline' ensures your descendants for the next three generations, maybe more, will have four stars." The Librarian says. Then Bri remembers Carlotta had told her about that and now it starts to make a *little* more sense.

Bri asks her, "So if a 'Direct Bloodline' were to marry a commoner with no stars, does their children lose stars *then*?"

"Not necessarily. That's why we go through the painstaking efforts of detailing genealogy."

Bri notices Carlotta and Millicent have three stars as does Peter and Phillip. "So, David and Lawrence would maintain three stars. Oh! Jack's father has two and his mother has four?!" Bri thinks about Vivian and sees she's right there for all to see but no one has noticed. Bri asks, "Can I snap a picture of my little one's place?"

"Of course, Ma'am! Here..." she lays some books one either side to make sure it's flat. "No flash, please." She requests. "We'll make sure there are no shadows on it..."

Bri makes sure the flash is off and lines up the picture to covertly include Lawrence's lineage in the picture. Then she takes another for good measure.

"Thank you so much!" Bri says, shaking The Librarian's hand. McMasters, David, Jack, and Mitchell also shake her hand and thank her.

Walking out of The Main Library, Lawrence is walking towards them. "Just the wonderful family I'm looking for!" He kisses her on the cheek and shakes everyone's hands. "What are you all up to?" He asks, as McMasters and Mitchell step away and take up their more protective positions.

"Well," she throws her thumb over her shoulder and gestures to The Library doors, "we just finished in there." She tries to change the subject. "What are you up to?"

He gives her a skeptical look. "Is this about what we talked about earlier." David and Jack are intrigued.

"Yes." She tells Lawrence, then explains to Jack and David, "This will be something you'll all know in the very near future, only *not right now.*"

He smiles. "Alright, Darling. Then is there anything I can do?"

She hesitates. "Anything?" She bites her lower lip with nervousness.

He laughs a little. "Yes, *anything!*"

"Um...How difficult would it be to set up a meeting for me to meet with your father?" She shyly asks.

"Not very. *Why?*" Lawrence is trying to push down his annoyance. "If all this is about getting my father and me on better terms, *drop this now.*" He states firmly. "*This won't end well.*"

She folds her arms and raises her eyebrow. "If I'm talking 'The King,' *STOP IT!* If I'm talking to Lawrence, then I'll remind you if that simply were the case, I would respect our previous agreement and none of this," she gestures, "would be an issue!"

"Fine, but you *will* fill me in later." He *tells* her.

She raises here eyebrow. "I promised *after* I checked into some things, I would tell you *everything*. I believe I heard that you trusted me *completely*...did I misunderstand something?"

He gives her a reluctant look. "Fine. Let me text Father and see if he can come to The Apartment?"

"No!" Vivian interrupts.

Bri jumps a little and looks at Vivian. "*No?*" Bri asks her. Lawrence pauses his typing and looks at Bri. He sees she must be talking to a spirit.

"Meet Phillip in The Conservatory." Vivian says.

Bri looks from Vivian to Lawrence. "Tell your father I'll meet him in The Conservatory." Vivian adds and Bri repeats, "By The Wishing Well." Lawrence raises an eyebrow. She looks at Vivian as she says, "I'm assuming he's already there." Vivian nods to confirm.

Lawrence is wondering who Bri is speaking to that *wants* to talk with his father?! They are walking to The Conservatory when Lawrence's phone chimes a text alert." Lawrence shows Bri the text that says his father is already there and he will wait for them.

Bri projects to Vivian, "That's your spot with him, isn't it?"

"It still is, I suppose." She replies. "He goes there when he misses me, which has been more than usual lately."

The Wishing Well is in the center of The Conservatory and it's pretty isolated. Bri asks McMasters and Mitchell to clear everyone out. She asks Lawrence to go with them, along with Jack and David, but Lawrence hesitates to leave Bri alone with his father.

"Please. *Trust me*. I'll be alright. What you *can* do is tighten security with Abby and Seth..." Bri suggests.

"I did right after your attack, as well as Genevieve's security." He replies.

Bri hugs him firmly. "I love you, Ace." She gives him a little kiss then starts walking the path.

"I love you." He says. She turns her head and smiles at him.

Lawrence watches her until she disappears, *struggling* not to be annoyed with her. Bri walks the few twists and turns down the path to The Wishing Well. When she sees Lawrence's father, he is leaning and looking down at the water; he doesn't hear her approach.

"Your Majesty?" Bri quietly says.

He quickly stands up straight and turns. He has a soft smile and walks over to her, looking around for Lawrence.

"Please," he holds his hands out for hers, "call me Phillip and may I still call you Bri?"

"I insist!" Bri smiles as she takes his hands and he gently squeezes them.

"I was hoping we would've had a chance to talk the other night, but I have to say I'm confused. My son was so angry with me that night for just talking to you." He looks at her compassionate expression. "I swear I don't blame him, but I'm wondering why he set this up for us to talk, *especially alone?*"

"Well, he set this up because I asked him to trust me that there was a reason and he *would* know why, only not right now. *He's not thrilled I'm here.*" She tells him. "Wait. Did he say something to you later that night?" She asks, a little irked. He's confused, but nods. She rolls her eyes, exhaling a bit of anger saying, "Ugh! I told him to leave you alone that night or we'd have issues!"

Phillip is concerned. "*Please*, don't be upset with him. He made a statement and that was it. His anger with me is what Millicent has done to him, as well as what she's done to Seth and Abby, all these years."

She gives him a faint smile and nods. She gestures to the bench and chairs. "Shall we?" They walk over and sit on the bench together. Bri looks around and lowers her voice to almost a whisper. "I have a couple of things I need to tell you. First, I've read one of Vivian's diaries."

His face drains of color, and he whispers, "*H-How...? Where did you find the diary?*" He asks. "*I searched and searched, but when I couldn't find any, I assumed Millicent had found them and destroyed them.*"

Bri gives him a kind smile and reaches over to squeeze his hand closest to her. "I can understand why Millicent would and why you'd think that. It says what you think it does. Well, about Lawrence. I haven't read them all yet, but given Abby looks so much like her..."

"*Oh.*" He whispers in relief, holding his breath as his emotions overtake him. He looks up, "*Thank you,* God! Millicent has had me between a rock and a hard place *all these years.*"

"I've felt there was more to all this." Bri says. "Then I read the journal and I knew I was right."

He is pleasantly surprised. "*You're perceptive.*"

"*Sometimes.*" She replies. "I was right about you since our dance, well, partial dance anyway...I felt there was something on your mind, like wanting to reconcile, and that things weren't as they seemed to be..."

He explains, "Millicent was going to raise Lawrence as hers, or she would have Abby and Seth killed. If I ever told them who their mother really was, she would have them killed. She would know it was me because she had everyone killed who knew the truth."

"Well, 'The Dragon *Lady,*'" she winks and he chuckles, "can't stop this now. *I'm* not under Millicent's threat to you and, as long as we keep this quiet, she can't threaten me beforehand." Bri looks more seriously at him. "Lawrence *needs* to know, as do Abby and Seth! When they calm down, things will make sense! And I think you'll find some forgiveness on their side."

"Make sense of this? How?" He's stunned. "I didn't intervene! Hell, I didn't even know the severity of what she was doing to Lawrence! *God forgive me...*" He chokes up and tries hard to push it down. "I'll *never* forgive myself!"

"For starters, a *real mother* couldn't do, nor allow, what was done to him!" She explains. "It doesn't justify anything, nor condone it, but *that much* will make sense. At the very least I'd think he'd be relieved!" Phillip hadn't thought of it like that and his eyebrows go up as he nods in agreement. Bri squeezes his hand again. "*You* should be the one to tell him, *but you can't.*"

"It may be better coming from you, Bri, and your compassionate heart..." he says in a matter-of-fact tone. He looks at her with his own sweet smile surrounded by sadness and regret. "You remind me of her, you know?"

Bri smiles, about to say something when her phone chimes a text from Lawrence. She says and types, 'I'm fine and all is well.' This way Phillip knows what she's texting to Lawrence. She looks back over at him. "Phillip, another thing I need to tell you is something no one knows outside of close family."

"Your secret is safe with me." He pats her hand.

"Thank you." She replies with a nervous smile. "My secret is I can see spirits and ghosts." He freezes as he takes that in; then his eyes fill with tears, they almost roll out of his eyes. "Vivian and I talked for the first time today. She agrees your kids need to know and the gift I can give *you* is to help you all see her when the time is right." His mouth opens a little in shock.

"*You saw her*?!" He can barely whisper.

"I did. I want to help you and your children rebuild relationships that were destroyed by that evil, vindictive, miserable shrew!"

"It's interesting..." he gives her a small, grateful smile, "during our dance that night, I was hoping to discuss the possibility of your help to find some sort of peace with my sons and daughter."

"Well, it seems like you're getting help from 'both sides of the veil' separating mortality from eternity." She notes, "Hopefully, it'll turn out better than you expected." He smiles in appreciation *and relief.* Bri suggests, "I think we should do this in Newhaven, bringing all four of you to a more neutral and loving place for this to unfold. Until then, I suggest we go about our days like we always have?" He agrees.

He takes her hand and squeezes it, but before he can thank her or say anything else, they hear Lawrence's footsteps. They turn in that direction and watch Lawrence's face drop as he stops, taking in their friendliness.

Lawrence's voice is monotoned. "Father." Bri pats Phillip's hand which he finds aggravating. He raises his eyebrow to Bri.

She tries to brush it off. "Ready?" Lawrence nods. She turns back to Phillip.

"*Thank you.*" Phillip whispers.

Bri smiles a little nod. "Take care of yourself."

"You two as well." He says and Lawrence scoffs.

Bri turns her head to the side and looks down with her eyebrows furrowed. She sees a rock along the edge of a bush that seems fake. She goes over and picks it up. When she realizes what it looks like, she glances at Phillip who sees it too. She gives him a weak smile before she turns to follow Lawrence, but he is taking longer strides in anger as he thinks things over in his mind.

"Lawrence. Please, slow down." She calls out. "I promise you'll understand."

"*Understand what?!*" He stops and pivots to her. "How you won't tell me, but," he waves his arm in the direction of his father, "you obviously had *no trouble* telling my father about whatever is going on?!"

"Lawr—."

"Shut it!" He brings his hand up. "Just stop." He walks away with Bri following at a distance.

When she sees McMasters, she hands him the fake rock, whispering, "*Is this what I think it is? Some sort of listening device?*" She explains where she found it as he looks it over.

"I'll look into it." He slips it into his pocket.

She walks the rest of the way without Lawrence. He had disappeared, and she wouldn't see him at all that night. She lets him be and decides to focus on some quality time with David and Jack before they leave tomorrow.

CHAPTER 56
Imperfectly Perfect & Royal Mistakes

The next morning, Lawrence was still nowhere to be seen and he wasn't answering his phone, nor returning texts either. She decided if he wanted to play this sort of game, then she would just go back to Newhaven with David and Jack this morning. She was ignored by David not too long ago and it didn't feel good! *Now* she is nauseous at the thought of having to go through it again!

Bri is quiet as she stares out the helicopter window. Jack takes her hand and squeezes it. She looks at him and gives him a sweet smile.

"Want to talk about it?" He asks.

"I can't yet." She looks back out the window. "I can say I'm nervous. I asked Lawrence to trust me about not knowing something *yet*, but that he *would* know. He said he trusts me, *completely*," she scoffs, "but after I spoke with his father in private, he stopped talking to me. I didn't hear from him last night, nor this morning. He's not returning my calls or texts..." she wipes a tear off her cheek with the side of a curled finger. "Being ignored is the second worse feeling in the world."

"What's the first?" David offhandedly asks. Bri gives him a bit of a sad look. He remorsefully replies, "*Ah*, right. When I left you behind at the office..."

She lays her head on Jack's shoulder. He kisses her head, but before he says anything, they hear soft whining. David pulls Kahla out of her carrier and sits her in his lap.

Bri points, "There's some treats in my bag." Jack grabs the bag to get them.

As David cuddles Kahla, he remembers Lawrence telling him and Jack there was an international meeting of some sort in the south of France. Jack figures he left early for it and tells Bri.

David comments, "I don't know why he didn't just tell you that?"

"He's hurt and angry." Bri quietly replies, looking out the window again.

"A bad combination." Jack notes.

"Yeah." She exhales. "That's what I'm afraid of."

David leans forwards and squeezes her hand. "Remember, he loves you; he just needs a little space."

She looks at him. "I wish I could get rid of this sinking feeling..." Jack and David know her sinking feelings never turn out 'for the best.' They leave it there for now and play with Kahla for a bit.

When they arrive at The Manor in Newhaven, she asks for Jack's help to arrange for Abby, Seth, and Genevieve to fly to The Manor in a few days. Bri wouldn't tell David or Jack why, but they understood when she says that Lawrence deserves to know first. Jack left it at that and jumped right into making arrangements for the three. Bri asks David to arrange for Lawrence's father to fly in one day sooner, if possible.

David asks with concern, "Does Lawrence know his father will be here when he arrives?"

"Depends on if he's talking to me by then..." She replies.

Bri had a point and David was annoyed *for her* because Lawrence was there after David treated her horribly, that included not returning her texts and calls, as well as when David left her behind at the office. Lawrence saw how hurt she was, how it broke her heart, and here he was breaking it again... He shakes his head and jumps into scheduling The King Father's arrival.

Lawrence had, in fact, flown to France to get away. Something about Bri being friendly with his father *infuriated* him! He wasn't sure how to process that and decided to leave early for his international meeting.

The meeting started promptly that next morning and went on all day. His phone was still silenced from yesterday. There was a formal dinner in The Grand Ballroom of the hotel he was staying at and he would bump into Karl Morley and his new wife...Dominique.

"Ah! Your Majesty!" Karl bows to Lawrence. "So good to *finally* meet you! Dominique says nothing but wonderful things about you!"

"Earl Morley." Lawrence shakes his hand. "*Dominique.* Good to see you again." He taps a kiss to her cheek.

Dominique has always been attracted to his kingly side; she like to control it, especially in the bedroom. She smiles like a child would upon finding a forgotten toy. "Karl, would you be a dear and get us some more drinks?"

"Of course, Darling! Champagne, Your Majesty?"

Lawrence needs something stronger. "Scotch. Neat."

Lawrence and Dominique watch Karl walk towards the bar. She turns back to Lawrence. "And where might your new little consort be?" She asks, looking around for her.

Lawrence had been reading Bri's texts, just purposely not answering them. "Newhaven."

"Oh?" She playfully smiles with a devilish smile. "Better for us to..." she pretends to fix his tie, "reconnect..." Lawrence feels the pull he has had with her in the past, but it isn't as strong as it once was... People stop by and shake his hand with a few friendly exchanges. When they're alone again, Dominique smiles with a desire in her eyes, "Maybe we can——." She stops as Karl gets close enough to hear. "Thank you, Dear!" She winks at him as she takes their drinks, then turns to hand Lawrence his dink and he takes a pretty big drink when he feels himself getting drawn into her again. She smiles to herself thinking she still has him wrapped around her finger.

Later on, after dinner Lawrence starts off dancing cozy with Dominique, after her husband starts groping his dance partner. Things get pretty heated between Dominique and Lawrence, who is 'classy drunk' at this point. He decides to skip out on the rest of the evening before he loses the 'classy.' He starts to walk down the hallway towards the elevators and Dominique comes up next to him with other ideas.

In the elevator, she pushes the button. "My room. I'll be alone *aaallll* night." She runs his hands down her body giving him a sultry and seductive look.

In an instant, he's kissing her and they begin making out like old times. The ding of the elevator makes them stop but once inside her room, they start kissing again. She tries to take control like she always did, but when he doesn't let her, she gets frustrated.

She angrily pushes him back saying, "What the hell's gotten into you?!"

Suddenly it hits him, and what he's about to do! He starts picking up his clothes and putting them back on saying, "*This is a mistake!*"

"*Wait, Luv,*" she starts to panic, "if you want control..." She tries to stop him from buttoning his shirt. "You don't have to go!"

"Yes, I do! This is already a *big* mistake!" He tells her.

"This isn't a relationship, Lawrence, it's just s——."

"*SOMETHING* that could ruin my marriage!" He forces himself not to panic in front of Dominique, at the thought of losing Bri.

She snorts. "You don't have a marriage! *It's a two-year contract!*"

He gets in her face and has the angriest look she's ever seen; it makes the hairs on the back of her neck stand up. "*Watch it, Dominique...*you might sound like a jealous slag!" She angrily raises her hand to slap him across the face for calling her a whore, but he grabs her wrist before her hand hits his cheek. "I just about threw the love of my life away for *meaningless* sex..." he pushes her wrist away, "*nothing* is worth that," then says with disgust, "*not even you!*" He turns to leave, but she's right behind him.

She sharply says, "*You don't mean that!*" She gets in front of him and stops him, her hands on his chest.

He grabs her hands with an intense look. She sees loathing in his eyes as he angrily tells her, "*DON'T touch me again.*" He steps around her.

"*WE'RE NOT DONE!*" She yells as he walks down to the elevators.

She follows him inhaling deeply and angrily yells, "LAWRENCE!"

"*No,* Dominique!" He pushes the button to bring the elevator to that floor and some of his guards join them. "With Bri it's the real deal! I love her! And even though she isn't here, I'm not interested in anyone *but her*. Being drunk had me losing sight of that!" That was all she needed to know. He kicks himself for being angry with Bri...he said he trusted her; *he should've trusted her*! He failed her then and keeps failing her...

"YOU'LL REGRET THIS!" She angrily threatens.

He snorts a humorless laugh stepping into the elevator. "*I already do!*" He presses the code for his floor. She says something to that but he is too focused on kicking himself for what he almost did, that he doesn't hear her. "*Goodbye, Dominique.*"

As the doors closed, a couple of guards stayed behind to block her. She unleashes an angry string of French swear words with British slang.

The following morning David and Bri are getting ready for the day. David is tying his tie and Bri is putting her heart-diamond earrings in. He walks over to her and pulls her into a hug. He hears and feels her take a deep breath as she relaxes into his arms and hugs him back.

"I love you, Macushla."

"I love *you*, My Love..." She hugs him tighter.

He pulls back to look at her as he asks, "How are you holding up?"

"Fine, I guess." She shrugs a little. Her stomach growls and she smiles. "I've learned that's baby 'sound language' for 'we're hungry.'"

David laughs. "Well, then, let's get you two some breakfast!" He takes her hand and they walk down to breakfast.

Peter and Carlotta are walking out of The Dining Room; no one would know that they're hiding the few newspapers that they would normally have on the table for anyone to read. This is because Lawrence and Dominique are front and center of the gossip columns and they want to spare Bri the shock of seeing them. They'll talk to David and Jack about discussing it with Bri. Hopefully *before* she sees the articles.

"Good morning, you two!" Bri happily smiles and hugs them both.

"Good morning, Sweetie!" Carlotta smiles. "Sorry we missed you, but we have to get going this morning."

"It's alright!" She puts her hand on her lower abdomen. "This little one and I are starving so I'll be more focused on eating than talking anyways."

Carlotta smiles at the thought of the baby. "How are you feeling, Sweetie?"

"Wonderful!" Bri turns towards The Dining Room saying, "Love you both!" They say 'I love you' to her, too, and all go their respective ways.

Bri sits and starts eating her food as David sits next to her. He's about to start eating when he hears Jack talking to him just before he turns into The Dining Room. "David! Have your seen the paper this—." He rounds the corner and stops when he sees Bri.

"No, I haven't." David looks around for one. "Odd. There isn't any here." Jack carefully tucks the paper he brought into the back waistband of his pants. David reaches his hand out for it saying, "Guess we'll have to see yours." He sees Jack's hands are empty, puzzling David because he could've *sworn* he saw a newspaper in his hands. "Why don't you come over to The Cottage after we eat here?"

"Or you could just tell him." Bri suggests, then eats another bite.

"Oh, it can wait." Jack tries to play it down.

Of all days he doesn't want her to look at a newspaper, *or any media*, today would be one of them! When he sees her shrug her shoulders, he's relieved and changes the subject. They talk about The Mill and The Wool Farm, as well as The New Beginnings Foundation, then discuss Jack's clients, The Worthington Corporation, even Lawrence's jewelry.

When they're finishing their breakfast, Bri's phone rings. It's someone from City Hall and she answers it as she heads upstairs to her office.

David looks at Jack, raising his eyebrow seeing him fidgeting. David asks, "*What's wrong with you this morning?*! You're acting all jittery and nervous!" Jack pulls out the newspaper he hid. "I thought you had a newspaper! Why—."

Jack hits him on the shoulder with it. "Shhh! Just open it!"

David opens to the front page of the gossip section and is stunned by the images of Lawrence making out with the woman he's dancing with. The headline reads: 'The Honeymoon's Over!' David skims the article and it's enough to make his blood boil.

"*Isn't that Dominique?!*" Jack asks David.

David clenches his jaw. "Dominique must've paid someone off not to name her in these pictures."

Jack agrees, then asks, "*What are we going to do?!*"

David shakes his head as he stands up and wipes his mouth. "I'm not sure...I need to think about it before we can discuss it with Herst because right now, all I want to do is slosh him!" He throws his napkin on the table and walks away, lost in his own thoughts and walks outside to the helicopter.

Over the next couple of days, Bri has been working in Kingsbury and buries herself in work there. She still hasn't heard from Herst and doesn't know what to do. She notices strange looks from people every now and then, but she shrugs them off. She finishes Appeals Court a little early and is going to The Cottage House office to try to work a bit more.

At her desk, she is going through the mail and talking on speaker phone to Gabriel. She gets to the bottom of the mail pile and sees one last big envelope. She opens it and pulls out a bunch of photographs of Lawrence and an unfamiliar woman.

"I'm going to be sick!" She says to him, hanging up. Gabriel just thinks it's 'morning sickness.'

Bri is bent over the trash bin throwing up when she hears Jack and David walking into The Cottage House. She quickly pulls a tissue out of the box and wipes her mouth, then works fast to put the photos back in the envelope. She is bent over tying the trash bag when they walk in; they see she has thrown up.

"Amore Mia!" Jack says as they walk over to her.

"Do you need anything, Love?" David glances at her desk and sees the envelope; he puts it together.

"I think I need to go change my clothes after I take this out." She replies.

Before she pulls the bag out of the bin, Jack puts his hand on hers to stop her. "Let me. David can go with you upstairs." Bri nods with an appreciative little smile, but there is a hint of sadness to it.

"Of course." David grabs the envelope and follows Bri upstairs.

As she changes her clothes, David holds up the envelope asking, "What's in this envelope that has you so upset?"

Bri closes her eyes and holds them closed, softly answering, "Pictures." David exhales a little frustration, swearing under his breath. Bri studies him. "*You knew?!*" Jack walks in and Bri turns to him, "*And I suppose Jack does, too?!*" Jack holds up his hands, not sure what is going on.

David pointedly says, "Yes, *we knew* and *we* weren't sure *how* to tell you." *Now* Jack was caught up! "*We weren't even sure if we should be the ones* to *tell you*! We are hoping when Lawrence arrives tomorrow you two will sort this out."

"*Sort this out?!*" She points to the envelope of pictures. "I can't say anymore...*I'll deal with you two later on this*! Lawrence hasn't spoken to me in days and I figured he was still acting out from the other day when I met with his father, but *now* it could very well be out of guilt! *Ugh*! We need to go greet Lawrence's father before dinner." She turns to both of them and has her finger angled upwards telling them, "Not.a.word. *Do you two hear me?!* You don't get to say anything about this to anyone, and that includes not saying anything to Lawrence, *or his father!*" They have compassionate looks on their faces as they nod in agreement.

That night, Bri wanted to stay at The Cottage in case Lawrence shows up at The Manor tomorrow like he is supposed to. She can't sleep and she doesn't want to wake Jack with all her tossing and turning, so she goes downstairs to the couch. She takes the pictures with her and lays them all out on the coffee table. While she quietly cries at certain ones and is angry at others, she does look at each of them. It takes a little time but then she begins to see it...the extent of how far it went, *or didn't*, go. She's able to take a couple deep, calming breaths and she relaxes some. She lays on the couch to rest and eventually she is able to drift off to sleep.

CHAPTER 57

Imperfectly Perfect & Royally Secret

Lawrence flew in early that next morning to talk with Bri while Jack and David were exercising. Bri starts to feel like someone is there and begins to wake up. She sits up expecting to see Jessica, but Lawrence is sitting in her overstuffed chair watching her sleep. He leans forward looking from her to the coffee table with a lot of guilt on his face. When he looks back at her, he sees her looking at the pictures, too.

"Bri, I *swear* I didn't sleep with her! I—."

"I figured that part out already!" She lightly snips at him. He is confused on how she could know. She takes a deep breath and explains, "I couldn't sleep last night, so I came down here and laid them all out." She gestures to the table. "It wasn't easy, but I studied each one and kept asking *why* someone would send *all* these pictures to me? Then I came to the realization they wanted me to *believe* you two slept together, but in reality, you hadn't." Lawrence is surprised, still staring at the pictures. "Lawrence," she takes a deep breath to calmly say, "had you two actually had sex, *those pictures* would be in here! They didn't have those because it didn't happen, so they're using these to try to convince me that you did sleep with her, or at least to cast a 'shadow of doubt' when you claimed that you two never slept together that night." She watches him a minute before she asks with annoyance, "Why are we talking about this now?"

His eyes dart to her. "I didn't know about those pictures also being sent to you! I honestly was going to tell you what happened, but I wanted to do it in person. *I owed you at least that much!*"

"If that were the case, then you should've flown here right away *and not let this much time go by!*" Her anger gets ahold of her, "*AND YOU SURE AS HELL SHOULDN'T HAVE LET ME FIND OUT LIKE THIS!*" She motions the pictures on the table.

He shamefully admits, "*You're right.*" He goes and sits on the couch with her. "Bri, I left this woman with the freest feeling from the hold she *used to have over me!*" Bri's eyebrow goes up and she gives him a skeptical look. "I swear! *Unfortunately,* I drank a few more that night in my room knowing what I almost did and the next morning I was nursing a *huge* hangover because I don't drink nearly as much as I used to anymore. The hangover lasted all day and I have even more empathy for you when you have a migraine!" He goes to hold her hand, but she pulls it away; he knows he deserves that. "I pictured this discussion about a million different ways, but they all ended one way...*badly*. Then I got an envelope just like this last night when I got back to The Palace. Not being under my mother's control anymore, I refuse to be blackmailed, which is what I thought they were going to try to do. I came here first thing to take away that kind of manipulative power over me! I've had that all my life! Since you...the freedom of having your love and loving you has given me..."

"*First of all*, let's back up a bit. You left without a word that evening, yet Jack and David had an idea of where you were? *Not.*okay!" She tells him.

He moves closer to her. "I'll move back, but please let me look at you when I say this." His expression is a heartfelt pleading one and she does feel he would back away if she insisted, which she is grateful for, but all she can manage to do is nod and shift more to face him better. "I was mixed up with feelings of seeing you with my father. I was upset you were talking with him, getting close to him *after all he's allowed to happen* and you end up telling him whatever is going on *before me*. I wandered around the gardens outside, then I decided to go to France early. The meeting lasted all day and then..."

She looks down at the pictures. "A party."

He closes his eyes as he takes a deep breath, then he looks her in the eyes again. "This woman has always had this sexual hold on me since we first met...*until you*!" She looks away to blink because she knows blinking will push the tears out of her eyes and she didn't want him to see them. He takes his finger and pulls her chin towards him. "I'm grateful for you, Bri, for too many reasons to count and one of those is because somehow a surge of love squeezed my heart and snapped me out of it." He points to the pictures. "Dominique was angry when I told her I didn't want to ruin this," he gestures with his finger back and forth between them, "*if I haven't already...*" He sees a tear on her cheek and he wipes it with the back of a finger. "*Please*, Darling, tell me I haven't ruined it..."

Bri shakes her head, wiping her cheeks as she looks at him. "If you had, Ace, you wouldn't be here. I'm not going to lie to you, those pictures hurt—."

"*So much so she threw up!*" Jack inserts as he walks in from working out up at The Manor with David. Bri's eyebrows come together. "Amore Mia, it wasn't

589

difficult for David and me to figure out that's why you threw up. You confirmed it later when you were angry, we knew about this and never said anything to you." He looks to Lawrence, his tone is stern, "*We hoped* you would've told her and straightened this out *sooner!*"

Lawrence replies, "I thought she deserved to have this discussion in person."

"I suppose that's fair." Jack agrees. "But then you should've had your *aaa*— you should've been here straight away!" He stops himself from swearing.

Lawrence has a small, reluctant smile, "You're right. I should've nursed the hangover on the plane."

Jack nods a little. "I'm going to give you two more privacy and take a shower over at The Manor." Before Bri can say it, Jack does. "I won't say a word to anyone, not even David." He kisses her cheek.

"Jack, I don't want you to lie, so if someone asks just give them the shortest answer possible." She tells him.

"Will do!" He waves to both and leaves.

Lawrence stares in awe when Jack leaves. Bri sees this and asks, "What is it?"

"I'm surprised I'm still standing!" He turns to her. "I thought he would've sloshed me!"

"There's still David...*and he still might.*" She states.

Lawrence admits, "And I'd deserve it!"

"Perhaps...then again, had you actually slept with her, *I'd do more than slosh you myself!*" She admits to him.

"I'd deserve worse!"

"You're right." She plainly states and the point is taken. "Lawrence, we need to go back and address your feelings towards me and talking with your father *before* I tell you what all this is about."

He blows out his exhale as he takes her hand in his hands and stares at it. "I know it'll sound ridiculous—."

"It won't." She tells him and his head snaps back up to look at her. "*I'm* sorry I didn't think about your feelings with that situation. I asked you to blindly trust me, but I hadn't considered how my meeting with your father might have looked, let alone how it might've felt for you *because of your history with him*." She squeezes his hand a little. "I swear to you, Lawrence, it *was* necessary to talk with your father first, before you or anyone else!"

"*Why?!*" He whispers loudly, with frustration. "I know it sounds childish but it feels unfair, which is so damn frustrating because I *do* trust you!"

Vivian appears when Lawrence has closed his eyes for a few seconds. "Bri, you *should* tell him now, *away* from everyone else."

Bri replies, "I was wondering if I should..." Lawrence looks at Bri, then looks where she's looking, not expecting to see anything, it's just more of a reflex. Bri watches Vivian disappear. "That was Vivian."

"Who's Vivian?" He asks.

She holds up her finger, "Just a sec," she says as she runs up the stairs to grab the journal, "I need to show you something." She comes back down saying to him, "I finally read this journal Jessica wanted me to read and I found out it was written by your father's Royal Consort, Vivian Brown."

"*Right! Vivian...*" He says to himself as he thinks back, trying to remember.

Bri pauses in mid stride before walking back over and sitting back down next to him again. She realizes he doesn't remember her name because he would've called her 'Mom,' well, 'Mum', in this case.

"Why were you led to her journal?" He's curious.

She holds Lawrence's hand. "You *will* be angry, upset, downright furious, and part of your knee-jerk reaction will be to charge right at your father. *Don't.*" She looks at him sternly, "Do you hear me?" He nods. She adds, "There's only a little bit we'll discuss here, but at the meeting we'll get everything out in the open." He nods. "Lawrence, once the dust settles, you'll have some answers that may make sense of a few things."

"*Like what?!*" He's becoming impatient.

Bri starts to explain, "Well, Vivian was your father's Royal Consort and she's the only woman he's ever loved. He's still mourning her every single day, after all these years since her death."

"My father? In-love?!" Lawrence scoffs. "He'd have to have a heart for that!"

"The Wishing Well in The Conservatory is their special place." She tells him. "The place he goes all the time because he's still grieving for her and *all* that was taken from him."

Lawrence is surprised, but then realizes, "That's why you met him there! That's why you discussed things in this journal with him first?!"

She nods. "Jessica led me to this book the day I, um, *toured* The Dungeons and was coming out of your office after our, uh, *row*." She sees a bit of humility coming over him. "Anyway, with everything going on, I had forgotten about the book until a few days ago. When I opened the book, it was clear it was a journal and it took only a few entries before I realized *who* was writing it. Later I would ask Jessica for the name of this 'Royal Consort.' In here," she pats the book with her hand, "Vivian talks about the wonderful relationship she has with your father. How they rarely fought, they just had mostly disagreements. When they did fight, it was usually about his cruelty and horrible actions as 'The King' against, well, everyone. However, he was a completely different person when he was with her."

"*Much like me...*" Lawrence whispers in awe to himself.

"No, Lawrence. Much like you *were*." Bri emphasizes. "The men you both were I suspect has a lot to do with Millicent." He gives her a little grateful smile. "There are two entries that are going to be a shock to you..." she opens to a page and reads to him:

> "*I told Phillip I was pregnant and he was thrilled!*"

Lawrence's mouth falls open.

> "*I've never seen him so happy and excited; he had tears and all he could do was kiss me and say he loves me! I'm thrilled too...to have a baby with the man I love more than anything in this world, it's a dream come true...but Millicent could prove to be a nightmare. She would be the type of mother who would eat her own young! What would she do to my child?!*"

Lawrence snorts and nods with that comment. Then asks, "So, does this mean we have a brother or sister out there? Er, wait! *Did Mother kill them?!*" He says with anger.

Bri flips to her next marked page. She goes to read, but is a little choked up and she swallows hard so she can push through:

> *"I gave birth to our son, Lawrence Alexander Heathherst, this morning."*

Lawrence's eyes go wide and fill with emotions across the board.

> *"He's such a beautiful baby! He has his father's eyes and my dimples. I've never been so happy and Phillip is the sweetest man I've ever seen with a baby!"*

He takes the journal and looks at the page; his fingers lightly touching the words his actual mother wrote on the page. She holds his face and wipes his tears on his cheeks with her thumbs.

"Lawrence, *your true mother* loves you!" She hugs him tight. She feels his arms hug her just as tight. She pulls back and explains, "I was hoping your father would help me understand why you three didn't know in the first place! He agreed to come to this family meeting that David and Jack helped me organize. *But* David and Jack don't know why we organized a family meeting. I told them you needed to know first."

Lawrence whispers, *"Thank you...I don't deserve that consideration after the way I acted."*

"That's a separate issue," she tells him, "and one *we will* discuss later."

He looks at Bri with so many tears. "I don't deserve you, Bri! After everything—." He gestures to the table, but he can't talk. He swallows hard and manages to suppress it. "She'd creep into my thoughts over the years and I'd always brush them off, but she was, *IS, my mother!*" Lawrence says in more wonderment than anything else as he processes. "If you have Abby and Seth coming; does that mean..."

Bri nods, "They are your full brother and sister." Bri opens up the photos on her phone. She shows Lawrence the pictures she took of The Official Royal Ancestral Tree.

"*It's been there the whole time?!*" He's flabbergasted. "How did I miss that?! She's right there!" He points to the screen and the connection of Vivian to *her* three children, with Millicent having none.

"I'm assuming the person who put the information there was killed and those who came after never thought to look at it or study it." Bri throws out there. "If anyone had brought it up, I'm sure they would've been killed." She points to the screen, "The stars are wrong, but that has to be Millicent's doing as well."

"Which is why she needed you! Being a 'Direct Bloodline' would give your children 'four stars' for multiple generations, it wouldn't matter what my stars were!" His face is angry again. "I knew she was a piece of work, but..."

"Lawrence, come upstairs while I get ready for our family meeting." He absentmindedly follows her, still looking at the picture on her phone in one hand and his mother's journal in his other hand.

She quickly changes her clothes and pulls back her hair into a low bun. She adds her favorite 'Heart Diamond Necklace' and earrings he made for her, along with the more casual, two-toned watch David had gotten for her. Lawrence had stepped out onto the small balcony and is looking out towards the field of sheep grazing. Bri joins him, hugging him from behind.

He asks, "How?...*Why?*" Bri steps to the side and they face each other. He sees the wind blowing a small strand of her hair across her face and he gently tucks it behind her ear.

"Lawrence, I need you to think about how devastated you might be if you lost me. Do *not* judge your father for decisions made *during* his grief, *but* he does need to, *and I think he wants to*, own all those decisions and choices! I think that's why he wanted to discuss some sort of reconciliation when he asked me to dance the night of The Midnight Ball." She tells him. "I'm not sure how we'd accomplish that if I hadn't stumbled onto the truth?"

He takes a deep breath and slides a hand to the back of her head. "I love you, Bri. I'm sorry for Dominique. I'm so very sorry for hurting you."

"Like I said, we *will* discuss that later. Right now, we need to head over to The Manor." She says and he lightly nods.

They go back into the bedroom where she grabs her things. Bri thinks about what happened and wants to make a point with all three men about the photos. As she descends the stairs, she sees the pictures on the coffee table and gets an idea.

She asks Lawrence, "Will you pick up the photos and put them back in the envelope for me?" He's relieved to get them out of their sight!

Bri goes into the kitchen and grabs some matches, then slips them into her pocket. She grabs the envelope of pictures from Lawrence's hand, then holds her other hand out for him...she sees his gratefulness in this as he takes her hand. She leads him out the back way to the path that goes between The Cottage House and The Manor.

CHAPTER 58
Imperfectly Perfect & Royal Confessions

Lawrence and Bri walk around to the front of The Manor and go. Jack sees them and gets up from The Sitting Room to go greet them; David is coming down The Main Staircase. Bri smiles at Jack and turns to greet David just as he punches Lawrence. Lawrence stumbles backwards and he braces himself with the wall. His guards go to help but hear the tone in Bri's voice and freeze.

"DAVID CHRISTOPHER WORTHINGTON!" Bri snaps as she goes to Lawrence and checks on him. David is shaking out his hand.

Lawrence stands up, waving his guards off, and wiping the blood from the corner of his mouth with the side of his hand. "It's fine, Bri. I deserved it."

"*No. You didn't!*" Bri exhales angrily as people start to venture towards them. Bri points, "Get into The Sitting Room," she glares at David, "*all of you!*" Once everyone is reseated, Bri walks over to the fireplace with the envelope and says, "I was going to talk about this with David, Jack, and Lawrence later, but I think I need to address this now. I'm sure all of you have seen a media picture, or few, of Lawrence with a woman who wasn't me. The details of which are *not* everyone's business," she glances at David and then everyone else, "but I will say this much to our whole family; while they were hard for me to stomach, I did notice something was missing..." she looks pointedly at David, "*not one of them* had the two of them naked, let alone actually having sex. Which only supports Lawrence when he said he never slept with her. If they had slept together, *that picture* most certainly would've been in this envelope!" She holds up the envelope. Then she turns to Lawrence, "You need to consider Dominique was either behind this, or at the very least, she was in on it. Either way, this was planned, *in advance*, to be used against you because some of these look like they're inside a hotel room. My guess is it was her room?" She could see Lawrence's guilt.

"She did say I'd regret walking away from her and unleashed a whole lot of anger when I left..." He thinks about it, "And she's *not* above something like that." He motions the envelope.

Bri looks at Lawrence with intensity. "The rest of this night is between us. *However*, Lawrence, this is the only one *any of you* get! If you so much as dance with any other woman when none of us are around, not to mention your lips on a woman in a way that's meant for me, this *will* become a family matter *and more than your jaw will hurt!*" She purposely looks below the waist and back up to his eyes, then she looks to David and Jack. "This goes for the two of you as well!" She looks back to Lawrence. "Then, I'll personally lock the three of you in a room and let the other two have a go at the one! And remember, if there's no body and no crime scene, then basically there's no proof that a crime even happened! Plus, I know people who'll help with the tricky forensic pieces! That saying of 'fool me once, shame on you; fool me twice...' well, let's just say there *won't* be a third chance given!" She enunciates, "*Am.I.understood?!*" Everyone's mouth drops. Sweet BriaLynn saying all that was surprising, but it also made her that much more serious, *almost scary*.

"Yes, Ma'am." They all three say.

Bri adds, "Perhaps to make it easy for us to keep things simple is having the general rule that we're never alone with the opposite sex unless it's necessary, or *trusted* family, assistants, or guards." The three nod in agreement. "However, if there is a situation where you're alone with the opposite sex, a simple text, at the very least, explaining what happened *is expected*."

Bri hears Carlotta whisper to Peter, "*That's a good rule.*" He agrees.

David realizes, "Just like *you* already do!" Jack looks at him and it clicks with him, too; *she has been doing that all along!*

Bri nods as she pulls out the matches from her pocket. She holds a lit match to a corner of the envelope with the pictures inside. When the fire gets all the way across the short end, she puts it in the fireplace. "Lawrence, I expect you to do the same to your set when you get home."

"I brought them with so we can take care of it later." He replies.

"Good. *We're* done with this topic at the moment, but the rest of you will forget that this ever happened!" Bri looks around the room and pauses at David, who nods, before moving on. Everyone agrees.

"Honestly, Carlotta and I are just happy it's getting worked out between you two!" Peter gives Lawrence a loving, fatherly look.

"That's all we need to know!" Carlotta adds.

Lawrence shyly mouths to both of them, '*Thank you.*' They smile and nod.

Both Peter and Carlotta go sit in some chairs that aren't central to the room; they are there for family support. James and Amy would be there, but they're in DC for the final countdown to the wedding.

Bri sees Phillip walk into the room and gives him a small smile. She says to everyone, "Now, the reason we're all here. Phillip," she gestures him, "Lawrence and I had a small *discussion* this morning. He doesn't know all the details yet, only one *very* important piece." Phillip looks at Lawrence and for the first time Lawrence *really looks* into his father's eyes and sees the pain in them. Unfortunately, Lawrence isn't ready to let go of his anger just yet. Bri looks at Seth and Abby. "This began when I was led to a journal..." she explains the journal and that their father's Royal Consort is the author.

"That was so long ago!" Seth comments.

"Yes, *but* with a heartache that comes from losing the woman you deeply love *and so soon in life*," she looks to Phillip, "I bet it feels more like yesterday." Phillip nods and looks down to hide the tears in his eyes and pushes his emotions down.

Vivian appears and says to Bri, "Show them the envelope with that test..."

Bri had forgotten about that envelope. She goes over and pulls it out of her bag. Everyone is now looking at it and Bri says to Lawrence, "McMasters had a suspicion, so he covertly sent samples off to DC to have a DNA test done between you being 'John Doe, Jr.' and Millicent being 'Jane Doe.' Here," she hands him the envelope, "*you* should open it."

Lawrence takes the envelope. "A DNA test?!" She nods. He's trying not to get angry, but it's difficult.

Phillip says to Lawrence, "I'm not sure how they got her hands on a test like that so quickly, but if it's accurate..." Phillip motions to the envelope.

"Wait." Seth furrows his brow and asks, "Why would Lawrence need to see a DNA test?"

"Bri, how long have you had the results of this test?!" Lawrence asks, getting a bit angry.

"*Look closer.*" Bri quickly answers. "*No one* has opened it."

"HOW LONG?!" He raises his voice.

Jack goes to step in, but Bri holds her hand up for a 'stop' at him. She replies to Lawrence, "Watch your tone, *Your Majesty*!" He winces and takes her hint. She says, "I found out about it the same day I asked you to arrange a meeting with your father in The Conservatory. The night *you left*." She adds pointedly. "And this is the first time *since you left*, you're speaking to me!"

He rips the envelope open and unfolds the paper. He skims it until he finds, "...Jane Doe is NOT a match..." he trails off as he reads the rest to himself. Lawrence stares at it and his anger builds.

Seth asks, "Jane Doe? Is that saying mother isn't your *biological* mother? Then who is? This Vivian?!" He's obviously upset for Lawrence. Abby gasps and looks at their father in shock.

"Please, Lawrence, Seth, Abby," their father says, "Bri is innocent in all this. She found out and just wants this news to have the least damage when you three were told." He looks at Seth and Abby, "Millicent—."

"NO!" Bri purposely interrupts. "*You* can't say anything!" She looks from Phillip to Seth and Abby. "*Millicent isn't your mother either.*" Carlotta lets out a soft gasp. As Seth, Abby, and the others take that in, Bri tells them, "I found out through the journal and knew the three of you deserved to know the truth. When I met with Phillip in The Conservatory a few days ago, he told me that Millicent threatened to kill Seth and Abby if he ever told anyone the truth about who your mother really is." She looks at Phillip. "Now we can honestly say *you didn't* tell them; *I did*!" Phillip sadly nods.

"That horrible woman isn't our real mother either?!" Seth exhales loudly. Bri and Phillip shake their heads.

Lawrence looks at his father, the anger finally wins out and he yells, "THAT-THAT WOMAN *ISN'T* OUR MOTHER! AND YOU WERE NEVER GOING TO TELL US?!"

Bri's face is pained and she gently says, "*Lawrence*—."

"*WHY?!*" His eyes are locked on his father and Bri notices Vivian appear. "WHY DIDN'T *YOU*, OF ALL PEOPLE, TELL US THE TRUTH?! WHY DID YOU PUT US THROUGH A LIVING HELL IN OUR CHILDHOOD AND *FAR* INTO ADULTHOOD?! *AND YOU WERE*

NEVER AROUND!" Lawrence crumples the paper and throws it at him. His tone is now low and loathing, "*I.hate.you!*"

Bri whispers, "*Lawrence, NO!*"

"*NO, BRI!* NO AMOUNT OF VISIONS YOU'RE GIVEN WILL GIVE YOU THE FULL SCOPE OF THE TORTURE THAT WOMAN INFLICTED ON ME!" Lawrence pointing angrily at his father. "AND THAT MAN COULD'VE PREVENTED *EVERYTHING!*" He looks at his father. "THAT WOMAN WASN'T FIT TO RAISE *ANY* CHILD AND *YOU KNEW IT!*"

His father takes in the significance of Lawrence's statement...he looks at Bri with pained eyes and Bri knows it's like he *just* lost Vivian and his family all over again. Bri feels more for this man who has never gotten over his grief, barely able to push it down to even function. Bri hears Phillip's breath catch when Vivian puts her hand on his cheek.

Bri asks him, "You can feel her, can't you?" Phillip nods. "She has her hand on your cheek right now." He holds his hand up to his cheek, smiling fondly and teary-eyed.

Lawrence looks to Bri and has a bit of desperation in his voice, "*I* want to see her!" He walks over to Bri.

"Please?" Phillip asks.

"NO!" Lawrence points to his father angrily again. "*YOU* DON'T GET TO SEE HER! YOU DON'T DESERVE IT! YOU DESERVE TO SUFFER FOR THE REST OF *YOUR MISERABLE LIFE—.*"

"LAWRENCE ALEXANDER HEATHHERST, YOU STOP THIS RIGHT NOW!" Bri stands right in front of him.

"YOU'VE GOT TO BE KIDDING ME!" He snaps back.

She says sternly but softly, "*Look at me!*" When he looks at her, she has such love and compassion in her eyes for everyone and the situation, his face softens. She cups his cheeks and says in a soothing voice, "I asked you this earlier but we didn't get very far, so I ask again: *try to imagine* for one moment, something happening to me!" He truthfully shakes his head at the thought. "If you can't, think about how close David and Jack came over a year ago!" She sees the pain in Lawrence's eyes as he considers this. "Ace, your father is *still* in that 'Hell' *right now*! That same 'Hell' you'd be in if you lost me; the 'Hell' *I'd be in* if I lost any one of you! *Really look at him!*" Lawrence looks at his father. "Hear me when I say he *couldn't* say anything to *any of you*, or Millicent would've had Seth and Abby killed! That's why *I'm* telling you! Hopefully, this keeps Seth and Abby safe..." Bri looks over and Phillip is so emotional his jaw shakes.

Phillip shakes his head thinking. "I'm not sure what she'll do at this point." Bri gives him a 'there's truth to that statement' look.

"Let her come after me, I don't care!" Abby replies.

Seth states, "I'd rather die knowing the truth than live one more day thinking that woman is our mother!" Abby agrees.

Bri continues, "I'm sure your father would've given *anything* to tell his children that the woman he loves is their mother," Phillip barely nods, "but instead, he was forced to give the three of you up to save Abby and Seth! Have compassion for a man who was in an *impossible* situation; who's still in so much unspeakable grief and he deals with it the best way he can! *Look at him, Lawrence!* You *don't* hate him!" Lawrence's eyes flick back to her. "You hate that he was never there for you, that he didn't protect you from what that woman did to you every day! *BUT HE COULDN'T!* He's your father who loves your mother so much, that when he lost her, he also lost his children and losing his entire family *all but destroyed him!* You need to seriously, and honestly, ask yourself, *could you have done any better?!*" Bri looks around, "Would any of you have done any better?" She looks back at Lawrence. "Let's pray we never find out..." She takes a deep breath.

Bri gestures to the furniture where Lawrence sits in a chair, furthest from his father, his father sitting in the other chair opposite him, with a coffee table in between them the long way. Bri exhales, shaking her head as she walks over to the couch and sits on the side closest to Lawrence. She pats the cushion next to her for Vivian to sit next to her. There is another couch across from Bri and Vivian where Genevieve, Seth, and Abby are already sitting together. Jack and David sit over by Peter and Carlotta and they listen.

Bri looks to Phillip and asks, "How old was Lawrence when his mother, *Vivian*, died?"

His mind is slowing down from spinning. "Uh, five maybe."

Lawrence scoffs, "You can't remember how old we were when your *greatest love* died?!"

Bri's head snaps to him. "*Lawrence Alexander, so help me—!*"

Lawrence is disgusted. "Who side are you on, *BriaLynn*?!" Peter and Carlotta put a hand on Jack's and David's shoulders to keep them sitting.

Bri stands up and leans down in Lawrence's face with a hand on either arm rest. Everyone can see she is *incredibly angry*. Her voice matches her anger but with a scary coolness to it. "I'm on *yours*! I love you and if you EVER question my motives and my loyalty again, *so help YOU*! I knew as soon as I had this information you *had* to know! I couldn't, *and wouldn't*, keep this from you," she looks over her shoulder at Seth and Abby, "from any of you!" They quickly nod. She looks back to Lawrence. "Had you never left or had come back earlier from France you might have found out *sooner!*" She stands up. "At the same time, *I'm not stupid!*"

"*No, you're definitely not.*" He quietly says more to himself.

"*But you're acting like a foolish child!* You don't *see* what I know, Lawrence, none of you see it; *but your father does!*" She tells him.

Lawrence's eyebrows scrunch together as he thinks back to what he might've missed. His eyes look from Bri to his father. Phillip looks at his son with compassion and understanding, but there's added sadness and a lump growing in his throat as he nods and his heart breaks for Bri.

He struggles to tell his son, "I *couldn't* tell you, *but Bri did!*" He stresses. Lawrence looks back to Bri.

She replies, "Simply stated: I've just signed my own death warrant...but more likely it's for someone else I care about!" His face shows his surprised reaction to what he hadn't considered. "When Millicent finds out *I'm* the reason the truth of her well-protected secret came out, she'll seek revenge! I'll deal with whatever she throws my way but," she points to his chest, "don't you *EVER* ask me who's side I'm on again, *Your Majesty*," he cringes again, "because it's *always* yours, Jack's, and David's! And all those I love!"

"You're right." He takes and kisses the finger she is using to point to his chest. "I'm *truly* sorry." She nods a little as she inhales to try to calm herself by exhaling slowly. He adds, "We'll address everyone's safety after this."

Lawrence stands up and hugs her firmly, the comforting way he knows she likes and she takes a deep relaxing breath...

"Bri," Vivian says, Bri steps back from Lawrence and looks at Vivian. She's looking so lovingly at Phillip and asks Bri, "Will you let them see me?" Then Vivian looks at her children.

"Vivian is wanting *all of you*," she gives Lawrence a pointed look, "to see her. I have the power to do it, but only if you're ready and," Bri looks to everyone, "if you're able to handle it." Lawrence nods, then Seth and Abby, as the others in the room nod, too.

Phillip dries his eyes. "I need to see her! I feel like we never got a chance to say goodbye."

Bri goes over to him and drops down to her knees next to his chair. She holds his hand and stresses, "Phillip, *this isn't* goodbye either! But this *can heal* the bleeding in your heart that happened when she died, then maybe you can help heal three other hearts?" He looks at Bri with such sadness in his eyes, yet hopeful, too. He looks at Lawrence, Seth, and Abby, before looking back to Bri. She squeezes his hand and nods before she stands up. "Vivian, are you ready to be seen?"

Her smile is huge and she looks full of love. "Oh, I'm ready!" She beams.

Bri steps back and concentrates. She brings up her hands and swoops her two fingers on each hand around in a circle. They all watch as a woman appears before them.

Phillip can barely whisper, "*Oh Viv...*"

Lawrence sits back down and leans forward with his elbows on his knees to marvel at his mother; trying to take in every detail of her. Bri steps over to him and she drops to her knees next to him.

She puts her hand on his and softly says, "*That's* your *real* mother, Lawrence. The mother who loves you! All three of you!" He nods and smiles tearfully. She says to him, "You have her smile *and dimples!*" Bri looks over at Seth and Abby. "Seth has her eyes *and Abby!* Abby is as beautiful as she is!"

"She definitely is!" Lawrence agrees, smiling at Abby. Seth nods, patting Abby's knee.

Vivian cups Phillip's cheek again and he can feel the sensation of it. "I've missed you, My Love!"

"And I miss you, Love!" Phillip tearfully and lovingly smiles.

Bri remembers, 'The love of a true mother' and smiles as she sees Vivian with this love. She can touch Phillip and her children, but they can't touch her...*odd*, Bri thinks but doesn't want to interrupt their moment to ask Vivian. Then Bri feels that it has to do with her gift.

Still wanting to give Phillip and Vivian a moment, Bri turns to Seth and Abby. "The day I...'*challenged* The King'..."

Lawrence has a faint smile. "Hard to forget."

"I'll say!" Seth says. "It was the day he *literally* became a king!" Gen and the others in the room snicker and lightly laugh.

"You're our hero, you know that?!" Abby tells Bri as she gets up to hug her sister-in-law.

Bri slightly smiles, hugging Abby back. "Remember that for my tombstone, will you?"

"*Not funny*, BriaLynn!" Gen chimes in.

"*Agreed.*" Lawrence's tone of voice is commanding.

"Well, we can come back to that later." Bri says.

"*No. We won't!*" Jack states.

David's just as determined, "We're *not* going to talk as if we already lost you!"

Bri clears her throat of a lump forming and gets back on track. "Vivian's diary spoke of how much your father loved her. The first diary I read took place over the course of a couple of years. It was towards the end when she would write about having her first baby, 'Lawrence Alexander Heathherst,' and how happy your father was!"

Vivian tells them more. "Your father was 'over the moon' and I could barely get him to put Lawrence down! All three of you actually! Each one was harder and harder for him to put down!"

Phillip had walked over to Seth and Abby. "I was *never happier*, than when I was with *my family*!"

"And the difference showed!" Vivian says to them, Phillip humbly agrees with her.

"She felt I was like 'Dr. Jekyll and Mr. Hyde.'" He has a small smile on his face looking at her. "She was right."

"I can relate," Lawrence adds. "I didn't want Bri seeing that awful 'kingly' side of me!"

Phillip walks over to Lawrence. "Oh, Son, I know life was cruelest to you and it started with the death of your *real* mother."

Bri says to him, "Lawrence, you know better than anyone, Millicent having the upper hand." He nods. "After poisoning Vivian, she killed anyone and everyone who knew about Vivian being the mother of Phillip's three children, leaving only Millicent and Phillip with the truth."

Phillip continues where Bri pauses. "She told me that if I told you three the truth about your mother, she would have Abby and Seth killed."

You can hear the loathing in Lawrence's voice adding, "They were *always* expendable to her."

"I just *couldn't* let that happen!" Phillip tells him.

Vivian states. "And if no one else knew the secret, she would *know* Phillip was responsible if any of you found out."

Bri mentions, "Let's not forget that Phillip was happiest with his family, so Millicent would use that and make sure he *wasn't* happy; to keep him miserable and compliant. If she killed Phillip, she'd be reuniting him with Vivian and she wouldn't want that either."

Phillip looks adoringly at Vivian. "Oh, Vivvy...*it wasn't supposed to be like this*!"

"Phillip, on this side it's seen a wee bit differently, Love." Her accent is a little thicker with that sentence. "To refer to our wonderful daughter-in-law when she quotes, 'everything happens for a reason,' Phillip, all *is* as it should be! You'll see!"

"*What reason*?! Why did you have to die so young?" He asks. "Our children *needed* their mother! Instead, they were raised by that, that—."

"Evil Dragon?" Bri helps.

"Yes!" He scoffs at the thought of Millicent. "That old *hag*!"

"Phillip," Vivian lovingly smiles, "look around at the wonderful people here for support. The Worthington's were a welcomed escape for Lawrence with Peter and Carlotta showing him how a family should be and he passed that on to Seth and Abby. David and Jack giving him the best of friendship, of brotherhood and 'The Three Musketeers' all these years! And if things had gone any differently, our Lawrence wouldn't have Bri." Vivian looks at Bri and Phillip looks over at her, too. "She's meant to be here and her children, *our grandchildren*...Oh Phillip, there *is* a grand design to all of this, to mortal life and in eternity! It'll be even better on this side when the time comes for you to join me!"

He looks at Bri again and smiles softly. "She reminds me of you, Viv..."

Vivian smiles as she remembers, "Well, *her love* inspires Lawrence to be a better man! Like you said mine did for you!" Vivian looks at David and Jack. "Just as I'm sure she inspires you two to be better than you already are?"

"That's definitely the case with David!" Jack says, nudging David. "Bri just makes me better than I already was!" He gives her his signature grin and she laughs, as does everyone else.

Phillip looks at his son, proudly. "Lawrence *already is* a better man than I could ever be! He was raised by that Evil Dragon *Lady*," he glances at Bri with a smirk, "and beat the odds! And, with the power of the love of a great woman behind him, he is well on his way to becoming an even better king than *any of us before him*! He is strong getting more self-assured, and has the best qualities of a great king! Oh, Viv. *He's your son through and through*! Lawrence..." he walks over to his son and Bri steps back, "I'm *so* sorry I wasn't there for you. I let all three of you down when you needed me most!"

Phillip's face has so much pain and remorse, "What she and her uncle did to you, I've wanted to rip her throat—."

"Tell Lawrence *why* you sent him to a plastic surgeon in California and *why* you stepped down." Bri interrupts to help. She remembers something and wants to redirect their conversation a bit.

Phillip gives Lawrence a look of love. "I swear I didn't know the extent of what they were doing, but I should've looked into the rumors. She *hated* being in the same room with children, even you three. I thought these 'lessons' were extreme versions of things like etiquette training, or watching others being punished in The Dungeons. I was also deeply mourning your mother and I lost myself, barely able to get out of bed. I failed my children more because I let that grief *consume* me." He tells him. "When you came to me that one morning after killing The Duke, I figured some lesson with Millicent's uncle got to be too much and you retaliated; I figured you had enough and stopped it. I wanted to protect you and ordered you to *never* speak of it again because we needed to keep it quiet for your safety! Even though you're my heir, Seth and Abby were *always* vulnerable." Lawrence nods as more pieces slide into place. Bri was right. He didn't have an adult perspective on what had happened. Phillip rests his hand on Lawrence's shoulder. "When I saw the scars on your back during a fitting of your uniform for your wedding, I was in shock seeing how far her sick and twisted mind went with you! I looked into the matter deeper and was appalled. *You were a child!* I wanted to fix what I could! Obviously, there was no way I could fix the psychological damage, but at the *very* least I could send you *secretly* to a plastic surgeon for the scars. She had way too many loyal guards and staff, so I couldn't have her killed without risking her finding out about it first and retaliating against Seth and Abby. The next best thing I knew I could do was to take her power away *before* she could stop me!"

Lawrence inhales at the realization. "*That's* why you arranged my wedding to Genevieve to also be our coronation..."

"*Precisely*. I knew, outside of you being married, she'd try to find a way to assign herself as your regent, but she still found a loophole... Well, as you know, her threats have serious follow through with any number of dedicated men and women at her disposal."

Lawrence nods and says, "She's threatened Abby and Seth numerous times and she's *brutal* in her follow through! The last time she 'punished' Abby, we weren't sure if she'd ever walk normally again! She got her way with me nearly every time after that for a long time until..." Lawrence looks sweetly at Bri who had sat down and waited patiently for them to talk things out.

Phillip looks Lawrence in the eyes. "I'm so very sorry, Son. I'm relieved all this is out in the open and you three finally know you have a *wonderful* mother!" Lawrence hugs his father and both men shed a few tears. Everyone in the room is emotional especially when Abby and Seth join the hug.

> Bri secretly texts McMasters: "How difficult would it be to get the autopsy and police file on The King Father's Royal Consort, Vivian Brown, from way back when?"

> He responds: "I'll see what I can do!"

Bri knows McMasters made trusted friends with people within The Royal Police Department in London who would send him whatever he asked for, no questions asked, especially with McMasters now The Grand Marshall of The Royal Guard.

Bri asks Vivian, "In your journal, you mentioned that it seemed like Millicent was always one or two steps ahead——."

"Yes! Phillip and I would talk about things, or make a plan with the kids, and she was always ready with some sort of plan of her own to interfere with whatever we wanted to do."

"Why do you ask, Love?" David asks Bri.

"I'm not so sure yet." Bri answers, walking to the archway of the room. "Mitchell, are you out there?" She waits and then hears footsteps. "Did McMasters show you the unusual rock I found the other day?"

Mitchell thinks out loud, "The listening device?"

"Well, that answers that part, but was it still working?" She wonders.

"No. It looks like it hasn't worked in years." Mitchell tells her. "By the age of that thing, it had been there for decades!"

"Is that what you picked up right before you left The Conservatory that day?" Phillip asks; the look on his face is beyond angry.

Bri sees the fury. "Phillip, *please* think about this. A swift sword can come through here and *try* to deal with Millicent, but we both know that won't work. We need to be smart about this, or this country will be divided for, or against, King Lawrence! However, if it's done in phases—."

Vivian catches on, "Like ruin her credibility and reputation, then the people will start to distance themselves from her!"

"Exactly!" Bri says.

Phillip is curious. "How do you suppose we do that?"

"Phillip, I think Lawrence needs to do this next part." She replies, then looks at Lawrence.

"*Oh?*" Lawrence looks at her with a raised eyebrow.

"What's the one thing Millicent values most, but it has to be given *by The King?*" Bri asks.

"*Her title!*" He answers.

"Right! *Aaand* all the *perks* that come with it. *The King* can strip her of her title, her royal status, and officially banish her from The London Palace. But first, assuming you all are not exaggerating on my popularity, you'll need to get the people angry with her for hurting me, and the baby," she puts her hand on her lower abdomen, "by officially naming her as the one who not only ordered my physical assault, but she is also personally responsible for striking me several times in the abdomen with a club of sorts. This will infuriate people more because of my pregnancy."

"Fantastically *brilliant* idea! I'll get right on this!" Lawrence kisses her temple before he steps aside and starts the arrangements for a press conference with his assistant, Spencer Brewer.

Bri takes a deep breath and looks around. Love is very much present in this room. Love is what all three kids needed to hear and feel from *both* their parents. Eventually, Vivian needs to go and says her goodbyes, promising she can visit anytime; Phillip being the most relieved.

The rest of them all gather around and settle in, finding places to sit and drying their eyes. McMasters steps in and sees Bri's bag; he gestures slipping the large thick manila envelope in it.

She mouths, "That was FAST!" He winks at her. Then Bri understands...he was already looking into everything because of his suspicions and was investigating on his own!

Lawrence sits next to Bri. He lovingly caresses her face with his fingertips. "This is such an amazing gift! Thank you!"

"OH NO, Lawrence. This is your family. *Your actual mother!*" Bri smiles. "A mother doesn't have to be biological to be a 'real mother!' A 'real mother,' a true mother, loves her children and is constantly thinking about their well-being and doing right *by them*! Selflessly sacrificing a lot of their own needs and wants without a second thought for the sake of their children. She constantly worries about doing a good job so her children will grow up to be whoever they want to be; who they were meant to be!" She adds, "I think we can safely say *everything Millicent wasn't.*"

He nods and gives her a loving look. "Adding babies to our family and making you The Queen will top this!" He kisses her cheek and then holds his cheek to hers for a moment.

Gen whispers, "*Did I overhear correctly? Your Majesty!*" She smirks at Bri.

"You did!" Lawrence says before Bri could respond. "But her coronation can't be this year, or New Year's..."

"With you acting out and all this," she gestures the room, "it slipped my mind. I hadn't had a chance to talk to David or Jack about it *first*!" Lawrence feels bad about that and apologizes to Bri, then Jack and David.

They talk for a little while longer before they leave and go their own ways until dinner. Phillip is one of the last to leave and stops Lawrence before he gets up. Bri goes to give them privacy, but he stops her, too.

"What I need to say, I can say in front of you, Bri. I doubt you two have secrets, even about what really happened with The Duke of Devonridge." Bri gives him a faint nod. "Lawrence, Millicent never knew I knew of her relationship with her uncle. There had been rumors and those were confirmed at different times when I would see him leaving her quarters, or her leaving his quarters, late at night. I never knew you were so severely abused! It never occurred to me they'd involve you in *anything* like that! It's hard for me to imagine people could do that to anyone, *let alone a child!* When you told me what you did that night to protect Seth, *I wanted to protect you!* I only wished *I* had done it so you didn't have that burden of taking someone's life at such a young age. I said we'd never speak of it again because I didn't want Millicent finding out it was you and striking back at any of you!"

"I was a stupid kid and blurted it out when I was angry at her one day." Lawrence admits.

Phillip looks at Bri. "Lawrence always ran interference to protect his brother and sister and he paid a high price." He cups Bri's cheek. "I'm glad the reward is so great a love for him. Thank you for that!"

Bri hugs Phillip and she could feel him hug her firmly in return. She says next to his ear, "I think Lawrence is just like you...a tough kingly exterior to protect himself against Millicent, but a *huge* heart underneath." He squeezes her a little more.

Before Phillip leaves, he asks, "Could I have the diaries when you're done?"

She sweetly smiles. "If Vivian wants you to, I'll definitely give them to you! I feel they're not mine to give and while I don't see why not, I still want to give her a chance to make that decision."

"I can agree with that." He says. "Where on Earth did you find them?!"

Bri faintly laughs. "She said you teased her about knowing The Palace better than you," he smiles fondly and nods, "well, it's some sort of secret room I was led to by Jessica, my guide. Vivian kept them hidden in case something happened to her, knowing if Millicent had found them, she would destroy them. I guess maybe she does want you to have the journals, but I still want to ask her."

He nods. "I understand."

Bri suggests Lawrence take Phillip to the press conference. She thought it would be best for them to show a united front and for Bri to be removed from the public view while it happened. Millicent will know Bri told Lawrence, Seth, and Abby, that she isn't their mother soon enough, and this next step will only intensify her lividness with Bri. She didn't need to be seen publicly, front and center, accelerating things with Millicent.

CHAPTER 59
Imperfectly Perfect & More Royal Secrets

During the press conference, Bri hides in The Living Room of their top floor residence in The Manor. She cuddles up with Kahla on the couch and opens the manila envelope McMasters gave her. She is looking through everything with two specific objectives: first, she wants to see the crime scene for herself; second, she wants to know if the right 'cause of death' was recorded. With Millicent being Queen at the time, she could have *easily* had something covered up.

She finds the pictures of the crime scene and lays them out, carefully reconstructing the room the best she can. She is not even halfway through the pictures when she recognizes the room as The Royal Chambers. It's the same 'bay window area' where it looks like she was having her tea and looking out at the beautiful view of the city. Bri softly smiles when she thinks of Lawrence and it's the same view he likes; he even has a chair permanently positioned to look out over the city.

When the poison causes her to collapse, Vivian falls out of her chair and onto the floor. Bri notices that for being poisoned, there is quite a lot of blood. She searches for The Medical Examiner's autopsy report to read their findings. It takes her a minute to find it in the file McMasters gave her; she reads it carefully.

The M.E. did find that Vivian was poisoned and with the help of a forensic toxicologist, they determined the poison was something called 'crimson powder.' Bri looks at Kahla and pets her, thinking about what she has heard about this poison, but all she can remember is that it is common in a particular part of the UK. She looks it up on her phone...

The crimson flower is a red flower that is poisonous in its dried state. It's typically ground into powder and used for rodent control. Inhaling would cause the throat or nose to bleed almost immediately and the lungs would try to push out the particles by violently coughing; and coughing up blood.

Consuming the powder, even half a pinky-nail size amount, would not only cause vomiting, but the victim would bleed out their eyes, nose, mouth, ears, etc...

'That explains all the blood in the crime scene photos.' She thinks to herself.

Most victims bleed out internally before anyone knows what is happening. Once internal bleeding begins, death is incredibly painful, even with high doses of morphine, as organs begin to liquify.

There is a cure, but the problem is getting it into the victim in time. The poison works so fast that by the time it is discovered it is crimson powder poisoning, it is usually too late.

Bri wants to check if The Medical Examiner was able to determine how long into her pregnancy Vivian was. She reads out loud, "...fourteen weeks..." and she can barely read through her tears, "the uterus was just starting liquify prior to death."

Bri gathers up everything she had spread out on the coffee table, then turns the top folder over to hide Vivian's name. She curls up on the couch with Kahla thinking about everything she has read and learned.

Bri dozed off; the next thing she knows, she feels a kiss on her cheek. She slightly smiles hearing Lawrence whisper, *"Darling, it's me..."*

Her eyes start to open, then she sits straight up worrying about, *"Kahla!"*

"She and her carrier are with Mitchell." He says as he sits next to her. He reaches for the folder on top of her stack on the coffee table asking her, "What's this?"

Bri quickly pushes the file out of his hand and back down onto the stack. She shakes her head. "This isn't for just anyone to see, Lawrence."

He points to the stack. "Is this about my mother, *Vivian*?"

"Lawrence, you hadn't noticed but since the moment I read the truth, I refused to refer to Millicent as your mother! From now on, when we discuss 'your mother,' it will *always and forever* refer to Vivian. Deal."

He rests their foreheads together. "This is one of the *countless* reasons why I love you so deeply!" He lifts his head and taps a kiss to her lips. "I was going to ask my father this, but I just couldn't bring myself to ask him..."

"What is it?" She asks.

"I could be wrong because I was so young, but I seem to recall she died in The Royal Apartment...is that right?"

"Yes." She replies.

"Don't tell me specifically where, or I may avoid that spot for the rest of my life!" He takes a deep breath. "I never asked about her before because I didn't think it mattered." He sits back and rubs his hands on his face. "I'm *such* an idiot! How could I not remember she was my mother?!"

"*How would you?*! *Why* would you?! Like you said, you were so young. Plus, you were told Millicent was your mother and you were still young enough those memories of Vivian *naturally faded*; Millicent used that to her advantage as well!"

"Why did he go along with it for so long?! Couldn't he come up with *something*—I can't imagine losing you, but basically to take away your children in death...like you never existed to them? That's just..."

Bri shifts to face him and cups his face. "First of all, comparing apples to coconuts!"

He has a small snort of laughter, which is what she hoped for to ease the tension. "Coconuts?" He asks.

"*Yes*! They've got stringy stuff and a hard shell on the outside and not much to look at!" She grins. He chuckles some more. "Seriously though. Short answer is *you're.not.in.your.father's.shoes*. Lengthier answer: the sorrow and pain your father went through, and keep in mind *he was still going through up until today*, takes its toll. Unfortunately, that grief opened up the door for Millicent to manipulate and restructure the family. You said it yourself not too long ago about your father, something like 'he changed around that time' when his Royal Consort died." He nods. "My guess is Phillip was so consumed with grief and devastated at losing your mother and ultimately his children, he probably would've died himself, of a broken heart, if someone wasn't tending to his basic needs!"

615

He says, "I tried to imagine losing you but I *couldn't...*" the last word is a whisper. "When we've been together as long as they had, with children and bonded even deeper..." he hugs her close and a hand goes to the back of her head. He whispers, "*I love you so much! For everything you do and for what you've done for me and my family.*" He smiles sweetly. "You've managed to do what I thought was impossible to do and a complete waste of time to try! You've managed to help our family heal." He hugs her tighter. "You helped me not to hate my father *and* I even have respect for him that I never had before." He pulls back. "How do you do it?"

She shakes her head asking, "Do what?!"

He smiles. "Do such magnificent things?!"

"I love you, Lawrence, but I can't take the credit!" She cups his cheek. "This is all The Lord's doing, *not mine!*" She sees his next question. "*Why* wasn't life better for you or your siblings? Because everyone has the *freedom* to make their own choices...even choices making everyone else's life a nightmare." She softly smiles. "I've felt for a very long time that we all choose to come into the life we live; knowing what our lives would be like and we still chose to come because it'll be worth it on the other side! That's why spirits, like your mother, can basically say 'everything is as it's supposed to be.'" She thinks about the coma she was in last year and that she chose *a second time* to live in mortality...

"I did say that your love *more* than made up for what happened to me and I stand by that *now, more than ever.*" He holds her face, looking at her with so much love. "If I chose to come into this life, it's because of you!" He looks into her eyes and sees something in them. "What is it?"

She shakes her head and smiles wiping the tears away from the corner of them. "I'll be fine. It's sad Vivian had such young children when she..." Bri chokes up, relating to Vivian being a mother and her children, along with being pregnant.

"Straddle me so we can talk better." He says. As she does, he moves the hair away from her face. "I know with my most recent history—." He takes a deep breath and holds her hand. "I'm indebted to you, BriaLynn Worthington!" She gets teary-eyed. He has a sad look. "I hurt you—."

She covers his mouth. "Stop. Stop. Stop." She sits up straighter, shaking her head. "*We will talk about it* because there are things we need to straighten out, but not now. *Please.*"

"Then talk to me about these files." He gives her a pointed look.

Just then David and Jack join them. "Are we interrupting?" David asks.

"*Not at all!*" She looks pointedly at Lawrence. "You're saving me actually."

Lawrence waves them in with a smirk. "She was about to tell me about this stack of files." He gestures to the coffee table.

"Lawrence," she takes a deep breath, "it's not that easy!"

"*Try.* What did you find out?" Lawrence encourages her with a knowing look.

She looks at him and says, "That stack has Vivian's case file from the police, *including* the autopsy."

"Then I want see—."

"No, Lawrence." She quickly grabs his hand and pushes him back with her other hand on his shoulder telling him, "*I mean it!* No." She is stern and his eyebrows come together. She explains, "Somehow, I've always been able to compartmentalize things like this. I don't know why, but things that would bother most people to see and have nightmares, don't bother me in that way. I was able to look at some of the most gruesome things all through my studies for my degree and was able to keep it separate. Now, if I saw some of those crime scenes in person, that may not be the case. Aside from that, Lawrence, you *don't* want to see the pictures of your mother in this file. As a mother, I wouldn't want any of my children to see me in crime scene photos, nor in autopsy photos. *Please.* If you trust me as much as you say you do—."

"*I do!*" He asserts.

She holds his hand against her and has a pleading look on her face. "Then trust me now. *Don't look!*"

"If she was poisoned, she wouldn't...I mean she'd look norm—." He starts to say, but she quickly shakes her head. His emotions threaten to overtake him, and he holds his breath.

She explains more. "A dead body wouldn't look the same even when someone dies of 'natural causes.' Personally, I think it's because their spirit is no longer there, which is why I describe the human body as a shell, for lack of a better word. Vivian was already dead when your father found her. Finding her like that," she points to the stack and squeezes his hand, "seeing those images of how he found her are what he has had to live with. I don't think I could do any better losing any of you." She wipes her cheeks and feels his hands on her hips.

He studies her again. "If you're able to look at these images and they don't bother you like most people, then what *is* bothering you?"

"What do you mean?" She asks and then points to the coffee table adding, "All of that *is* on my mind."

"There's something more, Bri. I can see it in your eyes. It sounds weird, but I want to say *I feel it!*" He says with a hint of frustration.

She closes her eyes and holds them closed, before opening them again. "I knew when I found out in those journals that Vivian was your *biological* mother, *you had to know!* If I didn't tell you and you found out later that I knew, you'd resent me and hate me for not telling you."

"Hate you? No. Would I be hurt and upset? Absolutely!" He admits. She goes to stand up, but his hands hold her hips. "Darling, there's obviously something weighing on you."

"There is, but only because I don't know if Vivian wants this to be known...your father was already at a 'furious' level that could shoot straight up to 'homicidal' if he knows this last piece, or worse, he could end up getting *himself* killed!" She holds her breath and unknowingly rubs her lower abdomen. Jack and David catch this.

Lawrence breaks the pause and tells her, "Bri, just tell me. I promise *I* won't go on a murderous rampage." He holds the back of her neck. "We can all shoulder the burden together."

"Your father doesn't know...she died before she was able to tell him." Bri tells him.

"*What?*" He sounds a little exasperated towards her.

David and Jack look at each other and say it together. "She was pregnant."

"*Hhhow...?*" She looks at them with a confused look.

Jack smiles lovingly and points to her hand on her lower abdomen, saying, "You unknowingly put your hand on your lower abdomen."

Bri looks down at her lower abdomen. She thinks of Vivian being pregnant when she was poisoned. She can barely manage to whisper, "*There were two that died that day...*" Her tears start to drip down her cheeks.

Lawrence stares at Bri's hands resting in her lower abdomen. He whispers to himself, "*She was pregnant?*" Then he hugs Bri close.

Still hugging him, Bri explains a little more. "Vivian had told me about a conversation not too long before her death where Millicent says Vivian's usefulness had just about ended. She was finishing up or had finished with nursing Abby and three was a decent number of children, or rather, 'ghastly creatures' she called you three."

Just then Bri suddenly sits up. She inhales through her teeth; putting one set of fingers to her temple and holds up a finger with her other hand for them to give her a minute.

> Bri's vision takes her to a dark, dreary place...into a 'back-alley' type of doctor's office. There was a beautiful dark haired young woman on a table with her feet in stirrups. Bri looks around and finds a chart open revealing the name 'Lady Millicent Marie Luxton Devonridge.' Bri's eyes go wide. She didn't even recognize Millicent! This young woman is incredibly beautiful with black hair, dark brown eyes with no dark circles around them, nice cheekbones, full lips. Bri thinks to herself, '*Something psychologically must've happened to Millicent to have her physically change so drastically?!*'
>
> The doctor's frantic voice brings her back into the moment and she gathers enough information to hear an abortion had gone wrong and she was needing a hysterectomy or she'd bleed to death. Bri's heart sinks for Millicent as a woman; to go through life and say you choose not to have children is one thing, but when it happens like this, Bri's heart breaks that Millicent no longer has a choice. Bri has a feeling

come to her that she'=has had multiple abortions and her uncle didn't give her a choice in those either.

When they were finishing with young Millicent, Bri wonders around and finds she is in a home and sees a young version of Millicent's uncle. He is almost exactly the same, only a bit thinner around the waist and more hair with less gray. Interestingly enough, he is nervous for young Millicent, pacing almost like a husband for his wife...as twisted as he is, though, it could be more of a concern for *a pet... Bri feels sick to her stomach.*

Bri follows Millicent's uncle when he goes to see young Millicent. She sees the gentleness he has with her, but Bri notices Millicent's eyes are no longer the same as they were just a few minutes ago. It's like there is some sort of 'disconnect' in them, like they still are today...Bri gasps thinking to herself, '*THIS is the significant turning point psychologically for Millicent; the moment she chose to 'disconnect,' allowing the darkness, the evil, to seep deep into her soul...*'

She hears another voice, a sort of echo, add, "To deal with the pain and agony of this moment...the moment she can no longer have children...*because all of her babies were ripped away from her!*"

Bri looks at Millicent being embraced by her uncle and she just lays there, staring at nothing in particular. She turns her head towards Bri and stares, like she can see Bri. It's eerie and she shivers, not only in the vision, but Lawrence, David, and Jack see her shiver, too.

The vision ends and Bri is weak. Lawrence catches her before she falls over and off his lap. He pulls her to him, hugging her firmly until she gains some strength back. She thinks about her vision and the significant turning point for Millicent...when she no longer could have children of her own. She hears and feels, '*She turned her feelings off to cope with her hysterectomy, convincing herself over time she hates children and never wanted any anyway. Her uncle will convince her to marry Phillip and use Phillip's Royal Consort to have The Heir she could raise as her own!*'

When Bri is able to, she sits back again and looks at Lawrence, then she looks at Jack and David who came over and sat next to them during her vision. They are concerned, but relieved when they see she is okay.

"Are you alright, Darling?" Lawrence asks.

"It was a vision of a young Millicent around sixteen years old..." she wipes her cheek where a tear skipped down it. Lawrence is almost frowning at her for shedding a tear over that woman. She sees this and puts her hand on his cheek. "Her childhood wasn't all unicorns and rainbows, Lawrence."

He reminds her, "You said most people who were abused don't become abusers themselves, that statistics—."

"But there's still a *small percentage* that do, and Millicent would be in that small percentile. I feel her childhood—." She starts to say.

Lawrence interrupts, "I don't care what that woman went through! She had NO RIGHT to do what she did to me!"

Bri says calmly, "You're right, Lawrence, it doesn't excuse it away."

His eyebrows stay furrowed but the rest of his face softens when he studies her. He sarcastically asks, "What was so awful in your vision that you took pity on her?"

Bri kindly replies, "I take pity on and feel for *the teenager* who was dealt the terrible cards she was given."

He gruffly asks, "Such as?"

"Aside from Millicent being sexually forced as a child to be with her uncle?" She gives him a pointed look. "Whenever her uncle got her pregnant, she was taken to have an abortion whether she wanted to or not. They always had to '*take care of it.*'" Bri's disgust is heard. "My vision was of her last abortion, and it went sideways." She replies and watches Lawrence's eyebrow go up with 'sideways.' "She had an abortion that went *horribly wrong*, in fact—."

"GOOD! She deserved it!" Lawrence sneers.

Bri folds her arms. "Do you want me to get up so you can go stomp around like a child and finish your tantrum?!"

He humbles himself a little and says, "No."

"This next part is something that will rightfully upset you!" Bri informs him. "I don't want to be pushed off when you have the reaction I expect when you hear it, so I'm going to move."

He stops her. "No, no. I promise. You're fine. You're in a good place to talk to all three of us." She raises her eyebrow in skepticism and nervousness. He kisses her hand. "Promise."

She takes a deep breath and exhales slowly. "The botched abortion caused them to have to do a hysterectomy."

"*What?!*" Lawrence whispers in shock as his face starts to show his fury.

David blurts out, "*She couldn't even have children?!*"

Lawrence slams his fists down on the cushions of the couch on either side of him. "She knew she could never have kids and married my father anyway! *He never would've married her if he knew*! Hell, he wouldn't have been allowed to!"

"*Exactly!*" She says. Lawrence's swirling thoughts pause and he looks at her. She explains, "Which is why she never pushed him to even *try* to have a baby with her. She needed kids to keep The Crown going herself and since she and your father both have three lines, it's recorded that you have three, but it shouldn't be because Vivian only has one line."

"This just keeps getting better and better." Lawrence sarcastically says.

She raises her eyebrow. "Are bloodlines really a problem at this point?"

He gives her a quiet, "No."

"What if she *did* have a child? The entire United Kingdom of Provinces would be different! *Newhaven would be different!*" She tells them. "My being a 'Direct Bloodline' guarantees all my children have four-stars for *however many generations*. This could've been a secret for quite some time! This is another place we can be glad there is a larger, 'grand design' for everything! The reason for her not having children is so you'd be born with a different bloodline, *one that can truly change the course of The Monarchy for the better*, not the worse like she has fought so hard to do!" The guys soak that in a minute.

Lawrence squeezes her hand asking, "What else is there?"

"Um...nothing really..." She thinks for a moment. "A couple of reasons I went through all that," she points to the stack, "was to see how thorough the autopsy was and to see if anything was covered up, at least compared to what I already know from Vivian."

"Was it accurate?" He asks.

 She nods. "It was determined Vivian was poisoned by crimson powder." She jumps up and grabs a file, then sits on the loveseat. "I didn't see *how* she was poisoned..." She tells them as she flips through the file. When she finds it and says, "It looks like the crimson powder was in her chamomile tea."

Jack is barely audible, "*Daaamn...*"

David quietly says, "The crimson flower is one of the deadliest poisons out there when it's dried out and the petals are ground into a powder."

"That's right!" Lawrence says and then it occurs to him, "*There is no cure!*"

"*Actually,*" Bri says, "there might as well not be a cure because by the time they administer the antidote, the poison is usually too far advanced that it wouldn't work anyway." She stares at an autopsy photo of Vivian's face.

"There's more." Lawrence states.

The lump closes up her throat and her lower jaw shakes. "*Lawrence,*" she whispers, "*please don't make me tell you. It was, and is, an absolutely horrible way to die! A swift death would be merciful...*"

Lawrence says in an angry, loathing tone, "Sounds like a perfect way for that *miserable shrew* to die."

"After what I saw in here," she gestures the file, "I'd *almost* agree with that..." she closes her eyes and holds them closed to push out the image of Vivian dying in the agony of *horrible* pain, but also the panic feelings a mother would have for her unborn baby. Bri isn't sure if it's another type of vision, or her empathy, but it's nothing she wants to keep thinking about regardless. She opens her eyes and sees they are watching her and are concerned. "I'm fine. I just wanted to push an image out of my head." They nod a little.

"How long did she suffer? You said once internal bleeding..." Lawrence starts to say but can't finish. "I need to know. I can read it if you'll point me to the right place." He waves his arm towards the stack she has in her lap.

She puts it down and goes back over to them and straddles Lawrence again. "Lawrence, *why* do want the visual of her death?"

He lightly shrugs, "I can't explain it, I just have to know..."

Softly nodding, she takes a calming breath. "Internal bleeding is said to be very painful and to bleed out, I logically conclude that would mean the pain would be intensified collecting inside her body. The crime scene photos show a lot of blood, but I honestly didn't stare too long at them. I now know that it didn't look right for being poisoned because her organs were in various stages of liquifying." She closes her eyes again and holds them shut as she holds her lower abdomen, "I think of Vivian and how her thoughts must've gone to a mother's fear for her unborn baby; to have that realization that she was going to die and so was her baby! Then she would be thinking of her children she would be leaving behind and how much she loves them, and of course Phillip..." Bri's lower jaw shakes and tears pour down her cheeks at this point. "Lawrence, I can sense some of her agony and fear...she was in so much pain!" She takes a deep breath to push down her emotions. "Your father blames himself that she died so horribly *and alone*! I can't imagine how he would feel if he knew there was a baby, too!" She hugs Lawrence and silently sobs.

When she is quiet, Lawrence agrees, "My father should be spared this, except the part about Millicent's hysterectomy at sixteen; *he deserves to know that much*!"

"Agreed." The guys say and she nods in agreement for the compromise.

"If your mother wants him to know about the baby, she can tell him." Bri says. "Otherwise, I'd like to picture him finding out at a distant future date when he's reunited with Vivian on the other side."

"You should tell him about your vision of Millicent and her hysterectomy." Lawrence says. "Maybe you can put a stop to his fury before he does end up getting himself killed."

"*Great.*" She says with sarcasm.

He hugs her close. Jack and David slip into the study and small library, which has a balcony they retreat to, giving Lawrence and Bri a moment in private. Lawrence and Bri hug for a few minutes, then go find David and Jack.

David asks for a moment to talk with Bri. Lawrence and Jack head outside and walk the trails before dinner; Lawrence wants to clear his head. David gives Bri a small apologetic smile. She folds her arms and leans her backside against the desk as she listens to David.

"I feel like I should apologize for sloshing Herst." He leans against the wall in between the patio doors and a window, across from Bri.

"Wait. *'Feel like you should apologize?'*" She asks for clarification.

"I wasn't planning on punching him. I saw him and thought of how hurt you were and then my anger..." She unknowingly nods. "Bri, I can't say I'm sorry because, while I'm relieved for you that he didn't actually sha–er, sleep with her, which would've hurt you worse, he shouldn't have been in that kind of a position to begin with! *However*," he inhales, "I *am sorry* for crossing a line into yours and Herst's relationship." He takes one step to her.

She looks up at him. "Thank you for that. For the record, Lawrence said not too long ago that the three of you do answer to each other. If the three of you are good, then so are we." She playfully tugs on his tie for him to come closer and kiss her. He does and she deepens it. She smiles against his lips when she feels his hands on her body. "Hold that thought and we can have some fun in a few days..." She playfully grins.

"Deal!" He kisses her again, then she takes his hand and he laces their fingers as they walk down to dinner together.

CHAPTER 60
Imperfectly Perfect & Royally Darker

Lawrence and Bri stay the night at The Manor so everyone can travel together to DC tomorrow for James and Amy's wedding. Standing at the foot of their bed, Lawrence says to her, "I don't have the words to describe how much I love you!"

"I love you, too, Lawrence." She is sitting on the edge of the bed. "I wish I could say that you not having sex with Dominique makes it all okay, but it doesn't. It *really hurt* to see those pictures! The one with you dancing with her is stuck in here," she points to her head, "and you kissing–UGH!" she stands up angrily, "it cheapens those moments *we shared* because now I know *that's just what you do with women*! It wasn't because of anything special we had! Why?! *Why* didn't you just trust me?! *WHY* weren't you more aware——." She gasps and looks at him across the room almost whispering, "You were *in–love* with this Dominique, weren't you?!"

"*Hold on!*" He goes to walk towards her.

"*Don't come near me!*" She warns, then glares stating, "*But please*, tell me how much you cared about me that night with your hands all over your '*forever girlfriend!*'" He clenches his jaw.

He's annoyed, but more at himself, because, "You're partly right."

She scoffs and rolls her eyes. "Partly?"

"Yes. *Partly!*" He replies and she rolls her eyes again. "Bri, I felt *you* betrayed *me!*" Her heart squeezes. "Here you were, confiding in my father, who at that moment I hated because I thought he supported *that woman*! I was hurt you told him whatever it was BEFORE ME!" His blood is running hot. "YOU'RE WRONG about Dominque! She *isn't* my girlfriend! *Never was!* There's a descriptive phrase to describe her, but I won't use it because you're a lady!"

"Fine. Use 'sex partner' because that's *so* much better!" Her words are thick with sarcasm.

Lawrence exhales, "*Damnit!*" He runs his hands up through his hair, then turns and walks about half a dozen steps towards her and she backs up just

626

as many. He sees that she will back right up against the wall behind her, so he uses that to stop her from continuing to put distance between them. They both stand across from each other, breathing hard, and staring at each other. "The techniques of flirting *are mine*! But Bri, *nothing* about being with you is the same as anyone else! Wouldn't you agree?" The weight of his smoldering look has her stepping back, but he takes a step, then another.

"Stop coming closer to me!" She tells him, but he only pauses. "Being with each of you *is* different," she tells him, "but I *stupidly* thought you and I were different from your other relationships!"

He takes a few more steps towards her as he asks, "What is it you say about love and lust?"

She rolls her eyes in annoyance. She steps backwards until her back hits the wall. He swiftly closes the distance. She is looking around for an escape but she is boxed in with a wall behind her, furniture on either side, and Lawrence right in front of her.

He puts his hands on the wall, one on each side of her, boxing her in more. She looks at him with annoyance. He gets right up to her lips so she can feel the heat of his breath and looks right into her eyes. "I *never* had her heart and she *certainly* never had mine! Nor did she ever surrender herself to me like you do!"

She raises her eyebrow and ghosts his lips right back saying, "I *won't be* surrendering to you tonight!" She abruptly stops with a defiant look.

Before she can do anything else, he immediately runs a hand into her hair and lightly pulls her hair so her head tilts back. "*Yes.* You *will.*" In a husky tone he whispers, "*I'll prove it!*" When she scoffs, he holds her hair a little firmer, "But first, because of your sassiness, *I'm going to mark you as mine...*"

She is confused at first; she doesn't know what he means. She feels her shirt being pushed off her shoulder and his warm lips press against the front part of the curve of her shoulder. For some strange reason, maybe it's the pregnancy hormones on top of everything else, this teenage 'mark' actually drives her hormones crazy! Her hands are white being pressed into the wall as hard as she can.

When he is done, he kisses her neck and down her jawline. When he is face-to-face with her again, she doesn't let him say anything. She kisses him passionately, wrapping her arms around his neck. He reaches down, picks her up, and carries her to the bed...

Lawrence holds Bri's cheek and tells her, "You're the only woman I've ever loved, Bri! For me to walk away from Dominique and her, we'll call 'lustful death grip,' it had to be an extremely powerful love!" He pulls her in for a kiss, kissing her so lovingly, so tenderly, all her anger and hurt melts away. He whispers, "You're mine, BriaLynn," she nods, "but I'm very much yours!" She holds his jaw and sweetly kisses him.

The next morning, the guys exercised a little earlier than usual. Lawrence is waiting for Bri in The Dining Room where David and Jack have joined him. They each read a different newspaper, but they all have similar headlines. David skims the first few sentences or so of their local paper...

NEWHAVEN NEWS
CHRONICLES

The Queen Mother Behind Assault of HRM The Princess Imperial!

By: Francis Chapman

His Majesty, King Lawrence announced late yesterday afternoon that the second to last person known to have been involved with The Princess Imperial's assault was The Queen Mother herself. She planned it all out and personally saw to the details of the attack. She personally used some sort of club on The Princess Imperial's abdomen! ...

The King also announced that The Queen Mother is now stripped of her title, as well as any family titles and lands. Millicent Devonridge has been banished from The London Palace, and *all* royal residences. ...

"Curious..." Jack says, "wonder if there's anyone out there who'll turn her in now that she's a commoner?"

Lawrence shrugs. "I don't know, but right now I'm just glad Millicent knows she didn't get away with any of it!"

"Things are about to get darker..." David notes and the other two nod.

Up on the top floor of The Manor, Bri is walking out of the bedroom she shares with David after going to get a couple things she almost forgot she needed to bring with her. When she is ready, Mitchell helps carry her things downstairs, including Kahla and her carrier. She goes into her bedroom with Lawrence to grab her purse and phone.

On her way back through the living room, Bri stops in her tracks! She is frozen as she takes in the spirit she is looking at, *dropping everything in her hands to the floor*. She can't move; *she can't even breathe* with a lump growing so large in her throat, it's physically painful. She starts to shake her head when she realizes *why* she sees her daughter's spirit in front of her...

She struggles to whisper, "*No...*"

"Mom, you need to get to Natty at Riverside Hospital *right now*!" Emmie tells her and disappears.

Bri jumps a little when her phone rings. She looks down at the floor and sees Henry is calling her. She bends down and picks it up.

Shaking, she answers it, "Henry, what ha-happened?!"